BEST KEEP QUIET, AND NOT TALK ABOUT THAT! AND TAKE WHAT YOU KNOW AND HEARD, TO THE GRAVE!

DERRICK D. CALLOWAY

Library of Congress Control Number:		2016919416
ISBN:	Hardcover	978-1-5245-6222-9
	Softcover	978-1-5245-6221-2
	eBook	978-1-5245-6220-5

Print information available on the last page.

Rev. date: 08/03/2017

To order additional copies of this book, contact:
Xlibris
1-888-795-4274
www.Xlibris.com
Orders@Xlibris.com
712187

To my Brother in Harold Walker
Christ Jesus.
May God Continue to
Bless And Keep you
Always. Minister [illegible signature]

Chapter One

(Life of the Callaway's Negro Property their Slaves!)

I always heard stories while growing up at China Grove Missionary Baptist Church in Lynwood Park Georgia. I heard many tells of White men in the Churches of the Colored. And now I fully understand the stories told to me as a young black boy growing up around the company that my grandfather kept. I worked with my grandfather digging graves and building extra rooms and digging footings for the foundation of the houses of neighbors that called upon him. I worked alone side of powerful Black Men that were of the Masonic Order and heard many stories of the older generations of Black Georgians. And to have the opportunity these seventeen years of research It was verified and a clearer picture unfolded before my eyes of the Slaves in the church and during Reconstruction the White men living as Blacks that were in the Black Churches after the Civil War in the 1870's up until the late 1890's.

The Slaves who had privileges in the church are the Slaves that I am about to introduce you to played a very important part on the plantation and served the social elite and powerful of society in Georgia at that time! Aaron's life in the beginning will set the pattern of life that will be laid out for his children as it pertains to the white families he was enslaved to that being the Callaway's and their extended families!

Aaron Calloway, what can I say about the cloud of confusion surrounding this man who is well trusted in the White community and who passes as a white man. The question of their ethinicy will play out in the lives of Charlie Calloway in Athens Clarke County and in Oglethorpe, also with Robert who never really showed up anywhere but in Greene in 1880 and as early as 1872 on the farm of P.M. Stephens in Oglethorpe County and once or twice in Wilkes County when he gets married. But never during Aaron's son Charlie situation between 1895 and 1899 with William Eberhart and never in the tax digest at any time in Clarke or in Beaverdam, Oglethorpe County, Georgia, did Robert ever show up, but only in 1899 and 1900 in Oglethorpe County, Georgia, for stealing a pair of pants! And his ethnicity was still a mystery like so many of the mixed raced men in Georgia at this time when the disenfranchisement of blacks began. One in particular is Rev. Collins H. Lyons. This question of their color and how 1806 Aaron Calloway, as I call him, has given his children favor in the white community as you will see this at Sardis Baptist Church in Wilkes County between 1816 and 1822 when I first found Aaron at Church!

Aaron

The first name Aaron is a name that was very popular in Wilkes County; it appears on both sides of my family. It is on the paternal side of my grandmother Georgia Mae Jones's . Aaron on my grandmother's side had a son named Willis Jones. Aaron is the name that intertwines in the whites and the blacks of Wilkes County, Georgia. I don't know if Willis or Aaron Jones had any dealing with Aaron Callaway, but it is more than likely they did! Being the alpha name of both sides of the black Callaway and the black Jones. I am sure they might have passed by each other at one time or another while doing their work as slaves on the two most popular family names in the South!

So Aaron Callaway is in the Sardis Baptist Church in Wilkes County where he comes to join in 1806! He joins about the time the Callaways are arriving in Georgia in the later parts of the 1790s. I do not know how old Aaron is at the time of his arrival at Sardis, but I do think he is in his late teens or early twenties. Let's start with the estate of Isaac Callaway and his wife Winnifred in 1820, where the young Aaron appears in Isaac's estate. Mr. Isaac had property in Wilkes County and in Greene County and Oglethorpe, so Aaron would live between the three or many plantations that drove the industry of slavery. Isaac Callaway is the son of Job Sr. and Mary Ann Carter. His brothers are Job, Joshua, Joseph, his two sisters are Mary and Eunice. Isaac brother Joseph married Nancy Ragan of Oglethorpe County. These are the two families that have ties to Aaron.

The church minutes at Sardis stated that Aaron's wife was sleeping around and Mr. Henderson said that Aaron had a good reason to leave her because of the things that she was doing to her husband. these are the Blacks that joined Sardis about the same time as Aaron. Silvey joined Sardis on the same day as Nanny. This is the same year that Hannah became the slave of Mr. Harper. Hannah left her husband and Jeremiah Reeves and Pete Milner had to go and see Hannah. John H. Milner was the church secretary at this time, December of 1811.

In the year 1811, Negro man Jesse Callaway joins Sardis. This is the only time that I find a colored Jesse Callaway in the minutes of Sardis. I do not know if Reverend Jesse R. Callaway of Penfield in Greene County is a descendant of this Jesse Callaway in 1811 or not. This is the same year that Joshua S. Callaway makes his confession at Sardis.

Milly joined August 25, 1810. Nanny joined June 27, 1812. I had a great interest in Mr. Joshua S. Callaway and his confession to the church. Joshua confessed that he was doing things that he didn't approve in himself and in others. It took him seven years to come and make this confession. Joshua came back just when Judy Callaway came in 1811 or maybe it was 1812. Judy came back under the last name of Callaway. August 21, 1812, the conference proceeded to appoint Brother M. Reeves as moderator of the church. Brother Dickens being charged with the sin of drunkenness by several, and being found it is ordered that the brethrens Joseph Henderson and Claybrook Williamson see him to the next meeting. Brethren absent last conference annulled from the charge of absence Brethren John Callaway, Job and John Chaney. Could it be that Job Callaway and John Callaway and John Cheney are moving in the same circles? They have been moving in the same circles from Bedford and Loudoun Virginia. This relationship will eventually led to the unification of the Callaway and Cheney buisness. I also wonder if Mr. Joseph Henderson is a sheriff or a justice of the peace.

Job is the side of the family that Isaac Callaway is descended from and John is the father of Rev. Enoch Callaway, whose daughter marries a Cheney. The three families are very much in my well house of people of interest!

I do know that Joshua Callaway and Joseph Henderson would govern the whites that ventured into the Indian territories and were stealing and intermarrying with the Indians, wrote letters of the offences that occurred to the government. Could this situation very well describe his own misbehaviors at this time? All men can sin! Is this the thing that he found within himself that was not pleasing, and in others as well? Yes, I believe that it very well could be! You will see this question of ethnicity raised quite often in the families of the South, both the blacks and the whites, and the Jews and Native Americans as well! Pride, which festers hate and loathing of other races, built upon secrets and lies has no value to the truth and the true history of our nation. We should learned to walk not after the flesh but after the spirits, for we know not man by the flesh but by the spirit! So walk after the spirit and live above the lies and secrets that still fester hate and pride even today, the weak carnal selfish mind cannot comprehend the true meaning of the spirit of love or the meaning of love thy neighbor as thy self and to walk in love towards all men and to hate is to commit murder Christians!

February 24, 1813, brother Mercer is moderator; the brother who stands charged for cursing Joseph Henderson still fails to attend and make any acknowledgments for which cause he is excluded. Brother Joseph Henderson Jr. brought forward a charge against a black woman of his named Beck for quarreling with and threatening to stick a knife in one of her fellow servants and cursing him.

Here I will introduce Isaac Callaway's wife Winnifred Ragan's father Johnathan Ragan of Oglethorpe County, Georgia. Johnathan Ragan died April 6, 1813 (Will book B. pages; 96 and 97). I am going to introduce Hannah, the slave of Winney Callaway. Winney became the wife of Isaac Callaway November 29, 1796. Hannah would be about three years old at this time, 1813. Young Hannah the slave of Mrs. Winnifred Callaway could be the daughter of old 1806 Aaron and Hannah at Sardis I am just speculating this however I have a strong inclination because of Mr. Ragan whose a member at Sardis at this time.

The Ragan family married into the Callaway family three times. Joseph Callaway married Nancy Ragan in Onslow, North Carolina, September 21, 1754. They had one child, Mrs. Elizabeth R. Callaway, born in Wilkes County, November 20, 1807. However, I found the will of Isaac Callaway and his second wife Mary Polly Barrett and Elizabeth is mention as the only daughter and not the daughter of Joseph Callaway and Nancy Ragan. Unless she is the adopted daughter of Joseph and Nancy. I also found the estate record of Isaac the husband of Winnifred Callaway and Mary his second wife and John P. Barrett are listed as having Lewis B., George W., Humphrey Tomlison, William A., James H. and Merrell P. Callaway between 1837 as their children on the same estate record as Isaac and Winnifred Callaway! However, I found that Joseph and Martha had more children. David Callaway, Joel Callaway, Almeda and Abraham Aaron Callaway, and Willis Ragan Callaway and Nancy Ragan Callaway. Eli Ragan Callaway married Martha Lumpkin. Martha is buried in Atlanta with her son Eli H. Callaway, who died in 1856 they are both in the Historic Oakland Cemetery in Atlanta. The other children of Eli R. Callaway and Martha Lumpkin are Anne Eliza Callaway and Thomas P. Callaway. Martha lived in Atlanta in the Third Ward near or on Cherry St. while her children lived in Oglethorpe County in or near Bowling Green and Bairdstown near the Cheney family before relocating to Lexington.

The Third Ward of Atlanta where Martha Callaway resided will become the place where majority of the colored Callaway's will come to reside called Summerhill. One in particular is Robert C. Callaway or Robert Charles Callaway. Thomas P. Callaway and his sons might have traveled between Atlanta and Oglethorpe County quite often and so do the Callaway slaves as well. My Grandfather even comes to reside in the Third Ward called Summerhill with his second wife Racheal in 1930.

Let us turn our attention back to Church! May 25, 1816, like I said before, they reported that Aaron was caught in immoralities, drinking and being with more than one woman, I assume. Aaron was having problems with his wife so they ordered that J. H. Milner and Callaway see Aaron and report to the next meeting. *The only reason that they would compel these two men, J.H. Milner and Callaway, without mentioning the first name of Callaway is that it might disclose the true relationship of the master and the slave or cast a perception of bad conduct that is happening on the plantation of Mr. Callaway because of the behavior of Aaron! The only tie between a Milner and a Callaway is through marriage, purchasing of land in Greene County, as I will show you later on.*

In June, they asked only Brother J. Henderson about Aaron's wellbeing. John Milner and Joshua wouldn't report of his wellbeing to the church, so they asked Joseph Henderson to do it, this went on for quite some time. And on June 22, 1816, they asked about him again.

The Church at Sardis accused Silvey of leaving her baby. Silvey had only been in the church four years. (Later on in my investigation Aaron Cheney who is (Robert Callaway) names his daughter Silvey while living in Clarke County in 1870).

Aaron might have been a free half white man until he made his way to Georgia in 1806 when he joined Sardis church, maybe by way of North Carolina, and they reminded him of his place in the colored social structure in the society of slavery in Wilkes County after he exercised his free will, and took it to the extreme by being involved with two women at the same time. Whether they were two white or two colored women, the minutes did not disclose the fact of his actions. I believe they were Native American myself. Aaron was only doing what the rest of the men, white and half-breed and black, were doing, and not only the males at this time but the white women as well. Why did Aaron have such freedom, I don't know, but this favor will be upon his children and grandchildren in 1899! This lifestyle will have a tremendous affect in both white and black lives after the Civil War because of the many families that these men who lived so freely with women both black and white and would have more than one family in the South. I have heard many times how certain men had more than one family in the community.

August 24, 1821, the White folks at Sardis asked Brother Joseph Henderson again to write a letter to inquire into Aaron's standing. And this is what the church wrote about Aaron in the church minutes: "Aaron our black brother who has been removed away for a considerable time out." *Now, this is what I don't understand about their inquiry of Aaron. They would mention his name as being immoral but they don't mention the names of the other parties he was immoral with. This is the beginning of things to come that would portray blacks in the South as being beasts. However, what is this desire of the whites at Sardis for Aaron's wellbeing all about? It does not portray Aaron as a nigger who is out to devour the pure white virgin woman as they are portrayed in the movie in 1916 by W. D. Griffith* Birth of a Nation. *Remember these are the culturevated and destinquished of society in the south and their human property that they valued above all other property on the plantation.*

As I had stated before, it was not just the white men having their way with the black women. The white women got close to mulattos and *mestizos* and negroes and half-breeds just as well as the white men in the height of the drink, and their social functions on the large plantations or in the slave cabins among the negro row houses late at night the white masters whether they be male and females would desire and devoured their slaves. You will see these social acquaintances take place during the 1870s, 1880s, 1890s, called the "Hot Suppers." This is where the liquor flowed and the swine roasted over the pit and the hay beds were kept warm by the body heat and sweat of the mixed company that was kept! While on my many quests to these three counties, an old deacon of Oglethorpe County named Burgess told me about the hot suppers. "You could get three f——ks and a fight at the hot suppers where both whites and blacks attended along with blind tigers furnishing the white lightning." His words confirmed what I had already read in the old newspapers. At this time the names of the white men and blacks were kept secrete to hide the identity of those that attended these "Hot Suppers". This was an ordanace in the legislation in Georgia to not needlessly expose those in attendance.

These relations cause me to think of a great conspiracy from the state government to the federal government in not disclosing the 1890 census that would reveal these relationships before and after the disenfranchisement of the Blacks in the south, whites and Jews and blacks had to make the decision of living as a white man or be reduced to serfdom in this great disenfranchisement era between 1890 and 1900! Both blacks and whites had to make a social decision that would have a detrimental and devastating effect on their two families!

For it didn't matter whether you were white Baptist or Methodist or black Baptist or white Jew or black Jew or whatever or whoever you considered yourself to be or where you were from. What is done in the dark was never to be brought to light! Best keep quiet and let's not talk about that, take it to your damn grave! I would experience this with my grandfather. He never talked about his family and he died with this secret. I also experienced this situation among the blacks and whites in the South that I visited. This is one thing that the whites and the blacks do agree upon, this *secret*! One troubling experience happened to me in Elbert County. I was visiting the Callaway family there and an older mother at first would not talk to me face to face but only behind the front door of her house. At this same house is where I met a Mr. Callaway, whom I ministered to through my nonprofit organization. He told me before he left that he was moving to Alabama. I don't know why he lied to me, and this wouldn't be the last time that I would experience such treatment!

I say up until the 1890s black codes were beginning to truly be enforced and not only upon the Negro but also the whites that lived in both worlds! The lives that these mixed societies coexisted in would never and can never be brought to light, and this causes me to believe that there is a conspiracy in the United States Federal 1890 census today! Between the 1870s during Reconstruction and the 1880s, interracial marriages increased because of the war and newly gained freedom of the Negroes in the South and the whites that found there was money to be made in the exploitation of the blacks at this time, so they intermarried. However, the whites of the old Southern plantation owners were perplexed about what to do with the Negroes, who were making designs against them since the war's end.

Because of Winnifred Callaway and her husband Isaac and their children, Aaron might have lived in Clarke, Lee, Troup, or Henry counties, and many of the other counties, just as well as far south as Columbus, Georgia, and Terrell and Monroe and out of the state as well. Who knows where Aaron might be! He even could be in Indian territory! All I know is that they didn't have a noose for his neck! Nor did they have him tied to a tree and his body riddled with bullets and burned and his members quartered. Did Aaron's father fight in the Revolutionary War to earn his son so much status at Sardis? What is this affection for their Black Brother Aaron!

But between October and December, as Aaron might have recollected if he was telling the story, 1824, a white woman prayed and the church received her into the house again after Brother Reeves and others went to see Brother Willis to resolve the case. Young Masta Enoch was the writer of words in the church at Sardis at this time. That same year, in February, Brother Enoch Callaway reported that Mr. Wemmse Mason, a colored member, left his wife for another woman, and they investigated the problem and found out it was true. So the church kicked him out in March at the next meeting. Aaron might have remembered this because it was a few months before Milly left the church with Mrs. Lee in July. However, they all came back in December when John Milner was the writer of the words. Now, let me finish telling you about Aaron and his experience at Sardis of Old Wilkes County, where everyone or anybody born in Georgia might have derived from.

In August, on the same day, they asked about Aaron through Masta Henderson again. The church took into consideration the remembrance of two sisters also that day who have been a long time out of the church. But they were capable of attending the meetings and their memory is endearing to the church. You know who these two women were, because Aaron might know them! So they agreed that Brethren M. Reeves, J. Henderson, D. Carrington the drunk, and E. Callaway with others as may see proper go and visit these sisters and have some religious exercise with them, and at some convenient time report to the church their practices. It was on March 23 of 1822 that Aaron had made up his mind that he wasn't going back. Aaron might be feeling liberated from the church and enjoying his liberty and a new lifestyle outside Sardis! Because it just was not right, all this time, and now they would call him black and treat him in such away. But they are still asking Masta Henderson how he was doing.

"It was the first place of business, Aaron," Joseph Henderson might have said to Aaron. Moreover, the church took into consideration the care of our brother Aaron, a *black* member, and appointed Joseph Henderson to write and ask about him again. Like I said, Aaron ain't going back! It will be a cold day in the pit of hell before Aaron decides to step foot in Wilkes County, Georgia! Yes, I am sure he's angry. But Aaron had to take into consideration that all of his family are there in Wilkes County, at Sardis, wherever he is at this time, and make his way back home.

On the twenty-fifth day of October 1822, Aaron was to join the church in the end of the month. I have not found out where Aaron was located during his absence from Sardis Baptist Church in Wilkes County, Georgia. I do know one thing, about this time state and federal land lotteries were taking place in the state of Georgia. Again, on October 27, 1822, Edward and Jesse Callaway applied for letters and it was granted. It was not just the Negroes who were having lascivious relationships and not only the white men as well. As I had stated before, the white women too.

On the twenty-third day of April 1823, at one conference meeting, Sister Willis and her husband accused Mrs. P. Davis of being with a colored man. Yeah! Mrs. P. Crane was a witness to it all. She stated that it was true! And stated that Sister Davis said to her that she knew him too well for her good. Then changing it, saying she knew him too well for her own good. The church also found just blame of reporting Brother Willis for wanting the Negro brought to justice. *Like I said, young Aaron might be the prodigy of such a relationship as well.*

However, Aaron might have been the child of these white rich slave owners and their children that lived much different lives than that of the common white men. Patsey Davis was excluded with one voice of the church.

Rose, a member of color belonging to John Spratling, came forward and reported to the church that Reubin, her husband, also belonging to Mr. Spratling, had, without any provocation, left her and taken up with her own daughter. Therefore, notwithstanding a letter of demission granted them by the church, should not have given in to their passion. The conference appointed the following brethren, Daniel Carrington, Joseph Henderson, and Tyre Reeves, to look into the affair and report to the next conference.

> May 22, 1824. John Spratling, Reuben Heard, the brethren reports which was sufficient to fasten the character upon him; wherefore he is no longer to be considered as one of us . . . for as much as Rose remains in our hands, we thank proper to take back her letter and consider her as in her former state. Enoch Callaway was the clerk at this time.

In conference, April 23, 1825, recorded a note from Brother E. Callaway stating the immoral conduct of Juda, a woman of color belonging to Sister Bethany Callaway, where upon the church appointed the brethren M. Reeves, J. Henderson, and I. Adams to inquire into the case and report to the next conference.

In conference on the twenty-first day of May 1825, Brother Reeves, the moderator the brethren appointed to see our sister Juda, belonging to Sister Bethany Callaway, reported that they found no case of dealings wherefore the church is satisfied. Juda is the slave of John and Bethany Callaway. The first name of Juda is in some way related to Aaron because the two claim Wm H. Callaway as their son. Juda in DeKalb County in

1870 and in 1880 Wm. H. is in Greene County listed as being insane and Juda was in Puryears District of Clarke County. Aaron claims Wm. H. as his son in 1900 in Beaverdam, Oglethorpe County, on Mr. William Eberhard's plantation.

The first time I see or ever saw a C. Callaway is on November 22, 1828. He is mentioned in this manner in the minutes of Sardis: "Appoint C. Callaway, D. Callaway, L. T. Irwin and in case of failure, Joseph Henderson as delegates for the (unreadable)." C. Callaway is to write the letter and report it to the next conference on the twenty-fifth day of October. Nancy, a woman of color belonging to Abram Callaway, received by experience. Aaron, belonging to C. Smith, joined by experience on the thirteenth day of November 1828. Harriet Hoof, Timothy Carrington, May, belonging to J. T. Irwin, all joined the church. Abraham Aaron Callaway might be his full name. He is the son of Joseph Callaway and Nancy Ragan and the brother of Eli R. Callaway and his wife Martha Callaway of Fulton County in Marthasville. His slave Nancy might be named for his mother.

So Aaron decided to go back to Sardis in June. Aaron is to join the church at the end of the month on about the twenty-fifth day, 1822. He might be over there on Isaac Callaway's plantation with Hannah. That's one place Aaron could be, however. Masta Edward and Masta Jessie left the church at Sardis in October of 1822 after Masta Joshua and his wife Isabella, and Aaron had already left five years before. Maybe it's because we all had business in Monroe, Forsyth, and Lee counties due to the death of Joseph Callaway about this time. If this is the situation, then Hannah, the slave girl of Winnifred, could not have been born in 1810.

> In Aaron's words: So we took our leave and left for South Georgia to the other many plantations the Callaways had in Monroe and Lee and Dougherty counties and other plantations down there. Masta Joshua Callaway joined the county line church down there and this is where we stayed for a while, 1816 to 1822.
>
> Well, Joseph left everything in the hands of Masta John Irvin. Masta Ervin was placed in this position in 1821 in October.

Well, Aaron could have heard this while in Monroe Forsyth in 1821 during the death of Joseph Callaway. Yeah!

> Many of the old men were dying. Now, I hated to see them all leave. However, we all got to make these plans to leave this here world. I pray that we all live our lives in truth and established in righteousness. We all must meet our blessed Lawd Jesus one early mo'nin'! Yes! I will hear the angels calling my name one of these old days.

> I mentioned Juda, didn't I? Let me tell you this. Well, Juda was the property of Daniel Carrington. She was given to Nancy, the daughter of John Callaway. Juda was a Callaway before she left and lived on Masta Daniel's place. Well, Juda joined Sardis in about, um, let me see, March of 1828. I recollect it was about the twenty-second day of March. Now, I don't know if Aaron had a relationship with Juda, but her name appears in Dekalb County in 1870 and the children of Aaron of Clarke County and Greene County appear in her house in the old town of Panthersville. With William and Berry Callaway, she relocated to Puryears district of Clarke County in 1880 and yet resided in the house of George W. Calloway in Oglethorpe. His daughter will have the grandson of Aaron and the son of Charley and Emma Callaway in the house with her as whites. Berry might later on become Berry Truitt. I believe that Juda is Jude, the younger or older sister of Aaron and the daughter of Hannah off of Isaac and Winifred Callaway's place in the 165th District of Wilkes County and Greene County.

> In conference, June 27, 1835, open door for the reception of members received by experience, Pemelia Newman. Took up the case of Jim and his wife Tefe from last conference. They both came forward and made a satisfactory acknowledgment to the church and on motion and second they were forgiven. Brother Henderson stated that Charles, a man of color belonging to himself, had been guilty of the sin of theft. Brother Henderson was

> appointed to cite him to the next conference. The church thought it proper to call a conference on the fourth Sunday evening of next month for the purpose of the members of color belonging to the church. Bro. L.J. Callaway stated that there were some difficulties regarding John, belonging to L. Weems, and Samuel, belonging to Bro. Appling; therefore, Bro. L.J. Callaway and J. Carrington were appointed to cite them to attend conference on Sunday evening at our next meeting. I have read the estate records of Joseph Henderson and his wife Hellen and there is no mention of either an Aaron or a Charles on his estate. Joseph Henderson had quite a large estate and property in other counties in Georgia that he left his children. This tells me that slave that are under the control of other white men are leased out to them.

However, there was no mention of an Aaron. This tells me that old Aaron is off the plantation of the Callaways.

Mr. Henry Pope, the neighbor of Winifred Callaway, in 1820 had in his family one white male under ten, one white male between the age of sixteen and twenty-five, and one white female under the age of ten and one white female between the age of sixteen and twenty-five. *Henry Pope had three slaves between the ages of fourteen and twenty-five, and seven slaves between the ages of twenty-six and forty-four. The number of persons engaged in agriculture is four.* I do not know what the relationship Mr. Henry Pope had with Oglethorpe but I do find in Oglethorpe County Mr. Burwell Pope in Lexington, Oglethorpe, in 1820. His first name is the same first name that Aaron gives to his son Burwell. The other tie that Henry Pope has with Oglethorpe County is the Barrow family in or near Maxey. In the year of 1830, Mr. Henry Pope was still located in the 165th of Wilkes County. He was over the estate of Isaac Callaway while Mrs. Winifred Callaway was in Clarke County. Mr. Charlie R. Carter was marshal. Mr. Henry Pope had three male slaves under the age of ten. He had four male slaves that were over the age of ten and under the age of twenty-five. He had four that were over the age of twenty-four and under thirty-six. He had three that were thirty-six and under the age of fifty-five. The female slaves were as follows: five female slaves under the age of ten, two female slaves from ten to under the age of twenty, four female slaves that were twenty-four and under thirty-six. He had one female slave that was thirty-six and under the age of fifty-five. In the year 1832, Henry Pope was the guardian of Mary Ann Callaway, the minor orphan of Isaac Callaway. The slaves that were in the charge of Henry Pope in the 165th district were Harry, a fellow hired by Henry Pope himself for fifty-six dollars; and Isaac, a fellow to Nathaniel Truitt for fifty-six dollars. In 1830, Nathaniel Truitt had a total of thirty-four slaves listed on the tax digest in the 165th District of Wilkes County. William was a boy that was in the care of Henry Pope to be hired out to Purnal Truitt in 1832.

Later on, William, a young boy, is hired out again to Mr. John Wilkerson for twenty-eight dollars, along with Siney and her three small children as well for four dollars and thirty cents. *I do not know if this is the same William Callaway that is in Oglethorpe under the name of Burk Callaway and then ends up in Morgan County under the name of William with his wife Mary in 1880. Or maybe he is the same William Callaway that is arrested in Clarke County for registering to vote in the 1870 elections along with other colored men trying to vote. I assume that William is some kin to Aaron and Oliver and Manda, the children of Hannah and maybe Mike. William might be the son of 1806 Aaron, who is the husband of Hannah as well. I am referring to 1837 estate records.* Penney and her child were hired out to Thomas Pullian for thirty-one dollars and twelve cents and Chloe and her two children were hired out to Winifred Callaway for twenty-five dollars. Thomas Pullian hired Sabrey, a small girl, as well for three dollars and seventy-five cents. The only plantation that I see the older Negroes of Isaac and Winnifred Callaway on is the plantation of Job Callaway's senior's estate.

As you may have noticed, there is no sanctity of marriage for these slaves mentioned. In some estates, they list the ages depicting the Negro family in some slave master's estate, but not here! For example, take a look at the following year of 1833. I have noticed one more thing and that is never do they mention Hannah as having a husband! I see Mike in the same estate but he might be a son of Hannah rather than her husband.

In the estate records of Isaac in 1837, *Mike and Hannah and one child* *ere on the plantation of Henry Pope for 180 dollars,* Oliver and Aaron was Seaborn Callaway place for 225 dollars. Shadrack went to Nathan Hoyt for 125 dollars. Ellen, a girl, to Nathan Hoyt as well for 50 dollars. Delila, a girl, to H. Holtzclaw for 30 dollars. Milly and her child went to W. Woodruff for 50 dollars. Lydia went to Charles Boswell for 30 dollars.

(These are the Negro slaves that were hired out to support Mrs. Martha H. Callaway as you may well know by now.) I must say that the Negroes names change in the later years as to who Martha Callaway's slaves are hired out to. One in particular is Mr. Charles Boswell.

As I had stated before about where Isaac and Winnifred Callaway inherited their slaves were from, it was old man Jobe or Job Callaway, who settled in Oglethorpe County near Greene County, Georgia, line! I kept wondering where I saw the name Mike before. It was on Job's estate. Job left his wife Mary, a Negro Will and his wife Lous, Sam and his wife Dinah. Gabe, Solomon, and Lady Crease, Big Doll, and Abbey and three boys, Feds, Hanson, and Bill all stayed on the plantation with Job's wife Mary. Job's son Jacob was already living on a plantation that his father had left him before he died. His father also gave him five hundred and fifty acres and the slaves Jack, Talbot, Charst and her child Henry. All of them went with Jacob. Like I said before, the slaves did not go too far from each other from Wilkes to Oglethorpe and to Greene County, Georgia. Joseph Callaway received five hundred and forty-five acres and Negroes, Mark, Dave, Spencer, and Rachel. And if and when his mother Mary died, he would get Gabriel as well. Job Junior received six hundred and fourteen acres, which he had in his possession. He received the following slaves, Sam, Charity, Silvey, and her child Minty. And after his mother's death he was to get little Bill. All are young children.

Joshua got the land he was already living on, which was six hundred and sixty-six acres. Joshua got Negro Moses, Nelson, Beck, and Tom. He would get boy Fed after his mother's death. Young Isaac would get a third of his father's land, which he already lived on, and after his mother's death he would receive the remaining property. Young Job was left John White's lands adjoining his home tract with his two biggest stills, also with the following Negroes, *Mike,* Sealy, Harry, and Sam, after his mother's death.

Job wrote that if his wife and Isaac could not get along, his sons Joseph and Job should divide the property. Job left his daughter Unice Griffin, seven Negroes, Lele and her children Lewis, Stephen, Patience, Milly, and also Big Doll after Mrs. Mary's death.

Mary, the daughter of Job, married a Mr. Parks. Job left the lands he bought from Isaac Millican and William Park. Job and Joseph are to dispose of the land to take good care of his daughter Mary Parks. Mary will receive Little Doll, Joseph and Henry, Crite, and Cato. And after the death of Mary, her mother, she will receive the Negroes and land. I was taken aback when I found out where one of the properties of Job Callaway was located in 1796. Job Callaway purchased this land in Oglethorpe County from Pilman Lumpkin, who is buried in the Penfield Cemetery of Greene County, Georgia. Job paid three hundred and twenty-one dollars for the property. Job also received land from David Whittle in Oglethorpe just as well. In April of 1800, he received 207 acres more or less from Jessie Whittle. Isaac, the son of Job Callaway Sr., married Winifred Regan Callaway and received from Mary Ramsey 793 acres and John Ramsey 793 acres of land along Fork Creek in 1807. Mary, the daughter of Job, received from John Milner after his death one share consisting of 247 acres and 8/10 of land in Oglethorpe County. Elie R. Callaway received from George Lumpkin in 1821 some eighty-two acres on Little River in Oglethorpe County just south of the city of Lexington. Eli R. Callaway also received land from Elijah, John, Amy, Smithfield, and Sarah Martin in 1827 in Oglethorpe. Rev. Francis Callaway received from William South 150 acres of land on Clouds Creek in 1827.

(Absolon Janes in the 605th District of Taliaferro): One of the men who is the Executor of the Estate of Isaac Callaway.

Yes! I always thought that there were no ties to Taliaferro County, Georgia, other than that of Mr. Charles Callaway and Louisa, his wife out of Wilkes County who comes to reside in Taliaferro in the 1880s. Mr. Absolon Janes had fifty-three slaves on his property in 1840 and he was the only white man listed in his family in the 605th District. His son T. P. Janes was in Greene County with forty-eight slaves and his wife. Elizabeth Janes was in the 605th District in 1840 with eleven slaves and five whites in her household. Let us start in the house of Absolon Janes in Taliaferro. *So I surmised that while Absolon Janes was in Taliaferro County over his own property there. His son T. P. Janes is over the estate of Isaac and Winifred Callaway property that was in Greene County. So I also surmise that these same slaves of Winnifred Callaway and Isaac Callaway were working on the plantation of Absolon Janes and T. P. Janes in Taliaferro.*

In Taliaferro County in the year of 1840, I found out that the white families that resided in Taliaferro County come to reside in Greene County later on or their children did. I see a close relationship between the two locations, such as these families in the 605th District with Absolon Janes, David Daniels, Lowe Fluker, William Lancford, Edward Meadows, L. B. Freeman, John Griffith, William Nichols, and Lewis Taylor. In 1840, Absalon had eight male slaves under the age of ten, thirteen male slaves between the ages of ten and twenty, eight male slaves between the ages of thirty and forty. He had eleven female slaves under the age of ten, six female slaves between ten and twenty, seven female slaves between the ages of thirty and forty years old. Now, remember Absolon is the only white male over these slaves located in the 605th in Taliaferro. However, Elizabeth Janes is living right next door to Absolon Janes and she has living with her, her children. There are no boys, only girls living with her. The youngest girl was under five, two were ten and under twenty, two were twenty and under thirty. Elizabeth's male slaves were listed as follows, three under the age of ten, one ten and under twenty, one thirty and under forty. The female slaves are as follows, one under the age of ten, two ten and under twenty, and three twenty and under thirty. Their sole purpose to owning these slaves was for agriculture. Absolon Janes had thirty-two of his slaves in agriculture and Elizabeth had only six in agriculture.

Winifred Ragan and Isaac Calloway

The property or plantation of Isaac Callaway was in the 165th District of Wilkes County, Georgia. I am going to pay a visit to the plantation of Winifred Callaway in Wilkes on the seventh day of August in 1820. Mrs. Winifred has one white male under the age of ten, one white male between ten and fifteen, two white females under ten, and two white females ten to fifteen. Mrs. Winifred is between twenty-six and forty-four. Isaac Callaway is not mentioned at this time. Isaac might have already been dead before the census of 1820. *The two younger females are Mary and Martha.*

Mrs. Winifred's slaves are nine males under the age of fourteen, eight male slaves between fourteen and twenty-five, six male slaves between twenty-six and forty-four, and seven male slaves forty-five and over. Her female slaves are six females under the age of fourteen, six between fourteen and twenty-five, seven female slaves between twenty-six and forty-four, there are thirty of these slaves engaged in agriculture. Mrs. Winifred has a total of forty-nine slaves that are located on her plantation in 1820. Mr. Henry Pope lived right next door to Winifred Callaway in 1820 and Aaron and Hannah and Oliver and Amanda are all here in the 165th District of Wilkes County along with the rest of the Negro slaves of Isaac and Winnifred Callaway under the watchful eyes of overseers of Absolon Janes and Henry Pope! However, at this time *Mike* is on Job's plantation before he died, the father of Isaac and father-in-law of Winnifred Callaway.

Another of Winifred's neighbors is Drury Griffin, who lived on the opposite side of Mrs. Winifred Callaway. Drury might be the husband of Unice Callaway. I do not know if this Griffin family in Wilkes County has any relationship to the Griffin family that was in Greene County. However, I do believe they are because of the plantation that was in Oglethorpe County that belonged to Mr. Isaac Callaway. Mr. Thomas Evans's place was between Nathan Burgamey's and Henry Pope's. The Hays brothers were in this district as well. They were Gilbert Hays and William Hays. They too also appeared on the estate of Isaac Callaway. As a matter of fact, let us take a look at who visited the estate of Isaac Callaway in 1820. Edward Callaway received more than just slaves from Isaac Callaway's estate. Joseph Henderson even stopped by the place in the 165th District of Wilkes County at this time in 1820. Remember in 1822 Edward and Jesse will be leaving the Sardis Church and will be in Monroe County Georgia while Joseph Henderson will traveling between Jones and Wilkes County alone with Joshua and John Milner relaying to the church about Aaron's wellbeing.

The Negroes on Isaac Callaway's plantation were very industrious, I believe. S. Echols and A. W. Janes, John Render, J. D. Lennard, J. Gresham, Joseph Render, W. Lacky, J. Wilburn, G. Tomlin, James Render, Seaborn Callaway, John Callaway, Enoch Callaway, William J. Callaway, T. Pool, Henry Pope, T. G. Monday, John Sherman, Rhoda Holtsclaw, T. Hillard, G. Jenkinson, and Thomas Rhodes all paid visits on Isaac's place. From the sixth to the eight day of December 1820, again on the same days, L. C. Toombs, P. H. Janes, Isaac Dickens, Robert Parker, and William J. Callaway came by the place of Isaac Callaway. Mr. Richard Peteet came by. He may be some kin to Parker and Seaborn Callaway's wives Susanna and Delphi. F. Thurmond, *Charles Smith,* and *Henry Pope* came by the house again on the same day, as well as James King, James Sherly, Charles

Strozier, Jesse Heard, Benjamin P. Wooten, *John Ray,* John Hurling, Jeptha Callaway, John T. Mitchell, John Wooten, Noah Callaway, *James Stephens* and Drury Callaway and Jasper T. Howard. Alabama is representing at this time in the estate on Isaac Callaway estate. Mr. Drury Callaway, Jeptha Callaway and Noah Callaway as well yes, the three will or are now living in Alabama and are visiting Isaac and Winnifred Callaway estate in Wilkes and Greene County Georgia. Henry Terrell got a wagon. A. R. Booker got cutting knives, *and Thomas Cooper stopped by the next day and got 40 gallons of gin. E. Smith and l. Mulkey got 60 gallons and 50 gallons of liquor. Joseph M. Callaway and William Brooks made it to the house to buy some things as well.* James Brown, Charlie Smith, and Washington Dickson, Leroy Sales, and James Armstrong and John M. Hanson with William Cameron bought some items from the estate. On the third day of business on the estate of Isaac, Absalon Janes and Henry Pope, the men in charge of Isaac's property, sold off and rented the slaves. *Winifred Callaway, the wife who is never mentioned as the wife of Isaac Callaway in his estate, got Hannah and her three children, Oliver, Aaron, and Manda. Alleck and Shadrack, Jude, Betty, and Matilda all stayed with Mrs. Winifred in the 165th District of Wilkes County until her death, after which they were sent in all directions. At this time in the estate, Mike is not mentioned.*

Mr. Joseph Callaway and Isaac Callaway Jr. in Wilkes County on or near Isaac and Winifred Callaway's place in the 165th District

Mr. Joseph Callaway resided in the same district as or near Mrs. Winifred Callaway, along with Isaac Callaway Jr. Mr. Joseph Callaway, in 1820, had one white male between sixteen and eighteen, one white male between sixteen and twenty-five, and Mr. Joseph was listed as being over forty-five. There were only two white females in his house and they were between ten and fifteen. Mr. Joseph Callaway's slaves were as follows, *six male slaves under the age of fourteen, four male slaves between fourteen and twenty-five, two female slaves under fourteen, two female slaves between fourteen and twenty-five, two female slaves between twenty-six and forty-four, and the number of person's engaged in agriculture were nine. I do not know if this is the Isaac Callaway that will come to leave his estate in the hands of Absalon Janes and Mr. Henry Pope. I do know he is living just two farms down from Mr. Joseph Callaway in 1820.* His household consists of the following numbers of whites, three white males under the age of ten, one white male between ten and fifteen, one white male between sixteen and eighteen, and one white male between sixteen and twenty-five, and one white male forty-five years old. The white females are one under the age of ten, two between the ages of ten and fifteen, one white female that is between twenty-six and forty-four. *The slaves of Isaac Callaway Jr. are four male slaves under the age of fourteen, one male slave between fourteen and twenty-five, and three female slaves under the age of fourteen; one female between fourteen and twenty-five, and the number of persons engaged in agriculture is five.*

Absolon Janes and Henry Pope the administrators of the estate of Isaac Callaway. This is the same year that the slaves were mentioned on the estate of Isaac Callaway.

An account of the hire of the Negroes and rent of the land of Isaac Callaway, deceased, on the seventh and eighth of December 1820 to the highest bidder until the twenty-fifth of December 1821 at a credit of twelve months by the administrators. The first to receive from Isaac Callaway's estate was Mrs. Winifred Regan Callaway. Winnifred hired a Negro man named David and a man named Alleck, and a boy named Shadrack and a woman and child named William. *One Negro woman Hannah and her three children Oliver, Aaron, and Manda. One Negro woman named Betty, Matilda, and little Harriet. Rolly, a boy, and Old Amy; Isham, a boy.*

In 1822, Nicholas Wylie hired Bill; Mr. Wilkerson hired Negro boy Matt. John Barren hired a Negro woman named Rose and little Beck. Jeptha Callaway hired Charles. William Reeves hired little Rena and two children, Darrell and Clara. William Brooks hired Negro woman Sarah and Negro woman Clary and child Rachel. Robert Parks hired Negro woman Nelly and two children, Ned and Mahala. *Ned and Mahala's last name will become Parks and eventually will acquire their freedom. Ned in 1870 is living in Greene County and Mahala is living under the last name of Callaway in the house with Martha Callaway in Atlanta in the third ward on or near Terry Street. Yes, Mahala and Ned are sister and brother. Mahala is fifty years old and Mrs. Martha is seventy-three years old. She is the mother of Thomas P. Callaway of Oglethorpe County, Georgia. Ned will go on to marry Ms. Sidney Harris in 1870. Before Ned marries Sidney Harris, he is living with Anderson Parks, a sixteen-year-old boy. I want to show you how easy it was to change your name at this time being a Negro in Georgia. You and your brothers and sisters could be under different last names after the Civil War. This is why I think Ollie went under the last name of Willingham because of the relationship between Charles Callaway and the Willinghams in the 1840s or the 1850s when he was living in Wilkes County, Georgia, and his cousin Mrs. Willingham was living in the house with him!*

In 1824, December 25, an amount of one hundred dollars for Harry to Richard Kingston, fifty dollars for Isaac to John Wooten, twenty-seven dollars for Linia to George Johnson, seventeen dollars and fifty cents for Penny to Emanuel Smith; *Chloe and her children William, Sarah, and Lousia to Winifred Callaway for support. Winifred swore to the correctness of the account on May 10, 1825. From Chloe's side of the family will come Green Callaway!*

Henry Pope is now the guardian of one of the young girls in the house of Winnifred Ragan named Martha H. Callaway, minor orphan of Isaac Callaway, deceased, direct for the hire of her Negroes between 1826 and 1827, Mike to Nicholas Wylie, for 129.50 dollars. Hannah and two children Ellen and Adeline to Henry Pope 1.50 dollars. Shadrack to Winifred Callaway for 35 dollars, Oliver to Purnell Truitt for 8.12 dollars, Aaron to Henry Pope for 3.12 dollars. Milly to Winifred Callaway for 12 dollars.

In the year of 1827, Mike to Nicholas Wylie for 5 dollars, Shadrack to Henry Pope for 25 dollars, Oliver to Purnell Truitt for 25 dollars, Aaron to Purnell Truitt for 1 dollar. Milly to Purnal Truitt for 5 dollars (Hannah and three children's names are scratched out). *However, in 1826, Aaron and Oliver and Amanda have two more siblings, Ellen and Adeline, who were on the property of Henry Pope.*

Henry Pope, in the same year between 1826 and 1827, is still over at the estate of Mary Ann Callaway, the orphan daughter of Isaac Callaway. Harry to Henry Pope for 70 dollars, Isaac to Nicholas Wylie for 61.06 ½, Liney to George W. Johnson for 35 dollars, Penny to Henry Pope for 1.25 dollars, *Chloe and her two children to Henry Pope for 10.06 ½. Here I believe that the child of Chloe in 1870 is named Green and there is another Green Callaway in Lincoln County in 1870 with Charlie and Clayborn and daughter America and the Reed family. Green was born in 1840.* William went to George Eastery for his board and clothing. Henry Pope and Martha H. Callaway were listed again in the same year, in 1826, on a credit of twelve months. Ike to Joseph Callaway for 136 dollars, Oliver to Purnal Truitt for 100 dollars, Aaron to Purnal Truitt for 85 dollars, Shadrack to

Archabel Little for 100.12 ½, Hannah and two children to Henry Pope for 26 dollars, Ellen to W. Callaway, Adaline to E. Dodson, Delia to W. Callaway for board and clothing. In consequence of a sour leg, Milly to T. Sutton. *(I can say that Hannah has had two more children, for now Ellen and Adaline and Delia are rented out besides the two she travels with going over to the plantation of Mr. Henry Pope. She now has eight children since 1820.) Let's see if I can name them all. The first three were Oliver, Aaron, and Manda, then Ellen, Adeline, and Delia. And now in 1827, Hannah had two more children born into slavery while under the care of Henry Pope and for the care of Martha Henrietta Callaway, the child of Isaac Callaway. I have noticed that certain slaves work for Martha H. Callaway and certain slaves work for Mary A. Callaway. Never do any of the slaves of Hannah go to work for anyone else. At this same time, in 1827, lands in Lee County were opening up to the rich white large landowners!* I might as well mention the Lee County land lottery, and that Mrs. Winnifred Callaway was located here too in 1827 in Lee County with William Cain, Richard Cain, Ranson Cain, Andrew Cain, Bethany Callaway, J.M. Callaway, and Elijah Callaway. Oh yeah, I also found Mr. Drury Callaway in the Popes District in Number 336 in the Twenty-Eighth District in Lee County. The Cates that were in Lee County, Georgia, were William Cates, and Charles Cates. *This is why Winifred Callaway does not show up in the estate of Isaac Callaway in 1827. She is in Lee County with Drury Callaway, who was in 165. I believe that Drury is in-law to Winifred Callaway.*

Hannah and the three children, Oliver, Aaron, and Manda. Alleck and Boy Shadrack, Jude, Betty, and Matilda all stayed with Mrs. Winifred. But in 1831, Mike and Hannah and three children went to work for Isaac Callaway's son Felix for $170. Shadrack worked for Seaborn Callaway for $70, Oliver and Aaron went to work for purnal Truitt for $88.60. Milly went to work for James A. Bowen for $32, and Ellen went to work for Henry Holtzclaw for $18. Did you notice Jude in the lot of Mrs. Winnifred Callaway as well?

Thomas Gresham was the guardian of Frances Callaway, another child of Isaac Callaway, on the tenth day of 1822. Masta Thomas Gresham had Sam, Nelly, Ned, Mahala, Matt, Big Sarah, Rolly on his property to hire out for the care of Francis. Sam left with Isaiah T. Irvin. Nelly, Ned, and Mahala left with Mrs. Isabella Henderson Callaway, the wife of Joshua. Matt left on this day with John Wilkerson, Big Sarah left with William Brooks, and little Rolly went with William Brooks too.

In 1827 again, Harry to Henry Pope for 50 dollars, Isaac to Nathaniel Truitt for 60 dollars, Penny and child to Henry Pope for 10 dollars, Chloe and two children to Henry Pope for board and clothing. Leney to Winifred Callaway for 10 dollars, William and little Sarah to Henry Pope for board and clothing. *(These are the slaves that are to support Mary A. Callaway, for Chloe and Penny are always going for the care of Mary.)*

Henry Pope, the guardian of Martha H. Callaway, minor orphan of Isaac Callaway, deceased, to said orphan for the hire of said minor orphan Negroes for the year of 1828. Mike to Henry Pope for 126.06 ½, Hannah and three children to Henry Pope 50 cents. Shadrack to Henry Pope for 30 dollars, Oliver to Purnal Truitt for 21 dollars, Aaron to Purnal Truitt for 5 dollars, Milly to David Pendergrass for 8 dollars. Shadrack who went to Henry Pope could be the kin to Aaron Callaway who took the last name Barrow.

For the year of 1829, Mike to Nicholas Wylie for 115 dollars, Shadrack to Henry Pope for 34 dollars, Oliver to Purnal Truitt for 31 dollars, Aaron to Purnal Truitt for 9 dollars; Milly, a girl, to David Pendergrass for 11 dollars. Hannah and her four children, Ellen, Adeline, Delilah, and Lydia, to Henry Pope for 7.25 dollars. *Lydia is now listed as a sister of Aaron and daughter of Hannah, the personal slave of Winnifred Ragan Callaway. I noticed a pattern evolving that the slaves of Mary and the slaves of Martha stayed and remained in a setting of relationship pertaining to the colored matriarch.*

Henry Pope, guardian for Mary Ann Callaway, minor orphan of Isaac Callaway, deceased. Said orphan direct to hire of said orphan, Negroes for the year of 1830 on a credit between months.

Harry to Henry Pope for 52 dollars, Isaac to Joseph Callaway for 55 dollars, Liney and her two children to J. W. Johnson for 10 dollars, Penney and her two children to Woodson Callaway for 23.68 1/2. Chloe and her four children to Winifred Callaway for their board and clothing. William, a boy, to S. C. Potson (?). *I believe that Chloe is the oldest child of Hannah and this is the reason she abides with Winnifred from the estate of Mary.*

Henry Pope guardian for Martha H. Callaway minor orphan of Isaac Callaway, deceased, to said orphan for the hire of said orphan Negroes for the year of 1830 on credit of twelve months, January 1, 1830. Mike to Nicholas Wiley for 100 dollars. Shadrack to Seaborn Callaway for 40 dollars. Oliver to Purnal Truitt for 37 dollars. Aaron to Henry Pope for 26 dollars. Hannah and her three small children to N. Wiley for 8.75 dollars. Milly, a girl, to Newton Armor for 27 dollars, and Ellen, a girl, to Stephen W. Hood for 9 dollars.

By 1830, Mrs. Winifred rented Hannah and the children to Henry Pope for the care of Martha H. Callaway. In 1830, Winifred had lost control over her daughters Martha and Mary, and Mr. Henry Pope was in charge of the two young ladies while Winifred was living in Clarke County in 1830. *Now, the tax digest suggests that Henry had in 1830 the following slaves on his property, and Hannah and her children are on his property at this time. I could now put an age on these slaves of Martha H. Callaway. Henry had three male slaves under the age of ten, four male slaves of ten and under the age of twenty, four that were twenty-four and under the age of forty, three that were thirty-six and under the age of fifty-five.* Now, remember that in 1820 Henry only had a total of ten slaves on his property, three that were fourteen and under twenty-five, and seven that were twenty-six and under forty-four. That means that the slaves that were on the property of Henry Pope in 1820 ranged in age from twenty-four to forty and thirty-six to fifty-five. The children of Hannah ranged between the ages of three under the age of ten and four that were ten and under twenty. I believe that Hannah would be about thirty-five years old. The female slaves on his property in 1830 are five under the age of ten, two ten and under the age of twenty-four, four that were twenty-four and under the age of thirty-six, and one matriarch female slave that is thirty-six and under the age of fifty-five. Hannah is the oldest female slave at this time on the plantation of Mr. Henry Pope in 1830.

In 1831, Masta Henry Pope was still the guardian for Ms. Martha Hennretta Callaway. On the first day of January, Mike left to go with Felix G. Calloway and so did Hannah and her two children. Shadrack left with Masta Seaborn Callaway. *Oliver and Aaron went with Masta Purnal Truitt. Milley was a little girl at this time. She went with James A. Grover. And Ellen was a little girl and she went with Masta Henry Holtzclaw. Adaline was about the same age as the other two girls, Milley and Ellen. She went with Masta John Jones.*

Masta Henry Pope also was the guardian for Mary Ann Callaway, the sister of Martha, and she had her own slave that Masta Henry Pope hired out on the first of January as well. Harry went with Masta Henry Pope, Isaac went with Masta Nathaniel Truitt, Siney and her two infant children went with Masta David Callaway for board and clothing. Penney and one of her children went with Masta Robert Huff. Willa was a small boy and he left with Masta Solomon V. Paterson. *Cloe and her four children went with Mrs. Winnifred Callaway for their board and clothing.* Sabrey, a small girl, left with Masta Woodson Callaway. Henry Pope, guardian of Mary Ann Callaway, minor orphan of Isaac Callaway, deceased, to said for the hire of said orphan Negroes for the year of 1832. Harry, a fellow, to Henry Pope for 56 dollars. Isaac, a fellow, to Nathaniel Truitt for 56 dollars. William, a boy, to John Wilkerson for 28.75 dollars. Siney and three small children to John Wilkerson for 4.30 dollars. Penny and one child to Thomas Pullian for 31 dollars and 12 pence. *Chloe and two children to Winifred Callaway for 25 dollars.* Sabrey, a small girl, to Thomas Pullian for 3.75 dollars.

Henry Pope, guardian for Martha Henrietta Callaway, minor orphan of Isaac Callaway, deceased, to said minor orphan for the hire of said minor orphan Negroes for the year of 1833. Mike, a fellow, to James M. Callaway for 136 dollars. Shadrack, a fellow, to Henry Pope for 75 dollars. Oliver, a large boy, to Purnal Truitt for 65 dollars. Aaron, a boy, to Purnal Truitt for 60 dollars. Hannah and three children to Henry Pope for 30 dollars. Milly, a woman, to Simeon Brook for 40 dollars. Ellen, a girl, to Henry Holtzclaw for 20 dollars. Adeline, a small girl, to Presley Aycock.

Here, in this section of the book, I want to establish that Aaron was not born on Reverend Enoch Callaway's place nor his father John's plantation as well. I found his estate or will and not one time is Aaron or Charles or Jesse Calloway mentioned. How Aaron ended up on Reverend Enoch's plantation in 1859, I don't know. John's wife Bethany Arnold got the dwelling house and every other house on the plantation. John left his wife Bethany the following Negroes, Scipio, Anthony, Lewis, Jude, and Cate. Now, this is the mindset of the Callaways' businessmen. This shows the relationship between his children, himself, and others around him. You had to have a business mind in this Callaway family, even in dealing with each other. Listen to what he left his son Job. Job Callaway got certain bonds or obligations he gave his father John for six hundred dollars in 1810 on the twenty-third day of August. It seems that it was all about being prosperous from selling the

Negroes and the selling and buying of goods. John gave his son John the Negroes Georgia and Ailsey, and a plantation in Madison County next to George Janes's consisting of 100 acres. John gave Enoch a slave named Milly and two-thirds of the land he was living on and the rest when his wife Bethany dies. He left Nancy Carrington, the wife of Daniel Carrington—the lawyer and son-in-law of John and Bethany Callaway, and a big mean drunk—received the Negroes Big Jude and Percilla. He left little Jude to Bethany Talbot and Bob with Mrs. Bethany as well. Now, Aaron Callaway in 1859, when Rev. Enoch Callaway dies is given in the lot of slaves to be sent off to William Owen Cheney will alternate or often change his name from Aaron to Bob and later to Robert Callaway after the Civil War ends. I wonder if Jude is his mother and Bob is his father or is Bob. I say this because Jude and Bob are left to Enoch's sister Bethany Talbot and in 1870 Judy or Juda comes to reside in Puryears where Aaron or Bob is located and in 1900 Aaron is on the plantation of William Eberhart and I do believe it is old Robert (Bob) Callaway with William H. as his son the grandson of Judy or Juda out of Panthersville in DeKalb County Georgia in 1870. I know that I might be reaching just a little but why not it's still a mystery! To Betsy Jerrell he left Negro Eveline and Diley. To Phreoby Strozier he left Henretta and Fanny. Mrs. Mary Thrash got Rachel and Simon. Lydia Thrash got Doll and David, and Adda Milner got Sammy, Washington, and Cloe. They were all divided up among the family members of John. *The brother-in-law of Rev. Enoch Callaway, Mr. Daniel Carrington, was having many difficulties in his family, and I believe that the John mentioned in the next situation is the slave of Rev. Enoch Callaway.*

In conference, August 27, 1842. First, invited brethren and sister churches to sit with us. Received corresponding brethren from sister churches. Third, open doors for the reception of members Abner Callaway. Fourth, called upon the case of Mr. Jackson. Brother Jackson came forward and acknowledged the charges against him were true and accepted that he was sorry that he had acted so un-Christian. On motion and second he was forgiven. Fifth, Brother Carrington reported that Sister Cordelia Carrington had been guilty of the sin of cohabiting with John, a man of color, the Negro (unreadable) also being a member with us and she having a child of color with him. On motion and second they were both excluded from the church.

It was January 11, 1843, when the courts in Greene County ordered that the following persons be appointed to appraise said estate of Mrs. Winnifred Calloway: Samuel Greene, Benjamin Brantley, William F. Willborne, Peter Northern, and Benjamin E. Spencer. But just in time,

Masta Absalon Janes, Mrs. Winnifred's son-in-law, went into open court and stated that he was qualified as executor of said will, and letters testamentary proved him as such. They adjourned that day and Masta Janes was back in court the next day. The courts said that on the application of Absolon Janes, executor of Winnifred Callaway (deceased), for leave to sell the land and Negroes belonging to said estate. It is ordered that he have leave to sell the land and Negroes of said estate according to law. This might be how Aaron ended up on Enoch Callaway's place in 1843. I wonder if the men Samuel Greene, Benjamin Brantley, William F. Willborne, Peter Northern, and Benjamin F. Spencer had control of her estate then my story might have gone in a different direction. Mrs. Winnifred can rest in peace now. They buried Mrs. Winifred Callaway in Penfield Cemetery in Greene County, Georgia, right next to Mr. Jesse Mercer. Winnifred Callaway had as her witness Mary F. Anderson, Cornelia M. Janes, and Carol S. Anderson on the twenty-third day of December 1839. Winnifred could not write her name, so she made her mark with an X. If you did not notice the last name Anderson in reference to the same last name of Sarah Anderson, the second wife of Isaac Callaway.

The last place I have Mrs. Winnifred Ragan Callaway is in Lee County, Georgia, in 1840, just a few years before her death. She was in the 139th District of Lee County, Georgia, in 1840. Winnifred was living alone and had her slaves around her. She had three male slaves under ten, three male slaves twenty-four years to thirty-four years old, and one male slave that is thirty-four to fifty-four years old surrounding her in her old age. Mrs. Winnifred Callaway is between the ages of sixty and seventy in the year 1840. The oldest slave might be the slave Isaac, whom she desired to set free after her death. I don't know if Isaac is the father of Hannah the mother of Aaron or not but there is some kind of depth to this affection she has toward Isaac, her oldest slave.

Mrs. Winnifred also had lands and a house in Lee County in Palmyra. Mrs. Winifred Ragan Callaway's brother James H. Ragan would make out his will in Lee County in 1864. I don't know how long he arrived here in Lee County from Oglethorpe, however he does leave a will that I will mention later on in the chapter. I am going to surmise that James H. Callaway the son of Isaac Callaway and Mary Polly Barrett named their son James H. Callaway after the brother of Winnifred Ragan. And if so what is this affection that these two women have between each other? Aaron might have visited this plantation while he was living in Jones County with Joshua Callaway and while Hannah was visiting with her slave master Mrs. Winnifred from Wilkes and Greene County to visit her brother James H. Ragan. I am sure that Aaron of 1805 was in Jones

County when Henry Pope died in Monroe County or Lee County or Bibb County; I just couldn't get an absolute where he died. But I do think Mrs. Winnifred was there to see about her children slaves that were in his care and under Henry's supervision. Just like everything I have ever investigated I come up short of a definite place or even a burial or a long standing place of residence even now for Mr. Henry Pope as well! I couldn't even find the Will of Mr. Pope! The mystery at the time of his death was in Monroe or Lee County Georgia in or between 1838. Now I am sure that this is about the time of his death because of the estate records of Isaac Callaway that left me confused as well in and about this time because Mary Polly Barrett and George W. and others shows up in Isaac Callaway and his wife Winnifred Ragan Callaway estate records. Maybe Henry Pope didn't want anything else to do with deception. Or It was Mrs. Polly time to make sure her children had a part in their fathers estate as well! I am just assuming this family and friends! She was living alone at this time before her death. Mrs. Winnifred was between the ages of sixty and seventy. However, Mrs. Winnifred might not be traveling alone at this time her slaves were with her. She had three male slaves under the age of ten, three male slaves between twenty-four and thirty-four, one male slave between thirty-six and fifty-five, and her female slaves were one under the age of ten, three between the age of ten and twenty-four, and one female slave between fifty five and one hundred years old. This cannot be Hannah her beloved and trusted servant from her father in 1813. The neighbors at this time in Mrs. Winnifred's life in Lee County, Georgia, were Saluda B. Mercer, the wife of Jesse Mercer, Robert C. Gibson, James V. Grier, John Ferrell, and Mrs. Winnifred Callaway's house. Then the house of John Goodbright, Armstead Hurst, Albert Gilbert, and Tena Sutton, Tom T. Thompson, Mr. E. E. Sanders, John F. Truett, Thomas Griffin, Wm. Griffin, Mr. Edward Jones or Janes, Joseph M. Roberts, and a few others not mentioned.

The Death of Winnifred Callaway in Greene County, Georgia

I wanted to show that Aaron and other slaves of Winnifred Callaway had already been divided among other families of the Callaways. I did not find Aaron nor Hannah on her estate or in her will. I assume that they stayed with the children Martha and Mary until the two children are come to govern themselves. The two daughters and the slaves that they own were mainly in the care of Henry Pope. Eventually all will come to know the Barrow family because of this relationship between Mr. Henry Pope. This section signifies that Winnifred and Isaac Callaway resided in Greene County and the Janes took over their estate in and near Bowling Green and Bairdstown in Oglethorpe County near the Greene County line.

I wonder if this is the same property that Joel Hurt bought from Luke J. and William A. Callaway for $275 in January 18, 1840. They sold him a tract or parcel of land situated on the water of Fishing Creek in the county of Greene. Beginning at a buckeye corner on said creek, thence due east seventeen chains and fifty links to a black-haw corner, thence south seventy-eight east, twelve chains and forty links to a stake, thence to a hickory corner on the old Academy line and bounded on the line by Mrs. Brockman and McWhorter's land, thence along said line to a hickory corner. These lines bounded on the north by McWhorter and said Hurt lands. Thence to a hickory corner on Fishing Creek at the ford, thence up the creek to the beginning buckeye corner containing one hundred acres more or less, etc.

Let us look at who might have had this land prior to Mr. Luke J. Callaway and William A. Callaway in 1840. *Luke J. Callaway is the son of Joseph H. Callaway and has close ties to Walton County and Joshua Callaway and Jesse Callaway in Whitfield County, Georgia.* I went further into investigating this section of town and found that Isaac Callaway in the grantees' book of Oglethorpe County, Georgia, might have had hold of this land. In the realty mortgages and deeds book, Isaac bought property from Mary and John Ramsey. Both sold Isaac Callaway 793 acres of land that was on the Sills Fork Creek, not too far from Little River on the twentieth day of the eleventh month of 1807. I say this, for another child of Winnifred Callaway and Isaac Callaway bought property here as well, Mr. Felix Callaway! Felix bought property from his brother-in-law Absolon Janes, the son-in-law of Winnifred and Isaac Callaway. This was on the twenty-eighth day of the seventh month of 1830.

It was in the eleventh day of the ninth month of 1830 that Felix Callaway bought land from John Rupert. The land that he purchased from Absolon Janes was 3/7 of 98 acres and 118 acres on Sills Fork Creek of Little River. This is not too far from the property of D.C. Barrow Place. It is also in the Bowling Green district and not too far from Woodstock of the county. Felix Callaway also bought property from Acrel Moody on the second day of the fourth month of 1832. It consisted of 700 acres on the fork of Little River. And James M. Callaway bought from Felix Callaway on fourteenth day of the ninth month of 1832 on Fork Little River 800 acres of land. You can see where the Moody

Cemetery is located on the cemetery map of the county of Oglethorpe just east of Maxey at the end of Center Church Road, just east of the North Fork of Little River. In fact, it is between Raiden Creek and North Fork of Little River.

Hannah, the mother of Aaron, Oliver, and Manda, was last seen on the property of Purnell Truitt. Hannah had had two or three more children later on. This signifies that Hannah was in her late thirties or early forties. By the time of the death of Mrs. Winnifred, Hannah had one child left to care for. The rest were all sent off in different directions. At one time I also noticed that Mrs. Winnifred had up to thirty-four slaves. By the time of her death in 1842, she was left with eight or less. The slaves is in the hands of Mr. Absolon Janes because Mr. Henry Pope was dead by this time. Mr. Absolon Janes is now in Greene County after migrating from Taliaferro. Mrs. Winnifred was located in several locations after the supposed death of her husband Isaac. I found her in Clarke County, Lee County, and mostly in Greene County, where she is buried.

Mr. Absolon Janes and what is the relationship he and his family have with Job Callaway and his estate and the estate of Isaac and Job Callaway Jr in Taliaferro County Georgia. The Janes family of Taliaferro, what can I say the Janes have a long relationship with Job Callaway Senior side of the Callaway family. The two families have ties to Job Callaway in Taliaferro County Georgia and the settling of his estate there. Edward Janes Robert C. Gibson, and Thomas G. Janes are witnesses over the estate of Job Callaway Jr. in 1827. Mr. Job Callaway Jr. dies and is buried in Alabama. However, he has property both real estate and personal property in Taliaferro. When I read this will of Job Callaway the only Job that I knew about died about this time in Alabama and his family has ties to Janes in Taliaferro. The courts in Taliaferro county handle his estate at this time. However in Alabama I found the estate of Job Callaway who dies about this same time in 1827. Job Callaway Jr. is the brother of Isaac Callaway the husband of Winnifred Ragan. Job Callaway Jr. married Rebecca Ragan. Job Callaway junior children are Milinda, Jeptha, Jesse. Amasa, Samuel, Matilda, Milton, Alford, and Ebenezer. I know that I have mentioned this before. However, I want to go a little bit deeper into the family of Job junior and his wife Rebecca Ragan Callaway. I'll start in 1850 when I can truly say Rebecca Ragan is still alive and doing well. She's in Sumter County Alabama with her forty year old son Milton and Caroline his wife at thirty six years old. Caroline was born in South Carolina and named her oldest daughter Rebecca A. who is thirteen at this time and Sarah E. is nine, Olivia C. is seven, Anne E. is four and even young Mr. M. Augustus a two year old all are born in Alabama and she has now been a widow for twenty three years. Mrs. Rebecca is seventy nine years old. I was so glad to get so much clarity at this point of the welfare and the use of their Slaves and finding Mrs. Rebecca now I can thank God for long-Gevity. I am sure when Mrs. Winnifred visited her sister and the family of Isaac Callaway her husband, their slaves that were in her care after the death of her husband Isaac followed her on such long journeys to Sumter and Greene County Alabama to visit their children and their mothers and fathers that they longed to see. And Now I can see why Hannah would make her way to Alabama now, and I can say what a find! In 1840 in Greene County, I wanted to see was Rebecca living with her son. I found that Milton is the head of the house hold and he had one white male under the age of five, one white male between twenty and twenty nine, one white female under the age of five, and one white female between twenty and twenty nine and Rebecca was still living with her son Milton and was between the ages of sixty and seventy years old. Alford Callaway the brother of Milton had a few names that were very interesting to me. They were Mary Williams, Wm. Williams and nearby. I mentioned their names because of the company that Aaron was in on the steamboat leaving Virginia toward Louisiana.

Milton had nine slaves six in the field and three to see to the needs of the house and his aged mother Rebecca. The year is now 1860 and Milton M. Callaway is living in Whorton Texas with fifty eight year old Lem Callaway a planter born in Georgia. L. L. a twenty year old male and M. S. an eighteen year old female and S. F. a fifteen year old female, C.A. an eleven year old, W. A. a nine year old female. M. M. Callaway the head of his house is now twenty nine year old planter from Alabama and his wife is twenty one years old with the initials M. S. born in Louisiana. Now, S. D. Callaway is a female planter from Alabama, with her children E. Thomas an eleven year old boy, born in Texas and Anna a six year old girl also born in Texas. This tells me that this might be the reason for Milton making a voyage from Louisiana on the twentieth day of December 1856 with John Watson a thirty year old slave, and from the looks of his family. Meaning, Eleanor his thirty year old wife and their children Maranda ten, Laura eight, Eliza six, Jane four, and John Henry a one year old boy. Now, Hannah Callaway of Tuskegee, Alabama 1870 on the second day of August. Hannah is sixty years old and is living with York Callaway who I believe is her son at the age of twenty one and a young man name Clark Callaway at the age of twenty five. York and Hannah were both born in Georgia and Clark was born in Alabama. Now if both young men are her sons then it shows what type of life Hannah was living! And if she was living it with Aaron tells me that the old boy, was visiting Hannah at one time or another in Alabama. This is an assumption! Or Hannah was the one in travel mode and having her children in two different states. However, this shows me that both young men were born in the 1850's about the time Aaron was in transition. The name York Callaway in Georgia shows up in the southern part of the state. First in Randolph County in April 18, 1867 in the 11th district, I found another York Callaway in Middlebrook Georgia in Fayette County in 1870 working for J. M. Chambliss alone with York were Julius Clarke and Green Clarke two colored men working down the road on W. M. Clark plantation. The last time I find York in Georgia was in Bibb County in 1870 on the 11th day of July. Now, York in the house with Hannah was twenty one on the 2nd day of August of 1870. York of Bibb County in 1870 has a family. His wife Martha was twenty, Cary his son was four, and James was two. Living in the house was fifty year old Harriet Huckeby and seven year old Edie Huckeby. Now, the strange thing that has a tie to Alabama is thirty six year old Jerry Sander and forty five year old wife Caroline and their children, Allen P, William J., Mary J., Nancy E., Thomas J., and Eleanor, Frank and Jane. I mentioned Mr. Sanders who more than likely have York on his plantation being so close, I mentioned him because of Sanders in Alabama over the estate of Job Callaway junior. Oh! the ties that bind? Now, Hannah was in Macon Alabama as early as 1870. I have another white family that ties Hannah and he has a familiar last name that fits in the mystery of Aaron and Hannah. His name is Dr. Chandler Mercer Pope. The son of Henry Pope and Urania Callaway. In 1850, Urania Pope is living in Athens Clarke County in the 216th district alone. Now this is the mystery concerning these men. Henry Pope is listed in the census in 1840 in the same district that Urania Callaway Pope in 1850. However, Henry Pope is settling his estate in 1837 which is in two counties of Bibb County and Monroe County Georgia and again he supposedly dies in Lee County. In Athens Clarke County Urania could be on the property that her mother Winnifred was living on in 1830. Urania was listed as fifty, William H. Pope was twenty eight, Mary J. was seventeen, Chandler M. was sixteen, Sarah was fourteen, Celestia Pope was at the tender age of eleven. While Dr. Chandler M. Pope was starting his practice in Alabama in 1860, his mother whom I had a hard time locating in 1860 I believe was under the name of Sarah K. Pope at the age of sixty four years old. Her son William H. Pope was in Jasper County about this time. Now Hannah residing in Macon Alabama is not by chance. Hannah neighbors are Charles Hugely a twenty five year old born in Georgia and his wife Carrie who was twenty and was born in Alabama with their daughter Cettie at the age of one years old. And another neighbor is Mike Pinkard a fifty year old colored man from Georgia and his wife Rebecca who is thirty four, John is eighteen, Stephen is six, Mike is three and Robert who is three months old. Another colored family from Georgia is Alexander Goode a fifty year old came with his wife Eliza at the age of forty five with their children Ameas thirty, Malinda twenty, Mary four and John who is two years old. A few more heads of families from Georgia were Levi Holland, Jeff Johnson, William Hugely twenty, Nett Hugely twenty two, Georgiana is two. The Hugley family were neighbors of Rev. Enoch Callaway in Wilkes County in 1850 and married into Dora McKinney family of Buckhead. The tie to Rev. Enoch Callaway was very significant. Mr. Jake Dyer, Edmond Barrow, a forty seven year old from Georgia, and his forty nine year old wife Kay, and John their sixteen year old son and Wallace at the age of thirteen, Robert is six, and Susan is a baby at one years old. I must mention the next families that relocated from Georgia and they are the Stafford families that were in Macon Alabama at this time. Anna L. Stafford is fifty six, and is white, Anna is thirty two, Clara is thirty, Dana is twenty two, Lon is nineteen, William is seventeen, Thomas B. is thirteen, and a young boy by the name of Robert Boykins at the age of three years old and Alafa an eighty five year mother from Georgia is here as well. Lewis Callaway a forty five year old black laborer from Georgia is with his forty year old wife Martha and sixteen year old daughter Amelia, and twelve year old daughter Mary, ten year old daughter Susan, eight year old Sue, six year old Sarah, four year old son Mac, and two month old son Bob. Living next door is two sixty year old husband and wife, Matt and Oney Pinkard. And thirty one year old John Pinkard and his wife Caroline twenty nine and Jane nine, Lucy seven, John four, and Mary is two. Harry Barrow is forty six, and his wife Judy is forty, Angeline is fourteen, and July is twelve. Even Dr. William H. Crawford the physician at the age of thirty six married his wife M. a twenty six year old Alabamian. Another white man and family is Mr. A. C. Barrow a Baptist minister from Georgia at the age of twenty seven. As you can see, Macon Alabama in 1870, Hannah Callaway a slave from Georgia must have felt at home with all of the men and women from Georgia residing in Alabama, especially Dr. Chandler M. Pope and Lewis Callaway! Now, I am going to spin this so you may understand why I am assuming this next statement. It's the family of William Bunkley a forty year old Georgia man from Georgia and his wife Mariah twenty five and young daughter Francis at the age of eight, Alice is five, William is three and Hester is one. Francis Bunkley the eight years old daughter of Williams shows up the house of W. T. Burton and his family with Isaac Callaway at the age of eighteen years old in 1880 in Greene County Georgia. This is the same family Bob Callaway or Robert C. Callaway is working for. The Bunkley family has one more tie and that is the marriage of Vina Bunkley and Claiborne Callaway in 1885. The mystery still eludes me! However, there is still a little light that breaks through yonder sky. It being on five years after the Civil War or as the Southern Kinfolks say's "The War Between the States for there was nothing civil about that war."

The Pinkard family that is living near Hannah Callaway my interest peaked when I found that the last name that is located near her at this time I have seen before during my research. It was in the family of Edward Callaway who I found on a cemetery search. Edward Callaway was born December 27, 1781 and died June 11, 1857. His wife was named Sarah Spratlin Callaway Pinkard. Sarah was born June 30, 1807 and died June 14, 1878. I think that they had a daughter by the name of Sarah as well. They are both buried in the Tuskegee City Cemetery in Macon County Alabama. During my physical paper work at the State of Georgia Archives when it was located in Atlanta on Capital Avenue. When I was in the estate record of Isaac Callaway, Edward Callaway was one of the first to appear on the estate of Isaac Callaway in 1820. The only other time I found Edward he was living in Monroe County Georgia, now I know why the church at Sardis was asking Joseph Henderson Jr. to inquire of Aaron between 1816 and 1825. It is Edward Callaway and his relationship between himself and the Henderson family and why Aaron and Oliver in 1837 about the time Henry Pope death is last recorded as being on the plantation of Seaborn Callaway. Edward I found in the Sons of the American Revolutionary records. Edward William Callaway was mentioned in the statements of William Ewing Cooper junior. Mr. Cooper is the great fourth grandson of Edward William Callaway and his wife Elizabeth Spratlin and the great fifth grandson of Joshua Callaway and Isabella Delphia Lea, and the next statement that he made was about Mr. Joseph Henderson who served in Capt. John Ashby's third Virginia Reg. during 1777. And he is the father of Isabella Graves Henderson who married Joshua Callaway, and Delphy Henderson who married Richard Peteet, and who had a daughter who married Seaborn Callaway. And Joseph Henderson junior who married first Margaret Reynolds, second Helen D. Dearing and third Hannah Shaw. These are the ties of Old 1805 Aaron Callaway and why the church at Sardis is asking brother Joseph Henderson how Aaron wellbeing is. Old 1825 Aaron of Greene County has a tie with Monroe County and that is

Peter Callaway as you can see that old Aaron of 1805 is well entrenched on the side of Edward William Callaway. Now Hannah is on the plantation of Isaac Callaway the son of Job and it's because of the wife of Isaac Callaway, Winnifred slave, that Aaron might have met the young lady Hannah. This is why old Aaron is not mentioned as a slave on John Callaway place nor is he mentioned on Job Callaway's place as well. I could not find the will of old Joshua S. Callaway or maybe he died after slavery. Now, Hannah has a son by the name of York at the age of twenty one and twenty five year old Clarke and a neighbor whose last name ties them with Edward William Callaway and his daughter Sarah Spratlin Callaway Pincard. I must mention the son that ties Aaron Callaway in Greene County to Hannah Callaway in Tuskegee Alabama. His name is Jesse Mercer Callaway lived in Monroe County Georgia where Peter Callaway who came to visit Aaron and left his son Wash Calloway in Jackson County Georgia who married a lady name Emma Watson. I have another name that ties Hannah to this side of the family that she is living with in 1880. It is the Hugely family. In 1880 in Tuskegee Alabama Hannah is still sixty years old the same age as she was in 1870. Hannah is living with forty year old Jack Hugely and his twenty eight year old wife Cealy and Jacks niece name Sarah Hugley. I am assuming that Cealy might be her daughter. I saw the last name of Hugely a few years back when I first started my research. It was as if they were two men on the will of Hellen Dearing Henderson in Wilkes County. They were John Hugely and Ransom W. Hugely. I know you may think that I am grasping at the wind. But that's the way my mind reason. The day I started to put the pieces together and the answer that I waited for since I started writing who is the Master of 1805 Aaron at Sardis Baptist Church. They never mentioned him as being the slave of anyone at that time. So I assumed that he might have been a Free Black Man! I believe that Jesse Mercer Callaway was the slave master of Peter Callaway. G. W. Chambless is the son of Arena Callaway Chambless the daughter of Edward and Elizabeth Spatlin Callaway Arena Callaway married Joel Chambless. Joel is thirty one years old and is living with J. E. Stevens a twenty two year old young man. Now let me get to the point of this relationship between 1805 Aaron and the man that was asked to inquire about his wellbeing. Mr. Joseph Henderson and his tie to the Callaway's I finally figured a part of the mystery to this old man named Aaron! Remember Isabella Henderson, she married Joshua Callaway and they are the father and mother of Edward William Callaway who was living in Wilkes County in 1820 before moving to Monroe County Georgia near Jonathan and Josiah Callaway. Now when I go back to Monroe County

1830 guess who I find Mr. John Chambless (spelled Chamness) living a few house and on the same page as his father-in-law and living right next door to Mr. Edward William Callaway is Mr. William Henderson, and living a few houses away is Mr. William Pinkard. The year is 1850 and William Callaway is still living in Monroe County Georgia at the age of sixty four years old, his wife Sarah is fifty six years old, Livica Edwards is a sixty seven year old woman living with William and Sarah Callaway in the 559th district of Monroe County Georgia at this time. Living in the same house is forty seven year Ann Callaway. However, there is a name that just does not elude me and that is the last name Hugely. Living right next door is twenty eight year old Mason Hugely and his twenty eight year old wife Henrietta and their children, William, Catherine, Mary Ann, Elizabeth, Susan H, and Zachariah the youngest. William Callaway was born in Maryland and had close ties still with that northern state. Holly Grove Primitive Baptist Church Association some great stories grew out of tradition take note. The minority is recorded as Edward Callaway and wife, Johnathan Collins and wife, Francis Colbert, A. D. Steele, W. M. Clark, J. W. J. Taylor, Gilbert Clark, Mary E. Clark and Harriet Harmon. These are called Brother and Sisters from Mount Zion Forsyth (Georgia).

Also, Mr. Felix G. Callaway will is made out in Taliaferro County Georgia in 1836. With Susan S. Callaway and James Peek and Absalon Janes over his estate. James M. Callaway makes out his will in Taliaferro County as well on December 20, 1838. Malcolm Johnston, Sam Johnson, Isaac Moore and George Tilly are over his estate at this time. Both men are the sons of Isaac and Winnifred Callaway and grandchildren of Job Callaway Senior. Now, here's a reason that Mrs. Winnifred Callaway is in Lee County. Winnifred might be down there for the purpose of settling the estate of her slaves. At first I thought she might just be in Lee County because of her father's death. However, she might be in Lee County because of her slaves that were under the care of Henry Pope. Mr. Henry Pope married Urania Callaway the daughter of Isaac and Winnifred Callaway. I believe that Mr. Henry Pope died in 1838 in Lee County Georgia. However, I could never find any estate record on Mr. Henry Pope. However, I did notice something strange about the estate record of Master Isaac Callaway between 1834. Received of John P. Barrett and Mary Callaway executors of the estate of Isaac Callaway deceased the sum of two hundred and seventy nine dollars and twenty eight cents being my part of the estate given off this 15th day 1834. George W. Callaway, Lewis B. Callaway was on the first day of January in 1834, Humphrey Tomlison, William A. Callaway, James H. Callaway, Merrell P. Callaway, were all on the 12 day of December of 1834 they received from Isaac Callaway's estate with John P. Barrett and Mary Callaway as the executors. Now two supposedly different Isaac Callaway's having the same estate record. Now, in 1820 I found Mary Callaway in the 168th district living near John Barrett and Winnifred Callaway living near Mr. Henry Pope. However I only found one Isaac Callaway living in Wilkes County in 1820 and one living in Madison County Georgia. None of these two women were covered by Isaac who supposedly had died in 1820 or the one Isaac who died in 1822. This is the only will that I could find in Wilkes County on Isaac Callaway in 1823 with Polly as his wife or Mary which is her real name and one daughter by the name of Elizabeth R. Callaway his daughter who married Amasa her first cousin. Amasa is the son of Job Callaway Jr. who died in Alabama and is buried in Elmore Alabama. Mary Polly is his executrix and John Barrett and Josiah B. Holmes are his executors. The other children are never mentioned in his will in 1823. Now I have a question that needed to be answered. How does George W. Callaway and Lewis B. Callaway who are to be the children of Isaac Callaway and Mary Polly Barrett Callaway end up on the property that once was owned by Mrs. Winnifred and Job Callaway senior and his son Isaac in Greene County and Oglethorpe County? I came across the estate of James H. Callaway of Fulton County in Atlanta and what a great find! This find carried me over into Alabama as well. James H. Callaway is the son of Isaac Callaway and Mary Polly Barrett. He died June 1, 1876. The executor of his estate was W. O. Tuggle the lawyer out of Troup County Georgia. This is the same man that had dealing with colored man Charley Callaway and the railroad as far as leasing property for Charley. I will start at the forth Item of business in Fulton County in Atlanta. It is with Hattie the daughter of William A. Callaway, she received one thousand dollars, the same as Louisa Carlton now Rochelle. He gave or left W. O. Tuggle land in Troup County known as "Wilkerson-Holderness Place". It was about eight hundred and forty acres. He left the niece of his wife Sarah Eades Goolsby the wife of Isaac Goolsby all received money. John Callaway the nephew of James H. Callaway's brother George Callaway the balance of his estate which is divided among the other nieces and nephews of the Goolsby's. The executor is to include the following person's two children of his brother George Callaway to wit; (1) his son William and his youngest daughter named Lucy, and also John, the son of his brother George. (2) each of the children of his brother William A. Callaway to wit; Hattie who has already received one thousand dollars in addition to her father share, the following children of his brother; Lewis, "Mit", Francis, Lewis is to also be included,

(4) includes the children of his brother Merrell P. Callaway, (5) includes the children of his sister Lucy Tomlinson, the share of Joseph Tomlinson, (6) includes the children of his sister Harriett Low, Newell her son is to receive one note share of three thousand dollars already given to him. (7) includes and goes to his sister Eliza children, Isaac's share to go to his child. John T. Cooper was the clerk of courts in Fulton County in Atlanta. And W. O. Tuggle signed his name alone with David Pittman as well. This was on October 17, 1876. However, in November in Bullock County Alabama on November 13, 1876, appeared in court before the Probate Court William O. Tuggle the copy of the will of James H. Callaway of Fulton County Georgia. And to the satisfaction of the court, Mr. Tuggle was given a bond in the sum of ten thousand dollars as the executor over his estate in Alabama. Fleming Law, W.O. Baldwin, William Youngblood, as his (unreadable). Fleming Law was the attorney for Mr. W. O. Tuggle. W. O. Tuggle wrote a letter to honorable Judge of the Probate court of Bullock Co. Ala. And state that James H. Callaway died June 18th of 1876 appointing his as his executor of his estate. Warrant to Appraisers document that was made on the 13th day of November by Judge Black in Union Spring in Bullock Co. Ala. listed that James had six mules and one horse and farm utensils totaling $540.24. R. G. Wright, S. T. Frasier and N. H. Frasier and Lewis Session bought seven hundred and forty six acres from Tuggle in the Township 13 range 22 the sum being $5.37 ½ an acre. Making the sum come to be at $4,900. 76ct. Here's a few names that are on James H. Callaway's estate in Bullock Alabama. T.J. Kennedy a Peace Officer on March 2, 1876. These are the legacies that are entitled to the estate of James H. Callaway to wit; Mary A. Brown at Hampton State of Ga., William Lowe at Atlanta Ga., Mrs. Sarah Zachary of Conyers Ga., Lucy Johnson of Stephens Ga. in Oglethorpe Co. Ga., Harriet Sims of Washington Ga., Martha Low of Hampton Ga., John Low of Hampton Ga., Merrell C. Low a minor about 20 years old of Atlanta Ga. Merrell Calloway of Americus Ga., Henry J. Calloway of Albany Ga., James Callaway of Camilla Ga. J. Tucker of Albany Ga., John Callaway of Austin Tex., J. M. Callaway of West Point Ga., Mary Davis a married woman, Eufaula Ala., T. M. Callaway of Murry Co. Ga., S. P. Callaway of West Point Ga. ("here I thought this might be Stewart B. Callaway of Atlanta Georgia living as a black man married to Annie V. Smith Callaway"). W. A. Callaway of West Point Ga., Hattie Calloway of West Point, Abbie Callaway of Atlanta Ga., Edward H. Calloway of Galveston Tex. F. Callaway a minor about 19 years old, said Edward H. F. Callaway children of H. V. Callaway to one share, Charles M. Callaway of Austin Tex. Lula

Trayham of Austin Tex. M. Griffin of San Marco Tex. F. N. Douglass of San Marco Tex., and Dawson Calloway, Benjamin Callaway, Selina Callaway, Orr Callaway minor children of W. D. Calloway and Whoseagers not known. William Calloway of Stephens Ga., Lucy Weatherly, of Athens Ga., John D. E. Calloway a minor about 17 years old of Lake City Fla., Mrs. E. Dorsey of Jonesboro Ga., C. Abbie Milner of Jonesboro Ga., R. H. Tomlinson of McDonough Ga., and Joshua Tomlinson, Loyd Tomlinson, Eugenia Tomlinson & Jarvus Tomlinson minor children of J. P. Tomlinson ages unknown with their father at McDonough Ga., Annie Calloway a minor about 17 years old of Griffin Ga., Mrs. M. Varner of McDonough Ga., Lucy Knott, of McDonough Ga., G. W. Calloway of Ala. Virginia Goolsby, Isaac L. Goolsby, James C. Goolsby & Sarah E. Goolsby minors over 14 years of age, Clarance W. Goolsby, Ellen B. Goolsby, & Wm. L. Goolsby minors under 14 years of age all of Washington Ga. in Wilkes County. Upson L. Goolsby, of Washington Ga., Mary E. Goolsby, of Washington Ga., Thomas C. Burch, Elberton Ga., James J. Burch of Elberton Ga., John Durham and Hattie Durham, ages unknown of Shreve Port La., Mrs. Lou Rochelle of Keechi La. Mrs. Mary Rebecca Rogers of Centre Tex. William W. Carlton of Shreve Port La., Henry Carlton, Edwin Carlton, ages unknown, of Shreve Port La.

At the end of his estate record, the recorder listed the families and how they are related to James H. Callaway. Harriett Law his sister and her husband John W. Law, and their son Merrill Law, William Callaway his brother and his daughter Hattie Calloway his niece, H. V. Callaway of Atlanta his brother and his son Edward Calloway and his daughter Fannie Calloway, W. D. Calloway his brother and his children Selma Calloway his niece and his nephew Orr Calloway, George Calloway his brother and his children, John Calloway, William Calloway, Lucy Calloway Weatherly. This is George W. Callaway of Oglethorpe County Georgia. Henry J. Calloway brother, Lewis Calloway brother and children, Francis Calloway his nephew, Mel Calloway nephew and William Callaway his nephew. Sarah E. Goolsby is the niece of his wife, Isaac Goolsby her husband and their children. Virginia, James C., Sarah, Clarence, Ellen B., Wm. L., Upson and Mary E. Goolsby. Merrill P. Calloway brother, Lucy Tomlinsen sister and her children; R. H., Joshua, Lloyd, Eugenia, Eliza his sister, Henry Carlton, Louisa Carlton Rochelle wife's niece. I wanted to go back and look at the names mention on Isaac Callaway's estate when Mary "Polly" Barrett is over his estate in Georgia. Now, the question that I have is that if the husband of Mary Polly Barrett dies in 1822, how can

James H. Callaway have brothers and sister after his death? And again I say that Isaac Callaway the husband of Winnifred Ragan has one more woman in his marriage and she is Mary Polly Barrett. Take another look at his estate record when his wife Mary Polly Barrett takes over. Received of John P. Barrett and Mary Callaway executors of the estate of Isaac Callaway deceased the sum of two hundred and seventy nine dollars and twenty eight cents being my part of the estate given off this 15th day 1834. George W. Callaway, Lewis B. Callaway was on the first day of January in 1834, Humphrey Tomlison, William A. Callaway, James H. Callaway, Merrell P. Callaway, were all on the 12 day of December of 1834 they received from Isaac Callaway's estate with John P. Barrett and Mary Callaway as the executors. The other question what is the secrets that has to be kept between Georgia and Alabama? Is it that Isaac Callaway himself? James H. Callaway resided in the second ward in Atlanta in 1870. He's fifty eight years old, and his wife S. D. is fifty seven. James is a retired merchant $50,000 dollars is the value of his real estate and the value of his personal estate is $3,000 dollars the both of them were born in Georgia. James H. Callaway was located and registered in precinct number four of the election district of 1026 on the 29th day of July of 1867.

H. V. Callaway was living in Lee County in Palmyra between 1866 and 1867 with Nick Callaway working for him. H. V. Callaway was in the same district as Robert and W. E. Ragan. H. V. Callaway took his oath in Lee County alone with Colored man Jesse Callaway (spelled Calaway). There is a last name that has a tie with Charlie and Mary in Terrell County is the Davis family. Joshua Davis, M. C. Davis, Vincent Davis, Cass Davis, Robert Davis, Daniel Davis, and Andrew Davis. All the Davis family was black. William A. Callaway died in Troup County Georgia where Isaac and Winnifred Callaway owned property there and Henry Pope handle his estate there before he died. William Anderson Callaway first wife was Martha Pope the daughter of John Pope and Eliza Smith, their children were John Isaac Callaway, Rev. Jesse Mercer Callaway of McDonough, Mary Elizabeth Callaway of McDonough Ga., George Wiley Callaway of McDonough, Henry Varner Callaway of McDonough, Andrew Fuller Callaway of McDonough, Thomas Merrell Callaway of McDonough, Samuel Pope Callaway of McDonough, Martha Abigail Callaway and William Anderson Callaway of Troup Co., Harriet Eliza Callaway of Troup Co. Ga. she is mention in James H. Callaway estate and will. Rough and Ready Callaway of Troup Co. Ga. I am now sure that the families of Isaac Callaway and Winnifred Ragan Callaway and Mary Polly Barrett might know about Aaron of 1805 and the slave of Rev. Joshua S. Callaway and the children of negro slave Hannah the slave of Winnifred. Maybe someone will inform me after the publication of this mystery.

HENRY POPE DIES, ABSOLON JANES IN CONTROL OF CALLAWAY'S ESTATE!

Mr. Absolon Janes is now in total control of Winnifred Callaway's estate after the death of Mr. Henry Pope.

Where can I start first? I wondered what Absolon Janes wanted with his subscription with Benjamin F. DeBorn esquire –of New Orleans in Louisiana he was the publisher of the Commercial Revier. Mr. Herman Lucas was the notary public witnessing of the account from July 1846 to July 1847. Could this be the reason I find old Aaron Callaway in Louisiana in New Orleans. Is this 1805 Aaron was on the ship with the slave trader John Hagan and Thomas Bourdar of Virginia who was at this time was living in the third ward of New Orleans.

Penfield Ga. August 3rd 1847 Col. A. Janes. Please pay to the Executive Committee of the Georgia Baptist Convention the sum of one hundred and twenty nine dollars for value received by us in part for tomb stones. Atkinson& Tate and Roberts.

On and before the last of December next I promise to pay Malcomb Johnston the sum of three hundred and sixty dollars as a donation together with other funds in his hands, to be invested in a Negro woman which he is to secure to his Sarah Ann Janes and family wife of Archibald G. Janes my brother Penfield September 1st 1847. Absolon Janes. November 28th 1847, Absolon Janes To the building committee for the Coloured Church. To his subscription for building church for the benefit of the coloured People in the town of Penfield $50.00 Georgia, Greene County. In person appeard before me Lemuel Green (One of the Committee appointed by the Baptist Church in Penfield) for building a church in said for the benefit of the beloved People, that Absolon Janes Subscribed the account stated in above account with his own proper hand, and this deponent saith upon oath that the above account as it stands stated just and true. Sworn to before me this 29th of November 1847. James M. Porter Justice of the Peace. Lemuel Green.

Now, there are two ties to the Williams family that are in A. Janes estate.

Absolon Janes to Jeremiah Nichols for building wall around Graveyard eight Graves and building Chimney in Penfield $159.00 Dec. 21, 1847. Paid Anderson Williams for services of overseer, for the year of 1847 with interest from the first of January last. June 13, 1848. James Sanders

Rec. Atlanta August 2nd 1848 of the Executive of Absolon Janes deceased by the hand of B. M. Sanders, ten dollars the amount of his Pledge for Building Baptist meeting in Atlanta. D. G. Daniel Agt. Exec. Com. G. B. C.

Rec. of Absolon Janes J. R. Sanders and T. P. Janes 75 shares of Georgia Rail Road Stock it being the legacy left R. L. McWhorter Sr. of the said Absolon Janes in his last Will and Testament February 9th 1848. R. L. McWhorter Sr. guardian for child. Just two days ago James R. Sanders the executor of Col. Absolon Janes decd. Received two dollars and fifty cents for recording sale of A. Janes and Mrs. Winnifred Callaway decd. Of which estate Col. Janes was the executor. Feb. 7, 1848. John Hackney says the account stands stated is just and true April 14 1849 James D. Williams Justice of the Peace attested by Samuel Eley, the last name being the last name of Crawford Hurts grandmother.

Personally appeared before me R. H. Watts a justice of the peace. H. L. French the son-in-law of Joel Hurt remember arriving on the 19th day of November of 1849 Absolon estate to John Griffith September 1848 John C. Holtzclaw surveyor of A. Janes land for January 8th and February 14 and January 1 of 1849 William A. Wilson fixed the front porch of the dwelling house of A. Janes on November 28, 1849. I walked this property after Mr. Boswell invited me and my wife Sheila into their house and then drove me around and showed me where the graves of Thomas P. Janes and his wife were located the year was in or around about 2007 and he showed me the property that they owned as well. It wasn't far from Mr. Wilson property who was living just across the street from the Hurt and Callaway house. I was very much overwhelmed were I was standing and I realized I was standing on the same land where more-than-likely my great-great-great-grandparents once stood and was worked from sun up to son down as slaves. I cried because, there on the Janes property I got to see what my ancestors saw. I can't tell you much on how they lived. But one of the stories that Mr. Price told me that they worked very hard and where ever they fell dead and died that's where they buried them! I walked those woods until the sun had gone down and I was afraid because many times I got disoriented and had to stop and just gather myself. I can imagine getting lost while trying to run away from the harsh conditions here as slaves when the darkness was upon you, it can be very frightening and very overwhelming. On one occasion I had been chased by a young angry bull after stumbling and crossing his path. I tore my good shirt trying to make my escape across the old barb wire while trying to crawl under. It was exhilarating and frightening hearing the sound of his hoofs and bellowing and the ground trembling under my feet as I was trying to survey my escape!

February 8, 1849, received of T. P. Janes twenty dollars to see negro girl receiving fracture of arm and thigh and attention to care. Thomas P. Janes is now in charge of the Negro Property of Isaac Callaway and Winnifred. It has now been twenty nine years since the death of Isaac and only a few years since his wife Winnifred had passed away. In July on the 16 day of 1849 John Hackney was paid four dollars and thirty eight cents

For work on the saw mill. Samuel Eley attested to it. Albert King was paid for being an overseer and Jack the slave of Mrs. Lucy Lumpkin was paid for the hire of Jack digging the a well in September of 1855. I got ahead of myself again. I have to mention Holly Spring Mississippi on April the second of 1849. Absolon Janes the executor of Winnifred Callaway's estate. It mentioned that William B. Lumpkin and Olin Lumpkin and Mary Ann Lumpkin in Winnifred Callaway's estate in Holly Springs Mississippi. The Lumpkin family is established with Job Callaway buying land from Pilmon Lumpkin in 1796 in Oglethorpe County. I did find another Callaway on Mr. Janes estate named Dr. R. S. Callaway of the firm of Callaway and Cheney. I believe the Cheney mentioned in the firm is Dr. Franklin W. Cheney. This visit by Dr. Reuben S. Callaway was on the twenty first day of March of 1848. Now I know that Mr. Henry Pope is dead by 1848. Because on the first of March 1848 Urania Pope received of Thomas P. Janes and James R. Sanders the exec. Of the estate of Absolon Janes decd. who was the executor of the estate of Winnifred Callaway decd. Eight hundred and seventy nine dollars and forty nine cents it being a part of her legacy from said estate this the first of March 1848. If Mr. Henry Pope was still alive, he would be representing his wife Urania. James R. Sanders paid six dollars and sixty one cents for freight on tomb stones from Marietta Ga. to Woodville on October 25, 1847. In the same year he sells lot of land in Crawfordville and H. l. French the son-in-law of Joel Hurt shows up again for a note of two hundred and thirty one dollars and thirteen cents owed to him for sell of cotton on February third 1855. Hiram L. French lives in south Georgia now with his brother and his young bride or does he? If Hiram French is in Greene County with the Janes his young slave Dinah is still on Mr. Hurts place. Received of T. P. Janes exec. Of A. Janes for the two minors heirs of said deceased five dollars for taking up negro man Charles this 12th day of July 1856. Now let's get to the sell or the dividing of the Slaves! To Mary E. Janes Slaves one negro boy Jack, Sophy, Judy, Katy, one old negro woman Nelly. Nelly being the mother of Ned and Mahala Parks. To Felix W. Janes, Susan H. Janes, and Cordelia F. Janes; negro Randle, Lile, Ausborn, Charles, Hannah, Sarah, Riley, Delia, Betsy, Jesse, MillerTom, Sally Lydia, Lewis, Rhody, Big Charles, Eli, Cherry, Little Henry, Peter, Levi, Lucy and child, Easter, Raney, Famous, Rachel, Charles, Anna, Sophronia, Nathan, Dice, Maria, Stephen, Rose, George, Sam, Jane, Delphy, Almyra, Bob, Mark, Adam, Hixy, Caroline, Child, Sarah, Joe, Adah, Willis, Edmond, and old Lizzie. To. Cornelia M. Sanders slaves as follows one negro man Ace, Mariam, one negro boy Abe and old Ritter. To Thomas P. Janes as follows; Henry, Barbara, Lewis, Eliza, Caroline and child, Primas, old Mose at minus one hundred dollars.

Cordelia F. Janes lot was number three continued; Liddy and two children, Polly and Sally, Levi, Ada, Jane and two children Sam and Creacy, Elmira and child Primus, Mariah and child Thornton, Joshua, Hixy and child Charlotte. Here I am going to surmise that Hixy is the wife of Jesse because the oldest daughter of Hixy is named Charlotte in 1870 in Penfield. Charlotte is eighteen years old. At the time of the making of this delivery of Slaves in 1860 Charlotte would be just seven years old. The rest of the slaves in lot three are Eli, Edmond, Randle, Charles, Rose, Easter, Lizzie and Same valued at minus on November 26, 1860. These are the slaves of Cordelia F. Janes daughter of Absolon Janes witnessed by William Tuggle, John G. Holtzclaw, Cordelia N. Daniels and Peter Northern.

In lot two Sarah Ann and child Thorn, Riley, Big Charles, Cherry, Mack, Raney, Ary, Anny, Sophronia, Famous, Peter, Adam, Slaves for Cordelia F. Janes and slaves Hanson, Jacob and Randle went to Cordelia F. Janes as well. Lot number one, Randle, Lite, Jesse, Hannah and three children to wit; Indiana, Sarah, Julia, Betsey, Henry, Rachel and her three children Sidney, Thornton, and Silas. Titus, Harriet and Susan, Bob, Miller Thomas, Thorn, Sally. I did get a few of the ages of these slaves that were in the care of Thomas P. Janes and James R. Sanders. Randle age fifty two, Lile forty two, Osborne nineteen, Charles 13, Charles is the same age as Charlie Callaway who marries Louisa in Green County in 1880 and moves down to Taliaferro County. I surmise this because where Charlie and Louisa moved to in 1880 and that is the same place where the Janes and Job Callaway owned property and that is in Taliaferro County Georgia. Back to the ages of the slaves of Absolon and Winnifred Callaway's slaves.

Hannah is fifteen, Sarah eleven, Riley ten, Delily, eight, Betsy six, Jesse three, now the only other Jesse this could be is the son of Hixey and Jesse Callaway and their daughter Charlotte and now their son young Jesse at the age of three years old. Miller Tom forty seven, Sally forty five, Lydia nineteen, Lewis seven, Rhody two, Big Charles forty two, Chery forty five, Ely fourteen, Little Henry four, Peter eighteen months, Levy twenty eight, Lucy and Tarlton twenty and three months, Easter four, Ramey thirty one, Famous fourteen, Racheal eleven, Big Charles seven, Anna five, Sophronie one, Sophy forty five, Jack fifteen, Judy nine, Katy seven, Sam fifty eight, Jane ten, Big Caroline and child twenty three and six months, Nancy twenty three, Joe thirty six, Adah forty, Nathan thirty one has a deformed hand. Dice twenty eight, Mariah ten, Delphy thirty five, Almyria ten, Adam thirty eight, Stephen forty three, Edmond thirty two, Willis twenty eight, and Mark at the age of twenty three.

Little Moses age is twenty one, Primus is thirty six, George is fifteen, Hixy is eleven, Bob is thirteen, Bob would have been born in 1847, I thought that he might be my Robert Callaway. However my Robert Callaway is still the same age as Aaron Callaway off the plantation of Rev. Enoch Callaway in 1859 and is now the property of Mr. William Owen Cheney in Bairdstown of Oglethorpe County. Back to the ages of a few of the slaves of Absolon Janes in 1860. Abe is thirteen, Ellick is twenty six, Lewis is twenty three, Patsy Caroline is sixteen, Eliza is twenty six, Sarah and her child Eliza is two, Barbary is fifty, Henry is twenty Abe is thirty one, Rose is seventeen, Mariam is eleven, Lizzy is seventy, Nelly is seventy and old Mose is fifty two, Ritter is sixty, witnesses are B. M. Sanders the preacher of the First Baptist Church in Atlanta and a donor of the Black Baptist Church Sanders Chapel in the old town of Penfield, Peter Northern, William Daniel and H. H. Watts are three more witnesses.

May 24, 1834, right after church at Sardis, Daniel Carrington came forward and made a number of false statements relating to the difficulties that had taken place between the Appling family and others. Together with deceptive drinking and using un-Christian language, which he acknowledged in some degree. But they took up some reports against him and said slander and un-Christian conduct are a part of his family and others. Deceptive drinking, denying it, threatening to shoot on condition a number of persons, striking his wife and denying it, pointing a gun at his wife and threatening to shoot. The church sent Joseph Henderson, R. Strozier, S. Callaway, James. J. H. Ragan, and William Brook to visit Daniel Carrington. *Now I believe that J. H. Ragan is the brother of Winnifred Ragan.*

The conference was in June 1834, Joseph Henderson, R. Strozier, S. Callaway, James J.H. Ragan, and William Brook stated to the church that two witnesses saw Carrington with certain Negroes and was drunk, so he was excluded from the church that same day. That same day, Seaborn Callaway reported his slave Sharon had left her husband and was with another man. Now let us look at two of these men that were sent to look into the allegations against Daniel Carrington. Joseph Henderson Jr. had property at this time in Walton County; Reuben Strozier was the son-in-law of John Callaway. Also in 1834, John Jarrell was accused of being drunk by T. Tuck and others at the conference. Now I believe that T. Tuck was a member of the Methodist Church that was located on Highway 78, or the "big road," as my grandmother called it. Mr. Tuck was one of the founding fathers of the Methodist church that was located just outside of the Callaway property going toward Oglethorpe County.

My wife Sheila and I went to Lee County again in my little red truck that was ready to break down at any time and did leave us stranded on the side of the road seeking assistance many times. We went to find any relationship that might tie Winnifred Callaway's slaves to the county. I found Mr. James H. Ragan. The slaves that he left his wife, L. A. Ragan. Abraham and his wife Fanny and their child were valued at $7000 dollars, as well as John Omer, and John Jule were both valued at 7000 dollars, all other Slaves that I am about to mention are all valued at 3000 to 4500 dollars. Lewis and Jule and child Nora, Hagar, Tim, Jeff, Aaron, Betsy, Clary and her infant child, Jane, George and John were both valued at 500 dollars. Jones and Josh were sold for 500 dollars as well. After these slaves of Mrs. Ragan were chosen by her the rest were sold off to Mary A. Long.

They were Seth and his wife and their infant children, sold for 8000 dollars, and so was Mark and his wife Susan, and their child Julia. Ira, Joe, Sarah and her child Louisa, Joshua, Artha, and Park, Harriett and her child, Big Mary and her child, these women and their children were sold for 7500 dollars. Green, Lucy, an old woman cost only 300 dollars. Henry and his wife Elvira and their three children went for 8000 dollars. Negro man Abram was forty-two years old and his wife Fanny was twenty. Old woman Viney was sixty-five years old. Lucy was fifty-five, Negro Seth was twenty-eight, his wife Mary was twenty, they had two children between them. Negro woman Mary was forty-twoand her son Green was one, Anthony was five, Negro girl Chany was nineteen, Harriet was twenty-two, with an infant child. Betsy was twenty, Haga was fourteen, July was forty-two, and her daughter Nora was about two years old. Henry was forty, Evlina was twenty-four. Their daughter Patrina was a mere five years old. Henry and Evlina son was named Anderson who was a little boy at the age of two. Milly was at the age of fifty-five. They considered Milly and John to be infirm.

I thought Hannah Callaway might be under the last name of Parks, However I found Hannah Parks living in Alabama with her son Albert. Hannah and Albert relocated soon after the death of Ned who had died June 1, 1870 at the age of eight four years old. His occupation was being a carpenter he built many caskets for the dying slaves. I know one in particular a slave of Mr. Henry English. Albert Parks is eighteen, Willis is ten, James is seven, Columbus is five, and Hannah is sixty, and Lucy is twenty-five, and all are living in the 163rd District of the county on the twenty-second day of October 1850. They are all living two houses down from Mr. Thomas P. Janes and Emily E. Fish Janes, his wife, and both are twenty-five years old. Their children are Emma, who is three; Fannie, who is two; and Poleman, who is six months old. If you are wondering what happened to Nellie the wife of Ned Parks she remained under the watchful eye of Thomas P. Janes while Hannah and Ned lived together as husband and wife. Back to the estate of Isaac Callaway.

Francis Callaway received from William South 150 acres on Clouds Creek. Francis is Rev. Francis, who moved to Giles, Tennessee, and then over into Alabama outside of Troup County, Georgia. Rev. Francis Callaway will preside over the Saparta Association as moderator, before moving to Tennessee. Saparta Association is the same Association that William Eberhart and J. R. Haynes are members of in the 1890s. Elie R. Callaway and Eli H. Callaway received from Elijah, John, Amy, Smithfield, and Sarah, all of their last names being Martin. They sold Eli Callaway in 1827 this property. So did William W. Edwards. All of this happens in Oglethorpe County. Eli did not live long after this. Before 1830 came, Eli would be dead. His wife Martha would be a widow. Eli owned property in Henry County, which became Fulton County. He followed his brothers. As a matter of fact, their children would buy and sell land that their fathers had bought and lived and work their Slaves while living nearby. These four brothers owned land in just about every county in the State of Georgia. In addition, just about every state in the country! Martha, after the death of Eli, would divide her time between Marthasville (Atlanta) and Oglethorpe County. Her two children, Thomas and young Martha, would live on this property before Thomas P. Callaway moved into the city of Lexington and young Martha moved to Atlanta, where Eli and his mother Martha are buried in Oakland Cemetery. They lived in the Third Ward near what is called Terry Street of southeast Atlanta that was called Summer Hill and

Peoples Town, where the majority of the colored Calloways or Callaways will come to reside at one time or another. One colored man and his son in particular was Robert Charles Callaway and the son of Robert Callaway of Clarke County, Mr. William A. Callaway alone with Indiana Callaway out of Fayetteville and her son Jesse.

In Aaron's words after his escapades at Sardis Church: "I might just be in Walton County on Masta Felix Henderson or Joshua S. Callaway's place, the two preachers, and Joshua S., the surveyor of Walton. We are all family. It was more than likely on Masta Felix's place in Walton County, because of the plantation that Masta Henderson had down there. In addition, Masta Joseph and his brother Simon Henderson had property in Smith, Elbert County, in 1820, and I could be up there staying on his plantation with him there with their brother Edward.

I must say that Aaron is hard to understand because of the favor he has at Sardis in 1816. And the reward of being a good black man as from what I was told and read that as long as you stayed out of trouble the plantation owner could keep you out of jail and you could have all the women and liquor you wanted! As long as you were the obedient Negro!

In 1830, in the 175th District, Masta Joseph Henderson had more widow women living near him than men. By 1831, Henry County was coming into its own. I would make my way to this county as well because this is where some of my family was relocated along with John Callaway and William J. Callaway and George W. Callaway. With the trade of cotton and other things they would send down the many rivers in Henry. Fulton and DeKalb County would come out of Henry County and that is why you can find some of the Callaway men and their family and friends living in Fulton and DeKalb counties. One of Aaron's family members, a sister named Juda, comes out of Henry County, now DeKalb, in Panthers Ville near John Callaway, where I found Martin Mathew Callaway residing With his family. Juda is living here she is forty five years old in 1870 in Panthersville, Georgia. William Callaway is four years old and Berry Callaway is listed in the house as being insane. In 1880 I cannot find her living in Panthersville. However, I do find Judea living in Puryears district in 1880 with her grandson Willie Howard. Judea is sixty years old and Willie Howard is ten, Gilbert Arnold is a boarder at the age of twelve and Fannie Grissom is at the age of two. Willie Howard will play a major part in the arrest of Charlie in 1899 as being a witness on J. R. Haynes complaint against Charlie for selling liquor and he will be living in the house of Aaron Callaway on the farm of William Eberhart as his son in 1900'd.

Now, I am in a conundrum about Aaron Callaway born in March of 1825 and is seventy three years old and living with his wife Harriet a young woman born in March 1862 who I believe in his daughter and the both of them states they have been married for five years and Willie Howard at the age of 22, born April 1878 and a grandson born May 1892 named Howard and a grandson name Willie born March 1894 is six years old. Their all located closer to Edward A. Carter place. Harriet states that she has had three children and one died. The grandchildren in the house of Harriet and Aaron are not the children of Mary and Charlie. If, Willie Howard is the grandson of Judea in Puryears in 1880 this would make Aaron Callaway born in 1825 the son of Judea. Now the question is this, who is this Aaron Callaway on the farm of William Eberhart near E. A. Carter place? Is it Aaron Cheney of 1870 who is thirty two years old, living with twenty six year old Letitia, and eleven year old Charley, and seven year old Cleveland and three year old Sis his daughter living near twenty one year old Fell Johnson and his companion Mose Cheney of Bowling Green? Or is he Aaron Callaway living as Green Callaway in Lincoln County in 1870, where he is thirty year old and Laura is forty years old and their daughter Euran is sixteen, Charles is twelve, Clayborn is nine, Jane A. is five and Elizabeth is three and America is one years old. And eighty year old Caleb Reed. The family of Clarke is here and so is William Reed at the age of twenty five and Alfred Reed thirty nine and Edna who is thirty.

Now, when the 1880's come around Aaron Cheney is now Aaron Callaway at the age of 55 and Tissue is fifty four and at the age of twelve is Siss who is now named Hattie! However, they have a close friend from Bowling Green living and covering them now and his name is R. T. Callaway at the age of thirty four. R. T. Callaway is the son of George W. Callaway and Elizabeth Betsy Milner Callaway and the brother of Lucy who marries W.A. Weatherly September 26, 1876 with Charles D. Campbell as the minister. Aaron Cheney to Aaron Callaway in 1880 and living in the company of R. T. Callaway of Bowling Green and has changed his name and age at the same time Major Callaway and wife Hagar are under the last name of Slaten or Sladen in Bowling Green on Jake T. Patton place near Mr. Joe Epps. What has happen in 1880? I'll ask myself time and time again this question? Aaron Callaway in Puryears district in 1880 age has doubled from 1870. I have a lot of questions because of R. T. Callaway presence in Puryears. Robert and his family and mother Elizabeth B. Callaway and their father George W. who died in 1879, have a presence in Puryears together with Aaron and Letittia and Charlie of 1899. I say this because in the house of W. A. Weatherly the brother –in-law of

Robert T. Callaway and his sister Lucy. Mr. W. A. Weatherly in 1900, was born Aug. 1850 and was fifty years old and have been married twenty five years to Lucy who was born in 1855 and was forty five years old. Their children were Earnest, Malcom, Ruth, Earl, Eugene and a sister name Emma Callaway born May 1860 and was forty years old and was a widow, and her son William listed as the nephew born April 1888.

Emma was first listed as the mother-in-law but was scratched out. William was twelve years old the same age as the son of Mary and Charlie Callaway. Now this is the problem with Emma and William her son living as whites in Mr. W. A. Weatherly and his wife Lucy house in 1900 near Mary Reed and her grandson Robert Callaway born in 1891. Emma is not the sister of Lucy because in 1870 in the house of her father George W. Callaway there is no Emma as his daughter. Emma was born in Tennessee alone with her father and mother as well. However, Lucy was born in Georgia and so was her father and mother. Mr. Weatherly was born in Georgia and so were his parents as well. Emma Callaway and young William is Mary and her son William that is missing. Them being listed as being out of Tennessee brings to mind Mr. Peg-leg-Williams of Tennessee and who has ties to Ohio. Again, this could be the very thing that William Eberhart fears of Dinah in hiding Brantley from him in 1900. While I am on this section of 1900 in Clarke County, I am going to Just start my rebuttal now, I have or will mention Aaron in Beaverdam, in Oglethorpe County. Aaron as I have state before is not Aaron out of Greene County Georgia and the children Willie and Howard Callaway is not the children of Mary and Charlie Callaway. I found this out because of the World War One records of Howard in Atlanta. Howard after marring seventeen year old Mary Harvey Callaway Howard moved in with her parents on Vine St in Athens, Clarke County. Howard was twenty two years old in 1910, making him to be born in 1888, Howard and his wife moved to Atlanta where he joined the Army while working for the Atlantic Steel at the Atlanta Plant near Brookwood. His younger brother Kator or Arthur Calloway will come to work for the same steel company in the thirties. This place was located where the Atlantic Station is now located. I found only one Will Callaway that came close to being my grandfather's brother.

Will was living in Jacksonville Florida at 1819 west Ashley in Jax Fla. he was born june 12, 1886 however he state that he was born in Albany Ga. and was working for the Atlantic Ice Co. as a driver and was supporting his mother. William was thirty one years old. He was medium in height and weight, brown eyes and black hair. The Atlantic Ice Company was owned by Ernest Woodruff and his brother-in- law Joel Hurt that owned and ran the electric trolleys the Atlanta and Edgewood Street Railroad. Woodruff ran and restructured the Atlantic Steel Company that is now the site of the Atlantic Station the same place where his brother Howard worked for as well! Now to further my suspicions that this is Emma and William Callaway that was in the house of Mr. W. A. Weatherby and Lucy Callaway living as whites now living in Jacksonville Florida!

They might have arrived here in and around about 1914 with Jewett S. Callaway and his wife Gussie. Jewett was located in Jacksonville Florida up until 1920 before moving down into Miami Florida. Jewett is the brother of Robert Lee Callaway and the son of Thomas P. Callaway and grandson of Martha and Eli Callaway of Fulton County. Jewett was charged with attempted murder upon his brother R. Lee Callaway in 1901. While on a train from Atlanta he brandished a pistol and shot his brother Robert and was carried off to the Federal Pen. Another suspicion to why I believe that Emma and her son Will are in Jacksonville Fla. is that at the same time Jewett made his home in Jacksonville so did a Charles Callaway. Colored man Charles Callaway resided at 1329 west Monroe and was living with David Loyd. By 1915 Emma Calaway made her home at 1208 ½ West ½ West Ashley. What makes this significant is that Will Callaway lived and supported his mother while going into the First World War while living at 1210 West Ashley street. There might be another tie and that is Rachel living at Bruce Street in Jacksonville Florida. And Lillian who came to live with Rachel in Atlanta in 1940. Lillian lived at 1204 ½ West Ashley with William Wright in 1930. I thought that it was ironic that Lillian would be living near the same place where Emma and her son William were living in 1918. I know that this is not the daughter of Rachel the second wife of my grandfather I just thought it was ironic. Lillian was only fifteen years old in 1940 while living in Atlanta with Rachel.

While Joel Hurt and Earnest Woodruff out of Atlanta had their Atlantic Ice Company and this company sold liquor and beer as well as there was Mr. R. M. Rose in Jacksonville as well. He was located at 626 West Ashley manufacturing and selling his liquor as well. Ashley Street was a black community known as "Harlem of the South". And R. M. Rose and Joel Hurt and Earnest Woodruff and others profited off the Black souls that once resided on Ashley Street. Ashley Street was where Black entertainers performed the Blues and Jazz concerts in the Black Mecca on West Ashely Street in Jacksonville, Florida. Now, don't forget this is one of the places where the S&L R.R. has a terminal as well. They could have very well sent Charlie down the rail to Jacksonville from Elbert County Georgia.

I'll try and tell which Callaways were in Henry and also some of their other family members and friends and how many slaves they had with them. William W. Callaway was living in the Second District near Towaloga River. I think he had about 202 acres of land and about twenty-one slaves on his property at this time. Over in Captain Griffin District was living William A. Callaway on 202 acres of land in the Third District of Henry County in 1831. William Anderson Callaway had about six Negroes on his property there helping him. Luke Gipson was living next door to William A. Callaway and had one Negro on his property. William A. Callaway was living near Cabin Creek in Henry County.

Over in the Rawford Captain section of Henry was Joshua E. Calloway, in the Third District of that county. He was living on the Towaloga River.

Elisha H. Calloway was living in the Captain Fields District of Henry County in 1831 in the Sixth District. Elisha had 204 acres of his own. If you haven't figured it out by now, 204 acres was just about as much as they were given in this land lottery. Elisha was more than likely renting his Negroes from someone else to work his land.

At the time of Isaac's death, white men and white women and Negroes alike of the Callaway family and other white friends of the family came to hire the Negroes for the wellbeing of his children.

Winnifred Callaway is a woman that I'll talk about once more. Masta Isaac and Mrs. Winnifred Ragan married down in Oglethorpe County in 1796. But when Masta Isaac died, she hired the following Negroes, Daniel, Alleck (who was just little boy at that time), Shadrack, and a Negro woman and her child William. William was a mulatto boy. Now, you know that the white folks name our chilun's when they are born, and more than likely they would name them after their own kin in their family. Like a brother or a sister that was close to the family. Hannah, Aaron's wife and her three children—*Oliver*, *Aaron*, and *Manda*—and a Negro woman named Betty also went with Mrs. Winnifred. *Mrs. Winnifred Callaway also hired out Negro woman Jude. She ended up in Oglethorpe County with George W. Callaway working as a servant.*

In the month of September, Job Callaway left Sardis in 1822, and it was on October 27, 1822, that Edward Callaway and Jessie Callaway applied for letters, which were granted. Joseph Callaway died. Joseph had married Sabrina Morgan. Unice, his daughter, married Willis Jerrell. All left for Monroe County, Forsyth, Georgia, near Macon in 1822. *This also could be the place where Aaron went missing during his transgressions at Sardis Baptist Church.* Imagine if Aaron was conversing with us now, "They divided up his Negroes and it was a sight for sore eyes. I'd see sons and daughters being torn from their mothers' and fathers' arms, not knowing where they are headed. Most of the time I realize that they are just on the plantations of the children of the slave masters when they leave. But just imagine hearing the wailing go'n' on, it makes the strongest Negro weak when he sees his wife and chillum leaven. Lord, have mercy on all of us, both masta and we slave". The slaves of Joseph went more than likely to Wilkes or where he had property in Oglethorpe County. Some more than likely went to Alabama to live with family as well.

Masta Edward Callaway was there. He was appointed as guardian for Masta Joseph's little ones. John Dyson received a letter for guardianship. They hired out blacks to help Masta Joseph's children. Cato was hired out to Edward Callaway, the uncle of the Callaway children. Bill and Mary went to the brother-in-law of Joseph Callaway, John Milner. John Milner was a preacher. Masta Milner married Eunice, the daughter of Joshua and Isabella Callaway. Little Ordicia and Elizabeth were the children for whom the Negroes were hired out in 1822. They paid John Dyson and Howel Short and Joshua S. Callaway in 1824 for this very reason. Joshua Callaway hired Will for $1. John Milner Callaway hired Bill. Bill and Mary later resided in Morgan County, Georgia.

Edward Callaway hired out Cato again. Willis Jerrell hired Mary in January. And in 1825, Ordicia Callaway hired Negro boy William and Elizabeth hired out Cato and little Mary. It was in March of 1825 to be exact. By 1827, Edward and the adopted daughters of his cousin Joseph Callaway were living in Wilkes County with Aaron nearby. John H. Dyson was sending papers up to Wilkes for Masta Edward to sign and eventually Masta John Dyson came to Monroe County. Edward and others had left Monroe County, Forsyth, Georgia, with the two misses and came up to Wilkes.

Let me tell you some more about the people of Monroe Forsyth and Lee and Terrell counties who were there at this time. William Proctor settled in the Moore district of Lee. Hannah Cooksey was a widow at this time in Lukes District of Lee County. William A. Callaway Jr. came into his own on March 22, 1827, in the lottery. He was in the Wootens District of Carroll County. By April 9, 1827, Abner Calloway was there with him in Carroll. In May 5, 1827, Bethany Calloway was in Amasons District of Lee County District 9.

Edward Callaway, who hired out Cato, is the son of Joshua and Isabella Henderson Callaway and I believe he married the daughter of James and

Winnifred Monday Spratlin, his wife name is Elizabeth. Caroline Callaway is the daughter born in 1808 in Monroe County, Georgia. An indenture made on the eighth day of January in the year 1827 between Joshua S. Callaway of the county of Jones and state of aforesaid of the one part and Josiah Chatham of the county of Wilkes and etc. Joshua S. Callaway for and in consideration of the sum of four thousand dollars to him in hand paid and to Chatam. That tract or parcel of land situated in the third district of Monroe County number one hundred and two and a half acres. In the presence of Davis Ray and William Paxton(?), March 24, 1827. Let me remind you again what happen about this time in referring you to page nine paragraph three, at the church at Sardis in Wilkes County six years prior on the twenty fifth day of October 1822, Aaron was to join the church in the end of the month. It was in the same month of October on the twenty seventh day of 1822 that Edward and Jesse Callaway applied for letters and it was granted. On the same page nine in the first paragraph it mentioned the men who were to visit the two women for their practices. They were M. Reeves, J. Henderson, Daniel Carrington and E. Callaway. I believe that E. Callaway might be Edward Callaway himself and not brother Enoch Callaway. I believe now that Aaron is off the plantation of Joshua S. Callaway. Other Callaways in Monroe County are Joel Callaway and Jesse M. Callaway in 1840. Jesse M. Callaway sold to John H. Thomas the following Negroes, Negro man Bob, a twenty-four-year-old man; a negro girl named Maria, about ten years old; and a boy named Henry, about fifteen years old. On the third day of October 1840, Jesse M. Calloway, for a thirty-dollar note unto McCurdy Sparks, two Negro girl slaves named Mariah (twelve) and Perlina (about seven). On the third day of April 1841, in consideration of five hundred dollars to him in hand paid Arthur Foster the following Negroes: Charity, a woman, about thirty-five dollars along with two horses and a grey mare and another gray mare. Another family that is in Monroe County is that of Mr. Aquella J. Cheney, the executor of the last will and testament of Aquella Cheney late of Monroe County, deceased. Can you say Aaron Callaway?

Before I go further on about Monroe County, I must mention the 1154th District and mention Peter Callaway and Jenny and Charlie Callaway on the tax digest. They are all working together on the place of Mrs. R. A. The two names other than Charles that I am interested in is Mr. Peter Callaway and Jenny. The name takes me to the district of Evers in Monroe County, Georgia. Peter Callaway is seventy-five years old and Mary, his wife, is forty-seven years old. Their eldest daughter in 1880 is named Martha, aged twelve. Their eldest son is named Allen, aged eleven. Amos is eight. Laura is their granddaughter, aged nine. Young five-year-old Jim

Callaway is living in the same house with Tote Watson, a twelve-year-old, and Butler Watson, his ten-year-old brother. Living in the next house is Mr. Jesse Callaway, a sixty-seven-year-old white man, and his wife Nancy, who is fifty-eight. Willis is their forty-eight-year-old son. Pitt is thirty-three. Nettie is thirty. Sallie is twenty-eight. Allen is twenty-six. William is twenty-two, and Columbus is twenty. The next family is composed of Richmond Nobles, thirty; Delia, his wife, twenty-five; *Charlie Nobles, six years old; and a one-year-old baby girl named Babe. In 1900, in Evers District, Mr. Columbus Callaway was the head of the house and was born in December of 1859. Pitt M. Callaway was born March of 1846, and was listed as his brother. Allen, his brother, was born August of 1853. William was born in May 1858. Marie McLeod was born in February 1847, and is a widow. Dora McLeod, his niece, was born April 1879. In 1910, Pitt M. Callaway is now sixty-four, Allen C. is sixty-two, Robert L. is fifty-nine, William is fifty-five, and Nettie is fifty years old. Eddie McLeod is a nephew, aged fifty. Lula, a niece, is thirty-five. The only tie to this McLeod family is in Terrell County, Georgia.* Also, the mystery is that none of the Callaway men ever married and Columbus Callaway changes his name to Robert L. Callaway and is the farm manager in Evers. Robert L. Callaway was supposedly living in Atlanta at one time. There is no telling of how many white Callaway men lived as black men and had black wives or mistresses. As I had stated before, the McLeod family that was in Terrell County was the same family located in Monroe County, Georgia. Mary E. Callaway married William McLeod in Terrell on the twenty-third day of July 1857. I believe they were out of Alabama. However, in the year 1860, in the Crowder District of Monroe, the family of Jesse Callaway had himself at forty-five, Nancy Callaway is forty-two, John is twenty-four, Willis Callaway is twenty-two, Mary is nineteen, Martha Callaway is seventeen, Sarah Callaway is fifteen, Pit is thirteen, Allen is eleven, David is nine, Edward Callaway is seven, Billy is five, and an infant at the age of two. The infant is Columbus C. Callaway. I believe that Jesse might be the son of Edward Callaway of Monroe County. In Captain Middle Brooks District, I found Edward Callaway. Edward Callaway was polled with twenty-five other people in his house. Edward was out of some place called Rum Creek, maybe because I can't make out the spelling but it is some place in Monroe County. While in Monroe County, Edward is living on 300 acres and maybe even more land as well. He also has a large spread in Wilkerson County, Georgia. His property backs up to Mr. Richard Fletcher's land. Edward is the guardian of Ms. Elizabeth Callaway, who was polled with two occupants in her house. I believe that Peter Callaway came off of Jesse M. Callaway's place in

Monroe. In 1870, Colored man Peter the sixty-five-year-old and his wife Mary (thirty-eight) and *Wash Callaway, his twenty-year-old son, who would come to live in Jackson County, Georgia,* Peter's daughter Dolly is eighteen, Delia is sixteen, Clara is ten, Jack is eight, Martha is four, and Allen a few months old. *Peter and his son Wash would live with Aaron in Oglethorpe County before Peter would return to Monroe County without his son Wash would would eak out a living in Jackosn County Georgia.*

In 1870, Eddie Callaway was a hotel clerk for James B. Camp before coming to Atlanta. This is while his brother Pitt Milner Callaway was the jailer in Monroe at the age of twenty-three. In 1900, Edward Callaway was living at the hotel at Twelve North Pryor Street, working for James E. Hicks. Edward was born March 1857 and was forty-three years old. He is the son of Jesse and Nancy Callaway of Monroe County, Georgia. I wondered how many black Callaways followed him because of his popularity in Atlanta.

Peter's son Wash Callaway married Ms. Emma Watson on May 4, 1882 with the Reverend A. S. Jackson presiding in Jackson County. When Wash arrived in Jackson County, he went to work for A. H. Brock alongside of Wesley Carter.

In 1900, Wash is fifty years old and Emma is forty-four. Alonzo, their son, is twenty-one. Minnie is seventeen, George is fourteen, and Newman is twelve. Nero is nine and Rena is six years old. In 1910, Wash Callaway is fifty years old and had been married to Emma now for twenty-five years. Emma is forty-seven now and Nerva is eighteen, Sermon is sixteen, and George is now living with his wife Elma. George is twenty-seven and Elma is twenty-five. Minnie now is under the last name of Burns. Her husband is Primo, aged thirty, and she is twenty-seven. Ivey is four and Bertlin, her sister, is three. Jefferson D. is two, and Fred S. is one year old, all on Athens Road in Jefferson, Jackson County, Georgia.

In the year 1920, Wash Callaway was now fifty years old and a widower. He is sharing a house with his two daughters, Rinda and Neva. Rinda is twenty-one and Neva is twenty-four. Also living in the house is three-month-old Harold Carithers, his grandson, and his seven-year-old granddaughter Matilda Burns. Wash Callaway is still living on Athens Street. In 1930, he is living on College Street with his forty-five-year-old daughter Mise Burns.

Wash was now seventy-three years old and Mise has four children living at home on College Street in Jackson County. Jesse, her eldest son, is twenty. Mineta, her eldest daughter, is twenty. Mitchell is her nineteen-year-old son, Emaline is her fourteen-year-old daughter, and Morris is her six-year-old son. Mise has her two grandchildren living with her as well. Martha McColough, her seven-year-old granddaughter, and Sadie her five-year-old granddaughter, and a lodger by the name Dolphus Carithers. He is seventeen. I assume he is kin to Mise Burns and Wash. Fonzo Johnson is living in the house as well. Fonzo is forty-nine years old. I do not know if Wash Callaway has any relationship with Gibson Callaway and the family of Hagar and Major Callaway that relocated here in 1910. Could this be the reason for the departure from Oglethorpe and Greene County, to be close to Wash's side of the family that arrived in Jackson County by way of Monroe County with his father Peter, who resided with Aaron? Here ends the family of Wash Callaway in Jackson County. *I must say this, that the mystery of Jackson and the liquor trade and the fact they forced a portion of blacks to relocate elsewhere in the 1920s leave me with many questions that still need to be answered. I might find some of these answers when I mention Mr. R.B. Russell and his friend Henry C. Tuck, the Methodist deacon and ex-mayor of Athens, of Clarke County.*

Early stages of Indentured Servants or Peonage in Oglethorpe County Georgia!Bureau agents for the United States government enter the names of the employees and the employer. This causes me to conclude the general area where these men of the United States government is working is in Oglethorpe and in Greene County, Georgia. These are some of the black children under contracts in Oglethorpe County in 1866, only a year after war's end. Travis Steven was a young colored boy about six years old, contracted out unto Mr. John A. Jewel on the twenty-ninth day of September 1866 along with Lina Stevens, a colored girl about four years old. John Finch was bound over to Cuthbert H. Smith until he became twenty-one years old.

On the twenty-ninth day of August 1866, Jane Neeson, with the help of Joseph McWhorter, bound her three children out to Joseph McWhorter as an apprentice. The boys were supposed to work for McWhorter until they turned twenty-one years old. The girls were contracted out until they were eighteen years of age. Ellick, her son, was twelve. Weavell, a young girl, was ten. Lety, a girl, was seven. Mr. Twepson Cox and Ms. Sarah Cox contracted with Sallie Janes, who was bound over to T. H. Cox, with Anderson who was twelve years old, and Aaron, the son of Sallie Janes, was eleven. All are off the plantation of Mr. Janes, who would become the first man to head up the agriculture department of Georgia. E. C. Shackelford to Mr. Thomas Callahan a colored boy named Frank, ten years old. Also contracted out Joe, another young colored boy who was about seven years old, to Mr. Callahan. I surmise that the young boys did not have a last name and they would go under the last name of Mr. Callahan. On the third day of August 1866, between Salley McWhorter for her two children, Buckhannan and Lucinda. They were nine and seven. The contract was with Mr. William McWhorter. Sally was afflicted seriously and Lucinda was to work for McWhorter until she was eighteen years old and Buckhannan was to work for him until she was twenty-one. They were to live in the house with McWhorter while McWhorter took care of their mother. Jabey M. Britain was to take care of young Luke Britain, a colored boy. The boy said that he was born in September of 1853 and was thirteen years old. Luke's parents were both dead just like the many orphans that resided in Oglethorpe County. Luke would have to come to the age of twenty-one before he could leave the plantation of Jabey M. Britain on the twenty-first day of August 1866.

Now, his first name is Charles; his indenture was made out like this! This is the format of all the contracts just mentioned and that will follow. This Indenture made this twenty-second day of February 1866 between Patrick M. Stevens of the one part and Joe McWhorter and agents A. F. and A. L. for a colored boy Charles of the other part both of the counties and state aforesaid. To wit: that Joe McWhorter and agent of the bureau of R. F. and A. L. acting in accordance with orders from the acting assistant commissioner for the State of Georgia does by the consent and doing of Charles. *Said Charles, having no parents in the county or natural guardian,* was sent out as an apprentice to the said P. M. Stephens to live with continence. And serve the said Stevens or his family the full term and space of eleven years. Charles, being now ten years old during all of which the said, does consent with the said Stevens that the said Charley will faithfully demean himself as an apprentice, observing and obeying fully the commands of the said Stevens and in all things deporting and behaving himself properly nor at any time leaving or neglecting the benefits of the said Stevens. And for and in consideration of the services faithfully and in as aforesaid by the said Charley said P. M. Stevens doth covenant and agree and faithfully instruct in his duties and also to read and write the English language and in the common miles of arithmetic and shall also allow furnish and provide his said apprentice with meat and drink and clothing during the said time. Pay said apprentice twenty-five dollars and a full suite of clothing. Mr. John J. Daniel and Mr. R. E. Moss witnessed this. Mr. P. M Stevens and Joe McWhorter and agents R. F. and A. L. signed the bottom of the contract just as well. Mrs. Celestia Stephens was a forty-two-year-old white woman living next door to John Jewell, a thirty-one-year-old white man in the census. Celestia Stephens is the wife of Patrick M. Stephens the same one Charlie is working for at this time in Maxey, Oglethorpe. In this same area is the plantation of the Hurt family. Now the most intresting thing is that I come across about the P.M. Stevens place is that in the same year that young Charles would come to work for Mr. P.M. Stevens Mr. Robert C. Callaway would come to work for Mr. P.M. Stephens himself. Charles and Robert on the same place at the same time!

The contract system started controlling the Negro during the reconstruction period right after the Civil War and at this time was controlled by the Federal government and the former slave owners, and after the withdrawal of the Union forces the contracted Negro was in the hands of the white Southern landowners again! Now the question is this is young Charley or Charles the servant of P. M. Stephens the son of Robert Callaway who comes to work for P. M. Stephens later.

Now, the question is this is Robert Callaway the father of Charlie who is the former slave of Rev. Enoch Callaway's place. Or is he the son of Aaron and Harriet Callaway. Or is he the son of Robert Callaway and Latitia Hardeman Callaway. I believe he's the son of Robert (Bob) Callaway because his father goes under many names! have the first name Aaron Calloway of Greene County, who never has a Charlie or Cleveland in his family in Green County. Aaron Cheney of Clarke County only appears one time in Oglethorpe near Beaverdam and Puryears in Clarke County in 1870.

Aaron is first listed in 1867 with Jesse Callaway and Henderson Calloway in Greene County. Now, Robert who is playing the role of Aaron travels in the same circles as his son Charlie even to the point of working for the Epps in 1880 the same family that his grandson or the son of Mary and Charlie Callaway would eventually work for as a servant in 1900. Now, Aaron went to work for Mr. William Jewell in the 1870s as well. I found how Robert playing the role of Aaron are moving in the same circles in the tax digest in the 1880's. Mr. Epps calls Robert Callaway, Bob Callaway. I always wondered how Mr. William Jewell comes to play a part in the life of Aaron. This indenture made the fifteenth day of December 1882 between Celestia Stevens and John J. Jewel, for and in consideration of the sum of 6,000 pounds of lint cotton to them in hand by Thomas L. Epps, the receipt of which is hereby acknowledged has remised, released, granted, bargained, sold, and forever, etc., to the said Thomas L. Epps his heirs and assigns a lot of land situated and lying in Oglethorpe County one mile south of Maxey's Depot known as part of the Hudson tract adjoining lands of John T. Hurt, Celestia Stevens, and others. Containing two hundred acres more or less. To have and to hold the said premises with all the privileges and appurtenances thereto pertaining to Thomas L. Epps, his heirs, and assigns so that neither the said Celestia Stevens, John A. Jewel, Sallie F. Jewel, their heirs, nor any person or persons claiming under them shall at any time, etc. Remember the contract between J. A. Jewell and young colored boy Travis Steven, six years old? *I asked myself this question. Aaron is in this area at this time. Major is in this area at this time in 1866, Jesse as well. The only one that is not listed here is Bob Callaway. Bob will come to work for the Stephens in Oglethorpe County later on in the 1880's was this the reason that Charlie was listed as being in Oglethorpe without a parent. .*

In 1870, Aaron is forty-five years old and his wife Harriet is forty years old and their son Burrell is fifteen, Matilda is twelve, Julia is eight, Ellen is seven, Margie is four, and Mollie is two years old. And they are living on the property of fifty-one-year-old Zachariah Freeman and living near William Ray. You must remember the last name of William Ray. Well, I might as well say it. If you want to know the truth about what happened in 1968, take a good look at what happened in the past! Remember that Aaron has an older sister named Matilda. Their mother being Hannah on the plantation of Isaac and Winnifred Callaway place. He must have been very close to name his oldest daughter after a close sibling of his mother Hannah.

This property where Aaron was living in the 147th District of Greene County, Georgia, is called Scull Shoals. In 1872, in the 147th District of Scull Shoals, Aaron was not on the property of Zack Freeman with George Barnett and Bob Maxey. Zack Freeman is kin to Thomas Finley and is mentioned in his estate. The property that Zack Freeman owns was once the property of the Finleys. The colored men listed as being on his property were Thomas Fambrough, Columbus D. Hurt, Berry Mitchell, Dick Smith, Ben Butler, Thomas Watson, and Sterlin Poulian. Augustus Brightwell had Booker Bugg, Cambridge Bugg, and Sandy Moody on his place.

Colored man Aaron Callaway is listed among the whites in the tax digest docket book of Greene County in the 147th District of Scull Shoals in 1872. Along with the following whites in the 147th District of Oglethorpe County, he is over at the property of William B. Campbell: Mrs. Mary Anderson, R. T. Asbury, Augustus Asbury, M. B. Arnold, John Brodenax, G. B. Brightwell, W. Bradshaw, Wm. Burges, J. D. Burges, R. L. Burgess, A. C. Burgess, A. T. Brightwell, W. B. Bowdain, L. B. N. Crochran, W. J. Coffield, Thos. Cofield, and John Cooley. Aaron Callaway had employed three hands between the ages of twelve and sixty-five years old. Aaron was working a 430-acre lot in the 147th District valued at thirteen hundred dollars. This will not be the last time

Aaron's ethnicity or color will be brought into question, or Charlie and Robert Calloway's as well!

Other whites at this time in the 147th were William Campbell, Joseph Campbell, J. M. Colclough, Joseph Davis, J. W. Edwards, Chesley Epps, A. W. Epps, Thos. N. Fambrough, trustee Boss Wilson, and children Gordon for L. and G. Fambrough, J. L. Fambrough, Zack Freeman, A. L. D. Freeman, J. J. freeman, James Gann, B. Goodue, Nathan Glosson, Andrew Gillem, S. N. Harper, Clayton Johnson, Wm. Jewell, Thos. P. Janes, Thos. Pleman Janes, John E. Jackson Sr., L. M. Maxey, G. W.. Maxey, R. Masey, Franklin Moore, J. W. Moore, Miss E. R. and F. G. Moore, John Memort, J. N. Milton, T. C. C. Cain, T. S. Miller, W. A. Moore, M. Loins (Lyons), W. A. Noel, J. M. Nosworth, Charles Potter or Porter, James Porter, T. E. Philips, J. w. Potter, W. A. Partee, agent for Mrs. E. Partee, Thos. N. Poulain, agent for Fountnoy Mills, J. R. Porter, W. A. Pew, Wm. Pitman, B. F. Ray, John Redman, S. Simpson, Arch Shaw Sr., Arch Shaw Jr.,

Samuel Shaw, John Wood, J. D. Williams, W. M. Wray, Silvanus Wray, James Watson, W. A. Williams, and Lawrence Wheeler. The fact that Aaron is listed among the white population at this time tells me of the influence that Aaron might have in the white community that I see with his children, especially Charlie and Robert! I loved walking this section where I knew my ancestors resided and work to make Georgia become established in its former glory before the war between the states. Oh! The many trails I crossed and creeks I waded through and enjoyed the scenary of the Oconee River and watching the deers at Falling Creek.

Before going into the year of 1873 with Aaron, I want to talk about the Hurt family in 1872. The Hurt family is the same family that Charlie Calloway will marry into. He will marry Mary Hurt in Clarke County in 1884. This is the Hurt family listed with the whites in 1872 in the 140th District of Greene County, along with E. F. M. Callaway and J. W. Johnson. In the 138th section of Greene County in the colored tax digest, James Davison hired Bob Edmonson, Albert Davison, Joe Daniel, Jerry McWhorter, and others. Owens Cheney's place consisted of Oliver Jordan and Alfred Swann, and E. R. Cheney had Henry White and Moses Cheney at his place. Mose Cheney will travel with Aaron to Beaverdam, near Clarke County, and a few others from Bowlingreen and Bairdstown. Remember this is Robert or Bob Callaway living under the first name of Aaron while in Clarke County with Mose Cheney. This pattern of migration for work still continues today between the two counties. Aaron came to know Mose Cheney when he arrived from the plantation of Enoch Callaway in 1859 to live on Mr. William Owen Cheney's place after the death of Reverend Enoch Callaway.

In the 137th, Ned Parks located on his 160-acre farm. This property has been in his possession since the early 1840s. Ned Parks Jr. is working for H. J. Bowles. *Mr. Parks's place will become the property of Emily Hurt, the wife of Richard Callaway, in 1916.* Esquire Hurt is located in the 140th District in Union Point with Albert Hurt. In the 142nd, C. C. Oliver has Richard Hurt, John Gunnell, and William Irwin on his place. In the 146th, Lindsey Hurt is working for Dr. Gresham, and in the famous district of 147th, Columbus Hurt is working with Berry Mitchell, Dick Smith, Ben Butler, Thos. Watson, and Sterlin Poulain on Thos. Fambrough's place. Zack Freeman had George Barnett and Bob Maxey at his place

In the 148th of Penfield, Terrell Blocker and Charles Champion were on J. D. Champion's place, Isaac English was on J. H. English's land, and Daniel English was working for William English with Young Geer. Jesse Callaway, George Lawrence, and Marshall Daniel, who are all black men, had their own property. I feel it necessary to mention a few of these names because of the marriages that took place between the families that might reveal the mystery behind Charlie and Mary Callaway's death, Charlie who supposedly had been lynched and left hanging from a tree as an example and Mary who supposedly had died in child birth with my grandfather this occurred in 1899 in the height of the disenfranchisement era, white men had to choose between living as a black man and be destitute in Georgia with his black children and black wife and the black who were passing had to either flee the south or stay and hope that their true identity would never be revealed. They had to make the ultimate decision of leaving their mixed families. They would go to extreme measures to deceive the public by saying they are dead when they just left everything they had and their family in the South! Some of the high-profiled white men and high yellow mulatto men did what they wanted when they wanted with their influential family background and power.

The first family that I am going to mention is the family of Mr. Albert Parks. Mr. Albert Parks's family has been a free family of color since the 1840s. Albert is the son of Ned Parks whose parents were Callaways off the estate of Isaac Callaway and Winifred Callaway estate that went to work for Robert Parks. The Parks are tied really to the Ragan Family through marriage of Winnifred Ragan's sister who might have married a free black man from Lincoln County Georgia. The last name Parks still has ties to my family to this very day!

This property was in the 137th district in Greene County in 1871. J. H. Daniel had Whit Willingham, Sparks Bowles, Dick Drake and Thomas Daniel. Jesse Daniel is working for William Daniel. Albert Parks is at home and is the agent for his father Ned Parks and his estate. The Estate consists of 160 acres and he is the only colored that has property. His property backs up to James Griffin, who had Allen McWhorter, Umphy Bowles, Davis Southerland, Richard Bennett, Charles Drake, Burd Drake, George Drake, and Henry Griffin and the property of W. H. McWhorter, who had Joseph Fulton and Isaac Carter, at his place. *Jesse Daniel or Rev. Jesse Daniel is a close friend of Rev. Jesse R. Callaway and again you now have the description of the property of Emily Hurt and Richard Callaway who purchased the place in 1916. .*

Not far from this district was the 138th District where Mr. James Davison has James Daniel, David Tuggle, Billy Wilborn, Jack Lunsford, Jerry Smith, Albert Davison, Harry Stubbs, Steven Murden, Cane Malone, Jack Barrow, Handy Barrow, Peter Barrow, Jerry McWhorter, Richard Daniel, Joseph Daniel, Alfred Haley, Columbus Park, Jordan Royden, and Reuben Lunsford. *Mr. James Davison will have a great influence over Richard and Emily Hurt Callaway's lives. They would purchase the Parks's property in 1916 with the help of the Davisons, and she will live on this property up until the 1920s. Eventually Emily would be brought back here to be buried on this same property after living in Atlanta after returning from Florida in 1930, where I find her and Richard!*

I have made many visits to this section of Greene County, walking for miles and through cow pastures and avoiding snakes and sometimes getting lost and I have not located her gravesite yet! Now, remember the Anderson family that was a witness on the will of Winifred Callaway in 1839? Well, the Anderson family owned property near the Oconee River. Again,

David C. Barrow the kinsman of Henry Pope who married Isaac Callaway daughter has working on his property the following Negroes: Reuben Pope, Sandy Moody, Barton Barnett, Walton Eberhart, Mingo Barrow, James Lumpkin, Isham Pope, Henry Barrow, and the only person working for Zack Freeman is Aaron Callaway, my great-great-grandfather. Thomas Fambrough had Thos. Watson and Frank Barnett, Ferdinan Barnett, Milton Fambrough, Ben Bugg, and Dick Smith at his place. Thomas Watson and Frank Barnett were the only coloreds who owned property. Thomas Watson owned forty-five acres and Frank Barnett had 150 acres. Mr. David C. Barrow might be the Dean at the University of Georgia, one *of the most powerful white man in Greene County and Clarke County as well. He more than likely has great respect in the colored Community. I noticed this in how the blacks lived on his land. I am assuming this.*

On the commissioner of agriculture, Mr. T. P. Janes's property I found Aaron's kinfolk, the Barrows, working there: George Barrow,

Perry Barrow, Ben Barrow, Henry Gresham, and Bill Freeman. John E. Jackson Sr. place, where Charlie and his brother Clayborn would make their escape to Atlanta fleeing Ed Jackson place in 1889. John E. Jackson farm consisted of colored men Booker Watson, Albert Oliver, and Amos. Z. Poulian. At Augustus T. Brightwell's place the colored help consisted of Cambrige Bugg, Samuel Gilham, and Booker Bugg. L. M. Maxey had Mark Williams on his property. Barnett Moore had Hixon Daniel on his place. *W. A. Partee had Henry Christopher on his land. James Watson had Booker Watson and Sampson Jackson.* Arm Gresham was at W. A. Wilson's place. The Wilson place is near the Calloway-Hurt house in the 147th District. I visited Mr. Wilson and informed him that I visited the colored Wilson Cemetery. Before I could get the word *colored* out of my mouth, he stated very curt that the cemetery was a white cemetery! I didn't argue. I just shook my head and said, "Yes, sir," out of respect, for he would know. *And again the question comes up: are we dealing with whites or blacks that are buried in a cemetery? What kind of secret am I looking into that even a cemetery is brought into question of its ethnicity? It tells me of a very close relationship that existed between the blacks and whites in this area.*

I came across a lot of cemeteries that could be a white cemetery or a black cemetery. Now remember, in 1872 Aaron is listed as being in the white section of the tax digest of Greene County in the 147th District. Aaron Callaway had a number of hands employed and under his supervision. They are between the ages of twelve and sixty-five years old. The oldest person that I can think that is living with Aaron on Mr. Campbell land is Judy and the two children that arrived with her from DeKalb County in Panthers Ville.

I also think that the hired hands of Aaron Callaway could very well be members of his own family! I am amazed by the fact that Aaron is in this capacity of trust in the white community and how he and Rev. Jesse R. Callaway are held in such high esteem. This also shows me that Aaron is under many names, as Green Callaway in Lincoln County and Aaron Cheney in or near Beaverdam and Puryears districts of Clarke County. Aaron and Jesse are operating in the midst of men of the Secret Order of the Clavern or the Klan. Now I can see why my grandfather kept quiet for so long and never talked about his family! It wasn't just Arthur alone that kept these secrets. One being old man W.B. Brightwell.

As I had stated before, Aaron has property listed at 430 acres. This property will be turned over to Mr. William Campbell. William Campbell had nothing listed beside his name in 1872. However, in 1873 Aaron is not listed among the white but there is a Hartwell Cornwell and W. L. Campbell who had the 430 acres that Aaron once had in the 147th District. This is the time that A. W. Epps shows up, and moreover, in the colored section of the tax digest in 1873 there is an Anderson Callaway on the property of Zach Freeman with a Peter Sheppard. I will mention Mr. Anderson briefly out of Atlanta by way of Randolph County where he was sixty one years old in 1880. Anderson was working for the Old Rolling Mills and being in business with Mr. Holmes. This was in 1877 and I believe that Anderson Callaway before coming to work in Atlanta in 1870 in the Rolling Mills Factory left briefly and visited to Greene County as early as 1872 and worked on Zachariah Freeman's place while Aaron was working as a white man on Mr. Campbell's place. Who knows that Anderson could just be the man working alone side of Aaron while being listed as a white man over William Campbell's place.

In the 148th District of Penfield, Bob or Robert Callaway, a son of Aaron Callaway that might be Charlie Callaway, is working for J. F. Erns with Thomas McCommins and Abram Moody. Abraham Moody is the father of Francis Moody the woman that my grandfather Arthur would take up resident in the same apartment in Techwood in 1930. In Bowling Green in 1900 Francis is at the same age as the brother of my grandfather Charlie who is in the house with Mr. Epps as a servant near Bairstown. R. L. McWhorter has Lee McWhorter, Dave McWhorter, Tom Rutledge, Bill McWhorter, Ritt McWhorter, Bob McWhorter, Sam Jerrell, James Callaway, Joe Irvin, Nelson Wright, Mat Colclough, Josiah Holes, Jasper McWhorter, and Boss Colclough. As you may notice, ex-slaves remained on the place where they were once slaves either because they were treated very well by their masters in the south.

Even up unto 1875, in the 147th District, Wm. Campbell is gone, but the estate of G. B. Connell is still listed in the white section. However, on the property of Zack Freeman were George Barnett and Aaron Callaway resides. I found Wm. Campbell in DeKalb County during this time in Panthersville.

At this time, in the 147th, Willis Williams is arrested and is on the Alexander chain gang on the banks of the Oconee River. Aaron is not listed among the whites and now Anderson Callaway shows up. I went looking for Anderson Callaway I found Anderson Callaway in Atlanta in the 1870s working for the Rolling Mills. Willis Williams dies in 1874 while in the 147th District, where the first Commissioner of Agriculture Thos. P. Janes is located. The work done here by the Negroes that resided in the Scull Shoals District of Greene County is now under the State of Georgia Parks and Forestry and is a very high-profile area after only nine years after the Civil War. Thomas P. Janes was in charge of agriculture. This tells you what was expected of the colored men and women and their children as to the harsh conditions they were subjected to. Blacks owned little land here and the land was for agriculture, and companies would and still own the majority of land in Greene County and Oglethorpe and surrounding counties. At one time, the saw mills dominated the areas and now there are poultry companies. Remember, this is one of the very reasons for disenfranchisement of the Negro! General Farms dominated the area. Take a good look at the 1900 census and there is no mention of General Farms employers or employees. However, in 1910 it dominated the census. In some ways, McKinley manipulated the advancement of the Negroes in the South to appease the Southern landowners and its growth and the Negro families in the South will suffer.

Account Book of Convicts leased during 1872–1876

T.W. Alexander's Division

April 6, 1872

G.W. Braswell, Henry Burges, Julia Black, Arthur Chapman, James Christian, Charley Champion, James Christian, Isaiah Chafin, Eli Chamberlin, Dock Carter, William Cox, John Duke, Andrew Dorsey, Henry Dumas, James Epps, Carey Earley, J.N. George, Henry Green, Daniel George, Nathan L. Jones, Turner Jones, Robert Jones, Dennis Noble, George Rouse, Loney Robinson, Lewis Scott, Isaac Scott, Green Scales, Stephens Smith, *George Samuels*, W.P. Smith, Butler Smith, James Thomas Wash Terrell, Robert Redding, Wiley Redding, Charles Ramsay, Cesar Richardson. *Names that are interesting to me in the chain gang are the colored men that will play an important part in the liquor trade or the Blind Tigers. George Samuels and his close relationship with the colored Callaways. The Smith Brothers, the Jones Brothers, and Charley Champion will be in and out of the chain gang.*

January 6, 1873

T.W. Alexander's Division

Mary Jane Lester, Henry Love, G.F. Maxwell, Charles Champion, James Buggs, Ed Booker, Boney Bates, Lula Brooks, Loudon Broomfield, Benjamin Allen, Wiley Arnett, *Willis Williams, Wm. Williams, Moses Williams, James Williams David Williams,* Bruce Walker, Linus Ward, Paul Walker, and Madison Wynn. *Look and take notice of the occupants now that are in the Alexander Camp in 1873. Charles Champion again, with Willis Williams, the great-grandfather of the Rev. Martin Luther King Jr.; William Williams, the white man that he shares crops for in the 147th District called Scull Shoals; Mary Jane Lester and the Lester Family; Linus Ward; and Paul Walker.*

A.C. from October 1, 1873 to April 1, 1874

T.W. Alexander's Division

James Buggs, Jesse Bird, James Chastain, J.J. Castilo, Ida Blanchard, Cris Borders, Columbus Browning, Wiley Arnett, Sarah Autry, William Adams, Sol Arnold, Charles Champion, William Cox, W.N. Campbell, Doc Carter, Henry Carter, Lucius Daniels, Grantville Dennis, James Epps, Nelson Lester, Alexander Mathews, Jerry Morrison, G.F. Maxwell, Jesse Marshall, and Wash Terrell

A rebate a/c claimed by Grant- Alexander and Co.

Aaron Curry, Crease Combs, Berry Chamblee, Isah Brown, Amos Bone, Dennis Blackshear, George Maxey, Jerry Lumpkin, Frank Stark, Mingo Washington, Steve Riley, Henry Redd, Dinah Rush, Andrew Pierce, Henry Penn, and Austin Martin.

Monthly Report of Convicts of T.W. Alexander's Division

Smith Riddle and Co. leases convicts, 1874, to State of Georgia for four months' hire to firm to Smith and Taylor.

Charles Champion, Morgan Cody, Frank Chambers, Henry Burges, William Barnett, Joseph Buggs, Bristo Brown, Solomon Arnold, Lewis Ambrose, Alex H. Evans, Andy Echols, Green Evans, Sam Frazier, James Friday, Alex Hinson, Berry Shamblee, Wash Terrell, Jerry Thomas James alias John Thomas, J.T. Thomas Frank Stark, Rose Williams, William Williams, Joe Williams, and Willis Williams. *Willis Williams might have made it home after being on the Alexander farm. Or this could be how they might have silenced the Civil Rights Preacher of 1874? Willis Williams is listed as being sixty years old in 1870 in the 140th District of Green County in a section of Greene County called Union Point. However, I do not know if they took him back to Union Point or if he was buried in the Bethbara Cemetery churchyard, the only colored church and burial place in the 147th. I see that Mr. Henry Burges is on the farm alone with William Barnett, whom I believe might be the Revered William Barnett. Mr. Sam Frazier, Charles Champion from the Champion Family. I do not know if all are colored inmates or men that are infirm; however, I do know that something is going on about this time in 1874 in Greene County and Oglethorpe that Aaron would be listed in the white section of the tax digest book. His older sons Burwell and Charles or Robert are in Wilkes County working for the Callaways and this letter went out from the McWhorter brothers to Governor Joseph Brown. That might have produced the demise of Willis Williams in 1874, and the other major political actions that were taking place. Mr. T. P. Janes has become the first commissioner of agriculture. This is the beginning of the fight for a state-run government and a federal-run government and the white farmers and their state right and also what the state does not know as well. Oh! The colored legislators are being kicked out of the Georgia State senate about this time as well!*

District 147 in Greene County at this time in the early 1870s was made up largely of Mr. Alexander's convict Camp in Georgia.

You can also see the interest of the federal and state agencies in this situation as well. This area, with one of its largest chain gangs is hardly mentioned in the annals of Georgia. It is also where the first governor, Early, is buried. This harsh environment, with its prostitution and murder and Blind Tigers, saturated the Falling Creek District and Scull Shoals and Oconee and Walton County areas, as well as Wilkes County and others in the northeastern section of Georgia! But all this adversity and chaos brought forth one of Georgia's most famous civil rights leader and these who are mention are those who have paved the way for him to come! the families who have never had a voice in the history of Georgia because the sins of their fathers and their past actions and the whites who had control over them and the oaths that bound them to secrecy in their Masonic orders and churches that allowed murder and control through sex and alcohol, to promote the sinful commercial economic growth in Georgia. Now, they have a voice, by one who is not ashamed of the past sins of the for-fathers ignorance and sinful desires cast upon the weak among them, I am the great-great-grandson of Aaron Callaway or Robert (Bob) Callaway. And I have searched and is still searching and is now wanting to know the truth!

I found this information about the true written document where the prominent white men of their areas stated what they did to drive out the carpetbaggers in their area and Georgia. I had read this partial statement that was presented in the public library of Oglethorpe and what was not mentioned shocked me to the core! They didn't mention the question of the Negro problem. The Negro problem that was spoken about in the letter written to the governor would answer this question and bring on the solution that manifested into the chain gangs that Willis Williams would never return from like so many other Negroes, including Green Calloway and Charlie Calloway! Here's the true statement made by the McWhorter brothers to Governor Joseph E. Brown of Georgia.

Prominent Men of Oglethorpe and the South not only had a Capet-Baggers Problem and Scalawag Problem but a Secret agenda for the Negro Problem as well!

A letter on the present political situation

Penfield, Green Co., Ga., August 31, 1874

Gov. Joseph E. Brown Atlanta Georgia

Dear Sir:

In this hour of political trouble we would counsel your wisdom and political experience. In our opinion, the passage by Congress of the Civil

Rights Bill would inaugurate a spirit of antagonism between the Black and White races that could never be reconciled. To us it does appear impossible for any Southern gentleman to identify himself with any party who seeks to impose this measure upon our people. But trusting in your profound judgment and practical common sense we advise with you.

Yours very respectfully: R. L. McWhorter and James H. McWhorter

Atlanta, Georgia, September 2, 1874

Messers. R.L. McWhorter and James H. McWhorter, Penfield, Georgia

Gentlemen, in reply to your letter in reference to the political situation in which I understand you to ask my opinion of the Civil Rights Bill pending before Congress.

I have to state that I am not engaged in political strife nor do I intend to be in the future. I shall, however, maintain the position of an independent citizen and I shall not hesitate to express any political opinions which I may entertain. And to set and vote in such manner as in my judgment will best promote the interest of the State of Georgia and of the whole people of the Union. As you are aware, I was one of the first public men in Georgia to take position in favor of acquiescence to the reconstruction measures adopted by Congress. I did this because I clearly foresaw that the South, as the conquered section, would be compelled to submit to these measures: and if acquiescence was refused, that more rigorous measures still would be enforced.

But I thought by acquiescing at once and raising no issues with the colored people of the state we would retain their confidence and keep them out of the hands of the carpetbaggers and designing men who would come among them for the purpose of misleading them and exciting their prejudices against the native white population, who are in fact their best friends. Each of you took the same position, which I felt it's my duty to take upon these issues, and we passed through the period of persecution and ostracism seldom endured by those who have in view nothing but the best interests of the state in the course they pursue, and who labor day and night to save those who revile them from a fate such as the white people of South Carolina and Louisiana, who followed the advice of unwise leaders and made no effort to control the deliberations of their contentions are now compelled to endure. The result of our labors and of those who cooperated with us in and out the Convention gave to Georgia a constitution under so her native original citizens the control and management of their own affairs. In the other Southern states, where the whole mass of the white people, following the advice of their excited leaders, gave up their constitutional convictions to Negroes and carpetbaggers and made no effort to control them, constitutions have been fixed upon them which vest the government in the hands of their former slaves, under the guidance and direction of Northern men who, bankrupt in character and fortune at home, come to the South and take advantage of the folly of our people who were setting upon their passions and prejudices and not upon their judgment and common sense, alienating the Negroes from their white neighbors and friends and obtaining complete control over them.

It was thirty to forty thousand white men in Georgia who acted with us, subordinating passion and prejudice to judgment and reason, and who contrary to the advice of honored leaders, voted in the election for delegates to the convention and sent such men as McCoy, Safford, Miller, Parrott, Trammell, Waddell, McWhorter, Bell, Angiel, Bigby, Bowers, Flynn, Foster, Irwin, Maddox, Shropshire, and a number of others, all able honored citizens of Georgia, who with the aid of some influences outside, controlled the counsels of the convention and secured our present constitution, who saved Georgia from the sad fate of some of her Southern sisters.

Suppose the whole white population of South Carolina, immediately after the passage of the Sherman Bill, had proclaimed to the world that they acquiesced in the measure and each had gone to work to influence and control as many colored men as possible, making no issue with them but informing them that their right to vote was conceded, and suppose every white voter in the state had gone to the polls and voted for delegates to the convention, who believes that they could not have carried colored votes enough with their own to have controlled the convention and made their constitution as good as that of Georgia?

This could have been done by them if they had acted promptly, in defiance of all the efforts that carpetbaggers could have made. If no issue had been made with the colored people, probably each white voter in the state could have influenced and controlled one colored vote. Some could have controlled a much larger number. But if only one in every five had controlled a colored voter it would have given the white people the control of the convention. And as a consequence would have given them a good constitution. The property intellect and intelligence of any state can govern it when it unites in a determined effort to do so. And if they had made no issue with the government or the colored people on their right to vote. There were strong reasons why their former owners could have exercised more influence and control over the colored people than the employer can usually exercise over the employed owing to the kind of relations which had formerly existed between them and the dependence upon the white people which the colored people had habitually felt during their past lives. But so soon as the sole mass of the white people proclaim their eternal hostility to the reconstruction acts and declared that they would never submit to Negro suffrage, they drove the Negroes from them, and as any other race who did not feel competent to control their own affairs would have done under like circumstances, they naturally looked around for somebody to lead them. And at this critical moment the carpetbaggers came among them, announcing that their mission was to see that the acts of Congress were carried into effect, and the rights for suffrage secured to the colored race.

Having no one else to lean upon, their former owners and neighbors having, as they considered it, become willing subjects of those who came through with flattering promises, and were soon bound to them by ties too strong to be easily broken. But the reconstruction contest is in the past and today we see the white people of Georgia coming up to the position of acquiescence that we took in 1867, and indeed going far beyond it. We then acquiesced in the Fourteenth Amendment and the Sherman Bill. They have since added an amendment added which might have been acquiesced in the Fourteenth Amendment and the Reconstruction Act, known as the Sherman Bill. But at this period we are met with much more dangerous issues than any presented in 1867; and it becomes us to meet it fairly and squarely, and to do all in our power to avert the enactment of a measure which will be productive of the most ruinous consequences throughout the entire South. It was a hard enough fate upon us for our conquerors to abolish slavery, and wrest from us, without a dollar of compensation, the billions of dollars invested in that property which had descended from generation to generation as the patrimony of several ages; and then to compel us to stand upon terms of legal equality with our former slaves, and meet them as equals at the ballot box.

This, however, the conqueror dictated and those who were most fiery and denunciatory in their warfare against it accomplished nothing of good for our people. At this stage, however, with a view no doubt to the next presidential campaign, and for the purpose of making the colored voters more enthusiastic in their support of the Republican party, certain leaders of that powerful organization bring forward what is called the "Civil Rights Bill" which is now pending on the calendar of Congress, and which in fact is intended, not as a Civil rights bill, but a social rights measure; for the purpose of compelling social equality between the white and colored people of the South. This can never be done, and if attempted should not, and what they may, God has created the two races different, with different tastes, capacity and instincts for social enjoyment, and no human legislation can ever compel them to unite as social equals.

Those who urge this measure in Congress, with view of bringing up the Colored voters to a more enthusiastic support of their party, are putting themselves in a position to do the greatest possible injury to the colored race. Suppose this bill should pass at the next Congress, what will be the result? The legislature of each Southern state, as soon as it is called together, will at once repeal all laws by which public schools are maintained at the public expense, and leave each man to educate his own children as best he can. This will leave the colored people, who are without property, to grope their way in ignorance, with no means of educating their offspring. And it will necessarily leave a great situation.

But be this as it may, we will never submit to mixed schools, where our children will be compelled to unite with those of the colored race, upon terms of social equality. I have been president of the Board of Education of Atlanta since the organization of our system, which is now working most admirably, under which we have separate schools open to white and colored children, and every child belonging to either race can find its way into a good school if the parent thinks proper to send it. These schools are maintained by taxation of the whole people and their burden falls mainly upon those who have most wealth and who often have no children to educate. I am proud of the system and of the great benefits which are resulting from it, and I feel as our white people generally do that since the colored people are made citizens, if they act in their proper social sphere, it is our duty, as well as our pleasure, to aid them in the education of their children.

But I do not hesitate to say that I should favor the immediate repeal of all laws on this subject and the disbanding of the schools as soon as the Civil Rights Bill shall become a law. It cannot be said that we violate any provision of the Constitution of the United States when we repeal our school laws, as that constitution requires no state to maintain any public school; and we make no discrimination on account of race, color, or previous condition of servitude when we refuse to maintain any public school at the public expense for the children of either race. But this is not all. The attempt to force equality between the races on railroad cars, steamboats, and especially in hotels and churches will produce constant strife and very frequent bloodshed that will probably soon lead to a war of races and produce a horrible state of things throughout the entire South, terminating in general anarchy, which will end in the extermination of the Negro race.

Much as I depreciate and oppose all mob law, I cannot doubt that in the excited state of the popular mind which would follow the attempt to enforce such a measure, it would soon be found that white juries would not convict white men for killing Negroes who undertook to intrude themselves upon them as social equals. And if the government of the United States attempted to coerce the white people of the South into submission to Negro social equality, they would find that the white troops who might be called into the field against us to fight for such Negro social equality would generally lay down their arms before they would perform the task. In a word, if they drove us to submission at the point of the bayonet, the bayonet would generally be in the hands of the Negro, and our people would have to defend themselves against it as best they could. The result would not be doubtful. All prosperity would be destroyed, and general confusion, bankruptcy and ruin would prevail, until the struggle between the races terminated, which would, as I have already said, in the end result in the extinction of the weaker race. But I do not care to pursue this theme. The consequences of this measure would be too horrible for contemplation, and we can only hope that the evil will be averted by the good, practical, common sense of the American people, and that the political organization which attempts to force this state of things upon the country, or any section of it, will meet with overwhelming defeat in every issue. I have no hesitation, therefore, in agreeing with you that the passage by Congress of the Civil Rights Bill would inaugurate a felling of antagonism between the white and black races that could never be reconciled; and, in saying most unequivocally that no Southern gentleman, I care not whether he be Republican or Democrat, ought, in my opinion, to identify himself, or continue longer to act, with the party who seeks to impose this measure upon our people.

In my judgment, there are but two contingencies which can avert the evil: one is the overwhelming defeat of the Republican Party in the elections this fall upon this issue. They are determined to make the issue, as already announced by some of their leaders upon the stump, and my sincere hope is that every state, county, city, town, village, and hamlet throughout the entire Union, where an election may be held, will give the Democratic Party an overwhelming majority. To this end, I shall cheerfully contribute my humble might. This would check the passage through the country of the horrors consequent upon its passage. If this should fail, and I trust it may not, the only remaining hope is in the exercise of the veto power by the president of the United States. I know nothing of the intentions of the president on this question, but I trust a sense of patriotic duty may compel him, if the measure should ever come before him for action, to save the county from anarchy and ruin by the use of this great conservative power which is wisely placed in his hands by the Constitution. If it should come to that point and General Grant should veto the measure and throw the vast weight of his executive power and personal influences in the scale of peace and harmony, he would be entitled to, and I believe would receive the thanks and applause of the entire white population of the South and of a vast majority of the people of the Union. I have no wish to thrust my opinions before the public on any political issue; but on account of the magnitude of this question, and the fearful results which may follow, I think it the duty of every citizen to speak out and state his position in terms too unequivocal to be misunderstood. I therefore authorize you to make such use of this letter as you may think proper.

I am, very respectfully, your obedient servant,

Joseph E. Brown

This is a good argument; however, it had great influence in the political realm in Georgia. Klansmen infiltrated the political and social fabric of Georgia. Look at what I found in the Atlanta History Center. There have been many times I have read the paper in Greene and Oglethorpe County boasting of the fact that their white citizens were infamous in running out the carpetbaggers in Georgia. However, they never mention this fact here concerning the larger question in dealing with the Negro Problem! Why did not these men boast about this act of influence against the colored community in Georgia and only the carpetbaggers? This is a good argument; however, it had great influence in the political realm in Georgia. Klansmen infiltrated the political and social fabric of Georgia. Look at what I found in the Atlanta History Center. There have been many times I have read the paper in Greene and Oglethorpe County boasting of the fact that their white citizens were infamous in running out the carpetbaggers in Georgia. However, they never mention this fact here concerning the larger question in dealing with the Negro Problem! Why did not these men boast about this act of influence against the colored community in Georgia and only the carpetbaggers?

In 1874, in the 147th, Aaron is on the farm of Zack Freeman and Bob Callaway (Bob is Robert Calloway, whose son Robert will own a large number of acres near the Epps; he is also the father of Will Calloway in Penfield in Greene County) is on the property of Williams Burton with Henry Kidd, Daniel

English, and Young Geer. The year 1880 on the property of Mr. William Burton I found George Callaway and Isaac and Francis Bunkley. I think that Francis is little Miss Vina Bunkley who will marry Mr. Claiborne. And living right next door is Mr. sixty year old Henry Kidd and his family. However there is no Bob or Robert Callaway but there is a sign that he has been on the property of Mr. Burton. George Callaway and Isaac are the brothers of Charlie and Clayborn or Cleveland Callaway and Sis or Silvey. While George was in Bowling Green district of Oglethorpe County. George was working for Mr. J. S. Cheney with Manuel Cheney and Allen Craddock while Charlie was on the property of Enoch R. Cheney. The two pair will go one to work together in Beaverdam. George would go to work for Mr. William Eberhart alone side of Mr. Scott Cox and Charlie his older brother would go to work for Mr. B. B. Williams working alone side of Stoney Colbert. While young George Callaway was on the property of Williams Eberhart place. Eberhart had Mr. Albert Boykins on his place living near a Mr. L. F. Edwards. I mentioned Mr. Edwards for this reason Mr. William Burton had in his house in Bowling Green had his sixty year old mother-in-law Mrs. Hannah Edwards. I know, I may be reaching but why not! George not only worked alone side of Charlie his brother. George was in Beaverdam with Aaron Callaway as well. While Charlie was on William Eberhart in the earlier days of 1880. Aaron Callaway was working next door to William Eberhart on the property of John Winter. I have established that this is not 1820 Aaron Callaway it is Mr. Bob Callaway or Green Callaway or Robert Callaway. However you want look at him, I know in 1870 he is under the last name of Cheney the same property that his two sons are living on in Bowling Green. The same Cheney family that young Aaron was given to in 1859 by the late Rev. Enoch Callaway of Sardis Baptist Church. *I do not know if Robert is the son of Major Callaway or is he the son of Aaron Callaway.* However, I really do believe that there are two Robert Callaways, one is white and one is black. The white Robert Callaway is the son of George W. Callaway; Mr. Robert T. Callaway who follows or whose land both Major Callaway lives on or near before moving to the town of Lexington. Aaron Callaway or Bob Callaway lived near him as well at one time or another.

In 1875, in the 147th Scull Shoals District of Greene County, Mr. William Campbell is gone. At Zack Freeman's place, George Barnett and Aaron Callaway still resided. The year is 1878. Robert Williams, the son of Willis William and husband to Matilda Callaway, the oldest daughter of Aaron named for his sister, were married by the justice of the peace R. L. Burgess on December 14, 1878. This is four years after the death of Willis

Williams. It seems like that none of Aaron's children besides Burwell are being married by colored preachers!

Let us see who and how they are living in Greene County in 1880.

J. W. Miller is the enumerator of the 147th in Scull Shoals on the fifteenth day of June. The family that I want to talk to you about is the house of Adam Williams, an eighteen-year-old listed as being white. However, he is a servant in the house of Mr. Barney Maxey. Adam William is a laborer at his place in the 147th with Creasy, who is four, and Eve, who is eighteen. Lou Williams is a nine-year-old servant and is listed as being black, and John is a two-year-old boy listed as being black. I believe that Mr. J. W. Miller listed Adam William on page seven as being white and on page eight listed the rest of the Williams family as being black because nine-year-old Lou and two-year-old John are in house number 56 with A. D. Williams. Adam William, as I had stated before, is in the house of Barney Maxey, a forty-five-year-old farmer, and his wife Sallie, who is thirty-nine. Clarence is their ten-year-old son, Julia their nine-year-old daughter, and Cora their seven-year-old daughter. Jesse is their two-year-old son and a cousin named Ben Maxey, who is twenty years old and is a farmer on the place of Barney. *I remember sitting on the porch of Mrs. Susie Armstrong enjoying the country view of her place and also the company of Mutt Geer. Mrs. Susie told me that A. D. Williams left there with a Mr. Burgess to Atlanta. I do not know if it is the same Burgess that married Bob Williams and Matilda Callaway in 1878. However, I will say that it was him because he was a justice of the peace. I believe that this same Burgess had family that came to reside in DeKalb County and has his name on the old jail house on Memorial Drive in Decatur, Georgia. And he was a judge in DeKalb. This will also let you know that this is the reason Rev. Dr. Martin Luther King was arrested and held in DeKalb County on a simple speeding ticket by honorable Judge Mitchel, and was killed by a well-known name in the Scull Shoals district, the Ray family!*

In the 148th District of Penfield, the McWhorters addressed a letter to Governor Brown in 1874 concerning the "Negro Problem." Was a wealthy landowner in Greene County. W. H. McWhorter had Joseph Fulton and Isham Carter at his place. William L. Tuggle had George English, Isham Tuggle and John Tuggle on his land. In the 138th section of Greene County called Baird's town, I found Tom Barrow and Gilbert Phinizy working for Baker Daniel. J. R. Boswell had Jerry Jennings and Moses Haynes, who will in some way become kin to Robert Calloway, the son of Major Calloway who is very close to Aaron. Aaron Janes is on J. R. Boswel place as well. W. F. Devant had Washington Evans, Jerry Lott, and Charles Dorsey working for him. Now, Mr. James Davison, whose family is close to Richard

Callaway and Emily Hurt, employed freedmen Charles Burk, Mike Reed, Washington Bowles, Joe Edmondson, and George Brisco. In the 140th district of Union Point, the Georgia Railroad hired these freedmen: Allen Parham, Columbus Hurt, Joe Carlton, Dolphias Phelps, Henry Kimbrough, Henry Briscoe, Dolphos Burley, Tom Harris, Albert Mitchell, Dovy Ellen, George Rhodes, Crawford Peek, and Esquire Hurt. *I must pause here and say that I found Esquire Hurt that was in Union Point in the third ward of Atlanta with the mysterious Emily Hurt Callaway and her family in the 1900s and now I find him working alongside of Columbus D. Hurt in 1872.*

Moving on, in the 145th District, I found ties to Henry Callaway and Morgan County Georgia! William Callaway is working for F. M. Loverett alongside of Cook Laborn, David Laborn, Wilson Wheley, Frank Swinney, John Robinson, Shandy Jerrell, Robert Speers, John Speers, Peter Perkins, and Ransom Edwards. It was told to me by Ms. Ruby Finch at Oconee Chapel Church that Labon or Laborn families were kin to the Calloway family. I know I am mentioning a lot of names, however, I want to show the scope of the large population of Blacks that lived in this area and the scope of the situation after the departure of these large populations of Blacks and I might show some families that might not know what happen to their family members.

Now, I know that Aaron will never become Will or Bill Callaway in 1880 in Morgan County. And yes, Richard Callaway and Emily Hurt married in 1877 but by whom and where they got married, I don't know. Richard might be the son of Birk Callaway, who is on the farm of G. W. Callaway in Bowling Green.

In the 147th, David C. Barrow hired Reuben Pope, Sandy Moody Barton Barnett, Walton Eberhart, Mingo Barrow, James Lumpkin, Isam Pope, and Henry Barrow. While Aaron Callaway was located on the property of Zack Freeman. Thomas Fambrough hired Thos. Watson, Frank Barnett, Ferdenos Barnett, Milton Fambrough, Ben Bugg, and Dick Smith. Clayton Johnson hired Berry Mitchell. Hurt Plantation had Young Partee at his place. *William Wilham had Peter Hurt on his property.* Thomas P. Janes hired George Barrow, Perry Barrow, Ben Barrow, Henry Gresham, and Bill Freeman. This is where Aaron and his wife Harriet and children would reside. Peter Hurt is kin to Dinah Hurt English, the wife of Abraham English.

I also found an older Charlie Calloway in Wilkes County in 1870, where Aaron originally came from before arriving in Greene County onto the Cheney place.

The 1870s in Wilkes County Georgia

The 1874 tax digest in Wilkes County is the only time that I found Charlie Callaway and Burwell, the two sons of Aaron, working together. There were a few more colored Callaways that I found, and I will try and mention a few of their names in this section as well. In the 174th District of Wilkes County Flem Callaway was making his home in this part of the county of Wilkes. J.W. Callaway hired George Daniel and Henry Williams. C. A. Alexander hired Henry Terrell. *Ned Callaway worked for Seaborn Callaway.* James Austin and Nathan Austin and Jack Brown and George Brown, Bob Evans, Sam Moss all worked for E. C. Austin. Aristides Callaway hired Allen Callaway and Calvin Callaway, Felix Smith, and William Arnold. C. M. Callaway hired Joe Booker, Isham Jones, and Steven Penn. M. B. Moss hired Henry Mays, George Moss, William Harris, Aaron Jones, who is the great-great-grandfather of my grandmother Georgia Mae Callaway. William R. Callaway hired Cyrus Lumpkin, William Booker, Burwell Callaway, Albert Hanson, Thomas Dunn, and Joe Lumpkin. *As you can see Aaron must have had a closer relationship to the Callaway's in Wilkes County send his son Burwell to work in Wilkes County for William R. Callaway. Remember, when Aaron left Sardis with a letter from the church and was accused of stealing prior to receiving the letter in 1866, William R. Callaway was the clerk of the church at Sardis.*

B. M. Callaway or Brantley M. Callaway hired Tom Sherrer, Joe Hanson, Allen Norman, and John Bankston. Sang Callaway worked on the property of J. Freeman with Step Norman. Jim Callaway was on the property of J. C. Tyson and Dr. Fred Hunter had Mack Callaway working for him right alone with Lewis Caldwell in the 167th District. *In the 177th District, George Samuels and Jeff York and Ned Floronoy were on S. Booker place. Ned and Allen Booker and Alfred Callaway, D. C. Callaway, and Willis Weems, Henry Harris, Henry Paschal are all on the property of T. H. Strozier.*

In the 179th District of Wilkes County in 1874, I found working for Mr. W. H. Lindsey, Mr. Charles Callaway, and Alfred Eberhart, Joe Crane, John Mulligan and Felix Cofer. A. Cohen employed Elias Jones, John Jones, Harrison House on his property in the 180th district of Wilkes. In the same district was Jesse Callaway as well as Mr. Ralph Jones, Nathan George Charles McClendon, Fred Sutton, Carter Turner who were all working for H. S. McClendon.

In the year of 1875, in the 164th District of Wilkes County, I found Mr. Willis Anderson, Harry Anderson, Jack Andrews, Bob Bonner, Edward Bonner, and Betsey Bonner, Peter Colman, Allen Crane, John Stokes, James Strothers, Jim Jackson, William Jones, and Ester Jackson, George O'Neal, William Wingfield and Cyrus Wingfield.

On the property of Levi Callaway was Alfred Favor, Jesse Hurly, George Daniel, and Henry Williams. Wilson Callaway was on the property of the Hillsman brothers. Austin Callaway was on the lands of T. T. Hunter with Mose Hill, Scot Hill, Calvin Hill, Charles Burns, General Favor, and Andrew Callaway. Flem Callaway was on the property of S. G. Pettus.

In the 165th District, Aristide Callaway hired Charles Hillard, Allen Callaway, Sandy Winfrey, Peter Jones, Calvin Callaway, Wylie Norman, Nick Callaway and Jack Williams, Felix Smith, James Butler, Rice Turner, William Johnson, William Arnold, Berry Arnold, Henry Furlow, William Callaway, and Lewis Murphy.

Aaron Jones is still on the property of M. B. Moss with Henry Mays, George Littleton, William Harris, James Walker, Edd Walker, Tom Bolton, and Jerrett Fortson. *W. R. Callaway's hired hands were Cyrus Lumpkin, Tom Dunn, Burrell Callaway, Sam Callaway, Alfred Callaway, Sanders Barrett, and Joe Barrett. B. M. Callaway hired Squire Irvin, Abram Callaway, Charles Callaway, Allen Callaway, John Bankston, and Tom Sheerer. George Willingham was on the property of Mr. R. Simms.*

In the 166th District, called Derbyshire, was Lewis Norman, who was on the property of William Lunceford. Sang Callaway was at J. Norman's place. Dick Callaway or Richard Callaway was on the property of S. B. Wingfield with Albert Hanson.

Joel Hurt's Will and his slave Dina

The first place to start at is the will of Mr. Joel Hurt. What I found it was a surprise to see how close the black Hurts stayed near or on the property of Joel Hurt when some of the Callaway slaves were more mobile and is hard to find, the Hurts are centralized in one spot in Georgia.

I Joel Hurt being of sound mind and disposing memory, ordain, declare and publish this to be my last will and testament, thereby revoking all other there before made by me.

Item-1st The Property herefore given to my children who have married, I consider equal except H. L. French's wife and I hereby give said French's wife the labor and use of Kate a Negro woman from the time they have had her until I call for her the use of her without hire until my death.

Item 2nd I give my wife Mary a negro girl named Harriet and her child, also Jenny a mulatto girl, also items and crops from his estate for her support as a life time of his estate except; Harriet and her child, and the girl Jenny and her increase.

Item 3rd I will to my son James the boy Henry and the woman Dilly and her children, and all her increase, and to my son Augustus the boy Tom, and the woman Sally and her children and all future increase. To my son John the boy Squire, and the woman Lizzie and her children and all her increase. And should either or any of the negroes become worthless or depreciate in value before going into their possession respectively it is my will that the lose be made up to him or them out of the remainder of my estate before any distribution herein after made shall take place.

"To even think that a human being as being worthless and to decrease in value as being a Christian is beyond my scope of reasoning. Maybe some of the sins of the fathers were passed to the children of these men or ethnic groups of so-called high society whose family got rich off the backs of these same worthless Blacks, still do reason like this man Hurt! I say this now, to the more intelligent generation today and to those who earnestly believe in the Holy Scripture, we are not to look down on the down trotted or weak willed man. Scripture says; Romans Chapter 15; 1st verse; We then that are strong ought to bear the infirmities of the weak, and not to please ourselves, 2nd verse; Let every one of us please his neighbor for his good to edification. 3rd verse; "For even Christ pleased not himself; but, as it is written. The Reproaches of them that reproached thee fell on me". I read this 3rd Item and I was floored and amaze at the ignorance and Pride of man!

Item 4th To my wife Mary I will and bequeath all my lands and the following negroes, - viz. Crawford and his wife and her eight children, also Franky and her six children, also Peter and his wife and her youngest child, also Griffin, Hal and Ned. Etc.... for and during her life time for support and maintenance and at her death the lands is to go to and rest in my three sons and the negroes mentioned in this clause at her death is to be equally divided between all of my children under the same conditions as the remainder of my property in the next item of this my will.

The Slave that Mr. Hurt left his wife Mary are Crawford Hurt and wife and children, Franky and her six children, Peter and his wife and her youngest child, also Griffin Hurt, Hal Hurt, and Ned Hurt. Are all living near each other where they all were slaves on the 6th day of October 1864. Griffin Hurt would now be fifty four years old, Peter and Mary his wife are both seventy years old in 1880 in 148th district of Greene County.

Oh! Crawford Hurt and his wife Harriet are in their forties, he is forty six and she is forty four. Dinah English and her husband Abe will live among Dinah's family the Hurts before moving onto Felix E. Boswell place.

Item 5th My will is that the remainder of my estate of all kinds whatsoever to be divided to be divided into eight equal parts to be distributed as follows; to each of my three sons before mentioned, I will one part respectfully and to each of my daughters viz. Caroline Wynn, Emily French, Mary Johnson, Josephine Stevens, and Cordelia Stevens, I will and share and share alike, of the five remaining parts free from the debts and contract of their present and future husbands and at their death respectfully to get to their respective child or children and should either or any of them die, without leave any or such child or children, then it is my will that her or their portion go to the surviving brothers or sister or their children.

Item 6th I hereby appoint my three sons James, Augustus, and John and constitute them executors, giving them full powers to carry into effect my last will and testament and leaving to their discretion whether they shall make returns of appraisement and distribution or not. In witness thereof I have hereunto set my hand and seal this sixth day of October 1864. Joel Hurt.

Witness to his will are; Addison A. Bell, Joseph B. Stevens, and Jeramiah Maxey.

As you can see the name of Dinah is not mentioned in Joel Hurt estate. This tells me that she is on the property of Hiram L. French his son-in-law place. I know what brings me to this decision it's the first name of Dinah French that is living near Abe English and his wife Dinah. Dinah French is always living a few houses away from Dinah and Abe English. Mr. Hiram L. French hails from New York City. And I just had to look a little bit further into Mr. Hiram L. French and his slave Dinah! The year is 1840 in Oglethorpe County Georgia in the house of Hiram French. Hiram has another male in the house with him that is about the same age as he is. This person I believe is William French. The two white males are between the ages of twenty to twenty nine. And one white female between the ages of fifteen and nineteen, one white female is the daughter of his father-in-law whose name is Emeline. Hiram has a male and a female slaves between the ages of thirty six and fifty five, one female slave under ten and one female between ten and under twenty nine.

Before I go into the census I want to see if I can understand and reveal to you the relationship between Dinah the wife of Abraham English and seventy year old Peter Hurt and his seventy year old wife Mary and Peter Hurt Jr. and his wife Laura Campbell. Well, Dinah French I tried to tie to Dinah English, However, Dinah the wife of Abe English names her oldest daughter after the wife of Peter Hurt Sr. and Peter Hurt Jr. is working alone side of Abe English on J. T. Hurt place in the 1880's while young Mary was coming of age. I am assured she might have called Peter Hurt Jr. with an endearing tone in her voice, "Uncle Pete".

Now Dinah and Abe is neighbors of Mr. Lewis Kinnebrew and his wife Dilla whose name might have been English. Dinah and English are in their middle twenties. And living in the house of Lewis Kennebrew is a black young twenty year old man Richard Hurt the brother of Dinah and Dinah French at the age of forty six years old. Now, remember this is the year of 1870 and ten years later in 1880 Dinah French still resides near Abe and Dinah English. Dinah French was the servant of John T. Hurt and his son Lewis alone side of another servant by the name Augustus English. Augustus English is twenty nine years old and the former slave of Hiram L. French, Dinah is now at the age of fifty six years old. Living in the house on Mr. John T. Hurt place is Abe and Dinah English and their children Mary thirteen, Nannie ten, Anthony seven, Lucy five, Henry three, and Charles the youngest at the age of two. I wasn't surprise at the names of his children because it looks like all of their first names are after the Hurt side of the family. Dinah is naming a few of her children after familiar and white family members of her slave master and his children! And Abraham is doing the same. I believe Lucy is named for his mother. Abe names his six year old son Anthony after his father as well.

Now where was Augustus English prior to coming to work for Mr. John T. Hurt. Augustus in 1870, was living with his forty year old father Anthony and his siblings, Daniel was twenty one, Mealia is sixteen, Ann is twelve, Nancy is eight, Augustus the twenty year old, and Oliver Hurt at the same age as his brother Augustus. I believe that Anthony lost his wife during the war or before the Civil War. However, she is not listed in the house with her husband. Let's go and see if we can find Anthony's wife in the estate of Henry English in Greene County Georgia! I would love to know her name! The year is January 25, 1858 and Mr. Henry English daughter Ann E. English comes to age and is now ready to receive from her father's estate. John D. English her brother is now the guardian of Ann E. English and is over his father Henry estate. Ann receives the following negroes; a man named Thomas valued a $1000, a negro woman named Lucinda at the age of twenty two and is valued at $900., a negro boy named Jonas valued at $425., a negro girl named Ella age ten, valued at $525., a negro boy named Augustus at the age of six valued at $325., Augustus is the son of Anthony and Tom is Augustus grandfather and Lucinda is Augustus mother. I believe William is still living in the house with his mother Elizabeth at this time in 1854. Prior to John D. English becoming the executor of his father's estate A. I. Watson was the executor on December 19, 1846. H. L. French and Omar Pinkerton were the witnesses. Hiram L. French is the son-in-law of Joel Hurt from New York. Now I know that Dinah is in the house with her mother in the house of Hiram L. French and the daughter of Emeline Hurt French. I asked myself was Dinah French the personal slave of Emeline Hurt. Now the first name Emeline has another slave named after her and she is the daughter of Griffin Hurt who is named Emily. However, Dinah French last days are spent living in Clarke County the last place I find the mother of Dinah English is in Athens Clarke County in 1900. Emeline Hurt French last known residence was in Sumter County Georgia.

Anthony English fell under the lot of James N. English while James was in the house of his mother Elizabeth. Anthony was always hired out under the lot of slaves of James N. English with another slave named Jacob and Minerva and Tom. Old Tom who had been sick about a year between 1860 to June 19, 1861. John D. English paid Ned Parks to build a coffin for old Tom for six dollars. I might as well say what I am thinking! Anthony is standing by the grave side of Tom his father with his sons Abraham and Augustus and his wife Lucinda and others saying goodbye for now! I am overcome with emotions that as I am writing this information I wonder If I came across his grave on one of my many walks through Bairdstown and in the old Harmonia cemetery near Maxey, Oglethorpe County. Or he could be buried in the Wilson Cemetery that once was named the Hurt Cemetery at one time that was located on Callaway Road where a large number of Hurts are buried. The closest Jacob English I could find in 1870 was in Liberty County Georgia. I don't quite know how he fits into Anthony's family but he is mentioned in the lots of his family. Jacob English was living with Delia and their children. Jacob was thirty four, and Delia was twenty seven, and Seabright was eight, Tilly was four and Georgianna was two.

The Hurt and English Families

The confusing part of the tax digest that I have come across in dealing with Greene County and the southern part of Oglethorpe County was that the 1880s one does not give me definite answers. And the relationship between Aaron and Charlie Callaway while in Greene County never materializes. However, I do know that Charley married Mary Hurt in Clarke County and George Callaway married Nannie Hurt in Oglethorpe County, so I will mention the Hurt family again here in the 1880s. The Hurts could very well pass as whites.

The year is 1870, the sixth day of June, and the assistant marshal is J. H. Brightwell.

I will attempt to put the Hurt family in the perspective that will show the relationship between the White privileged and the Negroes that could pass as white. I do know that the Hurts that I have met are and can pass as whites! The first family of Hurts that I will mention is the family of Crawford Hurt, a colored forty-six-year-old mulatto man, and Harriet Hurt, the forty-four-year-old wife of Columbus D. Hurt. Their son Jesse Hurt is eighteen, Charlie is sixteen, John C. is twelve, Addie is ten, Millie is twenty-four, and Lula is three.

The next family of Hurts is made up of Lila Hurt, a seventy-old lady living with Henry Hurt, who is a twenty-six-year-old man. Also Catharine nineteen, Lymon Hurt twenty-two, Jennie Hurt seventeen, and Callie Hurt, who is nine.

Madison Hurt is a forty-year-old mulatto living with Sophia, his thirty-year-old wife. James is eighteen, Jasper is sixteen, John H. is twelve, Savannah is eleven, Hiram is nine, Symms is seven, Julia is five, and Betsy is two.

I do not know the relationship between the colored Hurts and the white Hurts. However, I do know that they are very close. The colored Hurts will come to reside on the property of the white Hurts in Oglethorpe County in Maxey. While I am on the subject of the white Hurts, let us visit them as well. T. L. Hurt is forty-one years old, with his wife L. M. Hurt, who is thirty-eight. They have two daughters, Harriet and Louisa. T. L. Hurt has four sons, John T., Joel, Emory, and Earl F. Hurt. The father of T. L. Hurt is John T. Hurt, a seventy-four-year-old man. The white Hurts are living at the corner of West Main Street and Zion Street in Maxey. Also living in the house of T. L. Hurt is Anna Butler, a twenty-eight-year-old colored servant. The white neighbors of the Hurts are M. E. Harper and C. B. Bryant. In addition, Will McLain had two colored servants in his house. The servants are Sam Norwood and John Taylor. Sam might become the husband of Aaron's daughter Della.

Crawford Hurt's house is listed as being house number 98, Lila Hurt's house is numbered 99. Madison Hurt is a forty-year-old colored man living at the house that is numbered 100. Living in house number 101 is forty-year-old Anthony English and Daniel, a twenty-one-year-old, and Mealia, a sixteen-year-old. Ann a twelve-year-old, Nancy an eight-year-old, Augustus a twenty-year-old, and Oliver another twenty-year-old mulatto man.

Living in house number 102 is Eliza English, a forty-year-old woman, and Sarah, eight years old. The next house belongs to my grandfather's grandparents. *In house number 103, Dinah Hurt English is listed as being the head of the household. Dinah is twenty-five and Abram is twenty-eight. Mary, my grandfather's mother, is eight years old, Nannie is ten months old. Dinah and Abram are listed as being black.* Richard Hurt is living in the house with Lewis Kennibrew, a fifty-year-old black man, and his wife Silla, who I believe is off the farm of Isaac and Winifred Callaway. Silla is fifty as well. They have a daughter name Ellen and she is twenty years old. I believe that Richard is in the Kennibrew house because he is courting Ellen, their daughter. Richard is a mulatto man. The Kennibrews have another daughter by the name of Lotty, and she is four years old. The Kennibrew house is numbered 104, the last house before you get to the house of James Hurt. James is thirty-eight years old and has Howard, a four-year-old son, and Mamie, who is two. John is thirty-four years old and is with his son Gladden, who is one years old. Imagine having the oportunity to walk the place and through this very same house! And to know that your family whom you have never known anything about would come to life as you set in the setting of this place and know that as the land looked was the same view that they were apart of building with the sweat of their brow. An old white gentleman told me that the blacks who worked the land feel dead and majority of the time they were buried where they had fallen. I was surprised to hear such a statement and shocked of his casual expression on his face as he told me these words.

Mrs. Celestia Stephens is the wife of Mr. P. M. Stephens. However, she is living in the house of Mr. John Jewell, a thirty-one-year-old man, and his wife Sarah, a twenty-four-year-old. Kenah is a twenty-two-year-old domestic servant. Richard is their seven-month-old son, Francis is an eleven-year-old mulatto boy, and Joseph is a twenty-two-year-old black farm laborer. P. M. Stephens is who Charlie works for 1n 1866 and Aaron would work for Mr. Jewell as well. Now the house of Marshall Epps, a white farmer aged fifty-three, and his wife Elmira, a fifty-two-year-old lady. Oma is twenty-four, Ida is eighteen, Allie is sixteen, Hattie is fourteen, Haywood is eight, and their white male servant is named Mr. S. Haden, a twenty-four-year old. Aleck Bryant is a thirty-seven-year-old white farmer living with his wife Lizzie, who is twenty-two; Kate, their two-year-old daughter; and an infant just a few months old.

Mr. Daniel Stevens is a thirty-seven-year-old colored farmer and his wife Harriet is twenty-one. Their children are Nancy, twelve; Eliza, eleven; Parthenia and Queen, twins, seven; Lula, five; Dora, three; and Daniel, one. The next house is Mr. T. L. Epps, a thirty-three-year-old white farmer and his wife N. C., who is thirty-four. Effie is nine, Lemar is seven, Darah is five, Celestia (spelled Selestia) is three, and John is one. *Living next door is Mr. Robert Callaway, a thirty-two-year-old black farm laborer and his wife Anna, who is a thirty-year-old mulatto woman, and William, their four-year-old son. I always wondered during my research what happened to the young son of Robert and Anna Callaway. He was born in 1876. However, I did find a Will Callaway born at this time in Chamblee, Georgia, in 1876, but I thought he might be the son of Martin Mathew Callaway in Lithonia. Will showed up with Martin Callaway in 1901, working for the road gang in DeKalb County. Will Callaway of Penfield was born the son of Robert Callaway. I traced him moving from the place of Robert Callaway in Oglethorpe county to Penfield alone. William Callaway would also be living as a white man and a colored man as well.*

The community that surrounded Abraham and Dinah Hurt English in or near Maxey during the 1878 tax digest in the town of Bairdstown with J. T. Hurt, hired Abe English, and Gus or Augustus English, Hamilton Hines, Ned Kidd, Ban Lumpkin, who was over sixty, Edmond Lawrence, Charles Lumpkin, John Hurt, Tom Haynes, and Anthony Haynes, J. L. hurt hired Crawford Hurt, Aaron Johnson, Josiah Hurt, and Henry Gresham. Charles is in his early twenties and Mary is about eleven years old growing up on the Hurt place with her younger sister Nannie and brothers Henry and Charles and John. The Hurts that are on the plantation of J.L. and J. T. are the relatives of Dinah and Peter Hurt her brother and Griffin Hurt, who I suppose is the father of Dinah.

In the year 1879, in Bairdstown, Oglethorpe County, Georgia, Bob Callaway or Robert Callaway was working for the Georgia Railroad. This would put Mr. Robert Callaway in the city of Atlanta while working for the Georgia Rail Road. Mr. J. T. Hurt hired Abe English and Guss English as well. J. L. Hurt hired Hoss Hurt, Jordan Hurt, and Bath Hurt in 1879, while in Falling Creek Mr. A. T. Brightwell hired Shade Barrow, Wyly Bell, Rich Britain, Alfred Bell, and *Burrell Callaway, kin to Shad Barrow.*

Mr. Ferdinand Phinizy hired York Phinizy, Joe Phillips, Dock Phillips, and Oliver Patrick. Mr. William Gilliam hired Jobe Finch, Mose Finch, Dock Freeman, Marsh Freeman, John Gresham, Elijah Goolsby, Josh Goolsby, Sam Givens, Peter Hill, Sims Hunter, William Harris, Red Hatton, Aaron Gains, Walt Johnson, and Wes Johnson. *As you may have noticed, Mr. A. T. Brightwell is now in Bairdstown. Relocating from Scull Shoals to make a living after leaving the property of Mr. Finley in Scull Shoals out near highway 15 and north of Macedonia Church Road. I believe that it is more pleasant living in the town of Baird than in Scull Shoals and out near the Oconee River and the chain gang.*

In 1880, in the town of Bairdstown, T. L. Epps hired Bob (Robert) Callaway. In 1881, in Bairdstown in Oglethorpe County, J. L. Hurt hired Ed Crawford, Abe English, Harrison Thomas, and James Thomas, who was over sixty years old. All were on the property of J. L. Hurt. Robert is missing at this time in 1881. I believe that Robert Callaway is in Wilkes County. *Robert Callaway marries Lettie Hardeman on January 5, 1881, and is married by Rev. Brantley M. Callaway. However, I never find any records of Robert Callaway in the tax digest nor in any courthouse records besides him getting married to Lettie Hardeman. I must digress, I did find him once in the tax digest in Taliaferro County near Wilkes.*

In 1882, in Bairdstown, Bob (Robert) Callaway has left the property of T. L. Epps and has moved onto the property of Mr. T. E. Birchmore in Falling Creek in Maxey. About this same time in 1878, Aaron Callaway has born unto him and Harriet a child named Birchmore Callaway. *I must say that every white landowner Bob or Robert or Aaron Callaway has associations and aligns himself with the same white plantation owners has associations with Aaron's children. He also has associations with the same white plantation owners that Abraham and Dinah English are associated with as well.*

In 1882, J. T. Hurt has Guss English, Charles Labor, Edd Crawford, Anderson Smith, and Put Wright on his land. J. McWhorter has Charles Lumpkin, John Lumpkin, Nelson Armstrong, and Bob Shaw on his land in Bairdstown. I could not find Bob or Robert Callaway anywhere in Bairdstown at this time.

J. B. Crowley's list states that Elic English, in 1881, was in the Wolfskin District and he failed to pay his taxes, while Gus English and Abraham English were both in Bairdstown. Gus English failed to pay his taxes in Bairdstown in the years of 1883, 1886, and 1887. Abraham English failed to pay his taxes between 1885, 1886, and 1888. Joe Edward was here at this time as well and he failed to pay in the years of 1887 and 1888. And Clem Edmondson failed to pay in the year of 1882.

Now, let us take a good look at the old historical section called Scull Shoals at this time and at its finest. You will get to see the inner workings of a large land holder and those who married into his family or have a close relationship to the family of Mr. Finley in 1882. The Hurts that worked close to the Finleys were the colored Hurts that lived in Partee District near the Moore plantation. This plantation also puts Aaron here as well. Maybe his name does not appear but those whom he associated with do appear, even the Johnson family! Even Willis William as well, who had a close relationship with the white Burgess family. I went down this road toward Macedonia many times looking for the place where my great-great-grandfather and his family resided, just looking across the fields that used to be, hoping to find a sign of a burial plot or something in the Scull Shoals area, not knowing that with the dignity and prestige that came within this family they are just not buried wherever they fell while working in the field. The church in Scull Shoals is the Bethabara Colored Church and I could not find the cemetery the second time I went there after realizing my negligence the first time I walked through the woods trying to find a family member. It was very disheartening when I failed to realize how important the cemetery of Bethabara Colored Church was to me because of its location. However, I did enjoy few times there one Sunday morning as I saw Mr. Callaway sitting there with his legs crossed in a position that I have seen my grandfather so many times. He had the same complexion as my grandfather as well; you can imagine the nostalgia that I was experiencing! Yes, I was having a sentimental longing and affection for my times with my grandfather Arthur!

At this time in 1882, the property of James T. Findley was being handled by Mr. A. T. Brightwell. It was in April when cash went to Mr. O. P. Findley for $115. His estate sold for $2111 in June. W. B. Brightwell, the father of A. T. Brightwell, received money. Mr. Nicholson, on July 5, received property. On December 9, Mr. Nicholson's property would become the place where Burrell, the eldest son of Aaron, would come to reside. P. A. Walden and W.C.B. or the Boswell brothers received notes. December 30, Ms. M. J. Harris, Doc Findley had notes for rent and so did Henry Hurt. And in September, R. L. Burgess paid notes along with R. A. Maxey, Jessie Maxey, W. A. Burgess, W. T. Cochran, Columbus Hurt, and J. G. Nunnally.

Also, on August 2, W. H. Tuggle paid attention to illness to Mr. Findley. The next day, Catherine Hurt was paid for her work as a cook. O. P. Findley paid for his burial. On March 22, O. P. Finley to Mrs. Nancy Maxey. On March

26, W. A. Burgess and Margaret Freeman received money. On March 27, Ann Fambrough, James Johnson, Naomi and Lina Maxey, and Nancy Maxey. On April 13, John Michael and Mrs. Eliza Sims came by. On May 7, Eliza Johnson, an heir, and Mr. Raibon Johnson, the guardian. On June 1, A. T Brightwell received pay for his work as administrator. In May, Catherine Hurt, services as cook for four months, personally came before me as justice of the peace in and for said county, Catherine Hurt, colored, etc., Catherine X. Hurt made her mark. Catherine is the wife of Henry Hurt of the house that I had the opportunity to walk through and it is also called the Callaway house.

I never knew how closely Aaron Callaway and Abe English were living near and so close to each other. Aaron was in Greene County and Abe was in Oglethorpe right across the county line. It was just a walk down the Macedonia Church Road to Abe's house, which was located on the Hurt plantation, where you would find Mary, Charlie's wife, and his sister-in-law Nannie, her younger sister growing up with the eyes of Charlie fastened upon the young thirteen-year-old girl. In little community outside of Maxey called the Scull Shoals district, this estate record shows you a majority of the families in Scull Shoals and how closely related they were as family and friends and at one time slaves.

In the 1879 tax digest of Greene County, Georgia, in the 147th District I found Columbus Hurt, Henry Hurt, Doc Finley (founder of the Finley Chapel Church), and William McWhorter all working for James T. Finley. Thrasher Callaway was on R. L. or Robert Ligion McWhorter's property, with Mike Reed and Dan Reed. Now, there is no Aaron Callaway or Burwell Callaway in Maxey or Partee 147th Greene County. However, every time they are missing out of the district a strange name appears. *Thrasher Callaway* is a very unusual name that would appear just like Anderson Callaway appeared when Aaron was living as a white landowner over the estate of Mr. Campbell in the 147th. Oh! Jesse is still located in Penfield and gaining more property. *I walked the woods up near the Christopher place and up near the Oconee Colored Baptist Church where I played the piano under the watchful eye of Ms. Ruby Finch. After every service I walked up a large hill and came first upon a hunting camp. It was quite a sight when I came across the carcasses of small deer and animals. On this journey, I wanted to experience and did experience what it was to be a young Burrell Callaway and being with his new wife Mitt. Burrell and Mitt Callaway had five daughter and one son. The oldest daughter was named Francis, then Sis, Vessie, Sarah, Morset and Ozie would grow up around this area where I found it to be one of the most intriguing place as I made my way to the Oconee River. Ozie the youngest child mention was born the same year as my grandfather Kator (Arthur) I can see them playing and hunting and fishing and their names being called by either Mary or Mitt Callaway their mothers. As I walked these old grounds I found many foundations that once supported the dwelling places of the families that lived here. Walking up and down these roads, I was excited to notice how far one had to travel to get to their neighbor's house. I walked where all of Aaron Callaway and Abraham English children would play and grow up together and attended this church and is buried along the hill side of the large cemetery located on the side and behind Oconee Baptist now old church yard. What a vision I can see in my mind the young child that I called granddaddy running to meet his cousins and friends at the Church that now sits empty but once you could hear the songs resounding through the air as you made your way to the church that set way back in the beautiful wilderness. We Love you Miss Ruby Finch rest in Christ Jesus!*

Not knowing anything about my grandfather Arthur, I can be sure now that Kator left the Hurt property with his older brother Charlie and made their way towards Scull Shoals to visit his cousins and his kin. I can just only imagine the fishing adventures the cousins taken bait and sinkers to go fishing and swimming in Sandy Creek over to Falling Creek to the banks of the Oconee River. I got to walk all the way to the Oconee River from the Oconee Baptist Church to the place where Falling Creek emptied into the Oconee River. At the intersecting of the two I saw again foundations where houses once stood. Can you imagine how I was feeling right then and there? When I got down to the Oconee I saw the wire bridge that once crossed the river. This is the bridge that Mrs. Ruby told me about while having choir rehearsal at her house in Athens. Mrs. Ruby said that this was the quickest way to get to Athens from that place. You had two roads that led to this bridge called the Upper and Lower Wire Bridge Roads. Ms. Ruby was the child of Starling Finch and Elizabeth Brightwell, who were married on February 21, 1890, by Rev. E. J. Holland in Oglethorpe County. Ms. Ruby's grandfather was named Henry and her grandmother was named Emily and she had an aunt by the name of Sarah. I found them on the 1880 census living near Mr. Jacob Finch and his wife and children. By the year 1930, Ms. Ruby was at the age of thirteen and living with her mother Elizabeth, who was now at the age of fifty-nine and is a widow. Moses, her eldest brother, is twenty. Betty, her sister, is eighteen; Starling Jr. is fourteen. Ms. Ruby and Richard are twenty-one, and living next door is Henry, who is named for Starling's brother, and is thirty-eight years old. His wife Emma is thirty-three. The choir held rehearsals at Mrs. Ruby's house and I must say what a beautiful home she made there in Athens, Clarke County, Georgia. I saw her father's picture with the family, and I must say he looked almost white! And as she spoke of him, her voice gave way to emotions and it was in a very endearing way that brought me to tears as well. With great care and love and carefully reminiscing, did she take me back to Falling Creek. I enjoyed being in her home and in her presence as she poured out her memories to me and my wife Sheila. When I left, I knew that we would always be welcomed back to that house in Clarke County and not only by her but also by the beautiful family at Oconee Baptist Church! Thank you all, so very, very much! I not only got to play at Oconee but also at the church at Penfield, Sanders Chapel. Thank you all as well for your kindness and love toward us.

In the 1880 tax digest I found in the 147th District, Maxey, Aaron Callaway working for Thomas M. Fambrough with Dick Smith, Jim Barrow, Dawson Barrow, Davis Maxey, Phil Griffith, Tom Watson, and Frank Barnett, who has their own property, as well as Tom Finch.

In 1881, T. M. Fambrough had Thomas Watson, Albert Fambrough, Monroe Fambrough, John Fambrough, Felix Fambrough, Dick Smith, Giles Finley, Aaron Callaway, Ale Fambrough, Alonzo Fambrough, and Howard Fambrough. Columbus Hurt is on his own land.

In the year 1882, for the first time Richard Callaway is in Woodville in the 138th District.

In the year 1883, Dick Callaway or Richard is still in the 138th District, on the property of J. L. Young. Aaron was at the place of Zack Freeman in the Partee District. I found Henry Callaway on the farm of J.M. Griffin working alongside Dick Gray, Allen Whirter, John Tiller, Isham Carter, and Alfred Swain. *James M. Griffin is the marshal over at the 137th District in 1880, the same district where Mr. Griffin Hurt resides in the house of a white man, Mr. Benjamin Collins. This would put both Richard and Henry Callaway in the same place in the 137th District near Bairdstown.*

Now, Aaron was working on the farm of R.A. Maxey in the Partee District. Aaron was working alongside Bob Maxey or Robert Maxey and Bob Williams. *However, in April 15, 1884, Aaron was accused in Clarke County for trespassing. The warrant was issued for Aaron on the thirty-first of July 1884 by R. T. Pittard, the justice of the peace. However, R. T. Pittard resides in Oglethorpe County. The courthouse of Oglethorpe is not quite established, so the cases of Oglethorpe might be held in Clarke County, Georgia. I state this because the property of the accuser of Aaron is in Bowling Green in Oglethorpe County. Aaron was arrested and in the custody of Sheriff John W. Weir and J. H. Willingham. Aaron pleads not guilty to the charges and H. C. Tuck would be his attorney to plead his case in 1884. All of this took place on the sixteenth of October 1884. They charged him with simple larceny. The witnesses for the state were F. T. Pittman, P. B. Johnson, H. H. Crenshaw, R. H. Mathews, and Henderson Tyler, a colored man from this section of Oglethorpe County. Felix T. Pitman said that Aaron, on the thirtieth day of July 1884, took a watermelon that was valued* *at ten cents. Aaron was bailed out of jail by John Winter for $50 on July 31, 1884. Aaron was to personally appear at the city court on the second Monday in October and then he made his famous and very notorious ignorant mark, the famous X. H. D. McDaniel was the governor of the State of Georgia at this time I would like to elaborate on this Aaron Callaway. I believe that he is non-other-than Bob or Robert Callaway of Aaron Cheney of 1870! I say this because of this fact, Mr. R. T. Pittard goes his bond in Clarke County. It also shows me the relationship that Bob or Robert or Aaron Cheney Callaway has with lawyer Henry C. Tuck as his attorney at this time and the relationship he will have with Charlie his son the brother of George and Cleveland or Clayborn Callaway.*

Remember, I told you Aaron was in Clarke County and was working on the plantation of the Tuck brothers. Maybe this is the reason the young Henry C. Tuck came to be his attorney.

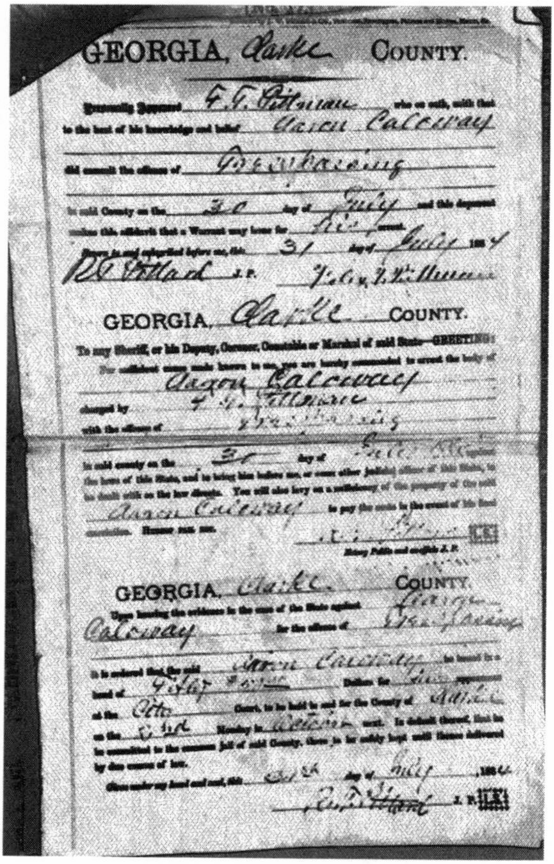
GEORGIA, Clarke COUNTY.

Aaron Calaway

did commit the offense of Trespassing

In said County on the 30 day of July

31 day of July 1884

R T Pittard J.P.

GEORGIA, Clarke COUNTY.

To any Sheriff, or his Deputy, Coroner, Constable or Marshal of said State—GREETING:

Aaron Calaway

charged by

with the offense of

in said county on the 30 day of

Aaron Calaway

GEORGIA, Clarke COUNTY.

Calaway for the offense of Trespassing

Aaron Calaway

Fifty $50

City

31st day of July 1884

R T Pittard J.P. [L.S.]

Aaron in Clarke County in the1870s to the 1880s

Aaron worked in Clarke County on Williams H. Dean's property after he left Mr. Winters' in 1873. You can see why Mr. Winter would go bond on Aaron Callaway's or Bob Callaway's behalf in 1884. Major Cheney is with Aaron Cheney both are off of the Cheney plantation in Bairdstown in the 1880's. Major and Dick Hargrove and Isiah Landrum and Tonie Tiller and Spence Winfrey and Wash Winfrey were all on Mr. Dean's property in 1874 over by the Georgia factory in the 217th District of Clarke County. Mr. W.H. Dean and his brother Joel M. Dean had property they were leasing out to Aaron and others to work their fields. Squire Cooper and James Cooper were on Joel Dean's property while Allen Cooper was working over on W.H. Lester's property. At this time, J.F. Morton had hired the Barnet's Toney, Jack, Mat and Tiller, and the Billups brothers, Luis and John and Lindsey Dean and Dub Martin, Wash McRee, Hill McRee, Alex White, and Perry Walker to work on his property. The McRee brothers came up with Aaron from Scull Shoals and so did the Barnet brothers, all came out of Maxey, Oglethorpe, Georgia, down between Greene County and Oglethorpe County.

Mr. W.P. Vancey had a lot of work for the coloreds to do on his property. Mr. Vancey had at least forty-four families on his property at one time. Some were the same families that were working on Mr. Lester's and others' land. Fed Buggs and Edward Billups, Solomon Billups, Clarke Barnet, Sandy Crawford, Cyrus Coleman, Willy Cole, Albert Graves, Frank Daniel, Hawkin Dean, Thomas Sanders, Gager Moss, Aaron Mason, Emanuel Jones, Clem Johnson, Dan Simmons, Henry White, Green Wingfield, Sully Williams, George Washington, Andrew Smith, Burrell Roberson Senior and Junior, Anderson Pope, Mell Roberson, James Wayne and his brothers Hampshire and Anderson Senior and Junior were some of the men and their families on Mr. W.P. Vancey's land near the Georgia factory in 1874.

Mrs. M.A. Kittle had Bill (William) Callaway on her property right along with Mike Henderson and James Harrison and Thomas Marble in 1874 as well. Mrs. Kittle's husband William owned a bar room in Clarke County. Mr. W. R. Tuck and his brother took on the task of taking on as many colored families as they could for the factory in the 216th District in Clarke County. Henry Clayton, Frank David, Green Ellis, Jack Ellis, George Johnson, Jack Lee, Armstead Louis, Edmon Morton, Louis O'Kelly, Willis Pope, Oliver Rucker, Elijah Arch, Charlie Callaway, Cleveland Callaway, John Austin, and his wife and sisters and their children, Armstead Barnett, Jordan Billups, James Billups, William Billups, Mary Brown, William Cary, Carter Daniel, Dave Daniel, William Fir (Fur), Norman Green Samuel Johnson, Richard Jones, Simon Mack, George W. McRee, Judge Morton, Abram Morton, Jack Oliver, Clark Dinson, Nelson Rucker, Anderson Thomas, Joe Humphries, Ale Barner, Bill Ware, Harry White, Miles Winfrey, and Cato Wiley.

In the year 1876, Thomas and Mary Epps are colored living in the 216th District of Athens. And Aaron Callaway is still moving back and forth on Mr. William H. Dean's property on Lexington Road with John Dean and Sandy H. Harris. William Morton has Edmond Jones and John Austin on his place during the years of 1877 and 1880. About this time, Aaron didn't come up to Clarke County and Robert shows up on the Epps Property in lower Oglethorpe County near Maxey.

Aaron must have had to return back to Clarke County to take care and watch over his children that were living there and were underage. Aaron was living near Robert T. Callaway. Aaron, with his wife, came back to Clarke County in 1881. You might as well say this was his second home. R. T. Callaway is a white male at thirty four, Aaron Callaway is fifty five and Tissue is fifty four, and Hattie is twelve. Remember in 1870 Aaron was under the last name of Cheney with his sons Charlie and Cleveland and his daughter three year old daughter Sis who is Hattie in 1880. Now the question is Aaron in 1900 on the property of William Eberhart? It couldn't be but non-other-than Robert Callaway. I don't quite know the relationship between Robert (Bob) Callaway and Aaron Callaway of Schull Shoals, but there's got to be something there between the two men! Now, concerning Robert T. Callaway the thirty four year old young white man. I have him coming off of the property of George W. Callaway in Bowling Green. However, he could be from Paulding County as well. Oh! the mystery of this man Bob or Aaron!

I found that on *June 18th 1870 in Paulding County Georgia P.O. Box Dallas Ga. Black woman Julia Callaway a fifty years old. Her son Robert is twenty five and Ida her daughter is nineteen years old. The only other colored family is that of Mr. Moses Jones a twenty five year old and his wife Eluda who is nineteen and their children Mary who is three and Joseph who is ten months old. The strange thing is that I can't find a husband that would tie Julia to a Callaway man. However, I might have a tie to Monroe County South Georgia and Alabama! That is the Pinckard's. Sarah Pinckard is a seventy year old white woman born in North Carolina, and her son or grandson Thomas who is sixteen, and William who I believe is her son living next door. William is thirty two, his wife Linda is twenty six, Mary is ten, Noah is eight, John is four, and Martha is two.*

1880 in Paulding County Georgia in Dallas I found thirty three year old Robert and his wife thirty year old wife Sally and their mother Julia Ann Callaway at the age of fifty five. Miss Julia has gotten younger instead of getting older! Robert and Sally has a daughter by the name of Savannah and she is a mulatto while both of her parents are listed as being black. Robert is living next door to Noah Pinkard a thirty eight year old and his thirty eight year old wife Sarah J. and their son John who is fourteen, and James who is eleven, and Zaro their daughter at the age of eight, William C. who is six and Peter who is four.

The only other blacks on this page of the census is Isaac Janes twenty five and Charley Pool who is twenty four.

In the year of 1900, Robert T. Callaway was now forty five years old and was born in November, and his wife Sallie A. was born in December of 1850. The strange thing is their ages does not match the year of their birth. Robert T. born in 1845 is forty one, and Sallie A. born in 1852 is forty nine. There is two black families that are neighbors of Robert and Sallie Callaway and they are Lewis Bryant forty five, and Austin Butler and his wife Evie and their niece Laster C. Harris. And yes, there's the Pinkard family. Lewis C. Pinckard is fifty seven and was born August 1848, and his sister Ellen H. Smith born November 1845 and was fifty four and single, and grandson Malcomb Pinkard born April of 1879 and was twelve years old. The strangest thing is Charles D. McGregor the enumerator of this district in Paulding County couldn't write in whether Robert T. Callaway was a colored man or a white man. He first listed him as being colored and then wrote over the C for colored with a W for white. The only other colored family was right next door to this mysterious man Robert T. Callaway of Dallas. Mr. twenty nine year old Austin Battle and his nineteen year old wife Evie and a niece named Lastor C. Harris who was eleven years old. Oh! There was Mr. Lewis Bryant a fifty one year old colored man living in the house before you came to the house of Mr. Battle. I must mentioned the Pinkard's who are always living nearby. Lewis C. who is fifty one is living with his sister Ellen H. Smith who is fifty four, and grandson Malcomb who is twelve years old. I felled to mention that Lastor C. Harris the niece of Austin Battle whose last name is Harris has the same last name as a white family living next door of the family of Robert F. Harris.

In Paulding County 1910, T. Luther Williams the enumerator stated that Robert T. Callaway a black man is sixty five years old and his wife Sarah is fifty nine and their niece Effie Wright is eighteen years old. Sarah had been married twice and Robert only once before. They've been married now for thirty seven years. And again I have to mention the Pinkard's that are always living nearby. Mrs. Lucy Pinkard is the heard of the family at the age of sixty four and is a widow living with her sister Ellen Smith who is sixty six and their niece Dessa M. Smith who is at the age of twenty six. Now, Williams A. Johns and his wife Mattie A. and their two sons Arthur and Benjamin F has a step brothers named Eugene Pinkard thirteen, Doyal eleven, and Clarence nine, and a father –in-law at the age of sixty six named James Brown. There is another familiar last name that comes to mind, it is Hawthorne. Grover C. Hawthorne is a white man at the age of twenty, and his wife Flora V. is nineteen, and a infant daughter one month old. As you may see, Robert T. Callaway neighbors are always or in the majority of the time are white. I only found Robert T. Callaway twice in the tax digest in Paulding County Georgia. So I might as well mention a few black or white men working as freedmen that were living and working by his side. Peter Adair, Jeff Cobb, George Deavours, Robert Elsberry, Thomas Lynch, J. Mathews, Wesley Marony, Robert Calloway, Moses Jones, George McConnell, Richard Lee, Isaac Gresham, N. Griffin, Isaac Shelton, Peter Turner, Andy Lester, Sirus Darby, Robin Scott, Alford Mullins, Washington Webb, Littleton Florence, Robert Cooper, Toney Glays, Charles Moon, Samuel Poole, Stewart Miller, Sandy Turner, Anderson Florence, Wm. Florence, Samuel Clonts, Solomon Chambliss, Mack Davis, Green Middlebrooks, Bob Holloman, Bob Farmer, Flemming Stoveall, Simon McElvey Jr. I couldn't find Robert T. Callaway and family in 1920, however, I found Marie Callaway an adopted daughter of Eleck C. Clonts. Young Marie was eight years old and Mr. Eleck C. Clonts was fifty two and his wife Marie was thirty three, and Earnest their son was nineteen. I also found a few marriages in Paulding County that were interesting as well. John R. Calloway a person of color married Sarah Pitman December 26 1872 by the Rev. John Moore. George Lester married Mary Sewell on the 15th day of March 1871 by the Rev. John Moon. L. B. McGregor is the ordinary. Neodemis Griffin and Idea Callaway married on the 29th day September 1870. Mr. Jim Reed married Dora McGregor Callaway in August on the 31st day of 1877 and Wade M. Graham was the minister.

About this same time, Aaron is back in Clarke County to meet Juda who has just relocated to Puryears with Willie Howard who is her son and the son of Aaron as well. Young Willie Howard as I have stated before is on the farm for the insane.

Aaron would go to work for Robert Tuck and John Austin was working right alongside of Aaron with Matt Barnett and his brothers Armstrong,

John Jr., and Toney, Jack, Francis, Charles, and Bivion. The Billups brothers were there as well. They were John James and Jamie L. Peter, and Billups Billups, Edmond Boss, and Wiley Coleman, William Coleman Squire Cooper, and John Cooper. All went to work for Mr. Robert Tuck. It seems that if you got into any trouble the landowners would be the ones to come and bail you out. William R. Tuck worked at the Clarke County Courthouse and was very influential to the things that went on in Clarke County at this time. By 1882, Mr. Robert Tuck only had six families on his property. Aaron Callaway, John Austin, John Barnett Jr., and Robert Dean and Linsey Dean and Andrew Austin. In 1882, I could not find Charlie Callaway on the tax digest in Clarke County at any time.

At this same time in 1882, Milly was killed on James Monroe Smith's place for armed robbery. She was thirty years old, a Mulatto woman with a nine-year-old son, Willie. Milly stood five feet tall and weighed 165 pounds when living in the Glade District of Oglethorpe County. Milly had a two-year-old daughter named Mary, who moved into the house with her uncle Robert, who was on the property of Mr. Epps in Maxey. Milly was close to the Johnson family, so was Charlie Calloway.

In 1883, Eliza Epps came to live in the 216th District of Clarke, with Thomas and Mary. Andrew Austin was working for Albert H. Weeks with Frank Bailey and Albert Barnett, whose nickname is Tiller Barnett. John Barnett, their brother, and Charlie Bostwick came to live with the Billups brothers, Joseph, James, George, and their sister Ann. Lewis Fletcher and Peter Brown are working on Joseph Epps's place down in Barber Creek.

Aaron came back to his second home in Clarke County in 1881. Aaron would go to work for Robert Tuck and John Austin will be working right beside Aaron with Matt Barnett and his brothers Armstrong, John Barnett Jr., and Toney, Jack, Francis, and Charles Bivion. In 1882, William R. Tuck has only six families on his property. Aaron Callaway, John Austin, John Barnett junior, Robert Dean, Lindsey Dean, and Andrew Austin. In 1882, Charlie and Clayborn and Cleveland Callaway could not be found in Clarke County, Georgia. However, I found them working on the Jackson's place in Bowling Green. Cleveland was working on Mr. S. Jackson's place and Charlie was on Mr. Ed Jackson's place. Here is where I would like to shed a little light on Cleveland or Claiborne Calloway the brother of Charlie. I have one tie to Bob Callaway or Robert Calloway with Claiborne and that is the last name Bunkley. Claiborne marries Vina Bunkley. Vina is the daughter of Adeline Bunkley in 1870. Adeline is twenty six years old and Vina is three, and Vina brother Grant is one years old. Mrs. Adeline is living near Mr. John English and his family in 137th district. Abraham named his oldest son John after this white landowner the son of old man Henry English. Young Miss Vina is the same age as Mary English who is in Bairdstown on the Hurts Plantation there with her mother Dinah Hurt English.

Mr. George English a colored man and his wife Isabella and their children one year old Eliza and one month old son John. The two brothers are side by side from Lincoln County to Clarke county to Greene County alone with Robert Callaway in just enough time to marry Letitia Hardeman in Wilkes County in 1881 by Rev. Brantley Callaway who now has a relationship with Robert Callaway the man by many names. I don't know if Adeline Bunkley is her married name or her birth name. I say this because of the family of Mr. Charles Bunkley living nearby in on Mr. James Brooks place a white farmer and his family. Charles Bunkley is fifty seven years old and his wife Sarah is forty three, the children are William eighteen, Mathew fourteen, Franklin is twelve, Martha is eight, Green is six, Robert is four, Mary is one, Richard is fifteen, and Betsey one years old. Now there was a son living near Mr. Wm. Burton he was Green. Charles son Green is eighteen, and a young girl name Julia is four, and young two year old William are servants of Mr. F. M. Cheney. Now a look at who might be the father of Isaac and George Callaway. What is going on, on the property of Mr. Burton place. I know only one Callaway that showed up on this property with his young son Claiborne Callaway and that is Mr. Robert or Bob Callaway who has been with Aaron and near the mother of Mary Hurt English and her father Abraham. As you can see Mr. Bob or Robert Charles Callaway and even Green Callaway is a very busy man. Because of his mystery within Aaron and Major Callaway's families I must take a better look at his activities through the tax digest and see what relationships that he established with the whites that were in each county he was in. In 1870 I know Robert or Bob Calloway is under the name of Aaron Cheney. It is not old Aaron born in 1820 but Bob Callaway and Lettitia Hardeman under the last name of Cheney in Oglethorpe County. I say this because of the neighbors he is surrounded by. Aaron is thirty two, Letitia Hardeman is twenty six, Charlie is eleven, Cleveland is seven, Sis or Silvey is three. Jerry Hudson is thirty six, Susan his wife is thirty four, Lemuel is ten, and living in the same house is Lee Hales a twenty two and his wife Jane is eighteen, living next door is Thomas Cheney at twenty two, Susan his wife is twenty five, and Lucinda their daughter is eight, Molly is six, Roll is four, Fred is two and Major Cheney is fifty and Sarah his wife is forty, William their son is twenty and Mary is eighteen, and Thornton is ten, living next door is Esquire Cheney at thirty two and Harriet his wife is thirty, Robert is eleven, Esquire is four and Watson is one, next door to Mr. Esquire Cheney is Mr. Watson Geer twenty five and his twenty two year old wife Martha and their children Edmond four and Mary their one year old daughter. Now, the most important part of this situation is who they are living by in this section of Oglethorpe County. Now, I know that this is not old Aaron Callaway from Scull Shoals area of Greene County Georgia! It is Bob Calloway or Robert Callaway and Letitia Hardeman. They are all living in the Beaverdam Section or the part of Athens Clarke County on the property that he will come to own in the 218th district of Clarke County Georgia! I say this because of this next neighbor that I am about to mention. Mr. Dean tucker a seventy year old white landowner and his wife Betsy at the age of seventy six, their house hold consist of Lucy D. Hales thirty five who will come to own the property I presume. Mary E. her twelve year old daughter, William T. Hales her ten year old son, Robert her eight year old, and Nancy Nicholson at the age of seventy three. Nancy might be from Falling Creek. Mr. Dean Tucker and wife Betsy both were born in Virginia and living on property valued in the thousands and personal property at two hundred dollars. I can't express how long Aaron, Bob, Robert, Green Callaway lived on this property and how he come into it. However, I know that between 1895 and 1900 this property was highly valued by evil undisclosed white men! Aaron has personal property valued at twenty five dollars and Esquire Cheney has personal property valued at sixty dollars they are the only Cheney or Blacks that have personal property to be taxed at this time in 1870. What else can I bolster my claim that Aaron Cheney is young Bob or Robert Callaway! I would have to take you back to the estate of Rev. Enoch Callaway and look at the age of Aaron Calloway off of his estate to bolster my claim! Now, George is working in Beaverdam for William Eberhart and his brother Charlie is on the place of B. B. Williams and they are located in Bowlingreen Oglethorpe County together again. Charlie the older brother of George is on Enoch R. Cheney place while George is on the place of J. S. Cheney place. Now a look at their father Aaron Calloway of Rev. Enoch Callaway place. I know you say How Aaron Calloway off of Rev. Enoch Callaway place could be Robert. Well take a good look at the age of Aaron Callaway in 1859. I can truly say that the 27 year old Aaron on Enoch Callaway's plantation is not Aaron Calloway from the Estate of Isaac Callaway place because of Reverend Enoch Callaway's will. Take a look at a portion of his will. *It was July 23, 1859 that Reverend Enoch Callaway resigned. Brothers Seaborn Callaway, J. Arnold and J. R. Crane were all sent to persuade Rev. Enoch not to resign.*

These are all the Negroes that were left Martha Callaway the wife of Rev. Enoch. Wylie was fifty three, Old Moses and Abram were both twenty nine, Randal was twenty eight, Little Wylie was twenty, Solomon and Charlie were both eighteen, Green was seventeen, Luke was fifteen, Sang was thirteen, Scott was eleven, Little Scott was nine, Milly was fifty three, Mealy was forty seven, Sarah was twenty seven Melvina was seven, and Fanny was four. Now the Negroes that were sold off in 1859 were Elijah sixty five, Lewis was thirty five, Aaron was twenty seven, (If Aaron is twenty seven years old, he was born in 1834 a long ways from being born in 1820 or 1825). Milly was sixty, Lem was twenty five, Nick was fifteen, George was fourteen, Pete was thirteen, Jack was eleven, Henry was eight, Penny was forty five, Nace was thirty seven, Melvina was nine, Parthenia was six.

Numbers were written on a piece of paper and put into a hat and names of the slaves into another. The lot fell like this. Number one was Mr. T. N. Rhodes, number two Mr. S. Callaway, number three Mr. F. M. Callaway, number four Mr. C. Binns, number five, Mr. William O. Cheney, number six, Mr. B. M. Callaway, number seven, Mr. J. F. Geer, number eight Mr. W. R. Callaway, number nine, J. H. Spratilin, number ten, Mr. A. R. Callaway. Lewis and Parthenia went with T. N. Rhodes, Rena and Jack went with S. Callaway, Nance went with F. M. Cheney, Simon went with C. Binns, Aaron went with William O. Cheney, Lem went with B. M. Callaway, Nick went with J. F. Geer, George and Elijah went with W. R. Callaway, Penney and Henry went with J.H. Spratlin, Peter went with A. R. Callaway, Rev. Enoch Callaway left Sardis Church July 23, 1859. This is part of the mystery of Aaron that I can say I come mighty close to solving.

Between the years of 1881 and 1887, Aaron stayed in Greene County. Mean while in the 216th District, where Aaron was once residing, Eliz Epps and Thomas and Mary Epps came to reside. Andrew Austin was working for Albert H. Weeks with Frank Bailey.

Insolvent Tax Payers of Clarke County, 1871 to 1875

Aaron failed to pay his taxes between 1871 and 1875, and is listed as being an insolvent tax payer of Clarke County, Georgia. The only other Callaway that I found with Aaron was John Callaway. I do not know if this is John out of Atlanta or John out of Henry County yet. However, I believe that it is John out of Henry County, Georgia. All this time I never found an Aaron Cheney, only Aaron Callaway! For Aaron to use the last name

Cheney, shows me who Aaron is and his character to change his name to Cheney and Major in 1880 to change his last name as well shows me the length they were willing to go to deceive! These men that can pass and they are using every advantage they can.

The names that are listed as being insolvent tax payers show who Aaron Cheney really is, and his real name is Aaron Callaway! However, I somewhat believe that Aaron is really Robert or Bob using the first name Aaron. The names are Major Cheney (who will reside in Bowling Green, Oglethorpe County), Dick Haygood, Tyler Barnett, Nathan Barnett, Jack Barnett, Henry Bugg, Scott Dean, John Dean, Spencer Winfrey, Zack Huff, Reese Smith, Wash Smith, Frank Smith, Charles Watson, Anderson Crawford, Jim Crawford, Jack Crawford, Ambrose Crawford, Jake Bugg, Alfred Smith, Ben Elder, Alex Smith Reese Smith, George Marshall, Jordan Bostwick, Sam Bostwick, Harrison Harden, Frank Huff, Hinson Edwards, John Billups, George Brown, Lewis Billups, John Jackson, Bart Lowe, Willis Lowe, Perry Walker, Jerry Thornton out of Greene County, Jim Thomas, Alfred Johnson, John Scott, Armsted Powers (might be A. C. Powers from the will of Jesse R. Callaway in 1901). George Glenn, Zip Barrows, Tolbert Barrows, Moses Sims Sr. (one of William Eberhart's men), and Mose Sims Jr., Ned Lester, Joe Holsey, Henry Harvey, Peter Johnson, Richard Johnson, Charles Johnson. William Reid, Uriah Osborn, Eli Porter, George Grissom, Charles Laster, William Jones, Pleasant Jones, A. P. Mack, Jordan Grisham, Thomas and George Jones, Susan Hunter, Thomas Glenn, and Dave Oglesby, and Anthony Richardson.

I want to try and see what was the relationship between Henderson Tyler the only black witness against Aaron Callaway and him stealing a watermelon and trespassing on place of Felix T. Pitman. The price of a watermelon which was ten cents will cause him to go to work in Beaverdam for Mr. Winters. J. T. Pittard had his store in Bowling Green and this is while he is on the other side of Pitman farm which Aaron had to cross. I don't know why J. T. Pittard went his bond however it will cause the honorable young lawyer Henry C. Tuck to defend him. How did this young lawyer come to defend Aaron or Bob Callaway or Aaron Cheney? The only relationship or tie that I could show between the only two black men in this indictment is a marriage license between Henderson Tyler and Janie Read of November 27, 1887. This marriage led me back to Green Calloway and William Reid in Lincoln County and now here on the insolvent tax payers list in Clarke County is William Reid the father of Jane Reid and the daughter of Mary Reid who in 1880 was living in Puryears district with Cheney their twenty one year old daughter, William was fifteen, major was fifteen, Jane was ten, Lila was eight, and Missie was seven and Henry was a mere two years old. They were living a few houses up from sixty year old Judea Callaway and ten year old Willie Howard her grandson and Gilbert Arnold a boarder at twelve and her two year old granddaughter Fannie Grison. Now I am sure that Aaron Callaway in 1900 is Bob Callaway or Aaron Cheney and Robert is the father of young Willie Howard who will be the black witness against his brother Charlie in 1899 with being charged with selling liquor by J. R. Haynes. I knew with all the other indictments and how the accuser of the one who made the complainant had sway over a friend of the accused or family member of the accused as a witness against him in court. The tie between Henderson Tyler and Callaway is some kind of relationship that ties them to the Reid family! I always thought this was a maniacal ploy to pit the friends and family members against each other in the Black community. This ploy will and has caused a mistrust in the community and have a long lasting effect even today! This was the same tactic that has been practice since the beginning of slavery!

In the year 1874, I found Clara Barnett, Fed Bugg, Sandy Crawford, Albert Graves, Anderson Pope, Bill Callaway (who will come to reside in Morgan County, Georgia), Thomas Marable, Dennis Marable, Charles Findley, Phillip Walker, Earl Strickland, Armistead Lewis, Anderson Carter, Cicero Brown, George Washington, Sally Williams, Oliver Rucker, Bill Ware, James Reed, Nelson Reed, Major Callaway, Aaron Callaway, Scott Ware, Dick Haygood, Mack Haygood, Isaiah Landrum, Tom Tyler, Elizabeth Blakeley, Lucy Schley, Jerry Poullian, Aaron Fambrough, Gus Finley, Isaac Ray, Henry Thompson, James Thrasher, S. C Livingston, William Flagg, John Lowe, Jerry Harris, Thomas Harris, John Lumpkin, and George Achols.

In the *Clarke County Tax Digest 1874 through to 1877, I found that in the 217th District Aaron Callaway was working with Major Callaway, Dick Haygood, Mack Haygood, Isiah Landrum, and Tom Tyler. Spence and Mark Winfrey are all working for W. H. Dean. As you can see, Major Callaway and Aaron are again side by side. Both are on the insolvent list for Clarke County and both have a relationship with Mr. Robert T. Callaway, lower Oglethorpe County and Henry County, Georgia.* Mr. Tom Tyler is traveling alone side of Aaron from Bowling Green and Mr. Pittman will influence Henderson Tyler to be a witness against Aaron for tresspassing on his property. Mr. Pittman might have gotten tired of Aaron taking his hands to Clarke County and leaving him with the labor that he needs to sustain his farm. You can see that this would be a problem for Blacks were jumping contract and the white farmers were now trying to enforce their will upon them now!

In the year 1876, Aaron Callaway is still moving back and forth on Mr. William H. Dean's property on Lexington Road with John Dean and Sandy H. Harris. William Morton had Edmond Jones and John Austin on his property in 1877 through to 1880. John Austin, in 1880, had Charles and Clayborn Callaway in his house during the census. This is the first time that Aaron brings Charles and Clayborn with him. While in Greene County his two sons are living in Bowling Green. Aaron could have been tresspassing on Pittman place to visit his two sons Charlie and Cleveland.

The insolvents' list listed the two in Clarke County in 1874. Aaron and Major, Dick, and Mack Hargrove; Tom Tyler; Lindsey Dean; Bill Callaway, who was working for Mrs. M. A. Kittle, with Mike Henderson and James Harrison and Thomas Marable in the 218th District of Puryears. Now, it was in the 1871 tax digest that I found Bart Callaway working for G. W. Callaway and Major Calloway was working for Robert Callaway the son of Elizabeth R. Callaway out of Henry County. Major was working alongside David Gresham and Gus Gresham in 1871. They were all in the 228th District of Oglethorpe County. I believe that Bart Callaway is Bill or William Callaway who is on George W. Callaway's place before he relocates to Morgan County with his wife Mary. Bill Callaway had company when he was listed as an insolvent tax payers in Clarke County alone with Emanuel Jones, Thos. Marable, and Ivey Austin and Ned Lester.

I cannot put Aaron directly in Clarke County or directly in the northern section of Oglethorpe County or Beaverdam, Oglethorpe District, or the Dam, as my Aunt Anna called it. Is located between the two counties. This is a common factor in dealing with the colored communities in the state of Georgia that were living in Greene County and Oglethorpe but working in Clarke.

The 1880s in Greene County, Georgia

The confusing part of the tax digest that I have come across in dealing with Greene County and the southern part of Oglethorpe County for the 1880s is that it does not give me a definite answer on the relationship between Aaron and Charlie Callaway while in Greene County.

In the 1879 tax digest of Greene County, Georgia, in the 147th District of Greene County, I found Columbus Hurt, Henry Hurt, Doc Finley founder of the Finley Chapel Church, and William McWhorter all working for James T. Finley. Thrasher Callaway was on R. L. or Robert Ligion McWhorter place with Mike Reed and Dan Reed. Now there is no Aaron Callaway or Burwell Callaway in Maxey or Partee 147th, Greene County. However, every time they are missing out of the district a strange name appears. Thrasher Callaway is a very unusual name that would appear just like when Aaron and Burwell were not located in this district, as you will see in 1882, and that is when Richard Callaway would appear in Woodville, not far from Aaron and Burwell. Oh! Jesse is still located in Penfield. He never changes. Rev. Jesse R. Callaway is well connected with the Ebenezer Colored Baptist Association in Atlanta. Who knows the relationships that Rev. J.R. Callaway has come to know while passing through the city.

In the 1880 tax digest I found out that the 147th District was now called Maxey and Aaron Callaway is working there for Thomas M. Fambrough with Dick Smith, Jim Barrow, Dawson Barrow, Davis Maxey, Phil Griffith, Tom Watson, and Frank Barnett (who has his own property), as well as Tom Finch. The only family that I know that mightbe kin to Aaron are the two Barrows Jim and Dawson.

In 1881, T. M. Fambrough, had Thomas Watson, Albert Fambrough, Monroe Fambrough, John Fambrough, Felix Fambrough, Dick Smith, Giles Finley, Aaron Callaway, Ale Fambrough, Alonzo Fambrough, and Howard Fambrough. Columbus Hurt is on his own land.

In the year 1883, Dick Callaway or Richard is still in the 138th District, on the property of J. L. Young. Aaron was over at the place of Zack Freeman in the Partee District near the Williams. I found Henry Callaway on the farm of J.M. Griffin, working alongside Dick Gray, Allen Whirter, John Tiller, Isham Carter, and Alfred Swain. *James M. Griffin is the marshal over at the 137th District in 1880, the same district where Mr. Griffin Hurt resides in the house of a white man, Mr. Benjamin Collins. This would put both Richard and Henry Callaway in the same place in the 137th District near Bairdstown.*

In 1885, Aaron was back on the farm of R. A. Maxey with Bob Maxey and Bob Williams, his son-in-law. Bob married his daughter Matilda, who later made her home in Ohio, a city frequently visited by Mr. Peg-Leg Williams.

I cannot put Aaron under the last name of Calloway in the earlier days of the 1870s directly in Clarke County or directly in the northern section of Oglethorpe County of Beaverdam, Oglethorpe District, or the "Dam" as my aunt Anna called it. The place is located between the two counties of Clarke and Oglethorpe. This is a common factor in dealing with the colored communities in the state of Georgia that lived on the county lines.

In the census of Oglethorpe County and Clarke County, Aaron and his family are under the last name of Cheney. Charley was eleven, Cleveland was seven, and Silvey was three. Aaron and his family were living next door to Jerry Henderson or Hutchinson, a colored man and his wife and son. Lee Hale was in the house with them at this time. Also under the last name of Cheney was Thomas, who is more than likely an apprentice to Seaborn Coles. It is important to say that Aaron and these three children are never in the same house in Greene County with the other children. I assume that Aaron has two families, which is not uncommon due to slavery. I wondered if Aaron and Green Callaway were one and the same, because I have two Charlie Callaways in the 1870s, one in the house of Green Callaway in Lincoln County and Aaron Cheney (Callaway) in Clarke County. Claiborn never shows up in Green County, only Cleveland and Charlie.

Major Callaway in Clarke County, . Major was fifty years old, his wife Sarah was forty, William their son was twenty, Mary was eighteen, Thornton their youngest was ten. I forgot to mention that Thomas and Major were under the last name of Cheney alone with Aaron. Watson Geer was living next door in Beaverdam section of Oglethorpe County, Georgia, near Winterville, about five miles out from Athens Clarke County. Watson Geer will be a witness for Aaron's son Charlie in 1899.

Watson Geer was a twenty-five-year-old colored man. I do not know if he is part of the Geer family that was on Geer Road in Penfield; however, he ends up in Penfield. Mr. Dean Tucker was next. Dean was seventy years old and his wife Betsey was a little older than her husband. Mrs. Lucy Hales and her daughter Mary and her brothers William and Robert. James Pittard had the next house. James was thirty-three years old and his wife Ella was twenty-five. They had one daughter named Susan who was seventeen.

I always thought there was tension between William Eberhart and Mr. Hal Johnson for one reason or another. When Hal or Henry Johnson sent his son to get Charlie Callaway off the property of William Eberhart during the time Charlie was to show up in the Federal Courts in Fulton County. I just knew that there had to be some kind of prior bad experiences between the two families. Hal Johnson sent his oldest son A.R. Johnson to remove Charlie off the Eberhart's land, which was south of the property that he owned in Oglethorpe County. Harry H. Johnson was his younger son, who went with A. R. in a wagon to rescue my great-grandfather in 1899. Mr. Carter, the commissioner of Beaver Dam, Clarke County, mentioned this to me while I interviewed him in the Clarke County Courthouse. He quoted without even knowing the full facts of what I had found in the Oglethorpe County Courthouse in 2001 of the charges brought against A.R. Johnson in 1899. Read this and you'll see what might be a reason for the friction between the two families.

Under an application for partition of certain lands by Whitston G. Johnson, Attorney for Martha Eberhart, Francino O. Williams, by and through B.B., which appears to be regular in every respect, the Commissioners B.H. Barnet, L.G. Johnson, Isham H. Pittard, W.J. Fleeman and D.A. Barnet, made their return to the Court, in which it is recited: "By virtue of the Commission to us directed, dated the 6th day of May 1876, last past, directing and requiring us to enter upon a certain lot of land in said County on the waters of Beaverdam Creek, containing 1,000 acres, more or less, belonging to Martha Eberhart, and make partition of said lot of land between the said Martha Eberhart, F.O. Williams, Martha E. Eberhart guardian for William Eberhart and M.E. Eberhart, joint tenants of said lot of land, after having been sworn to the faithful execution of said Commission, and having given the parties in interest due and legal notice and having employed Luke G. Johnson as surveyor, we proceeded on the 22nd day of July last past, to make partition of said lot of land; the following is the result: In the first place we find the land deficient in number of acres, 66 acres; we, therefore, for good reasons have run off to Lot #1 two hundred and twenty-two acres; Lot #2 two hundred twenty and three quarter acres; No. #3 two hundred nineteen and one-half acres; No. 4 two hundred twenty-one and one half acres, or less as the original plat will further show from lines, courses and distances marked thereon within and outline and boundaries which we have given as follows: (giving the courses and distances of the plat.) We assign Lot #1 to Martha Eberhart guardian for M.E. Eberhart . . . we assign Lot #2 to Martha Eberhart guardian for William Eberhart; we assign Lot #3 to Martha Eberhart; we assign #4 to Ethel Williams. All of which will more fully appear from annexed plat of survey which is made a part of the return of the undersigned . . .

Martha Sims Grantor

Martha Eberhart and her three children, F.O. Williams, M.E. Eberhart, William Eberhart

Warranty Deed, March 7, 1873, natural love and affection. (of said daughter and her three children). Deed Book W. Page 390-391. Oglethorpe County, The young boy William Eberhart is becoming a man. This will is separating him from Charlie and his brother Cleveland who might have played with young Eberhart as young boys on his grandmother's place near George W. Callaway place near Bowling Green.

All that tract or parcel of land situated lying and being in said state and county on the waters of the south prong of Beaver Dam Creek, known as the Bailey Place, bounded on the east by Mangus Carter, by Holly Carter on the south, Dean Tucker on the west, on the north by Clark Martin and Martha Sims' dower, containing 1, 000 acres more or less.

Now the land that Hal Johnson and his wife Mary Lena Johnson owned was a tract of land lying and being in said county on the headwaters of Clouds Creek and being a portion of the Nathan Johnson home place and adjoining lands on the north and west of James M. Smith, Capt. Barnett's old place and others, and on the south and east by lands of N.D. Arnold and H.A. Hayes's mill tract, etc. Hal G. Nowell is the brother-in-law of Hal Johnson and is also the attorney for the claimant, who is R.T. Johnson vs. H.O. Johnson and Mary Lena Johnson. In this situation A.R. Johnson is made legal guardian of his younger brother and their sisters, Annie Belle Johnson, Ethel Claire Johnson, Mary Zella Johnson, and Grace C. Johnson, and Harry H. Johnson being the younger brother. This is all because of the death of Hal O. Johnson, who took his life in 1899. This situation at the courthouse with Hal Jones and his family, will be occurring at the same time as Charley is going thru his situation in the Federal Courts and supposedly his death in Elbert County.

Chapter Two

Green Calloway
Aaron Cheney
Robert Callaway
(Bob Callaway)
Aaron Callaway

Greene Callaway is a mystery in Lincoln County in 1870 and was there during 1867 taking an oath of allegiance to the Union. He is working for a lady out of Elbert County that has a tie to the Truitt family out of Wilkes County. And after only about two or three years in Lincoln Green, Callaway just disappears in 1880.

In 1870, I found Green Calloway residing in Lincoln County, Georgia, just outside and north of Wilkes County, Georgia. The only older Callaway that resided in Lincoln County were Nancy Callaway and Rev. Francis Callaway, who relocated to Giles, Tennessee, and to Chambers County, Alabama, west of Lagrange, Georgia.

Alabama, west of Lagrange, Georgia. There is one family that resided here in Lincoln County and his name is twenty three year old Allen Callaway and his twenty two year old wife Betsy and their twenty two year old neighbor Henry Grissom that will have a tie to the house hold of Juda Callaway in Puryears and her two year old granddaughter Fannie Grissom.

In the year 1870, Green Calloway was living in Lincoln County, Georgia, in the district of Goshen, with his wife Laura. Laura was ten years older than Green, who was thirty years old. Eurar, their daughter, is sixteen. Charles is twelve, Clayborn is nine, Jane is five, Elizabeth is three, America is one, and Caleb Reed is eighty years old. Green and Laura were living next door to twenty-five-year-old William Reed. William Reed was living next door to Simeon Colbert, a fifty-year-old, and his forty-year-old wife Jane. Twenty-one-year-old George Howard and his twenty-one-year-old wife Louisa and one-year-old daughter Elizabeth. Alfred Reed is in the Goshen District of Lincoln County, Georgia, in 1870. Alfred is thirty-nine and Edna is thirty. This is the only time that I have found Clayborn and Charlie at the same time other than in 1880. Not at any time have I found Clayborn on any tax digest in 1890s. I did have a marriage license between Clayborn Calloway and Vina Bunkley on June 26, 1885, by Justice of the Peace John F. Smith, an N.P., and Thos. D. Gilham, the Ordinary in Oglethorpe County, Georgia. I was at the library in Clarke County and I was introduced to a Callaway man that was looking for the Callaway that changed his name from Callaway to Reed. The other family that is in Goshen in 1870 is the Clark family. Robert Clark is sixty-eight and Mary is fifty-two, and Thomas is twenty-seven and Adeline is twenty-six and Bennett is seven.

I had to get a little bit more information on Mr. Green Callaway and his family, so I turned to the tax digest in Lincoln and I found him in Lisbon working for Sallie E. Thomas and working with William Reid, William Mattox, Nick Mattox, and Simon Colbert. At one time on her property, working for her were Alfred Reed, William Reed, William Henry, Simon Colbert, James Jackson Sr. and Jr., Ben Harrison, James Dye, and James Andrews. Working for Liston House were Jerry Bone, Burnett Mahoney, Clark Mahoney, Alfred Tate, Sim Goss, James K. P. Norman, Alexander Moss, and Solomon T. Sadwick. Green stayed on her property only two or three years. I only found this lady not in Lincoln County but in Elbert County, the same county that Charlie will be sent to in 1899. Ms. Sallie E. Thomas's age is not listed. She is living in the house of Drury B. Cade and who I am assuming to be his wife Julia A., as well as Eliza Jackson, Eliza Hulon, Darissa, and a young boy named Charles. The only other family that I might be interested in is the family of Ann A. Almand and her husband John and her children Lucinda, Calvin F, and Henry Thompson and his wife Rosabell; John H. and Nancy S. I do not know why they do not mention her age. So I turned to the county of Oglethorpe.

I found Joseph T. Thomas, a fifty-year-old man, and his forty-five-year-old wife Mary Ann, his nineteen-year-old daughter Sallie E, his eighteen-year-old son John, fifteen-year-old son George, thirteen-year-old son Robert. Joseph A., their nine-year-old son; Jesse, his six-year-old; and Mary E., their three-year-old daughter.

In 1880 in Elbert County in Petersburg District, Sallie E. Thomas was forty-four years old and her father Drury B. Cade Sr. is now seventy-seven. Eliza Jackson is a colored seventy-one-year-old woman, Cora Isam is a seventeen-year-old, Lewis Hughes is a twenty-one-year-old, Archers Hughes is a nineteen-year-old colored young man, Pauline Thomas is an eight-year-old mulatto girl, Salline Jackson is six years old, all in the house with Mrs. Sallie E. Thomas and her father Drury Cade.

Green Callaway, in 1870, is living in Goshen but was working for Mrs. Sallie E. Thomas and her father Drury B. Cade's estate in Lisbon. Mrs. Sallie E. Thomas was found on the tax digest as early as 1868 and could have been located there much earlier. In 1868, in Lincoln County, Georgia, in the 188th District, there is another family that was living here as well that gives reason for Green Callaway being in Lincoln. They are the Barksdales! Benjamin F. Barksdale is the administrator of the estate of Shelton Oliver and the agent for Mary Barksdale and James W. Barksdale.

Between 1873 and 1877, I found in Lisbon District of Lincoln County, Georgia, the business of *Pharr and Callaway. The agents for the company are B.B. Brown and W. M. Brown*. In the years between 1873 and 1877, William M. Brown was the agent for Pharr and Callaway in Lisbon, Lincoln County. Benjamin W. Brown was in the district as well. I am also keeping an eye on Mr. James W. Barksdale, who is the guardian of Anderson Jones. He is also the administrator of the estate of H.M. Sale.

The Barksdales are close to the Jones family in Wilkes County, as well as the Callaway family. The family of Benjamin F. Barksdale was living near Purnell Truitt and Truitt had as his servants the colored Cade family. Jane being the head of the house at thirty-five years old and having been born in Virginia. Living in the same district and on the same page was Eda Callaway and her family. Eda is thirty years old. Harriet is eight, Mary is two, Nace is fourteen, and Minty is fifteen. *As I have stated before, both sides of my family, the Callaways and the Joneses, being my grandmother's family, are tied to Wilkes County, Georgia, and even the Barksdale.* In 1870, Wade Jones, twenty-four, and Aaron Jones, thirty, were living with thirty-year-old Catherine Barksdale and her children: Antownett, twelve; Moses, three; and Jackson Barksdale, four months old. *In the 179th District of Wilkes in the 1870s, Aaron Jones and Arch Anderson worked for Mr. B. F. Barksdale. Another time during the 1870s, in the 179th District* Aaron was on another plantation with Lewis Parthone and on the place of B. F. Barksdale was Wade Jones and Mike Jones and Arch Anderson and Austin Jones. B. F. Barksdale was selling land and these are the only freedmen that owned property while on his estate: Mike Jones, 250 acres; Gilbert Blakley, thirty acres; King Barksdale, forty acres; Wade Jones, fifteen acres; Tom Robertson and Aaron Jones no acreage; and Edmond Tate, one hundred and fifty acres. I don't know if Aaron eventually received land in Wilkes County or not. I don't think so, because he eventually moves out of this section of Wilkes County. Now, I might have come across Aaron's mother and father. They are living a few houses away in the 179th while Aaron and Wade and Catherine Barksdale are in the house together. Michael Jones is fifty-five and his mother and Aaron's grandmother is Charity, aged seventy. Along with six-year-old Wade, they are all living together in the house before you get to thirty-eight-year-old Nathan Barksdale and his large family. The grandfather of my grandmother was named Willis Jones. I don't know if he had an A for his middle initial or not. Willis is the stepson of Amos Walton and his mother is named Eliza in the year of 1880. Willis is twenty-two years old and his mother and Amos are fifty years old. I don't think it would be right if I didn't mention Willis's step-brothers and sisters. Mitchell Walton is eighteen, John is thirteen, Francis is ten, Mary is eight, and Emma is six. Francis is seventy years old and is the mother-in-law, Isabella is a thirteen-year-old niece, and Mathew is a one-year-old nephew. They are all farm laborers on Clarke D. Cosby, Julia A. Cosby, or John H. Cosby's land in the 179th District in the year 1880.

One September 22, 1881, D. Jones presided over the wedding of Willis Jones and Eugenia Wingfield. At this point, Willis Jones had been living near or on his wife's father's place in the 179th District, called Anderson or Hydeville. In their marriage certificate, Willis and Eugenia were not listed as being colored. And for this reason I am assuming that they were married by a white minister. And the only D. Jones living in the 179th District at this time was Dudley Jones! Dudley Jones is fifty years old and his wife Mildred A. Jones is the same age. Their daughter Mary W. is eighteen years old. I pinpointed them on the 1901 map of Wilkes County living near Wm. W. Hugley.

Eugenia Wingfield in 1870

Eugenia Wingfield grew up in the 179th District of Anderson near the property of Andrew J. Newsome and his family. Jesse was thirty-eight years old and his wife Reah was thirty-three years of age. Their children were Easter, fourteen; Eugenia, twelve; Jacob, nine; Charles, seven; Stephen, four; and Newby, two years old. Clay Wingfield was a seventeen-year-old young man living next door in the house of Abram Simpson and his family. Abram had a sixteen-year-old daughter named Cynthia. Then there is three-year-old Sixt, as well as a colored man named Nelson Wingfield and his family. Then comes twenty-eight-year-old Nathan and his family. At this time, I visited the tax digest and Nelson Wingfield had 371 acres of land in the 179th. Willis Jones, Jesse Wingfield, William Wingfield, Sim Wingfield, and Bob Anderson all worked for Mr. John L. Smith. While Nelson had Newby, Henry, Jack, Nick, and Isaac Wingfield on his place near E. A. John's, this was between 1884 and 1889 in Anderson 179th. Newby is the son of Jesse Wingfield. In the year 1880 the census taker W. J. Callaway listed the household of Jesse Wingfield and his siblings living nearby.

Jesse is forty-five and his wife Rhea is thirty-eight. Eugenia is now twenty-two, Jacob is twenty, Charles is eighteen, Stephen is fifteen, Newby is thirteen, Caroline is eleven, Martha is nine, Lucy is six, and Jesse Jr. is two. Also living in the house with Jesse and his family are William Tiller and Miles Smith, two farm laborers. Alex is his five-year-old nephew and Harriett is his five-year-old niece. Lula is his two-year-old granddaughter, and there is a two-month-old daughter that has not been named. Living next door is twenty-three-year-old Daniel Wingfield. Jesse's brother William is living in the house before you get to his. William is thirty-eight years old, his wife Puss is thirty, his son William is fifteen, Scott is thirteen, George is eleven, Harriett is nine, Dolly is seven, Holland is five, and Edward is two. The next house is his brother's, twenty-eight-year-old Nicholas and his wife Sophonia, who is twenty-eight. With them are their children Minerva, eleven; Mary Lou, ten; Elijah, eight; Harriett, six; Daisey, five; Jane B, four; and Albert, four months old. Taylor Hollins is a farm laborer and Archibald Wingfield is a seventeen-year-old nephew living with his uncle Nicholas. Next comes the old patriarch himself, Mr. Nelson Wingfield at the age of sixty-five, and his wife Mary at the age of sixty-two. Their children living at home are Elijah, eighteen, and Rebecca, twenty-six. With them are Rebecca's children, Anna, who is eleven, and Minnie, an eight-year-old. Henry Wingfield is living next door to his father Nelson, and he is twenty-four and his wife Anna is twenty. Their son Robert is eleven months old and his sister-in-law is twelve-year-old

Emma Hardin. They all lived on Nelson's 370-something-acre farm in Anderson in the 179th District of Wilkes County, Georgia, in 1880.

However, in year 1870, Amos is thirty-five years old and his wife Elizabeth is the same age. Stepson Willis is twelve and Mitchell is ten, and John Walton is three years old. I don't know how long ago Martha Elizabeth Jones left Aaron, but I do know it was before 1870. Maybe during the Civil War she decided to separate. Aaron and his daughter Martha were both living in the 176th District near white landowner Henry Wynn and his family. Aaron was at the age of forty-two and Martha was at the age of twenty-three. They were living with a black man named Charley Anderson, who was twenty-five, and his wife Sarah, twenty-one. Their two daughters were Anna, four, and Julia, two years old. I mentioned the family of Charley Anderson because Aaron would later, on May 13, 1876, marry Loney Anderson. J. H. Fortson was the minister. Aaron and Martha are listed in the 167th District in Malloryville, Wilkes County, near Willis and Millie Anderson. Living in the same district were Jim and John Anderson, as well as Reuben Walton. In the 167th, Aaron was over at the property of his first wife Martha or Elizabeth, or he had stock like Wylie or Willis Jones and Frank Walton as well.

I also found Mr. Robert Wallace here as well. Mrs. Sallie E. Thomas is over at the estate of Drury B. Cade and William G. Cade.

John S. Callaway shows up between 1878 and 1882 in Lisbon District in Lincoln. He is over the estate of his wife Posey, the daughter of James Barksdale. James is the guardian of Samuel S. Fortson, Anderson Jones, and H. M. Sale. James W. Barksdale in 1883 and 1887 is now the guardian for Minus H. Sale and agent for Mrs. Posey Callaway. I found one familiar family and that is Mr. George Haralson. While Mrs. Sallie E. Thomas and her family were living in Lincoln, they had property in Elbert County in Petersburg as well. Now, James W. Barksdale's property was in Lisbon, Lincoln County. However, the property of his daughter was in the district called Goshen, the same district that Green Callaway was living in during their short stay in the 1870s. The district is numbered 187 and these are the white landowners that were there. They are familiar last names that are out of Greene County and the southern parts of Oglethorpe County, Georgia. Benjamin Finley and James Finley were agents for Mr. C. C. Cary. Also living here was James. P. Thomas. Now, I just had to go to Whitfield County, Georgia, in 1880 to investigate Mr. John J. S. Callaway and his wife Posey. John is thirty-six years old, and Posey is thirty-three. Their children are Lucy, Chardion, Quinn, Augustus, Pollie, Annie, and Frank. Also living in the house is Simmon Sale and Hick Sale, his stepsons. However, to my surprise, there were two colored Callaways, Henry and Nancy, both seventy years old, with them. They were born in 1810.

I just had to find Henry and Nancy Calloway in 1860. I found them in Wilkes County, Georgia. Henry was born in South Carolina while Nancy was born in Georgia. This particular area is on the county line toward Lisbon, Lincoln County. The names of the families are all aligned toward Aaron Calloway, who was on the estate of Isaac and Winifred Ragan Callaway in Greene County and my grandfather Arthur Calloway Sr. I call this the Anderson section of Wilkes County, Georgia, and these are the names that are so close to my grandfather Arthur. I found fifty-five-year-old Henry and forty-one-year-old Nancy in Washington, Wilkes County, Georgia, with Wm. J. Callaway and the assistant marshal. I believe that they are on the property of Julia A. Anderson. Toney Calloway in a sixty-five-year-old in the house of Solomon Boren and his wife Harriet. In this section of Wilkes County is Harden Woodruff and his wife Viney, and Matilda Williams, a white family. William Cade is sixty-three years old, living alone and next door to Crammer E. jones, Jarratt Jones, Robert Johnson, Tolliver Johnson, and colored men Aaron Cade, John Cade, and Willie Cade. As you can see, Sallie E. Thomas's family of slaves are located in Wilkes in the district of Anderson on the road leading to Lisbon, Lincoln County, Georgia.

Moving on down the road to Mr. James W. Boyd's place and then to George W. Fortson and Joseph Fortson, as well as Augustus A. Neal and Benjamin W. Fortson, the white landowner, with James W. Boyd. The next house is the place of John S. Callaway, the school teacher, at the age of twenty-eight, and his wife Eliza at the age of twenty-four, and four-year-old Robert M. Callaway and their daughter Kate at the age of two. I believe that John is on the property of Dr. William D. Walton and his wife Martha and a young girl named Maria C. Favor. Along with them were Cesar Noble and wife Emiline, Alex, Kitty, Charles (who is a year old), Isaac, Daniel Noble and his wife Molsey, Thomas, and Samuel. I really loved visiting this section of Wilkes County on my many visits. I enjoyed playing for the Lyonsville Baptist Church Choir and meeting Pastor O. C. Daniels of Walton County, I met members who were well up in age and educated, also they were very pleasant to my wife and I.

Back to the neighborhood in Wilkes County, Mr. Love Stone is sixty. George Aaron, Eliza A. Williamson, Alice Williamson, Francis Carter, Martha Callaway and Jesse Rhodes a white child, were all in his colored household. Twelve-year-old Lucy is in the house of white farmer Mr. Greenburg Rhodes. David McCloud is sixty years old and Matilda, his wife, is fifty. Their daughter is six-year-old Matilda. Samuel McCloud is forty-five, Cariline is forty-three, Lucretia is sixteen, Amy is fourteen, David is twelve, George is ten, Emily is eight, Elsey is six, Dicy is three, and Elubra is four months old. Now, sometimes I think some things are just too obvious that these two families, judging by their location, were well acquainted with each other. Mr. Frank Barnett is forty-two, Lucy is thirty-six, Peter is eighteen, William is sixteen, Matilda is fourteen, Jane is eleven, Silvey is nine, Louisa is ten, Luinda is five, Frank is three, Phillis is two, and David is six months old. Joseph McCloud is twenty-two and Dicy is twenty-one. Mary is two, while Daniel is four months old. Clifford McCloud is a one-year-old in the house of Stephen Heard and Felix Cofer. Stephen Calloway is two years old in the house of Aaron Derrocott and Scilla, his wife, and their children. Not far is the house of Mary A. Callaway, sixty-five, and Dr. James J. Callaway, who is thirty-one. The next two families are white. The Mahoneys are Eliza J., sixty; Micajah, twenty-seven; Charles M., nineteen; John, eighteen; Finnie E., twenty-one; and Mary L., fifteen. Hiram F. Mahoney is a sixty-three-year-old retired school teacher in the house with a colored man, Andrew Leslie.

Now, just to mention why I am interested in the relationship between the McCloud and Barnett families is that my grandfather's cousin Maggie Barnett married George McCloud. Maggie's son told me that they met in Augusta, Georgia, when they married. Guiliford C. Sale's is the next family. Mr. Sale is forty-nine, and Delaney his wife is forty-one. They live with their children. Mr. Sale's last name is over at the Baptist Association in Georgia. James A. Slaten is a thirty-two-year-old and his wife Mary is forty-nine, and William is eight years old. This is the last name in 1880 Major Calloway was listed under in Bowling Green. White man William Sutton is fifty-eight, Amanda D. C. is forty-nine, James is twenty, Emma W. is sixteen, Blakey is nine. His son is Mose G. Sutton, aged thirty. Mary A. is twenty-six, Martha V. is five, Robert L. is three. Mr. Benjamin Holtzclaw is sixty-five, and Jesse is nineteen, living next door to William H. Freeman, a seventy-two-year-old farmer, and his wife Susan, forty-five. Their daughter Sarah F. is twenty-five. James W. Freeman is twenty-one, Thomas H. is nineteen, Robert S. is seventeen, George W. is fifteen, and Anderson Z. is twelve. Mr. Meriwether L. House is thirty-six and his family. John Mahoney is sixty-two, Sarah is fifty-eight, and Santa Anna is fourteen. You must remember the Mahoneys. This is the same last name that will be mentioned in 1899 as a witness in the case of Charlie Callaway.

Young white man Henry Holtzclaw, at the age of twenty-six, is in the house of Mr. Job R. Hinton. Mr. John W. Rhodes is a white farmer at the age of forty-eight, and Rhoda A. is forty-four. The next family is colored man John H. Baldwin at the age forty-two, Mary Ann at forty-five, Augusta at twenty, Stephen at seventeen, Tombs at fourteen, John at ten, and Randall Hurling, a twenty-year-old. Mr. Aaron Cohen is thirty-seven, Mary E. is twenty-one, and Sarah is one. He is a country merchant out of Prussia. Richard C. Sale is a forty-year-old white man and his wife Susan is thirty-eight. Mary E. is six, James D. is two, and James W. is forty-five. James T. Aycock is a thirty-six-year-old white farmer, and his family, and Edmund W. Anderson is a fifty-nine-year-old white farmer. Simpson Callaway is twenty and Ralph Callaway is sixteen, and both are in the house of Mr. Alfred Perteet. Mr. Anderson Sutton is forty, his wife Elizabeth is thirty-three, Julia is sixteen, Mary is thirteen, Frances is eleven, Leanty is ten, and James, her brother, is five. Anderson is living a few houses from Violet Sutton, a sixty-eight-year-old, and Ellen Saffold, who is thirty-eight.

The next families that I am about to mention have ties to Aaron going back to the 1820s. In this same district in Wilkes County is Mr. Purnell Truitt. I was very lucky to catch him in 1870 at the age of seventy-four years old, and his son James R. Truitt, who is forty-seven, and Sarah, who is twenty-three. Purnell is a retired farmer with property valued at $2000. He is living next to Jane Cade, a thirty-five-year-old colored domestic servant. Her son is Henry, who is twelve, Martha is ten, George is nine, Joseph is five, and John is two. John T. Adams is a thirty-two-year-old teacher with his wife Georgia A. Percy H. is seven, and Zolotes Adams is seventy-one, with his daughters Georgia, Emma, and Ellen. Mr. Thomas Daniel is forty-one and his wife is Susan. Mary E. is sixteen. Mr. Benjamin F. Barkesdale is a thirty-seven-year-old farmer whose property is valued at $8000, and his wife Nancy E. is thirty-three, Nicholas G. is twelve, Richard O. is ten, Mary is eight, Thomas J. is four, and Pauline is their youngest at the age of two.

Now, in the house of fifty-five-year-old Allen J. Paschal and his wife Almeda is Georgiana Murphey and twenty-year-old Martin D. Burgess and his wife Mary T. and George C. Samuels, who is twenty-two. In the next house are twenty-five-year-old David C. Callaway and his thirty-year-old wife Eda and daughter Harriet who is eight, and Mary is two and Nace is fourteen. Minty, his sister, is fifteen. Shadrach Callaway is twenty-one years old and is living in the house with twenty-seven-year-old Peter Jones. Henry Pope was a forty-year-old black farmer. Willis Weems was a twenty-eight-year-old colored farmer. And then comes the house of twenty-one-year-old Taylor Callaway and his wife Chloe. Bella, their daughter, is sixteen, and Alfred is forty, Rebecca is thirty-six, and Silla is thirteen. I believe that they are on the property of Thomas H. Strothers. Alfred Callaway is the father of Taylor Callaway.

I had to go to the year of 1860 in Wilkes County and visit the house of Purnell Truitt, who is sixty-four, and his wife Nancy Callaway Truitt who is sixty-three, and J. Riley is thirty-eight. Nineteen-year-old Nancy E. is married to Mr. Benjamin F. Barksdale. Now, the other name that is close to Purnell Truitt is the household of George W. Moore, a forty-three-year-old white farmer in 1860, and Mary E. Moore, his thirty-one-year-old wife. Eugenia C. is their five-year-old daughter. Oscar Hill Moore is three and Milton Robert Moore is one. And there is a Mary L. Barnett who is twenty-nine who is in the house with Emma Barnett, who is thirty-two years old. These two women live between the Truitt and Pope families. Hunter C. Pope, Alex Pope Sen., out of Virginia. The house of attorney Robert Toombs, who will become a general in the Confederate Army. His house is near Mrs. Mary A. Jones and Margret E. Combs, who is fifty-one.

Richard Callaway is sixty-three and his wife Matilda is fifty. George is seventeen, Eda is twelve, and Henry Seals is three. Eda is seventy-five years old. Next is the house of John Pope and family. John is a forty years old, colored man and his wife Sarah, who is thirty. Martha is twelve, Cain is ten, Nancy is four, Kitty is three, and Coral lee is one. And the next house is twenty-two-year-old Allen Callaway and his wife Elizabeth, who is eighteen. Jesse is five months old and Jessie Hill is nine years old. They are all living near or on the property of Johnson Norman, a sixty-one-year-old farmer near James W. Norman, a colored farmer at the age of thirty-five, and his wife Sarah.

I must prove my statement that Aaron knew the Truitts when he was a little boy in the 1820s or even earlier. I don't think that I need to mention the other names that I think might be the father of Aaron Callaway, Bob or Aaron Cheney, or Robert, because I believe that Aaron is living between two families or maybe even more! His humble beginning as a young man on the plantation of Rev. Joshua S. Callaway and his exploits in the church at Sardis and his lying with Hannah on the plantation of Isaac and Winnifred Callaway who had property in Wilkes County and in Greene County Georgia as well. I believe that Isaac might have been living between two families as well!

This was not an uncommon standard in the Southern culture. You will see this in the Aaron Callaway that I will mention first. He joins Sardis in the years between 1805 and 1806.

This portion of the first chapter shows the relationship that young Aaron experienced while on the property of Isaac and Winifred Callaway in Oglethorpe County, Georgia. One relationship that I am very much interested in is the one he has with Hannah, his mother, and how Hannah would come to live under the last name Barrow or Parks or even Willingham. Due to the marriage between Henry Pope and the Barrow family. I will show you the relationship that appears in the tax digest and census at the time of the adversity between the years of 1899 and 1900 in Maxey, Georgia, that shows Hannah Barrow with Harriet in Oglethorpe near Greene County.

I will try and build a relationship between this Aaron that was in the church at Sardis and the Aaron that might have fathered children with Hannah Callaway on the plantation of Isaac, who had property in the 165th of Wilkes and in Greene and partially in the County of Oglethorpe. Aaron, who was born on Isaac Callaway's plantation, was born between 1819 and 1820. I found him being hired out to Mrs. Winnifred Callaway, who is the wife of Isaac. However, Mrs. Winifred Callaway is never mentioned as being the wife of Isaac Callaway in his estate in Wilkes County.

Henry Pope, guardian for Mary Ann Callaway, minor orphan of Isaac Callaway, deceased, to said for the hire of said orphan negroes 1832. Harry, a fellow, to Henry Pope for 56.00 dollars; Isaac, a fellow, to Nathaniel Truitt for 56.00 dollars; William, a boy, to John Wilkerson for 28.75 dollars; Siney and three small children to John Wilkerson for 4.30 dollars; Penny and one child to Thomas Pullian for 31.12 dollars; Chloe and two children to Winnifred Callaway for 25.00 dollars; Sabrey, a small girl, to Thomas Pullian for 3.75 dollars.

Henry Pope, guardian for Martha Henretta Callaway, minor orphan of Isaac Callaway, deceased, to said minor orphan for the hire of said minor orphan Negroes for the years of 1833. Mike, a fellow, to James m. Callaway for 136.00 dollars; Shadrack, a fellow, to Henry Pope for 75.00 dollars; Oliver, a large boy, to Purnal Truitt for 64.00 dollars; Aaron, a boy, to Purnal Truitt for 60.00 dollars; Hannah and three children to Henry Pope for 30.00 dollars; Milly, a woman, to Simeon Brook for 40.00 dollars; Ellen, a girl, to Henry Holtzclaw for 20.00 dollars; Adeline, a small girl, to Presley Aycock.

Henry Pope, guardian of Martha H. Callaway, for the hire for her Negroes for years of 1837 to 1838. In 1837: Mike, Hannah, and one child to H. Pope for 180.00 dollars; Oliver and Aaron to S. Callaway for 225.00 dollars; Shadrack to Nathan Hoyt for 125.00 dollars; Ellen, a girl, to Nathan Hoyt for 50.00 dollars; Delila, a girl, to H. Holtzclaw for 30.00 dollars; Milly and one child to W. Woodruff for 50.00 dollars; Lydia to Charles Boswell for 30.00 dollars.

In 1838: Mike, Hannah, and one child to H. Pope for 150.00 dollars; Oliver to Charles Wooten for 157.00 dollars; Aaron to Purnell Truitt for 127.00 dollars; Ellen to Miss M. Thomas for 70.00 dollars; Delia to B. Norman for 67.00 dollars; Milly and two children to A. Norman for 59.00 dollars; Adeline to John C. Dodson for 70.00 dollars.

In July 1831, Brother Joseph Henderson reported that his girl Sealy, a colored woman of the church, was guilty of theft and lying. Enoch Callaway also reported that Monroe, a member of color belonging to him, was guilty of adultery and lying. They kicked him out of the church that same day. Sealy's last name will eventually become Callaway or she might have been a Callaway all along before becoming the property of Joseph Henderson. On May 24, 1834, right after church at Sardis, Daniel Carrington came forward and made a number of false statements relating to the difficulties that had taken place between the Appling family and others. Together with deceptive drinking and using un-Christian language, which he acknowledged in some degree. However, they took up some reports against him and said slander and un-Christian conduct are a part of his family and others. Deceptive drinking, denying it, threatening to shoot on condition a number of persons, striking his wife and denying it, pointing a gun at his wife and threatening to shoot on condition a number of persons, striking his wife and denying it pointing a gun at his wife and threatening to shoot. The church sent Joseph Henderson, R. Strozier, and S. Callaway, James, J. H. Ragan, and William Brook to visit Daniel Carrington. *Mr. J. H. Ragan, who was down in Lee County, is in the church at this time. I do believe that he is the father of Winifred Ragan Callaway or the brother, I do not know. However, the slaves that are located on his estate or property are similar to the slaves that Winifred Callaway had. The most important thing is that I find him in the minutes of Sardis at this time.* In June of 1834, the committee went to see Mr. Carrington and he was excluded from the church. On the same day, Seaborn Callaway reported his slave Sharon had left her husband and was with another man. Now I was surprised to find a Tuck in the minutes of Sardis! However, T. Tuck reported in 1834 that he saw John Jarrell as being drunk. The last name Tuck will become very prominent in the whereabouts of Charlie Callaway in 1899. His family is very closely tied to the Methodist Church that is in Rayle, Wilkes County, where the Callaway family is located and the Callaway family that is in Gwinnett County as well.

In Conference, June 27, 1835, the church thought proper to call a conference on the fourth Sunday evening of the next month for the purpose of the members of color belonging to the church. Bro. L. J. Callaway stated that there were some difficulties regarding John, belonging to L. Weems, and Samuel, belonging to Bro. Appling; therefore, Bro. L. J Callaway and J. Carrington were appointed to cite them to attend conference on Sunday evening at our next meeting. Brother Carrington reported that sister Cordelia Carrington has been guilty of the sin of cohabiting with John, a man of color, the Negro (unreadable) also being a member with us and she having a child of color with him. On motion and second they were both excluded from the church. *Answer me these questions, what can you say about the free will of a man or a woman when they are put into an uncompromising position? What is this man of color to say to this white slave holder? This proposition from this woman might cause him his life if refused. Joseph in the Bible when he was in the house of Potiphar and was entrusted with all that was in Potiphar's house. However, Potiphar's wife was persistent to sleep with Joseph, and when he refused her advances she charged him with rape and Joseph was thrown into prison.*

In 1840, Charlie left his wife and took up with another woman. Charlie was the property of Joseph Henderson. I believe that Charlie was once the property of Isaac and Winifred Callaway in Greene County, Georgia, or maybe out of Lee County as well. In Conference, January 21, 1843, received by experience Aaron, a boy, and Jenny, a member of color, the property of J.T. Irvin. Sister Helen Henderson applied for a letter of dismissal for herself and Winney, a woman of color, the property for herself. Mrs. Helen is the wife of Joseph Henderson. What I am about to write about and try and impart unto you is how close the families are that are rich and powerful and how Aaron and Charlie fit into these fragile pieces of the puzzle called their extended families.

On March 25, 1843, the church received members of color. George came to join at this time at Sardis. He was the property of Jessie Spratlin. Joe joined while he was the property of Mr. Stenson and the church restored to the fellowship Dennis, who was the property of Jessie Sparatlin. This is the same year Sardis sent missionaries to the general meetings on the third Sabbath

On April 22, 1843, Aaron and Jerry, both men of color, joined Sardis as being the property of J.T. Irvin. Both probably being from the estate of

Isaac Callaway or Winnifred Callaway. All I know is that whenever any of these wealthy landowners died J.T. Irvin was there.

In 1846, Sardis sent to the general meeting at Fishing Creek the following alternates: Isaiah T. Irvin, William R. Callaway, James Arnold, and John R. Tolbert. The church sent to the county line Dolford Silvey and Reuben Tolbert.

In June 1846, colored members joined Sardis, including Dick, the property of Thomas Favor. This was while George was characterized as being willfully lying and spouting falsehoods. Dick, Sang, and Burwell were to cite him to the next conference. Dick, Sang, and Burwell are of the colored deacons. Enoch Callaway, J.T. Ervin, Jessie Spratlin, Mr. Jackson, and F.G. Henderson, who was the secretary of the church. He wrote about the colored members joining Sardis in 1846 in the month of June. Dick, the property of Thomas Favor, joined the church while the church characterized George as of being willfully lying and falsehood. Dick, Sang, and Burwell were to cite him in the next conference. It is ironic that Aaron would come to name one of his oldest sons Burwell.

It looks like things were just as wild then as they are today and probably wilder! In June of 1846, B.B. Reeves and Daniel Carrington were seen off in some intoxicating place with a Negro and on a Sunday of the conference meeting. The church appointed men to inquire into the matter. Sang and Dick and Burwell were sent to the colored conference in the same year. Thomas Favor charged George, the property of Jessie Spratlin, of willfully lying and falsehood. A second committee of colored members of three were sent to look into the matter.

In August of 1846, members were coming back to Sardis. A total of sixty-five members joined Sardis this day. It must have been amazing, the outpouring of love for Sardis. On October 24, 1846, J.R. Tolbert reported to the church that a colored sister, Viney, the property of Jarrett Newman had quit or left her husband John, a colored brother and the property of Enoch Callaway. Viney was probably tired of John and also making the long journey from Jarrett Newman's property and decided to find another man during her lonely nights by herself. So she decided to find another slave on the property where she lived.

The church also sent messengers to Beaver Dam Church: Mr. J. T. Irvin, William R. Callaway, Nelson Vaughn, and Richard Gilbert. To Indian Creek in DeKalb County, they sent James D. Arnold and Mercer Spratling. This is the first time that I see a relationship between Wilkes and DeKalb County.

Sang and Dick and Burwell were sent to the colored conference in the same year. I believe that these three men are on their way to Augusta, Georgia, where the colored conference was being held.

Thomas Favor charged George, the property of Jesse Spratlin, of willfully lying and falsehood. A second committee of three colored members were sent to look into the matter. It seems that this is the time that the churches in the north argued about slavery and these were the men that left to go to the convention in Macon. Mr. Reeves, Rev. Jesse Mercer, Mr. Mercer argued that it was scriptural and that it recognized the relation of Christian master and Christian servant. And also that he spoke for the Southern Baptist that any attempts to disturb the quiet existence of such relation to be fanatical and unauthorized by the Holy Scriptures. It was in 1840 that the Ebenezer Association had expressed utter detestation for the sentiments abhorrent to their views that constituted threats against them or for them being slaveholders. The meeting took place in Macon, Georgia, in August of 1845. The Christian index stated that 158 white men were there from Georgia, and South Carolina sent 106 men. Virginia sent thirty-one men, Alabama sent twenty-three. Maryland, North Carolina, Kentucky, and the District of Columbia were all represented at the meeting.

This situation in Macon is the beginning of the echo of war and the death that would soon follow! The war would not restore or bring an end to slavery in the South, but a new form of slavery in dealing with the contract and the ignorant newly freed Negro servant! This new form of slavery would start soon after the war between the states, or the Civil War!

In June of 1847, Isaiah T. Irvin applied for a letter of demission for Jane, a woman of color. She is now the property of Merrell Callaway. In July 1850, Wiley was accused of stealing and he would not come to church to answer the charges against him. However, on August 25, 1850, he confessed to the charges with tears and the church at Sardis did not forgive him. The church excluded Wiley. This was the same year that Rhoda became a member. Rhoda was the property of Richard Dowdy.

In September of 1852, Mose, who was the property of Rev. Enoch, joined the church. Mose was a boy at this time. Burwell, a boy of color, and was the property of Moses Arnold. Daniel Carrington was restored into the church this same year. In the same year, the slaves of Enoch Callaway, Lewis and Tom, would become members of Sardis in September. Jerry, the property of J. D. Willis, joins as well. Sarah, the property of Mr. Rhodes. John, the property of Mr. Sherrer. Aaron, the property of I. T. Irvin. Wiley and John were restored back to the church, both being the property of Rev. Enoch. Jim, who was the property of William R. Callaway, was restored. N. T. Rhodes stated that Bob, a boy belonging to himself, was guilty of theft. The boy, being there at the church, was asked to answer the charges against him. Bob was given until next conference to explain. In 1853, Rev. Enoch was the pastor. America, a colored woman, was the property of Isaiah Irvin. John Talbot said that Aaron, a colored brother and the property of Mrs. Derricott, had been guilty of theft.

On September 23, 1853, J. T. Irvin reported that his boy Aaron had left his wife for what he considered just cause, and the next day Aaron came to church and the church forgave him. In the same year, 1853, Aaron, Charles, and Nancy were all the property of T. J. Irvin. *Now, listen. Mary Hurt Callaway's husband Charlie Callaway would be born at this time between 1854 and 1859.*

Even though Georgia did not mention Sardis as having a pastor in 1859, the Sardis minutes stated that Rev. J. J. Butler was the moderator of the church at Sardis in Wilkes County. It was July 23, 1859, that Reverend Enoch Callaway resigned. Brothers Seaborn Callaway, J. Arnold, and J. R. Crane were all sent to persuade Rev. Enoch not to resign.

These are all the Negroes that were left Martha Callaway, the wife of Rev. Enoch: Wylie was fifty-three, Old Moses and Abram were both twenty-nine, Randal was twenty-eight, Little Wylie was twenty, Solomon and Charlie were both eighteen, Green was seventeen, Luke was fifteen, Sang was thirteen, Scott was eleven, Little Scott was nine, Milly was fifty-three, Mealy was forty-seven, Sarah was twenty-seven, Melvina was seven, and Fanny was four. Now the Negroes that were sold off in 1859 were Elijah, who was sixty-five, Lewis was thirty-five, Aaron was twenty-seven, Milly was sixty, Lem was twenty-five, Nick was fifteen, George was fourteen, Pete was thirteen, Jack was eleven, Henry was eight, Penny was forty-five, Nace was thirty-seven, Melvina was nine, Parthenia was six.

Now I am glad that I found this bit of information of the estate of Rev. Enoch to verify the age of Aaron Callaway and who might have been on the plantation of Isaac Callaway. Numbers were written on a piece of paper and put into a hat and names of the slaves into another.

The lot fell like this:

Number 1 Mr. T. N. Rhodes

Number 2 Mr. S. Callaway

Number 3 Mr. F. M. Callaway

Number 4 Mr. C. Binns

Number 5 Mr. William O. Cheney

Nmber 6 Mr. B. M. Callaway

Number 7 Mr. J. F. Geer

Number 8 Mr. W. R. Callaway

Number 9 J. H. Spratilin

Number 10 Mr. A. R. Callaway

Lewis and Parthenia went with T. N. Rhodes. Rena and Jack went with S. Callaway. Nance went with F. M. Cheney. Simon went with C. Binns. Aaron went with William O. Cheney. Lem went with B. M. Callaway. Nick went with J. F. Geer. George and Elijah went with W. R. Callaway. Penney and Henry went with J.H. Spratlin. Peter went with A. R. Callaway. Rev. Enoch Callaway left Sardis Church on July 23, 1859. The church sent to inquire of his decision Mr. S. Callaway, J. Arnold, and J. R. Crane. In 1860, Sardis Church began preaching to the slaves at the church once a month. They appointed Brother Butler. He agreed to the third Sunday of each month. This passion to preach to them is all about the war that was coming to the South! Why now are they afraid that the Negroes left behind during the war would attack their white women? On the third Sunday of every month they would organize a Sunday school. They said they have a sensation to preach to the Negroes! The Abolitionist groups were angered the bondage and the conditions of the Negroes in the South. In May 1860, resolution was read and adopted, unpleasant rumors were reported about Joe, property of Richard Dowdy. The Church came together as one to resolve the situation for the purpose of looking into the state of the colored part of the church. They talked about this situation the next Sunday. Mr. William R. Callaway was the writer of the secretary.

On June 23, 1860, a colored man was over at the house of the colored conference. His name was Mr. Burgess, and the first business at the colored conference was the business of Joe. *I wonder if the Mr. P. F. Burgess that is over at Sardis Baptist in 1862 has any influence on the fact that there is a colored Burgess over at the first colored conference at Sardis.* Joe had joined another church with a letter from Sardis. Joe also was guilty of adultery and the church said that they put emphasis on the fact that he was carrying a letter from Sardis. I guess they did not appreciate the fact he had a letter and they wanted to know who issued the letter on his behalf. The men who investigated the complaint stated there was no other matter among the colored members. William R. Callaway resigned as the secretary. John Binns was elected into this vacant position. Joe, who was the property of Richard Dowdy, still was under the church's watchful eye. They sent W. R. Callaway, Seaborn Callaway, and J. R. Crane in February to investigate the matter at hand. The white men and women said that the coloreds could have the third Sunday in the month of May and August and November for conferences only if there were seven white male members present. (This type of control the whites and landowners had over the colored church carried well over into and well after the reconstruction period.) Colored brother Burgess opened the doors in the first conference at Sardis in 1860. Levi, the servant of Master Moses Arnold, joined Emily, the servant of W. W. Favor, and Mark, the servant of Master Robert Barrett. This is the same day that Isaiah Jackson was excluded after he admitted his sins and asked to rejoin Sardis. Colored brothers Elkin and Sherrer tried to patch up their misunderstanding. However, Brother Sherrer was still angry and refused to reconcile. He treated the church with contempt. So they sent some colored men to labor with him. In 1861, Sophia came to join Sardis.

Sophia was the property of Mr. Hudson. Mr. Crane said that evening that he was sorry for cursing at Mr. Moore and Dr. Schmidt. He was so sad, and the church believed he was sincere and forgave Mr. Crane. On the fifth Sunday in June, a motion was carried in the church to observe the first and second days of next month as days of fasting and prayer in view of the present disturbed condition of our country as recommended by the Baptist Convention. This was on the same day that Penney asked for a letter to leave the church. She was the slave of F. M. Cheney. Penny was the slave of Rev. Enoch Callaway two years ago. I believe Penny was sold because she was left for Martha, the wife of Enoch. F. M. Cheney was a doctor and his plantation was in Covington, Georgia.

Let me talk about Aaron Callaway, a colored Confederate soldier. Aaron enlisted as a private in the Twenty-Third Regiment of the Georgia Volunteer Infantry in Cobb County, Georgia. His brigade was called the Henderson Brigade. I do not know if Aaron's patronage to the cause of the Confederacy had an influence in the decision that the white community had on his son Charlie's life or the murder that might have occurred; however, I really believe his relationship might be the reason such an elaborate trial took place and not a quick death for Charlie!

Back to the church at Sardis in 1861, Matilda left her child, which had died. I noticed during my readings that this was more than likely due to a rape that had occurred. However, due to the death of her child, she was terminated from the church of Sardis. They were ready to give the colored people the use of the church house. Brother H. Spratlin, William R. Callaway, and Christopher Binns were sent to preserve order in the church in August. However, the church reconsidered the resolution passed and they granted the use of the house for them in the future. This was only if a white minister in good standing preached. I really wonder if this is due to the fact that Negroes could not congregate during this time of war! Randolph, the slave of Mrs. Martha Callaway, was caught stealing. Brantley, her son, charged Randolph to the church. W. R. Callaway reported Ms. Strozier for fornication and she was excluded from the church. I wonder whom she was sleeping with. J. S. Callaway asked for a letter of demission on the same day. The church has written the term *free white* in the minute book because for some of the coloreds you could not tell if they were white or black! Also, coloreds who want to join up at Sardis were to be allowed the same privileges and rights as were formerly enjoyed by slaves. I believe that this treatment compelled the coloreds to want their own place of worship!

Slaves in the Sardis Church and the Georgia Association

These are the male slaves in the Sardis Baptist Church in Wilkes County in Rayle, Georgia. The Sardis minutes states that these are the property of the Irwins or Irvins in Sardis. Charles got a letter by experience on September 26, 1874. Lewis, in 1882, could not be found. Colman received a letter on May 23, 1874. Moses received a letter on August 21, 1874. Bradford was dead. Coffee died on January 17, 1865. Anthony was lettered on September 23, 1882. Romie was lettered on August 26, 1874. Spephum was lettered on August 26, 1874. Peter went to Texas. George was dead. Esau was gone. Isaiah, the property of J. F. Irwin, was received by experience on June 21, 1821, and got a letter on May 28, 1874.

These are the male slaves in Sardis under the last name of Barrett. Billy died in August 1881. Joe was received by experience on October 21, 1870, and was lettered on November 7, 1875. Mark received a letter on June 28, 1874. Sanders Barrett was received by experience on September 27, 1873, and received a letter on May 23, 1874.

The only person listed under the last name Talbot was Howard, who was dead.

The names listed under the last name of Favor were Sang, who was dead in 1882; Burwell; Dick, who was listed as being dead on June 12, 1868; George was excluded March 1864; Lewis was listed as being dead on November 14, 1875; Charity was dead or gone; Lucy was dead; and Winny was gone or dead.

There were only two names listed under Turner: Nero, who received a letter on March 24, 1866; and James, who received a letter on August 28, 1865, and on October 26, 1873.

The Jacksons were Jacob Jackson, who received a letter on October 27, 1877; and Chany and Charity Jackson were listed as being dead. The only name listed under Colley was Billy and he was dead.

Names listed as the property of the Willis's were Isaac, who was dead; Jim Walker, who was under the last name of Willis and received a letter on April 25, 1865; Emily, who was received by experience on June 17, 1868, and was the property of N. T. Willis; Ben, who was received by experience on February 27, 1865, and was lettered out of the Sardis Church on September 24, 1869, and was the property of J. B. Willis; Charles, who was received by experience on April 23 1863, and was owned by Sister N. T. Willis and excluded on June 21, 1873. Jennifer was the property of J. R. Willis and was received by experience on December 26, 1863, and received a letter on December 26, 1868. Charles Willis was received by experience on February 28, 1873, and received a letter on April 26, 1874. Celia Willis was dead, and Juda Willis was listed as being dead. *Juda is buried in the colored section of the city cemetery of Wilkes County. Her headstone reads "In grateful memory of Judy, faithful servant of Francis T. Willis, the nurse of himself, his children, and his grandchildren. Called to a higher service, July 1878, in her 80th year. 'She hath done what she could.'"*

There was only one name listed under Johnson, and his name was Jacob. I do not know the status of his welfare in Sardis.

The slaves that were listed under the last name of Callaway were Seaf, who was dead; Tom, who was dead; Lewis Callaway, who received a letter on December 26, 1874; Wiley, who was dead; Jim, who was dead; Simon Callaway, who received a letter on May 23, 1874; Moses, who was excluded on February 25, 1860; Randolph, who was the property of

Martha Callaway, the wife of Rev. Enoch, and was excluded from Sardis on December 23, 1865, restored on October 27, 1866, and lettered out of the church on August 22, 1868. *Juda Callaway was listed as being dead.* Kate Callaway was lettered out of Sardis on March 24, 1866. Nancy Callaway was lettered out of the church at Sardis on August 25, 1882. Milly was dead. Amy was left blank, along with Mariah. Penny was lettered out of Sardis on May 25, 1861. Jane Callaway or N.C. Arnold was lettered out on September 25, 1875.

These are the names under the last name of Dowdy: Ben was gone, Joseph Walker was under the last name of Dowdy and was lettered out of Sardis January 21, 1860; Willis was listed as being dead, Hooper was lettered out or dead in November 26, 1859. Evolin was lettered out on November 26, 1859, and Rhody was lettered out on April 25, 1860. The only Aaron that I had in Sardis was under the last name of Derricot. He was lettered out of Sardis on September 22, 1866.

I put the beginning of the Sardis minutes here after the estate of Isaac and Winnifred Callaway to show that all the time Aaron was having trouble in Sardis, his wife Hannah was all alone, listed as the property of Isaac Callaway and his wife Winnifred in the 167th District of Wilkes. Hannah was left alone on Isaac's place and in the care of Winnifred Callaway while Aaron was under the watchful eye of Joseph Henderson and John Milner in the minutes of the church at Sardis.

The Slave man Aaron, The inquire Joseph Henderson, Rev. John H. Milner, and slave master Rev. Joshua S. Callaway leaves for Jones County Georgia.

Let us start at Sardis in August 1810. I found another older Negro that joined Sardis, and her name was Milly. Milly joined on August 25, 1810. In December 1811, Hannah got into trouble. Hannah became the servant of Mr. Harper, neighbor of Isaac and Winnifred Callaway in the 167th in Wilkes County. She left her husband, and Jeremiah Reeves and Peter Milner had to go and see her about the situation. John H. Milner was the secretary at Sardis at this time. Now this is the infidelity that I come across, not just with this young Callaway preacher but it is a structure that I found in the relationships in every hamlet, country, town, and village. "Yes, it took a village to give race to a child!"

The first time that I found something about Aaron was in December 1811. The church minutes at Sardis stated that Aaron's wife was sleeping around and Mr. Henderson said that Aaron had a good reason to leave her because of the things that she was doing to her husband. I do not know what the relationship was between Mr. Henderson and Aaron, or even whether Aaron was a colored and Mr. Henderson a white man. Aaron might be an Indian. You will see the relationship between the two men unfold and tell what even happens in 1816 five years later.

Joshua made his appearance at the same time Judy Callaway came to Sardis between the years of 1811 and 1812. She came with the last name written in the minute book as a Callaway. Jessie joined at this time as well. I do not know what plantation or county or state these two Negro Callaway slaves arrived from; however, they arrived shortly after Joshua S. Callaway returned to the church.

Conference, July 23, 1814: Mary King received by experience, Brother Joshua Callaway absent; adjourned.

Now, let us move into the year 1816, on May 25. The church has reported that Aaron had been caught in immoralities. The church elders ordered that J. H. Milner and a certain Callaway go and see Aaron.

Milner and a certain Callaway go and see Aaron. July 23, 1814, Joshua Callaway is absent and in May on the 25th day of 1816, J. H. Milner is the first person to inquire of Aaron immoral practices. Who is this J. H. Milner? In 1816 in the tax digest John H. Milner is in Jones County Georgia on about 202 acres of land. He will soon have company Mr. Joshua S. Callaway. John H. Milner I believe married the daughter of John Callaway and is the sister of Rev. Enoch Callaway. Now the mysterious Callaway has two Callaway's that could have been asked to enquire about 1805 Aaron our black brother! Mr. John Callaway whom I don't think so because he was excluded from the Church at Sardis for being intoxicated. I believe it is non-other-than Mr. Joshua S. Callaway the brother-in-law of Joseph Henderson Jr. Aaron is in the company of these three men. John H. Milner was the first to arrive in Jones County Georgia in 1816. In 1834 John H. Milner was in Monroe County in the 78th district with Pitt W. Milner whose land bound each other. I just had to find where Mr. Joshua S. Callaway at this time. John Spratling was in the 8th district of Monroe County and had property in Lee County as well. Mr. Thomas H. Pinckard, Mr. John Henderson, Pitt Milner Sr. was living in Monroe County Georgia on the waters of Rockey Creek his lands backs up to John H. Milner as well. Nancy and John Lovett and James Ray, Mr. Green

English, Mr. Aaron Sutton, Thomas Lyons and Hiram Phinizee, Aaron Talmadge and Wiley Jones, I feel like I am getting close to Evers District even though its named Colliers district. I say this because of the names of Phinizee and Aaron Sutton, and now Mr. Fredrick L. Crowder. Now Mr. John H. Phinnizee, Mr. John Chambless, Mr. John Pinkard and Samuel B. Baldwin, Mr. Samuel Patton, Mr. James Pinkard, Mr. Hiram Lester, Douglas and William Watson, Mr. Isaac and Henry Carlton, Mr. Reuben Nolan, Mr. Edward Callaway was in Clarks district on the waters of Rum Creek in the 5th district of Monroe and he has property in Pulaski in the 13th and 19th district of the county. Mr. George Turner is his neighbor alone with Thomas Lawlis. Another last name nearby is John Pitman, this is Rum Creek in Monroe County where Aaron and Hannah the colored slaves came to live and raise their family before the end of the great war. Here is a familiar family that is on Rum Creek with Edward Callaway and Hannah in Alabama. Mrs. Sarah Pinckard she's the guardian for Sarah C. Pinckard and Charlotte C. Pinckard of Rum Creek. Mr. John, Thomas and Robert Finch are on Rum Creek, William Pinckard is guardian for John F. Pinckard. Jesse S. Clark agent for William, Lucy and Rebecca Clark and John C. Baldwin are all in Rum Creek District with Mr. Edward William Callaway the son of Joshua S. Callaway who is living in Henry County about this time. Now comes Mr. Jesse M. Callaway in Clark district Jesse is not far from Mr. Amos Nobles and John Pope. Now remember this tax digest is in the year of 1834 and the last family that I am going to bother writing to you about is that of Mr. Henry Pope in the Ross District of Monroe County Georgia. Mr. Wiley H. Pope who had property in Lee County Georgia was over Mr. Henry Pope estate in Monroe County Georgia in 1834. Now this is strange to me because if Henry Pope is dead in 1834 who is the Henry Pope over the children and slaves of Isaac and Winnifred Callaway in Greene and Wilkes County. Could it be young Henry Pope junior who was living with his mother in Clarke County who had this responsibility after Seniors death? I wonder if Cadesman Pope and the other Pope are the children of Henry Pope. Excuse me I found another Pope by the name of Walter R. Pope with Mr. John R. Raines does not the names mentioned remind you of the rich landowners of Wilkes, Oglethorpe and Greene County Georgia! Captain Wiseman Ross is over the district where I even find another Pinckard by the name of John H. Wait one second Mr. Thomas L. Pope is here as well, near Mr. George Clower and Jonathan and John Shockley. In the Brewer's district lives Mr. John T. Pope a neighbor of Mr. Robert Brown and Arthur and Thomas Redding. There is a number of Redding's family located in Monroe County. Mr. William Smarr is located in the Brewer's district and has property in Dekalb County as well. Here's another family that has ties with the Callaway and they are William, John, Travis and Jane McKinney. Mr. Grisham McKinney, Now here comes Columbus Pope and Josiah Hudgins and Aquilla Cheney the neighbor of Henry C. and William A. Slaton the name that Major Callaway changed his name to hide for some reason or another in 1880 in Oglethorpe County. Aquilla Cheney and Isaac Cheney and the Slaton family were in the Lester District of Monroe. I found another name that ties to Oglethorpe and the children of Aaron or Robert Callaway. It is Edmond and Henry F. Jackson and family. The tax digest keep jumping from district to district and it is very hard to pin-point exactly what district they are in it is only when I go back to the top of the page. I left the Lester district and went into the Brewer district and now I am back in the Lester District again. This is where I found Josiah, Jonathan and William Callaway living next door to William W. Breadlove and Charles Evans. The next district is called Capt. Butts district where I found Mr. Zachariah Hugely the executor of Jesse Morgan who had property in Lee County and his neighbor Mr. Levi Stroud. Hansel Williford is over a minor Cullon J. Pope in Butts District. Zachariah Hugely has another property near Mr. Henry Strickland who is the guardian of a free colored man named Samuel Jones. James Lyon, William Findley, Mr. Alexander Russell, William Jernigan, William Samuels, Augustus H. Findley, Charles W. Haynes, Thomas McGintry was over the colored man Asa Summerland. What is the occupation of Joshua S. Callaway and John H. Milner? They are minister of the Gospel. I believe that they were close enough that John H. Milner, while making out his will had this endearing word to say about Rev. Joshua S. Callaway in Item five of his will. I will my executors sell in any way they seem first at either public or private sale any lands I may own except my Home plantation near Zebulon in Pike County except my interest in lands in Randolph County Alabama which last I have given to my Old Brother Joshua S. Callaway. Let me repeat myself and that is let me take you back to the earlier years at Sardis Baptist Church. The church minuets at Sardis stated that Aaron's wife was sleeping around and Mr. Henderson said that Aaron had a good reason to leave her because of the things that she was doing to her husband. Silvy joined Sardis on the same day as Nanny, this is the same year that Hannah became the slave of Mr. Harper. She left her husband and Jermiah Reeves and Pete Milner had to go and see Hannah. John H. Milner was the church secretary at this time December of 1811.

How can I pin point where Aaron was located and narrow it down. I can narrow it down to where the three men that were asked to inquire about him. The place is Jones County 1811. The Jones County tax digest of 1811 Mr. Williamson had two hundred acres in the fourth district his property was next to or boarded Mr. Callaway and he also had property in Franklin Co and Wilkes County as well. In the year of 1820 about the time Aaron was missing from Sardis I located Joseph Henderson in Jones Co. with John H. Milner in Captain Grens district of Captain Jefferson's District alone with William B. Mercer James Davison, Umphia Cooper and Jesse Chambless. Ocmulgee Baptist Association held at Walnut Creek Meeting House. Jones County from the third to the sixth September 1825 exclusive. Line One; The introductory sermon was delivered by Bro. Pace at the stand. Line two; The association required to the house when Bro. B. Milner was called to the Moderators seat,(Bro. Talbot being absent) and after devotion proceeded to business. Line four: Bro. J. Milner was chosen Moderator and Anthony Clerk. Bro. J. S. Callaway to preach the sermon next year and in case of this failure, Bro. Henderson; and Bro. Cooper to write the Circular Address. Line five; Appointed committee consisting of Jonathan Nichols, James Henderson, Richard Pace, I. L. Brooks and B. Milner to unite with any two from Walnut Creek Church, and arrange the preaching from day to day during this meeting. Line six; Brethren J. S. Callaway, t. Cooper, I.L. Brooks, P. F. Flournoy and E. Brantly, were appointed a committee to arrange the business to come before this Association. Adjourned until Monday morning o'clock. I found Mr. Joshua Callaway in the same year of 1820 in Capt. Gresham District of Jones County Georgia. This is while Joseph Henderson was in Grens or Jefferson Dist. Let us see who is in this same district with Rev. Joshua S. Callaway that I might know. Before I see who is in the district with Joshua Callaway in Jones County at this time in 1820 I want you to know that it took me almost seventeen years today to answer this question. Where did Aaron of 1805 in Sardis go and who was he with that day is April the 14th 2017. I had to get up and shout for joy at 6 am in the morning! Well, let's see who is in this district with Mr. Joshua Callaway in 1820 Jones County. I tell you the truth I've had a hard time trying to find anything on Mr. Joshua S. Callaway. It is the Gresham District of Jones County. Joshua is on the first page of five and the second from the top that mean his first neighbor is John R. Moore and then Joshua and then Mr. James Griggs. The next names just have familiar last names. Robert Middlebrooks, Robert Baldwin, Noah Mercer, John T. Pope and Jesse M. Pope, John Pinkard is in the Griffith district with Daniel Henderson. Isaac R. Pope was in the Hansford district. Mr. Asa Gammage was living in Mulkeys district. Elijah M. Callaway is in the Phillips district with a Mr. William Russell and a William Rose, Jonathan Callaway, Littleberry Champion, Mr. Thomas and James Stephens, William Williams is in the Rossers district with Sarah Williams. Jonathan W. Carrington was in the Clinton District, in a non-stated district I found David Blanton, and Benjamin Samuels. I thought this was the greatest find because it took me so long to answer the question of the absence of 1805 Aaron Callaway in 1816 at Sardis Baptist Church! I wanted to see what the household of Joshua S. Callaway, John Holmes Milner and Joseph Henderson in Jones County looked like in August 7,1820. I was very surprise to see that Joshua and his oldest slave in his house were between twenty six years old and forty four years old, the only white female was under ten years old and he had three white male under ten years old. Joshua Callaway's wife is missing from the household in Jones County Georgia. Remember he married Polly Milner nine years ago in 1811. The slave that is the same age as Joshua whom I am assuming is Aaron grew up together on Old Joshua and Isabella Henderson Callaway place in the old county of Wilkes. The ways of the boy hood friendship show the character that Aaron has as his master he grew up with. Aaron is located in the slave role or slave cabin with two slaves male under fourteen, two female slaves under fourteen, and one female slave between fourteen and twenty five. If this is the wife of Aaron she would have been born between 1806 and 1795. The four younger slave children are too young to work in the fields. Let's look at Mr. Joseph Henderson house hold at this time in Jones County. Joseph was in Grens District and was listed as being over forty five years old, Mr. Henderson has no slaves and has two son under the age of ten, and on female under the age of ten and one female between twenty six and forty four years old and that is the household of Mr. Joseph Henderson and now I visit Rev. John H. Milner's house at this time in the Jefferson District. John is between the ages of twenty six and forty four, he has two son under the ages of ten, one son between ten and fifteen, and one male in the house that is over forty five, one female under ten, it does not mention him as having a wife with him. He has two male slaves under fourteen, one between fourteen and twenty five, and one female slave under fourteen years old with five of these in agriculture. These four men Aaron, Joseph, John and Joshua are fairly close in age and all four were raised in Wilkes County Georgia. Aaron followed the preacher and his escapades that he did or were doing even from Wilkes County to Monroe County to Henry County Georgia to Chambers County Alabama where he was listed as having any slaves.

It will be only about four years from now in Chambers County Alabama that Joshua S. Callaway will be listed as being dead in Fayette County Georgia. I have yet to find a will or an estate record on Rev. Joshua S. Callaway anywhere!

However, I could estimate the age of Aaron in 1806 by the age of his childhood master Joshua S. Callaway. Joshua was born in 1789 in 1805 he would be sixteen years old. So, Aaron in 1805 would join Sardis at the age of sixteen. Also, if Aaron is in Jones County with the preacher Joshua S. Callaway he is also in Monroe County as well. Monroe County is the same place where Mr. Henry Pope dies and John Milner, and the Callaway's in Evers District in Monroe who has ties to Alabama. When Henry Pope dies the slaves of Isaac and Winnifred Callaway that was in his care were in Monroe County. Aaron and his ties to Peter and Mary and Wash Callaway and last but not least in the 1154th district of Terrell County Georgia Peter, Charles and Jennie Callaway. Terrell County, the last place where Charlie and Mary Callaway resided. Oh! Can you say mystery!

The next time that I find the members of Sardis asking about Aaron is on August 24, 1821. I wonder what charge they had against Aaron that would cause such concern at Sardis. Could it be that after exercising his free will by being involved with two women or the drink, acts that were common among the white men and coloreds and even Indians and half-breeds? Was there a change in the social structure and in the enlightenment of Joshua Callaway that brought all the lasciviousness and debauchery to light, because this is the lifestyle of the men of this time? Women were property along with slaves. Well, I did not find this to always be true. Women also exercise their free will, as you can see in the minutes of the church. Now, the question is where was Aaron living between 1816 and 1821? He was not with Hannah on the property of Isaac and Winnifred in Wilkes, nor was he on their property in Greene County. Could he have been down in Lee County or over on the property located in Troup County in LaGrange? Could it be that he left with Rev. Joshua S. Callaway in 1816?

CHAPTER THREE

THE FORCED CONTRACTS UPON CHARLEY AND FAMILY AND DEATH OF CHARLIE

1884

I found Charles Callaway using his real name in Union Point, the railroad town. He went to work for Union Point in Crutchfield, Greene County. Anthony Hurt and Jeff Hurt were with Charles Callaway at this time. The only name that I do not find on any tax digest is Richard Callaway. The question is, when Charlie married Mary Hurt, did he return to Union Point with his new bride?

This is also about the same time that he marries Mary Hurt, the daughter of Abraham English and Dinah Hurt English. When Mary married Charley Callaway, she used the last name Hurt, and I had a hard time trying to find their marriage license for this very reason. They were married in Clarke County in 1884 by Minister William Coile, the bother-in-law of William Eberhart. While down in Crutchfield, Greene County, Charlie Callaway was in the company of some good colored railroad men. They were James Lunceford, Reuben Lawson, Harrison Dowdy (whom he probably knew from Wilkes County), Jim Armstrong, Alec Wilson, Carey Moncrief, Bose Watson, Bill Thomas, Bill Tuggle, John Edmonson, Web Lumpkin, Bob Thornton, Barney Johnson, Rance Hill, Jerry King, Luke Banks, Sam Daniel, Joe Ranson, Wes Curry, Avery Mitchell, Sam Heard, Charles Williams, Henry Howard, Asa Thomas, Thore Kent, Elam Bailey,

James Pollard, John Jones, Warren Daniel, Ran Roberson, Ea Kent, Amos Fambrough, Ea Statham, Reuben Jones, Henderson Evans, Dan Jones, Joe Mitchell, Sam Mitchell, Will Green, Ples Perals, Henry Mitchell, Allen Wilburn, George Gordon, Jim Reynolds, Jesse Pinkyard, Frank Nesbit, Mose Cheney, Pat Anderson, Dan Curry, Calvin Jenkins, George Henry, Lee Roberson, Sam Carlton, Red Mitchell, Sammy Lamtrum, Sam Moody, Lucius Harris, Alfred Parham, John Cody, Sank Hillman, Ea Nesbit. These are all railroad men for the Southern Railroad.

In June 21 1900, Abraham and Dinah and family are living on the property of Thomas L. Epps in Oglethorpe County. Lucy is a twenty-six-year-old whom my grandfather said was caught up in a tornado and never seen again. He also said she was crazy in the head. His aunt Sallie is in the house at the age of fourteen and so is John. He is at the age of twelve, and another daughter, born in 1889, is eleven. She is my aunt Anna. Lizzur is six. They have three grandchildren living in the house with them: Brantley at the age of four, Rosa at the age of two, and my grandfather Kator at the age of one. Kator is listed as being born in January of 1899. Kator is my grandfather Arthur! Two months later, they are selling property to go to court with William Eberhart to save their grandchildren and the children of Charlie and Mary.

MY AUNT ANNA B. DANIEL SAID. "KATOR DADDY, CHARLIE WENT A MISSING FOR A LONG TIME, FOUND HIM HANGING IN A TREE ONE EARLY MORNING

I was in the care of my aunt Anna because my mother was named for her sister namesake. I would be captivated by her long braided grey hair and her hard demeanor that had been nourished from being in the constant work she performed on the farm in Greene, Clarke, and Oglethorpe County, Georgia. I was so cared for while I was in her care while my mother was gone as a little boy without a father in my life, and alone she took up the time to talk to me. I was sitting here writing and thinking the day when she died was the first time in my life I felt lost and afraid and alone!

STATE OF GEORGIA, Oglethorpe County.

THIS INDENTURE, Made and entered into this 29th day of September 1900, between J. J. Bacon, ordinary of said County, and Dinah English the Grand Mother of Cato Calloway aged Fifteen months

all of said county.

WITNESSES, That the said J. J. Bacon, ordinary as aforesaid, hereby binds and apprentices to the said Dinah English the said Cato Calloway until the said Cato Calloway is twenty-one years of age, upon the following terms:

Said Dinah English agrees to take into his custody said Cato Calloway, teach her the business of husbandry, furnish her with protection, wholesome food, suitable clothing, necessary medicine and medical attention, teach her habits of industry, honesty and morality, cause her to be taught the elementary principles of Mathematics and to read English, and shall govern her with humanity, using only the same degree of force to compel her obedience as a father may use with his minor child, and when said Cato Calloway shall arrive at the age of twenty-one years to receive from the said Dinah English one hundred dollars in cash. In consideration of all which said Dinah English is to be entitled to the services and earnings of said Cato Calloway until he is twenty-one years of age.

Witness our hands and seals, this 29th day of September 1900

Dinah English (L. S.)

J. J. Bacon ordinary (L. S.)

Sealed, signed and delivered in duplicate in the presence of

Dinah goes to the Oglethorpe Courthouse to get custody of Kator

State of Georgia, Oglethorpe County Maxey, Ga., August 13, 1900

For and in consideration of the sum of Fifty Dollars to me in hand paid by A.T. Brightwell, the receipt whereof is hereby acknowledged do hereby bargain sell and deliver to the said A. T. Brightwell the receipt whereof is hereby acknowledged do hereby bargain sell and deliver to the said A. T. Brightwell the following described property to-wit: All my undivided one half interest in 30 acres of Cotton now maturing and matured 20 acres of

Corn and other produce grown by me on land of T.L. Epps being worked by me on halves for the year 1900. To have and to hold the said property unto the said A.T. Brightwell. And to hold the said property unto the said A. T. Brightwell. And it is agreed by the said Abe. Dinah English that they are to hold and gather said bargained property subject to the order of said A. T. Brightwell at any time.

Witness my hand and seal this 14th day of August 1900

Witness: F. A. Hurt, J. W. Patrick J. P., Abe X English his mark

State of Georgia } Maxeys, Ga. Aug. 13th 1900
Oglethorpe County } For and in consideration of the sum of
Fifty Dollars to me in hand paid by
A. T. Brightwell, the receipt whereof is hereby acknowledged,
do hereby bargain, sell and deliver to the said A. T. Brightwell the
following described property, to wit: All my undivided one half
interest in 30 acres of Cotton now maturing and matured 20 acres
of Corn and other produce grown by me on land of T. L. Epps
being worked by me on halves for the year 1900 To have and to
hold the said property unto the said A. T. Brightwell. And it
is agreed by the said Abe & Dinah English that they are to
hold and gather said bargained property subject to the order of
said A. T. Brightwell at any time.
Witness my hand and seal, this 13th day of August, 1900.
Witness F. A. Hurt Abe his x mark English L.S.
J. W. Patrick J. P.
Filed in Office for Record Dec 1. 1900 at 3 15 O'clock P. M.
T. U. Lester Clerk
Recorded This Dec 1st 1900
T. U. Lester Clerk

Filed in office for record Dec. 1. 1900 at 3:15 P.M.

September 26, 1900, William Eberhart enters the courthouse at Lexington to file a complaint against Dinah English, a grandmother trying to protect her grandchildren Charley and Brantley Callaway. William shows the following facts.

1. That on the 22nd day of August 1895 Charley Callaway did bind and apprentice his two minor children to wit Charlie Callaway and Brantley Callaway to him the said William Eberhart until the said Charlie and Brantley Callaway should each become twenty-one years

of age; that said minors were duly and legally apprenticed to him and that letters of apprenticeship were duly recorded in Book B. of Indentures pages 57 in the ordinary's office of said, a copy of which letters are hereto attached and made a part of this petition-

2. Petitioner also shows that said Charlie and Brantley Callaway are illegally detained from the custody and control of your petitioner and by one Dinah English under same pretense unknown to your petitioner that the place of detention is in the neighborhood of the town of Maxey's, in said County-
3. Petitioner alleges that the detention of said Charlie and Brantley Callaway by the said Dinah English is illegal and that your petitioner desires to assume the custody, control, maintenance and education of said minors-

Wherefore he prays, Your Honor, to issue the writ-of-habeas corpus requiring the said Dinah English to bring the said Charlie and Brantley Callaway before you at such time and place as you may direct that what is right and proper may be done in the precise this September 26, 1900.

To Dinah English, you are hereby commanded to produce the bodies of Charlie Callaway and Brantley Callaway alleged on the sworn petition of William Eberhart to be illegally detained by you, together with the cause of such detention before me on Saturday, Sept. 27, 1900, at 10 o'clock at my office in Lexington, Ga., then and there to be disposed as of the law directs-

William Eberhart comes before the undersigned and on oath says that he has reason to ascertain that Dinah English will remove Charlie Callaway and Brantley Callaway beyond the limits of Oglethorpe County or conceal them from the offices of the law unless the bodies of said Charlie Callaway and Brantley Callaway be brought before the court. Sworn to and subscribed before me, September 26, 1900.

To George J. Cunningham, Sheriff of said county, or any Deputy Sheriff or constable of said county, William Eberhart, the applicant for the foregoing Writ of Habeas Corpus, having made oath in terms of the law, that he has reason to assert end that Dinah English will remove Charlie Callaway and Brantley Callaway beyond the limits of said county or conceal them from the offices of the law. You are hereby commanded to reach for and arrest the bodies of the said Charlie Callaway and Brantley Callaway, and bring them before me to be disposed of as the law directs. Herein fail not. Given under my official signature and seal of office this 26th Sept. 27, 1900.

I have this day received a copy of the written Writ of Habeas Corpus on Dinah English personally and have arrested the bodies of Charlie Callaway and Brantley Callaway and have them before the court this Sept. 27, 1900.

Geo. J. Cunningham, Sheriff O. C.

Now this statement by George J. Cunningham is written in the same handwriting. Oh! The manipulation of this writ of habeas corpus.

By September 29, 1900, about 10:00 a. m., trouble will come to the house of Abraham and Dinah English under the name of William Eberhart, who would file for custody of Charley Callaway and Brantley Callaway in Oglethorpe Courthouse in Lexington, Georgia. Dinah was served with a copy of the writ of habeas corpus and Charley and Brantley were in the custody of the sheriff. It also appears that there is no answer or contest filed in the petition filed in said case and it further appears from the evidence that said William Eberhart is entitled to the custody and control of said Charlie and Brantley Callaway under and by virtue of an indenture of apprenticeship duly executed by the parents of said minors. It further appears that said William Eberhart is a fit and proper person and that the best interests and welfare of said minors who are now orphans will be promoted by his having the care of them. And it was ordered that the sheriff deliver Charley and Brantley to William Eberhart, to wit: Charlie Callaway and Brantley Callaway, unto the custody and control of said William Eberhart in accordance with the said indenture of apprenticeship. It is also ordered that William Eberhart pay the cost of this proceeding.

J. J. Bacon Ordinary

On the same day, Dinah respectfully shows the following facts:

- That she is the maternal grandmother of Cato Callaway, a boy fifteen months old and orphan child of Charles and Mary Callaway, deceased
- That the said Charles and Mary Callaway, the mother and father of said Cato Callaway, are both dead and that said Cato has no

one that is legally bound to care for him or provide for his wants in his tender years, and that he has no means at all

- And that for and in consideration of the natural love and affection she has and cares for her grandchild she desires to assume the legal custody, maintenance and education of said Cato Callaway until he shall arrive at the age of maturity

Therefore, she prays, Your Honor, to bind and apprentice the said Cato Callaway to your petitioner in terms of the law.

Sept. 29 1900, Dinah X English, her mark

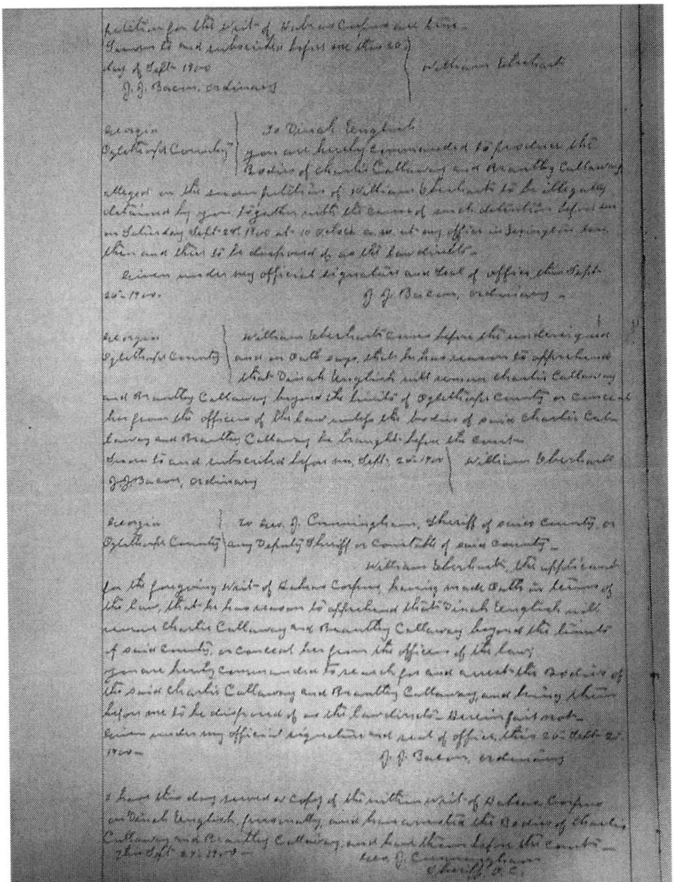

The foregoing petition read and considered, and it is ordered that citation issue and be published in terms of the law calling upon all persons concerned to show cause, if any they have, at the Oct. term 1900 of the court of Ordinary for said County why said land should not be sold as prayed for.

J. J. Bacon, Ordinary–

Court adjourned to next regular term–

J. J. Bacon, Ordinary

Georgia
Oglethorpe County } To Hon. J. J. Bacon, Ordinary of said County–

The petition of William Eberhart a citizen of said County, respectfully shows the following facts–

1st That on the 22d day of August 1895, Charley Calloway did bind and apprentice his two minor children, to wit: Charlie Calloway and Brantley Calloway to him, the said William Eberhart, until the said ~~Will~~ Charlie and Brantley Calloway should each become twenty one years of age; that said minors were duly and legally apprenticed to said Eberhart and that letters of apprenticeship were duly recorded in Book B. of Indentures, page 57 in the Ordinary's office of said, a copy of which letters are hereto attached and made a part of this petition–

2d Petitioner also shows, that said Charlie and Brantley Calloway are illegally detained from the custody and control of your petitioner by one Dinah English, under some pretense unknown to your petitioner– that the place of detention is in the neighborhood of the town of Maxeys, in said County–

3d Petitioner alleges that the detention of said Charlie and Brantley Calloway by the said Dinah English is illegal, and that your petitioner desires to assume the custody, control, maintenance and education of said minors–

Wherefore, he prays your Honor to issue the writ of Habeas Corpus, requiring the said Dinah English to bring the said Charlie and Brantley Calloway before you at such time and place as you may direct that what is right and proper may be done in the premises–

This Sept. 26th 1900–

William Eberhart–

Georgia
Oglethorpe County } Personally appears before me, William Eberhart and on oath says, that the statements made in the foregoing

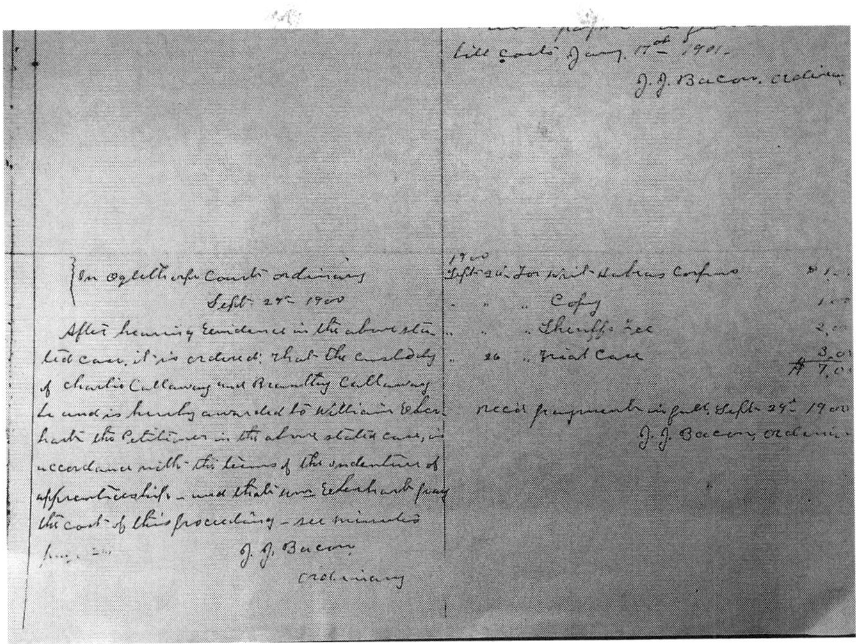

bill costs Jany. 17th 1901.
J. J. Bacon Ordinary

In Oglethorpe Court of Ordinary
Sept. 29th 1900
After hearing evidence in the above stated case, it is ordered: that the custody of Charlie Callaway and Bramlitty Callaway be and is hereby awarded to William Eberhardt the Petitioner in the above stated case, in accordance with the terms of the indenture of apprenticeship - and that Wm Eberhardt pay the cost of this proceeding - see minutes
J. J. Bacon
Ordinary

1900
Sept 29 For Writ Habeas Corpus $1.00
" " Copy 1.00
" " Sheriff fee 2.00
29 " Trial Case 3.00
$7.00
Recd payment in full Sept 29th 1900
J. J. Bacon, Ordinary

The above petition read and considered and the statements made therein appearing to be true, and it also appearing that said Dinah English is a colored woman of good moral character and of industrious habit and a fit and proper person to assume the custody and control of said Cato Callaway, and that she is the nearest of kin to said Cato Callaway, and henceforth there is no necessity for the extensive proceeding as set forth in section 2605 of the Civil Code of 1895, Vol. 2-

It is therefore ordered: That said Cato Callaway be bound and apprenticed to his said grandmother Dinah English until he shall arrive at the age of twenty-one years, and that letters of indenture issued to her in terms of the law, this Sep. 29, 1900.

J. J. Bacon Ordinary

Let's take a closer look at the family Dinah and her husband Abraham English.

In re
application of William Eberhart for custody
of Charley Callaway and Brantly Callaway

Before the ordinary of Oglethorpe County, Sept 25th 1900.

It appearing that Dinah English has been duly served with a copy of the writ of Habeas Corpus in the above stated case, and that the minors named in said petition are now in the custody of the Sheriff – and it also appearing that there is no answer or contest filed to the petition filed in said case, and it further appearing from the evidence that said William Eberhart is entitled to the custody and control of said Charlie and Brantly Callaway under and by virtue of an Indenture of apprenticeship duly executed by the parents of said minors, and it further appearing that said William Eberhart is a fit and proper person, and that the best interests and welfare of said minors, (who are now orphans) will be promoted by his having the care of them; It is therefore ordered, that the Sheriff deliver said minors, to wit; Charlie Callaway and Brantly Callaway into the custody and control of said William Eberhart in accordance with the said Indenture of apprenticeship –

It is also ordered, that William Eberhart pay the costs of this proceeding –

J. J. Bacon, Ordinary

Georgia
Oglethorpe County

To Hon. J. J. Bacon, Ordinary of said County –

The petition of Dinah English respectfully shows the following facts –

1st That she is the maternal grand mother of Cato Callaway, a Boy, fifteen months old, and orphan child of Charles and Mary Callaway, deceased.

2nd That said Charles and Mary Callaway, the mother and father of said Cato Callaway are both dead, and that said Cato has no one that is legally bound to care for him or provide for his wants in his tender years, and that he has no means at all; and that for and in consideration of the natural love and affection she has and bears for her said grand-child, she desires to assume the legal custody, maintenance and education of said Cato Callaway until he shall arrive at the age of maturity – wherefore, she prays your Honor to bind and apprentice the said Cato Callaway to your petitioner in terms of the law, Sept 29th 1900 –

Dinah her mark English

The above petition read and considered, and the statements made therein appearing to be true, and it also appearing that said Dinah English,

The year is 1860 on the plantation of Joel Hurt in Oglethorpe County, Georgia, on the Oconee River and many surrounding creeks. Joel Hurt has thirteen house slaves, and I can see the fourteen-year-old Dinah Hurt and her thirty-year-old mother and her siblings. She has a twelve-year-old brother, ten-year-old brother, eight and seven, five, and a two-year-old boy and two ten-year-olds, one of them a mulatto, and a two-year-old female in the house of the thirty-year-old. I had to find out if I had the right family that Dinah was in. I found four-year-old mulatto Dinah in the house with her twenty-one-year-old mulatto mother and two-year-old mulatto brother. This is a pattern that is consistent with 1870 as well as in 1860.

Maxey, Oglethorpe County, Ga., June 6, 1870, J.H. Brightwell, Asst. Marshal

Crawford Hurt, forty-six mulatto man

Harriet Hurt, forty-four

Jesse Hurt, eighteen

Charlie Hurt, sixteen

John C. Hurt, twelve

Addie Hurt, ten

Millie Hurt, twenty-four

Lula Hurt, three

Lila Hurt, seventy and living with Henry Hurt, twenty-six

Catharine Hurt, nineteen

Lymon Hurt, twenty-two

Jennie Hurt, seventeen

Callie Hurt, nine

Madison Hurt, forty-year-old mulatto living with Sophia, thirty

James, eighteen

Jasper, sixteen

John H. Hurt, twelve

Savannah Hurt, eleven

Hiram, nine

Symms Hurt, seven

Julia, five

Betsy, two

Buy of A. T. BRIGHTWELL & SONS and Save Money on Your Purchases.

STATEMENT

Maxeys, Ga., Oct 5 1907

A. T. BRIGHTWELL & SONS

Merchants and Cotton Buyers

BOUGHT OF Lum Hurt

2 BALES COTTON

MARKS	BALE NO.	SINGLE WTS	TOTAL WTS.	PRICE		AMOUNT	
			523	58	84		
			541	61	31		
						120	15

Under the picture that Lum Hurt owned his own property next to R. A. Maxey who hired Bob Williams the husband of Matilda Callaway the daughter of Aaron and they are living in the 147th district of Greene County Georgia. As a matter of fact they are living near Adam Williams the grandfather of Martin Luther King Jr. who is in the house of Barney Maxey. Adam is listed as being a white servant of Barney Maxey alone with his siblings as well and Bob and Matilda the daughter of Aaron are living next door and Bob Williams and his wife Matilda's father is just a few houses away in 1880.

Living next door is Mr. Anthony English, a forty-year-old black man and his son Daniel, twenty

Mealia, sixteen

Ann, twelve

Nancy, eight

Augustus, twenty

Oliver, twenty

Eliza English is a forty-year-old mulatto female living with Sarah English, an eight-year-old mulatto

Now my great-great-grandmother Dinah English is at the age of twenty-five, her husband Abraham English is twenty-eight. Mary, my great-grandmother, is three, and Nannie is ten months old.

Mr. Lewis Kennebrew, a fifty-year-old farm laborer, and his wife Silla, who is fifty as well. Ellen, their daughter, is twenty-four. Lotty is four, Katie is a forty-eight-year-old domestic servant, Richard Hurt is twenty years old, Dinah French is a forty-six-year-old domestic servant. I might be mistaken about this statement that Richard Hurt might change his last name to English. I believe that all are on the property of Mr. James Hurt, a thirty-eight-year-old farmer, and his son Howard, who is four, and Mamie, who is two. John Hurt is at the age of thirty-four and has a Gladden Hurt who is a year old. They both have land valued at $3,000 and their personal property is valued at $2,000. *Joel Hurt bought property from Luke J. Callaway and Wm. A. Callaway on July 4, 1867. This document was witnessed by T.W. Cheney and James A. Davison, the justice of the peace. Joel Hurt also bought property from H.C. Bugg on the same day, July 4, 1867, and was witnessed by F.A. Hurt and W.A. Partee, the justice of the peace.*

On the ninth day of June 1870, J.H. Brightwell, Asst. Marshall, Maxey, Ga.

Peter Hurt is a fifty-year-old farmer who worked alongside Abe English on the property of Mr. Hurt. Peter Hurt's wife Mary is fifty years old, and Oliver Hurt, their son, is eighteen. Delia is fourteen. Jane is ten. James Shaw is a twenty-five-year-old white man, and his wife Josephine is twenty-two. Their son William E. Shaw is eight months old. Mr. Henry Barnett is a nineteen-year-old white man living with his twenty-four-year-old black woman named Mariah and Mary, a fourteen-year-old or nineteen-year-old colored woman. Wash Barnett is a sixteen-year-old black man and Parthenia is a one-year-old black female. I am amazed at the fact that I missed this household and this situation that was not to be but was. And I am more amazed by the fact that the McCloud brothers told me the picture of a white woman hanging on their wall was of Mary Barnett or Mariah, their great-grandmother. They mentioned Mrs. Parthenia as well.

Living next door to them is the Mitchell family: Robert R. Mitchell, a forty-one-year-old; Martha W. Mitchell, forty; William, eight; Bell, five; Ida, three; Wiley Bell, a forty-year-old farm laborer; Margana Hudson, a twenty-five-year-old domestic mulatto woman; Julia, two; and Mary, three months.

In 1880, in Woodstock, 230th District, Oglethorpe County, M. B. Milner is the enumerator on the twenty-ninth of June. Abram is thirty-seven, Dinah is thirty-three, Mary is thirteen, Nannie is ten, Anthony is seven, Lucy is five, Henry is three, and Charles is two. All are living on the property of John T. Hurt, a white landowner at the age of forty, and his son Lewis G. at the age of eleven, and living in the house as servant is Dinah French, a fifty six-year-old, and August English, the twenty nine-year-old brother of Abram. James Hurt and his son Howard are a few houses down the road. James is forty-seven and Howard is fourteen. There might be two more families on the Hurt place and they are the families of Aaron Johnson and Anderson Smith.

In the tax digest between 1870 and 1880, J. T. Hurt employed Abe English, Tom Clark, and Ed Crawford. While Abe was on J. T. Hurt's place, his brother was on W. Brant's property next door. Now, in 1900, Abe and Dinah will go to work for T. L. Epps's place but for now he has Charlie Jewell on his place. Sy Jewell, the father of Charlie, was on Mr. J. McWhorter's place. Rich Callaway was on W. H. Cheney's place, right next to J. T. Hurt's place at this time. A few years earlier, in the tax digest Abe was still on J. T. Hurt's place in the 232rd District of Bairdstown. J. T. Hurt employed Marshal Hill, Jordan Hurt, Aaron Johnson, Crawford Hurt, and Henry Gresham. Now, the last man that accused Charlie in 1899 of selling liquor was J.R. Haynes. J.R. Haynes employed Allen Evans, Francis Allen, Nathan Armstrong, and Tom Moore Jr. In the earlier 1870s tax digest, he was still on Mr. Hurt's place with Peter Hurt and Richard Huff, and Gus Hurt was on F. A. Hurt's place. J. L. Hurt has Anthony English, the father of Abe and Gus English, next is Lewis Kinnebrew, Jordan Hurt, and Crawford Hurt on his place. Preacher Tom Moody was on Mr. McWhorter's place. Rev. Tom Moody represented Penfield with Rev. Jesse Callaway as being students in the Atlanta Baptist in Atlanta. Between 1875 and 1877, Abe was still on the Hurt property with Ned Johnson, and Peter Hurt Jr. was next door on the property of Marshall Hurt. On H. McWhorter's place was Anthony Haynes, and Bob Callaway was on P. M. Stephens's place with Steve Daniel, who was just married by Rev. Jesse R. Callaway. Robert Callaway or Bob is an employee of Mr. P. M. Stephens the same landowner in 1866 only four year earlier Charles or Charley would become his indentured servant. The age of young Charlie or Charles is the same age as the son of the oldest son of Aaron Cheney also known as Robert Callaway or Bob or even Green Callaway as well.

Now, I have a pattern, grouping certain colored Hurts and white Hurts in Bairdstown in Oglethorpe County. Again here is another year that Abe is still living upon the plantation of J. T. Hurt and his father J. L. Hurt. Abe and Peter Hurt is on white landowner J. T. Hurt's plantation, and Crawford Hurt and Henry Hurt and Lewis Kinnebrew are on J. L. Hurt's place. These are families that are very close. Rev. Tom Moody is on W. Moody's place. At this time, Bob Callaway is not on Stephens's place. In the census, Tony English was sixty years old and his wife Brach was fifty. Alice is their nine-year-old daughter and James is their seven-year-old son. All were listed in the census on June 14, 1880, by Ligon McWhorter. Now, remember in 1870 Anthony was forty years old and living with Daniel, twenty; Mealia, sixteen; Ann, twelve; Nancy, eight; and Augusta, his twenty-year-old son, and Oliver, his twenty-year-old son in house 101. Living in house 102 is Eliza English, a forty-year-old, and Sarah, an eight-year-old mulatto school girl. In house 103 is twenty-five-year-old Dinah, twenty eight-year-old Abram, three-year-old Mary, and ten-month-old Nannie.

Lewis Kinnebrew is in house 104. Lewis is fifty years old and has fifty-year-old Sila Kinnebrew as his wife. Ellen is twenty-four. Lotty is four. Kalie is a forty-eight-year-old domestic servant. Also in the house is twenty-year-old Richard Hurt and Dinah French. All are on the property of James Hurt, a thirty-eight-year-old farmer with a four-year-old son Howard and two-year-old daughter Mamie. With them are thirty-four-year-old John and one-year-old Gladden. Now I know the relationship between James and John. They are brothers sharing property valued at 6,000 dollars. Their property is right next to Celeste Stephens, the employer of Bob Callaway, and James Jewell, who employed Aaron Callaway. The properties of the Hurts lie in both Greene County and Oglethorpe County, Georgia. This is why I had a very hard time understanding the place where Abe and Dinah English resided and I have come to a conclusion that Aaron and Bob Callaway are the only two close relations to the Hurt and English families besides the Williams and Jesse R. Callaway.

I do know that when 1900 rolls around Kator Calloway will be brought up in the stable household of Abraham and Dinah English. I have noticed that they did not move from plantation to plantation often. They lived on the Hurt place for quite some time. I also noticed that they always lived in or Near Maxey even when they moved on to the Epps place. The only colored church in this vicinity was that of Harmonia Baptist. However, when they moved closer to the town of Penfield they attended Sanders Chapel. *All this time in Maxey and near Bairdstown they stayed close to the family of Hurts, on whose plantation Dinah grew up and might have had children by some white landowner. Mary must have been born out of wedlock and so was Nannie because they both married under the last name of Hurt and not English. You have to look at the mulatto color of the women in the pictures on the cover of my book to know that I am not lying!*

Now don't forget that Bob Calloway was on T. L. Epps's place in the 1880s while Abe English was on J. T. Hurt's place with Ed Crawford. I believe this is how Charlie Jr. met Emma Crawford while Jim Callaway was on J. H. McWhorter's place. I believe that Jim is the son of Rev. Jesse R. Callaway. Dick Callaway was on J. L. Wilson's place. Another time I found Bob Callaway (Robert) in Bairdstown is when he's working for the Georgia Railroad right on top of Mary Hurt and Abe and Dinah English, her parents. Bob or Robert got into a little trouble in Bairdstown in the 1880. He was charged with trying to kill Lumpkin Goolsby, who was on J. H. McWhorter's place with Thomas and Anthony Haynes and Henry Gresham and John Hunter. The charges were dismissed against Robert Callaway.

In 1900, Abe is now sixty years old. Abraham was born in March 1840. Dinur (Dinah) was born April 1850 and is now fifty. Lucy, their daughter, was born October 1873, and is twenty-six. Sallie was born May 1886 and was fourteen. John, their son, was born May 1887 and was twelve. Annur or my aunt Anna was born February 1889 and was eleven. Lizor, their granddaughter, was born December 1897 and was six years old. Brantly, their grandson, was born February 1896 and is four. Rosa, their granddaughter, was born May 1898 and is two. Kator, my grandfather, was born 1899 and is a year old. Dinah and Abe has all of their four grandchildren in the house with them and Charlie, my grandfather's brother, is in the house with T. L. Epps, the landowner whose property Dinah and Abe are on. Charlie was born February 1885 and was now fifteen years old. Dinah and Abraham's grandchild Lizor is not in the house of Dinah and Abe's in 1910 and can't be found.

Now we will look at what William Eberhart's writ of habeas corpus based on the contract between Charley and Mary and William Eberhart. This Indenture made and entered into on the nineteenth day of 1892 between William Eberhart and Charley Callaway and his Wife Mary Callaway, the father and mother of Charlie Callaway about six years old, and Howard Callaway about four years old, all of said county.

Witness: That said Charlie and Mary Callaway hereby bind and apprentice unto the said William Eberhart the said Charlie and Howard, until the said Charlie and Howard are twenty-one years of age, under the following terms, said William Eberhart agrees to take into his custody the said Charlie and Howard to teach them the benefits of husbandry, furnish them with protection, wholesome food, necessary medicine and medical attendance, teach them habits of industry, honesty and morality, and shall govern them with humanity using only the same degree of force to compel their obedience as a father may use with his minor children. And when the said Charlie and Howard shall arrive at the age of twenty-one years, they are to receive one hundred dollars in cash: In consideration of all which, said William Eberhart is to have and be entitled to the services and earnings of said Charlie and Howard, until they are twenty-one years old.

Witness on hands and seals, this 19th day of October 1892

Witness: George J. Cunningham and J. T. Carter William Eberhart

Charlie X Callaway, his mark Mary X Callaway, her mark

Personally appears G. J. Cunningham, who on oath says that he saw William Eberhart, Charlie Callaway and Mary Callaway sign the written paper for the purpose therein mentioned, and that he signed the space as a witness thereto sworn and subscribed before me, this 23rd July 1895.

George J. Cunningham comes back nine months latter and bears witness again and what for? Is it that they expect something is going to unfold that they need to cover their ——? J. T. Carter didn't come back and sign as a witness again. Why?

> This indenture made this the nineteenth day of October 1892, between William Eberhart and Charlie Callaway and Mary Callaway, his wife, all of said county.
>
> Witness: That said Charlie and his wife, in consideration of the promises and undertakings of the said William Eberhart hereinafter set forth do herby bind themselves, together with Robert Callaway, son of said Charlie for the full term of fifteen months from this date and at the expiration of said term. If the said parties have not paid

all obligations to the said William Eberhart, this contract shall continue from year to year, until five years shall have passed; and they herby agree and contract with said Eberhart to work faithfully under his direction, respect and obey all orders and commands of the said Eberhart with reference to himself herinafter set forth, and at all times demean himself and themselves orderly and soberly; And the said Charlie, Mary and Robert further agree to account to the said Eberhart for all loss of time, except in cases of temporary sickness. If such sickness should be of longer duration at any one time than six days then such loss of time shall be accounted for at the same rate per day as they are then receiving pay under this contract: And should this contract be terminated in part by the death of either of said Callaways or William Eberhart, then the compensation of the said Callaway that dies shall be pro-rated for the time completed for the year in which the death may occur; And the said William Eberhart, in consideration of the promises and undertakings of the said Callaways, agrees and contracts with said Callaways to furnish them with house room, and the usual allowance of rations. He further agrees to pay said Charley Callaway eighty-five dollars per year for himself, and twenty-five dollars per year for Mary Callaway and thirty-five dollars per year for Robert Callaway, the services of above parties are to be rendered on farm.

In witness whereof the said Charles and Mary Callaway, and the said William Eberhart, have hereto respectively set their hands and seals the day and year first above written.

In witness of this contract: George J. Cunningham J. T. Carter W. T. Carter.

Charlie X Callaway, his mark Mary X Callaway, her mark William Eberhart

Filed in Office for record July 25 1895 Recorded July 25, 1895

Why is the nineteenth day of October 1892 written? And also why does it take nine months before the ordinary filed this in his office?

> Now this is the argument of William Eberhart and the writ of habeas corpus.
>
> This indenture made and entered in this the 22nd day of August 1895 between Wm. Eberhart and Charlie Callaway, the father of Robert Callaway, age seventeen years, Willie Callaway, aged three years, Brantley Callaway, aged six months, and Annie Sib Callaway, aged six months, all of said county.
>
> Witnesses: That the said Charlie Callaway hereby binds and apprentices to the said Wm. Eberhart the said Robert Callaway, Willie Callaway, Brantley Callaway, and Annie Sib Callaway until they are twenty-one years of age upon the following terms: Said Wm. Eberhart agrees to take into his custody said minor children, teach them the benefits of husbandry, furnish them with protection, wholesome food, necessary medicine and medical attention, teach them habits of industry, honesty, and morality, cause them to be taught the elementary principles of mathematics and to read English, and shall govern them with humanity, using only the same degree of force to compel their obedience as a father may use with his minor child. And when said Robert Callaway, Willie Callaway, Brantley Callaway, Annie Sib Callaway shall arrive at the age of twenty-one years, they are to receive from the said William Eberhart one hundred dollars each in cash. In consideration of all which, said William Eberhart is to be entitled to the services and earnings of said Robert Callaway, Willie Callaway, Brantley Callaway and Annie Callaway until they are twenty-one years of age.
>
> Witness our hands and seals this the 22nd day of August 1895. Executed in duplicate and sealed, signed and delivered in presence of G. J. Cunningham and B. B. Williams N. P. Ex. off. J. P. filed for record Aug 24th 1895 J. J. Bacon Recorded aug. 26 1895
>
> Charlie X Callaway, his mark William Eberhart

State of Georgia,
Oglethorpe County.

THIS INDENTURE, Made and entered into this the 22nd day of Aug 1875 between Wm Eberhart- and Charley Calloway The father of Robbert Calloway age 17 Years Willie Calloway age 3 years Brantley Calloway age 6 Months and Annie Lib Calloway 6 Month all of said County.

WITNESSES, That the said Charley Calloway hereby binds and apprentices to the said Wm Eberhart- the said named minor children until the said Robbert Calloway Willie Calloway Brantley Calloway and Annie Lib Calloway until they are twenty-one years of age, upon the following terms: Said Wm Eberhart- agrees to take into his custody said named minor children teach them the business of Husbandry furnish them with protection, wholesome food, suitable clothing, necessary medicine and medical attention, teach them habits of industry, honesty and morality, cause them to be taught the elementary principles of Mathematics and to read English, and shall govern them with humanity, using only the same degree of force to compel their obedience as a father may use with his minor child, and when said Robbert Calloway Willie Calloway, Brantley Calloway and Annie Lib Calloway shall arrive at the age of twenty one to receive from the said Wm Eberhart- one hundred dollars each in cash. In consideration of all which said Wm Eberhart- is to be entitled to the services and earnings of said Robbert Calloway Willie Calloway Brantley Calloway and Annie Lib Calloway until they are twenty one years of age.

Witness our hands and seals, this 22nd day of Aug 1895

Charley his x mark Calloway L. S.

William Eberhart L. S.

Sealed, signed and delivered in the presence of

G. J. Cunningham

Benj B. Williams N.P.J.P.

As I sit and type this contract, I can see that it is written in a hurry and that Mary didn't sign it or was a witness. Charlie's signature X is forced. It is darker than the previous marks. J. T. Carter is not a witness to the contract this time. And last but not least, the ordinary of the court who filed the contract didn't take nine months, only two days. It was done in such a hurry. Why? I'll show you why. The only thing is that he has the year wrong in his statement or there was a conspiracy on the US attorney's part.

Charles is the third count leveled against William Eberhart on Indictment number 5357 in the United States Circuit Court.

The Grand Jurors Aforesaid, upon their oaths aforesaid, in the name and by the authority of the United States of America, do further present that William Eberhart, late of said Northern District of Georgia, within the northern district of said Court, on the 10th day of January in the year of our lord one thousand eight hundred and ninety-six, did then and there unlawfully, wrongfully, feloniously and with force and arms hold, arrest and return, and did then and there cause to be arrested, held and returned a certain person, to wit, Charley Calloway, a person of color, to a condition of peonage. That is to say that on or about the first of January 1896 the said Charley Calloway, who had been in the employ of the said William Eberhart, left the employ of the said William Eberhart and refused to work for him longer because the said William Eberhart had cruelly mistreated the wife of the said Charley, to wit, Mary Callaway, by unlawfully and cruelly beating, bruising and wounding her and by compelling her, the said Mary Calloway, at the point of a pistol and with threats to unlawfully yield her body to the lustful embraces of the said William Eberhart and compelling her to have sexual intercourse with him, the said William Eberhart.

The Grand Jurors charge that after the said Charley Calloway had left the said William Eberhart for the reasons aforesaid, to-wit, on the 10th day of January 1896, the said William Eberhart did then and there hold, arrest and return, and cause to be held, arrested and returned the said Charley Calloway to his farm and to a condition of involuntary servitude and did then and there place hand-cuffs upon him, the said Charley Calloway, and did beat him, the said Charley Calloway, upon the back, head, face and body and did compel the said Charley Calloway to enter upon a long period of involuntary servitude and did reduce the said Charley Calloway to a condition of serfdom and slavery, and did compel the said Charley Calloway to do any and all kinds of work and service for him, the said William Eberhart, and did compel the said Charley Calloway to remain upon the farm of his, the said William Eberhart, against his will. And in order to compel him to remain upon his farm, the said William Eberhart stripped naked the said Charley Calloway and did hand-cuff him to and with one Orange Neeley, the said Orange Neeley being then and there confined to his bed with sickness. And the said William Eberhart, in order to more cruelly and thoroughly and effectually establish the industrial and agricultural serfdom herein before described and to brutalize and terrorize the said Charley Calloway, did compel him, the said Charley Calloway, by holding a pistol over him, the said Charley Calloway, to pin his own beloved son, Robert Calloway, outstretched to the ground, and did make the said Charley Calloway hold his said son while the said William Eberhart did violently and unmercifully beat the said Robert Calloway with heavy sticks and other weapons to the jurors unknown until the blood gushed from his body and did wound and cripple him, the said Robert Calloway. All of which said cruel acts on the part of said William Eberhart were done unlawfully and without provocation, and the said William Eberhart, in furtherance of said horrible system of peonage, did compel by force and threats the said Charley Calloway to bind and apprentice his three minor children, two of whom were nursing babies until each of them was 21 years old to a condition of involuntary servitude, contrary to the form of the statute in such case made and provided and against the peace and dignity of the United States of America.

Previously, I presented to you the contract between William Eberhart and Charley and I made mention of the hurried process. But I didn't mention that Mary did not sign or enter into this contract. Charlie mentioned in March of 1898 that Mary had been sexually violated, threatened with a gun, and beaten. She couldn't have made it to the signing of this contract in her condition. Willie is three years old Brantley and Annie Sib is six months old, so I asked myself this question: what kind of work can they perform? They can't work in the house and serve. The children surely cannot work in the field, so why would Charlie enter them into servitude?

Let's look at the other people who were victims in this peonage Case against William Eberhart.

First count – Moses Sims

Mose Sims was in Fulton County when William Eberhart was held and arrested. William Eberhart claimed that Mose Sims was indebted to him for some amount. William Eberhart put handcuffs on him and forcibly carried him to Oglethorpe County. William Eberhart carried him before his brother-in-law Ben Williams, who was then the justice of the peace and did and there compel Mose Sims against his will by threats of prosecution upon some pretense and trumped up charge to enter into a contract with him to work for William Eberhart for a term of five years. He was also compelled to enter into a contract with William Eberhart to bind his five minor children, Weyman and Ned and Sarah and Ophelia and Richard, ages eleven, nine, six, four, and two years, all against his will.

Federal Judge Newman and District Attorney E. A. Angier *and how they came to their positions in the Federal courts.*

The Federal Judge and the U.S. Attorney

Atlanta, Ga., Aug. 2, 1886

To the President,

We the undersigned, who are practicing Attorneys in the Northern District of Georgia and who reside in Atlanta, do reside respectfully represent to your Excellency that we are well and initially acquainted with the personal and professional character of William T. Newman Esq. of the Atlanta Bar, and that he is eminently qualified by bearing and experience to fill the position of United States District judge. In our opinion his appointment would give satisfaction to the bar and people of the district. We have the honor to be your best obedient servants:

C. W. Smith

A. B. Culberson

Shelton Sims

C. T. Ladson

T. B. Redwine

T. A. Hammonds

R. S. Gordon

J. N. Milligde

Hoke Smith

Burton Smith

F. M. O'Bryan

J. R. Whiteside

Harroll Paynes

Piromis H. Bell

John B Goodwin

Jno——

Robt——

Aoolph Brant

T. P. Westmoreland

Jack J. Spalding

C. D. Hill

W. S. Tumhell

Henry Herlsey

J. C. Newman

Hamp Arnold

Alex. C. King

Samuel West

Henry Hillyer
Lewis S. Thomas
Luther Z. Rosser
Jas. W. Austin
E. A. Angier*
E. W. Martin
J. M. McAlpin
J. R. Hardy
Wm. H. Haggard
Milton A. Candler
Geo. S. Thomas
Wm. P. Hill
Wm. S. Thomson
Milten H. Rhett
G.H. Tolliver
J. T. Pendleton
Geo. T. Gray
Howard E. W. Palmer
M. Degraffengrid
W. D. Ellis
S. B. Tuner
T. S. Sawton
Harrison & Peeples
J. H. Lumpkin
Henry Tieley
Hooper Alexander
Parker King
Thos. F. Carrigan
Jno T. Glen
E. R. Angier

Atlanta, Ga.

August 4

To the President

Sir,

We herewith petition you for the appointment of the Hon. W. T. Newman of Atlanta to United States judge made in account by the death of Judge H. K. McCary. We testify cheerfully to Mr. Newman's high ability, Integrity and fitness. His appointment would be, in our opinion, the best that could be made. If you can see your way clear to make the appointment, we would be gratified and are sure a very large majority of the people would be.

With great respect,

H. W. Grady

E. P. Howell

To Hon. Governor Cleveland

President of the United States

Washington, D. C.

July 31, 1886.

We the undersigned members of the Marietta Bar would respectfully ask that Capt. W. T. Newman of Atlanta, Ga., be appointed to fill the office of United States Judge for the Northern District of Georgia, said office having become vacant by the death of the lamented H. K. Mckay. Capt. Newman is eminently qualified to fill said office, being a profound scholar and jurist, and if appointed, will be acceptable to the bar and people of Georgia and a credit to the bench.

Joe B. Alexander

H. M. Hunnicutt

J. E. Mozley

R. N. Holland

Will Winn

Clay & Blair

W. S. Cheney

W. R. Power

Oath of office

In Re, Hoke Smith Esq., Special Assistant U. S. Attorney: I, Hoke Smith, having been duly appointed, on the 24th day of November 1896, by the Honorable Attorney General of the United States of America, Special Assistant U. S. Attorney in and for the Northern District of Georgia, do solemnly swear that I will support and defend the Constitution of the United States against all enemies foreign and domestic; that I will bear true faith and allegiance to the same; that I take this obligation freely without any mental reservation or purpose of evasion; that I will well and faithfully discharge the duties of the office of Special Assistant Attorney for the United States in and for the Northern District of Georgia on which I am about to enter, so help me God.

Sworn to and subscribed before me this 14th day of December, 1896.

O. C. Fuller, U. S. Commissioner, Northern District of Georgia

Hoke Smith

Attorney and Counsellor at Law

10 1/2 s. Broad St. Atlanta, Ga.

My dear sir: I enclose you the oath of office made by myself as special assistant United States attorney to aid in the prosecution of the indictments against J. S. King, formerly president of the Merchants National Bank of Rome.

I understand that the bank will employ local counsel to aid in the preparation of the case. It will not, therefore, be necessary to change the usual custom of the department and to designate one of those men as representing the Department of justice.

Very sincerely yours,

Hoke Smith

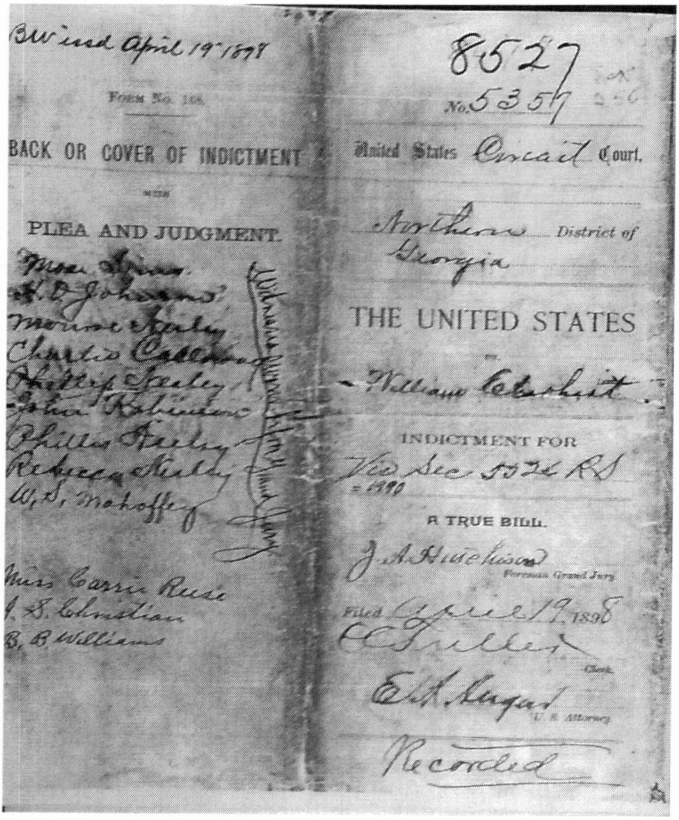
8527

No. 5357

FORM No. 168.

BACK OR COVER OF INDICTMENT

WITH

PLEA AND JUDGMENT.

United States Circuit Court,

Northern District of Georgia

THE UNITED STATES

vs.

William Eberhart

INDICTMENT FOR

Vio Sec 5326 RS

A TRUE BILL.

J. A. Hutchison
Foreman Grand Jury

Filed April 19, 1898

Clerk

U. S. Attorney

Recorded

Miss Carrie Ruse

B. B. Williams

Cases Against Eberhart and Others in 1898

Case No. 5363, U.S. Circuit Court Northern District of Ga., *United States Vs. William Eberhart and Albert Boykin* Demurrer to Indictment. Filed in Clerk's Office Oct. 31, 1898. This Indictment has the same argument in case no. 5357. And Demurrer has the same attorneys. Mr. William Eberhart's bond in this case is set at $1000.00 and Albert Boykins Bond is set at $600.00. The man who got Eberhart and Boykins's bond is Billups Phinizy, claiming the same property in Clarke Co., June 17, 1898.

(Opinion) *The United States vs. William Eberhart*

Peonage. Vio. Sec. 5526, R.S. Demurrer. The indictment charges the defendants with certain acts in restraint of the personal liberty of named persons of African descent, and characterized these acts as peonage, and charge the defendants with holding the persons named as peons and with returning them to a condition of peonage in violation of the Act of Congress of March 2, 1867 14 Stat. at Large, 546, (Rev. Stat. 5526.,1990–1.)

The Act of Congress, entitled "An Act to Abolish and Forever Prohibit the System of Peonage in the Territory of New Mexico and Other Parts of the United States," was aimed at a system. Its purpose was to abolish and forever prohibit the system known as "peonage" as it existed in New Mexico and elsewhere. A full discussion of this system and how it came to exist in New Mexico will be found in the case of *Jaremillo v. Romero*, 1 New Mex., Rep. 190. It came with the territory ceded to the United States by the treaty with Mexico after the Mexican war. It was part of the system of the people inhabiting that territory. The clear purpose of the act was to deal with this system by abolishing it and prohibiting a return to it.

An examination of the act will show that this is true beyond question. No such system as this ever existed in Georgia. African slavery existed, but this was the ownership of Africans and persons of African descent as chattels. There could not be, therefore, in Georgia, any such thing as holding persons under this system of peonage or returning them to it. It would be the merest perversion of this act to attempt to apply it to an ordinary case of restraint of personal liberty, and the case is not strengthened by the charge that the person so restrained is of African descent. However wrongful and illegal some of the acts charged in the indictment may be, they cannot be punished under the statute named. The purpose of this act, as stated, was to abolish this system of peonage, and to render null and void all acts, laws, resolutions, orders, regulations or usages in New Mexico or elsewhere which established or which sought to establish this system. The penal part of the act will not be enlarged beyond the scope and purpose of the act as above indicated. The penalty is for holding under or for arresting o returning to this condition of peonage. A person must have been held under this system or arrested and returned to it; that is, to a pre-existing condition of peonage.

It may be added that even if the Act of Congress on which this indictment is based could be held applicable in Georgia, the acts set out in the indictment are nothing like the old system of peonage. That system seems to have been, even as it came from Mexico, a voluntary system of labor and of servitude. The individual in the beginning at least voluntarily assumed this service. He was afterwards, it is true, held to the service against his will until his contract was discharged; and he could be held under it, or by the custom and usages of the country arrested and returned to it. Certain it is that by the act of the territorial legislature of New Mexico of 1852, which was probably in force when the Act of Congress was passed, the service must have been voluntarily entered into (*Jaremillo vs. Romero*, supra), so that both under the old system of peonage as it came from Mexico and also as it was embodied in the statute law of New Mexico, the contract was entered into freely and voluntarily by the servant.

The Act of Congress on which this indictment is based is inapplicable in Georgia, and even if applicable here, the facts set out in the indictment are not such as to make a case under the Act. to merely characterize acts in restraint of personal liberty as peonage is not sufficient to make them such, certainly not under this Act of Congress.

This February 24, 1899, Wm. T. Newman, U.S. Judge

Judge Newman went on to demurrer the case of conspiracy in January of 1899 for here is the demurrer in its brief.

The United States Vs. Eberhart et al.

The Indictment charges the defendants with the offence of conspiracy in that they conspired against Thomas Bush and others named in the respective counts to deprive said Bush and others of the free exercise and enjoyment of rights and privileges secured to them by the Constitution and laws of the United States, to-wit, the right and privileges of contracting and being contracted with, and the right and privilege of personal liberty, and the right and privilege of private property.

It is not alleged that Thomas Bush and the others said to be the subjects of the conspiracy are persons of color, and the presumption is that they are free white American citizens and always have been such. The presumption is that the pleader intended to charge two free white American citizens with conspiracy against other free white American citizen to deprive them of the rights and privileges enumerated in the Indictment.

We say in the first place that the indictments are demurrable because the rights and privileges mentioned in the indictment are not rights and privileges secured by the Constitution and laws of the United States, but are rights and privileges which American citizens have inherited as their birthright and which they and their ancestors before them have claimed and enjoyed for centuries. They claimed and enjoyed them before Magna Carta was obtained, for the barons did not demand their rights of King John as new rights, but as ancient rights. They claimed a confirmation of the ancient liberties of the subjects of the British Crown. If, therefore, these rights and privileges are invaded, the remedy is by proceedings in the state courts. The right to vote for Presidential Elector or Member of Congress is a right granted by laws of United States and a conspiracy to oppress or intimidate in exercise of that right is punishable under Sec. 5508. Yargrough's case 110 U. S. p. 651, so right to be protected while a prisoner in custody of United States Marshal for violation of United States laws. Logan Vs. U. S. 144 U. S. p. 76, so a person who informs a Marshal of U. S. of violation of internal revenue Laws of the United States is protected under this statute. In re Quales 158 U. S. 332, likewise a person who is a settler on land under homestead laws of United States. 112 U. S. p. 79.

But the right of life, liberty and property are fundamental rights not created by nor dependent on the constitution and laws of the United States, and must be protected and defended by the states. The Supreme Court of the United States in case of Cruikshank 92 U. S., pages 553–4 says: "Sovereignty for this purpose rests alone with the State. It is no more the duty or within the power of the United States to punish for a conspiracy to falsely imprison or murder within a State than it would be to punish for false imprisonment itself."

With his own hand he makes the decision after hearing argument and receiving the same. It is ordered that the Demurrer be satisfied in this case.

Wm. T. Newman, U. S. Judge

Judge Newman rendered his decision on January 9, 1899. And by February of 1899, Charlie Calloway and others where being charged in Oglethorpe in a systematic process of keeping them quiet or from appearing in court.

> *Athens Banner Newspaper*, February 1899: Yesterday after a warrant was issued against Charles Calloway, colored, charging him with selling liquor illegally in Clarke county. Calloway seems to be in plenty of trouble recently. He was sentenced to pay a fine of $50 a few days since on pleading guilty to the charge of carrying concealed weapons. Now

> he will have to face the charge of selling liquor, and if convicted he will not get off with a $50 fine.
>
> Let's look at others surrounding this manhunt of Charlie, my great-grandfather!

Henry O. Johnson, the Instigator

The white man is H. O. Johnson, the man the Clarke and Oglethorpe newspapers call the instigator in the peonage case.

> Oglethorpe County, in the name and behalf of the citizens of Georgia charge and accuse H. O. Johnson, of the county and state aforesaid, with the offense of misdemeanor. For that, the said H. O. Johnson, on the 6th day of January in the year of our lord one thousand eight hundred and ninety-eight, in the county aforesaid, did, with force and arms, unlawfully have and carry about his person, not in an open manner and fully exposed to view, a pistol.
>
> F. M. Coile, C. C. Fagan and S. 1. Gaulding are witnesses.

Also, H. O. Johnson might be kin to the U. S. Marshal in the peonage case, Mr. J. C. Johnson. And as one of the jurors in this sits William Eberhart, the man in whom H. O. Johnson is said to be decoying his hired hand away from the plantation. In April of 1898, H. O. Johnson was in court once more. The charge is that

> . . . he enticed and persuaded and decoyed and attempted to entice, persuade, and decoy one Mose Simms, a servant cropper and farm laborer of one Wm. Eberhart, after he had actually entered the services of the said Wm. Eberhart, his employer, to leave his said employer during the term of service knowing that said Mose Simms, servant, cropper and farm laborer, was so employed.

Witnesses are Wm. Eberhart and Mose Simms. The next court appearance is in April of 1899. The charge says that on the eleventh day of February of 1898, he (H.O. Johnson) was carrying a concealed pistol again. W. J. Smith is a lone witness.

E. H. & W. F. DO

121 Clayton Street, - - - - ATH

Horses Killed By Lightning.

Early Wednesday morning lightning struck a barn at the house of Mrs. F. Dillard in Wolfskin district and killed two horses, one belonging to Mr. Ben Dillard and the other to Judge R. B. Russell of Winder whose wife was on a visit to Mrs. Dillard, her mother. No other damage is reported to have been done.

A New Departure Store.

In this issue of The Echo a new departure in a store is advertised which we are sure the ladies will appreciate. Turn to the second page and see what it is. Mr. Stern the proprietor is well and favorably known among our people and will receive the liberal patronage from our people he merits. We predict that his new store will at once become a most popular place with the ladies. Read his advertisement.

Six O'clock Closing.

As will be seen from notice of merchants published elsewhere all the business houses of Lexington have agreed to close at 6 p. m., from May 1st to September 1st, public days and Saturdays excepted. This is done that clerks and "bosses" may have some time for recreation and it is the thing to do. Customers should bear this in mind that they may not be disappointed in expecting to make purchases after the hour named.

Will Rebuild Residence.

Judge McWhorter showed us the other day the plans and specifications he has had prepared for a new residence he will build on the site of his present home. It will be an exceedingly handsome house of ten rooms in the latest style of architecture and will contain all modern conveniences and comforts. It will cost not less than five thousand dollars. The Judge has not decided whether or not he will have the home built this summer.

Look at That Date.

This is not for delinquents but those who renewed their subscriptions last week. We ask them to compare the date printed with the address of their paper with their receipt and see if the two dates correspond. If not we want to be notified of the fact so that any errors can be rectified. We are more than grateful to the many who renewed and subscribed last week. It is encouraging to have our patrons be so prompt in extending their patronage.

Ministers' and Deacons' Meeting.

The above organization of the Sarepta Baptist Association convenes at the Crawford Baptist church to-day, the session continuing through Sunday. Besides the set program of exercises which The Echo gave last week there will be other

MR. HAL JOHNSON SUICIDES.

Sends a Pistol Bullet Crashing Through His Brain.

He Goes About the Act in a Deliberate Manner Showing that it Was Premeditated.

When the telephone brought the news to Lexington Sunday evening that Mr. Hal O. Johnson had suicided at his home in Winterville that morning the community was shocked but not altogether surprised. Not a few had predicted that recent trend of events in his life would drive him to some such desperate act.

It will be remembered that he was the chief instigator of the famous postage cases recently brought in the United States district court against several of our best citizens. This, of course, made him unpopular in his community and led to other troubles.

Last week he was indicted by the grand jury for carrying concealed weapons. After being arrested on this indictment he effected an escape from the officers and succeeded in eluding them until after court was over.

None who know his life and characteristics and are familiar with his recent conduct are altogether surprised that he should have taken his own life.

Mr. Johnson was of one of the very best families of our county or section, and has many relatives among our very best and most highly esteemed people, for all of whom, together with his estimable wife and children, universal sympathy is felt in this dark hour of trouble and deep sorrow.

The Athens Banner of Tuesday contained the following particulars of the suicide:

"Sunday morning at eleven o'clock Mr. Hal O. Johnson of Winterville ended his life by sending a bullet crashing through his brain.

"No cause is assigned unless it be that Mr. Johnson had brooded over certain troubles until he came temporarily deranged.

"Sunday morning Mr. Johnson appeared to be bright and cheerful. He dressed neatly as if going to church and chatted pleasantly with his family. He told his brother-in-law, Mr. Nowell, of Monroe, that he wanted to talk with him a while before he left for his home.

"Mr. Johnson went up stairs just before eleven o'clock, and in a few minutes the report of a pistol was heard.

"His family rushed up to the room, and when they opened the door they saw Mr. Johnson lying on the sofa with the blood oozing from a wound in his head.

"He had partially disrobed and had wrapped a towel around his neck. He

MEMORIAL DAY EXERCISES.

They Are Highly Entertaining to a Good Audience.

A Most Creditable Tribute Paid the Memory of Those Who Died for the Lost Cause.

The Confederate memorial day exercises at Meson academy auditorium Wednesday evening was rather a pleasant surprise to the fairly good audience that assembled to witness them. Few if any expected them to be so highly entertaining as they were, and Prof. Ballard and his pupils are being warmly congratulated upon the signal success of the occasion.

The stage was beautifully and appropriately decorated with flags and festoons of red, white and blue. Seats were placed on the stage for Confederate veterans, sixteen of whom were present to occupy them.

The program as published in these columns two weeks since was most admirably carried out, each and every feature being perfectly rendered.

After the school had sung "Hail Columbia," a most fervent prayer was offered by Rev. W. A. Farris.

Master Harold Reynold spoke "A Cry to Arms" in his usual good style.

Miss Pope Marwell recited "Music in the Camps" most beautifully and feelingly.

Then came the most touching feature of the program, the singing of "Camping on the Old Camp Ground" by a quartette composed of Mesdames W. M. Howard and F. B. Smith and Messrs. Wm. King and John Booth. So sweetly and feelingly did these excellent voices render this old song that it brought tears to the eyes of not only the veterans but to many of the audience as well.

"The Bivouac of the Dead" was splendidly spoken by Master Willie Stewart.

Miss L. E. Cunningham brought moisture again to the eyes of the old soldiers present by her touching recital of "Furl That Banner."

The school sang "Flag of Columbia."

Master [illegible] Faust, with marked ease and good oratory, spoke "The Stars and Stripes."

A trio composed of Mesdames W. M. Howard, F. B. Smith and E. T. Keene sweetly sang "Columbia, the Gem of the Ocean."

Then came the memorial address, which, having failed to secure a speaker from afar, devolved upon Prof. Ballard to deliver. In this, however, the audience was fortunate, for no orator could have made a more entertaining address or delivered it in a more pleasing manner than did the Professor. Lexingtonians were rather surprised to

GEORGIA, Oglethorpe COUNTY.

IN THE SUPERIOR COURT OF SAID COUNTY.

THE GRAND JURORS, selected, chosen and sworn for the County of Oglethorpe *to-wit:*

1 Joseph McWhorter Foreman.

2. Ed V Arnold	13. Columbus J Landrum
3. Ed B Clark	14. John W Moody
4. Thos W Crawford	15. Royal A McMahan
5. Jacob Eberhart	16. Wm H Reynolds
6. Wm Eberhart	17. Oconomus L Reynolds
7. John V Garbett	18. Jas C Gribble
8. Wm M Hawkins	19. Mark H Young
9. Frank R Howard	20. Andrew J Young
10. Elija W Johnson	21. J P Armstead
11. Henry A Lawrence	22.
12. Oscar L B Lester	23.

In the name and behalf of the citizens of Georgia charge and accuse H. C. Johnson *of the County and State aforesaid, with the offense of* misdemeanor *For that the said* H. C. Johnson *on the* 1st *day of* February*, in the year of our Lord, One Thousand Eight Hundred and Ninety-*eight*, in the County aforesaid did, with force and arms, unlawfully* have and carry about his person not in an open manner and fully exposed to view a pistol

While Mr. Hal Johnson was being terrorized because of his defense of Charley and other Negroes in Oglethorpe County that were on the property of Mr. William Eberhart. Mr. Henry C. Tuck was handling his court case that was before the judge in Oglethorpe and Clarke Counties. This is at the same time that Mr. Richard B. Russel is over the case of Charlie my great grandfather. I was in the retention room at the courthouse in Athens Clarke County and I was very much interested in the cases from 1896 to 1899 and not knowing what I was looking for. We found, I mean my wife and I found this letter to Mr. E. A. Angier's the United States District Attorney of the U.S. Circuit Court Northern District.

At Chambers
Athens Ga. Feby 10th 1899.

It being made to appear to the Court that Charlie Calloway (col) is confined in jail under an Indictment for carrying pistol concealed and being unable to give bond for his appearance, will be likely confined until April at expense to the County: It is therefore ordered that the Indictment against said Charlie Calloway be transmitted by the Clerk of the Superior Court of Clarke County, (together with all other papers appertaining to said case) to the City Court of Athens and there stand for trial or other legal disposition. Ordered further that this order be entered on the minutes of the Superior Court and said City Court

R B Russell Judge S.C.W.C.

Ent. #35 page 183
Ent #5 page 6

I found this letter with only two names other than Charlie mentioned on this mystery letter with the letter heading of the Commercial Club and the writer of the letter did not bother to write his name. He decided to remain anonymous for some reason or another. First, I thought that it was Mr. Henry C. Tuck who wrote this letter that is why I put a portion of his handwriting from the case he was handling for Hal Johnson and his family on the top of the letter however it did not match the mystery letter on Charlie's behalf. The only other person who could have written the letter was in the seat of authority for the State of Georgia, and that is non-other-than the Honorable Judge Richard B. Russell Senior. I don't know why he was afraid to write his name on the letter and then he wanted nothing else to do with the case so he threw the case down to city court.

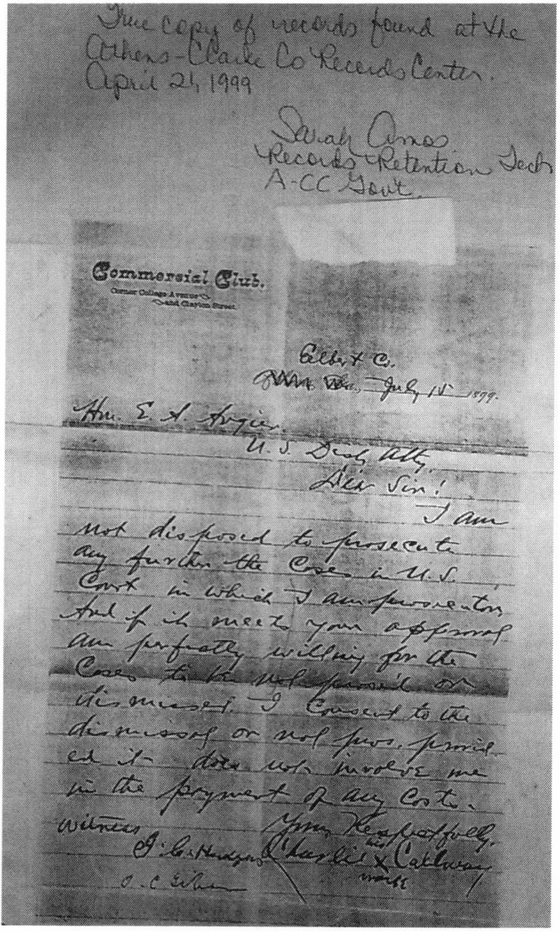

True copy of records found at the Athens-Clarke Co Records Center. April 24, 1999

Sarah Amos
Records Retention Tech
A-CC Govt.

Commercial Club.

Elbert Co.
July 15 1899.

Hon. E. A. Angier,
U. S. Dist. Atty,
Dear Sir!

I am not disposed to prosecute any further the Case in U.S. Court in which I am prosecutor And if it meets your approval am perfectly willing for the Case to be nol pros'd or dismissed. I Consent to the dismissal or nol pros, provided it does not involve me in the payment of any Costs.

Witness

Yours Respectfully,
Charlie X Callaway
his mark

I want you to see how I compared the two letters against the mystery letter that was found in the retention room in Athens. I compared the words (courts and the capital letter A and the A in the word attorney. And the spacing of his words, and if you take a good look at the C in courts they are the same and if you look at the last letter in how he slants and crosses his t's are they not the same. I wonder what plans did mister Richard B. Russell the judge in the high profiled case that in the federal courts and in the newspapers all over the state is going to do with Mr. Charlie Callaway my grandfather daddy Charlie! Would he ride to the Beaverdam district 226 with others and hang his forty year old body in the tree at night to make a statement to the Blacks that were waiting word of his long absence from his wife Mary who is with child. Did this high yellow mulatto mother who is carrying my grandfather Kator (Arthur) in her womb and is about to give birth find the man she loved and married that morning with her young sister Annie B. English by her side hanging from a tree! Can you just imagine the scene that early morning and how the sound of a distraught mother and sister voices pierce the early air awaking the older colored neighbors already know that Charlie was not going to return home when they arrested him in February. Maybe she knew that after her many visits to Elbert County to see her husband of sixteen years on the chain-gang of J. C. Hudgins. Now, when I went to the Federal Archives I found the carbon copy of this letter. I went to Elbert County to see could I find the original copy there and there was no such letter to be found in Elbert County. The original letter was at the Courthouse in Athens Clarke County. The Letter didn't even reach Elbert County it originated in Clarke and it was found by me and my wife on our many visits. Judge Richard B. Russell is one of the orchestrators of Charlie's demise or his new life elsewhere! Oh! the mysteries that have been hidden for so long and the men behind this orchestrated public deception that has left a stain and chasm between families both Black and Whites alike! The case Charlie Callaway was sent down to City Court and into the hands of Mr. Hoke Smith

Others Caught up in the Disenfranchisement in Oglethorpe

The next person is Rich English, Abraham's brother, who was living with Abraham at one time. I assume the relationship because of their age. Rich English pleads not guilty to a charge of selling spirituous and intoxicating liquors on the fifteenth of October 1897, but it is the April term of 1899. Why charge a man after two years? Excuse me, it is a manhunt! Robert Boyd is the lone witness in this matter and Rich English is found guilty but recommended to the mercy of the court.

Next case on Rich English is a charge of selling spirituous and intoxicating liquors on the twentieth of August 1897, but it is the April term of 1899. The manhunt is still on. Rich English pleads not guilty in this case also.

The next case against Rich English is a charge of enticement of Will Aubry, the servant and farm laborer of one Benj. B. William after said Will Aubry had actually entered the services of said B. B. Williams, to leave his said employer during the term of service, knowing that said servant and farm laborer was so employed by said B.B. Williams. Rich English was found guilty on the testimony of B. B. Williams and his servant and laborer Will Aubry. The date of the accusation is the third day of May 1898, but it is the April term of 1899. On the charge of selling spirituous liquors, Rich English was sentenced to twelve months and to pay a 100-dollar fine after the termination of sentence was already served, April 21, 1899.

Richard English is a person that is very close to Abraham and John English. I believe all three are brothers, for the oldest is Richard English, who is living on the property of William Boswell in 1870. Richard English is sixty-five years old and he is a farmer. His wife is named Mariah and she is at the age of sixty-four years. They are living in the 148 G. M. district of Penfield, Georgia. Jane Calaway (white) is three houses down from Richard English and she is at the age of eighty-two, living on the property of Augustus Phelps.

Richard English (I'll call him Number Two) was a man that knew how to farm. Richard and Abraham and John sold their produce and cotton to have an income and a place to live. Let's look at some of the contracts. We know that Abraham had property on T. L. Epps's place in Clarke County and now we will look at Richard English.

> May 28, 1891: On or about the first day of November next, I, the subscriber, of Clarke County State of Georgia, promise to pay to McAlpine and Pittard on order three hundred dollars. This note shall bear interest at the rate of 8 per cent. Richard English sold to McAlpine and Pittard of Winterville County and State of Georgia one bay horse named Bob, twelve years; one grey horse named John about fifteen years old. One red cow named Ider about ten years old; one red cow with white spot in the face named Sunday School about eight years old, one horse wagon made by Mathews and Hutcheson of Winterville, Ga. One old buggy (make unknown). Also, all the produce of fifty acres of land now planted and being cultivated by me, forty acres of which is planted in cotton and ten acres in corn, said land situated, lying and being in Clarke County, Ga., belonging to Jno. Hall and adjoining lands of J. E. Biggers, W. C. Baugh, J. T. Hale, and others. Receipt one thousand lbs. of cotton for rent, which property I declare is mine in my own right and in my possession and against which there is no judgement.

The next transaction between McAlpine and Pittard is with Richard English and Jack McLeroy.

> May 28, 1891: We, Richard English and Jack McLeroy, of Clarke County, Georgia, for and in consideration of the sum of one dollar to me in hand by McAlpine and Pittard of Winterville County, State of Georgia, the receipt whereof is hereby acknowledged, as well as secure the payment of our promissory note bearing date the 28th day of May A. D. 1891 for the sum of one hundred and twenty-five dollars and made payable to McAlpine and Pittard on the first day of November next do hereby mortgage, sell, lien, etc. the following described property to-wit: one Sorrell horse named Bob about twelve or thirteen years old, also the products of twenty-seven acres of land now growing and being cultivated by us, twenty acres of which is planted in cotton and seven acres in corn, said land situated, lying and being in Clarke County, Ga., belonging to J. W. Hale, adjoining lands of J. E. Biggers, W. C. Baugh, Mr. H. Lester, Dr. Hunnicutt, except eight hundred lbs. of lent cotton for rent, which property we declare is ours in our own right and in our possession and against which there is no Judgement or mortgage, lien, etc.

> May 28th of 1892: To McAlpine and Pittard all the products of twenty-three acres of land now planted and being cultivated by me. Fifteen acres of which is planted in cotton and eight acres in corn, said land situated, lying and being in Clarke County, Georgia, belonging to J. W. Hale, and adjoining lands of J. E. Biggers, J. S. Hale, Doctor Hunnicutt and others. Eighty-one thousand four hundred and sixty-seven lbs. lint cotton for rent which property I declare is mine in my own right and in my possession and against which there is no judgement or mortgage, lien, nor lien for unpaid purchase money nor homestead nor exemption lien nor other encumbrance as head of my family. I hereby waive and renounce all my rights and privileges under the Homestead and Exemption laws of this State as far as the above described property is concerned until the

> debt it is mortgaged to secure shall have been paid in full, including all cost charges and commissions and interest at 8 per cent per annum. Should I fail to pay above named note at maturity and the holder place the same in the hands of an attorney for collection by reason thereof, I hereby agree to pay 10 per cent attorney's commissions and in case of suit or of a sale of the mortgaged property to pay in addition all costs and expenses that may be incurred. And I hereby authorize the holders of this mortgage to foreclose the same in the usual manner as at their option by taking possession of the mortgaged property and selling all or any portion thereof, either at public or private sale, upon giving ten days' notice in writing to me, the same to be left at my usual place of residence of their intention to sell and such other notice as they may deem proper. And I hereby constitute the said McAlpine and Pittard or their assigned attorney to pass a good and sufficient title to such property upon making such sale.

Things are looking up for Richard English for right now, for they will get worse for he is being contracted with and trusting these men to make good on this agreement.

> Case no. 5360 Tom Erwin et.al. Indictment Witnesses: Rich English, Carter Daniel, Andrew Daniel, and Tena Mcleroy.
>
> We, the Grand jurors of the United States, chosen, selected and sworn in and for the Northern District of Georgia, upon our oaths do present that Ben Williams, Tom Erwin and Charley Johnson, together with diverse other evil disposed persons to the Grand Jurors unknown, late of said Northern District of Georgia, within said District and within the jurisdiction of said court, heretofore, to-wit, on the 1st day of January in the year of our Lord one thousand eight hundred and ninety-eight did then and there, with force and arms, unlawfully, wrongfully, fraudulently and feloniously combine, confederate, conspire, and agree together between and among themselves, and the said other evil disposed persons to

the Grand Jurors unknown, to injure oppress, threaten and intimidate one Rich English, a citizen of the United States, in the free exercise and enjoyment of a right and privilege secured to him by the Constitution and Laws of the United States, to-wit, the right and privilege of contracting and being contracted with, and the right and privilege of security, and the right and privilege of personal liberty and the right and privilege of private property, and did then and there combine, confederate and conspire among themselves and others to the Grand jurors unknown, to establish slavery and involuntary servitude, not as a punishment for crime, whereof the party shall have been duly convicted, but to obtain cheap, servile labor to conduct the farming operations of said conspirators Ben Williams, Tom Erwin and Charley Johnson, and others to the Grand Jurors unknown at a cost below that said farm laborers were entitled to, and Charley Johnson, with other to the Jurors unknown, did then and there deprive Rich English, and others to the Grand Jurors unknown, of their liberty, without due process of the law, and said Conspirators did make unreasonable searches and seizures of the person and property of said Rich English, and others to the Grand Jurors unknown, in order the more completely to reduce said Rich English, and others to the Grand Jurors unknown to a system of absolute vassalage and helpless agricultural serfdom.

For that, heretofore, to-wit, on the 1st day of June of 1895, the said Ben Williams, Tom Erwin and Charley Johnson and other evil disposed persons to the Grand Jurors unknown, conspiring together as aforesaid, for the purpose aforesaid, did with force and arms, and without any authority, arrest the said Rich English and did forcibly take and carry the said Rich English to the premises of the said Ben Williams, and did then and there tie and bind him, the said Rich English, hand and foot, and did then and there unlawfully and unmercifully whip, beat, bruise and wound the said Rich English with a buggy-trace, and with sticks and other weapons to the Jurors unknown, and did force the said Rich English against his will to enter into a pretended contract with the said Ben Williams to work for and serve him for

> the term of five years, and did then and there subject him, the said Rich English, to said long period of involuntary servitude and forcibly and against his will, and has continued and still continues to keep him in said servitude and to deprive him of his right of personal security and personal liberty and the free enjoyment of his own acquisitions, and did on the day and year first aforesaid, to-wit, January 1, 1898, compel him, the said Rich English, in pursuance of said pretended contract, which the said Ben Williams, Tom Erwin and Charley Johnson with other evil disposed persons, to the Grand Jurors unknown had so forcibly and illegally compelled him, the said Rich English, to make and enter into, to remain in said involuntary servitude. All of which said acts and deeds of said conspirators as aforesaid are contrary to the form of the statute in such case made and provided and against the peace and dignity of the United States of America.
>
> E. A. Angier, U. S. Attorney

Rich English is on the misdemeanor chain gang on the twenty-eighth of April, sentenced to thirty-six months for trying to lead Mr. Will Aubry from Benj. B. Williams's property. Richard English is on James M. Smith's farm in Oglethorpe County, the same place where Milly Callaway died and Mr. James Monroe Smith was the highest bidder in 1899. In the first term of the Superior Court, he paid Clarke County 50 dollars a head for each convict, so I ask myself why wasn't Charlie on his plantation instead of being in Elbert County. Listen to what the *Echo* newspaper of Oglethorpe County says about Rich English: "Rich English, a Madison County Negro, was jailed last week in Lexington for decoying hands last May from the plantation of Mr. B. B. Williams. He was tried before Squire W. T. Carter."

Let's look at the trouble the U. S. Attorney had with keeping up with the affiants in these cases, Charles in particular.

July 18, 1898 - Warrant sent to U. S. Atty. for approval

Aug. 2, 1898 - Continued case material witnesses for government absent defendant, enter temporary bond ($600.00) to appear August 6

Aug. 6 - Defendant on trial and held to bail ($600.00), continued absence of material witnesses for the government

A. R. Johnson	Winterville		
E. R. Carter	Winterville, 1 mile west	1 day, 12 miles	
Chas. Callaway	Winterville	"	"
Henry Geer	Athens, 2 miles east	1 day, 4 miles	
Armistead Strong	"	2 days,	14 miles
Gratlon Johnson	"		
W. R. Tuck	"	1 day, 19 miles	

The place where Charlie was living in Winterville is still a mystery for one of the court documents stated that he was 5 miles southwest of Winterville. The court system knew where he was but failed to seize his body. This document states that he is 1 mile west of Winterville, on the property of E. R. Carter, the overseer of William Eberhart.

The 1900 census shows that Aaron is living on the property of William Eberhart and being watched over by his overseer E. R. Carter. Aaron has in the house with him Harriett, aged thirty-eight. Aaron is seventy-three years old, so Harriett is his daughter or she's Mary the wife of Charlie. Remember, Aaron and Mary are to work for William Eberhart until then there is Willie Howard, the son of Aaron Callaway on William Eberhart's place and the accuser of Charlie for selling liquor in 1899. He is twenty-two. Also, there are Howard (eight) and Willie (six). William Eberhart (thirty-nine) married Ella Carter (twenty-two). Mattie is a daughter of William and Lucy Tucker, and she is at the age of nineteen. Travis is eighteen, William is sixteen, and Golding is fifteen. Nancy Tucker is William Tucker's mother, seventy-one. Edward R. Carter (thirty-four), his wife Lizzie (twenty-nine), Eugene (seven), Nettie (five), Magnolin (three), and Benny H. (one).

The first bench warrant is No. 5357, March term of 1898, *United States, vs. William Eberhart*, issued on April 19, 1898. William Eberhart in violation of Section 5526 of the Revised Statutes of the United States. William Eberhart came in on April 20, 1898, and made bond, according to U. S. Marshal W. H. Johnson and Deputy Marshal W. C. Thomas.

The second bench warrant is No. 5360, March term of 1898, *United States, vs. Tom Erwin and Charley Johnson and Ben Williams*, issued June 16, 1898. Charging all three with conspiracy. Tom Erwin was in custody of U. S. Marshal W. H. Johnson and Deputy Marshal J. C. Johnson, coming in on the seventeenth of June 1898, and Charley Johnson came in on June 20, 1898, and made bond. It doesn't look like Ben Williams made bond for the U. S. Marshals don't mention him doing so.

The third bench warrant is No. 5361, March term of 1898, *United States, vs. George Cunningham and Ben Williams and Tom Erwin*, issued one June 16, 1898, charging all three with conspiracy. George Cunningham came in and made bond on June 20, 1898. Ben Williams was arrested on the seventeenth of June. It doesn't look like he made bond for there is no mention of him doing so. Tom Erwin was arrested on the same day and it doesn't look like he made bond either. All had separate bonds made out to them under No. 5361, and the same for the others.

The fourth bench warrant is No. 5362, March term of 1898, *United States, vs. Ben Williams and Tom Erwin*, issued on June 16,1898. It is another charge of conspiracy. He was arrested on the seventeenth of June 1898.

The fifth bench warrant is No. 5363, March Term of 1898, *United States, vs. William Eberhart and Albert Boykins.* Albert Boykins is a colored overseer. It was issued on June 16, 1898. Both William Eberhart and Albert Boykins are charged with conspiracy. The marshal does not mention if either man made bond.

Now, let's look at who got bond for the men by viewing the bonds. The sixth document is an indictment for conspiracy.

> We, the Grand Jurors of the United States, chosen, selected and sworn in and for the Northern District of Georgia, upon our oaths do find and present that Tom Erwin, William Smith and William Eberhart, together with other evil disposed persons, whose names are to the Grand Jurors unknown, late of said Northern District of Georgia, within said District and within the jurisdiction of said court, on the 16th day of July, in the year of our Lord one thousand eight hundred and ninety-eight, did then and there unlawfully, wrongfully, fraudulently and feloniously combine, confederate, conspire and agree together, between and among themselves, and with other evil disposed persons to the Grand Jurors unknown, to injure a witness in his person, to-wit, Charley Calloway, on account of his having on the 15th day of April, 1898 before the Grand Jury of the Northern District of Georgia appeared in said United States Court before said United

States Grand Jury, the same being a United States Court in and for the Northern District of Georgia, as a witness in a case then and there pending, of the United States against William Eberhart and Thomas Erwin, charged in said United States Court for the Northern District of Georgia with the offense of conspiracy, and on account of his having testified to said matter pending therein before said United States Grand Jury in behalf of the United States. And in order to prevent him from testifying in the future in said case against said parties fully, freely and truthfully, the said Grand Jury being on the day and date aforesaid, to-wit, the 15th day of April, 1898 lawfully assembled as a Grand Jury, and having then and there taken an oath, administered by the Foreman of said Grand Jury, that he would testify fully, freely and truthfully in said case against the said William Eberhart and Tom Erwin as aforesaid, and the said Charley Calloway then and there testified fully, freely and truthfully concerning said case as aforesaid. And in furtherance of said conspiracy, so formed as aforesaid, for the purpose aforesaid, and to effect the object thereof, the said Tom Erwin, William Smith and William Eberhart, together with other evil disposed persons to the Grand Jurors unknown, on said 16th day of July 1898, within said District and within the jurisdiction of said court, did then and there hit, beat, bruise, wound and otherwise ill-treat him, the said Charley Calloway, and did then and there knock him on the head, face, and body with brass knuckles and with other weapons to the Grand Jurors unknown. All of which said wrongs and injuries the said Tom Erwin, William Smith and William Eberhart, together with other evil disposed persons to the Grand Jurors unknown, did then and there do to the said Charley Calloway because he, the said Charley Calloway, had attended the said United States Court as aforesaid and testified fully, freely and truthfully in said case pending in said court and in order to prevent him from appearing again in said case and testifying therein fully, freely and truthfully to a concerning said matters therein pending, contrary to the form of the statute in such case made and

> providing and against the peace and dignity of the United States of America.

A True Bill, October 19, 1898, U. S. Attorney. E. A. Angier. The witnesses are Chas. Calloway, Gratlen Johnson, Henry Geer, James Hall, Armstead Strong, John Seymour, and Henry Boykin. Both Tom Erwin and William Smith had warrants to apprehend them both to appear in court on August 6, 1898.

Next, is the subpoena in the case against Tom Erwin, Charles Young, Henry Gee, Clem Geer Armstead Strong, Charles Calloway, W. R. Tuck, E. B. Carter, and Gratlen Johnson.

Now, don't forget that Charlie said that on or about the sixteenth day of July 1898 he was beaten in Charles Young Stables in Clarke County. Also, he spoke to E. C. Kennibrew on the eighteenth of June. Let's look at who got bond for these men. How many time did these men beat my great-grandfather. He must have been a very strong man to endure so many beatings by the hands of so many people. What fear and torment ducking behind buildings and ally way in the town of Athens with his companion Graton Johnson. I must assume also that if by chance they could get away with murder they would! But to shoot a white man in Georgia, would automatically mean you would be lynched!

Tom Erwin's second bond was a temporary bond and John T. Pittard of Clarke County got his bond as surety by paying $600 on the second day of August 1898. He was to appear in Athens on the sixth of August 1898 for a hearing before E. C. Kinnebrew, the commissioner. John T. Pittard owned a bank, store, and a warehouse in Winterville. This was the final bond for Tom Erwin, who lived in Winterville, Georgia. For his signature, Tom Erwin makes his mark X. The Federal Courts were held in Athens, The unknown evil disposed men did not have to go far to find Charlie as he made his way out of the courthouse and passing the spiteful eyes as he left the office of E. C. Kennibrew through the narrow allies down to Clayton Street and then being cornered at Youngs Stables as he retrieved his horse. There stood in the way Mr. Tom Erwin and Will Smith the man who worked for Mr. James Monroe Smith of Smithonia.

Next, we will view William Smith's final bond on the sixth of August 1898. John T. Pittard got the bond as surety by paying $600.

Now, indictment.

5360 - Charlie Johnson and Ben Williams. Both are under this indictment, Charlie Johnson as principal. These are the men who got their bond: James Monroe Smith and George J. Cunningham, who is their attorney. Benj. B. Williams, as surer, is to verify his worth. James M. Smith's name is signed and scratched out. Ben Williams signs as Surety for $1000.00, claiming to have $15,000 in the County of Oglethorpe, Georgia, to-wit: 1,000 acres of land where he resides, about four miles north of Winterville, in District 226. This is more than lilkey his wife property in which she inherited from her mother Martha Eberhart.

Ben Williams is listed as principal and Billups Phinizy as Surety. Billups Phinizy claims to $50,000 in the county of Clarke, Georgia, to-wit: one warehouse, one block of stores, and other property in Athens. The bond is set at $1000. Mr. Billups Phinizy made his forturn in Savannah Georgia, However, he ran a merchantile store in Bowling Green near Thomas P. Callaway in Oglethorpe County. Like so many other names that I came across in Oglethorpe I came across the Phinizy's in Forsyth, Monroe County Georgia near the Callaway's. After leaving Oglethorpe Phinizy moved his buisnes to Athens.

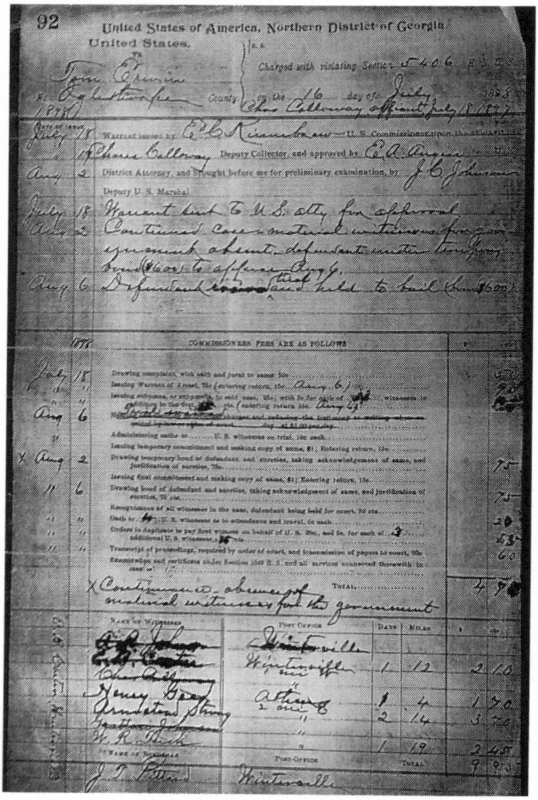
92

United States of America, Northern District of Georgia

United States, vs. Tom Erwin

Oglethorpe County

Charged with violating Section 5406 R. S.

on the 16 day of July 1898

Chas Calloway affiant July 18 1897

July 18 Warrant issued by E. C. Kinnebrew — U. S. Commissioner, upon the affidavit

" 19 Chas Calloway Deputy Collector, and approved by E. A. Angier

Aug 2 District Attorney, and brought before me for preliminary examination, by J. C. Johnson

Deputy U. S. Marshal

July 18 Warrant sent to U. S. atty for approval

Aug 2 Continued case material witnesses for government absent. defendant under temporary bond ($600) to appear Aug 6.

Aug 6 Defendant tried and held to bail (bond $600)

COMMISSIONERS FEES ARE AS FOLLOWS

x Continuance absence of material witnesses for the government

[Continuance of Case Charlie missing Aug. 6, 1898]

Indictment No. 5361 - Tom Erwin et-al. Conspiracy, March Term 1898. Northern District of Georgia, upon our oaths do find and present that Ben Williams, Tom Erwin and George Cunningham, together with other evil disposed persons to the Grand Jurors unknown, late of said Northern District of Georgia, within said District and within the jurisdiction of said Court, on the 23rd day of June in the year of our Lord one thousand eight hundred and ninety-five did then and therein, with force and arms, unlawfully, wrongfully, fraudulently, and feloniously combine, confederate, conspire and agree together, between and among themselves, and with said other evil disposed persons to the Grand Jurors unknown, to injure, oppress, threaten and intimidate one Henry Davenport, a citizen of the United States, in the free exercise and enjoyment of a right and privilege secured to him by the Constitution and Laws of the United States, to-wit, the right and privilege of contracting and being contracted with, and the right and privilege of personal security; that is, the free and uninterrupted enjoyment of life, limb, body, health and reputation, and the right and privilege of personal liberty; that is, moving and going wherever he, the said Henry Davenport, desired, without restraint or control save by due process of law, and the right and privilege of private property, or the free use, enjoyment and disposal of his own acquisitions without any restraint, control or diminution save by the process of law. Each and all of said rights and privileges being secured to him by the Constitution and laws of the United States, and the said Ben Williams, Tom Erwin and George Cunningham, with diverse other evil disposed persons to the Grand Jurors unknown, did then and there combine, confederate and conspire together between and among themselves, and with others to the Grand Jurors unknown, to deprive the said Henry Davenport of the rights, privileges and immunities aforesaid and to establish slavery and involuntary servitude, not as a punishment for crime whereof the party shall have been duly convicted, but to obtain cheap, servile labor to conduct the farming operations of the said Ben Williams, Tom Erwin and George Cunningham, and others to the Grand Jurors unknown at a cost below that which said farm laborers were entitled to. And in furtherance of said conspiracy, so formed as aforesaid, for the purpose aforesaid and to effect the object thereof, the said Ben Williams, Tom Erwin and George Cunningham, with other evil disposed persons to the Grand Jurors unknown, did on the day and date aforesaid deprive the said Henry Davenport of his rights and privileges aforesaid, and did then and there make an unreasonable seizure of the person of the said Henry Davenport, and did then and there reduce him, the said Henry Davenport, to a condition of vassalage and serfdom, and the said Ben Williams, Tom Erwin, and George Cunningham, with diverse other evil disposed persons to the Grand Jurors unknown, conspiring together as aforesaid, for the purpose aforesaid, did with force and arms and without any authority of law, seize and arrest the said Henry Davenport, and did compel him by force and against his will to sign and enter into a pretended contract with said Ben Williams to work for and serve him for a long period of time and did subject him to said involuntary servitude by force, intimidation and threats. All of which said acts and deeds of the conspirators aforesaid are contrary to the form of the statute in such case made and provided and against the peace and dignity of the United States of America. Tom Erwin was the partner of Mr. William Eberhart. He worked the property of William Eberhart located near Dr. Hutchinson south of Winterville and near Hal Johnson's fathers home place. This will not be the only time that Tom Erwin will be indicted on charges of Peonage. Tom will go to the extent of retrieving Peon's from the hideouts in Atlanta to the city of Chicago and Michigan.

June 16, 1898, E. A. Angier, U. S. Attorney

I find no claim for demurrer in this Indictment No. 5361, and the process of the cases and the argument of the attorneys of the defendants are ridiculous. And presentation of the prosecution side to help the witnesses are a joke!

Indictment No. 5361 - Tom Erwin, Ben Williams, and George Cunningham are all under this number. For Tom Erwin, on the seventeenth of June, Billups Phinizy of Clarke County got his bond since Mr. Billups Phinizy owned property in Athens, Georgia and easily paid $600. As you can see the lynch men such as Tom Erwin and Will Smith, George Cunningham, Charley Johnson working for the larger and rich land owners such as the big man Jim Smith of Smithonia and the great Mr. Phinizy these two big landowners could use their power and influence over the masses and crush whomever and buy whomever they wanted too!

The next two men, Ben Williams and George Cunningham, had men of importance get their bonds. George Cunningham had a letter written on his behalf by Mr. James Monroe Smith. George Cunningham is the Marshall or Sheriff of Oglethorpe County. I call him the enforcer or right hand man of Mr. James Monroe Smith. George place is located north of Winterville near Mr. James Monroe Smith in Pleasant Hill

Ben Williams and the man who got his bond.

Case no. 5361 - This man owned one warehouse, one block of storehouses, and other property in Athens, Georgia. The reason Ben Williams would call upon Mr. Billups Phinizy is because the bond was at $1000, on the seventeenth June 1898. Now, ten days after posting bail for Mr. George Cunningham, this man appeared in an article in the *Elberton Star*. Charlie Callaway had been on the chain gang since February in the Wyche District of Elbert County, on J. C. Hudgen's prison farm, in a conspiracy to keep him from testifying in said case.

> Elbert County, Georgia, 1899
>
> Hon. James M. Smith, the largest diversified farmer in the world, will deliver an address on farming Wednesday, which will be a most practical and valuable address. The farmer of northeast Georgia who misses hearing this wonderfully successful farmer will miss hearing one of the most pleasing and instructive talks ever given in Elbert County. The 23rd of August will be farmers' day. On that day, a farmers' institute will be organized.

Hon James M. Smith, the big farmer of Oglethorpe, will be here. Mr. Jordan, the agricultural writer of the *Atlanta Journal*, also agreed to make a speech on that occasion, along with other prominent speakers.

We'll come back to the news of this carnival in Elberton, Georgia. We will view the letter of James M. Smith for George Cunningham to the sheriff of Oglethorpe County.

> Know all men by these present that I, James M. Smith, of said state and county have been constituted and appointed by these present do hereby constitute and appoint George J. Cunningham of the county and state aforesaid my true and lawful attorney-in-fact for me and in my name to sign my name as security on two certain bonds for appearance of said G. J. Cunningham requiring him, the said G.J. Cunningham, to be and appear in the United States District or Circuit Court for the Northern District of Ga. to answer the charge contained in each of two bills of indictment the present week found true against said G. J. Cunningham

> by the Grand Jury in said court and also for me and in my name to sign my name as security on a bond for the appearance of Charles W. Johnson in the said court to answer to charges in a certain bill of indictment found true the present week against said Charlie W. Johnson by the Grand Jury of said Court and I hereby ratify and confirm all that my said attorney-in-fact George J. Cunningham may lawfully do in the pre—— as fully and confilab—— as if I were personally present and acting in witness of all which I have hereunto set my hand, affixed my seal and delivered in their presence this, the 18th day of June A. D. 1898.
>
> James M. Smith, signed, sealed, and delivered in the presence of us, David W. Meadow and J. A. Moore N. P., Oglethorpe County, Ga. Bond set at $1000.

Now, back to the carnival in Elberton, Georgia, and who was on hand in September 1899, a month before Charlie is killed on the third of October 1899. The exercises relative to farmers' day were celebrated in the courthouse. A good crowd was in attendance, but it was decided to postpone the organization of a farmer's institute to someday in the early fall. The speeches of Messrs. Jordan and Hunnicutt were well received. Hon. Ben R. Tillman and wife spent several days in Elbert County visiting relatives. The Hon. Tillman and wife resided with Solicitor H. J. Brewer near Elberton. Col. A. E. Thornton, the oil mill magnate, was at home with Elberton folks during the carnival and gave a big dinner to the farmers at the oil mill. His plant at this place is one of Elberton's foremost industries and its big president is always hailed with delight by Elbertonians. I was wondering why they had to get Charlie out of the way! Was it to further the farmers' club that would become General Farmers Club in Oglethorpe County, Georgia? And also perhaps the white landowners had to have him out of the way because of all this attention brought unto them by way of this colored Callaway who has some kind of high influence behind him! Someone had to die! Or did they get him out secretly by changing his age and under an assumed name?

> *Elberton Star*, 1899: We were shown a letter from Governor Candler to Hon. T. M. Swift in which he states that on account of the sickness of his wife he was unable to visit Elberton during the carnival. A similar letter has been received from Hon. James M. Smith as the reason for his

failure to speak Wednesday to the farmers. The speeches of Hon. W. M. Howard and Senator A. S. Clay were the events of Tuesday that drew the largest crowds and were most heartily cheered. Their efforts have received most unanimous praise. There are no statesmen in Georgia whose efforts, acts and conduct receive more hearty approval by the people of this section than do these two talented officials in Congress. Long may they live.

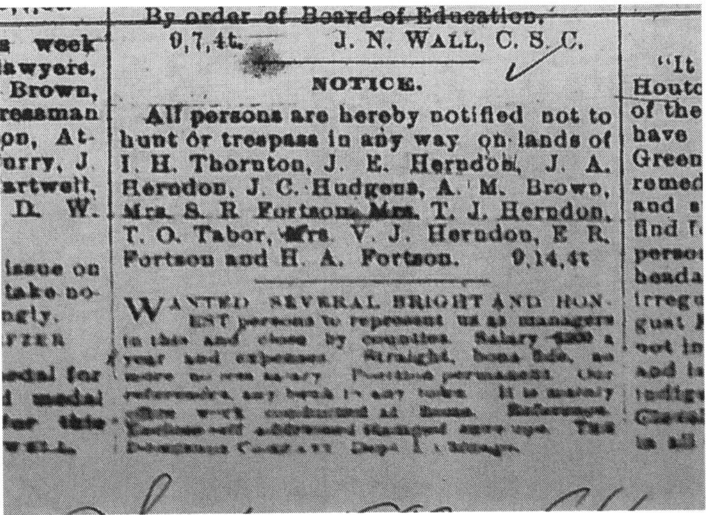

By order of Board of Education,
9,7,4t. J. N. Wall, C. S. C.

NOTICE.

All persons are hereby notified not to hunt or trespass in any way on lands of I. H. Thornton, J. E. Herndon, J. A. Herndon, J. C. Hudgens, A. M. Brown, Mrs. S. R. Fortson, Mrs. T. J. Herndon, T. O. Tabor, Mrs. V. J. Herndon, E. R. Fortson and H. A. Fortson. 9,14,4t

WANTED SEVERAL BRIGHT AND HONEST persons to represent us as managers in this and close by counties. Salary [illegible] a year and expenses. Straight, bona fide, [illegible]

The most fearful arraignment Georgia politics ever had was that indulged in by Senator B. R. Tillman of South Carolina. The elimination of the Negro from politics was his theme, and he used no poultice except genuine Ben Pitch Fork Tillman purgative. "The colonization of the Negro will not do," says the senator, even if they wanted to go and the whole people wanted them to go, as it would cost from $50 to $200 per head, which would incur a national debt equal to that of the civil war. The white primary will do for four or five years, until some scheming politician takes them to the mountain and whispers that he has money to turn loose against the organized democracy. *"Disfranchise them," cried the senator, by special clauses in the constitution. Make them ineligible by an educational clause.*

> *South Carolina, with 95,000 white votes against 140,000 Negroes, controls their elections that way. If they cannot read and write, they cannot vote.* The pitch fork was used in no uncertain language on politicians, and he declared that as long as the white people went to Negro cabins at night to plead and dicker with them for their votes, just so long would all the heinous crime being committed continue. No man ever swayed an audience more completely and while there may be some who differ with the distinguished speaker, he taught an abject lesson, and the truth of which no man can deny.

All this time Charlie is sitting in prison in this same county as a transferred prisoner from Clarke County in the Wyche District a few miles from town. I wonder could he hear the music and see some of the floats in the parade? Maybe he is thinking he is about to come to the end of his life after the speech of Ben Pitch Fork Tillman, a white supremacist who has boasted and has had a hand in killing blacks in South Carolina. I am sure that Charlie probably got word that Tillman was in Elbert County for some reason. The famous reputation of Pitchfork Tillman would proceed him causing Charlie's torment and as he set their in chains pondering his death while the praises are heaped upon the men outside this place where he is confined there in Elbert County in 1899. I can't help but ask myself did they really kill him after all they asked of him as to signing the statement that I know that he couldn't have spoken in the context that was laid out in the letter to E. A. Angier's.

There were many events happening in Elbert County while Charlie was in prison in the Wyche District of Elbert the granite capital of the world. On July 21, 1899, a preacher who knew Charlie, and his father Aaron being his father's property and slave, was to perform an ordination on the behalf of Rev. Phil W. Davis. Also another who would have known Charlie Calloway is J. F. Cheney. He led the ordination prayer. Also, Deacon W. E. Faust to act as Secretary. Rev. Weaver is the moderator. And last but not least, W. M. Coile, the brother-in-law of William Eberhart, who married Charlie and Mary. These events coincided with the fact that Charlie was a well desired man and a show of solidarity was needed to prevent him from testifying. These are the men that E. A. Angier called "other evil disposed persons to the Grand Jurors unknown who did then and there combine, confederate and conspire together, between themselves to deprive the rights, privileges and immunities aforesaid and to establish slavery and involuntary servitude," and they did!

Back to the case, the demurrer of Case No. 5362, the *United States vs. Tom Erwin et al.*, conspiracy.

And now come Thomas Erwin, Benj. B. Williams, and George J. Cunningham, the defendants in the stated case.

> . . . before arraignment and before pleading to the merits of said case and having heard said indictment read, say, first, that said indictment with the allegations in manner and form as therein set out are not sufficient in law, and defendants should not be arraigned or put upon trial thereunder. Second, that said indictment does not set out in what county the alleged offence is claimed to have been committed. Third, that said allegations as set out in said indictment do not charge any offence against federal law, and said defendants should not be required to answer thereto in said court. Fourth, that said United States Circuit Court has no jurisdiction over any offence that may be held to the charged in said indictment but that any offence that may therein be charged is within the jurisdiction of the proper state court of the State of Georgia in the county wherein said offence was committed. Each and every of the defendants was, at the time said offence is alleged to have been committed and also at the time of the finding of said Indictment, is now a resident and citizen of said county of Oglethorpe, Ga., and if it should be claimed that said alleged offence was committed in said county of Oglethorpe, then the Superior Court of said county of Oglethorpe, Ga., alone has jurisdiction of the offence charged. Therefore, these defendants, and each and every of them prays that this their demurrer be sustained, and that said defendants each and every of them be by the court hence dismissed and discharged foresaid indictment and the charges therein set out.
>
> David W. Meadow, defendants' attorney, filed in Clerk's Office the 20th day of December 1898, O. C. Fuller Clerk.

This demurrer does not mention George J. Cunningham, just B. B. Williams and Tom Erwin. Why didn't David W. Meadows argue George Cunningham's case under this demurrer?

> Indictment for Tom Erwin et al., Case No. 5362, United States Circuit Court, March Term, 1898. We, the Grand Jurors of the United States, chosen, selected and sworn in and for the Northern District of Georgia, upon our oaths do present that Tom Erwin, Ben Williams and William Eberhart [but his name is scratched out], together with other evil disposed persons to the Grand Jurors unknown, late of said Northern District of Georgia, within said district and within the jurisdiction of said court, on the 1st day of January, in the year of our Lord one thousand eight hundred and ninety-eight, did then and there with, force and arms, unlawfully, wrongfully, fraudulently and feloniously combine, confederate, conspire and agree together between and among themselves and with said other evil disposed persons to the Grand Jurors unknown, to injure, oppress, threaten and intimidate one Teney McElroy, a citizen of the United States, in the free exercise and enjoyment of a right and privilege secured to her by the Constitution and Laws of the United States, to-wit, the right and privilege of contracting and being contracted with, and the right of the free and uninterrupted enjoyment of life, limb, body health and reputation, and the right and privilege of personal security; that is, the right to go wherever the said Teney McElroy sees fit, without any restraint or control, except by due process of law, and the right and privilege of private property; that is, the free and uninterrupted use, enjoyment and disposition of her own acquisitions, without any restraint, control or diminution, save by due process of law. And the said Tom Erwin, Ben Williams and William Eberhart [his name scratched out], together with others to the Grand Jurors unknown, did then and there combine, confederate and conspire together between and among themselves, and with other persons to the Jurors unknown, to establish slavery and involuntary servitude, not as a punishment for

crime, whereof the party shall have been duly convicted, but to obtain cheap, servile labor to conduct the farming operations of said Tom Erwin, Ben Williams and William Eberhart [his name blotted out] without paying just compensation therefore. And did then and there deprive the said Teney McElroy of her liberty without due process of law, and did then and there unlawfully seize the person of the said Teney McElroy and completely reduce her to vassalage and serfdom. For that, heretofore, to-wit, on the 31st day of May 1898, the said Tom Erwin, Ben Williams, and William Eberhart [his name blotted out], together with others to the Jurors unknown, conspiring together as aforesaid, for the purpose aforesaid, did then and there, with force and arms, and without any authority whatever did seize and arrest the said Teney McElroy and her three minor children, to-wit, Tom, Nat, and Louisa, and did tie and bind each of them and did carry them to the premises of the said Ben Williams and did unlawfully and unmercifully whip, beat, bruise and wound the said Teney McElroy upon her face and naked body with leather straps, sticks and other weapons to the Jurors unknown and did then and there by means aforesaid compel her, the said Teney McElroy, and her minor children aforesaid to work, labor and serve the said Ben Williams and subject the said Teney McElroy and her said children to a long period of involuntary servitude forcibly and against her will. And in furtherance of said conspiracy, so formed as aforesaid, for the purpose aforesaid, the said Tom Erwin, Ben Williams and William Eberhart [his name blotted out], together with others to the Grand Jurors unknown, on the day and date aforesaid, January 1, 1898, in continuation of said conspiracy, still held and kept and continue to hold and keep the said Teney McElroy and her children aforesaid in said condition of bondage and involuntary servitude and continue to deprive them of their rights, privileges and liberties aforesaid. All of which acts upon the part of said conspirators are contrary to the form of the statute in such case made and provided and against the peace and dignity of the United States of America.

June 16, 1898, E. A. Angier, U. S. Attorney

Case No. 5357, U. S. Circuit Court Northern Dist. of Ga., United States Vs. William Eberhart Demurrer to Indictment. Filed in Clerk's Office Oct. 31, 1898, November 5, 1898.

1.

And now comes William Eberhart by his attorneys into court, and having heard the indictment read, says that the said indictment and the matters therein contained, in manner and form as the same are above stated and set forth, are not sufficient in law, and that he, the said William Eberhart, is not bound by the law of the land to answer the same; and this he is ready to verify.

2.

And for further ground of demurrer, the said William Eberhart says that the said indictment and the matters therein contained, in manner and form as the same are stated and set forth, charge no crime or offence of which the Circuit Court of the United States for the Northern District of Georgia has jurisdiction, and that the charges in said bill of indictment charge no crime cognizable by the Federal Courts.

3.

And the said William Eberhart by his attorneys further says that if any crime is charged in said bill of indictment, it is a crime of which the Superior Court of the State of Georgia for the County of Oglethorpe alone has jurisdiction. In this behalf, the said William Eberhart prays judgement, and that by the Court he may be dismissed and discharged from the said premises in the said indictment specified.

A. J. Erwin, E. T. Brown, Hamilton McWhorther, and T. W. Candler, attorneys for the defendant

The same demurrer under the same case number is filed in the October term of 1898 and filed in the Clerk's Office on the sixth day of December 1898.

Second Count

William Eberhart went on the property of Phillis Johnson and held and arrested her and placed handcuffs on her and took her to his property. William Eberhart falsely pretended to have a warrant against her for taking away from the employment of William Eberhart her children, which William Eberhart claimed had previously been bound to him until they were twenty-one years of age by her husband, Jesse Johnson. William Eberhart took her to Ben Williams, his brother-in-law. William wanted her to contract with him for a period of two years. William procured Tom Erwin to unlawfully whip, bruise, wound, and mistreat her. Phillis didn't want to contract, so she was beaten by Tom Erwin.

Third Count

My great-grandfather Charlie, which you have previously read.

Fourth Count

William Eberhart claimed that Monroe Neely, the father of Arthur Neeley, Arthur Neeley being a minor about sixteen years of age, was indebted to him, the amount being sixty-five dollars, saying Monroe Neeley would pay the said indebtedness. William Eberhart claimed Monroe Neeley borrowed sixty-five dollars from Phillip Neeley and agreed with Phillip Neeley to let Arthur Neeley work for him until the said sixty-five dollars was paid. Monroe Neeley took the sixty-five dollars in money and tendered it to the said William Eberhart in payment of the debt, which the said William Eberhart claimed against him. William Eberhart refused to accept the money and accused Monroe Neeley of persuading his laborers to leave him. The purpose of all this was to induce and compel Monroe Nelley to apprentice his son Arthur for five years

Fifth Count

John Roberson and William Eberhart held and arrested John Roberson with a false charge. William Eberhart put handcuffs on his wrists and whipped, beat, bruised, wounded him. William Eberhart beat John with sticks, leather straps, and other weapons and with threats of prosecution for some pretended and trumped up charge to compel John to serve him for three years on his farm.

Charlie's testimony was much more damaging, and that's why William Eberhart and others went after him for his testimony to E. A. Angier. I'll show you what I mean in the newspaper article of his beating in the newspaper in Athens, Clarke County.

Athens Banner, August 5, 1899

> Two Conspiracy Cases
>
> Yesterday Judge Kennebrew tried two white citizens of Oglethorpe County, Messrs. Tom Erwin and Bill (Will) Smith, on charges of conspiracy. They were charged by a Negro named Charles Callaway with having beaten him in this city for having testified against them in a case in Federal court. Judge Kinnebrew placed them under a temporary bond and the trial will be held Saturday.
>
> United States 0f America, Northern District of Georgia
>
> Personally came Charles Calloway, who on oath, saith that of his own personal knowledge he knows that on or about the 16th day of July 1898 in the County of Clarke, State of Georgia, Tom Erwin and William Smith did commit the offence of Conspiracy in violation of Section 5406. For that, on or about said date, affiant saw said Tom Erwin and said William Smith Conspire to inflict and did actually inflict great physical injury on affiant by beating the latter in the face and over the head with brass knuckles to deter affiant from being a witness and also for having already testified, in the case of said Erwin, Eberhart et al. now pending the Circuit Court of the United States for the Northern District of Georgia.
>
> Witness: Charles Young, Athens, Ga.; George Geer, Winterville; Charles Calloway, Winterville, Ga.

93

United States of America, Northern District of Georgia

United States vs. William Smith, Oglethorpe County

Charged with violating Section 5406 R. S. U. S. on the 16 day of July 1898

Chas. Calloway affiant July 18 1898

Date		
July 18		Warrant issued by E. C. Kinnebrew U. S. Commissioner upon the affidavit of
	19	Charles Calloway Deputy Collector, and approved by E. A. Angier U. S.
Aug	2	District Attorney, and brought before me for preliminary examination, by J. C. Johnson
		Deputy U. S. Marshal
July	18	Warrant sent to U. S. atty for approval.
Aug	2	Case continued until Aug 6 on account of absence of material witnesses for the government defendant put on temporary bond $600.
Aug	6	Defendant tried and held to trial (bond $600)

1898		Commissioners Fees Are As Follows	$	cts
July	18	Drawing complaint, with oath and jurat to same, 50c		50
	"	Issuing Warrant of Arrest, 75c; entering return, 15c Aug 6		90
	"	Issuing subpoena, or subpoenas, in said case, 25c; with 5c for each ... witnesses in addition to the first, 50 cts; entering return 15c Aug 6		70
Aug	6	Hearing and deciding on criminal charges and reducing the testimony to writing when required by law or order of court, 1 day at $5.00 per day	5	00
	"	Administering oaths to 12 U. S. witnesses on trial, 10c each	1	20
	"	Issuing temporary commitment and making copy of same; Entering return, 15c		
	2	Drawing temporary bond of defendant and sureties, taking acknowledgement of same, and justification of sureties, 75c		75
		Issuing final commitment and making copy of same, $1; Entering return, 15c		
	6	Drawing bond of defendant and sureties, taking acknowledgement of same, and justification of sureties, 75 cts		75
		Recognizance of all witnesses in the case, defendant being held for court, 50 cts		
	"	Oath to 7 U. S. witnesses as to attendance and travel, 5c each		35
	"	Orders in duplicate to pay first witness on behalf of U. S. 20c, and 5c. for each of 6 additional U. S. witnesses, 30 cts		60
	"	Transcript of proceedings, required by order of court, and transmission of papers to court, 60c		60
	"	Examination and certificate under Section 1042 R. S. and all services connected therewith — Swearing 13 witnesses for defendant	1	30
		Total	12	65

x continuance absence of material witnesses for the government

Name of Witnesses	Post-Office	Days	Miles	$	cts
Chas Young	Athens	2		3	00
Chas Gerr	Winterville	2	12	3	60
Chas Calloway	2 mi E	2	10	3	50
Fielding Johnson	3 mi E	1	8	1	90
James Hall	"	1	18	2	40
Alfred Gilmer	"	1	18	2	40
[illegible] Johnson	"	2	18	3	90
Name of Bondsman	Post-Office			Total	20 70
J. T. Pittard	Winterville				

UNITED STATES OF AMERICA, Northern District of Georgia.

Personally Came Charles Calloway

who, on oath, saith that of his own personal knowledge he knows that on or about the 16th *day of* July *, 189*8 *, in the County of* Clarke *, State of Georgia,* Tom Erwin and William Smith *did commit the offense of*

Conspiracy in violation of section 5406 R. S. U. S.

For that, on or about said date, affiant saw said Tom Erwin and said William Smith conspire to inflict and did actually inflict, great physical injury on affiant by beating the latter in the face and over the head with brass knuckles to deter affiant from being a witness and also for having already testified in the cases of Tom Erwin, Eberhart et al. now pending in the U. S. Circuit Court for the Northern District of Georgia.

Charles Young, Athens Ga } Wit
George ~~Charles~~ Gee, Winterville "
Charles Calloway " "

Affiant believes that defendant has property of the value of $ ______ *, and makes this affidavit that a warrant may issue for his arrest.*

Subscribed and sworn to before me, and read over to affiant by me this 18 *day of* July *189*8 *in presence of*

E. C. Kinnebrew
U. S. Com.

Charles his X mark Calloway

Post-office address Winterville

THIS AFFIDAVIT MUST BE READ OVER TO THE AFFIANT BEFORE ADMINISTERING OATH.

Chapter Four

The New Slavery by Contract with the Freedmen

Georgia Oglethorpe County

This indenture made and entered
into this 19th day of October 1892 between
William Eberhart and Charley Calloway &
his wife Mary Calloway father and mother
of Charles Calloway about 6 years old Howard
Calloway about 4 years old all of said County
witnesseth that the said Charley and Mary
Calloway hereby bind and apprentices unto
the said William Eberhart the said Charles
and Howard until the said Charles and
Howard is 21 years old under the following terms. The said William Eberhart
agrees to take into his custody the said
Charles and Howard to teach him the business
of husbandry furnish them with protection wholesome
food suitable clothing necessary medicine and
medical attendance teach him them habits
of industry honesty and morality and
shall govern him with humanity using
only the same degree of force to compell
his obedience as a father may use with his
minor child and when the said Charles and
Howard shall arrive at the age of 21 years
they are to receive 1000 in cash in conside-
tion of all of which said William Eberhart
is to have and be entitled the service and
earnings said Charles and Howard until they are 21
years old

Here it all started, in the year 1892, the year that Charlie makes his first contract with William Eberhart in Beaverdam, Oglethorpe County. Charlie is in District 226. The tax digest does not state who Charlie is working for at this time. However, the contract that he made with Eberhart put his children on Eberhart's plantation. Charlie is listed with these other colored men that paid their taxes in Beaverdam: Albert Boykin, Sam Bailey, Cato Eberhart, Gilbert Eberhart, Bob Eberhart, George B. Glenn, Daniel Glenn, Walt Glenn, John H. Glenn, Charlie Gates, Young Geer, Monroe Neely, Orange Neely, Ed Neely, Phil Neely, Jim Neely (who is over sixty), Jim Neely Jr., Henry Neely, Charlie Neely, John Roberson, Carrie Sims, Jack Sims, Henry Strickland, George Sim, Mose Sims, Bob Sims, Zack Sims, Cain Simmons, Sam Terrell, Charlie Thompson, Bill Turner, Henry Thomas, Lizzie Swain, George Malone, Dave Norman, Dock Mitchell, Osborne McCarrie, Lindsey, White, Croff White (who is over sixty), Will Warren, Uriah Wood, Wash Williams, Alex Wood, Hos Winfrey, Ambrose Winfrey, Will Winfrey, and Dock Winfrey. This area is known to harbor many of the Blind Tiger gang located in Falling Creek and in Clarke County, all the way into Atlanta. Bob Callaway is the only Callaway that is in Maxey in 1892. I could not find Burwell Callaway in Falling Creek. And Ben Callaway is in Sandy Cross in Oglethorpe County.

Who is William Eberhart? I heard my aunt Anna talk of him for many years during my short time that I had with her while feasting on sugarcane and raw corn in her room as a young boy. There were many very interesting conversations about Mr. Eberhart among other family members, who talked about my grandfather as well. And as I got older and they started to leave me, the desire to know my grandfather's past grew even more. I heard that my grandfather worked for him. I was told how certain white men came to harass blacks on his place and he said, "If five come, kill five. If ten come, kill ten. If twenty come, kill twenty. And if a hundred come, damn it, you kill as many as you can!"

William Eberhart, J.R. Haynes, and R. T. Pittard act as messengers from the Winterville Baptist Church in Clarke County, with W.M. Coile as the pastor. They are in the Saparta Baptist Association of Winterville in 1887 in Clarke County, Georgia. Pastor Coile is the same pastor that married Charlie Callaway and Mary Hurt in 1884. J. F. Cheney was located in Crawford Baptist Church in Oglethorpe County as the pastor. His messengers are himself, T.T. Herndon, R.A. McMahan, and J.P. Armistead. The other church that I am interested in is Black's Creek in Madison, and the messengers of the church. Mr. Jas. B. Smith, J.D. Chandler, and the pastor J.R. King. C.M. Callaway was a messenger with

G.J. Cunningham at Lexington Baptist Church in Oglethorpe County and Mr. A. E. Keese is the pastor. Now, at Falling Creek in 1899 is Mr. T.D. Thornton, the neighbor of Mr. J.C. Hudgins, who had altercations with Mr. Hudgins. T.D. Thornton is also the pastor of Falling Creek as well. Here I must quote, "A family that prays together stays together." However, I'll change the quote to, "A family that prays together can also kill together."

William Eberhart married a Carter and was very close to the Carters that were in Winterville, Clarke and Oglethorpe County, Georgia. The Carters are very intertwined with Charlie and Mary Callaway while they were on Eberhard's place. I had an opportunity to talk with Commissioner Carter of the Beaverdam District in Clarke County and he told me of the story of what was told him about a colored man on Eberhart's place and Hal Johnson in 1899. I sought to locate the Carters in Beaverdam only a few years before 1892, before Charlie and Mary entered into contract with William Eberhart. I was in Beaverdam, Oglethorpe. In 1888 in Oglethorpe County, near Winterville, some of the white landowners were young William Eberhart, who had 135 acres of land at this time. Wesley T. Carter, William Carter, Dr. W.D. Carter, Thomas R. Carter, Elbert B. Carter (who was over at the estate of Mary S. Carter), Ed A. Carter, John F. Carter, William T. Carter, Abel Eberhart, Mrs. M. E. Eberhart, F.J. Eberhart, and Ed Eberhart.

Major Callaway is living in Lexington and was working for T.H. Olive. T. H. Olive might be the brother-in-law or father-in-law of Thomas P. Callaway, the father of Robert Lee Callaway. George W. Willingham died in 1890 and was a member of the Beaverdam Alliance or the Farmers Alliance. William Eberhart, E.A. Carter, and W.T. Carter were on the committee. Workers for James Monroe Smith in Smithville are Alex Barnet, William Barnett, Reuben Barnett (who was sixty years old), Spencer Blackshear, Archy Bridges, and Jim Burton. B.B. Williams had Lige Butler, Strong Brawner, and Wylie Baugh (who was over sixty years old) on his property. B.B. Williams is the brother-in-law of William Eberhart. B.B Williams also had on his plantation Anderson Boykin, Strong Colbert, Joe Foote, William Flemming, Alex Wood, Parish Wood, Newton Warren, and Mansfield Watson. W.D. Carter hired Sherman Brown and E.B. Carter hired Pope Ellis and Rich English, the brother of Abraham English, in 1888.

Vouchers for the estate of Martha Eberhart in the year of 1890. Benjamin B. Williams and F. Ophelia Williams are not to contest her estate. Isham H. Pittard is the executor of aforesaid and guardian of William Eberhart, a minor.

> ... is hereby fully, completely and entirely discharged and acquitted of any and all further claim or demand of said estate. R. M. McAlpin and R. T. Pittard are witnesses for Benj. B. Williams and F.O. Williams in 1881.

Isham H. Pittard received payment of fifty dollars as of the legacy of Martha Eberhart on the tenth of December. On March 1, of 1880, Isham H. Pittard, the executor of Martha Eberhart, received $150 as part payment. He also received fifty dollars in March 4, 1882. Isham H. Pittard, on March 25, 1882, received $400 as part payment of legacy due M. E. Coile, the wife of preacher Coile of the Winterville Baptist Church.

General Farmers Corporation

This system of farming techniques went north after William Eberhard, the president of the Farmers Club in Oglethorpe County, moved with his wife to Cornelia in Habersham County. The farming techniques were that of James Monroe Smith. It consisted of terracing the land to keep the water from flowing off the terrain. You can see this very same system going up Highway 441 and 326.

Meeting held in the courthouse in Lexington, Georgia, on seventh Monday of 1905 for the purpose of organizing a farmers' club. The meeting was called to order by Wm. Eberhart and the object of the meeting stated. On motion, Wm. Eberhart was unanimously elected president of the meeting. A. T. Drake was elected vice president and Hamilton McWhorter Jr. secretary and treasurer. After which those wishing to become members of the association handed their names to the secretary. On motion of L. W. Collier, the above elected officers were made the permanent officers of the association. On motion of E. B. Carter, a committee of three was to draft bylaws. Following committee appointed E. B. Carter, J. McC. Bryan, and W. J. Crowley, on motion that committee on bylaws want until next meeting to report. A very interesting talk by L. W. Collier on how to voice ... (unreadable). C. A. Stevens made a very interesting and practical talk to the association. A very interesting talk was made to the association by Hon. Wm. Eberhart, the president of the association.

Now, Eberhart was to be residing in Habersham in Cornelia, Georgia. The Federal Courts stated that he was removed from the northeastern district in 1899. However, I only found him in the 1909 tax digest of Habersham. Eberhart was still located on his estate in Winterville in Beaverdam with his trusted colored overseer Mr. Albert Boykins. In 1910, he's forty-nine years old and a real-estate dealer for Georgia. He has been married for twelve years to thirty-nine-year-old Ella Carter Eberhart. They lived at 78 Academy Street in Cornelia.

By the year 1913:

> . . . the Hon. Wm. Eberhart in the Habersham Superior Court page 483, Exhibit A:
>
> To Robert McMillan, Solicitor General in Habersham County. You are hereby notified that in accordance with law that the Mayor and Council of Cornelia., Ga., called an election for the assurance of bonds to be held on the 15th day of February 1913, for waterworks and sewage in said town. Said election was held in said town, and that the election was in favor of using said bonds for waterworks. And sewage bonds shall be issued in the sum of $20,000 (twenty thousand dollars) aggregate, of which $15,000 (fifteen thousand dollars) shall be expended for the purpose . . .

WILLIAM EBERHART FLEES TO CORNELIA GEORGIA FLEEING PROSECUTION

In 1900, in Beaverdam, William Eberhart is the same age as Charlie. I don't quite believe that Charlie wouldn't have a deep hatred toward William. Having to listen and obey him knowing that he watched this young boy whom he played with and probably ran from the soldiers during the war. They might have fished and hunted as boys on Mrs. Sims's place near Bowling Green. And now he has to be subjected to his newfound power and a new owner of land. And now Charlie has to live and be subverted to this same young man. Eberhart has his father on his place in 1900, along with his wife and his two children, Willie and Howard. I don't know if Charlie is dead; however, Mose Sims is still alive and is living next door to his employer, or I might as well say, the new order of slavery of his owner, Mr. Eberhart. Mr. E. A. Carter is living between Mose Sims and Aaron and Hattie.

Albert Boykins in 1910 is now sixty-one and his wife Linda is seventy-three. Their son Robert is seventeen, and the three of them are living near Mr. William Carter, a fifty-six-year-old man in Beaverdam. Albert has been with William while he was a young man on his mother Martha's place. Now it was in April 1, 1918, that Sam Carter stated that William Eberhart was dead and had left an estate that was mainly in part a life insurance policy valued at 200 dollars. Sam is the father-in-law and father of Ella. George Echols is surety on the bond on April 1, 1918. *Now, you can see the true power of Mr. James Monroe Smith through his estate and the powerful influence he has over Oglethorpe County and Clarke and other parts of the state of Georgia! He swallowed up land and was feared by all that stood in his way! Blacks feared him and loved him and some whites hated him and yet feared him as well. I noticed this when he had the sheriff of Oglethorpe County appear in the Federal Courts on his behalf in 1899! William J. Smith was raised in Elbert County in Ruckersville and worked for non-other than Mr. James Monroe Smith. William J. Smith the other hand that beat Charlie olong with Tom Erwin worked for Jim Smith. Making his way across from Elbert to Smithonia.*

Thomas Erwin was born in 1861 and died in 1932 in Winterville, Georgia. Thomas Erwin was born in South Carolina. In 1880 he was living with his mother in Oglethorpe County. James Monroe Smith dies in 1917, according to the Winder News, September 20, 1917.

Winder, Barrow County, and look at the area where the liquor trade routes come right through the new county!

And this article is on none other than the great Hon. Mr. James M. Smith of Smithonia!

September 27, 1917, Thursday - The estate of Mr. Jim Smith and his properties in other counties other than Oglethorpe.

1). Grove Creek 51 acres in the town of Sandy Cross adjoining lands of the estate of Jim Steele, W.T. Cunningham, Stevens, Huff & Company, and W.T. Harris.

2). Lots in the town of Crawford, known as A.S. Rhodes Storehouse. Lot being 40 by 100 feet. On Depot Street, north by the Baptist Church, east by street on the south by J.G. Chandler, west by Depot St. being same lots or parcel of land deeded by T.J. Shackelford receiver of A.S. Rhodes to James M. Smith.

3). Undivided one half interest of land in Lexington District on the waters of Long Creek. Known as old Joel Bacon's home place containing two hundred and fifty-two acres on the north by Long Creek and lands of the estate of R.M. Bacon; on the east by lands of Mrs. E.B. Clark and W.S. Callaway, formerly known as the Hawkins Place. South by J.H. Smith, West by R.M. Bacon. Known as the Savings Place. Long Creek and lands of Hamilton McWhorter Jr.

4). ½ interest in Lexington known as the Savings Place, 186 acres north by W.T. Brooks and R.M. Bacon east by Long Creek land just above known as Old Joel Bacon place. And Mrs. Nora Smith, west by Mrs. Nora Smith and W.T. Brooks plat of the same made by M. S. Weaver.

5). Also the tract in Beaverdam district known as the Mitchell Place, 132 acres north and west by lands of Mrs. Sam Goulding; east by lands formerly of the estate of Hal Johnson; on the south by lands formerly of Tommie Johnson.

6). Also in Beaverdam district on Dunlap Road and Winterville known as the Mathews Place, 241 acres adjoining lands of the estate of Allen H. Talmage, H.J. Meyer, and others.

7). Land lying in the counties of Oglethorpe and Madison, in Pleasant Hill and Beaverdam, on the waters of Beaverdam Creek, Big Clouds Creek, and Hawks Creek known as Smithonia Plantation, 7,000 acres on the north by the land of Kidd Sikes and Pharr, Waggoner, H.H. Hampton, and Davison, on the east and north by lands of Holcomb, L.W. Collier, Chandler, Martin, J.D. Power, and J.H. Thomas. Southeast by M.V. Willingham, (deceased); J.D. Coile, and the old Johnson Place. South by George Crowley, Porterfield, Hayes, and W.J. Culbertson, southwest by T.J. Erwin, W.H. Gabriel, Lester, Freeman, and others.

As you can see, the property of Mr. Hal Johnson was in the eyes of the great Mr. James Monroe Smith. I believe that he would not have stopped until he had this property. Even if he had to murder for it and get all of the obstacles that might arise out of the way. This means if Charlie did not get on board, he too would have to be eliminated or relocated as well!

Estate of James M. Smith: Andrew C. Erwin, L.K. Smith, N.D. Arnold, administrators. J.O. Mitchell is the manager. Mr. James M. Smith had a somewhat relationship with Mr. N.D. Arnold. They both were members of the Farmers Club with Robert Lee Callaway the son of Thomas P. Callaway and Mr. William Eberhart of Oglethorpe County with Mr. Eberhart as the president in 1906. And in the *Atlanta Georgian* and *News Friday*, December 24, 1909, Col. Jas. M. Smith and Mr. Nat D. Arnold were mentioned together as being members of the Great Southern Accident and Fidelity Company that would open its offices to the world and take its place among the financial institutions of Atlanta with Mr. L. Carter of Jessup, Georgia; S.E. Smith of Atlanta, Georgia; H.H. Bass of Griffin, Georgia; J.M. Ponder of Forsyth, Georgia; Dr. S.F. West of Atlanta, Georgia; A.G. Campbell of Natchez, Mississippi; R.H. Cantrell, the president, who was located in Atlanta; Col. James M. Smith of Smithonia, Georgia; W.G. Chipley as the vice president, of Atlanta, Georgia; Judge David W. Meadow of Elberton, Georgia, the same man that defended Mr. William Eberhart with Hamilton McWhorter in 1899 in the federal courts; Mr. W.C. Pitner of Athens, Georgia; J.R. Duvall, the secretary and the treasurer, of Atlanta, Georgia; Ben F. Barbour of Birmingham, Alabama; and Mr. Nat D. Arnold of Lexington, Georgia. Could it be that Mr. James Monroe Smith has a hand in Charlie's demise or relocation and name changes to keep him from the Feds? There is a large number of Charlie's children who will come to reside in Atlanta, as you have seen, as I told you the relationship between the Cates and the Roses and Callaways in Atlanta and the liquor trade and the Blind Tigers! There is another man that needs to be mentioned as well, and he is *Mr. Walter H. Johnson, the U.S. marshal at the time of Charlie's demise and relocation during his trial, and who is located in Atlanta as well.*

Walter H. Johnson is on the farm of Mr. James Monroe Smith in 1900 and would become a permanent fixture there as well. It states in the Georgian that

> . . . Mr. Walter H. Johnson, the U.S. marshal for the northern district of Georgia, was born in Columbus, Georgia, and received his education at the schools near his

> home. When the war broke out between the states, Mr. Johnson, although quite young, joined the Confederate Army and enthusiastically gave his services to his county. Shortly after enlisting, he was made a lieutenant in the Fifth Georgia Reserves and all during the war he served with distinction. After the war, Mr. Johnson engaged in the mercantile business, and although he was successful, he decided to enter the service of the government. Mr. Johnson has taken an active part in politics and is now looked upon as one of the Republican leaders in the South. It is largely to aim and his knowledge of politics to Georgia that such acceptable appointments have been made to Federal offices in the state. He has been recognized as a leader in Republican politics in Georgia, and for that reason, he was one of the three references selected to pass upon applications for government offices in the state. He was appointed United States marshal several years ago and he has filled that position since then, administering the affairs of his office in a necessary that has called for words of praise. He has discharged his duties with fidelity. Has conducted his offices in a businesslike manner and has (unreadable).

Muscogee County, Columbus, Georgia, is where a few of the colored Calloways will come to be buried and a Robert or Charles Calloway, Robert Charles Calloway, will marry a Ms. Emma Stafford. I had this Robert Charles Callaway confussed with the son of Charlie the brother of my grandfather Arthur.

James Monroe Smith's place is in Pleasant Hill, Oglethorpe County, near Winterville, Georgia. This place is called Smithonia, Georgia, named for the man that kept and killed at will! I visited this place and walked the grounds and was overwhelmed at this large plantation,, knowing that my forefathers were housed here and I walked where the inmates were housed. And I was taken aback to see the conditions that my aunt Milly was housed in, in the women's section, and I was moved to tears standing in the place where she lost her life on Mr. Jim Smith's place in Oglethorpe County, Georgia. I stood on his porch and stood in the place where Boss Man Smith stood and watched the many Negroes call him "Yes, sir, boss" as he beamed with pride, knowing that he was living on his place where no man dared to cross him. And I mean no white man or especially any Negro! As Tom Erwin was the sidekick of William Eberhart, William J. Smith was an employee of Mr. James Monroe Smith. Will Smith resided in Elbert County, Georgia. In 1850, William J. Smith is a year old in the house with his father Hudson J. Smith and his mother Martha D. Smith and Jane Madden. Hudson was born in South Carolina. I moved on to 1870 and I found the Smith family living near the Craft family, whom the district was named for, in 1850. William is now twenty-one and now he has two sisters, Virginia and Tallulah, in Elbert County. William J. Smith marries Caldonia A. Crawford in 1880, and by 1900 they are in Ruckersville, Elbert County. James M. Smith father was named Zadock Smith from Virginia and his mother was named Ann of Georgia, and his older brother was named John L. at the age of twenty and Benj. Franklin at the age of nineteen and young eleven year old James was the youngest living in Wilkes County in 1850. By 1860 young eleven year old James Monroe Smith was living in Alabama in Cherokee County with his wife Lucinda. Lucinda as the story goes was a Colored woman for when James Smith ran for Governor of Georgia they called his constiuance Lucindites and he lost the election. James was now twenty one and Lucinda was was at the age of twenty three. Lucinda was born in South Carolina. There is only on name that I must mention. Mr. Dolphus Kellum, his last name was a surprise to me because I was told that the oldest mother at my home church China Grove First Missionary Baptist maiden name was Kellum! I don't know if this is any relationship however, Jim Smith faithful employee was Mr. Kellum and quite a number of residence where I grew up was out of Athens Clarke County. I enjoyed my time on Jim Smith place. However, the scenary is mired by the fact that my mind cannot get the imagases of Blacks being chained and beaten and worked to death and the Government turned a blind eye during McKinly progressive movement. Just as long as the country was prospering the death of the Negro Men and Women and Children will fade away in time!

Escape from Oglethorpe County with Help from Peg-Leg Williams, AKA Ransom A. Williams

Mr. Ransom A. Williams will have a profound effect on the blacks in the South. He will be the Moses to the Negroes that longed to leave the northern parts of Georgia and move to South Georgia or to Mississippi. He will also cause havoc in the families that are willing to escape while under contract.

These black men and women would have to change their names and ages and remain in seclusion under the names given by him to remain undetected by such men as William Eberhart and J. T. Irwin, B. B. Williams, and the great Hon. James Monroe Smith! He is very active in and around Clarke County and Oglethorpe County, and Greene and Madison as well. These activities that are happening to our ancestors have an everlasting effect on our families today! I come across men and women, both black and white, that still kept the secrets passed down from their parents and would not even talk to me in some of my interviews. The horror that they felt caused me to believe that these murderous men did this to them or maybe it was that the secrets they kept were not of the atrocities of these wicked and cruel men but maybe they were protecting those who lived as white men and women while being delivered by Mr. Ransom A. Williams! The Federal courts, as well, could not help them, as you can see by the relationship that W. H. Johnson, the Federal sheriff, had with the great Hon. James Monroe Smith. The other place that R.A. Williams had much business in was Ohio, and this is where the daughter of Aaron will come to reside along with other colored Callaways. Her name is Mrs. Matilda Callaway Williams, who married Bob Williams or Robert Williams out of Greene County. Yes! The Williams family.

Peg-Leg Williams is the worry of William Eberhart and a thorn in his flesh. Eberhart has every right to be worried that Dinah English is trying to get Charlie and Brantley out of the county by travel agent Ransom A. Williams out of Atlanta by way of Shelby County, Tennessee.

Georgia Division of Archives and History – Manuscripts: AC 1968–0606m

"Peg-Leg" and "Jim" Davison

> The Populist movement and the cotton mills afforded to the poorer white people of Greene some opportunities for expression and added income. In the meantime, R.A. Williams, known as "Peg-Leg," was taking Negroes from central Georgia to the new plantation sections of the Mississippi Delta and Texas. He had an office in Atlanta, and centered his activities in Greene, Morgan, and Putnam counties, where there was a surplus Negro population.

Farmhands for the Delta

Williams was asked by leading citizens of Greensboro to relieve the county of 1,000 "surplus" Negroes. He came to Greensboro, discussed his emigration plans with the city and county authorities, promised to cease activities upon request. Commenting on his work in the winter of 1899–1900, the *Augusta Chronicle* of January 14, 1900, said: "It is clear that fully 2,500 Negroes have gone from Morgan and 1,500 to 2,000 from Greene."

Greensboro businessmen, in getting rid of "surplus" Negroes, were not speaking for the planters, who soon found that when the Negroes left their plantations, the cost of farm labor tended to rise.

Luther Boswell, one of the county's largest planters, swore out a warrant for "Peg-Leg." The charge against him was failure to pay the emigrant agent's license, which the State Legislature in 1877 had fixed at $500 per county. The sheriff arrested "Peg-Leg." His bond was fixed at one thousand dollars and Dr. T.B. Rice signed bond. Williams took a roll from his pocket, counted out a thousand dollars, and handed it to Dr. Rice. Within a few days Williams paid the $500 fee in Greene County, and continued his operations here and in surrounding counties.

A couple of weeks later, Williams boarded the west-bound night train out of Greensboro, with a large number of Negro migrants he had corralled. Just across the Greene County line, the Morgan County sheriff boarded the train, and Williams was lodged in the county jail—where one of his co-workers had already been placed.

While the train was in the Madison station, angry whites strode through the crowded "For Colored" cars. When the émigrés learned that their "Moses" had been arrested, they left the train pell-mell. For a mile out of town, the railroad right-of-way was strewn with cardboard valises and bundles. Williams and his agent remained in the jail during the day; men were there from all over the county threatening them with lynch law.

Except in Greene County, Williams refused to pay the $500 emigrant agent's license. Charges were then pending against him in four counties. One court after another had upheld the law. Williams refused to concede its constitutionality, and took the case to the United States Supreme Court.

During the summer of 1900, he did public relations work in Memphis and Atlanta. He played both ends against the middle: gave the Memphis papers interviews in which he assured the delta cotton growers that he would bring into that area thousands of good workers; told the Georgia papers that taking the Negroes out of the state would leave room for the white families ex-governor Northern and other leaders were then trying to attract here. "I bet you never thought of the question in that light before," he said to a reporter of the *Atlanta Constitution* in July. "Peg-Leg" then stated that he already had requests for 5,000 workers the coming winter, but would probably double that number.

Most of the émigrés were Negroes, though he reported in Mississippi that "a lot of white people" were getting interested.

Williams confidently opened an office in Atlanta in the early fall of 1900. With an able lawyer, James Davison of Greensboro, in charge of his case before the Supreme Court, he repeatedly refused to pay the licenses in Fulton and the other counties. Attorney "Jim" Davison contended that a license fee of $500 per county was prohibitory, that this precluded freedom of movement and hereby impaired the right of personal liberty. He argued further that the $500 fee was in contradiction to the laws of the Interstate Commerce Commission, and that it was not a legitimate exercise of police power.

Most important of all was the possibility that the law might be interpreted, according to the *Atlanta Journal*, as "in the teeth of the 14th Amendment of the Constitution which clothes the Negro with the liberty of the citizen."

The case excited great interest, particularly among the larger farmers of central Georgia. Cotton farmers in

Morgan County estimated that their growing crop would be 1,000 bales off because of the loss of the Negro workers; planters readily said that if the $500 fee were declared unconstitutional, some sections of the state would be virtually depopulated of workers and that agriculture would be ruined. Then there was the possibility that the decision in the case might affect the legal status of the Negro as a citizen.

In early fall, the Supreme Court heard the evidence. An equal number of justices voted for and against the constitutionality of the Georgia law under which Williams had been convicted in the state courts. The tie automatically upheld the decision of the lower courts. Williams was liable for a $500 license in each county in which he operated. He paid the license in Fulton County, and forthwith notified the tax collector that he was filing suit to recover it. But once the U.S. Supreme Court had spoken, even if in a split voice, "Peg-Leg" Williams's activities in Georgia were done.

The section of Greene most thoroughly depopulated by Williams's activities was the "Lower Forks." Into this area came white families, most of them from north Georgia, first Ceiger, Hard, Tingle, R.K. Hoard, J.R. Statham, and a little later Phelps and Center. Here and there throughout the old plantation areas, new white families came in and took up residence as farm tenants or small owners. With a background of home ownership of family-size farms and a tradition of work, these newcomers soon demonstrated that a family could raise its food on the red lands of Greene. Said the grand jury of March 1902.

On one of my many visits to courthouses in Georgia, I made a stop in Barrow County and I was sent to the Historical Society of that county. However, before I left the courthouse, I found records of a liquor ledger like the one I found in Greene County and Oglethorpe County. When I got to the Barrow County Historical Society, I saw signs of the influence of the liquor Mr. Rose distributed through the railroad in the place. At this same place, I found old news articles from the Winder News, *whose editor was Mr. McWhorter of Greene County, Georgia. It was Friday, March 27, 2009. It was a few days ago and a while back when I visited.*

I found the information that might give Charlie another first name and that name would be Richard. Richard was married to Rachel Hurt the daughter of Griffin Hurt. The article read like this. October 11, 1928.

Death of Hon. R.E. Davison

> Judge R. E. Davison, chairman of the state's Prison Commission for many years, died Tuesday afternoon, of last week at a sanitarium in Atlanta after a short illness. Judge Davison was seventy-four years of age at the time of his death. He was a native of Greene County, Georgia, and lived at Woodville. The burial occurred there. He had represented Greene County in the legislature and was prominent in political affairs of state. Associated with him on the Prison Commission were Judge George A. Johns of this city, and Hon. E. L. Rainey of Dawson.

I am so glad that my wife convinced me to continue in the reading of these old newspapers in Winder because I might have an answer to my many questions as to who and where and how this political power and prisons and chain gangs moved Charlie from place to place. This is what I found in the prison office of commissioner's books at the Georgia Archives.

Prison Commission

> Robert Emmett Davison, chairman, merchant, farmer, born on October 14, 1854 in Woodville, Greene County, Georgia; son of James M. Davison, born in Ireland, resident of Woodville, Georgia, died 1860; and Margaret Moore Davison, born in Green County, Georgia. Grandson of Burnette and Rebecca Billingsly Moore of Greene County, Georgia. Attended Bairdstown, Georgia, high school. Married on December 22, 1875, in Woodville, Georgia, to Hattie Armstrong, daughter of Capt. James Armstrong (died 1863) and Caroline Edmondson Armstrong (died 1875). Children: James Emmett, Charles Julian, Margaret Carry, Annie, Ida, Henry, Sarah, Ellen, Allene, Baptist,

> Democrat, Mason. Member House of Rep. Greene Co., 1894–1895, 1896–97, April3, 1902, August 1907. Trustee, Eighth Congressional District, S.N.S., Aug. 27, 1901–Aug. 27, 1910. Member, Prison Commission 1911–date. Resident, Woodville.

1900 census, G. M. Supervisor District No. 8, Enumerated Dist. No. 34, Enumerator James L. Young, twelfth day of June. Robert E. Davison is forty-five, born October 1854. His wife Hattie was born December 1857. They have been married twenty-five years and have had nine children: Charles L., Carrie M., Annie, Eda E., Henry, Sallie, Eleanor M., Silve, and Pearl. Reid, a colored servant, a fourteen-year-old girl, and Rosetta Edwards, a servant born February 1850.

Why would R. E. Davison be the defense attorney for Peg-Leg Williams? Could it be his son, Mr. J. E. Davison, in Atlanta in 1901? J. E. Davison, et al., to return amount paid for licenses pg. 656 line 44/ J. E. Davison et al. for refund of amount paid for license. Pg. 727, line 36.; pg. 763, line 8; adverse upon petition of Traders Collection Agency for refund of license tax. J. E. Davison and the Traders Collection Agency Co. This is the same Trader Collection Agency that Mr. Peg-Leg- is a part of in Atlanta. Could this be the reason?

In 1870, James Davison was a thirty-four-year-old farmer whose land was valued at $15,000. His mother Margrett Davison was forty years old and her land was valued at $12,000. Joseph Davison was twenty-eight years old and was a railroad agent. William Davison was twenty-five years old and worked as an insurance agent. Margrett was a twenty-two-year-old young lady. Charles was a seventeen-year-old and Robert was a fifteen-year-old. George n. Boswell is the assistant marshal. It is June 18, 1870, and the PO box is listed as being Penfield. Charles will sell Rachel's property beginning in 1912 in Woodville, Georgia. Now, Peg-Leg Williams is in Colquitt County, down near Mr. R.L. Rainey. Both are friends too. Mr. R. E. Davison of Woodville, Georgia, was the attorney for Peg-Leg Williams. It also puts Robert Callaway, born in 1877 in Colquitt County, and then Ned Callaway in 1910 on the property of Peg-Leg Williams. It also puts Charlie and Mary Calloway in Terrell County with Mr. R.L. Rainey.

Now, Robert Callaway was in the house with Henry Wooten, a man born June 1864 and was thirty-five years old. Sarah, his wife, was born May 1871 and was twenty-nine. Ella was born October 1884 and was fifteen. Bozzy was born August 1888 and was eleven. Gussie Loften was born May 1879 and was twenty-one years old, a boarder in the house with Henry Wooten and Robert Callaway another boarder at the age of twenty-two. Others that are neighbors and about the same age as Robert is Will Watts, John Henry, George Williams and his wife Loula, William Nelson, and Lee Watkins.

Now, there is another person that Peg-Leg Williams could have had help from in Falling Creek or Maxey and that could be the son of William B. Brightwell, Mr. A.T. Brightwell, the KKK. On one of my many travels to Oglethorpe County, I heard how the Brightwells were liquor runners in Falling Creek and Maxey. I heard this quite often whenever I inquired of the name Brightwell. However, I did find that they did good deeds toward the colored community as a whole. The name Brightwell is in big bold letters on one of the largest mercantile stores in Maxey. I believe that this name in Maxey caused William Eberhart to trod lightly in 1900 while looking for young Charlie and Brantley in the care of their grandmother Dinah in 1900. This name also might have caused Big Jim Smith of Smithonia to tread lightly as well, because of the position of Wm. B. Brightwell of the high order of the K.K. K. I read about him and his exploits in 1870 as being of the Grand Order of the Secret Society in the 1870's. William Brightwell was returning from Atlanta after marching in the parade as the grandmaster.

Mr. William B. Brightwell had every reason to be feared by others. Being at one time the largest landowner in Maxey in 1870, his property in Falling Creek was valued at $50,000 and he owned two properties in Lowndes, Clinch; five properties in Thomas, Irwin; two properties in Dooly; two properties in Randolph; six properties in Baker; three properties each in Early, Wilkinson, Pulaski, Decatur, Gwinnett, Stewart; two properties in Cherokee, Cobb County. Nathan G. Brightwell was forty-eight, living with George Campbell, a twenty-two-year-old, and a colored thirty-year-old Jack Brightwell in 1870. Nathan was eight houses away from his brother William, and Thomas Epps was twelve houses away. In the year 1860, Wm. B. Brightwell had $30,000 worth of personal property and $10,000 in property. He was forty-two years old and his wife Elizabeth was the same age. Augustus was seventeen, Martha was fourteen, Anna was twelve, Eveline was ten, and William was seven. N. G. Brightwell, whom I assume is his brother, is in the house at the age of thirty-eight, both William and N. G. are out of Virginia. Now, William B. Brightwell has property in Colquitt County as well. I want to remind you that Aaron at a breif time was in the possession of the property of Mr. Campbell in 1872. This shows you the relationship and company that Aaron Callaway kept. His skills as a farmer and him being possibly as close as being white allowed him to keep company and have favor in this time of transition from slavery to being free and his last name being Callaway.

I made my visit to the Colquitt County and met a few of William Callaway's decendence and found this deed. The information that I got out of Colquitt County about Mr. W.B. Brightwell stated that Mr. Brimberry was out of Walton County, so I wanted to trace him and his son Marion. I traced them all the way back to Walton County, Georgia.

Now Colquitt County is where I found Robert Callaway (born 1877) in 1900 and Ned Callaway in 1910. I don't know if Ned could be Charlie or not but I do know that Robert is the son of Charlie Callaway and Ned was residing in Terrell County prior to being in Colquitt County in 1910. I wonder if Ned was looking for his son Robert, who went under the first name of Jesse in the tax digest.

Well, Mr. Brimberry is on Mr. William B. Brightwell's indenture made the twenty-third day of July in the year of our Lord 1853 between William B. Brightwell of the County of Oglethorpe, State of Georgia, on the one part and Rufus J. Hughes of the County of Walton of the other part.

> Witnesseth that the said William B. Brightwell for and in consideration of his heirs and assigns all that tract or parcel of land situated, lying and being in the County of Thomas in the Eighth District of originally Irwin now Thomas County. Known and distinguished in plan of said District by number twenty-one, containing 490 acres more or less. To have and to hold said tract or parcel of land unto him, the said Rufus J. Hughes, his heirs . . .
>
> Look and see where this indenture was recorded: Walton County, Georgia.
>
> Personally came before me W.H. Brimberry who being duly sworn deposeth and saith that he saw W.B Brightwell sign, seal and deliver the written order for the purpose therein contained and that this deponent the same as witness and say Nathan G. Brightwell do so also sworn to and subscribed before me this 14th day of November 1853.

> P.G. Murray, J.I.C., recorded March 2, 1898, G.W. Newton Clerk

In witness, the said William B. Brightwell set his hand and seal the day and year above written, signed, sealed, and delivered in the presence of Nathan G. Brightwell and W.H. Brimberry.

Eventually the county of Thomas ceded land for the county of Colquitt. I also found this indenture

> . . . made and entered into this sixteenth day of November in the year of our Lord one thousand eight hundred and fifty-two. Between Nathaniel H. Parris of the county and state aforesaid of the first part and William B. Brightwell of the same place of the second part. Witnesseth that the said Nathaniel H. Parrish for and in consideration of the sum of thirty dollars to him in hand paid at and before the sealing and delivering of these presents the receipt is hereby acknowledged had granted, bargained and sold and doth by these presents grant bargain, sell and convey unto the said William B Brightwell his heirs and assigns a certain tract of land situated lying and being in originally Irwin County now Thomas in said state in the Eighth District, number twenty-one containing four hundred and ninety acres more or less . . .

In witness whereof the said Nathaniel H. Parris both has set his hand and seal the day and year above written. Signed, sealed and delivered in presence of Hanry Parris, Sarah A. Parris and Franklin C. Campbell the justice of the peace

Now again take a look and see the year that this was recorded and It will blow your mind: recorded March 2, 1898, G.W. Newton, clerk.

What is the relationship between Brimberry and Brightwell in Oglethorpe County in Falling Creek? In Colquitt County, Georgia, in 1898 to settle the estate of Mr. W.B. Brightwell, the father of Mr. A.T. Brightwell. His name is Marion Brimberry. His name is on the plat of Mr. James T. Findley and he is a mystery in Oglethorpe Maxey Ga. . I first come across Mr. Marion Brimberry in 1860 in Maxey, Georgia, in the house of Mr. Thomas Fleming, who is thirty-eight years old and he is married to Mrs. Jane McWhorter Fleming, who is twenty-six. Their children are Maderah (nine), Joseph (seven), William (five), Hubbard (three), and Marion Brimberry, who is a seventeen-year-old clerk in the mercantile store of Mr. Flemming, who has land valued at $3,500 and his personal property is valued at $14,000. Mr. Fleming and his household are living next door to Mr. Kilpatrick Smith, a fifty three-year-old farmer born in Virginia and his daughter Jane, who is twenty-eight; Elizabeth, twenty-one; Thomas, twenty-one; Mariah, eighteen; Charles, sixteen; George, fifteen; and Sarah, fourteen. Living next door to them is the family of Mr. John Bushell, a thirty-eight-year-old shoemaker, and his wife Nancy, who is the same age as her husband. Their children are Henry (fifteen), Martha (nine), and Margret Ward (nineteen).

Mr. William F. Gilliam is a forty-two-year-old Georgia farmer whose land is valued at $3,000 and his personal property is valued at $2,200. William's wife Lucinda is forty and his children are Sarah (sixteen), John H. (fourteen), William (twelve), Robert (seven), Emma (five), and Franklin (four). William Martin is a fifty-year-old white clerk like Mr. Marion Brimberry. Caroline is a sixteen-year-old daughter and John is his fourteen-year-old son. Mr. John F. Wray is a twenty-eight-year-old overseer for Mr. William B. Brightwell, and Mary, who is thirty-three, is his wife. Harriet is five, John W. is three, Martha is one. Now, I don't know which way Mr. Benjamin Crawley is going down or up the road to Mr. William B. Brightwell's house but it is at the intersection of roads leading from Oconee Colored Baptist Church and the road leading from Macedonia Church Road.

I believe that the fear that Mr. William Eberhart had about Dinah English leaving with the children was real. As you can see, the newspapers were correct that a large number of Negroes were leaving the area. This is why Aaron is missing from his house and is not on the tax digest of Clarke County, nor is he in Lincoln, Wilkes, Greene, or Oglethorpe as well.

Grover Cleveland, the first Democratic president after the war between the states, was a guest of Atlanta at the Piedmont Fair of 1887 when Henry W. Grady was master of ceremonies. And again in 1895 during the Cotton States and International Exposition, of which Charles A. Collier was president. Because of Grover Cleveland's policies he was not well received by Ben Pitch Fork Tillman out of South Carolina. Tillman is the same governor that visited Elbert County during Charlie Callaway's detention on J. C. Hudgins Convict Camp.

The *Athens Banner*, Friday morning, February 2, 1900: Searching for a Murderer: Deputy sheriff Brooks, of Greene county, was in Athens yesterday in search of a Negro who is wanted for murder.

He had tracked him through several counties in this section of the state, and at one time ran him so close that he abandoned his pistol and some "Peg-Leg Williams" emigration circulars that he had been distributing. Mr. Brooks has these articles in his possession now. Deputy Sheriff Brooks left yesterday afternoon to continue his search for the desperate criminal.

The Athens Banner, Friday morning, March 2, 1900:Athens Negroes Leave, Over One Hundred Set Their Faces Towards Mississippi: Over one hundred negroes left Athens Sunday morning for different points in Mississippi, where they are to receive high wages as farmhands. While Peg Leg Williams has not been here himself, he has had a number of agents working secretly and has distributed a quantity of his literature in this city and county. The darkies have been holding meetings and discussing matters for several weeks. Some of them have sold their property in order to get money with which to start out comfortably in their new homes in Mississippi. Sunday morning, sixty-eight men and as many more women and children started out to the promised land. They went off on the Seaboard Air Line train, and just after the cars containing these darkies reached Atlanta, Peg Leg Williams came into the coach with the announcement, "This is Mr. Williams." This is not the last batch to go from Athens. There are others who have the emigration fever in their heads. No attempt is being made to stop them.

The Weekly Banner, established 1882 Athens, Georgia, Friday morning, March 9, 1900

Facts coming out from deluded Negroes

They have tasted of the emigration sweetness and are satisfied

Two darkies have returned, they tell their experiences in the Mississippi bottoms

No bed of roses

Along the pathway of those who have emigrated from this section strap and rifle carry out the orders of the overseer in many instances

At least two of the Negroes who went to Mississippi from this section have returned home and they give an interesting account of their treatment there. Mr. W.A. Jester, one of Athens's prominent businessmen, was in Watkinsville Tuesday and was talking with an intelligent darky who owns his own farm in Oconee County, about the exodus of Negroes from this section to Mississippi and other points. Then it was that this darky told Mr. Jester all about how two of his cousins had been duped into going to Mississippi and how they had got enough of it and returned home.

These two Negroes were among the crowd that recently left Athens for the Mississippi Bottoms. They say that the men out there pay regularly what they agree to pay, but that they treat the darkies outrageously. All are put to work at daylight and worked until dark with only twenty minutes allowed for dinner. They are worked in the ditches in water up to their knees. The overseer stands by with a strap in one hand and a rifle in the other and doesn't hesitate to use either on the slightest provocation. These two darkies watched their chance and slipped away from the crowd one evening as they had started home. They had a little money and with it managed to get to Georgia again. Despite these facts and the persuasion of the best element of their race, quite a number of darkies continue to emigrate . . .

The Athens Banner, Friday morning, March 16, 1900: Has R.A. Williams Violated the Law? There is diversity of opinion on this subject. The charge against him, he says he has not been in Athens in several years it is not claimed that he has personally solicited laborers to leave.

The arrest of "Peg Leg" Williams and his subsequent release by Sheriff Nelms has caused considerable talk in Athens. A great many are of the opinion that Williams has been guilty of a great crime in deceiving these Negroes concerning the work for them in Mississippi, and that the limit of the law should be given him when he is convicted. That brings up the question of conviction and a great many do not believe he can be convicted of the charge of being an emigration agent doing business in Clarke County without license. Williams himself says he has never done any business in Athens and says he has not been in Athens in several years. It is true that he has not personally solicited laborers to leave Athens, but has done so through his agents. In fact, one of them had a telegram from him on his person. The subject has been sifted carefully by the attorneys and they believe a prosecution of Williams will stick.

There seems to be no question of the prosecution of the Negro agents being successful. They were here on the ground and the evidence is against them. They will be tried soon on the charges against them. The Negroes are not the only agents of Williams in this city. There is one or more white men engaged in this work and the police hope to be able to get the evidence soon with which to convict them.

Railroad agents in Atlanta were listed in the directory as follows

Adiar & Peers Union Depot

D. W. Appler at 9 S. Pryor

F. D. Bush at 28 Wall St.

Jack W. Johnson at Wall and Pryor St.

T. F. McCandless at 36 E. Wall St.

W. McPherson at 28 Gate City Bank Building

J. Maloy at 28 East Wall

J. A. Sams at 26 S. Pryor St.

W. H. Trezevant at 28 S. Pryor

S. B. Webb at Ballard's Restaurant

R. A. Williams (Peg-Leg) at 28 East Wall Street

The only railroad that was on Wall Street was Richmond & Danville Railroad at 56 East Wall Street. *Richmond & Danville Railroad is the same railroad Charlie Callaway was accused of receiving stolen goods from and was sent to prison for. Also in 1890, Robert Callaway, a black man, worked for R&D Railroad depot. There are too many similarities between Robert and Charles Callaway.*

In the following year, at 28 East Wall Street, were these agents:

F. D. Bush

J. Maloy

B. F. Nevill

M. C. Sharp

R.A. Williams

C. N. Winner

A. B. Wrenn

In 1910, Ranson A. Williams is listed at the age of fifty-nine years old and is out of Tennessee. His wife is named Francis M. at the age of fifty-seven, and Dicy M. is twenty-three, and Dora B. is twenty-one. Beslie L., their daughter, is fifteen, and Paul H. is sixteen. And Mr. Ned Calloway is listed at the age of sixty-five years old. All are in Colquitt County, Georgia. They are in the militia district no. 1549, Monk District. Ransom A. Williams is listed as a farmer. And Ned or Edward has no idea where he's from and neither does he know where his parents were born. I failed to mention that there was another colored family living opposite Ned Callaway. It was Ed R. James or Jones, a thirty-five-year-old man and his nineteen-year-old wife Eula and their three-year-old son Wesley and Mr. Will Thomas and his family.

What is Ranson A. Williams doing in Colquitt County, Georgia, in 1910, with Ned Callaway out of Terrell County, Georgia? Or he could just be Ned Callaway out of Bowling Green in the 228th District of Oglethorpe County in Stephens. In 1880, R. A. Williams is living in Shelby County, Tennessee, with his twenty-one-year-old wife Fannie and his mother P. M. and grandmother S. Ward and aunty Ellen Ward. R. A. Williams is working for the P. as an agent for L. Railroad.

Also in Shelby County, Tennessee, in 1880, is W. A. Williams, a forty-eight-year-old lumber merchant and his wife L. M., who is thirty-four. W. H., their daughter, is eighteen. John S. Williams is their thirteen-year-old, and Eliza Mullsey is a forty-year-old white servant. Oh! Now, I see the purpose of Mr. Ransom A. Williams in Colquitt County, Georgia. Many of the Oglethorpe and Clarke and Greene County Negro population was carried to the southern counties of Georgia for the timber and turpentine industry.

In the Atlanta Directory, Mr. R. A. Williams or Robert A. Williams is living at 28 Wall Street as a train hand for W&ARR and resides in Cartersville, Georgia. I went to Cartersville in Bartow County, Georgia, and found Wm. A. Williams, a forty-two-year-old blacksmith, and his wife Sarah at the age of thirty-four. Elijah is their eleven-year-old son born in Alabama, and Mary is their nine-year-old daughter born in Alabama. Minnie, who is seven, was born in Georgia. Sarah, who is five, was born in Georgia. And their three-year-old son named Charles was born in Georgia. However, Ransom is in Memphis with his mother and grandmother and his wife Fannie.

In 1884, Robert A. Williams is still a passenger agent for M&L RR and resides at 28 Wall Street. Fannie is at 52 Johnson and is the widow of the many first names for her husband. This time it is R. in the year of 1890. Robert A. Williams is a passenger agent for M&L RR and resides in Memphis, Tennessee!

Williams's occupation and duties of carrying his Negro cargo from Georgia causes him to shelter his wife from others who do not agree with his profession, who might attack his family while in Atlanta.

Peg-Leg Williams had family in Morgan County and he was Mr. Sidney Rose's brother-in-law. He was born in October 1861 and has been married to Martha for thirteen years. Martha and Sidney will remain here until 1920. Their children are Ola (twelve), Alba, Beula, Maud, Annie, Norma, Hettie, and Nellie.

Chapter Five

CHARLIE AND NED CALLAWAY WHOSE WHO? AND PEG-LEG-WILLIAMS

Ned Calloway or Edward Calloway. I believe that Ned is short for Edward Calloway. The only time that I found Ned in Oglethorpe County is between 1878 and 1880, living on William Crammer's place in Bowling Green. Ned was working with the following Negroes. Manuel Cramer, Ed Clarke, Dinah Callaway, Mat Callaway, Ben Cramer, Phil Callaway, Peter Callaway (who is over sixty years old), Ned himself, Peter Drake, and Mr. Allen Dupree. Mr. William Crammer's plantation was near the following other white landowners: Mr. J. M McWhorter, T. D. Gilham, and Ferdinand Phinizy. *I do believe that he returned to Monroe after a short time before getting his affairs in order so he could return to Monroe County, and this is why I find him in Bowling Green near Bairdstown with Mat Callaway, the husband of Nancy, and a Dinah Callaway, who I believe is Dinah England who had been living near Dinah Hurt. Who knows, it very well could be Dinah English herself under the last name of Callaway. Her two oldest daughters Mary and Nannie married Charlie Callaway and George Callaway! Remember they changed their last names to work under contract with more than one plantation owner until the 1880s when the white landowner caught on to their deception. I myself would call it deception but a way to survive under such harsh conditions. Remember Dinah was just a few houses away on the Hurt brothers' place, who are friends of Klansmen Augustus T. Brightwell and his father W. B. Brightwell, who just a few years ago marched in the Klan parade in Atlanta and gave a railing speech to the white masses and instill fear in their counterparts. Peter, the seventy-five-year-old, made his way back to Monroe County and is living with the rest of his family after helping his son Wash get established in Jackson County, Georgia.*

I also found another Ned Calloway in Terrell County, Georgia, in the 1143rd District working for J. A. Davis alongside George Brooks, William Harris, Morgan Harris, Henry Addison, Ned himself, Dick McConnell, Frank Johnson, Henry McConnell, and Ned Epps in the 1880s tax digest. There are a few names that I am very interested in that are living in this district that might answer questions later on about Charlie and Mary and their children. One is named Mr. Lewis Byrd, another is Mose Austin. Within the same year, Ned is working for the company of Martin and Dozier in Terrell in the 1143rd with Moses Walker and Moses Austin. Also in the district is William and Rayburn Byrd and Wiley Maxey. Ned even went to work for Mr. E. G. Hill alongside some of the same men Charlie will come to work with while on Mr. Hill's place. I don't know if Charlie is using the first name of Ned while here on Hill's place because Charley Mitchell is working alongside Adam Brown, who will come to own a large estate in Terrell County. Ned, while on E. G. Hill's place, is working with Drew Jacobs, Andrew Johnson, Bill Jones, Sam Cutts, Ed Harper, and Isam Sherman. Mr. E.G. Hill's place is in what is called Brown's Station. The post office is in Powers. Colored man Alfred Huchaby is living at his place. Gilbert Steven is living in this section at this time in Brown's Station in Powers. Gilbert Stevens will marry a female Callaway near Charlie and Mary Callaway in Terrell. Two white men I have to name are T.N. Killen and J. T. Johnston. Gilbert Stevens owns thirty acres in land, lot number 149, in District 12. Joseph Brown lived in the Evers District in 1900, and Mary, at the age of sixty, and is Joseph Brown's mother-in-law. Martha, the wife of Joseph Brown, was married to a Crowder. So by this time Peter is dead and Mary is a widow that will live until she is 102 years old and is buried in the Tessie Hall churchyard.

Ned Callaway, while in the 1143rd District of Terrell, at one time worked on the land of E.G. Hill with Ed Harper, Adam Brown, Ike Ellis, Isham Sherman, Charley Mitchell, Sam Cutts, and Andrew Johnson. It was a year later that Bill Jones and Isaac Brown and Shead Stark came to share crop on Mr. Hill's place as well.

Charles Calloway shows up in the 1143rd District on July 29, 1867. *As long as I have researched Charlie Callaway in Terrell County, I haven't listed him with a family at anytime. In 1870, he was living alone in 1870, and in 1880 I could not find him living with anyone at all. In the 1900s I couldn't find either Ned or Charlie Callaway in Terrell. The only time Ned showed up was in Colquitt County with Peg-Leg Williams, and for the first time, Charlie.*

Now, in the 165th District of Wilkes County, the same district that Aaron was born on Isaac Callaway's property, I found Mr. Ned Callaway working with John Darden, Isham Thomas, Mat Richardson, John Richardson, Dan Mattox, Solomon Walker and Simon, George, and Jones Mercier. In this same district of 165 in Wilkes County is my grandmother's grandfather Aaron Jones working with Charles and Henry Mays, with Cyrus Wingfield, his kin, working on a plantation nearby. Also in this 165th District is George Willingham, Burt Sims, Bob Mack, and many others that are kin to the colored Callaways in Wilkes County, Georgia, even Mr. Willis Williams! I thought that it was ironic that I would find the 1927 death certificate of Jonathan (Calaway) in McDuffie County, Georgia. Jonathan was fifty-three years old when he died. He was working for Mr. Pla Gibson, who was a doctor as well. His wife was named Mira, and his father was named Ned Calaway out of Wilkes County. His mother was named Rachel Booker and the informant was Willie Callaway out of Mesena, Georgia. Ned was buried at Pleasant Grove in Thomson, Georgia. Could this Ned who has married to Rachel be the same Ned in 1910 living near Mr. Peg-Leg Williams or R. A. Williams or Robert A. Williams in Colquitt?

I might as well linger in Wilkes County for a while and investigate Mr. Ned Callaway and Rachel Booker, his wife. In the 177th militia district, I found Dave Callaway working for T. H. Strother and Ned Callaway working for Abram Franklin. Squire Booker is working for V. L. Booker. Mr. Sim Booker had Toney Booker and Pierce Booker at his place, while Mr. Virgil McKinney was at Mrs. E. Holliday's place with John Wright, Newton Frazier, and Turner Mercier. Ned later shows up in the 164th District with Fem Callaway, Jerry Roberts, Fielding Mays, John and Wylie Thomas, Felix Booker, and William Wright.

This northern section of Georgia has a very close tie to the elite of the white population because of the many slaves that they had during slavery. In the 177th District of Wilkes, Jones Callaway is working for A.J. Paschal with Shed Richardson and Davis Mabra. Ned is working with Allen Booker and Alfred and David C. Callaway and Henry Pascal on T. H. Strother's place with Henry Harris and Willis Weems.

Back over in the 165th District of Wilkes County, Ned Callaway is working with John Darden, John Richardson, Mat Richardson, and Sol Walker on R. H. Callaway place, while Chas. Callaway and James

Wallace is on H. L. Aycock place. Aristide Callaway has on his place Allen Callaway, Sandy Winfrey, Calvin Callaway, Nick Callaway, Henry Pope, Peter Jones, Ned Wingfield, and Adam Winfrey.

So I went back to Terrell County, Georgia, in 1900 and found Ned Callaway, born June 1839, sixty years old, and living next door to Mr. Rupert Roberts and his wife Lola and children Mollie, Roshie, Maud, Babe, and son Bill Perry, as well as the white family of Mr. Milton Gammage. The Gammage family is kin to the Jones family. I found them living together in Colquitt County. I mention this because there is a close relationship between the two counties. Colored man Joe Marshal and his wife Elizabeth and their children. On the opposite side of Ned is the family of Banner Williams and his wife Jane and their son Ely Gibson. Mr. Roberts might be kin to Mr. Charley Robert that was on the tax digest working for Mr. Dozier with Ned in the 1870s while he was working for Mr. J. N. Sanders. Ned, while in the 1143rd District of Terrell, was working for Mr. E. G. Hill with Drew Jacobs, Andrew Johnson, Bill Jones, Sam Cutts, Charley Mitchell, Adam Brown, Isam Sherman, and Ed Harper. Working on G. O. Hill's place, the kin of E. G. Hill, was Thomas Ransom, Nelson Ransom, Isaac Brown, and Anderson Raines. This is the family of Browns that Ned Callaway is kin with and one of his children in 1910 is on Mr. Peg-Leg Williams's place in Colquitt. As I narrow this down to a particular Brown family, it is in the same district that E. G. Hill has Adam Brown and Ned Calloway and Drew Jacobs and Alfred Huchaby and Sam Cuts and Andrew Johnson on his place. In this same district is Mr. T.N. Killen, who has Ben Still and John Cato on his place.

Not only is there a Ned Callaway in Terrell County but there is a Charlie Callaway as well. I found Charlie Callaway living and dying in this county. It is stated on his death certificate that he had resided in Sasser for forty years until his death, but I found information that does not coincide with the informant's words on the death certificate. Therefore, I will start with the 1901 through 1930 tax digest of Terrell County and prove my point! Also, Charlie Callaway had two death notices, one stating that he was born in Mississippi and the other stating that he was born in Atlanta. I believe the second statement that he was born in Atlanta because of the white Callaways and the Joneses that I found living here. The white Callaways were W. H. Callaway and Martha Callaway.

As I stated before, I wanted to see for myself if Charlie resided in Terrell for forty years, so in the 811th District, Terrell County, Dawson, the twelfth enumerated district, there was no Charlie or Mary Callaway living there in 1901. However, I did find Allen W. English and A.J. Freeman, last names from Oglethorpe County. *Now, I want to remind you that Terrell County has a large state-run chain gang and this is a place where families, both blacks and whites, just pass through.*

In 1902 up to 1904 in the 811th District, there is no Charlie or Mary Calloway in Terrell. However, Edd Calloway and Jim Calloway is in the fourth district of Doral Militia District 1150. Guss Callaway and Edd Callaway and Will Lumpkin are in the 1143. In the 1154th District, I found Bill Callaway and George Calloway.

In 1905, in the Brownwood District of 1143, I found Amos Calloway and Fallie Calloway. In the years 1906 and 1907, I found Charlie Cooper and Charlie Carter in District 811 in the town of Dawson. In the 1154th District, for the first time Mary Callaway comes on the scene. She's in the same district with Eli Callaway and Barlow Cooper and Oscar Callaway. In the Brownwood District of Terrell County, I found Joe Callaway and Tollie Callaway. In Dawson, I found Lewis Calloway and Baylor W. Cooper.

Now, though she's not mentioned in the tax digest, I found Mrs. Emma Callaway in the 1154th District. She was born January 1864 and is thirty-six years old. Her son Ely Callaway, born July 1886, is thirteen, and Olla, her daughter, born June 1884, is fifteen. George, who was born June 1890, is nine years old. Now, her neighbors are Edd Crawford, his wife Lonny, their son Allen, their daughters Bessie, Mammie, Daisy, Nettie, and sons Hubbard and Floyd. Sarah Daniel is the next colored woman and her family. Carrie, her daughter; Rufus; Rebecca; and Willie Lee, her daughter.

In 1908, Pink Callaway was in Dawson District 1150. In District 1154, Dawson Toll Callaway and George Callaway resided. Anthony Calloway made District 1143 his home in 1908. Cal Callaway, Anthony Calloway, and Charlie Carter lived in Brownwood District, while Charlie Carter also made his home in District 941. By 1910, everything remained the same as to where everyone was living in Terrell County. But in 1911, Charlie Callaway came on the scene. Charlie Callaway lived in the 811th District of Terrell County in Dawson. He had 20 dollars' worth of kitchen and household furniture, 3 dollars' worth of stock of all kinds, which comes to 40 dollars in all. *Now this might be the reason that Charlie shows up in the 811th district at this time. Charlie shows up one year later after Ned Callaway and Peg-Leg Williams show up in Colquitt. Ned is never on the tax digest in Monk District in Colquitt County, Georgia, after or before 1910.*

Charles remained in the 811th District up until 1922. J.H. Callaway moving into the 1150th District with Pink Callaway in 1912. Pink Callaway might be the same Pink Callaway that was in Oglethorpe County in 1870 and 1880. Ed and Lillie and Steve Callaway resided in 1154th District in 1912. In 1913, George Callaway moved to District 1154 with Ed Callaway, Lillie Callaway, and Steve Callaway. Charlie Brown moved to the district with Pink Callaway in the same year. This district happens to be the 1143th District. Charlie Brown lived on 2,260 acres of land in this district and had $735 in horses, cattle, and mules, and $125 in tools. All this time Charlie Callaway only held on to $50, and that was all that he had during this time.

Henrietta Callaway's estate was located in the 1154th District at this time. She was a colored woman. Mrs. Henrietta Callaway has the same name as the middle name of the daughter of Isaac and Winifred Callaway. I do not know if this is significant or not; however, this is the same place where I found Mr. Ned Callaway living in, in 1880.

Now, here's a name that ties me to DeKalb County, Georgia, Mr. Frank A. Ruggles. I first come across him in 1910 in DeKalb County. However, I found him in Terrell County in the Town of Dawson in the 1154th with Mr. Eugene L. Rainey. In the year 1910, Mr. Frank A. Ruggles was living at 175 North Howard Street with his wife Kate. Frank was fifty-eight years old and Kate was forty-five. Clarence was fourteen, Olive was nine, and Eli Callaway, a handyman, was fifty-three. Mary Callaway was twenty-two years old. Eli and Mary had been married twice. In the Atlanta Directory, I found the two of them living in a house at 167 Howard NE. I also found several other Ruggles in DeKalb County nearby at 1414 DeKalb Avenue NE: Elizabeth and Roy. Frank was a cabinetmaker. In the year of 1920, in DeKalb, at 73 North Howard Street, Frank owns his property and is now seventy-four years old. Kate is now sixty years old and Olive, their daughter, is nineteen. Living in the same house is Michen May and Johannah Vanderhide, a niece. Michen May and Johannah are renting from Ruggles and the two are from Berlin, Germany. Frank is from Michigan and Kate is from Kentucky. However, in 1910 Frank Ruggles states that he is from Massachusetts. In 1870, Frank is in Toledo, Ohio. Frank is twenty something and his father is named Levi, out of Massachusetts. Mary, his mother, was born in Ohio. Frank was born in Massachusetts. Emma is twelve, Charles is thirteen, and Clara is seven. Frank works in a chair factory. Now, I will turn my attention to Eli and young Mary Callaway, who were in the house with Mr. Ruggles in 1900, in Terrell County in the 909th District.

Eli Callaway was born January 1860 and was forty years old, and married to Francis for twenty years. Anna, their daughter, is fifteen. Boisie is twelve, Stephen is ten, John is eight, and Nellie is two. Living in the house is Henry Hall, a brother-in-law, at the age of thirty. Twice I found this family In the 1870 census, I found Eli as a young boy in the house with Reuben, a forty-year-old man, and Biddy his wife. Biddy is the same age as her husband. Their children are Mary (seventeen), Charity (sixteen), Reuben (thirteen), Eli (twelve), and Ella is, Emma (six), and Frank (four). Reuben and Biddy were both born in Georgia. and the year is 1870 on the 20th day of July. However, in the same year, 1870, on the twenty-second of July Reuben is forty years old and was born in South Carolina and his wife Biddy was thirty-six years old, and now Charity is listed as being older than Mary at the age of sixteen and Mary is at the age of fourteen, Reuben is eleven, Eli is ten, Ella is six, Frank is four, and Emma is a year old. Biddy was born on January 27, and she died July 2, 1901. She is buried at the Sardis Cemetery in Terrell County Georgia. The census was taken in Randolph County Georgia.

I know that this is the Eli that is in Terrell County because of his mother. I walked the Sardis Cemetery in Terrell County and I walked these hallowed grounds with pride as I had walked many before. However, this one meant so much to me after traveling four to five times to Terrell County. Sardis Cemetery is a mystery because I found James Calloway, Lavonia A. Callaway (born February 25, 1889, and died January 1, 1968), Geo. Calloway (born June 1870, and died June 2, 1954), and Lillie Calloway (died September 21, 1985). Now, there is a Mr. Joseph Callaway who died on November 16, 1907, at the age of seventy. Mary Callaway, his wife, died on November 20, 1907, at the age of thirty-eight. The only woman I found to be the same age as Lavonia was the wife of Will H. Callaway, the son of Aaron Callaway. William H. Callaway married Lavonia Turner in Athens, Clarke County, on February 9, 1909, presided by Rev. William Barnes. I am just assuming that this is the wife of Will. However, it does come pretty close to her, seeing that they are the same age.

I forgot to mention Mr. George Brightwell and his family in the enumerated district of 135. This county had been infiltrated with the men and women of Oglethorpe County, both black and white. George Brightwell had with him his twenty-six-year-old wife Almer and their children, Mary Bell, Sonnie, and Jessie B. Brightwell.

In 1915, I found living in the same district Edd, George, Lillie, and Steve Callaway. All this time Charlie Callaway was in the same district that W.H. Jones's wife was living in. Steve Callaway was out of Randolph

County as well. In 1870 Steve was living in Randolph County Georgia. Steve was twenty five and his wife Lou was twenty, Jessie their five year old son and three year old Ella Lou, and their youngest son Johnnie who was born in March of 1880 and was three months old.

By 1918 Charlie Callaway had made his home in the 909th District of Dawson in the twelfth militia district. Charlie owned $15 in household items and $125 in cattle, mules, horses. He also had $40 worth of tools to run his farm, all the time under the watchful eye of William H. Jones. I say this because William H. Jones has made his home in the same district as Charlie. By 1919, William H. Jones (white) had 50 acres of land in the 909th District of Terrell of the third militia district. The market value of improved land and buildings is $350. Charlie Callaway, in 1919, has $25 in household utensils, $105 in horses and cattle, and $25 in tools, which comes to a total of $155. Now, I don't quite know where Charlie came from. He is aliened with the Jones. Charlie might have come to reside here because of the the Jones.

By 1920, W.J. Jones is the agent in the 909th District, while William H. Jones has moved on. Charles Callaway is now without any property and I wonder why! Maybe it is because now that Mr. W.J. Jones is the agent over Mr. W.H. Jones's property that left Charlie without! Well, Charlie has a friend that has moved into the 909th District of Terrell County with him, Mr. Charlie Gratlin. However, his name might have been Mr. Gratlin Johnson and not Charlie Gratlin. I might just be grabbing at straws. The same man who was forced to take up residence in the same chain gang in Elbert County in 1899 and was charged with the same offence: carrying a concealed weapon.

Well, back to Terrell County. Charlie Brown, who had at one time 857 acres, has 0 acres to his name, but Aaron Brown has the acreage now. In addition, all of this is in the 909th District of Terrell County in 1920. By 1921, Charlie Callaway had left the area. I believe that he may be in Greene County with Mary Callaway to help take care of Dinah English, Mary's Mother. W.J. Jones is still located in the 909th District of Dawson or Terrell County. Charles stayed away until the year 1925 and still his name didn't show up on the tax digest in Terrell, only Mary Callaway's name did in 1925. I got a surprise when a certain person showed up in 1924. A Mr. Cornelius Lumpkin made a brief stay in the 1154th District of Terrell County. Cornelius Lumpkin is the same man that Julia Callaway and Nelson Callaway were charged in 1894 for beating him up in Clarke County in Athens. I was very surprised to find him in Terrell. I speak of Mr. Cornelius Lumpkin because of Will Lumpkin, my grandfather's cousin. They say Will was born blind and played the mouth harp and guitar at the local dances and gatherings in Greensboro, as I remember. I believe that Will is the son of Nannie Hurt, the sister of Mary who married Cornelius Lumpkin in 1884. However, I also have Nannie Hurt Callaway marrying George Callaway in Oglethorpe County as well.

Mary Callaway made it back to the 909th District before Charlie did. She lived near W.J. Jones and W.L. Jones in this section of Terrell. I do not know why Charlie did not use his name at this time, because Mary signed or made her X up until the year of 1928 on the tax digest in Terrell County.

Let us start in Terrell County looking for Charlie Callaway and Mary in the 909th District of Terrell in the year of 1920. I did find Charlie Callaway in his declining years, at the age of sixty, living with his wife Mary. Nevertheless, Mary is going under the name of Elizabeth Calloway and is fifty-three years old. They have a son by the name of Robert who is four years old, and a boarder in the house by the name of Ella Smith, who is twenty-three years old. *Charlie and Elizabeth are living on Harrison Place in the third district of the 123rd enumerated district of Terrell County. I would mention their neighbors but none of them looks familiar to me.* Therefore, I will just mention the Callaways and those in the section of Terrell County at this time. William I. or H. Jones is living at the beginning of the census taker's journey or his walk through the 123 sections of Terrell County. William Jones is living with his daughters Mayrel, Fannie, and Estelle; and his sons Clarence, Jerry, and Oubrey. These are the same Joneses that are buried in the Oakland Cemetery with Maud Jones out of Walton County where Mr. Rev. Henry Callaway is buried in what is called Jones Woods. Rev. Henry Callaway died in Tennessee where his wife Rosetta his wife lived and died as well.

Henry B. Jones is in the 909th District of Terrell Georg. The spelling of the name of the street escapes me. But it seems to read Hools Road. Both Charles and William are in the same district. And they've been here in the same district since 1911. William's house number is 17 and 18. Charlie Callaway's house number is 121 and 122. The neighbors of Charlie Callaway and his wife Elizabeth are Tobie Reed and his wife Bertha; Ella Holly and her children Jim, Annie, Camillia, and Louis (?); and Alex Haden and his wife Ellen and their children. They all are living on Harriston or Hamilton & Leary Road in the 123rd enumerated district of Terrell. In Enumerated District 124, I found Mariah Calloway, a sixty-five-year-old living on or near Pleasant Street. Mariah's neighbor is a white family named E.C. Gammage and his wife is Mrs. Katie. Mariah Calloway is the wife of Ned Calloway or Edd Callaway. *In my youth, I was under the leadership of Rev. Richard Gammage at the China Grove Baptist Church in Lynwood Park in Buckhead on the county line between DeKalb and Fulton Counties. Rev. Gammage is from this area.* Moreover, a Mr. Cooper Lowery and his wife Regina resided near Mariah Calloway. Also in the same district was Anthony Callaway, a fifty-two-year-old colored man, his twenty-eight-year-old wife Lena and their two sons David and Willie D. Callaway. Also living in the same house was Turner Wilkerson, an eighteen-year-old.

Jim Callaway was located in Enumerated District 126, living with his wife Sallie and their daughter Rosa, sisters-in-law Ida Toby and Maggie, and a boarder named Lizzie Solomon. Jim Callaway was forty years old in 1920 and his wife Sallie was at the age of thirty. Rosa was ten years old. Ida Toby was forty years old. Maggie was fifteen years old and Lizzie Solomon was twenty-eight years old. Jim worked for none other than the General Farms corporation. They all resided on a side road off of Loraine Street (?). In the same district was Mollie Callaway, the sixty-year-old mother-in-law of twenty-year-old Sea Hicks. Hick's twenty-year-old wife was named Minnie. They had one son by the name of W.D. Calloway. Their neighbor was named Jeff Bostick and his family.

In Enumerated District 127, I found Jim Callaway, a forty-six-year-old man renting his property and living with his forty-two-year old wife Sophilia. Also living in the house with Jim and his wife Sophilia was a twenty-four-year-old woman named Ella Patterson and her sixteen-year-old granddaughter Mattie Patterson. Jim was living near a white woman named Emma York, who was seventy-seven years old. Now, living in Enumerated District 128 was George Calaway, a fifty-one-year-old colored man that owned his own property and was living with his forty-year-old wife named Lilly. They lived on Ralan or Kalan Street in the 1154th District. In District 129, I found Thomas M. Callaway, a white male at the age of fifty-three. Thomas's fifty-one-year-old wife was named Mammie C. and they have three children that go by the names of Tom, Clayton, and Victoria. Now, check this out. The sister-in-law of Thomas M. Callaway was named Ella Bacon. So! He might have married a Bacon out of Oglethorpe County. Remember, J. J. Bacon he died in 1901, just after Aaron Callaway's contract was to expire or began with William Eberhart. J. J. Bacon's son took over as ordinary of the county after his death. Eighty-year-old Victoria, the mother of Thomas M. Callaway, was also in the house as well. Alma Young was their neighbor. He was forty-one years old and his wife Amanda was twenty-two years old. They had three children, Jimmy, Bertha, and James.

I found Sclodet Callaway in the 133th District in Terrell living with the family of Henry Johnson and his wife Hettie. Henry is forty-eight and Hettie is thirty-five. Their children are Ollie, Mamie, Millie, and Oscar. Sclodet is eighty years old. This district is named Sasser, the same district Charlie and Mary Callaway are living .

Wednesday, July 02, 2008

Coloreds Terrell County Marriages

Wiley Walker to Martha Callaway, April 5, 1879

Shadrack Reed and Mollie Callaway, March 15, 1879

Mr. Peter Harris is the minister of the gospel

Lafayett Williams and Alice Callaway, May 12, 1881

Elbert Walker M.G.

John Anderson and Eliza Callaway, February 14, 1883

Ike Hodge and Lizzie Callaway, January 4, 1886

Wiley Callaway and Suckie Williams, December 11, 1886

Charley Tooke and Anna Callaway, March 15, 1888

Gus Callaway and Mattie Mitchell, December 1, 1889

B.J. Jordan M.G

Joe Thomas and Sallie Calloway, March 19, 1890

G. W. Marching M. G.

Gus Callaway and Lucy Perry, December 23, 1892

A. S. Stamper M. G.

Ned Callaway (spelled Calaway) and Sallie Harris, January 7, 1893

George Callaway and Sallie Aikins, April 24, 1893

James W. Walker M. G.

Ned Callaway and Mattie Thomas, December 21, 1895
George Callaway and Mary Hall, March 14, 1896
C. L. Harris M. G.

Willie Callaway and Margaret Williams, April 28, 1894
W. S. Bates M. G.

Jim Jackson and Margaret Calaway, June 26, 1897
L. J. Mallard M. G.

Joe King and Lula Callaway, July 31, 1897
S. M. Clark M. G.

Major Crawford to Carrie Callaway, November 4, 1899
Rev. C. W. Maxwell M. G.

Dock Dismuke and Lillie Callaway, August 9, 1902
Henry Humphries and Orrie Callaway, September 2, 1905
Oscar Callaway and Sarah Gore, December 28, 1905
B. J. Jordan M. G.

Squire Dudley and Rebecca Callaway, February 10, 1906
Rev. L. R. Bridges M. G.

Tax Digest Terrell County 1915

White, 1143rd District Terrell

W.H. Gammage and James W. Gammage, Emmet C. Gammage, Mrs. Mary F. Gammage, P.H. Gammage, D.A. Gammage, G. M. Gammage, G.C. Holland, John M. Holland W.M. Holland, Mr. W. A. Jones, and J.D. Irwin and non-resident

Clint C. Rainey, Claude Rainey, Sidney J. Rainey, D.J. Roy, Thomas H. Williams, Henry T. Williams W. C. Williams

White, 1154th District

T.M. Callaway, Mrs. T.M. Callaway, S.L. Carter, Mrs. S.L. Carter, T. L. Cain, Bridges and Jennings, Clarke E. Bridges, J.C. Bridges, H.T. Bridges, A.C. Bridges, Dennis Bridges, J.R. Bridges, E.B. Bridges, Mrs. S.S. Janes, W.C. Janes, R.R. Jones, and Ms. T. Jones

Coloreds, Twelfth Militia District 1915, Dawson, Georgia

Charles Calaway, A.E. Carter, Ben Carter, Charlie Carter, Pete Williams John Wooten, John Watson, Wade Watson, Jim Williams, John Williams, Quallis Williams, Andrew Williams, Banner Williams, and Edd Williams

Coloreds, Sixth Militia District, 1143 PO Box, Brownwood

Amanda Cain, Ike Carter Cutts Carter, Tol Carrington, Jim Callaway, Anthony Callaway, Tol Callaway, John Cloud, Henry Jackson, Dan Jackson, John Jackson, Sol Jackson, Henry J. Jackson, L.C. Jones, E.T. Jones, Rich Jones, Will Jones, Sol Jones, William Jones, Ben Jones, Harrison Johnson, Sam Johnson, Will Johnson, Arthur Perry, Sam Perry, Chas. Perry, Beacham Perry, John Perry agt., Sol Perry, Ely Peeples, Will Pitts, Solomon Pierce, Clive Riley, Jelly Riley, Gabe Riley, Homer Riley, John Scott, Gus Sanders, Landis Sampson, Peter Robert, Babe Roberts, Jesse Roberts, William Roberts, Will Roberts, Luke Roberts, John Roberts, Levi Roberts, John Reed, Cornelius Reed, Bossie Reed, John E. Reed Wilson Reed, Jeff Robinson, Ross Robinson, Story Williams, Henry Williams, Gen Ed Williams, Dublin Williams, Andrew Williams Est., James Williams, Gene Williams, Alex William, Carrie Williams, Albert Williams, Clara Williams, Edmond D. Williams, Edmond Williams, Ransom Williams, Tom Smith, Isom Smith, Wesley Smith, Jesse Smith, John Smith, Gov. Smith, John M. Smith, Henry Smith

1150th District, Fourth Militia District, Dawson

Pink Callaway, Oliver Cato, Arthur Crawley

1910 Terrell County Tax Digest

Sixth Militia District, 1143 Brownwood

W.A. Jones, John M. Holland, George Holland, Mrs. Emma Harrison, John D. Irwin, Chas. S. Irwin, Mrs. Susie Johnson, J.C. Gammage, D.A.

Gammage, Jas. W. Gammage, J.E. C. Gammage, Gov. M. Gammage, P.H. Gammage, Mrs. P.H. Gammage, Holland & Hill, John C. Holland, Haynes & Kennedy, Clawd Harvey, WM. Holland, Mrs. Ada Holland, Kennedy Gin and Mill, J.S. Kennedy, J.A. Kennedy, C.B. Kennedy, W.S. Kennedy. J.V. Oliver, C.H. Price, Calvin H. Rainey, Clint C Rainey, Sid J. Rainey, J.C. Sampson, Green F. Smith

Coloreds, 1910, 811th District, Twelfth Militia District, Dawson, Georgia (no Charles Callaway)

1673rd District, Sasser: Tom Cloud, Dave Cloud, John Cloud, Ike Carter

941st District, Eleventh Militia District, Dawson: Bob Cloud I mentioned the Cloud family because of John Cloud. In 1930 in Techwood John Cloud lived near my grandfather in Atlanta.

1143rd District, Sixth Militia District, Brownwood: No Tol Callaway, but there is an Anthony Callaway, and an Evans Jackson, Will Johnson, Mathew Jackson, Ben Jones, Jesse Jackson, Sam Johnson, Henry Jackson

1150th District, Fourth Militia District, Dawson, Georgia: Oliver Cato, Pink Callaway, Jim Callaway, Henry Carter

1154th District, Dawson: Ed Calloway, B.W. Cooper (has 12 acres of land no. 226, valued at $200, city and town property is $350), John Craddock and C. Craddock, Susan Cato, John Carter, Willis Clark, Oliver Jackson, Bice Jackson, Louis C. Jeffiers, Georgia Jeffers, Eli James, Mack Jones, Eugene Jones, Samm Jessie, Luis Hightower or Levi Hightower, Crawford Hightower, Sam Jackson, Sherman Jackson, Henry Jackson, Mathew Jackson, James S. Nobles

1930, whites, Sixth Militia District, 1143: J.D. Irvin estate, G.L. Jones

1930, coloreds, 1673 Sasser: Jim Calaway, Dave Cloud, Howard Cloud, Tom Cloud Jr., Tom Cloud

909th District, Third Militia District: Charles Callaway, Albert Jackson, Silvey Jones, Gussie Jones, Arthur Jones, Will Jones, John Jones, Ida Jones, Dad Sims, Chas Sims, Jack Solomon, Chas Solomon, Louiza Terrell, Hannah Thomas, Mary Thomas, Will Thomas, Chas Thomas, Elbert Williams, Lige Williams, Will Williams, Ned Williams, George Williams

INDICTMENT. Form 107.

Georgia, Oglethorpe County.

IN THE SUPERIOR COURT OF SAID COUNTY.

THE GRAND JURORS, selected, chosen and sworn for the County of Oglethorpe to wit:

1 Joseph McWhorter, Foreman.
2 Ed. V. [illegible]
3 Ed. B. Clark
4 Thomas W. Crawford
5 Jacob Eberhart
6 William Eberhart
7 John V. [illegible]
8 Frank R. [illegible]
9 Richard L. Hargrove
10 Eliza W. Johnson
11 Henry A. Lawrence
12 Oscar L. B. Liston
13 Columbus J. Sanders
14 Royal A. McMahan
15 [illegible] P. Reynolds
16 Dr. Ed. L. Sanders
17 James E. Tribble
18 Mark H. Young
19 Andrew J. Young
20 John [illegible]
21
22
23

In the name and behalf of the citizens of Georgia, charge and accuse Robert Callaway of the county and State aforesaid, with the offense of larceny from the house; for that the said Robert Callaway in the county aforesaid, on the 1st Sunday of January in the year of Our Lord One Thousand Eight Hundred and Ninety eight with force and arms One pair of [illegible] of the value of Two & 50/100 dollars, being the goods and chattels of one William Humphrey in the Dwelling house of him the said Wm. Humphrey, Robert Callaway, [illegible] in the County aforesaid, being found the said Robert Callaway then and there, from the said Dwelling house, feloniously, wrongfully, privately, fraudulently and with intent to steal, the said Robert Callaway then and there did take and carry away he the said Robert Callaway then and there, having entered said [illegible] with intent to steal, contrary to the laws of said State, the good order, peace and dignity thereof.

Oglethorpe Superior Court, [illegible] Prosecutor.
April Term, 1897. R. H. Lewis [illegible] Solicitor-General.

Robert C. Callaway

From Being a Negro Laborer to Being a Negro Landowner with Tenants

Here are a few of the dealings of Mr. Robert Callaway while in Clarke County. He had an indenture with Selig Bernstein (exc.), book 11, page 22. (Robt. Callaway to Selig Bernstein.) Robt. Callaway to Mrs. Emma Edge Haynie, book 11, page 242. Robert Callaway to Edith A. Callaway (colored), 1914, book 14, page 464. Robert Callaway to Mary A. Hilsman,

1914, book 16, page 50. Robert Callaway to William Bates, book 17, page 254. Robert Callaway to S. Bernstein, book 30, page 144; book 32, page 16. I am praying that a few of these aquanteces of Robert Callaway might open avenues of other families to contact me and they may fill in a few of the blanks of the mystery of Charlie Callaway and my great-grandmother Mary.

I must mention Elsie Callaway et al. from James Brittain (est.) by administration book 58, page 288. Edith Anne Callaway from Robert Callaway (colored), book 14, page 627. Elsie Callaway from R.C. Callaway, 1921, book 33, page 297. Robert Callaway from Jake Joel Jr., book 37, page 67. Robert Callaway et al. from Mrs. Annie Jones, book 41, page 243. Elsie Callaway et al. and Annie Bell Callaway to Athens, book 81, page 476. Gibson Callaway from Independence Order of Good Samaritan, book 18, page 193. Gibson Callaway from Gospel Pilgrim Society, book 17, page 616. Gibson Callaway to Ida L. Chamberlin, book 34, page 390; book 34, page 549; book 21, page 146; and book 15, page 412.

H. C. Callaway from Robert L. McCombs, deed April 24, 1900–April 27, 1900, book SS, Page 531

Henry C. Callaway sold the land bought from Darricott to McCombs for $71 on April 25, 1900. J.R. Porter witnessed, with A. Graves as the notary public. Mr. A. Graves is Antoine Graves of Atlanta a very prominent Black realtor and first principle of the Gate City Colored Public School and was principle over the Storrs School as well. Jesse Callaway from King-Hodgson Co. Mtg. March 21, 1912–April 3, 1912, book 7, page 348, and book 7, page 367. There was nothing listed as being on these pages! Henry C. Callaway is the father of Will Callaway, who is a mystery in Atlanta starting in 1891, with Charles Callaway working for Finly Furniture Company. Let's look at Henry a little closer. *Henry C. Callaway is living between Atlanta and Clarke County after leaving Oglethorpe County with Charlie, fleeing to Atlanta in the 1890s.*

Robert Callaway (colored) married Lettie Hardeman (colored) on the fifth of January 1881. George Dyson was the ordinary. B.M. Callaway was the minister of the gospel. Charles Callaway married Fanny Wylie on March 13, 1880, and they are not listed as being colored. They were married by Thomas Andrews. Now Robert Callaway (colored) married Elsie Ann Harris (colored) on December 25, 1892. Mr. M. Hill was the minister of the gospel and he was colored. Minister M. Hill might be the pastor over at the Hill Baptist Church in Clarke County. *At the time of this marriage,*

Robert C. Callaway had to be living in the 220th District when in 1900 a row or fight or argument broke out at the house of the mixed family of Robert Callaway.

So one thing I know is that Robert Callaway did not originally come out of Clarke County. For him to be married by Mr. Brantley M. Callaway in 1881, I had to ask myself this question: what was he doing in Wilkes County in 1881? I know that the only ones of interest in Clarke County in 1870 were located in the Sandy Creek District of Clarke. This district is located just before you would get into Jackson County. This is where Gibson Calloway will own property and Hagar, the grandmother of Gibson, will relocate to in 1910.

The first family was Mr. James F. O'Kelly, a forty-five-year-old white man, and his wife Elizabeth, who was thirty-three. Thirteen-year-old James, twelve-year-old Dicey, six-year-old Robert, four-year-old Lewis A., and one-year-old Dedrick. Living in the house with them was a colored fifteen-year-old boy named Elijah Johnson. The O'Kelly's will play a great part in the story that will include Richard English and Abraham English the son Abe and Dinah English in 1901. They will play a role in the life of Charlie Lester of Rockbridge as well. They will sell him land in Gwinnett County and also establish the O'Kelly Chapel as well.

James W. Lester was a forty-year-old white man with his thirty-five-year-old wife Elizabeth, their thirteen-year-old son James, twelve-year-old Charles, nine-year-old Louis, six-year-old Pinkie, two-tear-old Lizzie, and four-month-old Thomas. I am very much interested in young twelve-year-old Charles Lester because he is to marry Ms. Missouri Tuck. James W. Lester has two colored people in his house in 1870: George Landrum, a fourteen-year-old man, and Mrs. Lizzie Langston, a fifty-four-year-old, working as domestic laborers.

Now Albert Binion is a forty-four-year-old colored man living next door to his brother Burton Binion, who is forty-seven years old

In Sandy Creek, Clarke County, Georgia, April 23, 1910, I found Hanson Calaway, a sixty-year-old colored man working for General Farms Inc. His wife is Annie and she is forty-four. Orrie is their daughter aged fourteen. They are living next door to a Colly W. Barnett, a twenty-one-year-old white man, and his wife Sarah J., who is twenty, with James G. Barnett, who is a year old.

On May 26, 1887, Riley Calloway married Anna Moore in Wilkes County. Will Henry Callaway married Lavonia Turner in Clarke County in February 1908, and Mr. Rev. Wm. Barnett was the minister of the gospel. In 1907, Riley Callaway married Susie Howard in Clarke County, and R.H. Johnson was the minister of the gospel. If anybody knows the relationship that Charlie and Mary might have had with anyone previously mentioned contact me on FB. You might have a story to tell.

The State of Georgia
vs.
Robert Calloway

Indictment for Larceny from the house
and Verdict of guilty

WHEREUPON, It is considered, ordered and adjudged by the Court that said defendant do work in a chaingang on the public works for the term of twelve months and that he be delivered to the authorities of Oglethorpe County, who are hereby required to deal with him according to this sentence:—Said term to be computed from the day said defendant is set to work (after the commutation of the sentence already imposed) in said chaingang, and said defendant to remain in the common jail of said county till put to work in said chaingang. Said defendant may be discharged from custody under this sentence at any time before the expiration thereof upon paying a fine of Fifty Dollars and the costs of this prosecution.

This, 21 day of April, 1899.

[illegible]

Henry C. Tuck and friend Richard B. Russell

These two men have been friends from childhood, growing up in Oglethorpe County, Georgia, just south of the Beaverdam District of Oglethorpe. I will show some of the Negroes that were defended by them and how the colored families that they defended were kin to the colored Callaways in this section of Oconee and Barrow County, and even Gwinnett over in Rockdale as well.

Henry C. Tuck

Here I want to show you the closeness of Henry C. Tuck and Mr. Richard B. Russell, and their beliefs in their politics during the 1880s, 1890s, and 1900s. I was at the University of Georgia Library and I found just what they meant when Charlie want to get off with just a $50 fine for carrying a pistol concealed in 1899. He was now in the hands of the State of Georgia after appealing to the Federal Court. Now we will get a good look at what is called state rights in the South! Here's a look at Oconee County during the reign of Richard B. Russell as judge and Henry C. Tuck as *pro tem* in Oconee County.

First, look at this prominent last name: Lester! The *State vs. Dick Lester alias Green Lester*, a person of color, simple larceny, horse stealing. Found guilty!

The *State vs. Thomas Jones*, a person of color. *Nolle prosequi* is entered on this bill for not enough evidence.

James Scott, intent to murder a person of color

Spencer Lester, a person of color, charged with a misdemeanor for using opprobrious language, assault and battery

Jerry Marable and Charles Sims, burglary, January 30, 1885, E. J. Brown, Sol. Gen.; Geo. C. Thomas and Henry C. Tuck, defendant's attorneys, plea of not guilty

State vs. Charles Sims, a person of color, misdemeanor charge for carrying pistol concealed. The defendant Charles Sims waives copy of indictment and list of witnesses and pleads guilty. George C. Thomas and H.C. Tuck, defendant's attorneys. Fined $20 and court costs and served six months from the thirtieth of January 1885. N.L. Hutchins, judge of superior court.

State vs. John Bush, adultery and fornication. Benjamin Bush was charged with burglary in January 31, 1885.

The State vs. Charlie Vincent, a person of color, simple larceny; James Frazier, foreman

State vs. Bob Sims, a person of color, assault with intent to murder

1886 to 1892

State vs. Charlie Sims (who might be white) and Ed Carter, a colored person, for burglary, case *nolle prosequi*

State vs. Columbus Barrow

State vs. Howard Sims

State vs. Will Broughton and Anthony Thrasher, persons of color, for obstructing railroad, plead not guilty; B. E. Thrasher, defendants' attorney

State vs. Mary Hightower, abusive language

State vs. Harrison Jackson, charge for retailing without a license, selling and furnishing liquor

State vs. Charlie Mayes (colored), carrying pistol concealed; James W. Lea, foreman

State vs. James Sharpe, a person of color, charged with rape; Asbury H. Jackson, foreman

Oconee County Superior Court

This day comes Richard B. Russell, Solicitor General of the Western Circuit, who prosecutes for the state, January Term 1891. N. L. Hutchins, judge.

Minute Book 1892–189——

State vs. Mack Lester, colored

The State vs. John Calloway, colored, assault with intent to rape; ordered to pay a fine of $30 and cost of prosecution, serve twelve months; January 27, 1894

1894, Richard B. Russell is solicitor general of Oconee County

Mit Johnson vs. James Johnson for divorce, July 24, 1894

James M. Smith and Wes Ridley, misdemeanor, 1894

State vs. Robert L. Lyle, selling whiskey; witnesses: John Griffeth, T.S. Bray, Arthur Langford, and William Belk

State vs. John N. Ridgeway, selling whiskey; witnesses: Y.W. Doggett and Jack Harper, January 1895

State vs. John Eberhart, assault to murder

State vs. Andrew Austin, assault; J.D. Price, foreman

State vs. John Eberhart, Ellis Foster, Stewart Thrasher, McCajah Thrasher, Buck Greenwood, aggravated riot

State vs. Andrew Austin, January term 1897

Coon Sims, selling whiskey

Conn and Weldon Sims, selling whiskey in 1897

J.M. Sims, selling whiskey

Jim Barnett and Frank Thompson, playing and betting cards

January 26, 1902

Mrs. Anna Vincent vs. J.H. Sikes, estate of John Sikes; Richard B. Russell is the judge

1892 term Superior Court Minute Book

State vs. Lon Ranson, burglary; Lon Ranson, larceny from the house

State vs. Will Lucas, Sidney Robinson Jr., Bob Brown, and Ed Anderson, playing and betting at cards

State vs. Charley Colquitt, assault with intent to rape, May 25, 1899; C.H. Brand, solicitor general; R.R. Burger, defendant's attorney. Charlie Colquitt is a person of color, twenty years old, and R.B. Russell is judge S.C.W.C.

Henry C. Tuck is representing John T. Anderson, the defendant, in the January term of 1900 and R.B. Russell is the judge.

January Term 1901, H.C. Tuck, solicitor general *pro tem*, and R.B. Russell is the judge S.C.W.C.

R.B. Russell is in his chambers on May 18, 1901, handling business from Winder over at the Oconee County Court.

Now the question is did Richard B. Russell just say that he sent Charlie Callaway's case to city court? Or did he just transpose it to Oconee County or Barrow County and allowed Charlie to live under a new name. I didn't know if Charlie is in their hands but I do know because of the relationship these two men. They must have had some heated debates in 1899 about what to do about Charlie Callaway!

Now, because of the relationship that Henry C. Tuck has with the Carter family and William Eberhart, did he put Charlie into the hands of Eberhart? Is this the reason that the courts of Oglethorpe have on their dockets that Charlie Callaway is dead by October 17 and Richard B. Russell doesn't know about the situation with Charlie! Because of the closeness of Tuck and Russell, I do not think that this would elude Judge Russell. Tuck is also close to the Callaway family that was in Gwinnett County near Rosebud Road. This situation concerning the Tuck family puts them in or near Walton County and Charles C. Callaway who lived in Rockbridge in Gwinnett.

July 28, 1902, R.B. Russell Judge

The State vs. Will Cusey and Mose Lester, colored burglary

Three charges against Joe Puryears for selling liquor, and Mose Lester and Will Cosey, on July 29, 1902, plead guilty.

J.H. and Mrs. Woodie Bishop vs. Central of Georgia Railway Co., the motion be and the same is hereby overruled; in open court July 31, 1902, R.B. Russell judge

Clifford Cheatham, January term 1903, selling liquor, three charges, case *nolle prosequi*; Richard B. Russell, judge

Minute Book (C)

State vs. Joe Colbert alias Jerome Colbert, for murder, said motion stand continued until the twentieth of February 1903, to be heard at Russell, Georgia, on that day at 10 o'clock to make out and file a brief of testimony without prejudice and without permission to amend within motion and that this under act as supersedes to stay execution of sentence in said case; L.B. Russell, judge S.C.W.C.

The State vs. Mose Lester, July term 1903

The State vs. John Henry Rains, selling liquor within three miles of a church

State vs. Alex Jones, Bob Johnson, Will Winbush, Munch Grimes, gaming, 1905

State vs. Adam Crawford, Gaines Heard, General Rogers, Frank Thomas, gaming, January term 1906

Sherman Richard, charged with selling liquor and beer

This is Oconee County, Georgia, and the criminal element that plagued the county. You will hear some more of the people that plagued this county later on but for now let us focus on Mr. Henry C. Tuck.

These are some of the names that Mr. Tuck had relationships with in his special papers that were located at the University of Georgia, his *alma mater*: Thomas S. Mell; H.H. Carlton; W.G. Brantley of Blackshear, Georgia; Joseph M. Snow of Waterville Douglas Co.; S.C. Anderson; W.W. Humphreys; Charles Z. McCord, 1889, at 811 Broad Street, Augusta, Georgia; David C. Barrow Jr.; Major J. Colton Lyndes; Marcus Beck of Jackson, Georgia; Robert L. Moye of the city of Cuthbert, Georgia Mayor's Office; W.W. Royston of Franklin, Georgia; George B. Cornwell in 1896; and James A. Royston.

Chapter Six

HENRY C. TUCK; A PARADOX A SELF CONTRADICTORY STATEMENT TO THE RELATIONSHIP TO CHARLIE DID HE HELP OR DID HE DECEIVE TO KILL

Mr. Henry C. Tuck was also elected as a member of the House of Representatives of Georgia. He was a member of the Clarke County United Methodist Church and taught a very elite Bible class. His book was praised by *The Atlanta Journal*, January 18, 1939. He spoke of the four years at his *alma mater* between the years of 1877 and 1881. He also wrote about his encounter with Mr. Henry W. Grady at a commencement in 1878.

Judge Tuck gives an interesting glimpse of a distinguished Georgian. "One man that attracted a great deal of attention at this commencement," he writes, "was Henry W. Grady, whom I found to be the drawing card on the campus. Everywhere he went or stopped a crowd would gather around him and such talking and laughing I never heard before, Grady's class, that of '68, had a reunion this year and no doubt laughing with him were old classmates. But, Henry Grady was the life of the party, for he did most of the talking . . ."

Part two of Judge Tuck's book consists of "Thoughts upon life and its various phases, and upon man with his varied manifestations, with numerous quotations from writers, both ancient and modern, presenting their views upon these. Here is that which has proved useful to the author in his legal and judicial work and as a teacher of one of the largest Bible classes in Athens. Themes discussed in this portion of the work are life, character, learning, truth, friends, enemies, personality, ambition, and aspiration, reserve energy, creeds, belief, fate, fortune, ancestry, and the future of man."

As you can see into the mind of the man that took control over my great-grandfather, I wonder what was his conversation with my great-grandfather in Elbert County or at the Courthouse of Clarke, where I found the original copy of my great-grandfather making his X, saying he was not going ahead in the litigation of the case that was in Federal Court. Did Tuck talk about fate, aspiration, ambitions, personality, enemies, truth, friends, character, fortune, and last of all ancestry to Charlie in his circumstance that he had with the farmers of Oglethorpe County? Oh! What theocracy that is blended with hypocrisy!

In the next section is the family of Mr. Henry C. Tuck living in Oglethorpe County. How did they get word Charlie was dead? Or did they all have a hand in his death on October 17, 1899?

The late Judge Henry Carlton Tuck, son of Robert and Louisa O'Kelley Tuck, was born in Buck Branch District, Clarke County, Georgia, on February 12, 1864, the youngest of ten children. In his early childhood, the family moved to Puryear's District of Clarke County, where his boyhood was spent. Judge Tuck received his early education in the old-field schools of the county with a year's tutoring by the Rev. T.A. Harris in preparation for his entrance examinations to the University of Georgia in the fall of 1877. Four years later, July 20, 1881, at the age of seventeen years and five months, he received from the university his AB with first honors. The following July (1882) he was awarded a BL degree, after which he began in Athens the practice of law, which was to continue until his death more than fifty-seven years later. In his early career, Judge Tuck was elected to the legislature of Georgia from Clarke County. Some years later, he became mayor of the City of Athens. The last twelve years of his life, he served as judge of the City Court of Athens, and a few weeks before his death he was elected for another term of six years.

For more than a quarter of a century, he was a teacher in the Sunday school of the First Methodist Church of a men's Bible class, which today bears his name. This class had a membership of about two hundred and throughout the years has been outstanding, both in personnel and accomplishment. Dr. N.G. Slaughter, in a recent history of the class, says that Judge Tuck was a teacher "of distinction and honor" and considered this work the crowning achievement of his life. His death occurred on December 17, 1939, at the age of seventy-five years and nine months, and he was buried in Oconee Hill Cemetery, Athens.

I do not know what happened to my great-grandfather, but I am going to mention the men that were in his class. In 1910, Judge Tuck's class was organized with F.B. Hinton, president; J. W. Eberhart, secretary and treasurer; with the addition of E.R. Harris, vice president. The organization is the same today. The class got off to a slow beginning, and it was 1913 before it began to function right. Forty persons were members of the class in 1913. The roll now includes one hundred names. Professor E.C. Westbrook of the Georgia State College of Agriculture is the oldest member of the class (not the oldest man). The name Smith, which is popular for its being common, is tied in the class by Dunaway, each appearing five times on the roll. Nineteen letters of the alphabet are represented here. Members have died. Others have left town. Still the class continues to function. Although some of the men leave the city, they continue to correspond with the class, and when in town, to visit the Sunday school. Two weeks ago, Henry M. Bacon of Virginia, who lived here several years ago, visited the class.

The Teacher

Judge Tuck is serving his second term as judge of the city court. When he was twenty-four years of age, he was a member of the Georgia legislature. When only twenty-seven years old, he was mayor of Athens. Colonel Tuck has never been defeated for a political office. He has been an Athens attorney for fifty years, etc.

Now let us look at some of the correspondence between Mr. Richard B. Russell and Mr. H.C. Tuck.

State of Georgia

House of Representatives Atlanta, Nov. 11, 1882

R.B. Russell Room 193 Kimball House Atlanta Ga.

Mr. H.C. Tuck

Athens, Ga.

Dear Henry,

Your favor of Nov. 10th was received this morning, for which I am much obliged. I have been as you may imagine quite busy since my arrival here. It is enough to keep a new man busy just to keep up with the new of business. A new man has no idea how much is to be learned until he comes and sees. I now see well how an old member can be so much more efficient than a green one. But do not misunderstand me when I say an old member. I do not mean an old man for this is the day of young men in Georgia politics. They do all the work of legislation and the old men vote. The recognition I have received at the hands of the speaker has been very flattering. I am placed on the special Judiciary, Education, Wild Lands (2nd on this committee), Privileges of the floor and Rules Committees. The Committee on Rules, which is the smallest and most important committee of the house, is composed of only five members, the Speaker (Garrard) as Chairman, Talligant of Chatham, Maddox of Chattooga, Rankin the Speaker Pro Tem of the House and Russell of Clarke. You bet I feel proud of that. I am on more committees than any other member except Maddox of Chattooga who is on six committees.

I was at "the meeting gorgeous and gay" called the Inaugural Ball, as you may have seen by the Constitution. The only bill I have introduced so far is one for the benefit of farmers. It is to punish as a misdemeanor, any violation of yearly labor contracts. You know it is very frequently the case that a man hires a hand and after furnishing him with $50.00 or $60.00 worth of necessaries the Negro gets dissatisfied and can go off and hire himself to his very next-door neighbor and the only redress the farmer has is to sue the person employing his hands for damages. In nine cases out of ten the judgment he gets is not worth a nickel. I wish you could have been here to witness the inauguration of Gov. A.H. Stephens. The De Give's Opera House was packed from pit to the second gallery until there was no standing room. When almost every prominent man in the state had taken his stand on the stage and the band began to play "Dixie," the little roller-chair rolled slowly forward amid loudest applause I ever heard. The whole building shook. Men, women and children stood up and cheered. The old man looked serene. His speech was not much after he got halfway through because he seemed to get confused but the first half brought down the house and don't you forget it. On account of Old Alex's past more than his present I shall always be proud that I was in the legislature that inaugurated him as governor of Georgia.

I have been to see him twice and he seems to like me first-rate and I am going to try to be "a power behind the throne." In regard to the papers of Jos. Jacobs. I will be at home on next Wednesday when I will see you about then.

I have written more than I expected to, so I expect it is about time to stop. Henry, I want you to write me at length in regard to Athens the state of public feeling and any expressions you may have heard in regard to me. I am always glad to hear from you.

I am as ever, your sincere friend

R.B. Russell

In the Athens newspaper about this same time there was an article that mentioned this same bill that was introduced by Mr. Richard B. Russell. Is it just a coincidence that this article appears the same time as this bill is trying to be passed or is Tuck behind the article while in Clarke County? What happened to my great-grandfather Charlie?

Now as you may know by now the court case that was to be held October 17, 1899, dealing with Eberhart in Oglethorpe County and the hands that worked for him, the witness Charlie Callaway was now dead and could not appear! And at the same time there was an uproar on J.C. Hudgins's place on October 17, 1899, with one of his convicts.

It was also stated in the Elberton newspaper that one of J.C. Hudgins's convicts took flight and could not be captured even after the hounds were set upon him in the same year. In one paper in Clarke County it was stated that at Christmas J. C. Hudgins set free his convicts.

I found this indenture in the papers of H.C. Tuck, and it was the only thing that pertained to the year of 1899!

> This indenture made this 20th day of October in the year of our Lord one thousand eight hundred and ninety-nine (1899) between George B. Conwell of the County of Wilkes of said state of the one part and Mrs. Sallie Conwell of the same place of the other part witnesseth that the said George B. Conwell for and in consideration of the sum of one thousand three hundred and twenty-nine & 50/00 Dollars ($1329.50) in hand paid at and before the sealing and delivery of these presents the receipt whereof is hereby acknowledged has granted, bargained, sold aligned, conveyed and confirmed and by these presents does grant . . . sell unto the said Mrs. Sallie V. Conwell, her heirs and assignees all that tract or parcel of land

> situated, lying and being in the County of Franklin said state containing one hundred acres more or less, joining lands of H.L. McCrary and R.L. Cauthen on the east; J.D. Veal on the west and lands of Shug Phillips on south and on the north by public road leading from Carnsville to Royston and known as the Franklin Springs place. The Mineral Springs Cattyes dwelling . . . being located on the same said trust made up of ten (10) acres conveyed by Jas. A. Royston and M. M. Royston admin. of W.A. Royston deed to J.B. Cornwell by deed dated Nov. 11, 1896 . . .

I must mention the fact that Francis Callaway lived in Franklin County at one time and I wonder does this and only this one deed have anything to do with Charlie being relocated during his trial in 1899.

July 14, 1899, Richard B. Russell wrote this letter to Henry C. Tuck.

Winder, July 14, 1899

Hon. H.C. Tuck

Athens, Ga.

Dear Henry,

I sent you by express today the papers in the case T.P. Vincent Adm & C. vs. I.V. Murray et al. with my decision thereon. Please see that they reach the clerk at once. I sent them to you because I knew you would want to know the decision but the other side the law requires me to notify and they may want the papers to except——

Yours Sincerely

Rich D. B. Russell

This is another piece of information in the papers of the Men's Sunday School teacher at the First Methodist Church in Athens, Clarke County. *However, before you read the letter he wrote. I want to mention this fact. Wherever you see the Methodist church you see the KKK. Do they think that we are oblivious to the fact that the liquor trade is aligned with both institutions, the church and the KKK? What a contradiction to the very thing the clan portrayed to these entire United States.*

Whiskey, Temperance, Prohibition

Whiskey like Strychnine (spelled Strichinine) is a medicine when used in appreciable doses, both are poison. Whiskey, though, is used more as a beverage, when no one would dare use Strychnine as a beverage. All spirituous or malt liquors, wine, or cider contain alcohol, a deadly poison, though in smaller percentage than pure alcohol. No one would think of using alcohol without diluting it. Whiskey or anything containing any percentage of alcohol, used by anyone as a beverage, is one of the greatest curses to mankind and the most powerful tool the devil has, awful to think of. Anyone who uses whiskey or any alcoholic stimulants as a beverage can and will be led to do anything immoral and wrong. Sin is nothing but doing wrong and wrong is anything, but what is right. No need of mentioning here the many things wrong that we human beings are prone to do. All who have attained the age of accountability know right from wrong. Were it not for our blessed Savior, Jesus Christ, ever ready to forgive our wrongdoings we would be in an awful situation, though we should not try the patience of good in continuous wrongdoings. Not under the influence of alcoholic stimulants people will and do abstain from many wrongdoings. The use of alcoholic stimulants affects the brain, heart, kidneys, and other vital organs. Continuous use of it even for a short while, a person will acquire an appetite for it, which seems to them impossible to quit the use of it. It becomes a disease with many. A good man took to drink. Thought at first he could control his appetite, instead it got the best of him. Like many others he drifted to poverty, his family to want and suffering. This man had a sweet little girl that he loved beyond expression. When all others deserted or shunned and gave him up as hopeless, this little child would go out after him at nights. It mattered not what kind of weather, she would bring him home from the saloon. At last this faithful little one, from exposure, sickened with pneumonia, was desperately ill for several days, though as long as conscious pleaded with her father not to drink any more whiskey, made a proposition and obtained a promise from her father that the next drink

> of whiskey he took would be from her hand. The little angel died with the hopes that her father would keep that promise by not taking another drink. He did as long as his child lived. The father was greatly grieved and distressed on account of the death of his child, but the appetite being so strong, he was unable to resist. He placed a glass of whiskey in the hand of his dead child, held it with his hand, and drank the whiskey.

This was told as a true story by a temperance lecturer in a lecture delivered at Athens, Georgia, some years ago. Many, many cases of this kind with truthfulness could be mentioned. He goes on to quote from Proverbs 1:1; 20:1; 23:2, 21, 29, 30, 31, and 32; Acts 24 and 25; 1 Cor. 9:25; Titus 1:7, 8:2, 3, 4.

> I am mostly interested in the societies dealing with temperance. Some years ago we had temperance societies, such as Sons of Temperance and Knights of Jericho. These were temporary pledges, binding while a member, but did a lot of good. In Athens, Georgia, there were two brothers, Bill and Bob Williams. They were good men, brick and rock masons. They ran a brickyard and made a lot of money. They took to drink, spent and wasted their money as fast as they got it. These two men were induced to join the Knights of Jericho. They took the pledge and soon built themselves up financially. There were temperance lectures at which many were induced to sign temperance pledges, then individuals by kind treatment got temperance pledges signed. There was another temperance society, the Independent Order of Good Templars, which had a lifetime pledge, as follows: Never to use, make, buy, sell, furnish or cause to be furnished to others as a beverage, any spirituous of malt liquors wine or cider and that in every honorable way discountenance the use of them in the community in which they resided. This society was composed of male and female, many took that pledge, many kept their pledge, no way of estimating the good that society did. In the year 1882, ye writer took this pledge, afterwards took may other obligations

in different fraternal orders, none of which is prized more than this lifetime temperance pledge, was in public office, connected with the courts for about twenty years, went though many elections, last office filled ten years up to 1901, have kept this pledge to date. I am now over seventy-six years of age, born in April 3, 1856. Some years ago there were prayers in churches and homes for temperance. O! How the victims to strong drink need the prayers of the good people and their counsel, which is the only way to get rid of whiskey as a beverage.

This is written by one who knows whereof he speaks, from actual experience and observation. He drank and dissipated heavily for four years, between the age of seventeen and twenty-one years. O! If those four years could be blotted out of remembrance.

What is prohibition? It is being butchered so that it is hard to tell just what it is. After all, it is simply a law on our statue books being violated just as well as any law. This is said with all due respect to those who claim that the prohibition laws are not being enforced.

Prohibition is intended to aid temperance and aid the victim to strong drink by making whiskey harder to get as beverage legally. It is doing this to a certain extent; and if we the citizens will do our duty by aiding, assisting, supporting and backing up the officers and prohibition agents in the enforcement of prohibition laws and all Laws which it is our sacred duty as true American citizens to support the constitution and laws of our government, then beyond any doubt the prohibition laws will have the effect and accomplish the purpose for which they were enacted, and not without the co-operation of we citizens will alcoholic beverages ever be under any more control than it now is. Some say yes that is true but can it be done? The answer to that is, nothing impossible with God. With His help this can be accomplished and not otherwise, to put over any moral question as important as this we will accomplish more by taking God as our partner.

Prohibition was brought about by temperance lectures, temperance societies, prayers in churches and homes;

in other words, communion with God. First by local option acts for different counties (spelled countys), then State wide acts, then Nationwide the 18th Amendment and many laws based upon this amendment. The Drys temperance lectures, temperance societies, prayers in churches and our homes, when then in fact, with the adoption of the 18th Amendment our work really had just begun. It is an evident fact the wets have never let up, have been and are still working, have succeeded in getting this great moral question into politics where it should never have entered, it being absolutely and strictly non-partisan. Whiskey can never be controlled through political measures or politicians, the only way that whiskey will ever be controlled as a beverage, is by moral suasion, educate the people to quit using whiskey of course the laws based on the 18th Amendment is a great aid, but let's try to keep out of the courts by doing our duty in supporting the laws. After all the person who uses whiskey as a beverage is the sole cause of it being manufactured and sold illegally. A good physician when called will first try to find the cause of the sickness before he can successfully treat the patient, unless we can remedy the cause no need of worrying about the 18th Amendment or complaining that the officers are not enforcing the laws, which they are enforcing the best they can and with our co-operation can do it better. No officer, no nation will ever accomplish anything without the co-operation of the people and that with God's help.

The wets say that there is more whiskey manufactured sold and drank than when we had open bar rooks, this is a great mistake. They ask for the repeal of the 18th Amendment. Why not ask for repeal of the Ten Commandments and other laws, all are being violated as well as the prohibition laws. They advocate compromise, light wine and beer, also advocate government control of whiskey, both compromise and government control has been tried and when we had open bar rooks than under present prohibition laws. The following is a clipping from a newspaper recently: "More illegal stills ran 40 years ago, Macon clerk says; Macon, Georgia, Sept. 29. Observing Tuesday the forty-second anniversary of his connection with the United States Government, George F. White, district clerk here, recalls the early '90s 'when there were more whiskey distilleries operated illegally than now, and we got forty-one in a single raid.'"

Mr. White was deputy United States marshal at the time, and Fred D. Dismuke Sr., father of the present deputy prohibition administrator, was deputy collector of internal revenue in this section of Georgia. In these days, Mr. White said, a whiskey distiller was required to register and pay the government a license fee of $1.10 for manufacturing the liquor. To sell it, a $.25 special license was charged annually. To avoid payment of the $1.10 per gallon to the government, hundreds manufactured it illegally—without registration—and subjected themselves to jail sentence if apprehended. Many more revenue officers were killed in the mountains of North Georgia and Western North Carolina then than now.

Compromise has been tried. Some years ago, on account of it being thought that whiskey was necessary as a medicine, Clarke County, Georgia, had a local option act passed allowing a practicing physician to prescribe whiskey and druggists could sell it under such prescription. At Athens, the county site, Dr. E.S. Lynden, a practicing physician and druggist, put in a stock of liquors and just sat and wrote prescriptions for a while, then had blanks printed. In a little while Palmer & Kinnebrew and Lowery and Rush opened two more similar drugstores and we had three very large bar rooms in operation, until we could get that act repealed. Government control has been tried in Georgia, North Carolina, and South Carolina, and failed to accomplish purpose intended.

At Athens, Georgia, we established a dispensary for the sale of whiskey under government control, had one big bar room. Pink Welch brought the Athens dispensary plan to Waynesville, North Carolina. We had one big bar room at Waynesville, North Carolina. At same time, there were dispensaries, operated under a little different plan South Carolina don't know how many. All during open bar rooms and dispensary operation there was any amount of whiskey manufactured and sold illegally, by bootleggers, then called blind tigers and blockaders. Wets advocate light wine and beer and say they are not in favor of bar rooms, when if it should be sold there certainly will have to be some place to dispense it. Matters not what that place may be called, it will be nothing more than a bar room or saloon, light wine and beer will not satisfy the appetite for strong drink, will only whet up the appetite. The name bar room is detestable. No wonder the name is objectionable, no one has been able to figure out how it got the name. "The Bar-He who named it named it well; a bar to hope a door to hell." There are now two organizations working for temperance: the Anti-Saloon League and National Woman's Christians Temperance Union. We will do well to give these organizations our Support. Following is clipping form Asheville paper recently: "No compromise on prohibition, says Sheppard, Washington, D.C., Jan. 16. Mrs. Ella A. Boole, president of the National Woman's Christians Temperance Union, told the Anti-Saloon League delegate tonight that jobs not beer were what men need and want. And that bread not beer is what women want. As a general program, she proposed: election of dry president and vice president on a dry platform. Support for dry congressmen and senators, governors and legislators, judges who obey the law themselves and deal out adequate penalties to convicted violators of the prohibition laws. In fact we need a campaign of education on law observance, promoted by the government as the liberty bonds were promoted. She said, 'We need the support of patriotic citizens rallying to constitutional government. Thus will we give prohibitionists chance.' Suggestions to legalize beer to aid finances was born of a desire for beer rather than a desire to solve the financial problem, Wets have forced us into politics, all should vote as they think right. Mrs. Boole's suggestions are for the best interest of our nation.

Wets make a to-do over the loss of the revenue that license to sell whiskey would bring to the government, do not seem to take into consideration the great harm the legalized sale of intoxicants will bring to victims of strong drink, their families and loved ones; the loss of one soul will over-balance all the revenue received for license, when chances are that many souls will be lost, they do not seem to think of the great expense and time wasted in taking the time of Congress and senate trying to repeal the 18th Amendment.

This is written by on who knows whereof he speaks from actual experience and observation, is written for the purpose of trying to save some victim of strong drink and for the best interest of our nation.

Respectfully and prayerfully

Joseph Keys Kenney

This is a letter to Mr. Henry C. Tuck from Mr. Joseph Keys Kenney in repealing the Eighteenth Amendment. I don't know how this letter affected Tuck; however, I do know Tuck and Russell defended a lot of Blind Tigers as attorneys in the beginning of practicing law in the State of Georgia! Especially in this section of Georgia, where even the last lynching occurred in Walton County not far from Oconee County, Georgia, and on and near Highway 78. The other thing that helps me establish this conclusion about this section of Georgia and the liquor trade and the KKK is that I only found the liquor ledgers in Barrow County, Oglethorpe County, and Greene County. Greene County is where the first boasting of the character of the McWhorters and others in the 1870s as running out the carpetbaggers out of Georgia and the letter that they wrote about what they are going to do about the Negro problem to the state government by appealing to the Governor of Georgia. I have read and seen with my own two eyes the lies and deception the two entities the KKK and the government at the city, state and federal level conspired to commit murder and manufacture liquor in high quantities to sell and to get rich by using the Negro to make them do their will. I have not only seen it I have experienced it as well.

Chapter Seven

Richard Callaway or Dick and Emily Hurt Callaway

The year is 1870 in Oglethorpe County, Georgia, Dick is fourteen years old and is in the house of Mr. Bart Callaway, a fifty-five-year-old man and his wife Ellen, who is forty. Adaline is ten, Fannie is five, and Phronia is four. James Callaway is thirty years old and his wife Jane is thirty and Ike is eleven. Amos is five, James is four, and Rose is one. One other family that I am very much interested in is the family of Mr. Dock Phillips, a fifty-five-year-old, and his wife Cresie, forty-five. John is seventeen, Coleman is sixteen, Jarred is fourteen, Fannie is twelve, Cora is eight, and Phil is six, and Austin is four. Bart or Bartley Callaway was born in 1815 and died between 1870 and 1880

Over in Greene County, Penfield, Georgia, George Boswell is the enumerator. I found Mr. Griffin Hurt, a sixty-year-old and his wife Mahala, a forty-five-year-old. Susan, their daughter, is twenty-one. Peter is seventeen, Leroy is fifteen, Emily is thirteen, and Daphny is eleven. They are all living near Mr. Enoch Cheney's place with Mose Cheney near Bairdstown and Woodville. About this same time in Oglethorpe County, Georgia J. H. Brightwell recorded on the mortality records that Bartow Calloway was a year old when he died in June on G W. Callaway's place.

In 1870, on the twenty-third of July J. H. Brightwell, the marshal of Oglethorpe County, recorded Richard Callaway as being twenty-two years old. His wife Pink is eighteen and another sixteen-year-old female named Sidney. The only other Calloway family living nearby is Steven's, a forty-year-old. Ellen is thirty, Marian is twelve, Jett is ten, Eliza is six, Susie is four, William is two. The only other family that I think is close to him would be the Willingham family. Warner Willingham is sixty-three, Silvia is forty-six, Presely is sixteen, Andrew is thirteen, Harrison is nine, Columbus is four, Cicero is one, and a Susan Hancock is seventy years old and from Virginia. Also in the house is eighty-two-year-old Dinah Shackelford. *Even though Brightwell does not state the district that Richard is in at this time, I can say by the people that he is living near and the tax digest that he is near Maxey and Bairdstown in Oglethorpe County. I had a hard time trying to figure out Richard Callaway in Henry County, who died in Tennessee, and Richard Callaway in Bowling Green and here Henry Callaway is in the house with his father Bart in 1870 under the first name of Dick*

In 1880, I found Dick Calloway living in Bairdstown in Oglethorpe County. Dick was twenty-two years old and Lily his wife was twenty-five as well. Daniel Brisco is a fifteen-year-old colored servant. I believe that Daniel Brisco is working for Mr. J. D. Solomon or Salmon. Sucky Johnson is forty-year-old female farm laborer living with twenty-four-year-old Susan and her twenty-year-old son named Samuel. Young C. E. Kinnebrew is twenty years old and his sister Lillian is fifteen. While Daniel Brisco was in the house with Dick and Lily Callaway, twelve-year-old Ida Brisco was in the house with a white farmer, Henry Cheney, and his wife Mattie and their family.

In the year 1880, Mrs. C. B. Callaway was sixty-five years old and Bartow was now sixty years old and Ellen was forty. Fannie is now eleven, Puss is eight, Johnathan is five, and Ossie is three, and Emmily Ann is seven months old. Matt Callaway is in the next house. He is fifty-five, and his wife Nancy is fifty. Daniel, their grandson, is seven. Susan is twenty, Abbie is eighteen, and Brooks, their granddaughter, is one. John Henry, their grandson, is six months old. They are on G. W. Callaway's place right next door to John Simms and his wife Mattie and Mr. C. C. Olive.

In the June of 1900, in Oglethorpe County in Bowling Green District, was Richard Calloway, born in August of 1854 and now forty-five. Emily was born May of 1859 and was forty-one years old. Their oldest son Nathan was born April of 1889 and was eleven. Mahalie was born January of 1894 and was six. Frank was born December of 1897 ad was two, and John D. was born May 1900 and was eight months old. George Simms was a grandson born March 1897 and was two years old.

In the year 1910, Richard is fifty-three years old and Emily is fifty-one. Mahaley is fifteen, Johnson is ten, grandson George is eleven. Bob, a grandson, is eight, and grandson William is six.

Coloreds, 137th District

Employer: J.H. Bowles

Freedmen: Toney Haynes, Henry Haynes, Toney Parham, Ned Parks

At home: Albert Parks, agent for Ned Parks's estate, 160 acres in District 137, valued after deducting $200, $520; aggregate value of property $720 (Albert Parks is the only colored owning any property in the 137th District)

138th District COLOREDS

Employer: J.R. Boswell

Freedmen: Jerry Jennings, Moses Haynes, Aaron Janes

Employer: James Davison

Freedmen: James Daniel, David Tugler, Bill Wilborn, Jack Lunsford, Jerry Smith, Albert Davison, Harry Subbs, Stevan Murden, Cane Malone, Jack Barrow, Handy Barrow, Peter Barrow, Jerry McWhorter, Richard Daniel, Joseph Daniel, Alfred Haley, Columbus Park, Jordan Royden, Reuben Lunsford

Employer: Enoch Cheney

Freedmen: Moses Cheney, John Hart, Henry White

140th District

Employer: Ga. R. Roads with Houters

Freedmen: Allen Parham, Columbus Hurt, Joe Carlton, Dolphias Phelps, Henry Kimbrough, Henry Briscoe, Dolphos Burley, Tom Harris, Albert Mitchell, Dovy Ellen, George Rhoads, Craford Peek, Esquire Hurt

145th District

Employer: J.W. T. Cotchens

Freedmen: Charles Terrell, Peter Swenney, Harrison Cobb, Green Charleston, Perry Kuntright, Marshall Terrell, Jordan Swenney, James Lee Swenney, Cornelius Swenney

Employer: W.H. Crawford

Freedmen: Elijah Anderson, Shed McWhorter, James Terrell

Employer: F.M. Loverett

Freedmen: Cook Laborn, David Laborn, Wilson Wheley, Frank Swinney, William Callaway, Jon Robinson, Shandy Jerrell, Robt, Speers, John Speers, Peter Perkins, Ransom Edwards

147th District COLOREDS

Employer: Zack Freeman

Freedmen: Aaron Callaway

Employer: Thos Fambrough

Freedmen: Thos. Watson, Frank Barnett, Ferdenos Barnett, Milton Fambrough, Ben Bugg, Dick Smith

Employer: Clayton Johnson

Freedmen: Berry Mitchell

Employer: Hurt Plantation

Freedmen: Young Partee

Employer: Wm. Wilham Plantation

Freedmen: Peter Hurt

Employer: Thos. P. Janes

Freedmen: George Barrow, Perry Barrow, Ben Barrow, Henry Gresham, Bill Freeman

Employer: John E. Jackson Sr.

Freedmen: Booker Watson, Albert Oliver, Amos Poulian

Employer: Augustus Brightwell

Freedmen: Cambrige Bugg, Samuel Gilham, Booker Bugg

Employer: L.M. Maxey,

Freedmen: Mark Williams

Employer: Barnett Moore

Freedmen: Hixan Daniel

Employer: W.A. Partee

Freedmen: Henry Christopher

Employer: James Watson

Freedmen: Booker Watson, Sampson Jackson

Employer: W.A. Wilson

Freedmen: Arn Gresham

Coloreds in 1872

138th District

Working on Owens Cheney's plantation are Sam Johnson with Oliver Jordan and Alfred Swann. E.R. Cheney has Henry White and Moses Cheney at his place.

James Davison has Bob Edmonson, Albert Davison, Joe Daniel, Jerry McWhorter, and others.

In the 137th District Albert Parks has the estate of Ned Parks 160 acres still. *Remember Ned Parks is off the plantation of Isaac Callaway in 1820. He eventually became the property of Mr. Robert Parks, who hired a Negro woman named Nelly and two children, Ned and Mahala. Robert Parks is and has been a free colored in Greene County for he was once the property of Joseph Callaway or Jacob Callaway, then they ended up in the estate of Isaac Callaway and Winifred Callaway. Robert Parks ended up living in or having property in Coweta County.*

I believe that young Ned Parks is working on the place of H.J. Bowles. There are no Hurts listed in this section of Greene County. Esquire Hurt is living in Union Point in the 140th District with Albert Hurt. In the 138th District, I found Henson Callaway working with Jerry Jennings and Tom Brown, Lem Janes, Aaron Jones, Ned Parks, and Moses Haynes on the property of J.R. Boswell. In the 142nd District, on the property of C.C. Oliver, I found Richard Hurt with John Gunnell and William Irwin. In the 143rd District, I found Alfred Lester, John Irwin, Essix Maddox, Sol Norris, Bob Craddock, Frank Terrell, Tom Red, Eldrege Red, Green Barnett, Freeman Colesby, William Barnett, Stehpen Bonner, Augustus Barnett, Lewis Brown, and Andrew Park. In the 146th District, I found Lindsey Hurt working for Dr. Gresham with Lewis Maxey. In the 147th District, I found Columbus Hurt working with Berry Mitchell, Dick Smith, Ben Butler, Thos Watson, and Sterlin Poulain on Thos Fambrough. And Zack Freeman had George Barnett and Bob Maxey on his place. No Aaron Callaway anywhere.

In the 148th District, Terrell Blocker and Charles Champion were on J.D. Champion's place. Isaac English with J.H. English, and Daniel English was at William English's place with Young Geer. Jesse Callaway and George Lawrence and Marshal Daniel had their own place.

1873, Greene County Coloreds

138th District

John R. Boswell has Jerry B. Jennings, Thos. Borrow, Aaron Janes, Ned Parks, Jefferson Harris, Lem Janes, Mosses Haynes, and Henderson Callaway on his land. Nat English is on the land of T.C. Carlton. Moses Cheney, Moses Martin, and Peter Chivers are on E.R. Cheney's place and living on James Davison's place is Albert Davison, Lumm Park, Cane Malone, Berry Lankston, Alfred Haley, Young Partee, Lewis Hurt, Elijah Hurt, Andrew Bryan, Dock Daniel, Henry Watson, Reuben Lunsford, and Adron Partee. Living on James Edmonson's place is James Edmondson and Lewis Edmondson. Living on T.J. Malone's place is Moses Finch.

1874, 137th District Coloreds

Albert Parks is still over at the estate of Ned Parks and Bob Watson has his own place. Adam Hurt is working for James Davison, and so is Hack Willingham. Whit Willingham is at the Reed and Daniel place. In the tax digest, I could not find Richard Callaway; however, I did find Dick Callaway in the town of Bairdstown in the 232th District on J. L. Wilson's place with Nathan Burham and Biill Bunkley. He had very interesting company in Bairdstown at this time. Bob Callaway was at T. L. Epps's place. Jim Callaway was at J. H. McWhorter's place. Abe English was at T. L. Hurt's place and white landowner Jasper Haynes had Nathan Armstrong and Frank Armstrong at his place. Now, this puts Robert (Bob) Callaway and Richard (Dick) Callaway and James (Jim) Callaway in the same place as the Hurts in the 1870s.

Also, while in Bairdstown, Dick Callaway stayed on W. H. Cheney's place, while Gus English was at W. Bryant's place and Abe English was at J. L. Hurt's place. P. M. Stephens had John Hardeman at his place. By 1880, in Bairdstown, Abe is located on the place of Mr. Hurt in Maxey. And this is while Gus English is still on Mr. Bryant's place. Dick Callaway is on W.H. Cheney's place in Bairdstown. R. M. Callaway comes on the scene in Bairdstown, Georgia. Dick will remain on W. H. Cheney's place the next year with Ben Anthony.

While in Bowling Greene, Dick Callaway was at G. W. Callaway's place with William Striplin and Lee Arnold. By the time that Major had changed his last name to Statem in the tax digest, he was on Mr. Smith's place in Bowling Green, Georgia with John Johnson and Dick Callaway. Burt or (Bert) was on G. W. Callaway's place with Andrew Stevens. Also at Smith's place was Bob Hunter, Bill Dalton, and John Wealer (Wheeler).

1875, Greene County, Georgia, Coloreds

Albert Parks still has his estate. Whit Willingham is in the 138th District on the property of James K. Daniel. Columbus Parks is on the place of Jas. Davison. Hock Willingham is on the place of Joseph Davison with Jeff Harris, and C.C. Davison has Meat Edmonson. Neal Hurt is on the place of John R. Young with William Nelson, Charles Ware, and Bob Veazy. J.L. Young has Jim Neeson and Clark Harris on his place.

E.R. Cheney has on his place Moses Cheney, Peter Chivers, Sam Geer, Smith Craddock, Anderson Potts, To Pain, Oliver Jordan, Alfred Swain, and Jerry Craddock. *One name that is working on the plantation of E. R. Cheney is Mr. Peter Chivers. His last name solidifies the fact that W. O. Cheney, his father, was kin to the Chiverses that were living in Buckhead in Fulton County. This would show that Aaron more than likely made his way to Fulton County not far from DeKalb County to work for Mr. W. O. Cheney. The Chivers are the family that Mercier married into a Jewish heritage.*

In the 140th District, Albert Callaway is on the place of J.Y. Cox with James Lonsford, Isaac Mapp, and Wm. Wrisby. Albert Hurt is in Union Point on his own place. *I was confused to find Albert Callaway living in Union Point at this time so early. I found him in Atlanta and now here in Greene County in 1875.*

In the 147th District, Aaron Callaway is working with George Barnett on the place of Z. Freeman. T.M. Fambrough has Henry Smith, Sandy Moody, Bardon Barnett, Booker Bugg, Richard Smith, and Proffit Cammil at his place. Kit Mitchell has 200 acres of land and living with her is Lee Mitchell, Rubin, Mitchell, Sam Mitchell, and Berry Mitchell. Jessie Callaway and Jack Wright and Austin Daniel are at Penfield, Jesse has 55 acres of land.

In the 148th District, at Penfield, Sherrick Thomas and Henry Thomas and Columbus Hurt and Henry Hurt and Dock Finley are on their own land.

Coloreds, 1876, District 137

At home was Albert Parks on his 160-acre farm valued at $800 and is the only colored in this section with land.

In the 138th District, William R. Mullins has Harry Daniel on his place. Enoch R. Cheney had Moses Cheney, Tom Pain, Anderson Potts, Peter Spivers, Columbus Strozier, and Smith Craddock on his land. William T. Burlons has Hansfield Butler on his land. Cane Malone is on Chas. C. Davison's place, and Henry Moss has Dock Hoppy, John Hunter, and Mack Willingham on his land. Cullin Caldwell has Joe Jones at his place. Fannie and Lizzie Moore have Frank Aycock, Booker Bugg, Daniel Hixon, and Phil Griffeth on their land. George A. or H. Arthur has James

Callaway on his land, and James L. Young has Griffin Hurt, Jim Mason, and Lee Chivers on his land. Moody & Durham has Alex Adkin and Arch Agee on their land. William Mitchell has Peter Reed, Joseph Peek, and Thomas Lawrence on his land, John D. Beall has James Asbury at his place. James F. Geer has George Geer on his land. Charles Haley, a colored man, is on his own property. Joseph Davison has Moses Armstrong on his land. William B. Guill has Henry Daniel at his place. William Vibbert has Marshall Dandil, Spark Bowles, William Pinion, and Henry Geer on his place. Robert E. Davison has Mat Edmonson, Wash Broughton, Lewis Hurt, and Aaron Partee.

In the 147th District, Zachariah Freeman had Aaron Callaway on his property and Aaron had 75 acres of land valued at $225 dollars. Also on the same land was George Barnett, who owned 20 acres of land valued at $60. Robert Neel was on the same land without any property. Arthur Fambrough does not live in the 147th District but he has 300 acres of land valued at $1,500. Living nearby are Igge Fambrough and Middleton Fambrough. It is the same with Kit Mitchell, who has 200 acres of land valued at $1,800. Living nearby is Reubin Mitchell and Sam Mitchell and Berry Mitchell.

In the 148th District, Jesse Callaway has only 58 acres, Katie Barnett has 100 acres, Tom Watson has 50 acres, George Sanders has 10 acres, Henry Armstrong has 30 acres, Put McWhorter has 140 acres, Columbus Hurt has 50 acres. In the 160th District, Issac Jones is living on 404 acres of land and is the only colored man in the district with land. In the 161st District Mr. Joe Malery has 250 acres of land and Henry Malery has 30 acres of land, Washington Hall has 132 acres of land, and Frank Hall has 20 acres of land. In the 162nd District, Richard Jackson has 5 acres of land. In the 163rd District, Jack Heard has 49 acres, Jerry King has 15 acres, Sam Davis has 40 acres, Wash Rowlan has 150 acres, Richmon F. and Johnson has 130 acres of land.

1877 Coloreds, 137th District

Albert Parks is on his 160 acres of land located between M.J. Reynolds's place and W.L. Tuggle's land in 1876. He was listed before you got to James M. Griffin's place and Woodfin's place.

In the 138th District, George English is on J.H. English's place. Nat English is on G. English's place. Lewis Hurt is on R.E. Davison's place with George Billingslea and Charles Ware. Hal Hurt is on J.R. Young's place with William Neeson, Jim Neeson, Grif Hurt, and Peter Chivers. Wash Broughton is on C.C. Davison's place with Matt Edmonson and

Cain Malone. Henry Geer is on F.T. Ham's place. Mose Armstrong is on Joseph Davison's place. J.R. Wilson has Bery Lumpkin, Mose Lumpkin, George Veazey, Dick Callahan, and Henry Wilson on his place. G.A. Arthur has James Callaway on his place and Hinson Callaway is on J.R. Boswell's with Abraham Janes, Howard Harris, Mose Hanes Sr. and Mose Hanes Jr., George Geer, and Snap Martin.

1878 Coloreds, 137th District

Albert Parks is at home between Pippin Needham and T.D. Wilson and above Wm. L. Tuggle, and Daniel and Reed's place, and below Pippin Needham and Jas. M. Griffin and W.G. Wright and J.V. Durham. And John H. Bowles and Wm. C. Williams. P.A. Fluker, Daniel William, and William G. Woodfin.

In the 138th District, J.L. Young has Griffin Hurt, Bill Greene, Warner Neeson on his place. Hal Hurt is on the property of Wm. J. Newsom.

In the 140th District, Anthony Hurt and Albert Hurt are both in Union Point, Squire Hurt as well.

For the first time in the 147th District, called Fontenoy Mills, Burrell Callaway is working with his father Aaron on the Fambrough place with Dick Smith, Ned Landrum, General Poullian, Joe Clarke, Aaron Fambrough, and Charles Brawner. Living at home in this district was Tom Watson with 45 acres; Frank Barnett with 198 acres; Sterling Poullian, agent for Delia Poullian, with 10 acres; Arthur Fambrough with 240 acres; and Aaron Callaway, who has acreage but it is not listed. Mit Mitchell has 200 acres, Dick Hurt has acreage but is not listed, Frank Aycock has acreage but is not listed. Sam Stovall has acreage but it's not listed. Bob Maxey has property but it's not listed, Elbert Oliver has property not listed, George Gresham as well has property but it is not listed, Harry Durham has property but is not listed.

1879 Coloreds, 137th District

Albert Park has the same amount of land between Pippin Needham and James M. Griffin John H. Bowles is below him and William D. West is above him.

In the 138th District, Lewis Hurt is working for Mr. C. Cox or Cose. Jeff Hurt has showed up and is on the land of S. Brook with Bue McWhorter.

In the 147th District, Jut Hurt is with Doe Hurt and Mut Colclough on W. Colclough's place in Maxey. These are the colored Fambroughs: Albert, Howard, Arthur Milton, Martin, John, Frank, and Felix. Henry Hurt is on Jas. T. Finley's place with Columbus Hurt and Doe Finley and Wm. McWhorter. Thrasher Callaway is on R.L McWhorter's place with Lowery Jackson, George Jackson, Ann Griffin, Mike Reed, Richmond Harris, Henry Nelson, and Dan Reed. No Aaron or Burrell nor any Freeman that owned any property in the 147th District in Greene County in 1879.

This was the year before 1880 and something is wrong in 1879. Aaron and Burrell are both missing from District 147 in Falling Creek. Major Callaway has changed his last name to Slaton and Bob Callaway shows up in the Epps house. And young Green Callaway is in the Alexander chain gang in camp number three. What is happening in 1880?

In the year 1880, I found living in the 137th District of Greene County Mr. Griffin Hurt, who is now seventy years old. His daughter Matilda is fifteen and Lizzie six. Emily Hurt's father and Richard Callaway's father-in-law is in the house of Mr. Benjamin Collins, a white thirty-year-old man and his wife Mary L., who is thirty. Their son Robert W. Collins is ten, Pope Collins is eight, Lula S. is six, Sarah C. is four, and Harriet A. Love is his thirty-nine-year-old sister-in-law. They also have an eighteen-year-old female boarder named Lavern S. Tunnell, and a colored fifty-year-old servant named Francis Tiller. The only other colored families living nearby are Peter Hurt, thirty-five; his wife Martha, thirty; John H., eleven, and Berrmon, nine. Henry Reed, a colored fifty-five-year-old man, and Matilda, who is thirty-eight. Living with them is fifteen-year-old Eliza Willingham, Robert Reed (seven), Daniel Reed (three), Manda Reed (two), and George (one).

Between 1880 and 1883, Richard Calloway was in the tax digest in Woodville on W. R. Wilson's place with Anthony Geer, Jim Ray, Lee Chivers, Hamp Kinnebrew, Philip Moore, and Mansfield Butler. On the property of Enoch R. Cheney were Harrison Culbreath, Charlie Callaway, Nathan Taylor and Mose Cheney. Now here is Charles Callaway in the same district as Mose Cheney. Charlie is the son of Aaron Cheney or Bob Callaway and Tissue Hardeman Callaway. Charley Cheney in 1870 became Charley Callaway in 1880, as a little boy he grew up knowing Mr. Mose Cheney on William Owen Cheney's place in Bairdstown.

In 1890, Dick Callaway was living in Woodville, Greene County, Georgia, on Cheney & Co. land. At the same time, Charlie is in Beaverdam on B. B. Williams's place. He is with Lige Butler, Stony Brawner, Charlie Bell, Lewis Barnett, and Stony Colbert, while George Callaway was on W. Eberhart's place with Scott Cox, Albert Boykins, Wylie Ball, and Armistead Arnold.

Remember that between 1883 and 1887 Charlie and George Callaway were living in Bowling Green District 228 and the PO was Stephens. Charles was on E. R. Cheney's place and George was on J. S. Cheney's place. Also between 1887 and 1888, Charles was still in Bowling Green only he was on Ed Jackson place and Cleveland was on the Jackson place as well. Not at any time do I find Charlie or Cleveland living on the place of Aaron. However, Charlie gets his first experience with the newspaper in 1888, the paper was out of Kansas. It was called the *Fort Scott Daily Monitor*. It came out on Saturday, November 3, 1888. I downloaded the article on March 24, 2016 from newspapers.com.

The article read *White Slaves of Democracy*. The following extract is from a correspondence written to the *Cincinatti Commercial* by a laboring man who had been down South and spent a couple of years. Our workman should read it carefully.

> "The Democratic Legislature of Georgia passed a law making it a crime for a man for any cause to quit his employer, and any one thus offending is outlawed, and any giving the poor, outraged laborer food or shelter is himself liable to punishment."

That is the way things were going prior to the war. By the grace of the shotgun and Grover Cleveland, the old ways and old laws are fast being reestablished. This particular law was enacted to prevent the Knights of Labor. The good people of Georgia shot one Knights of Labor organizer so badly that he has never attempted to do any more work of that kind. In North Carolina and South Carolina Knights of Labor have been given about the same treatment as in Georgia. What is the result of the law in Georgia? Why, human slavery prevails to a large extent.

As a result of the working of the slave law in Georgia, the following specimens are given, taken from Southern papers:

> *Warning: All parties are hereby notified not to hire or harbor Charles Calloway (colored), as he is under contract with me*

> *for the year 1887. Any information as to his whereabouts thankfully received (Stephens, Georgia; Ed Jackson).*
>
> Runaway. All persons are hereby notified not to hire or harbor Arthur Cheney (white) or Henry Johnson or Lewis Glenn (colored) as they are under contract for me for the following year.
>
> M. H. Arnold of Crawford, Georgia

Crawford Georgia is in Oglethorpe County, as well as Stephens, Georgia. Oglethorpe County is a county that will become scrutinized because of contract labor and peonage, which started about 1886 with Jim Smith of Smithonia. E. C. Kinnibrew was also asking for help from the Federal government about this time because he stated that it was getting out of hand! The writer further writes, "Laboring men of the north, how do you like the picture from 'Way Down South in Dixie,' where you get Democracy pure and simple?" There the working man is made a slave, and in a more offensive sense of the old slave days. If the working man becomes unfortunate, he is put on the block and sold. If a laboring man makes a contract and the contractor treats him unfairly, he cannot pack up his "kit" and quit. Oh no. He is advertised and becomes an outcast, whom no man must assist without the risk of the strong arm of the law. This shows that the old feelings still exist down there. The aristocracy is not dead. It only bides its time. In the face of all men, this hellish doctrine that was thought to have been shot to death on the battlefield is still taught, held up, and believed. The Southerner is only waiting a little longer. He has shown you people of the north what he was capable of doing in the old slave way. Charlie Callaway, the son of Aaron, was well known by 1899 because of this publicity and exposure from the newspaper.

In Bowling Green, in Oglethorpe County, Richard Callaway (born August 1854) has been married twelve years to Emily Hurt Callaway (born May 1848) and has had seven children: Nathan, born April 1889; Neal, April 1897; Mahala, January 1894; Frank, December 1897; George Sims (grandson), November 1897.

Walton County comes to mind now. In the Richardson District in 1900, Henry Callaway was born March 1870. Rosetta, his wife, was born April 1875. Cornelius, their son, was born May 1892. Roy, their son, was born April 1894. Armstrong was born May 1899 and was a year old.

Henry Callaway and Rosetta in Walton County, Georgia

Walton County is a place that I thought was very close to Oglethorpe County and so was Morgan County, as well as Oconee County, as to dealing in the liquor trade, called the Blind Tiger gangs. I had to look into the court records of this county to find out who were the men and women that were dealing in the liquor and the Blind Tigers and how they were close to Falling Creek in Oglethorpe County. Remember the Blind Tigers have been around since the 1870s, right after the Civil War. And with Falling Creek in Oglethorpe County, not too far away from counties previously mentioned. Highway 15 has been a very active highway for quite some time!

State vs. Oscar Williams, page 409

State vs. Erskin Williams, charged with carrying pistol concealed

State vs. Oscar Williams, for shooting at another, August 31, 1899

> To Sol. Gen. stating in open court that this is a doubtful case and the defendant having served out a sentence of the court for carrying a pistol concealed and this case being part of the same transaction all accruing at the same time and place. It is ordered that this indictment the prosecution consulting be settled upon payment of cost but not otherwise.
>
> O. H. Brand, sol. gen.; R. B Russell, judge S. C. & W. C.

I just knew that the blacks played not the "yes'um" and "no'mam, sir" role in our black history. I say this because of the life that was told to me growing up. I was told that Arthur was a black gangster and a well-known liquor runner or blockade runner in his twenties. And that is the mystery that follows my grandfather. Between the years of 1921 to about 1929, I can find nothing about him in Atlanta. These secrets he carried to the grave, where he is buried at Mount Mariah Baptist Church Cemetery in Dekalb County, Georgia.

R. B. Russell, the friend of Mr. Henry C. Tuck, the mayor of Athens, is all over the place for being the circuit judge. In 1899, R. B. Russell, a man who once defended the coloreds with attorney Henry C. Tuck, was in Oglethorpe and Clarke County and in Oconee County as well. These counties of Walton, Clarke, Oglethorpe, Greene, Oconee, Jackson, DeKalb, Gwinnett, and the younger two counties of Barrow and Rockdale would be ruled by the liquor trade as well as having a large number of KKK power structure at the same time as having a problem with the mixing of the races due to the Blind Tiger gang! These two are bound to conflict and at the same time support each other in keeping the Negro in its place whenever the Negro was getting uppity! These two entities will culminate in the murders in Walton County, but the murders really happened near Oconee County. This conspiracy with the Blind Tigers in 1899 will not disclose the identity of the coloreds or the whites during this time because of the revenue that the liquor was bringing into the state. However, this also went back to the 1870s during the beginning of the Reconstruction Period. The question is what took place at the hot suppers and who visited these places of vice. You will never know. Because the Federal and state don't want you to know what took place! This kind of vice also affected the places of worship in both white and colored communities, because the church was also a place where social gatherings took place as well. And the pastors and deacons had many problems with vice outside the churches during this time and time to come after! This vice caused the KKK or the notorious white Blind Tigers to bomb colored churches without any for thought! The two communities were too close!

To further show you the relationship of the power that resided in Walton County, take a look at this indenture

> . . . made this the third day of March in the year of our Lord eighteen hundred and eighty-eight, between T. D. O'Kelly of the County of Rockdale and State of Georgia of the first part and T. L. O'Kelly of the County Gwinnett and State of Georgia of the second part. Witnesseth that the said Thomas D. O'Kelly for and in consideration of the sum of four hundred dollars in hand paid at and before the sealing and delivery of these presents . . . Unto the said Thompson L. O'Kelly his heirs and assigns on half undivided interest in all that tract or parcel of land situated being in the fourth district of Walton County known in the place of said county as part of lot number two hundred and seventy six. On the north by lands of Sarah D. O'Kelly on the east by lands of H. W. Hammock to have and to hold the said one half interest with all and . . . witnessed by J.F. Wallis and C.V. Lanford N. P., January 11, 1889.

The O'Kelly family is kin to Judge Henry C. Tuck. The O'Kelly family is the same family in Oglethorpe County that Richard English was working for before having all his crops confiscated and was sent to Mr. James Monroe Smith's chain gang.

Walton County Deed Book, F. Lewis C. Russell, the Russell manufacturing Co., pg. 559–560. R. B. Russell to the Russell Manufacturing Co., 561–562.

As you can see, the black man was of great necessity and still of great value to the ex-slave master in the South well after the war! Some say we should forget about where we come from but in order to know how you are being treated now, it's best to understand the system of the past to know the system of the present to affect the system that the black man or poor lives are under in this present age and in the future lives to come. A system that they lived under and made to live under was this very same system of the 1870s of drinking, sex, and violence. I thank God for the Spirit of Jesus Christ that helps me to understand the true meaning of being free!

Pg. 139.

> Walton Co. this indenture made this the 8th day of July in the year of our Lord one thousand eight hundred and ninety-nine between E. M Rockware first part of the county of the first and Louis Lucy, Pake Lester, Maurall Racker, Jack Puckett, Ben Plummer, Ike Hoise, Bill Flint trustees of Zion A. M. E. church and their successors in office of the county of the second part. Assigns all that tract or parcel of land lying or being in the county of Walton said state aforesaid containing one acre of land more or less lying and being in Walton County and bound as follows; road leaving form Rockbridge by Steven Brands, thence along said road leaving from 100 feet thence N. E. 233 ½ feet . . . running to the middle of the Rockbridge. Wit: by W. L. Floyd and S.A. Starr N. P. recorded July 26, 1899.

The first name that I came across was that of Mr. Willis Lester, a colored man, for selling liquor. The defendant Willis Lester waived a copy of the indictment and list of witnesses. He also waives being formally arraigned and pleads not guilty on October 14, 1903. *I was not too overwhelmed to find Willis Lester here because I found quite a lot of Lesters selling liquor in Clarke County near Oconee and in Gwinnett.*

Isaiah Callaway vs. Jos. W. Dalton

Upon motion of plaintiff's counsel it is ordered by the court that this case be continued until the July quarterly term of this court and that the security Jackson Arnold on the bail bond is received and relieved of all liability thereon this April 3, 1905.

Isiah Callaway is out of Morgan County out of Fairplay. He is out of Greene County, living there in 1880 in the 138th District on the plantation of W. T. Burton. Isiah was a mulatto male at the age of Fifteen and George was at the age of twelve. Isiah is the son of mysterious Robert C. Callaway I believe this because remember, George went to work for William Eberhart in Beaverdam, Oglethorpe County and Charlie went to work for B. B. Williams the brother-in-law of Eberhart in 1890. I am assuming young Isiah made his way to Morgan County near colored man William Callaway and his wife Mary Callaway.

Henry Callaway vs. Wm. (Cap) Jackson, demurrer dismissed, judgment for cost.

The only other time I have seen a Callaway having dealings with a colored Callaway is in Atlanta.

Robert Cameron vs. Thomas Calaway, debt, confession of judgment, appeal, bond

Aiken Callaway et al vs. the State, riot; no bill

Sallie Callaway et al. vs. the State, assault with intent to murder; true presentment

Sallie Callaway vs. the State, misdemeanor; true presentment, minute book 1907

Minutes August 26, 1919, Walton County Superior Court

The State vs. John Lucas for using opprobrious words and abusive language; accused by Charles M. Walker

The State vs. King Lester

The State vs. Buck Lester

When I turned to the pages in the docket book to find the case against Buck Lester, I found Roy Thompson charged by the state and indicted in Walton County Superior Court for making liquor, February term 1922.

The jury in this case stated after deliberating for several hours and coming into court and stating that they are unable to agree upon a verdict and that they will be unable to agree if longer kept together, and it appearing to the court that the jury will not make a verdict in said case and cannot vote and the same is hereby declared ordered and adjudged by the court that a mistrial be hereby declared and that said case be withdrawn from further consideration by the jury. This March 3, 1922. W. O. Dean, Sol. Gen., W. C. Blanton Fortson, judge S. C. W. C.

Minute Book 5

The State vs. Henry Callaway, page 15

The State vs. Henry Callaway, colored, true bill, having liquor. L. W. Howard is the prosecutor. Henry H. West is the solicitor general. Recorded February 21, 1938. John S. Dickinson is the clerk.

The State vs. Henry Callaway, colored, case no. 2744, Walton Superior Court, February Term 1938, having liquor, a true bill. Henry pleaded guilty to the charges with Paul H. Paschal as his attorney on the 25th day of 1938.

The state prosecuted Ed Henderson, a colored man, for having liquor; Will Preston, another colored man, attempting to make liquor; Daisy Thomas, a colored woman, for having liquor; Henry Briscoe for having liquor; John Smith, another colored man, for having liquor; and *Ollie Robinson* for having liquor.

The State vs. Louis Calloway, a colored man, a true bill for bastardy. R. P. Burson is the foreman. Mary Alice Williams, colored, is the prosecutor in the case on the twenty-first of August 1940.

Book Two: Page 218

State vs. Guss Williams for having a still and attempting to make liquor. The defendant Guss Williams waives copy of accusation, list of witnesses and being formally arraigned, also waives indictment by the Grand Jury of said county and pleads guilty.

The State vs. Earnest McElhannon and Obe Willingham, manufacturing liquor. On motion by solicitor general it is ordered within true bill be null, processed, as to Earnest McElhannon this August 28, 1924.

Henry Callaway, son R. W. Callaway or Roy Callaway, is buried in the Baber Creek Baptist Church yard in Barrow County. Roy died September 27, 1955. His death certificate could never be found in Barrow County or in

Walton County, or anywhere in the State of Georgia. Cornelius Callaway was at the age of twenty-four when he joined the First World War. He was living at 54 East Harris Street in Atlanta, Georgia. His birthplace was Woodville, Georgia, and he worked for Randolph Rose as a cook. Cornelius's date of birth was listed as being May 12, 1893. In 1900, in the Richardson District of Walton County, Henry Callaway had been married for four years, and was born May 1870 and had three children. Rosetta was born in 1874 and was twenty-five years old. Their children are Cornelius, born May 1892, and was eight years old; Roy Callaway was born April of 1894 and was four years old; and a young boy by the name of Armstrong, born May 1899, and was one years old. They were living next door to the Robinson family. Sarah Robinson was born April 1860 and was forty years old and was a widow.

Mat, her son, was born May 1882 and was eighteen. Willie, her son, born April 1892 and was eight. Sam was born April 1893 and was seven. Johnson was born February 1894 and was six. Ben was born January 1895 and was five. Brutus was born July 1896 and was four. *At this time, I must mention the fact that Henry might be closely related to Jesse R. Callaway because of the Robinson family that was his wife's maiden name. Remember when I found a Fannie Callaway that had the grandchildren of Jesse Callaway in the house with her in Penfield in 1900. Well, I came to some conclusion that the only way that Fannie could be tied to the family of Jesse was that she had to marry one of his sons. The only person that I found in Wilkes County to marry a Fannie was Charlie Callaway, who married a Fannie Wylie.*

The tax digest shows that Henry Callaway shows up in the Richardson District of Walton County in 1901, the same year that Dick or Richard Callaway has left Greene County. The PO box number for the Richardson district is Cut Off Pass office box Winder. The colored men that are in the Richardson District are Tom Allen, Reuben Akridge, Ransom Akridge, Charles Akridge, Alex Butler, Allen Butler, Book Boyce, Charlie Brown, Jesse Boyce, Pig Brown, Lit Brown, Lon Barrett, Joe L. Butler, Noah Brown, Will Calvin, Jack Colquitt, Howard Chester, Peter Nolan, Andrew Nolan, John Nolan, Robert Nolan, Tom Nolan, Jesse Nolan, William Robertson, and Henry Callaway.

In the year 1902, in the Richardson district a few more names are added to the tax digest along with Henry Callaway: Charlie Brown, Jim Johnson, Jasper Foster, Tom Davis, Jack Hill, Alford hill, Jim Heard, Morgan Hawk, Charlie Jackson, John and Jim King, Gee Malcolm, Lee Malcolm Tom Malcolm, G. Malcolm, John Malcolm, June Malcolm, Frank Malcolm, John Moore, Robert Malcolm, Pete Nolan, Tom Nolan,

John Nolan, Robert Nolan, Joe Pascal, Will Smith, Henry Tuggle, Ike Telmon, Florence Williams, Lee Williams, Pete Williams, Ike Williams, Will Williams, Fred White, Henry Watson Bailey Walker, and George Wiloby. *Also, 1902 is the year that Williams shows up in the district of Walton County.*

Let us move on to the year 1915, the year the draft was enacted for World War I. Will Baldwin, Arthur Brown, Lit Brown, Jake Brown, Ammous Brown, Cliff Branch and Bill Branch, Thomas Billups, Tom Barrett, *Henry Callaway,* and Johnston Callaway are all gone and are not in Good Hope in the Richardson District. Jim Colquitt is here still, with Charley Jackson and Charley Jackson Jr. Mattie Johnston is out of Atlanta, and Jim Johnston and Eliza Johnston, Man Jones and Walter Jones. In the year 1916, Henry Callaway is not in Good Hope. *Between the years of 1916 and 1917, Cornelius states that he is taking care of his father, mother, and his wife while living in Atlanta. However, Emily Hurt Callaway is purchasing the property of colored man Mr. Albert Parks in the 137th of Greene County.* In the year of 1917 Henry Callaway shows up again, but not in the Richardson District. However, Henry is in the 419th District called the Town District of Walton County. Henry Callaway shows up with Joe Cheney, Etna Carter, Ambros Carter, Jack Battle, Tom Cabin, T. J. Cantrell, Pinkey Brown, John Brown, Jess D. Brown, Cora Brown, Lucinda Billups, Walker Culbreath, Will Culbreath, Hill Culbreath, Emiline Culbreath, Easter Crew, Boyd Conyers, Brown Conyers, Jesse Conner, Henry Conner, Judge Colquitt, Anna Dunn, Charles Dunn, Jake Edmondson, Johnston Edmonds, Joseph Herndon, Mose Hammond, John Hester, Anna Haygood, Henry Haygood, Hosea Haygood, Jade Hill, James Hill, John H. Hill, John Hemphill, Sara Hill, George Hillyer, Jane Howard, Melson Howard, Emily Johnston, Boykin Johnston, Hope Johnston, India Johnston, Pauline Johnston, Sibby Johnston, Ella Jones, William Kilgore, Oscar king, Peter R. King, Ella Lumpkin, Tom Lumpkin, Mack Lumpkin, Bole Murry, Pleas O'Kelly, Henry Osby, George Williams, Guss Williams, Lear Williams, Pink Williams, Lizzie Wood, Man Wood, Will Wood, and Lizzie Williams.

In the year 1920, Ben Callaway was in the Richardson District called Good Hope. Ben was born May 23, 1892 and was living in Good Hope, his draft cards states. Ben was a farm laborer supporting his wife and child. He was a medium-built man with medium skin color, with black hair and black eyes. He was in precinct 559 with J. M. Thompson as the registrar. Ben Callaway was employed by E. H. Hester. I do not know what the relationship that Henry Callaway has with the white Thompson family in Walton County and I wonder why I can't find a marriage certificate between Henry Callaway and Rosetta Daniel in Morgan County. Now, the question is why Rosetta married under the last name of Daniel in Morgan County when her last name is Thompson. Was she married to a Daniel before she married Henry Callaway?

This is at the same time that Henry Callaway is still living in Town District on Lucy Street. A few of his colored neighbors are Levi Brown, Julia Brown, Jim Brown, Judge Brown, Tom Crawley, George Davenport, Verley Broughton, George Bugg, Elbert Burson, Tom, Caswell, and Henry Colquitt. Town District was in the city of Monroe. Henry was thirty-seven, Rosetta his wife was forty-two, Henry their son was eighteen, Mary their daughter was seventeen, Susie was thirteen, John was eight. John had a twin sister and her name I cannot quite make out in the census. There is another daughter by the name of Susie who is seven, and Anna A. who is five. Roy was the eldest son at the age of twenty-three. I was surely surprised to find that George Williams was the neighbor of Henry Callaway at this time in 1920. George's age looks like, he is thirty-seven and his wife Ida is at the age of thirty-four. They have three daughters who are aged sixteen, eleven, and eight. Their names I cannot quite make out in the census. It's strange that George would show up in the census but not Guss Williams. Remember I found Guss William in Falling Creek in Oglethorpe County in the house of Columbus D. Hurt. Maybe the reason that I cannot find Guss William in the census is because he is on the chain gang for trying to make liquor. I remember finding a book in the Hurt house in Oglethorpe County and it was a book on how to build your own still! This is Falling Creek, where the "hot supper" was frequently visited by many of the notorious "Blind Tigers." These are both black men and white men as well as women.

Between the years of 1921 through to 1925, Henry Callaway remained in the 419th district, the Town District. While for the first time in Loganville Pope Lester and Jams Lester and Robert Lewis and M. Lucas resided. Also, in 1922, Henry Callaway had some Cheneys to help him move into the district, Joe Cheney and Cary Cheney. In 1923, Ben Callaway is gone from the Richardson District of Good Hope, and Henry Callaway is gone from the town of Monroe. However, in 1924, Isaac Calloway of Fairplay, Morgan County, moves into the Richardson District of Good Hope. *Now, I have three situations that took place in the year 1922 among the colored Callaways that I have researched. One is in Terrell County Tax Digest with Charlie Callaway and Mary Elizabeth Callaway.*

They are missing in 1922. Henry Callaway and Ben Callaway are missing from the tax digest in Walton County, and Dinah Callaway is about to die in Greene County in Penfield.

I always wondered why Rev. Henry Callaway is buried alone in Jones Woods in Walton County. Why or where is his wife Rosetta? Now, Henry was in the cemetery with H. H. Nolan, born January 5, 1870, and died September 21, 1900. Francis Grimes Washborn was born March 5, 1850, and died October 21, 1900. Reverend Henry Callaway Sr., born May 1868 and died February 10, 1928. Sallie Mord or Maud Thompson, born March 22, 1883, and died September 7, 1901. And Dora Thompson died February 27, 1939. I found the death certificate of Mrs. Rosetta Calloway. Rosetta died February 23, 1947, in Hamilton, Chattanooga, Tennessee in the first district of the county. She lived at 2302 East Fifth Street and resided there for twenty-four years. She lived in this house from 1923 to 1947. Her date of birth only mentions the month of October and the fifteenth day, it does not mention the year. It mentions where she was born and that was Walden (Walton) County, Georgia, and Henry Callaway, her deceased husband. Her father's name was Sam Robinson, and her mother was Sarah Thompson, who was born in Walden (Walton) County, Georgia. Ben Calloway at 217 Clarke Street was the informant. They buried her at Pleasant Garden, Chattanooga, Tennessee. *I knew that Cornelius Callaway had to have some kind of tie to Tennessee. If he was a cook for Randolph M. Rose and Rose was relocated to Tennessee this had to be. The strange thing is while Henry Callaway is missing from Walton County in 1916, he and his wife Rosetta are never mentioned on the census in Atlanta and never are they listed on the tax digest. Well, from the time that they are missing from Walton County they are living in Hamilton, Chattanooga, Tennessee. What a wonderful eye-opening find! However, what would compel Rev. Henry C. Callaway to come back to be buried in Walton County, Georgia? Is it another family? Now the white family that owned the slave cemetery where Rev. Henry Callaway lived was Maud Jones, Banner Jones, Stafford Jones, and Walter Jones. I was told this by a long-time resident of the community. I believe that Henry is old Birk Callaway, not Bart Callaway, but the Birk Callaway who married Rosetta Daniel in 1887. The reason that he made his way back to Walton County was to be near his other family in Morgan County! Yes, we are talking about one thing the Callaway have in common and that is having more than one family!*

Rev. Henry Callaway of Walton County

In the year 1900, Henry Callaway was listed as being born May 1870 and was thirty years old. Rosetta was born April 1875 and was twenty-five years old. They had been married for four years and have only three children. Cornelius was born May 1892 and is eight. Roy was born April 1896 and was four. A young unnamed son was born May 1899 and was a year old. Rosetta was living next door to her mother Sarah A. Robinson. She was born April 1860 and was a widow at forty years old. Mat was born May 1882 and was eighteen. Willie was born April 1892 and was eight. Sam was born April 1893 and was seven. Johnson was born February 1894 and was six years old. Ben was born January 1895 and was five. Prostus was born February 1896 and was four years old.

MATT CALLAWAY AND PETER CALLAWAY FROM MONROE COUNTY

I found Mat Callaway and Nancy Callaway only in the 1870 census and the 1880 census and a few times I found them in the tax digest in Woodstock, Oglethorpe County, and in Bowling Green in Oglethorpe County. So I will start with 1870. Matt Calloway and Nancy stayed mainly in Woodstock in Oglethorpe County, Georgia. Matt Callaway stayed on Mr. Dalton's property while in Oglethorpe County. While working on Mr. Dalton's place he worked alongside Peter Barrow, Adam Daniel, Jim Roberson, Isham Daniel, Tom Glenn, Charley Glenn, Columbus Parks, Littleton Dalton (who was over sixty years old), Felix Dalton, Madison Dalton, Young Arnold, Josh Dalton, Ben Hull, and Hudson Clark.

Another tax digest stated that Matt Callaway was still on Mr. Dalton's place with Littleton Dalton and Sherly Glenn, Orange Canady (who was over sixty), and Web Willis. Beck Barrow was over sixty on Mr. D. C. Barrow's place with Calvin Barrow, Frank Barrow, Tom Wright, Jesse Oliver, Willis Bryant, Cain Barrow, Lum Bryan, Ben Thomas, Jim Reed, Charles Barrow, Lewis Watson, Tom Thomas, Reuben Barrow, Peter Barrow, Handy Barrow, and Daniel Gresham. All are kin to Aaron, as I was told by Mrs. Susie Armstrong.

Mat Callaway is in Bowling Green in Oglethorpe County on Mr. William Crammer's place with Dinah Callaway, Phil Callaway, Peter Callaway (over sixty), Ned Callaway, Peter Drake, Allen Dupree, Ed

Clarke, and Manuel Crammer. Pink Dalton was working on Mr. J. N. McWhorter's place. The place of Mr. Crammer's place was not far from Mr. Ferdinand Phinizy's place. One year Matt Callaway moved onto the place of Mr. George W. Callaway near Mr. Frank Winfrey and T.J. Callaway's place in Bowling Green. At this time, Aaron Haynes was on Mrs. Celeste Stephens's place, where Bob Callaway worked in the 1870s. Mrs. Stevens's property is near Mr. J. J. Sims's place.

Another year in Woodstock, Oglethorpe County, Matt Callaway stayed on Peter Dalton's plantation with Clem Fulton, Ellic Dalton, Felix Dalton, Madison Dalton, and Littleton Dalton (over sixty). I was told not only by Mrs. Susie Armstrong that the Daltons were kin to me, I was also told by Mrs. Ruby Finch that was true as well when asked. Matt has moved from Peter Dalton's place that was near Mr. H. Wright's place and onto Peter's place that was near Thomas P. Callaway's place with Perry Crattic and Hutson Clark. Henry Crammer was on T. P. Callaway's and Barrow was on D. C. Barrow's place.

Thomas P. Callaway still had property in Woodstock 230 District of Oglethorpe with Levi Lumpkin on his place. This is while Matt Callaway was on E. A. Dalton's place with Dillis Parks, Zack Parks, Thomas Carlton, Jerry Arnold, Eleck Dalton, Liddleton Dalton, and Sherly Glenn. Now I do not know if Matt Callaway stayed married to Nancy Callaway; however, I have Matt Callaway married to Emma Maxey on June 6, 1889. J. J. Bacon is the ordinary.

Matt Calloway has 100 acres valued at $300, and Floyd Callaway, his son, is on Mr. Dozier's place in Woodstock, Georgia. I don't know how long he held on to this property in Woodstock or even if he is buried somewhere on the property as some would be after they died.

In 1880, Matt Callaway was sixty-one years old and Nancy was fifty-eight. Susan is twenty, Daniel is now nine, and Rebecca was born in July and was one month old. They are living near Mr. Stephen English and his wife Martha. And on the other side of Matt and Nancy are Marshal Clarke and Anna, his wife; Eugenia, their sixteen-year-old daughter; and Mathew Clarke, their fourteen-year-old son. Remember now Matt Callaway is living in two places in 1880. He and Nancy are at the place of Mrs. E. B. Callaway after the death of George W. Callaway, with Bartoe Callaway and Ellen and Fannie, Puss and Johnathan, and Ossie and Emily Ann. Mat's age while on Mrs. E. B. Callaway's place is fifty-five and Nancy is fifty. Daniel is nine, Susan is twenty, Abbie is eighteen, and Beckie (his grandfather) is one. I believe that Matt came to reside on Mrs. Callaway's place because of the troubles that were happening. He made his way because what I discerned is that Matt and Major and Bart Callaway are brothers and Aaron and Jesse as well as Henderson Callaway and his wife Sallie are all family and kin to the Callaways in Wilkes County as well as in Monroe County, Georgia, and DeKalb, Henry, as well as many others.

Now I also found other Callaways that lived in Bowling Green and Woodstock, Oglethorpe County, Georgia. I found them in the list of tax defaulters. Two prolific names are of Cleveland Callaway and Charles Callaway in Bowling Green District. Charlie was in Bowling Green in 1885, 1886, and 1887. Cleveland was there only in 1886. Now the only names that reside in Bowling Green are Major Callaway, Matt Callaway, and Bart Callaway. Charlie and Cleveland and Clayborn are a mystery in 1870. Aaron Cheney is in Puryears District of Clarke County and Green Callaway in Lincoln County, Georgia, in 1870. In 1880, neither Aaron Cheney nor Green Callaway exist. Now, while Charlie and Cleveland were in Bowling Green they were on the Ed Jackson's place. This is the same place where I found Abe and Dinah working on the Jackson place as well.

I must put this bit of information in about Mr. U. G. Blanton, the man my grandfather Arthur Callaway mentioned as being his employer and helped him by giving him money to purchase his property in Lynwood Park.

> *April 25, 1922 J. H. Ewing of Fulton the first part and U. G. Blanton of the second part of DeKalb Co. in consideration of the first part received $650.00 for land lot number 309 of the 18th District of DeKalb. Known as track no. 8 Chamblee Ga. September 10, 1919 witnessed by Fletcher W. Laird and Ethel M. Ezell the notary public and Ben. F. Burgess is the clerk of the courts.*
>
> *This was three acres on Peachtree Road.*
>
> *On April 15, 1924, a contract between W. D. Wallace, J. W. F. Tilly, W. G. Tilly, C. D. Jones, J. E. Flowers J. L. Wallace and R. F. Bolton trustees of prospect M.E. Church South of DeKalb County Georgia, parties of the first part and U. G. Blanton of DeKalb of the second part. Witnessed by R. P. Rudasill the Notary Public and Jno. McKibben.*
>
> Robert Dorsey opened a "jot 'em down" grocery store around the end of the nineteenth century on the corner of Peachtree and East Paces Ferry roads. Groceries

were delivered to consumers in his horse-drawn buggy. Although Dorsey had many wealthy clients, not all of them paid their bills. Consequently, he went broke and closed his business around 1907. (Courtesy of the Atlanta History Center.)

JOHNSONTOWN BLACK COMMUNITY

Peachtree Heights Parks, Peachtree Hills, and Johnson Town were developed. Walter P. Andrews began developing the Peachtree Heights Park neighborhood around Peachtree Battle Avenue on the west side of Peachtree Road. Sixty-one acres of the Benjamin Plaster estate were sold in 1911 to American Securities Company of Georgia.

In 1890 and 1891, the Suburban, an improvement company established the Peachtree Park Subdivision across from the present Lenox Square and attempted to sell 243 lots. It met with poor success. In 1912, Columbus and Callie Johnson, a black South Georgia couple, purchased fifteen lots from D.N. Williams for $600 and in turn sold the lots to other blacks in the area. Columbus and Callie Johnson are not out of South Georgia but out of Oglethorpe County with Charlie and Mary Calloway and were under contracts just like Mary and Charlie. In 1920, Columbus Johnson is sixty years old and working at Fort Gordon. His wife Katie is fifty-five, Wilie is twenty-three, Pearl is twenty-one, Gertrude is five, Allena is two months, and Willie is six months. They were living on Fulton Avenue in Buckhead. *This is the same place where Mr. Willie Callaway came and he worked for Mr. D. N. Williams. The same D. N. Williams that sold land to Columbus and Callie Johnson that started the colored community near Lenox Square Mall. And a few more earlier Callaways showed up in this northeastern section of Fulton and DeKalb County. William Callaway was born September 5, 1876, and was forty-two years old. William and his wife Mammie were both living on Rt. 2 Chamblee, DeKalb County. Will could write his name and his occupation was as a farmer. However, I do not think that C. C. Mitchell is in the farming business. Mr. D. N. Williams signed as registrar of the district on September 12, 1918. It doesn't state where William was born. However, I do have a marriage that happened in Atlanta between William Callaway and Mammie Smith in book P, page 425. Mammie Smith's name is the closest name to that of William Callaway's wife in DeKalb County, Georgia.*

I found a Charlie, Willie, Howard, and Cornelius Charles Callaway in DeKalb County, Georgia, in Chamblee and in the Peachtree District so early. I believe I found Charlie and Mary Callaway, my grandfather's mother and father! Harriet, a teacher from Spelman, also came to teach in Doraville at a colored school that was located there.

The other family that I am interested in is the family of Charles Mitchell, a thirty-four-year-old man, and his wife Fanny, who was twenty-eight. Their daughter Lylie is eight, Willie is seven, Cora is five, Sophie is four, Fred is three, and Charlie is one. I mentioned the Mitchell family because it was a C. C. Mitchell that helped William Callaway in DeKalb County in 1918 on his draft card during World War I and I could not find anything pertaining to a C. C. Mitchell. I mention the Stark family, for they were close to the Callaways in Fulton County and DeKalb, but in Fulton while living on Alabaster Alley in the Fourth Ward of the city of Atlanta. I mention the Brown family because of the relationship that my grandfather had with Effie Brown.

The new community became known as Johnson Town, and before long it was filled with modest bungalows and shotgun houses built along unpaved streets. These houses on Oak Valley Road and Railroad Avenue were typical homes in the community, because there were no indoor plumbing privies located in the backyards. Both courtesy of the Atlanta History Center. Some of the members of the Johnson Town community were entrepreneurs. They operated grocery stores and nightclubs. One such enterprising resident was Henry Walker, who operated Henry Walker's Restaurant and Grocery Store at 937 Railroad Avenue. His popular nightspot provided music, dancing, and drinks for his patrons. Walker also owned apartment buildings and duplexes. He was considered one of Johnson Town's most prominent citizens. The Zion Hill Baptist Church served the religious needs of the Johnson Town residents and those living in the surrounding black neighborhoods. The white wooden building was built around 1912 and was located on Railroad Avenue. The church affiliation was originally Methodist. But it later became a Baptist Church. This church, called Zion Hill Baptist Church, has Rev. S.E. Sawyer on its marquee outside the front of the church. I wonder if this is Pastor Elder Sawyer that is over at the Holiness Church at the corner of Winsor Parkway and Osborne Road in Lynwood Park. *Bishop Sawyer was very instrumental in my conversion to the fullness of my belief in Christ! I would go to his house that evening and he would give me the keys to the church and I would stay there all by myself and would return the keys to him the next morning. I would here the loud music across the street where I ran the pool room for Mr. Ezzard. I got into many fights and almost lost my life over a pool game one late night, and the next day I almost killed the same young man that pulled the gun on me to take my life.*

I was blown away to find that the headquarters for the KKK located in Buckhead, Atlanta, Georgia, not far from the DeKalb county line. The Klan has had a watchful eye over the colored communities that were in North DeKalb and North Fulton, even over toward Gwinnett County Pass Stone Mountain. I was at the Atlanta Historical Society and found this passage about the colored communities in Buckhead and found this article on the KKK.

> Because of the Leo Frank case, the Ku Klux Klan raised its ugly head in 1915 after hibernating since 1877. Membership grew quickly, and Buckhead became its local headquarters. The Klan bought the Edward M. Durant property on Peachtree Road (now the Cathedral of Christ the King) in 1921 and established its command center in the beautiful two-story, antebellum-style home they called the Imperial Palace. (Courtesy of the Cathedral of Christ the King.)

A. Mr. Coleman built this three-story building on Roswell Road in 1920 in the heart of Buckhead, and deeded it to the Knights of the Ku Klux Klan. It became their sheet factory, where the members' robes and hoods were made. Upstairs, there was a secret room used to initiate new members. The factory operated until 1929 when Klan activity waned. Today it is the Cotton Exchange Office Condominium.

There was a well-known blind guitar player in Buckhead named Blind Willie. I thought this might have been Blind Willie the famous blues player. I also thought that this could be blind Willie from Greene County.

> From, *Buckhead: A Place for All Time* by Susan Kessler Barnard, page 138–139: There was the drive-in corner of Paces Ferry and Peachtree, where Buckhead Plaza now stands kind of back in the woods. Jack Spalding recalled, "You got curb service . . . There was a blind black man, Blind Willie, and he'd come out and sing, with his foot on the running board. He had a guitar, and he'd strum all these ballads. People would say, 'Meet you out at Blind's.'"

Camp Gordon in Chamblee, DeKalb County, Georgia

Camp Gordon was the first US military camp in Georgia and maybe the US, where its majority of soldiers were colored. I grew up hearing about Camp Gordon and the Negroes that started it came from this US military camp to settle in the Lynwood Park colored community in the early 1920s. I took the time to list a few of the occupations and the work that was required of the colored soldiers that occupied the camp during the First World War. You will take notice of a few of the soldiers that already resided in Chamblee and Doraville and Roswell. I also took the time to list the civilian workers as well. Enjoy! These are some of the most influential white men this area of Chamblee during the building of Fort Gordon

MR. JUSTANIAN EVANS-MR. JAMES CATES AND NANCES CREEK ROAD

Will Hood, his wife Senty, and their daughter Constance Hood lived in house number 79. Bose Allen, his wife Harriet, their daughter Charity, and their son Columbus are all mulattoes. They lived in house number 80, right next door to Justanian Evans and his wife Anna J. Then Mr. James Cates's property was next, with his wife Sallie and their son Charlie. The next house past Mr. James Cates was the colored family of Mr. Marion Harrison and his wife Susie and their children. Their son, whom I will call Paul, and Ella, Perry, and Margret. The next family is Malinda Porter's, a white woman with colored children. Her children are May, William, and a younger daughter named Inears. *The next set of colored families are living on Linnwoods Road in 1920. They are Will Julian and his wife Eva and their daughter Alice. Selma Bryant and her son Luther are living in the house next door. Living next door to Selma and her son Luther are Jim and Katie Nise. William Hutchins and his wife Julie are next with their large family on Linnwood Road. William and Julie Hutchins's family is composed of Evie, George, Sallie, May, Catlin, William, Betsy, Lee, John, Michelle, and Rosie Lee. The next family is Henry Kellog and his wife Laura and their daughters Cary, Ethel, and Artis. Charles King is the next family. His wife is named Lina King, and their children are Luther, Lillie, and Larry. Luther Wallace is living with his wife Elsie and their two daughters Sarah and Mollie.* I believe that what is called Linnwood Road is now called Lynwood Drive, the first section of the Lynwood Park Subdivision to be built! You will see this when the coloreds start to move into the Lynwood Park Colored Community and these very same coloreds on Linnwood Road are purchasing houses on the same road in the thirties.

Here are some of the property transactions with the Cates Family in DeKalb County in 1920. Now I just had to tie these two families together because of the fact that my grandfather and the Lynwood Park Community were given land by Mr. J.C. Lynn to the coloreds. However, the property belonged to the Cates family. The first road in Lynwood Community was Cates Avenue. My grandfather's first house was located on Mae Avenue and this is where my mother Mary Calloway was born.

> State of Georgia Fulton County No. 270838: This indenture, made this 1st day of October in the year of our Lord one thousand nine hundred and twenty between Mrs. S.C. Cates of the State of Georgia and County Fulton and J.L. Patrick and A. C. Blalock of the State of Georgia and County of Fulton. Witnessed: that the said party of the first part for and in consideration of the sum of nine thousand five hundred forty-five dollars in hand paid at and before the sealing and delivery of these presents, the receipt of which is hereby acknowledged, has granted, bargained, sold and conveyed, and by these presents does grant . . .
>
> All that tract or parcel of land, lying and being in land lot thirteen of the Seventeenth (17) District of Fulton County, Georgia and a part of land lot Two hundred Seventy five of the Eighteenth District of Dekalb County, Georgia, more particularly described as follows: Beginning at the southwest corner of land lot thirteen (13) in the Seventeenth(17) District and running thence north along the west line of land lot thirteen (13) seven hundred thirty-five (735) feet to Peachtree & Dunwoody Road; seventeen hundred and nineteen (1,718) feet to Justinian Evans or House Road: thence southeast along the Evans or House Road two thousand two hundred (2,200) feet to the east line of land lot thirteen (13); thence south thirty-five (35) feet, more or less to Rock Corner: thence southeast five hundred forty six (546) feet to an iron stake; thence east one hundred fifty-four (154) feet to iron stake in Evans Road thence southwest

along the Oglethorpe Road three hundred sixty (360) feet thence west two thousand six hundred ninety-two (2,692) feet thence south nine hundred thirty-nine (939) feet; thence west seven hundred seventy-seven (727) feet to beginning point. Containing seventy-six and thirty-six hundredths (76.36) acres, according to the survey of said property made August 1920 by J.L. Zachary C. E. . . . Signed, sealed and delivered in presence of B.J. Fuller and C.B. Copeland notary public, Fulton County, Georgia, filed 11:30 a.m. October 2, 1920. Arnold Boyles C.S.C. Hereunto set her hand and affixed her seal, Mrs. S.C. Cates.

Case # 382146, State of Florida, Duval County: This indenture, made this 11th day October, in the year of our Lord one thousand nine hundred and twenty-three, between James Ira Milton Christian of the state of Florida and County of Duval of the first part, and W.J. Fuller and J.C. Lynn of the State of Georgia and County of Fulton of the second part. Witnesseth: that the said party of the first part, for and in consideration of the sum of seven hundred fourteen and 26/100 dollars ($714.26), in hand paid at and before the sealing and delivery of these present, the receipt who of is hereby acknowledged, had granted bargain, sold and conveyed, and by these presents do grant, bargain, sell and convey unto the said party of the second part, their heirs and assigns, said undivided one-fourteenth interest all that tract or parcel of land lying and being in the County of Dekalb, bounded as follows: part of lot 303 and part of lot 275 and a part of lot 14, sometimes described as land lot 12 of the 17th district of Fulton County, Georgia. Commencing near Evins Old Mill at a post oak stump near the creek; thence down the creek to Nancy's Creek; thence down Nancy's Creek to G.F. Glazaner line: thence a line agreed upon running near east to the north and south line of Harrison and House: thence north to a branch near where a negro Anthony built: down said branch to the junction of another branch: thence on to the corner of the fence of Wilson's farm Survey said fence west of Cates House: thence to the north of Mill Lane;

> thence down Mill lane to the beginning corner, including one hundred and twenty-five (125) acres no more or less.
>
> This deed conveys all of Grantor's right, title and interest as an heir at law of Mrs. Louisa C. Cates: Mrs. Louisa C. Cates died leaving as her heirs at law her children, one of whom Mrs. M.I. Christian died prior to the death of Mrs. Louisa C. Cates and the within grantor and Mrs. Dessa Milton were the only children of Mrs. M. I. Christian and these two children of Mrs. Christian were living at the time of the death of Mrs. Louisa C. Cates. To have and to hold the said bargained premises, together with all and singular the rights members and appurtenances . . .

In the year of 1924 on the fifteenth day of April, a contract between W. D. Wallace, J. W. F. Tilly, W. G. Tilly, C. D. Jones, J. E. Flowers, J. L. Wallace, and R. F. Bolton trustees of Prospect M.E. Church South of DeKalb County, Georgia, parties of the first part and U. G. Blanton of DeKalb of the second part. Witnessed by R. P. Rudasill the notary public and Jno. McKibben. This is the town of Chamblee, Georgia, in DeKalb County. Mr. C.D. Jones is either a white man or a colored man and he comes out of the southern section of DeKalb County. I visited the Prospect Cemetery in Chamblee and did not find him buried there. No, I am not saying that he is not there; however, he might be, just under another name. Here is the property that he owned not too far from where the Old General Motors Plant use to be.

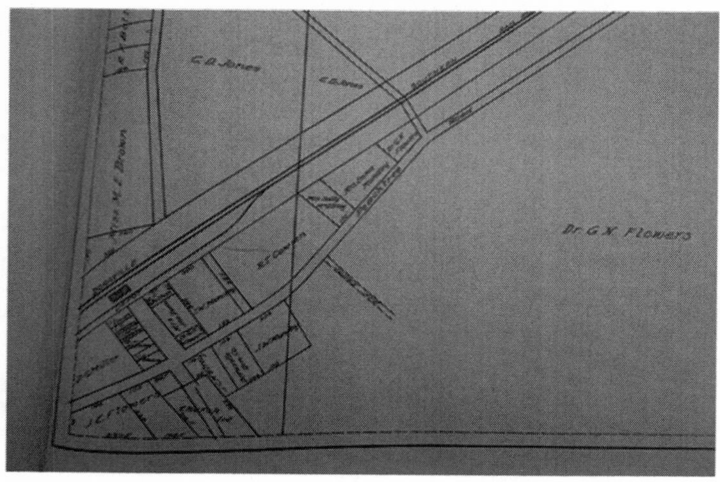

In this same place is where Harriet Callaway came to teach, and it is where you find the Colored Odd Fellows Masonic Order. However, in the book of Rev William J. White, pages 73 through to 77, I found the Jones in the minutes of the second annual session of the Sunday-School workers of Georgia held with the Tabernacle Baptist Church, Augusta, Richmond County, Georgia, on July 5 to 8.

Minutes

of The

Second Annual Session of the

Sunday-School Workers of Georgia

Held with the

Tabernacle Baptist Church, Augusta, Richmond County, Georgia

July 5, 6, 7, and 8, 1894

Time and place of next meeting, Mount Olive Baptist Church, Atlanta, Georgia, Thursday, before the second Lord's day in July 1895.

Officers: Prof. A. R. Johnson, president of Augusta; T. B. Garfield, first vice president of Athens; Rev. W. L. Jones, second vice president of Atlanta; Rev. W. A. Crittenden, third vice president of Social Circle; A. A. Blake, fourth vice president of Atlanta; J. S. Brandon, secretary of Atlanta; Rev. C. T. Walker D. D., treasurer of Augusta; Rev. E. P. Johnson, corresponding secretary of Madison.

The print made by the Atlanta, Georgia, Baptist Banner Print, 1894.

Minutes. First Day, Augusta, Ga., The Sunday-school Workers Convention of Georgia met with the Tabernacle Baptist Church, according to adjournment at Columbus Ga., July 9, 1893.

The meeting was called to order at 10:30 a. m. by Brother E. Jennings, by singing on page 99 in "Notes of Praise." Prayer was offered by Rev. C. O. Jones, of Atlanta. The 103 Psalm was then read. Sang "All Hail the Power of Jesus's Name." Bro. C. W. Newman led in prayer, then sang "My Soul be on the Guard." Rev. J. C. Center then invoked the blessings of the Lord upon us. The hour having arrived for the introductory sermon, the choir sang a beautiful anthem, "Holy, Holy is the Lord." Rev. J. H. Moon, of Greenville, Ga., then introduced the services by singing, "Stand up, Stand up for Jesus." Rev. T. M. Allen, of Marietta, then led in prayer. Rev. E. P. Johnson read a part of the first chapter of Nehemiah. Rev. R. T. Schell then lined "To the work to the work."

Rev. C. O. Jones was mentioned in the National Convention in 1898 to represent Georgia and its colored Baptist churches. J. S. Kelsey of Columbus, Georgia; Julius Goff of Buckingham, Georgia; E. K. Love D. D. of Savannah, Georgia; W. G. Johnson of Macon, Ga.; M. J. Morris of Cordelle, Ga.; W. H. Brown of Columbus, Ga.; Mrs. S. C. J. Bryant of Atlanta, Ga.; Mrs. Emma Della Motto of Savannah, Ga.; Z. A. Jones of Columbus, Ga.; and C. O. Jones of Atlanta, Ga. Courtesy of the Mercer University in DeKalb.

Rev. E. J. Fisher, of Atlanta, having been introduced by Rev. C. T. Walker, D. D., read the 19th verse of Nehemiah, 4th chapter. From this passage Rev. Fisher delivered a very able sermon full of instruction and interest. "Throw out the Lifeline," was then worded by Rev. C. T. Walker D. D., which was sung and joined in by the congregation. Prayer was then offered Rev. E. P. Johnson, of Madison. After prayer the choir was requested by the president to sing. The welcome address was then delivered by Ms. Lula Lamar, which assured the delegates that they had a warm reception from the hearts of the people of Augusta. The response by Rev. J. T. Russell, of Dawson, Ga., showed the people that all the expressions of their kindness were highly appreciated. A communication from the mayor of the city, Hon. J. H. Alexander was read showing regret for not being able to be present. A committee was then appointed on reading letters. The different committees were appointed. The following visiting brethren were introduced to the convention. Revs. G. H. Dwell, C. S Wilkins, A. Green, G. S. Johnson, T. J. Hornsby, J. W. Whitehead, W. H. Dunn, I. A. McNeal, Wm. Russell, J. B. Bunch, P. Walker, R. J. Johnson, and J. Campfield of Raysville, Ga.; A. L. DeAntignac, Noahs, Ga.; J. C. Carter, Hephzibah, Ga.; F. L. Bowie, Springfield, Mo.; D. McHorton, Gracewood, Ga.; G. W. Jones, Kiokee, Ga.; Mrs. J. C. Beall, Hampton Ga., Profs. H.L. Walker, T. M. Dent and M. C. Parker were appointed reporters for the different newspapers. Then adjourned until 3:30 p.m. Benediction by Rev. C. C. Jones.

Afternoon Session: At 3:30 the devotional services were conducted by Rev. R. T. Schell by singing, "At the Cross." Rev. J. H. Moore then invoked the blessings of the Holy Spirit. The 119 Psalm was read, then sang, "More Love, O, Christ! To Thee." Bro. W. Murphy then led in prayer. "Laborers of Christ, Arise" was sung. Prayer by Rev. R. T. Schell. The president announced the convention in order for business. The annual address was then delivered by the president. Rev. A. B. Murden motioned that the address be adopted and printed in the Baptist Banner, and also in the minutes of this convention. By motion Prof. A. R. Johnson was re-elected President. Rev. A. B. Murden motioned that all the present vice presidents be re-elected. Bro. J. S. Brandon was re-elected Secretary. Rev. R. T. Schell and C. T. Walker, D. D. were appointed to escort the newly elected president to the chair. Sung "All Hail the Power of Jesus's Name." Rev. E. J. Fisher, acting chairman, then introduced the president to the convention. The president made a few brief remarks, after which the treasurer, Rev. C. T. Walker made his annual report, which was adopted. By motion of Rev. J. S. Kelsey, Rev. C. T. Walker was re-elected treasurer of the convention.

A letter was read from Rev. D. D. Crawford, of Tennel, regretting his inability to be present during our meeting. By motion Rev. J. M. Jones, of Guyton, was appointed to preach at night, filling the appointment that was made for Rev. Crawford. A paper was then read by Prof. G. A. Goodwin, entitled "Origin and Progress of the Sunday School." Discussion was then engaged in by Revs. J. T. Russell, J. M. Jones, E. J. Fisher, E. P. Johnson, C. T. Walker, Bro. R. H. Thomas, Rev. A. B. Murden, and G. A. Goodwin. By motion of Prof. H. L. Walker that a vote of thanks be tendered Prof. Goodwin. By motion the papers to be read by Prof. C. Parker and J. S. Brandon be postponed until the most opportune time of Friday morning. The committee on letters then resumed reading. Report of committee on application was read and adopted, and those desiring to become members of the convention were introduced to the convention. Prof. N. L. Black, city editor of the Baptist Banner, of Atlanta, Ga., was also introduced to the convention and made a few remarks. After singing "Salvation," the benediction was pronounced by Rev. Gad. S. Johnson.

Night Session: The convention convened at 9:00 p. m. Services were begun by singing. After which Rev. C. T. Walker D. D., introduced Rev. J. M. Jones of Guyton, who read Mark 16th chapter. His text was taken from the 6th and 17th verses of the same chapter. After the sermon sang, "Why do you wait, dear brother." Prayer was offered by Rev. J. C. Center. A solo was then sung. Here are a few more that met July 5, 1894 in Augusta Georgia at the Tabernacle Baptist Church. Each person mentioned paid .25 cents to the cause. Mrs. S. C. Jones, Mrs. J. Dozier, S. W. H. Murry, Rev. R. T. Schell, Rev. C. McGahhee, Ms. Hattie G. Eskridge, Bro. Alfred Berrien, Mrs. Lydia Brown, Mrs. Berryan, Mrs. Eliza Thomas, Rev. R. H. Thomas, Ms. Viola Gilbert, Mr. Ned Beaton, Mrs. Clara Sells, Mr. Willis Washington, Mrs. Victoria Baity, Mr. R. M. Patterson, Mr. Allen Cole, Ms. Mamy Johnson, Ms. M. Yancey, Mr. W. Robinson, Mr. Charles Tilman, Mr. J. R. Stones, Mr. John D. Lakey, Ella Kelley, Josephine Smith, Mrs. Kittie Miller, Mr. W. M. Mack, Mr. S. H. Jones, J. B. Allen, Dempsey Shedric, a total of $20.00. Sang "Doxology," by Rev. J. S. Kelsey.

In the afternoon session Prof. T. M. Dent was then introduced, who held the audience in close attention while he spoke with eloquence.

I believe that Camp Gordon United States Military Reservation is a good place to start. I will mention the colored men and women that were located here and I was told me that these men and women started the colored communities.

Anna E. Williams is thirty-six years old, and is a cook out of South Carolina. Roger N. Cosby is a twenty-two-year-old out of South Carolina and works in the mailroom. Sara A.T. Jackson works in the mailroom. She was born in Georgia, and she is twenty-five years old. Aleck Smith is a thirty-year-old colored man born in Georgia and works as a cook in the kitchen. Albert Anderson is a forty-year-old born in Kentucky and he works as a cook. John Taylor is a twenty-four-year-old teamster. He was born in Georgia. Clifford J. Hardeman is a twenty-four-year-old man born in Georgia and works as a teamster as well.

Elmer Burch is a twenty-year-old colored man born in Georgia and works as a teamster. Charlie Hicks is a nineteen-year-old teamster as well and was born in Georgia, and works as a teamster, Samuel Lumpkin is twenty-four and was born in Georgia and works as a teamster, Augustine Hall is a fifty-four-year-old man born in Georgia and is a Feeder, *Kurmis W. Quesley is an eighteen-year-old mulatto man born in Georgia and works as a teamster and resides in Chamblee.* William McCaan is at the age of seventeen and is a teamster who was born in Georgia. *Albert Walker is a twenty five-year-old mulatto born in Georgia and is a teamster. Robert Carter is a twenty-two-year-old born in Georgia and works as a teamster.* Cyrus Gibson is a twenty-four-year-old born in Georgia and works as a teamster as well.

Adam Wade is a twenty-four-year-old born in Georgia and is a teamster. Cleveland Paxton is a twenty-six-year-old born in Georgia and works as a teamster. Luscious Smith is a twenty-three-year-old born in Georgia and is a teamster, Rutledge Teasley was born in Georgia and is at the age of seventeen and works as a teamster, Albert W. Rosser is a seventeen-year-old mulatto who was born in Georgia and works as a teamster, Arthur Williams is a fifty-year-old born in Kentucky and is listed as being a mulatto and is a feeder. Claude Phillips is a twenty-four-year-old mulatto born in Georgia and works as a teamster. These teamsters all work in the corral.

Eli Ward is a twenty-six-year-old born in Georgia and works as a teamster. Cliff Marshall is a twenty-one-year-old born in Georgia and is a teamster, John Coleman was born in Georgia and works as a teamster and is thirty-six years old. George Brown is twenty-seven born in Georgia and works as a teamster. *John Jett is a thirty-year-old man born in Georgia and works as a teamster who resides in Chamblee. Seaborn T. Jones is a thirty-four-year-old teamster born in Georgia and resides in Chamblee. George A. Hutchins is a twenty-year-old born in Georgia and works as a teamster and resides in Chamblee.* Frank Harvey is a twenty-six-year-old born in Georgia and is a feeder. Will Eaves is a twenty-six-year-old born in North Carolina and works as a teamster and resides on Pine Street in Atlanta. Ed Scott was born in Florida and works as a teamster. Sipe or Si Greene was born in Alabama and is twenty years old and works as a teamster. John W. Brown is a fifty-seven-year-old born in Georgia and works as a laborer in the garbage station with Ed Maxwell, a sixty-three-year-old born in North Carolina. Columbus Johnson is a sixty-year-old born in Georgia and works on the septic tank. William Stubblefield is a forty-five-year-old man born in Georgia and works on the septic tank as well. Thomas M. Sims is a thirty-one-year-old born in Georgia and is a laborer on the roads. Will Norells is a thirty-eight-year-old born in South Carolina and works as a septic tank cleaner, and so does Will L. Johnson, who was born in Georgia sixty-four years ago.

Early Brown is a twenty-three-year-old born in Georgia and works on the roads. *Wesley Parks was born in Georgia and is fifty-five years old and works as a laborer on the roads and resides in Norcross. Charlie Parson is a thirty-four-year-old from Georgia and works as a laborer on the roads as well. He resides in Doraville. Charlie Bul—— is forty-five years old and he was born in Georgia. He works on the roads and resides in Norcross. Oscar Trimble is fifty-five years old. George Trimble is forty years old.* I've got to mention Mr. Paul H. Jones, a sixty-five-year-old white man out of Marietta, Georgia, who is a fireman. Charles H. Purcell is a sixty-five-year-old born in Alabama, and he works on the roads as well. Will Nix is a twenty-five-year-old born in Georgia and works on the roads as well.

Sam Jett is a twenty-two-year-old born in Georgia and is a laborer on the roads and resides in Buckhead. Noah Bamer is a thirty-eight-year-old from Alabama and works as a laborer on the roads. Ison Smith is a fifty-five-year-old born in Georgia and works on the roads as well. Green Mathews is a thirty-five-year-old born in Georgia and works as a laborer doing plumbing. Paul Russell is a thirty-year-old mulatto born in Georgia and works on the roads. William Moore is a twenty-eight-year-old born in Ohio and works as a fireman in the boiler room. James W. Daniel is a forty-seven-year-old born in North Carolina and works as a laborer in concrete. Eugene Colbert is a thirty-year-old working with saddles. He was born in Georgia and lives at 201 Bell St. in Atlanta.

Will Scott is a twenty-four-year-old born in South Carolina and works on the wagon train. Lindsey Jones is a twenty-four-year-old out of Georgia residing on Currier Street in Atlanta. Virgil Smith is a thirty-eight-year-old born in Alabama and works on the wagon train. Mose Otez is a fifty-eight-year-old born in South Carolina and work on the wagon train as well. Edd Harris is a fifty-nine-year-old man born in Georgia and works on the wagon train. Luther Hosey is a fifty-year-old born in Georgia and his work consists of feeding the force. *Alonzo Howell is a twenty-two-year-old mulatto born in Georgia and works feeding the force. Alonzo resides in Doraville.* Harry Jones is a sixteen-year-old mulatto born in Georgia and works on the wagon train and lives in Atlanta. Floyd Daniels is a fifty-four-year-old born in Georgia and lives in Atlanta and works in the corral with sixteen-year-old George Daniel and sixteen-year-old farmer Daniel. All three reside at 67 Moody Street in Atlanta. *Charlie Appleberry is an eighteen-year-old born in Alabama and resides in Chamblee, Georgia.* William H. Long is an eighteen-year-old living in Atlanta. Ozie Cirtrunck is a nineteen-year-old living with William H. Long in Atlanta at 14 Bird Street. All are out of Alabama.

Jim Simmons is a forty-eight-year-old born in Georgia and living at 14 Bird Street as well. Millard M. Mapp is a thirty-one-year-old born in Georgia and works as a teamster. *Edgar Jones is a sixteen-year-old mulatto born in Georgia and resides in Chamblee, Georgia, and he works as a teamster as well.* Major Harris is a thirty-three-year-old born in Georgia and works in the corral and lives in Atlanta. George Gore is a nineteen-year-old born in Georgia and lives in Atlanta and works in the corral. Obee B. Brown is an eighteen-year-old man born in Alabama and works feeding the force. *Charlie Jones is a twenty-eight-year-old living in Doraville, Georgia, and he works feeding the force.* Robert Murry is a twenty-three-year-old mulatto man born in Georgia and resides in Atlanta and works feeding the force. Charlie Prather is a twenty-four-year-old man born in Georgia and resides in Atlanta and works feeding the force. *John Howell is twenty-nine-year-old living in Doraville Ga. John was born in Georgia and works feeding the force.* Clarence W. Weaver is seventeen-year-old mulatto living in Atlanta and is out of South Carolina and works feeding the force. Claude Marshall is living in Atlanta and was born in Georgia twenty-two years ago as a mulatto. Claude works feeding the force. Charlie Williams is a twenty-one-year-old born in Georgia and is living in Atlanta and works on the wagon train. Hinton Taylor is a twenty-two-year-old born in Georgia and works in the corral.

Charlie Core is a twenty-year-old living in Chamblee and is born in Alabama and worked as a teamster. Herbert Hope is a colored soldier born in

South Carolina and is a private in the United States Army. *Roy Bryant is a twenty-two-year-old colored laborer working in concrete.* William M. Bulkins is a twenty-one-year-old working in the warehouse. William Brown is a mulatto at the age of twenty-seven born in Georgia and working in the warehouse. Jack Stanley is a colored forty-year-old born in Georgia and works as a fireman in the boiler room. Lace Kelly is a thirty-six-year-old born in Georgia and works in the corral. Jim Hubard is a thirty-one-year-old born in Georgia and worked in the corral. Tellman Blake is a forty-nine-year-old born in Georgia who did the same kind of work as well. Morris Hudisan is a thirty-six-year-old, born in Montana, and works in the corral. *Willie Julian is a nineteen-year-old born in Georgia and is working in the corral. Willie Julian is a long-time colored resident in Lynwood Park and is now at this time living in Chamblee, Georgia. Mr. Lewis Jones is a twenty-four-year-old mulatto living in Chamblee as well. He was born in Georgia, and at this time he is working in the corral as well. Mr. John Peebles is a long-time member of the Doraville community as well and now Mr. John Peebles is at the age of twenty-one and is working in the wagon train as a teamster.* Mr. Jesse Zachary (spelled Zacery) is at the age of seventeen, was born in Georgia, and is a teamster as well. *Clifford Sutton is a close friend of my grandfather Arthur. Mr. Clifford Sutton is now at the age of twenty-six and he was listed as being a mulatto. He works as the foreman in the corral. Mr. Sutton was living Buckhead, Georgia. Mr. Sutton was living in the community of Buckhead, Georgia, and attends the Zion Hill Baptist Church in Johnsontown.*

Mr. Robert Kelsey is a forty-three-year-old born in Georgia and was now living in Atlanta, and he worked as a blacksmith I do not know if Mr. Robert Kelsey will become a preacher and have some kind of relationship with helping start Little Zion Baptist Church in Lynwood Park. Mr. John Hood was living in Chamblee and was a seventeen-year-old mulatto young man. John Hood was born in Georgia and was working as teamster. Archie Niceley was born in Georgia and is at the age of twenty-nine years old. Archie worked on the wagon train. Henry W. John was at the age of twenty-four years old and was born in Georgia and worked as teamster. Mr. Ernest Moore was born in Georgia and is at the age of twenty-eight years old. Mr. Moore worked on the wagon train. Lon Stokes was an eighteen-year-old mulatto young man born in Georgia and worked as a teamster. *William Fabere was twenty years old living in Chamblee, Georgia, and was born in Georgia and worked as a teamster.* Ervin Percey was a forty-six-year-old born in Georgia and worked in the corral. Mose Connally was born in Georgia and was at the age of sixty-seven years old and worked in the incinerator. I came across a few of the colored soldiers that were at Camp Gordon. Clarence

A. Laythne're was a thirty-one-year-old mulatto born in Kentucky. John B. Williams, at the age of twenty-three, born in South Carolina. William H. Treyman, a twenty-two-year-old mulatto born in Virginia. William E. Mathews, born in Virginia and a nineteen-year-old mulatto. Luddis B. Worrell a twenty-three-year-old born in North Carolina. Louis White a twenty-four-year-old born in Virginia as well. Joseph Ivey was a twenty-three-year-old mulatto born in Virginia. Layloy Thomas Was a twenty-seven-year-old born in Georgia.

Mr. Edward Hill is a twenty-six-year-old born in New Mexico. James A. Donaldson a thirty-one-year-old born in South Carolina. *Ben H. Williams is a thirty-four-year-old born in North Carolina,* Howard Cyceroe (?) was a twenty-one-year-old born in Mississippi and his Father was born in Jamaica and his mother was born in Mississippi. Napoleon Ramsey was a twenty-one-year-old born in Georgia. Griffin Martin was a twenty-three-year-old born in Virginia. James Russell is a twenty-seven-year-old mulatto born in Kentucky, and James W. Guthrie was a twenty-year-old born in Tennessee. George Baxter was a twenty-seven-year-old born in Arkansas; Will Robinson was born in South Carolina and was twenty-nine years old. Abner D. King was at the age of twenty-eight and was born in Arkansas. Willie Simon was a twenty-six-year-old born in Georgia. Sam Tatnall is a thirty-one-year-old born in Georgia. Barney L. Golden was a twenty-three-year-old born in Georgia. Louis W. Bryant was a twenty-nine-year-old born in Alabama.

Wilbur T. King was a twenty-seven-year-old mulatto born in Georgia. William A. Wilkes was a thirty-two-year-old mulatto born in Georgia. Judge Nelson was a thirty-year-old born in Georgia, and Ed Nishtigala was born in Georgia and was at the age of twenty-four. This section of the camp at Gordon was the sergeants quarters because all that were just mentioned are listed as being colored sergeants.

Will Spearman is at the age of thirty-four and is a private. Herbert Hope is a private as well and is at the age of twenty-four. Dave Hicks is a colored soldier at the age of nineteen. John Easley is a sixty-one-year-old out of Virginia working as a janitor in the civilian capacity at Fort Gordon. Bob Leslie is a forty-two-year-old mulatto born in Georgia and is working in the civilian capacity as well in the coal yard with twenty-one-year-old William Oxford, who was born in Georgia. Here are four young mulatto men born in Georgia working in the coal yard: *twenty-one-year old Earnest Summour,* twenty-one-year-old Fred D. Pascal, twenty-three-year-old Joe Benton, and John Watkins, a twenty-five-year-old. Carter Riley is a fifty-one-year-old born in Georgia. Britton Jordan is a sixty-four-year-old born in Georgia and he worked in the corral. Twenty-four-year-old George Rice was born in South Carolina. Fifty-year-old Allen Joseph was born in Georgia and Clarence Fall was a twenty-seven-year-old born in South Carolina. Harvey Pierce is a twenty-three-year-old born in Georgia. William Carter is a thirty-five-year-old born in Georgia. *Grady Ezzard is a twenty-year-old born in Georgia and works as a laborer in the coal yard. Mr. Grady Ezzard is living in Chamblee at this time in 1920.* William H. Jones is another colored man at the age of twenty-nine and was born in Alabama. Wesley Ellis is a fifty-year-old colored man born in Georgia. Willie Baker is a twenty-three-year-old born in Georgia. Charley Williams is a fifty-two-year-old born in Alabama and living in Atlanta. *Henry McDaniel was at this time at the age of twenty-four and was born in Georgia.*

Webster Maxwell was born in Georgia and was living in Atlanta. He was twenty-four years old. *Mr. Mack Smith in 1920 is at the age of thirty-three and a mulatto. He is living in Atlanta at 135a Bell Street and was born in Georgia. Is this the same Mack Smith that was living in the apartment with my grandfather in 1930 in Techwood?* Jim Cash is a forty-one-year-old born in Georgia. Leonard Bell is at the age of eighteen and was born in Georgia, and Pink Slack was born in Alabama and is at the age of fifty-three.

Now let's look at a few of the females that were working as civilians at Camp Gordon in 1920. Mamie Echols is a twenty-six-year-old mulatto. Annie Smith is a thirty-seven-year-old mulatto woman. Rose Carson is a twenty-four-year-old mulatto. Willie Wheeler is a thirty-one-year-old colored woman. Henrietta Barnett is a forty-one-year-old mulatto woman, and Annie Martin is a twenty-one-year-old mulatto woman. They all work in the laundry section of the camp. *Mr. Eugene Thompson is a mulatto living in Norcross, Georgia, and is at the age of thirty-six. He also works in the plumbing shop. Arthur Trimble is a twenty-two-year-old mulatto working in the plumbing shop as well and he too lives in Norcross.*

Erwin Hopkins is a colored man at the age of twenty-five and was born in Georgia. Dude Williams is a mulatto at the age of twenty-five and was born in Georgia. Len Harper is a sixty-year-old colored man born in Georgia. Rengo Martin is a twenty-year-old colored man born in Georgia. Roy Herndon is a twenty-one-year-old mulatto born in Georgia, *and Ed Huff is a thirty-four-year-old mulatto man born in North Carolina and works in the heating plant. I wonder if this is the first minister of China Grove Baptist Church.* James Herndon is a twenty-one-year-old mulatto born in Georgia. Ed Mayers is a forty-year-old born in Georgia, and Henry Blackwell is at the age of fifty-two and was born in Georgia. Sam Dougherty is at the age of eighteen and was born in Georgia. Jerry Howardworth is at the age of thirty-four and was born in Kentucky. Clem L. Hardy is at the age of eighteen and was born in Georgia. All worked in the plumbing plant at Fort Gordon.

Here are a few more colored soldiers from Fort Gordon in 1920. David Chamber is at the age of twenty-four and was born in Alabama. Durham E. Fergerson is out of Florida and is listed as a mulatto at the age of forty-seven. Julius or Julian Gibson is a colored soldier born in Florida and is at the age of twenty-four. Dock Jones is a mulatto colored soldier at the age of twenty-six years old and was born in North Carolina. Scott Razdell or Raydell is at the age of forty-one years old and was born in Kentucky. Lewis Washington was born in Virginia and was at the age of forty-three. Cosby Foster is a mulatto born in Georgia and is at the age of twenty-one years old. Carroll Jordan is at the age of fifty-four and was born in South Carolina. Walter Rose was born in Virginia and was at the age of twenty-eight.

BUILDING OF CAMP GORDAN AND THE HUDGINS FAMILY AND THE BLACKS OF CHAMBLEE GEORGIA.

> The State of Georgia, Fulton County: This indenture made this 18th day of June in the year of our Lord one thousand nine hundred and nineteen, between Gus Hudgins and L.P. Hudgins of the State of Georgia and County of Dekalb of the first part and the United State of America of the second part, to wit: That the said parties of the first part for and in consideration of the sum of three thousand nine hundred seventy-four in hand paid hereby acknowledged have granted, bargained, sold and conveyed and by these presents, do . . . parcel number 245-2 land lot 245 18th dist. DeKalb Co., Ga. Situated being part of land lot num. two hundred forty-five of the eighteenth dist. Beginning at an iron pin corner southeast corner of the Will T. Hudgins tract and southwest corner of L.P. and Gus Hudgins tract; thence 1 degree north five minutes thirty seconds east a distance of nine hundred twenty-seven and eight-tenths, feet to a point on the southern property line of the F.L. Hudgins tract, said point being

a common corner between Will T. and L.P. Hudgins, a distance of nine hundred twenty-two and four-tenths feet . . .

Being the same property conveyed by W.T. Hudgins to Gus and L. P. Hudgins by warranty deed dated October 28 1918, recorded in Deed Book 3-J page 373, DeKalb Co. Rec. at Decatur, Georgia. All of the above described property is more fully shown by blue print entitled Camp Gordon, Georgia, the L.P. and Gus Hudgins's property dated May 17, 1919, a copy of which is hereto attached . . . Signed, sealed, and delivered in presence of John D. Hightower, Capt. Q.M.C.; Hanson W. Jones, Notary Public, Georgia State at Large. My commission expires June 16, 1923. (I.R. Stamps $4.00)

3-J. page 373

This indenture made the 28th day of October in the year of our lord one thousand nine hundred and eight. W.T. Hudgins of the county of DeKalb and State of Georgia of the first part and Gus Hudgins, L. P. Hudgins of the county of DeKalb and State of Georgia of the second part, to wit: That the said party of the first part for and in consideration of the sum of four hundred dollars in hand paid at and before the sealing whereof is hereby acknowledged, has granted, bargained, sold, aliened, conveyed and confirmed and by these presents the receipt . . . the following property, to wit: commencing at an iron fence corner on the west side of Shallowford Road in front of the residence of A.P. Garrett running north nine hundred and thirty-six feet to F.L. Hudgins line to iron pin corner on east side of said road thence west nine hundred and thirty-five feet to G.N. Pierce line to iron pin corner then east nine hundred and thirty-one feet to beginning point containing twenty acres more or less being a part of the east half of the north half of land lot No. 245 in the eighteenth district t of said county of DeKalb and bounded as follows on the east by the land of A.P. Garrett on the north by F. L. Hudgins on the West by W.T. Hudgins on the south by G.N. Pierce . . .

> Witnessed by J.A. Sword and J.E. Munday N.P. W.T. Hudgins recorded Nov. 2, 1908 B.T. Burgess Clerk.
>
> Page 560 R.P. House
>
> The proceeds of said sale are to be applied, first, to the payment of said debt and interest and expenses of this proceeding, note for twelve hundred and thirty-six and 67/100 dollars dated Sept. 18, 1920. Land put up for this money was in the 15th district of DeKalb County, Ga. On the east side of Mayson's Avenue one hundred and fifty feet south of Oxford lane and running thence east two hundred feet and north fifty feet, being lot no. 30 of the Fannie J. Mayson subdivision also all that tract of land in land lot 239 in the 15 district of DeKalb co. being the west half of lot no. 2 of the Mayson subdivision, as per plat of record in deed book H.H. page 295. Z.D. Harrison land. Signed, sealed and delivered in presence of R.P. House, W.E. Talley deputy clerk.

About this same time Little Zion Baptist Church was being formed. I gathered this information from the secretary of Little Zion Baptist Church one Sunday afternoon.

> Now the Little Zion Baptist Church began as a little Sunday school in the home of Sis. Janie Gaither. Later she was given a place to have church service in a little courthouse on Cheshire Bridge Road, with Bro. Ed Dorsey as superintendent and others.
>
> In 1923, Rev. J.T. Dorsey, Pastor of the Second Mount Zion Baptist Church, and his staff of Deacons organized the Little Zion Baptist Church. The first revival was the second week in August 1923, and many joined Little Zion under its first Pastor, Reverend J.B. Davis. Baptism was the second Sunday in September 1923. Seven Brothers were set aside for Deacons: Bro. Raymond Akins, Bro. Will Banks, Bro. Wylie Akins, Bro. Alvin Wright, who in 1930 was living on Briarcliff Road and was thirty four years old and had been married to Annie for twenty one

years and she was at the age of thirty, and their children were Willie B. thirteen, Cartha L. ten, and John H. was two years old. I believe that Alvin was working for seventy year old Wm. C. Jones and his sixty nine year old wife Nancy. In 1920, Alvin was living in Clayton County on Stockbridge Road at the age of twenty five his twenty two year old wife Wutsie A Wright had born him two children William B. three and a few days old daughter named Cartha L. and Albert Williams a ninety year old grandfather. Alvin was living with nineteen year old Berry Wright and his wife Annie who was the same age as her husband. Living with Berry and Annie were one year old Berry W., forty six year old mother Etta, and his sixteen year old sister Katie. I even found fifty three year old Will Banks as well. I mentioned this part of Clayton County because this is where Indiana Callaway was located as a widow in 1900 with her son Jesse living near the white family the Adamson. This is the same place where I found Rev. Joshua S. Callaway and his slave Aaron and Hannah. I must mention the next family because this next family has a tie to the Jackson family. Tom Julian fifty five, Randy his wife is fifty three, Leilar is seventeen, Eddie is fifteen, Ada is twelve, Feddie and Henry are both eight years old, and their youngest is their daughter Francis at five. Mr. Oscar Julian is thirty and his wife Mattie S. is sixteen, and a brother living with him is named Luther at the age of twenty six. When I went to Clayton County after finding that Alvin Wright once lived here I was wondering who else was living near the Adamson family where Indiana Callaway left there to live in the third ward in Atlanta where my grandfather and a few more Callaway's lived. Arthur Callaway lived there with Racheal Callaway. Will Fleming, Bro. Randall Butler, and Bro. Will Glover.

The congregation served for a short time in that little courthouse but for some unknown reason was locked out and had to find another place to worship. With the help of the good Lord, the congregation purchased a piece of property on Piedmont Road that had a two-room house on it. Rev. J.B. Davis, first Pastor of Little Zion, and some of the members did not come back to church. Rev.

> Howard Irvin served as leader until Rev. T.H. Hurley was called to pastor. He, with the help of the members, built the first Little Zion Baptist Church. He then organized the Usher Board, ordained several Deacons and two Preachers (Deacon Will Banks and Bro. Virgil Oliver). He served for a short while. Rev. T.H. Ford, little Zion's third Pastor, organized the Willing Workers' Club, which did wonderful work for the church. He served a short while and resigned in favor of Rev. H.O. Hood.
>
> Rev. H.O. Hood, Little Zion's fourth Pastor, ordained two Preachers (Rev. H.B. Dix and Rev. C.C. Woods). Rev. H.B. Dix became the fifth Pastor; Rev. H. Hall became the sixth Pastor. He ordained one preacher, Rev. Jerry T. Johnson, and several Deacons.
>
> Rev. J.C. Carter became Little Zion's seventh pastor; R.L. Verden became the eight Pastor, Rev. C. Edwards became the ninth pastor, Rev. Edie L. Jones became the tenth pastor.
>
> A one-room New Hope Elementary School was built in the churchyard in 1910 and became an important element in Buckhead's black community; a second room was later added. (Courtesy of Elizabeth Few.)

Pleasant Hill Church was established on September 29, 1877 when William Brown deeded an acre of land on Paces Ferry Road at the intersection of Mount Paran Road. The church was renamed Paces Ferry United Methodist Church in 1957.

On September 19, 1899, the trustees of the Piney Grove Church, a place of worship for black members of the community, bought land on present Canterbury Road between Lenox Square and Lindbergh Plaza from John Mason for 50 dollars. The Piney Grove congregation worshipped under a bush arbor near an old slave cemetery on their acre of land until they later built a permanent sanctuary.

Piney Grove Baptist Church is in the New Hope Baptist Association. This is a profile of the Piney Grove Baptist Church between 1900 and 1902.

1. *Piney Grove, Fulton County. I. M. Murphy is the pastor, the clerk is E. Rhodes and the place in Fulton County is called Edwardsville.*

2. *Piney Grove, Fulton County. E.D. Smith is the pastor, the clerk is E. Hike and its post office is Atlanta.*
3. *Piney Grove Baptist Church, Edwardsville, Ga., Fulton Co.—Pastor, N. B. Blalock; delegates, Rev. N. B. Blalock and A. Williams. The Piney Grove Baptist Church relocated to Lynwood Park after some split between the membership.*

While N.B. Blalock was the pastor, the place where Piney Grove is located is still called Edwardsville. Here is an ironic situation about Rev. N. B. Blalock. He was the pastor of China Grove in Campbell County or South Fulton in Red Oak. China Grove is the name of the church that I grew up in, in Lynwood Park. Red Oak does not exist in the Red Oak section of Fulton County. In all of my studies on the New Hope Baptist Association, I never found I. R. Hall at any church in this association. What is his purpose for being in this association if he is not at any church? Is he a white man? Or like M. M. Kelly and Collins H. Lyons, will soon become a white man?

The City of Doraville, Georgia, and Its Colored Families

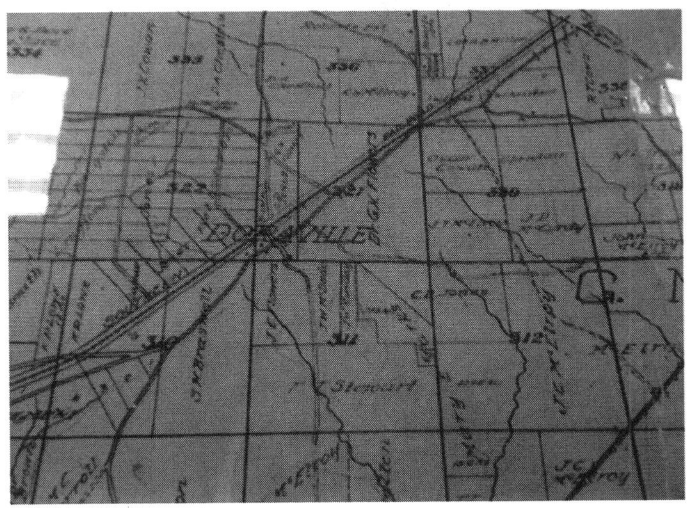

The first Callaway that I found that would have been in Doraville, Georgia, in DeKalb County is Ms. Hattie Callaway. She was a student in the Spelman Seminary College in Atlanta, Georgia, with another

Calloway named Lillie. This was at the beginning and between the years 1896–1897, in Class H.

Nenie Benjamin of Jacksonville, Florida; Beatrice Adams of Millen, Georgia; and *Hattie Calloway of and Lillie Calloway of Atlanta. We will follow the events of Harriet Callaway and Lillie Callaway in the Spelman College enrollment book. These are the children of Henry C. Callaway and his wife America. They have ties to Robert C. Callaway in Athens.*

Doraville is a colored community and its members are as close to me as family. I spent many Sundays in the churches here and buried many colored men and women from Doraville in Mount Zion Cemetery in Chamblee. My grandfather would rise up early in the morning and then awaken me early so we could get to the cemetery in time to dig the grave before the funeral procession was to arrive. Some days it was so cold, and we would just wait, wait, and wait. We waited because sometimes the funeral service would take longer with the colored Baptists and Methodists. It's not like it is today, just call it a celebration and we're done! People really took their time to express themselves in truth for the ones they valued so well.

1893 Doraville, Georgia

I also found these coloreds living in Doraville and the Shallow Ford District of DeKalb County at this time as well.

Doraville District 1416

Elbert Evans, Perry Golston, Dan Garrison, Charlie Hudson, Lewis Jackson, Anderson Jones, Berry Jones, Warren Johnson, Robert Kendrick, John Kinnon, Barto Lankford, Eli Middlebrooks, Daniel W. Morehead, Jonah Partee, Sam Stanton, C.C. Tucker

Perry Golston had 55 acres, Robert Kendrick had 1.5 acres, and C.C Tucker had 40.5 acres of land.

Doraville is a place where coloreds resided and prospered. This is the same place where Harriet Callaway, a graduate of Spelman, became a teacher after marring St. Claire Hardin.

> *Atlanta Historical Society in Buckhead:* The name which deserves mentioning in this connection is that of Mr. Clarence C. Tucker, who was in charge of the industrial training of the boys from 1883 to 1892. His impress is therefore upon the construction of the Knowles Building, in 1884, and upon the type of instruction which was given to

> the students in manual work. Himself an expert as an artisan, he was yet primarily a teacher. Important as was the product of the student's effort, and he was not the man to accept imperfect work, he yet regarded the one ruling purpose to be the development of the intelligence and efficiency of the boy himself. The teaching of Mr. Tucker was therefore in reality on a high academic plane, coordinating well with the literary studies of the same student.

In Doraville was a Colored Odd Fellows Building located between buildings owned by B. L.E. Sallerpeky and two buildings of B. N. Nuckles and J.E. Flowers and O. C. Cowan and D. G. Miller owned property on Depot Street where all the buildings reside. Now C. C. Tucker is a teacher at Morehouse College.

1894, Doraville District 1416

Elbert Evans, Perry Golston, Dan Garrison, Charlie Hudson, Lewis Jackson, Anderson Jones, Berry Jones, Warren Johnson, Robert Kendrick, John Kinnon, Barto Lankford, Eli Middlebrooks, Daniel W. Morehead, Jonah Partee, Sam Stanton, C.C. Tucker

Shallow Ford 524 district PO Dunwoody

Peter Bankston, Joe Butler, Miles Bryant, Bill Dilfre

Coloreds in 1899 in Doraville District 1416

Miles Bryant, Tinn Ford (who has thirty-five acres), Edmond Gholston (fifty-five acres), Dan Garrison, Charlie Hudson, Andrew James, Charity Jones, Berry Jones, Lewis T. Jones, Lewis Jackson, Bartow Lankord, Dan W. Morehead, Allen McDaniel, James Reeves, Sam Stanton

Shallow Ford District 524

Henry Bryant, Peter Bankston, Ed Bailey, Webster David, March Holmes, John Jones, Giles Young

Coloreds in 1899, Cross Keys 686 *Lynwood Park Community*

Bose Allen, Adell Bryant, Judge Couch, Sandford Favors, James W. Hood, Perry N. Hood, Ed Jones, Thomas Johnson, Titus Jett, Buck Johnson, Levi Jet, Sam Jet, Wilkes Smith, Tony Turner, C.C. Tucker, Lewis Zachry

As you can see, C. C. Tucker is in the Cross Keys District after he was first located in Doraville. This will become a trend with the coloreds that would come to reside in Doraville in the 1920s through to the 1940s. C.C. Tucker arrived at Morehouse in 1884 up until 1892. Where was Mr. C. C. Tucker between 1892 and 1898? The Tucker family were long-time members of the China Grove First Missionary Baptist Church in Lynwood Park.

1899–1900 *Spelman College*

Class I
Emma Tuggle of Atlanta
Ivernonah Wilkinson of Grantsville, Georgia
Eddie May Wofford of Cartersville, Georgia

Class H
Carrie Baldwin of Atlanta
Hattie Calloway of Atlanta
Lilie B. Callaway of Atlanta
Carrie Cash of Red Oak, Georgia
Carrie Bell Dixon of Columbus, Georgia
Addie Dupree of Atlanta
Annie Durden of Madison, Georgia

The next time that I find Hattie is in the first year of class at Spelman in 1912–1913. I found Hattie E. Calloway of Atlanta with Leila Adams of Watkinsville, Georgia. However, Hattie has the middle initial E. *Could the middle initial stand for Elizabeth, who is out of Alabama with Lillie B. Callaway?*

Seventh Grade class

Letitia Callaway of Vernon, Texas

Fourth Grade Class

Ethel Callaway of Vernon, Texas

Hattie E. Callaway was mentioned in the class of 1914 as being in this class and out of Atlanta.

High School English Normal Class of 1914: Dinah E. Brailsford is teaching in De Land, Florida. Lillian B. Brockenton is teaching at Lamar S. C. *Hattie W. Callaway is teaching at a school in Doraville, Georgia.*

Hattie W. Callaway is mentioned in the Spelman Almanac up until the time she is married while teaching in Doraville, Georgia. In the class of 1917, Ms. Rowena V. Holley was teaching in Palatka, Florida. Spelman also mentions still Ms. Edna A. Calloway of Union Springs, Alabama. *Ms. Hattie W. Callaway has now become Mrs. E. St. Charles Hardin of Atlanta, Georgia.*

I have these two surprising last names that are mentioned as living in Chamblee between 1919 and 1920 and they are Juanita Sharpe and Roberta Sharpe of Chamblee. In the fifth-grade class and in the sixth-grade class: Willie Bronner of Roswell, Georgia.

The names of the landowners in the 686th District of Cross Keys, such as the Hudgins family, are some of the ones that resided in Chamblee, Georgia, and sold their land to the Federal government to make way for Fort Gordon. Gus Hudgins was the defense attorney for Charlie Callaway as well. I do not know how he came to represent Charlie. Since finding Charlie Calloway born in 1859 on the Elbert county Chain Gang on the farm of J. C. Hudgins this is the only other time that I found a Charlie Callaway having any relationship with the Hudgins family again in DeKalb County in Chamblee of All Places! Remember I could not tell if his real name is Charley or Cornelius out of the Hope Well Association minuets and who would eventually come to resided in Decatur Georgia between 1930 and 1940.

1899 DeKalb County Georgia

Whites, Decatur 531

Ben F. Hudgins, Ms. Georgia Hudgins

Coloreds, 1899, Clarkston 1327

Aaron Aycock, Isaac Aycock, John Aycock, Thomas Chandler, Charlie Chandler, Robert Lester, Mathew Lester, Charlie Shaw, Carrie Stokes, Laura J. Stokes

Shallowford 524 district

Henry Bryant, Peter Bankston, Ed Bailey, Webster David, March Holmes, John Jones, Giles Young

The 1940 census of Doraville, Georgia, in DeKalb County

Doraville, Georgia M. D. 1411; Supervisory District No. 5, Enumerated District No. 44–48. April 5, 1940. John W. Chesnutt is the enumerator.

The first colored family I come across is living off of Winters Chapel is the house of Mr. Darling Warbington, a seventy-year-old, and his sixty-year-old wife Emma and their granddaughter Lori, who is twenty-one. Loush S. their grandson (twenty). Andrew C. is nineteen, Betty J. fifteen, Jarson is thirteen, Leon is twelve, Robert is six, Gwendolyn three, Perry Parsons is ten, Colquitt is nine, and Morris Hood is seven. All are his grandchildren. Mr. Darling Warbinton paid five dollars a month for his mortgage for he owns his property next to Mr. F. J. Wilson. Mr. Darling Warbinton is a farmer on his own farm.

Mrs. Lula Lankford is a seventy-year-old widow paying five dollars for rent of her place. She has her forty-year-old daughter June Peoples and her grandchildren William S. (twenty), Ruth (seventeen), Mattie (sixteen), Harrison (fourteen), Fannie (twelve), May (eleven), W. C. (ten), Gholston (nine), Floyd (eight), and Lucile (four). The whole family is living on Winters Chapel Road. William S. is the only one working in the house of Lula Lankford as a laborer in road work.

Moving on down the road I come to the place of Mr. Carly Smith, a fifty-year-old colored man and his wife Clyde, who is twenty-four years old. They are paying rent at five dollars a month. He works twelve hours a week working as a laborer in road work.

Living out on McClary Road is Mr. James Gholston, a fifty-two-year-old colored man, and his twenty-one-year-old wife Jasmine, their twenty-four-year-old daughter Irene, their twenty-one-year-old son Langston W., their nineteen-year-old son Hezekiah, their sixteen-year-old daughter Emma H., their thirteen-year-old son Tommie Lee, and their two-year-old step daughter Marian Williams. Mr. James Gholston and family are living at the intersection of McClary Road and Buford Road.

Living on Doraville and Tucker Road is the colored family of Grover Jackson, a twenty-five-year-old man and his wife Cleo, who is twenty-four, their twelve-year-old son Paul, and their four-year-old daughter Mayse.

Living a few houses down the road is Mrs. Lizzie Gholston, a seventy-five-year-old widow woman who owns her own property at one thousand dollars a month in mortgage. And living right next door is Essie Morrison, a fifty-year-old colored woman who pays one dollar in rent. Her daughter Alma L. is about thirty years old. Another daughter, Throston's age is blotted out. Overton, her son, is twenty and works in the filling station.

Mr. George Mosley is twenty years old and his brother John is eighteen and are lodgers in the house with Mr. C. W. Morris, a fifty-three-year-old white man, and his forty-nine-year-old wife, Mrs. Clara Morris. Mr. C. W. Morris runs a dairy farm and they are laborers on his farm. They are all living on or near Railroad Avenue in Doraville.

Moving on down Railroad Avenue, we come to the house of Mr. John Ramsey, a thirty-eight-year-old colored man, and his wife Fanny, who is thirty-nine. Elizabeth, their daughter, is twenty, Margaret is eighteen, Edwin is fifteen, Robert is thirteen, Sammy is ten, Otis is eight, and Barbara is three months old. Mr. John Ramsey pays five dollars a month for rent, and works as a farmer on a farm. Mr. William D. Hood does public work and pays five dollars for rent. His wife Cyonting is forty years old and their son Herbert is nineteen, Hurbert is nineteen, Barbara is seventeen, Willie Mae is ten, and the mother-in-law Mrs. Harriet Allen is an eighty-eight-year-old widow living in the house.

Mr. Adolpheus Jones is a sixty-six-year-old colored neighbor of Mr. William D. Hood. His wife is named Cora, who is fifty-seven. Their daughter Carrie is nineteen. Mr. Jones owns his property and pays one thousand dollars a month in mortgage. He is a laborer in public works.

Mr. John H. Hood is a colored fifty-two-year-old property owner of one thousand dollars a month in mortgage. His wife Ethel D. is fifty-two as well, and Ethel T., their daughter, is twenty-six. Mattie M. is twenty-five, Kenneth R. is twenty-three, Mariam L. is twenty, Lamon N. is eighteen. Mattie Lamar is the seventy-eight-year-old mother-in-law. Essie, the sister, is thirty-seven. Mr. John H. Hood works in public works as well. His neighbor is Thurmon Gresham, who is a seventy-four-year-old Negro, and his grandson Osburn is thirty-two. Ethel, his wife, is twenty-six. Their children are the grandchildren of Mr. Gresham. Mathew is eight, Willie is seven, Mary is six, Horace is five, Josh is two, and Virginia is a few months old. We are still on Railroad Avenue in Doraville, Georgia.

Moving on down the Railroad, I come to the house of Mr. Andrew Gresham, a twenty-eight-year-old, and his wife Mildred is seventeen. They are paying two dollars a month for rent. He's a helper in something that is spelled Juc-trash.

Lizzie Gresham is paying mortgage of two hundred and fifty dollars a month. Mrs. Lizzie is a widow at the age of forty. She's a washer woman and has her son Eugene, who is seventeen. Grady is thirteen. Mary Lois is twelve. Laura Ford, her daughter, is thirty. Henry Powell, her brother, is forty-nine years old. George Ford, her brother-in-law, is thirty-four.

Grier Ramsey is a sixty-year-old Negro, and his wife Margaret is forty-two. Grier and Margaret pay one dollar a month. He's a laborer in a private home and she's a cook in a private home. The two live at the end of Railroad Avenue. I also found these three women. one white and two coloreds. Dolly Holbrook is a wife at thirty-five. Martha Peoples is nineteen and Mattie is her sixty-five-year-old mother.

I hope that my writing about the many colored families in Doraville and in Chamblee and other places that my wife and I have traveled show the readers and generations to come that the men and women they call grandfather and grandmother or even great-grands are men and women that just should not go down in history as those people or Generation X. These are colored men and women that came through very hard and murderous and deceptive and manipulative trials, which led to the deception of their families, both black and white, that have something very much in common and that is relations!

The secrets that have been kept have driven a huge wedge between the two communities, which cause the same thing to happen today with the question of the race of our president. Many times I have stood in awe of the blank look when I have asked questions about the genealogy or question of their father's race or even their mother's race, then comes no response. The quietness or stillness in the room breaks my heart when I would get close to some of my lost family and they think just because my wife is white that she is really the Callaway and I am just an imposter! The response that never comes is due to the fact that the shame and fear that came because of the mixed relationship in the past generations that existed might have happened because of love or rape. It might be that they have been cautioned not to speak of the white ancestry to protect them or themselves from harm! We may never know why Arthur Callaway or Kator didn't speak of his family! However, I may get some kind of response from my generation who are freer in their understanding as we move far away from the guilt and ignorance of our past. And that is why I am writing names of the colored and a few whites that might have heard of this story in 1899! It is a large conspiracy and I may not come to a conclusion as to what really happened to Charlie and Mary. However, I do know that if the story was passed down to me and my family, it has to be passed down to another family as well.

The other coloreds that were in the 686 Cross Keys District were Mr. Pink Medlock, who was born May 1855 and was forty-five years old. He had been married for seven years to Sarah, who was born September 1847 and was fifty-two. Their children are Maggie (born September 1883 and is sixteen) and Ethel (born March 1887 and is thirteen). A grandson named Joe McFarlin was born May 1884 and is sixteen. Living next door is the colored family of Mr. Crawford Flowers, born March 1868 and is a widower at the age of thirty-two. His two daughters are Emmie (born April 1896 and is four) and Jewell (born September 1898 and is a year old). There is one white family that I will mention and that is the Baldwins that lived in the Cross Keys district. Mr. V. J. Baldwin was born March 1863 and was thirty-three years old. He had been married for twelve years to Sue Baldwin, born November 1863 and is thirty-four. Their children are Minnie (born October 1888 and is eleven), Angeline (born January 1891 and is nine years old), Lena (born September 1892 and is seven), Ezra (born March 1896 and is four), and Elnora (born April 1898 and is two). Mr. Baldwin had as a neighbor Jordan Phinizy, a colored man born February 1865 and is thirty-five years old. He had been married for three years to Mary Phinizy, who was born January 1868 and was thirty-two years old. They have one child, Laura, born April 1898 and was two years old.

1910

By the year 1910, the Cross Keys District had named roads. Living on Powers Ferry Road on the thirtieth day of June was Mr. Bailus Sutton, a twenty-nine-year-old colored man and his twenty-two-year-old wife Emma B. Sutton out of South Carolina. The two have been married for five years and both have been married only once and have one child named Peter S. Sutton at the age of four. March M. Holmes is a seventy-one-year-old colored man living next door with his seventy-year-old wife Emma C. They have been married for fifty years and have had nine children, only three of them still living in 1900. March M. Holmes and his wife Emma C. and Bailus Sutton and his family live near the property of Mr. Justonian Evans, a sixty-six-year-old white man whose property backs up to Mr. Cates, which was sold to the colored community of Lynwood Park. In the house with Mr. Evans is his wife Martha C. who is sixty-four years old. She has been married to Mr. Evans for forty-three years and have had eight children, seven of whom are still living in 1900. Anna, their twenty-year-old daughter, is living in the house with her parents. Mr. Robert H. Brown is a forty-five-year-old colored man living on the other side of Mr. Evans and the opposite side of Bailus Sutton and March M. Holmes and their families. Robert Brown lives with his wife Mandy M. Brown, who is thirty-five years old. They have been married for eighteen years and she had borne him eleven children, with only nine still living at this time. They are George W. Brown (eighteen), Robert A. (fifteen), Winston H. (twelve), Laura L. (nine), Julius O. (seven), Henry C. (five), James F. (four), Linda L. (two), and Lenna B. (three months old). Their nephew living with them was William M. Emory, aged nine.

Before I go on down the road to Mr. Bose A. Allen's house, I want to visit the tax digest of White County about this same time in 1910. Here I will attempt to show you the relationship that might have taken place between the Sutton and Callaway and even the Jones families that were in White County, Georgia. One major tie that might bind Charlie Callaway and Balous Sutton and the Joneses in DeKalb together is Mr. Ransom A. Williams, better known as Peg-Leg Williams.

Moving on down the road to the house of Mr. Boss A. Allen, a fifty-three-year-old colored man, and his wife Harriet, who was fifty years old. They have been married for three years and both have been married once before. They have had thirteen children between them, and in 1910 only eleven are living. *As you will now see, the Jones were kin to the Allen family as well.*

Boss Allen had a sixteen-year-old stepson by the name of Cyrus S. Jones and a sixteen-year-old stepdaughter, Cynthia L. Jones. Tolbert Jones, another stepson, is twelve years old. Harriet, his second wife, was born in Georgia; however, her parents were born in Tennessee. Living next door is Wooten J. Allen, a twenty-eight-year-old, and his wife Georgia A., who is twenty-six. They've both been married only once and have had four children while being married for eight years. Their children are Ethedge R. (seven), Mattison (five), Arthur E. (three), and Christine (one month old). Mr. James A. Cates is the white man that sold the property to start the Lynwood Colored Community. Mr. James A. Cates is sixty-two years old and his wife Sara C. is fifty-four. James A. Cates has been married once before, while it is the first time for Ms. Sarah. They have been married for fourteen years and have had only one child. However, there are three children living in the house at this time in 1910. Their children are May (twenty-six), Emma L. (twenty-five), and Charles A. (thirteen). There are a few more colored families that are one the Powers Ferry Road. However, Mr. Cates and Wooten T. Allen are living on the Atlanta Road. While Jasper Watson, a fifty-year-old colored widower, is living with his two sons Robert E. (eighteen) and Harold (fifteen). Jim Nix is another colored man on Powers Ferry. Jim is fifty-four and his wife Kate is forty-nine. They have been married for thirty-seven years and have had five children, with only three still living.

Mr. Luther Huie is a thirty-three-year-old man and his wife Lessie Huie is at the age of thirty-two. They have been married for nine years and have had two children: Eva (nine) and Zelma (six). The next family is the white family of Mr. James H. Smith, a thirty three-year-old, and his thirty-six-year-old wife Sara J. They have been married for twelve years and have had five children with only four living in 1910. Charlie J. is eight, Lawada is six, Margaret is three, and Charles L. is one month old. I believe that Mr. Smith gave the property to help start the Colored Methodist Church in Buckhead on Arden Road. Living near the Stone Mountain Road in the Cross Keys district is Mr. William J. Ford. Mr. Ford was living on Carroll Street in Chamblee, Georgia. Mr. Ford was a colored man at the age of twenty-four and his mulatto wife was named Leila, who was twenty-two. Their daughter Mattie was a few months old. Living on Peachtree Road was Mr. Walter McDaniel, a mulatto man at the age of twenty, He has been married to Carwina for one year and has a three-month-old mulatto son by the name of Edward M. McDaniel.

Also living on Peachtree Road is the family of Ms. Fannie New, a colored woman out of South Carolina who is thirty-three years old, and Corrie Shields, a thirty-year-old colored man out of South Carolina as well. Only nine houses away is the house of Mr. Tom Johnson, whose age is unknown. His wife Lucy's age is also unknown. Lucy was born in Virginia. Only two houses away is the house of Tom Coker a colored widower at fifty years old and out of South Carolina and his son Solomon who is fourteen and was born in Georgia.

On June 4, 1910, I found in the Cross Keys District of DeKalb County on Peachtree Road the DeKalb County Road Construction Camp Lines 53 and 77, with Pr. Leon P. Hudgins as the enumerator. I was told that there was a chain gang at Johnson Ferry and Peachtree Road at one time. As I look at the 1910 census, there were places for these men to reside and Mr. Jim or James Russell, a colored twenty-six-year-old man out of Kentucky, is the head of the camp. Jim Russell had Mr. Will Donald lodging with him, a forty-six-year-old married man out of South Carolina, as well as eighteen-year-old Jim Donald also from South Carolina. Out of North Carolina is twenty-year-old Ed Black. Norman Young is a twenty-one-year-old out of South Carolina. Frank Anderson is a twenty-eight-year-old out of South Carolina. Buford Williams is at the age of forty-five and has been married for seventeen years and is out of S. C., Jean Harrison is fifty-one and has been married thirty years and is out of South Carolina. Mr. Joe Wyden is a twenty-six-year-old out of South Carolina. Will Thomas is an eighteen-year-old out of South Carolina. Frank Madison is a twenty-eight-year-old out of South Carolina. Millroe Cook is a twenty-year-old out of Alabama. John Thomas is a twenty-seven-year-old out of South Carolina and has been married for eight years. James Henry is a twenty-one-year-old out of South Carolina. Knox Young is an eighteen-year-old out of South Carolina. Charlie Brown is a twenty-three-year-old out of South Carolina. George Donald is a twenty-two-year-old out of South Carolina. Mr. Ed Sanders a twenty-year-old from Georgia. All that were previously mentioned are colored men who working in the stone quarry.

The men that I am about to mention are all white. Mr. Lon Patterson is a twenty-four-year-old man, half Irish and half English, and is listed both the head and a laborer. John King is a thirty-six-year-old engineer out of California. James C. Betorbaysh is a thirty-four-year-old out of South Carolina and is an engineer as well. Sylvester Harper is a twenty-three-year-old from Georgia and works as an engineer as well. Earl Barton is a twenty-one-year-old out of South Carolina and works as a drill man in the stone quarry. Mr. Dave Hulsey is from Georgia and is twenty-three years old and works as an engineer. James Jones is nineteen, from Alabama, and works as a demolition man.

Here ends the enumeration of Cross Keys District. The majority of the coloreds in the road gang in Cross Keys are out of South Carolina and I wonder if these same men came through Elbert County, the Granite Capital of the World.

Living at the corner of Dunwoody Road and Harts Mill Road were these colored Families in 1910. Reuben Carter, a fifty-five-year-old colored man, and his wife, Tissue, who was fifty-three. They have been married for twenty-nine years. Their children are Eunice C. (fourteen), Carl (twelve), and Claud (ten). Wallace Underwood is a boarder at the age of fifteen. Homer C. Carter was twenty years old and had been married to Malarida for one year. Gip Hamady is a twenty-nine-year-old man and his wife Fannie is forty years old. They have been married five years. Fannie was a Mitchell before becoming his wife. Fannie's children are Rose Mitchell (twenty) and Pearl (seventeen).

Living on Shallowford Road in 1910 are these colored families. Trim M. Ford, a fifty-year-old, and Beatie, his forty five-year-old wife. Ola, their daughter, is thirteen. George is their five-year-old grandson. This family is located on Shallowford Road near James L. Wilson, William R. Wilson, and Mrs. Netty Huggins. Dock Pew is a twenty-four-year-old colored man married for five years to Willie, twenty-three. They have four children, Leola (four), Orrie (two), Otis (one), and William H. Pew (two months old). They have a boarder by the name of William Fair who is fourteen.

Moving on down the Shallowford Road to Mr. Miles Bryant's house, a mulatto man at the age of eighty-five and his seventy-seven-year-old wife Martha. They have been married for sixty-four years. Their neighbor is Levi Jett, a forty-eight-year-old widower, and his daughters Dorris (sixteen) and Gertrude (thirteen). All of Levi Jett's children are mulattoes. Oh! I forgot to mention his fourteen-year-old son Dent S. These colored families are living near the plantation of John B. Loyd and William E. Marchman in 1910.

Living on Powers Ferry Road in 1910 in the Heart of Buckhead

This is a wonderful find and shows me the relationship between certain coloreds that relocated to the Lynwood community in 1916 from Buckhead. The two white men are James A. Cates and Mr. Evans. Both owned property in the heart of the Buckhead Community on the road leading toward Chastain Park, where the chain gang was located for years. Like I said before, how the colored community was formed or run paralleled the chain gang system, and the men who furnished the liquor became filthy rich from this system! This is the elite of North DeKalb and North Fulton, Georgia!

Living on Powers Ferry Road is Perry N. Hood, *a mulatto fifty-six-year-old widower, and his mother Sallie Hood, seventy-five, who is a widow as well. Their house number is 84. They are living next door to a white man named Adam W. Philips. After you pass his house, you come to the house of Mr. Robert Johnson, a twenty-four-year-old colored man who has been married to his wife Anna for eight years. They have four children, Lula (five), Estelle (three), and a three-month-old daughter named Anna. One of their child died. The next house you come to is Mr. Ed D. Childer's, a thirty-three-year-old white man living with his family. The next house you come to is the house of a colored man named John W. Gibson, a mulatto man at the age of thirty-two; his wife Alm, a mulatto woman at the age of thirty-two; their twelve-year-old daughter Margaret; and their ten-year-old daughter Alma. The next family is the family of Smiths that are living on Powers Ferry Road in 1910. Mr. Wilkes Smith is a fifty-two-year-old man who has been married only once for forty years to Emaline. They have no children. The next set of Smiths is John Smith, who is forty-five years old, and his sixty-five-year-old mother Mandy. Living also in the house with John Smith and his mother Mandy is* Ms. Mary Nesbit, *a twenty-six-year-old colored woman. William M. Smith, who is eighteen years old, is in the house as a boarder. These are the relations of a certain colored Callaway man in Atlanta who ran a dance hall on Harris Street. His name is Mr. Stewart B. Callaway! And also the Smith family as well. What a find! Mary Nesbit does laundry for a hospital and William M. Smith is a farm laborer. This part of Powers Ferry Road is in what is now the heart of the Buckhead Community where Zion Hill Baptist Church was located and started before moving to Lenox Square in the 1940s. It is located near where Phipps Plaza is now and the White Baptist Church. I do know where Mary Nesbit and William M. Smith are living while at house number 90 and on what section of Powers Ferry Road. They are on Powers Ferry Road before crossing Peachtree or after crossing Peachtree. This is now the corner of Piedmont Road and Peachtree Road, across over an old road called Ivy Road headed toward Chastain Memorial Park and Nancy Creek. This was land lot number 61 near East Paces Ferry Road and Martina Drive and not far from Pharr Road.*

Mr. Robert R. Voyles and Alfred J. Martin are at the corner of Peachtree Road and Powers Ferry Road. This shows me that Ballus Sutton and Mr. Brown and Bose A. Allen are further down Powers Ferry Road near the intersection of House Road, which would become Winsor Parkway. This is where Nancy Creek is located and where I use to fish with my older cousin Robert Mayfield and my younger cousins.

Here is another colored man that was close to my grandfather Arthur Callaway. His name was Balus Sutton from White County. The census taker on April 30, 1910, was Mr. Leon P. Hudgins, and his last stop was at the house of Ballus Sutton on Powers Ferry Road. Ballus Sutton is a mulatto at the age of twenty-nine. His wife Emma B. is twenty-three. Both have been married for the first time and have been married for five years. Their son Peter S. Sutton is a four-year-old mulatto.

The only other colored family is before you got to the house of white man Justinion Evins, a sixty-six-year-old farmer, and his wife Martha C., who was sixty-four. The Evinses have been married for forty-two years. Their daughter was twenty-year-old Anna V. Evins.

Ballus Sutton's house number is 211 and Mr. Evins's house number is 213. The next house is the house of Robert Brown, a forty-five-year-old colored man, and Mandy M., his thirty-five-year-old wife. They have been married for eighteen years and have had eleven children, nine still alive in 1910: George W. (eighteen), Robert A. (fifteen), Winson H. (twelve), Laura L. (nine), Julius O. (seven), Henry C. (five), James F. (four), Lowde L. (two), and Lenna B. (three months old). Their nephew William M. Emory (nine) is also with them. The Brown family lives in house 214, the house before Mr. John F. Mabry, a forty-four-year-old white man, and his wife Loe L., a thirty six-year-old. Their children are Clore (sixteen), Rubie C (thirteen), John L. (nine), Roy H. (six), and Hollie Mae (two). This is who Mabry Road in Lynwood Park is named for. Another white family is located in house 216, just before you got to the house of Bose A. Allen. This was the Turners. Mr. Charles M. Turner is thirty-six and has been married for seventeen years to Loisa L., who is thirty-two years old. Their children are William E. (thirteen), Jessie M. (twelve), Rosa L. (nine), Charlie C. (two), and Bertha Turner (a few months old). The house of Bose A. Allen is number 217. Bose A. Allen is fifty-three years old. He had been married before, and Harriet, his fifty-year-old second wife, had been married once before as well. The stepchildren of Bose A. Allen are Cyrus S. Jones (sixteen) and Cynthia L. Jones (fourteen), and Tolbert Jones (twelve). The next house is house no. 218, the house of Wooten T. Allen, a colored man at the age of twenty-eight and his wife of eight years Georgia A. Allen, who is twenty-six years old. Their children are Theodore (seven), Mattis G. (five), Arthur E. (three), and little Ms. Christine (one year, ten months). They live next door to Mr. James A. Cates on the Atlanta Road that intersects Powers Ferry Road. James A. Cates is sixty-two years old and has been married once before and now has been married to Sara C. Cates for fourteen years. They have one child. Mrs. Sara C. Cates is fifty-four years old. The children in the house are May (twenty-six), Emma l. (twenty-five), and Charles A. (thirteen). I believe that the Atlanta Road is now called Ivey Street just before you crossed over Roswell Road. Here I will highlight a few of the families that were just mention because of the relationship to my grandfather. The first family is Mr. Columbus Jones, the earliest that I could find anything on Mr. Jones is in White County in Nacoochie Georgia. Columbus father was named Briton Jones born in South Carolina and so was his parents. Mr. Briton was born March 1854 and was at the age of forty six years old and has been married to Mr. Airy his for thirty years. Mrs. Jones was born in 1854 as well. Their children at this time were Ms. Augusta born February 1881 and was eighteen, Columbus was born July 1883 and was sixteen, Andy was born January 1887 and was thirteen years old and Katie was born February 1891 and was nine years old. In 1910 in White County Mr. Columbus is twenty eight years old in Nacoochie District of White County Georgia in 1910. His wife is named Anna at the age of twenty six and is a mulatto as a matter of fact her children by Mr. Jones are all mulatto's. Edward is six, Oscar is five, Wallace and Henry is three months old. Airy Jones is a fifty two year old woman and is living with her thirty year old daughter Augusta and her six year old grandson Brit Sutton and her fifteen year old nephew Reuben Jarrett. Living in the house before you get to the house of Mrs. Airy Jones is the house of eighteen year old Emory Dorsey and his fifteen year old wife Ivey. The house before you get to their house is forty year old Emma Dorsey and her children under the last name of Sutton. Ten year old Emma Sutton, nine year old Fletcher, eight year old Carrie, five year old Sallie, three year old Martha, and two year old James H. Sutton. Let me shine a light on the Sutton family and turn our attention back to the year before in 1900 in Nacoochee, White County. Mr. Balus Sutton was listed as being born in March of 1830 and was seventy years old, his wife is named Corrie born February 1836, and has been married to Balus for forty years. Bale or Balus junior was born June in 1879 and was twenty years old, Denia their daughter was born February 1881 at nineteen, Annie B. was born March 1882 and was eighteen, she will become the wife of Mr. Columbus Jones. Lou E. Sutton was born March 1887 and was thirteen, Piercy their daughter was born February 1890 and was ten, Mr. Clifford my grandfather running partner was born January 1892 and was eight, Stanton was born May 1895 and was five, Billie their daughter was born May of 1897 and was three, and Milton Fields a young man born January 1875 was twenty five years old. Thirty year old Eddie Sutton was living right next door with his wife Wildie at twenty five years old. I thought this was a wonderful find in White County where I found the Williams family and the liquor that came out of this county as well.

I cannot contain myself. I am very excited about my find! Right in the heart of Buckhead was one of the biggest secrets ever! Coloreds that could pass as white, Mr. Bose Allen, Mr. Balus Sutton, Mary Nesbit, the Jones and Smith families, as well as the mysterious colored Callaways. Even Mr. John F. Mabry, who moved from Powers Ferry Road and has a road named for him just outside of Lynwood

Park. The road was once called Capital City Drive. Capital City Club is the same club that Henry C. Callaway and George Truitt worked for in Atlanta in the 1890s. You can now see the hidden side of the Lynwood Park Community!

The Colored Citizens Moving into Lynwood Park

This is the layout of Lynwood Park in the year 1933, only three years after the 1930 census. This is why a large number of coloreds are living in Chamblee, Georgia, because the colored community of Lynwood Park was just in its beginnings.

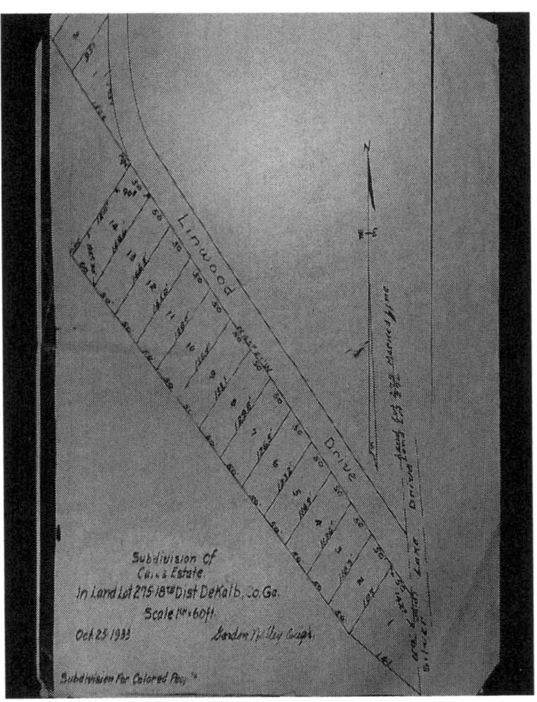

The only houses that were built at this time were on Lynwood Drive in Lynwood in 1933. They were all on the left side of the street of Lynwood Drive. Minerver Vaughn was deeded lot number 1 on Silver Lake Drive. Mr. Eddie Mimms was deeded lot number 4 on Silver Lake Drive. On Lynnwood Drive, Lucius Albert got lot no. 5, Dave Holland got lots 7 and 8, Major Wright got lot 12, Tommie Sutton got lot 13, Massie Jones got lot 14, Guy Chambers got lots 22 and 23 on House Road and Mae Avenue through a lien. Boley Gaither got lots 22 and 23 on House Road and Mae Avenue. Mary Wiggs was deeded lot 46 on Mae Avenue. Homer Gilliard was deeded lot 64 on Johnson Ferry Road and Victoria. Minerver Vaughn was deeded lot 64 on Silver Lake Drive and Lynwood Drive. Charles J. Cates deeded her lot 64.

In the month of June in the year of 1934, only one year after Gordon Nalley Engineer began on Lynwood Park Drive, we now have the houses on Mae Avenue, Victoria Street, and Johnson Ferry Road (Osborne Road) in Lynwood Park Colored Community. It was in 1937 that I found living on Mae Avenue Mr. W. M. Hamilton at lot 47. Love Jones et al. was located on Victoria Street at lot 95. Claude W. Scarborough was at lot no. 83 on Johnson Ferry Road. Mrs. Ora Wilcox moved onto House Road (Osborne Road) on lots 17, 18, 19, and 20. Will Johnson lived on lots 38 and 39 on Mae Avenue.

In 1938, J. W. Dickson bought one of the many pieces of property in the Lynwood Park Subdivision. Mrs. Ethel J. Brown lived on Mae Avenue. John T. Gilbert lived on House Road (Osborne Road). Mrs. Minnie Morgan lived on Lynnwood Drive. Arthur A. Gilliard Jr. also lived on Lynnwood Drive.

In 1939, Mr. Fred Haywood purchased property on House Road (Osborne Road). Mr. Oscar Jones purchased property on Johnson Ferry Road. Luke Holsey purchased property on Mae Avenue. Mrs. Lener Bell Holland purchased her property on Mae Avenue from Emma and J. Charles Cates on November 29. On December 11, 1939, they deeded land to John Jackson on House Road.

Miles Mosley et al. was deeded land on Johnson Ferry Road on February 21, 1940. Mrs. May Bertling was deeded land January 6, 1940 on Bradford Road. Harry Burton was deeded land on Mae Avenue on April 2, 1940. Jack Andrews et al. was deeded land on House Road on May 3, 1940. Balus Hood was deeded land in the Lynwood Park Subdivision on July 1, 1937, and April 2, 1940. J.W. Dickson was deeded land number 31 on Mae Avenue on May 7, 1940. William Wilcox was deeded land lot number 20 on House Road on June 5, 1940. T. J. Hood lived on Victoria Street on lot 98. Mrs. Viola Brinson got lot 55 on Johnson Ferry Road.

I enjoyed many good times in the place I called home. I loved the many people that made up the family of Lynwood Park. Deacon Luke Hosley, Mr. Will Sims, Mr. Jack Lucas, Mr. W. L. Edmondson, Mother Annie B. Truitt, and a host of many, many more. My membership was with China

Grove Missionary Baptist Church. I also fellowshipped with the Little Zion Baptist Church, the Mt. Mary Baptist Church, and the Lynwood Park Church of God Holiness Church. I practically grew up in my mother's friends' house, the Moore family on Mendel Circle and the Jackson family on Osborne Road. I had so many friends and family I may have not have known that they were even kin to me as well. Lynwood carried within it many secrets as well.

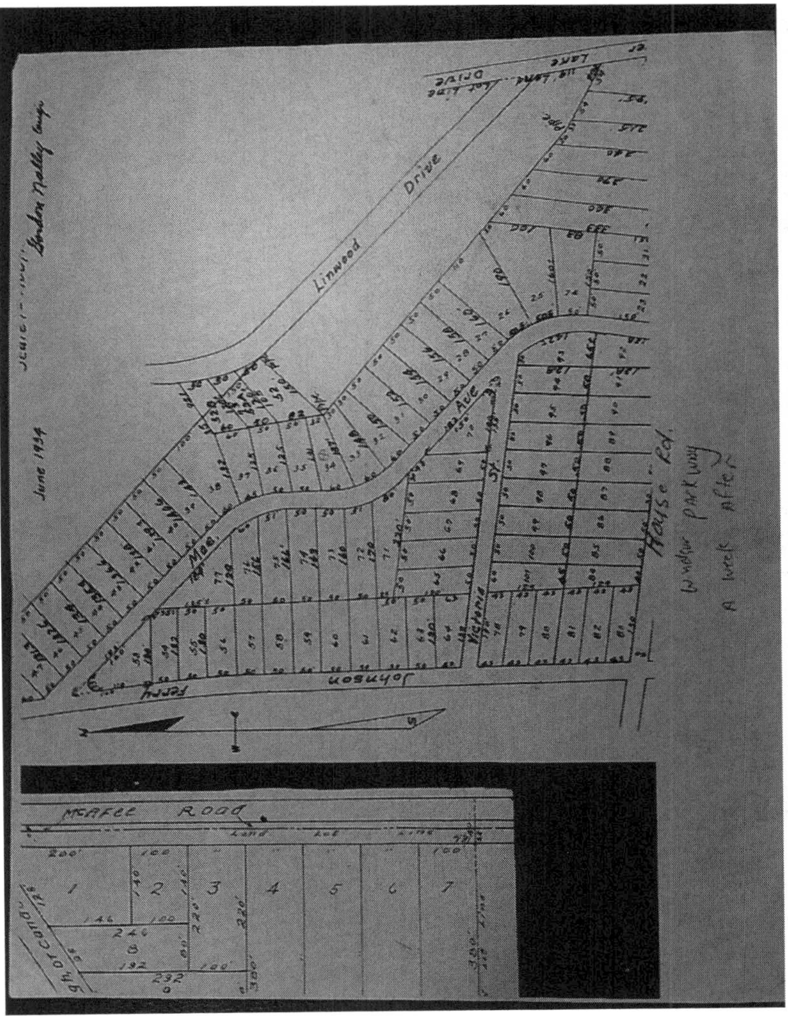

Photography by John Peeples

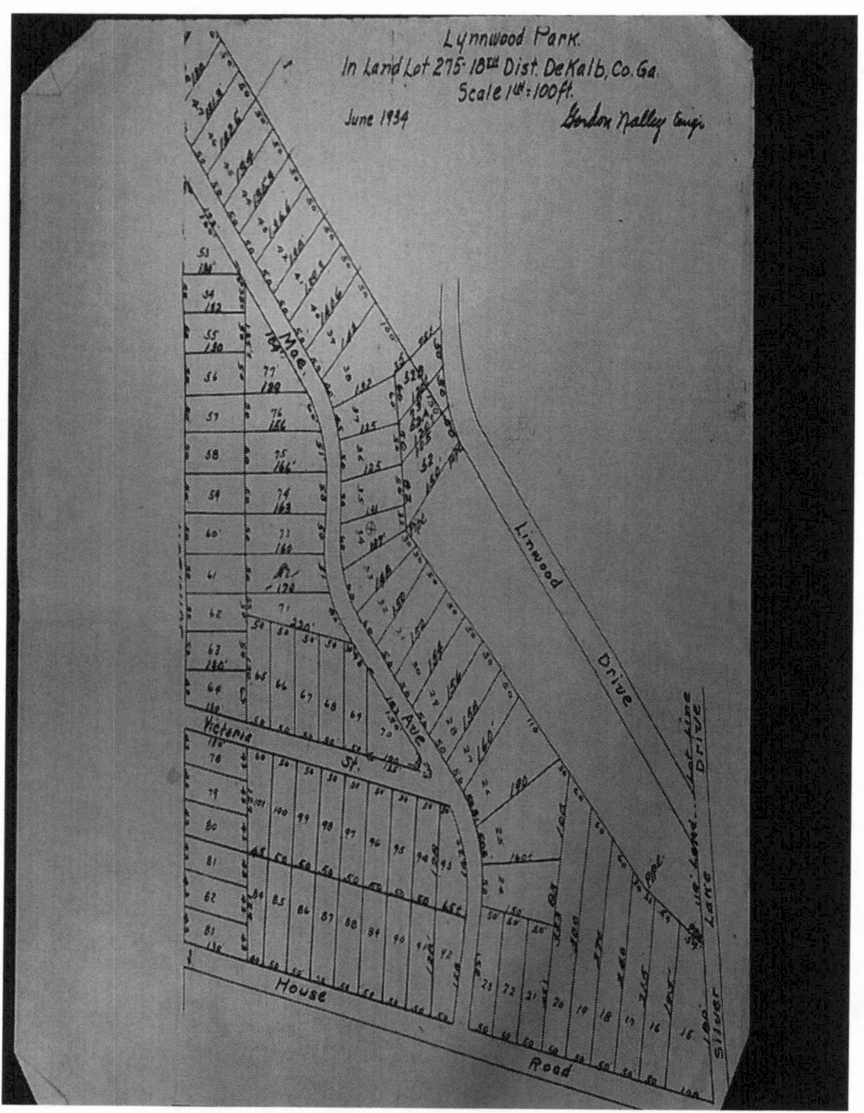

Photography by John Peeples

My grandfather, Arthur Calloway, purchased land lot number 71 on Mae Avenue in 1940.

I had a hard time tracking the life of my grandfather Arthur in Atlanta. I had heard many stories about his activities while living in Atlanta. However, I found little information on him. I first found him in 1930 on Hunnicutt Street in what used to be Techwood Homes. He was living in the house of his brother Charlie and his wife Emma. The two married in Clarke County, Georgia. Arthur had four people living with him. Silvey was too old to be his wife and I figured that it had to be Silvey his aunt, the sister of Charlie, his father. The other two people are Martisha Hawthorne and Mack Smith. The last two would come to live with my grandfather when he comes to live on Chestnut Street in Atlanta. In 1935, Charlie his brother dies and my grandfather signs his death certificate. At the time of his brother's death, my grandfather was living at 926a Grove Street on the northwest side of Atlanta with Rachel, his second wife. Charlie and Emma had a house at 270 Currier Street in northeast Atlanta in 1935. The first house Charlie and Emma lived in on Hunnicut Street in northwest Atlanta was the house that my grandfather occupied in 1930 while Charlie was in jail. Now, this house more than likely has been torn down to make way for Techwood Homes.

Just a year afterward, my grandfather Arthur was living alone at 332 Corput in northwest Atlanta. I know that this is my grandfather because his occupation is a steel worker. Rachel Callaway was doing laundry and had a house at 400 Wallace Street in northwest Atlanta in 1940. Also in 1936, Charles Calloway is residing at 66 Piedmont Avenue. His occupation is laborer at the United Iron & Metal Company. I do not know where this Charles comes from!

My grandfather, while living at 332 Corput Street, is living near or where I found a Charles Calloway working as a yardman for H. Meinert and residing at 17 Means Street in 1916. Means Street is located in the Fifth Ward and not too far from Corput Street and is located just north where North Avenue crosses over Marietta Street. Cherry Street is located in the same area and it is where I found Cornelius Calloway living. Cornelius is either the son of Richard Calloway or Henry Calloway out of Walton or Morgan counties. In this same area is where Springfield Baptist Church and Corinth Baptist Church, which separated from Springfield Church, were located before Springfield moved on to Jones Street and Corinth moved on to Bankhead.

In the year 1930, my grandmother Georgia was living in Washington, Wilkes County, in the house with her father George Jones, her mother Betty Mae Jones, her brothers and sisters Eulas, Eugenia, and little Ms. Lillie. Great-Grandfather George Jones lived with his family on Waters Street just about two houses before you got to the entrance of Oak Street. However, in the year 1940, the Atlanta Directory put people in the right perspective as to where they were living. I mean my grandmother and my great-grandfather both lived on Chestnut Street in northeast Atlanta between Courtland Avenue and Piedmont Avenue. However, I did not find my great-grandfather George with Betty Mae Jones. Betty Mae is now Betty Mae Fallin, who is married to Ludie Fallin and living at 121 Chestnut Avenue in northeast Atlanta. Ludie is forty-two years old and has a third-grade education. Betty Mae has a sixth-grade education and is thirty-nine. Uncle Eulas Jones is eighteen and has a sixth-grade education. Luginia is sixteen and has an eighth-grade education. Aunt Lille Jones is fifteen and has an eighth-grade education. And then there's my grandmother, who is under the last name of Robinson. She is nineteen years old and has an eighth-grade education and work with Lillie at St. Jude Hospital. Both Aunt Lillie, a fifteen-year-old, and my nineteen-year-old grandmother worked forty-nine hours as waitresses in this hospital.

Uncle Wallace is my grandmother's son and he is a year old. Now, my aunt told me that my grandmother took care of my grandfather after a car accident. He was paralyzed. My grandmother made her way across the street to visit him at house 128b. Arthur was living in the lower part of the house and Mrs. Ida Elligan, a twenty-seven-year-old divorcee, was living in the upper level of the house. Arthur is working in a steel mill and has worked twenty-seven hours for the week. My grandfather is under the first name Abe. I found him under this name before in the Atlanta Directory in 1935 while he was married to his second wife Rachel and living at a house on 926a Grove Street. He was also residing with someone at 58 Towns in Southeast Atlanta under the first name Abe. Abe was working as a laborer with the Southern Wheel Company. There must be a relationship between the Callaways that were in the Northwest section of Atlanta and the Callaways that were in the Southeastern section of Atlanta. I say this because I have found my grandfather in both parts of Atlanta and also Cornelius while both William A. and Mathew Callaway are either in the northwest or southeast section of Atlanta.

Mrs. Dora G. Odom visited the house of Arthur Callaway and his upstairs neighbor Mrs. Ida Elligan and listed the house as the 194th and the 195th house she visited on April 9, 1940. She visited Ludie Fallin and Betty Mae Jones Fallin and listed it as the 211th house she visited on the same day. Ludie Fallin and Betty Mae Jones Fallin paid nine dollars to rent this property while Arthur paid eight dollars. My grandmother and grandfather are living in the Third Ward of the City of Atlanta in 1940. In the same year, the two were married in DeKalb County.

State of Georgia, Dekalb County, Marriage License

> *To any Judge, justice of the peace, or minister of the Gospel, you are hereby authorized to join Arthur Callaway and Georgia Mae Jones in the holy state of matrimony, according to the constitution and laws of this state and for so doing this shall be your license, and you are hereby required to return this license to me, with your certificate hereon of the fact and date of the marriage.*
>
> *Given under my hand and seal this 21st day of September 1940. License obtained under oath by V. S. Morgan. I certify that Arthur Callaway and Georgia Mae Jones were joined in matrimony by me this 21st day of September nineteen hundred and forty. W. J. Langley, J. P. recorded September 25, 1940 V. S. Morgan, Ordinary. Colored Marriage Book (L).*

They are married six months later after leaving Chestnut Avenue. Now the Atlanta Directory have them living in Chamblee in 1940 and the deed that my grandfather signed or made his X on is in book 563 on page 262 and states that the deed was made September 6, 1940. I wonder who my grandfather is living with while he was in DeKalb County in Chamblee.

Hermon Quisley got lot 78 on Cates Avenue. Shelly Truitt got lot number 62 on Johnson Ferry Road (Osborne Road) in 1940. Shelly Truitt's house is located near where the China Grove Missionary First Baptist Church held its first meeting. The deed reads Shelly Truitt et al. My grandfather's property was located right behind the property of Shelly Truitt. They would eventually become neighbors on Osborne Road as well. This is after the building of China Grove Missionary Baptist Church. I was told where the church is located is the same place where the Truitt place was on Johnson Ferry road. Mr. Dan Hanson moved to lot 96 on Victoria Street in 1940. Otis Banton moved onto Johnson Ferry Road lot 35, and Mr. Elix Shiver to lot 226 on Francis Street. Hulon Dixon lived on lot 198 on Mae Avenue. Mr. Emerson Worthly lived on Cates Avenue lot 134. Mrs. Mattie Holland moved onto House Road, which is now Winsor Parkway. Mrs. Holland's lot was 39. Willie Mae Dix lived on Mae Avenue at lot 40. Ms. Hattie Cox lived on Mae Avenue at lot 34 in 1941. Nathaniel Baccus was at lot 16 on House Road. Cliff Sutton was at lot 88 on House Road (Winsor Parkway). Dewitt Young was located at lot 200 on Mae Avenue. Boley Gaither was living at lot 24 on Mae Avenue. Mrs. M. V. Lynn lived at Mae Avenue at lot number 173 and 255. James Perry lived at Johnson Ferry road at lot 256. Dave Holland was living on House Road at lot 103. J. W. Dickerson owned property on Cates Avenue and House Road at lot

119. J. W. Dickerson also had property at lot 80 on Johnson Ferry Road. John Gabriel had property at Francis Street at lot 184. Birt Putman lived on Francis Street at lots 185, 173, and 238. John Lester lived at lot 93. J. W. Dickerson also owned lot 201 on Mae Avenue. MaCeo Ruff was living at lot 238 on Mae Avenue. Lee Reeves et al. lived on Francis Street at lot 228.

George Wallace lived on Johnson Ferry Road (Osborne Road) at lot 167. In 1940 the Wallace family was living in the Nichols Bottoms community. Living at house number nine paying seven dollars a month at this time in 1940, George Wallace Senior was at the age of twenty eight years old and his wife Mary was twenty four, George G. was at the age of five, Jesse Mae was four, Johnnie Lee was three, Mr. Napoleon was two years old, as a young boy I watch this man get into his car an go golfing. His brother Eddie B. was eleven months old in Nichols Bottom a Colored community of Briarcliff Road. Mr. Luke Holsey et al. was deeded lot 45 on Mae Avenue in 1941. Mr. Luke Holsey was a very good friend to my grandfather Arthur. They would work and build and redo houses in the community of Lynwood Park. They went fishing and hunting quite often. Deacon Holsey lived to be quite old and was still in his right mind up until his death. Otis Oglesby et al. lived on Mae Avenue at lot 72. J. W. Dickerson had lots 41, 68, 151, 168, 180, 189, 168, and 171 in the Lynwood Park Subdivision in 1941. Mrs. M. V. Lynn was still living on Winsor Parkway in 1941. It does not show what lot she lived on in 1941. In the years between 1942 and 1946, some more of the families purchased more property in Lynnwood Park. Also, many more people moved into the Lynwood Park Subdivision. First in the years of 1942, Mrs. M. V. Lynn bought lots 106 and 108 on House Road. Phil Irvin bought lot 171 on Mae Avenue. Mamie Lee Chandler was deeded lot 160 on Cates Avenue. Ressie Gabriel was deeded lot 183 on Francis Street. Frank Panion was deeded lot 174 on Mae Avenue.

J. W. Dickson was deeded more property in this subdivision. Mamie Blake was deeded lot 67 on Victoria Street. Aaron James Johnson was deeded lot 197 on Mae Avenue. J. W. Dickson was deeded lot 25 on Mae Avenue. William hall et al. was deeded lot 221 on Johnson Ferry Road. Mrs. Bessie Mae Hogan was deeded lot 130 on Cates Avenue. Dan Hanson et al. was deeded lot 97 on Victoria Street. Florie Mosley was deeded lot 184 on Johnson Ferry Road. Henry Jones was deeded lot 53 on Johnson Ferry Road. Willie Gardner was deeded lot 196 on Mae Avenue. Mrs. Ida V. Walker was deeded lot 15 on House Road. Rev. O. C. Woods was deeded lot 36 on Mae Avenue.

I got to hear Rev. O. C. Woods preach many times at the Mt. Mary Baptist Church. I was blown away at his larger than life voice when he delivered his sermons. Mount Mary Baptist Church is the first church where I attended my first funeral and the preacher was Rev. O.C. Woods. His voice still today resonates in my spirit. I was a very young and scared boy. However, I was taken to experience the truth about living and dying.

Mr. Mathew Moore et al. was deeded lot 170 on Mae Avenue. Mrs. Susie Barnes was deeded lot 125 on Cates Avenue. Mr. Albert Williams et al. was deeded lot 110 on House Road. Mr. Harvey Parker was deeded lot 129 on Cates Avenue. Mrs. Mary Chaney was deeded lot 43 on Mae Avenue. Mr. John Gabriel was deeded lot 182 on Francis Street. Nellie Quisley was deeded lot 173 on Cates Avenue. Ozzie Lee Mayfield was deeded lot 208 on Victoria Street.

Mr. Ozzie Lee Mayfield is my cousin Robert Mayfield's relative, and Mr. Mathew Moore is the friend of my mother Mary.

Margarett Jackson was deeded lot 179 on Cates Avenue. Virginia Scott was deeded lots 230 and 231 on Francis Street. Sarah Flemming was deeded lot 195 on Mae Avenue. Mr. Cleveland Rucker was deeded lot 105 on House Road. Mrs. Ethel May Lane et al. was deeded lot 130 on House Road. William Austin was deeded lot 117 on House Road. Lena Burson was deeded lot 146 on Cates Avenue. Dorsey Rucker was deeded lot 217 on Victoria Street.

We used to call *Uncle Dorsey, Dorsey Rucker, a man with a long beard and a small truck that he gave anyone in the neighborhood access to or a ride in to their destination. I can just see him with his pipe in mouth and his gentle spirit and kind smile.*

Mrs. Estell Scott was deeded lot 56 on Johnson Ferry Road. Charles J. Summerhour was deeded lot 183 on Francis Street. Mrs. Ora Brown was deeded lot 225 on Johnson Ferry Road. Robert Morgan was deeded lot 27 on Mae Avenue. Mrs. Annie Flannagan was deeded lots 15 and 16 on Silver Lake Drive. Willie Roy Holland was deeded lot 218 on Victoria Street. Willie Lee Pryor was deeded lot 214 on Victoria Street. Mr. John Seagraves et al. was deeded lots 162 and 164 on Cates Avenue and Johnson Ferry Road (Osborne Road).

Mr. Seagraves's property was just across the street from my cousins and I can still see the two red houses set on this property. I was a young boy when he passed. The place seemed always vacant and empty.

Mr. William Banks was deeded lot 144 on Cates Avenue. Beatrice Smith was deeded lot 66 on Victoria Street. Bessie M. Wortham was deeded lot 135 on Cates Avenue. Mr. Henry Jett was deeded lot 240 on

Victoria Street. Lee Reeves et al. was deeded lot 239 on Francis Street. Mrs. Rebecca Ellis was deeded lot 77 on Mae Avenue. John Epps et al. was deeded lot 122 on House Road. Mr. George Usher was deeded lot 152 on Cates Avenue. Mr. Fred Haywood was deeded lot 86 and lot 84 on House Road. Mr. Joseph Lenard Curtis was deeded lot 235 on Francis Street. Mr. Dave Holland was deeded lot 104 on House Road. Howard Quisley et al. was deeded lot 137 on Cates Avenue. Martin Dyes was deeded lot 145 on Cates Avenue. W. T. McClendon was deeded lot 306 on Cates Avenue. Otis F. Allison was deeded lot 107 on House Road. Linton Sutton et al. was deeded lots 78 and 79 on Victoria Street and Johnson Ferry Road. He also was deeded lot 87 on House Road. William Banks was deeded lot 142 and 143 on Cates Avenue. Mr. John Seagraves was deeded lot 152 on Johnson ferry Road. Florrie Mosley was deeded lot 193 on Cates Avenue. Bosley Gaither was deeded lot 21 on House Road. Mr. Harvey Parker was deeded lot 128 on Cates avenue.

The Parker family was very close to my mother Mary. I grew up in their house and was welcomed as family. All that were just mentioned were deeded land from Ms. Emma Lou Cates between the years of 1942 and 1946.

My first experience away from my grandparents' house was to the little red schoolhouse in the back of China Grove. My second time away from the house as a small boy was at the daycare of Mrs. Bertha Jones across from the same little red schoolhouse. I could still smell the chicken noodle soup and imagine myself after lunch sleeping on the mats on the floor and leaving and grabbing my coat and hat from the clothes racks of Mrs. Bertha's nursery. The next experience was when I entered into the first grade at the Lynwood Park Elementary and High School and meeting my teacher for the first time. Her name was Mrs. Cheeley and the principal was Mr. Coleman. I only attended this segregated school in my first grade and left there to attend Jim Cherry Elementary, where I met for the first time a white person and some of my most closest friends. Years have come and gone and my heart is still thankful for this community that I called home. Even though I was alone, I still can write that the people in the Lynwood Park Community were my family and I loved them all!

Now, the place that I once new is almost gone and I am older now and have learned from the many mistakes and dark passions do not hunt me now. It is because wherever there was darkness there was also those who carried a light to lighten my way! I loved the times that I would make my way to Mother Truitt's house and one day for the first time I got to taste turtle from the shell. I got glimpses of the past whenever I played in her yard! The blackberries were plentiful, as well as the peachtrees and plums. Life was very good! God was instilled in the children of Lynwood. Now I know what it feels like to be saved from doing things I did not want to do but still did. I have true understanding and am now enlightened by his word as Bishop Elder Carter would exclaime, "I Heard!" Yes, I finally heard what thus says the Lord Jesus Christ!

Lynwood Park Colored Community

3290 Osborne Road

I was born a Grady baby at Grady Memorial Hospital in Atlanta, Georgia. I came home to 3290 Osborn Road in the Lynwood Park Colored Community. My grandmother purchased this property with her father George Jones. *My grandfather Arthur built a little wooden shack on the back side of this property after his second wife Rachel visited and gave him trouble at Mae Avenue, at the first house they occupied. Arthur, Georgia Mae, young Wallace, Eulas, Claudia, Mary (my mother), Eugenia, and Arthur Jr., the last two came later on. There was a fig tree planted there at that same spot where the shack was to remind us of the time spent in the shack. I was asked many times by my grandmother Georgia to work the garden and fight off the bees and birds trying to pick figs from this tree. There were many experiences that took place in this backyard! The beagle dogs or hunting dogs my grandfather had penned against in a fence, next to mother Truitt's place. I even experienced a hog being killed by Mr. Marvin. I even experienced the test of my faith when the death of my aunt Anna came in 1972. Aunt Anna B. Daniel told me the many stories that I could remember that I am trying to tell you now. I was ten years old when my cousin Luscious and I were in Mrs. Thomas's yard playing basketball. And as we were on our way home, we found Aunt Anna leaning against the back of the house. She had had a sunstroke while hanging laundry on the clothesline in the backyard.*

This lady that kept me and comforted me was dying and I didn't know what to do. I was a young boy and I was scared. So I yelled out, "Grandmama!" I left for home that night. I was living in Scottsdale in the apartments in the projects there. I asked my mother Mary for weeks on end if I could go and visit Aunt Anna. I loved the lady with her old clothes and apron and long braided hair and snuff between her lips. But she just told me I was too young to visit. So I cried myself to sleep that night and many nights to come! I didn't know I would have to cry even more the following two weeks at her funeral at China Grove Missionary First Baptist Church. Let me talk about my early morning rising to go to work with Arthur my grandfather. So when I was called by Granddaddy Arthur to gather myself to go to work some mornings to dig graves after a hardy breakfast he would cook for us. The whole kitchen was smoky from the thick fat back he had in the black skillet with the flat corn bread he fried in the same black pan with two eggs turned over lightly but hard on one side, I was in heaven! We were either digging graves at Mount Mariah or Chamblee at Mt Zion. At Mount Mariah, I would stop and visit my aunt Anna. I dug many graves after that with my grandfather and had many experiences too. I remember digging over into another grave and I jumped out of the grave that I was digging and ran. My grandfather calmed me down and told me, "Son, you don't have to worry about the dead. They can't do you no harm. The ones you have to really worry about is the living." We would wait and wait for the Cox brothers and Haugabrook Mortuary to show up. I got to know a lot of the men that worked for them and they knew me and my cousins who would help my grandfather as well.

These were some cold mornings but it never really crossed my mind that one day I would come to bury this old, tough man whom I had come to trust and respect and love as a father. But still I didn't know much about him except for the stories passed down from old family members. I couldn't be consoled that day. I never thought this day would ever come. I was loved! After all the houses we worked on and footings that we dug, strange white men we come across who knew him well, but they were strangers to the little dark skinned grandchild. I remember all the times I was a young boy watching him groom himself. Arthur would never leave the house unkempt. I watched him get very angry and watched him be patient and caring, especially when I had to give my dog away. He was there. He was the only one to come to my ROTC graduation, and as a World War I veteran they announced his name over the PA system. I was a very proud young man that day! However, I never thought the day would come when I would stand over an empty grave dug by me and his sons and grandsons. I had to say to my grandfather Arthur goodbye for now, I will see you again. I must say that he was not only my grandfather, he was my friend. This Is why I want to find out about my grandfathers father. And about my friend and this last name that I have in his honor.

> On May 24, 1949, between Lawrence P. Cobb of the state of Georgia *(a furniture dealer living on Piedmont Avenue in Buckhead),* first part, and Georgia Mae Callaway of the state of Georgia county of DeKalb. Sold all that parcel of land lying in Land Lot 303 18th district of DeKalb County starting at an iron pin located on the western side of Johnson Ferry Road fifty-eight and three feet northward from Johnson Ferry Circle and running thence northwardly along the western side of Johnson Ferry Road fifty ft. to an iron pin thence westward 150 ft. to an iron pin thence southwardly 50 ft. to an iron pin, thence eastwardly 150 ft. to and iron pin and the point of beginning being

lot 2 block b of Lawrence P. Cobb property according to plat on file in office of building inspector. DeKalb Co. Ga. Grandma paid $10 for this property.

Mr. C.J. Cofer and Mr. John J. Delamater Jr. was the notary public of DeKalb.

On June 30 1950 she was back at the courthouse in DeKalb County to correct some mistakes on the deed to this very same property. The lot number was 21 and it was located in block E. Mr. C.J. Cofer witnessed and Mr. John J. Delamater Jr. was the NP of DeKalb.

Now the only Cofer family that is living nearby is in Gwinnett County. When I think about any Cofer family and the Callaway family, my mind goes back to the county of Wilkes and the house of Mr. Charles Callaway and his wife Louisa in 1870, as well as Mrs. Nancy Callaway, who was in the church at Sardis and worked for the Cofer family.

Land Lot 275, which was part of Lynwood Park, was the land of Mr. Hugh Cockran of the Thirteenth District of Effingham County, Georgia. Mr. Cockran received this land in the lottery of Henry County in 1821 on the twenty-second of August by way of Mr. James Meriwether. Lynwood Park had a southern section that was called Land Lot 303 and it was purchased by Mr. Philip Pace from Stallings District of Jones County, Georgia. Mr. Philip purchased his land on August 22, 1821 as well. Section 303 will somehow become the property of Mr. Ivey.

Now, while looking through these papers pertaining to the Eighteenth District of Henry County, which became Dekalb County and what is now known as Buckhead and Brookhaven near the Oglethorpe University, I found Mrs. Sarah Callaway (spelled Calaway), a widow, of Kellons District of Franklin County. She was purchasing land in Fayette County District no. 7, lot no. 93, with lot 100 to the west and lot 68 east of her property. Mr. Wm. T. Davenport was the surveyor and Isaac Willett and Groves Colbert were witnesses. Now the strangest thing is that Mr. Isaac Willett is mentioned in the estate record of Mr. Isaac Callaway and Mrs. Winnifred Callaway, his ex-wife or his first wife while still married to Mrs. Winnifred Ragan Callaway. He took up with Mrs. Sarah. Now this property of Mrs. Sarah Callaway is located in Fayette County, Georgia, some parts of which will eventually become Fulton County.

What is the relationship that my grandfather Aaron have with DeKalb and Fulton County, Georgia? Did he come to reside with his master's second wife

Sarah and the slaves of Isaac that are now divided between the two women, Mrs. Winnifred and Mrs. Sarah? Also, is this why I find Mr. W.A. Callaway who is the son of Sarah and Isaac Callaway located very much in Fulton County with Mr. James H. Callaway as well? Now this puts two sets of Callaways in the Fulton County area. The family of Thomas P. Callaway and his mother Martha and her husband Elijah or Elisha, and the family of Mr. Isaac Callaway and his second wife Sarah. Sarah lived in Fayette County.

Chapter Eight

THE 1940 CENSUS OF THE LYNWOOD PARK COLORED COMMUNITY

I waited ten years for this 1940 census. I had great expectations; however, when it came to finding the information that I was looking for, it hardly played out like I expected. When I came down to Lynwood, I really thought that I would find my grandfather on his property; however, he was still located on Chestnut Avenue in Atlanta when he came to Terrell County. Charlie and his wife Mary couldn't be found.

The first house that John Frank Beal stops by on April 27, 1940, in the supervisor's district number 5 in the enumerated district 44-34 is the house of Lucious Scott, a twenty-seven-year-old road grader, and his partner Adell Blake, who is thirty years old. They are living on Johnson Ferry Road and paying rent of four dollars. After passing the three white families of H. Smith, Joseph Dutton, and Emmitt Dutton, is the house of Leslie Hosly, a fifty-three-year-old widow with a sixth-grade education and works as a housekeeper for a private family. Mrs. Hosly owns her house valued at $1,500. The sixth house that John visited was that of Roy Bryant. Roy Bryant is at the age of forty-one and has a fifth-grade education. *However, I do not take notice of the education of these men because his occupation made him well off in Lynwood Park, just like my grandfather and many of these colored men who did masonry work.* Roy Bryant was a brick mason. Celmay, his wife, is thirty-eight years old. Luther is twenty-one,

Leslie Mae is nineteen, Roy Jr. is seventeen, Howard is fourteen, Bachlor is nine, Henry is eight, Margrett is six, and Febe is three. Mr. Roy Bryant owns his property, valued at $500.

The next house is the house of Katie Mayfield. This is the seventh house that Mr. John visited. Mrs. Katie Mayfield owns her property and pays a mortgage of $300. Mrs. Mayfield is eighty-three years old and is a widow and has never been educated in school.

The eighth house visited by John is Mr. Willis Julian's, a forty-one-year-old plasterer who pays mortgage of $300. His wife Eva is forty-two. Both have a sixth-grade education. Their children are Willis Jr. (who is nineteen years old and has a sixth-grade education), Bootsee Elise (seventeen, with a seventh-grade education), Rosa May (fourteen, with a seventh-grade education), Geneva (ten, with a sixth-grade education), Buddie Alfred (eight, with a first-grade education), and Dessie (six, and has not been educated as yet).

The ninth house Mr. John visited was that of colored man Mr. Robert Jones, a twenty-two-year-old, and his twenty-two-year-old wife Alice. Lettie, their daughter, is two years old, and Robert, their son, is eight months old. Robert Jones does yard work for a private family. All are living on Johnson Ferry Road just before you get to Rosemont Road and the white family of Mr. E. A. Harper and Mr. James Hardegree.

The next house Mr. John Beal visited was number 15, the house of Mr. Christ Meta, a forty-year-old colored man, and his wife Essie, who is thirty-two. Mr. Meta has no formal education and was a laborer doing landscaping. Their children are Willis T. (fifteen), Florida (thirteen), Claud (eleven), Leysee M. (nine), Jennie c. (six), Velma E. (three), and Marion (one). Mr. Meta pays only one dollar toward his rent on Ashford Road near Chamblee Dunwoody. Mr. Oscar Julian's house was listed as the sixteenth house Mr. John visited. Oscar Julian is fifty years old and his occupation is farming. He pays five dollars for his room and board. His wife Effie is twenty-four. Elizabeth, their daughter, is eight. Oscar, their grandson, is four. Francis, their granddaughter, is seven. Joe Tom Julian is Oscar's father and he is seventy-one years old.

John listed Mrs. Nona Grice, thirty-eight years old, a maid from Washington Wilkes County, as house number 23. Mrs. Grice pays ten dollars for her rent on Chamblee Dunwoody and Ashford Road. She could be the maid of Robert Stephens, a thirty-five-year-old white man whose property is listed as number 22 on the visitation of Mr. John and he pays ten thousand dollars for mortgage on his property. He is out of

Tennessee and his last place of residence was in Atlanta as an executive salesman. Mrs. Nona Grice could also be the maid of Roy Durden, whose last residence was in Fulton County in Atlanta. He is the owner of a bank and property where he pays mortgage of $1,500. His wife is named Anne and she is thirty-five years old. They are living in house number 27. *Mr. Roy Durden is the man that my grandfather had dealing with when he bought his property in Lynwood.* Mr. Roy Holland is a cement finisher at house 25 and his rent is $7 a month. Roy Holland is twenty-seven years old and his wife Ida is twenty-eight. Elizabeth is eleven. Martha, the mother of Roy, is forty-nine, and John, his nephew, is nineteen.

Here are some of the white neighbors along with Roy Durden and Mr. Robert Stephens, who owns the mill. Robert is the largest landowner at the corner of Hart Mill Road and Ashford Road, which is closer to where the main road of Ashford and Johnson Ferry Road come together. Mr. John Stribling is a colored forty-nine-year-old from Tolbert County and so is his forty-three-year-old wife Lila. George Wingfield is a thirty-three-year-old man born in Wilkes County, Georgia, and his wife Iona is twenty-five. Roberta, their daughter is eight. John Stribling's house is numbered twenty-nine and George Wingfield's house is thirty.

In this section of 686 of the Cross Keys District in Supervisory District 5, and in the Enumerated District 44-37 on April 2, 1940, on the Tucker Road, which became the Chamblee Tucker Road, in starting in Chamblee, I found Mrs. Nora Barnes McTowns as the enumerator. Mrs. Nora numbered the house of Joseph Yancey on Tucker Road as number 7. Mr. Yancey was renting his place for four dollars a month. He was living with his wife Daisy, who was fifty-two years old, and he was fifty-three and worked as a share cropper alongside the family of Mr. Silas Johnson a forty six-year-old colored man and his thirty seven-year-old wife Minnie and Silas Jr. who was twenty-one, Rebecca his daughter at the age of nineteen, Emma was eighteen, Robert was sixteen, Lou Ellen was fourteen, James was eleven, Samuel is eight, George Johnson is five, and Maidee is seven months old.

On April 3, 1940, Mrs. Neva Barnes McTowns started her count on North Peachtree Road at the house of Mr. George D. Byrd and his wife Maude. Their house was numbered nine. Then the house of colored man Charles Johnson, who was forty-nine years old, and his thirty-three-year-old wife Dolly, daughter Anna (twelve), and son Lee (three). Mr. Charles Johnson and his family are out of Rockdale County. At the end of this census is the house of Callaway Latham, a forty-eight-year-old white man, and his wife Lily, who is forty-three, daughter Elizabeth (nineteen), and sons John (seventeen) and Charles (fifteen). Moving on down North Peachtree Road, the only other colored family besides the family of Charles Johnson is the family of Willie Lyman, a twenty-seven-year-old dairy laborer out of Atlanta, and his wife Pearl, a twenty-eight-year-old out of Meriwether County. Living in house number 41 is Matilda Lidell, a sixty-eight-year-old widow and a servant for a private family.

On April 5, 1940, Mrs. Neva Barnes McTowns stated that she was at the end of North Peachtree Road and was at the corner of Shallowford Road where she listed Mr. Thomas Harper, a white renter out of White County. His house was before you got to the larger landowner Mr. Carl Wallace. He is forty-five, his wife Jessie is forty-two, Catherine is nineteen, Betty is sixteen, Jean is fourteen, and Billie is five. Their colored neighbors are Mr. Armested Hamilton, a twenty-five-year-old man born in Georgia, and his wife Sara from Tallapoosa, Alabama, who is twenty-one years old. Mrs. McTowns is now at Chamblee Dunwoody Road and the only colored on this section of Chamblee Dunwoody is Nola Caine, a servant of Herbert West, a white twenty-five-year-old, and his mother Bonnie, fifty. Nola was thirty years old and divorced. Mrs. Nola Caine was out of Tennessee.

Moving on down Chamblee Dunwoody Road to the house numbered 68, the house of Mr. Fred Strickland, a colored thirty-one-year-old born in Georgia out of Pike County. Fred Strickland was a farm laborer. His wife Willie was thirty-three and his stepson Lee Dickerson was eighteen. Paul Harris was a lodger at the age of forty-three. Fred pays rent at two dollars a month. Going past the house of Oscar Lockhart, a white forty-nine-year-old man, and his wife Ella, who is forty-five. Their brother Thomas is thirty-three and a son-in-law named Albert Bean, a twenty-eight-year-old out of South Carolina, as well as a seventy-year-old lodger named Samuel Gentry are living with them. Oscar Lockhart's house is numbered sixty-nine and the colored family of Tom Thomas is in number forty-nine. His wife Christine is twenty-seven and they pay rent at a rate of two dollars a month. Mr. Robert Etchinson is forty-three. His wife Irene is thirty-nine, Charles is nineteen, Robert is fourteen, Ervin is twelve, David is ten, Horace is seven, Mary is four, Harold is two, Travis is three months old, and his mother-in-law Millie Hamilton is seventy-one. Robert Etchinson pays rent at five dollars a month.

On April 8, 1940, on Chamblee Dunwoody Road, Mrs. McTowns listed Odel Niles and Gussie Niles, both twenty years old and servants of Mr. Luther Fincher, a fifty-nine-year-old, and his wife Alice Fincher. On April 10, 1940, Mrs. McTowns was at the intersection of Chamblee Dunwoody Road and Mennenhall and Sexton roads. Living at the intersection of Sexton is the landowner Paul Tatum, a thirty-two-year-old, his wife Era (thirty), their ten-year-old son Calvin, and their nine-year-old daughter Ruth. Mr. Paul Tatum's mortgage is $3,000. Mr. Mack Allen is a colored man paying rent on his property. Mack Allen is forty-seven years old and his wife Lucile is thirty-five. Living next door in house 102 is Frank Cook, a colored thirty-eight-year-old, his twenty-nine-year-old wife Louise, children Sara (nine), Willie (eight), Ruby (two), and Agnes (five months). Living in house number 103 is Charlie Grasham, a sixty-three-year-old; Mary, his forty-eight-year-old wife; and Thelma Mackey, their daughter, who is thirty-one years old. Thelma was out of Atlanta and a nursing teacher who had her own practice.

Mack Allen and his wife are out of Atlanta and Frank Cook is out of California. He lived in Fulton County in Atlanta before moving to 686 Cross Keys District. Mack Allen did farm work and Frank Cook was a building contractor. Charlie Grasham was a farm laborer. Mr. James Sexton, for whom the street is named, is at the end of the road with his wife Nancy and their children. After entering onto Shallowford Road, the first house you come to is the house of colored man Mr. Henry Grimes, a twenty-nine-year-old man, and his wife Roberta, who is thirty-one. Their son Henry is ten. Their house is listed as 108 and he pays three dollars for rent. Henry was a farm laborer. Earl Johnson is thirty-three. Lucile, his wife, is thirty-one. Ula Mae is twelve, May is ten, Mary is nine, and the mother-in-law Millie Lunford is a fifty-nine-year-old widow. Earl pays four dollars for rent.

Mrs. Sallie Parson is a widow at the age of fifty-nine. Ella, her daughter, is forty, and both are widows. Willie Ruth Woods is her daughter at the age of twenty-three and is married. Sallie Parson's granddaughter Dorothy Reese is thirteen. Her two-year-old granddaughter Lily May Warbington is in the house as well. I forgot to mention that Mr. Earl Johnson is out of Elbert County and is a carpenter, and Mrs. Sallie is a carpenter's helper. Mrs. Ella, her daughter, does farm work. Living in the house that is listed as 111 is Mrs. Vorgia Moore, a thirty-nine-year-old man and his twenty six-year-old wife Katherine and their daughter Minnie Lee who is nine, Gladys Moore (four), Christine (two), and Mary (a few days old). All are out of Anderson, South Carolina. Still moving down Shallowford Road toward the intersection of Johnson Ferry Road and living next door to the Moore Family is Mr. David Hamilton in house 112 and paying five dollars for rent. Mr. David Hamilton is forty-four years old and his wife Bessie is twenty-seven. Mr. Hamilton was a carpenter's helper. Mr. Alex Gresham is at the age of fifty-two and his wife Mrs. Flora is forty-nine years old. Lola is twenty-three. Haywood is twenty-one. Jenette, Mr. Alex's granddaughter, is eight years old. At the very intersection is the property owner Mr. Columbus Jones at house 114. His mortgage is $2,000. Mr. Columbus Jones is forty-nine years old and his wife Mrs. Annie is forty-eight. Henry, their son, is thirty. Lillie Mae is twenty-six years old. Mr. Elijah Kelly is in house 115 on the other side of the intersection of Shallowford Road and Johnson Ferry Road. *This particular location at this intersection of roads puts colored man Mr. Columbus Jones right at the place where Black Burn Park and the Publix Shopping Center are now. I did not know Mr. Columbus Jones owned so much property. I wonder if he sold this property. Before coming to DeKalb County, the Joneses were in White County as well.*

In 1910, the White County coloreds in the Nacoochee section were Geo. G. Austin, John Austin, Tom Brown, Arondale Brown, Alfred Brown, Kale Bartley, Sam Brown, Charlie Brown, Geo. Crawley, Joseph I. Cantrell, Ed Dorsey, William Fagg, Rubin Janet, Lillie Janet, Bob Janet, Jesse Jenkins, agent for Henryetta Nicely *Columbus Jones, agent for Arie Jones, agent for Will Jones, agent for Maggie Jones, agent for Harry Richardson, Brit Jones, Andy Jones, Andy Janett, Wiley Nicely, J.H. Nicely, agent for Mary and Nicely, Balus Sutton, Sanford Sutton,* Fate Trammell, Tom Trammell, Alfred Trammell, Joe Trammell, Geo. Trammell, Alex Wells, Good Wells, Sherman Winn, agent for Jno. Blockwell, and agent for Martha Winn. *Mr. Columbus Jones had 10 acres of land, number 42 and 43, district 3. Arie Jones had 65 acres in 43 and 43, district 3.*

Mr. Elijah Kelly is forty-two years old and his wife Matilda is forty-four. Ira Lee, their son, is nineteen. Le Gree, their son, is sixteen. In the next house is Mr. George Perry, a twenty-nine-year-old, and his wife Julie, who is twenty-eight years old. Mr. Elijah Kelly and Mr. George Perry both pay six dollars in rent. The next house is Walter Taylor's, fifty-two, and his wife Sally, forty-three. Alberta (nineteen), Lucile (twenty-two), Alma Jean (thirteen), son-in-law Athel Anderson (twenty-two), and grandson Norris (four). Mr. Taylor pays six dollars for rent as well. William Rice is a colored thirty six-year-old and his wife Mary is thirty-four. Mr. Columbus Jones is a carpenter and building contractor. His son Henry Jones is a general handyman at the Golf Course County Club. Mr. Elijah Kelly is a farm laborer; Mr. George Perry is a section hand for the railroad. Mr. William Rice is a laborer in a garage.

Mrs. McTowns, on April 11, 1940, is still on Johnson Ferry Road and made the house of Lucas smith number 124. Lucas Smith is twenty-six years old. His wife Nellie is thirty-eight. Henry Smith's house is 125. He is fifty-two years old and pays two dollars a month for rent. Lucas Smith pays four dollars for rent. John Stribling is a forty-one-year-old with his wife Laura, who is thirty-seven. Roy Wingfield is a thirty-five-year-old and Irna is his twenty-six-year-old wife. Robert is their son at the age of eight. John Stribling and Roy Wingfield and their family are out of Wilkes County, Georgia. Henry Smith is a laborer for a private school. John Stribling is in road construction. Roy Wingfield is working for a private home.

The next enumerator in the 686 is Christine Garrett Crow of the supervisory district number five and enumerator district 44-38 of the Cross Keys District. The first colored house is the house of Herbert Dix. His house is number 3. Herbert Dix is twenty-six years old. His occupation is a track repair worker for the Southern Railroad. Willie Mae, his wife, is twenty-four years old. Elizaberth is eight, William L. is three, and Lonnie N. is a year old. Mr. Herbert Dix and his family are living on Peachtree Street. On April 11 the enumerator Christine Garrett Crow listed forty-three-year-old Daisy Johnson as the housekeeper of James W. Lindsey in Brookhaven Town.

On April 12, 1940, at the intersection of Candler and Candler Drive, at house 208, visitation number 92, is Mrs. Hattie Hood, a seventy-four-year-old widow who owns her property and pays mortgage of six hundred dollars. Mrs. Hattie Hood's daughter is named Emma Christian, a forty-nine-year-old widow. Her grandson James Christian is nineteen, and her forty-one-year-old daughter Francis Childs is in the house with her mother, as well as her eighteen-year-old grandson Johnnie Middlebrooks and her fifteen-year-old granddaughter Dollie Middlebrooks. Living in house 210 at this corner is fifty-nine-year-old James Hood and his wife Carrie, who is forty-eight.

From Peachtree to Candler Street and Candler Drive is Brookhaven Town. I think these two roads are near what is now the town of Chamblee. Was the town of Chamblee once called Brookhaven Town?

At the intersection of Candler Road and Decatur Road we come to the house of Charlie Vinson, who is paying rent at eight dollars a month. Charlie is thirty-five and his wife Anna is thirty-nine. I do not know if this Candler Road is now part of the DeKalb Peachtree Airport. Down on Briarwood Road I found the Wright family. D. M. Wright, Paul Wright, and Clyde T. Wright all own their properties. Then there is the property of Richard Randall, who is at the intersection of Briarwood Road and Decatur Road. And then there's the house of Mr. W. G. Grant, who is renting his property at twenty-five dollars a month. And then the house of Mr. Crichton C. Callaway, who is paying rent at thirty-five dollars. Crichton C. Callaway is twenty-nine years old and works as a clerk in paint. Richard R. Callaway is listed as his wife and she is twenty-eight years old. Crichton C. III is a few months old.

Living at the intersection of Decatur Road and Briarwood Road is the colored family of Ollie Culyer, a twenty-one-year-old, and his twenty-year-old wife Willie Mae Culyer. Their neighbor Leon Echols is a thirty-one-year-old colored man. Both are paying rent of four dollars. Mr. Culyer works on a dairy farm and Mr. Leon Echols works as a farm laborer.

Before I leave this street I want to mention that Mr. Crichton C. Callaway is out of Fulton County. Mr. Richard Randall is also out of Fulton County and is the president of a soft drink company. I also know that Mr. Randall is part of the family of liquor sellers in Fulton County, with Mr. Rose and Mr. Samuels. I also believe that Mr. Culver was a member of the Little Zion Baptist Church in Lynwood Park Colored Community.

Mr. James T. Cates is a forty-eight-year-old white man living on Briarwood Road with his forty-five-year-old wife Olla and their children Sarah M. (sixteen), Eamarly (twelve), Barbara (a few months old), and Eugene (three). At this intersection is the large twenty-thousand-dollar property of Mr. Sylvester E. Guess, a sixty-six-year-old white man. With him are his cook Dora Maddox and her son Eugene Jr. (fifteen) and daughter M. Rose (three months old). Mrs. Dora Maddox has Mr. Luie G. Graves, a gardener aged thirty, living with her. Mrs. Maddox and her family are all out of Atlanta. Mr. Guess's property on Decatur Road is at the corner of Candler Road, near Clairmont Road. Moving on down Candler Road, I come across the house of Thomas Graves, a twenty-eight-year-old. He and his twenty-three-year-old wife Thelma are renting their place for five dollars. Mr. Thomas and Thelma are working as a gardener and servant.

Mrs. Christine Garrett Crow, the enumerator, is now on New Buford Highway at the house of Lee Reeves, a sixty five-year-old, and his wife Anna, fifty-one years old. He is paying rent at three dollars a month. Their neighbor Mary Porter is forty-two years old, the head of her house, and has been married for seven years but her husband is not with her. Lee and Anna Reeves are both out of Gwinnett County. At the intersection of Clairmont Road and New Buford Highway Road is the property of Adam G. Lanier, a white man. However, there is a colored man who owns property right next to Mr. Lanier. His name is Samuel Jett, whose mortgage is five hundred dollars a month. Mr. Jett is thirty-eight years old and his wife Lettie is thirty-two. Rosetta is seventeen, Clinton is fourteen, Forrest is twelve, Curtis is ten, J. W. is eight, and Carolyn is four. Mr. Samuel Jett is a gardener for a private home.

The next house is that of Mr. Memphis Jett, a thirty-four-year-old colored man, and his family. Mr. Memphis owns his property as well and pays mortgage of five hundred dollars a month. His wife is named Odessa Jett, age twenty-nine. Charles E., their son, is seven. Alice M. is six, Bobby is four, Alton is two, and Francis Claudette is only a few months old. And now here comes the father of Mr. Samuel Jett and Memphis Jett. His name is Titus Jett. He is now a widower at the age of seventy years old. His son Harry (I will call him) is twenty-nine, and Marion Lewis is twenty-two years old. All of the Jett men are gardeners for private families.

Crossing over New Buford Highway and before moving onto Clairmont Road we come to the house of Mr. Charles D. Herren a white man and his wife Anna. Charles is sixty-three and Anna is fifty-two. Their Colored Servants are fifty-three-year-old F. L. Morris and thirty nine-year-old wife Clinissie. Mrs. Eula Smith is a colored servant of M. O. Sams. Mr. Jessie Hamilton is living on the corner of Hardee Road and Clairmont Road. Mr. Hamilton is thirty-three and so is his wife Flora. They pay five dollars for renting their place. Mr. Hamilton is a yardman and Mrs. Flora is a maid. Lenora Hamilton their daughter is twelve and Ruby Lee Hardeman is their niece at the age of nineteen.

Mrs. Cynthia Garrett Crow is now making her way down Clairmont Road on the thirtieth of April 1940 toward the houses of two white men at the corner of Hardee Road and Clairmont. They are Lewis Pirkle and Ray W. Pirkle. The two are renters. Two of the larger landowners are Kenneth B. Rice and Mrs. Beulah Young, both white.

On April 25, 1940, Mrs. Marie Gery Booth is the enumerator over supervisory district number five, enumerated district 44-38B. She started on University Drive at the house of Mr. Willis Zach Jones, a sixty-one-year-old, and his wife Margaret, who is fifty-four. Their daughters are Margurite (twenty-five) and Ori Sue (twenty-two). I want to get to the intersection of University Drive and Loraine Drive, where I found Mr. Clifford Hudgins, a fifty-four-year-old landowner paying mortgage of five hundred dollars a month. His forty-five-year-old wife Annie Mell Hudgins is with him, and their children Clifford Jr. (seventeen), Mary Frances (thirteen), and Robert Lewis (four). Mr. Clifford Hudgins Sr. is a disabled veteran. At the end of Loraine Drive you come to Colonial Drive.

On April 30, 1940, Mr. Booth was the enumerator on Cheshire Bridge Road. Floid (Floyd) Key was a sixty-seven-year-old who owned his property and paid $1,500 a month. He was living with his wife Mary Smith, a fifty-five-year-old. Next is the house of John J. Wallace, who paid mortgage at seven hundred dollars a month. Mr. John J. Wallace was thirty-one years old and his wife Ada was twenty-seven. Elsie, their daughter, was six years old. John J. Wallace was a yardman for Monroe Nursery. Willie Benjamin Smith is living at 424 while Floid (Floyd) Key is living at house 314 on Cheshire Bridge Road and John J. Wallace is at 425 Cheshire Bridge Road. I think something is amiss or strange here.

Willie Benjamin Smith is forty-eight years old and his wife Nellie is forty years old. Willie has had only five years of education and Nellie has had only four. Cody, their son, is twenty-two years old and has had six years of education. Harold has had twelve years and is twenty years old. Grace is eighteen and has had eleven years. Maudessa is fifteen and has had seven years. Velva is thirteen and has had five years of education. Vorcile is eleven years old and has had four years. Aubrey is nine and has had three years. Ethel is seven and has had one year. Martha is five years old. Willie B. Smith and his family are out of Atlanta, in Fulton County. I hope I do not get ahead of myself by saying this. However, I believe that this might be Will Callaway under the last name of Smith. I say this because of the name of Willie B. Smith's wife, Nellie. She has the same name as Will Callaway's wife and they are living in the same general area where Will Callaway was living during the First World War! He is a farm laborer.

Mrs. Margaret Green is a colored widow at the age of forty-two and has a boarder by the name of Willie Baidner, a twenty-year-old young man. They live at 420 Cheshire Bridge Road. Mr. E. D. Childress is a sixty-four-year-old white man living with his fifty-three-year-old wife Maggie. They are living next door to the colored household of John Gibson, a colored landowner who pays mortgage at $1,200 a month, while Mr. E. D. Childress pays only $500 a month. John Gibson is sixty-three and his wife Alma is sixty-one. Charlie Nelms is their son-in-law at the age of thirty-six, and Alma is their daughter, who is forty years old. They are living just before you get to the Natural Park Boulevard. The next property is of Mr. Leroy K. Smith out of South Carolina, a forty-six-year-old white man. His wife Mary is from South Carolina and is forty-two. Their daughter Margaret David is twenty-four. Preston David, their son-in-law, is twenty-two. Their grandson Charles Alexander David is two. Mr. Leroy Smith and his family are living on Rollins Road. The only colored man is at the end of the road, paying five dollars. This is Ben Rigsby, a fifty-year-old colored man born in Georgia and working as a servant.

On April 2, 1940, Mr. John Frank Bass is the enumerator of this section of the 686 Cross Keys District in the enumerated district number 44-35.

Ms. Mattie Segars is a colored maid at the age of thirty-two years old and she is in the house of Mr. Garland R. Harlerick, a thirty-six-year-old retail coal man and his family on East Club Drive paying mortgage of $7,000. Mr. Garland is at the corner of East Club Drive and Peachtree Road.

Living on Peachtree Road, just after leaving East Club Drive, is Mr. George H. O'Kelly, a white man aged thirty-six and a teacher in the public schools. His maid is a colored woman named Rosie L. Linder, a twenty-eight-year-old married woman.

Lula Rhodes is the maid of Mr. Albert Martin, a thirty-six-year-old white man out of Atlanta who is renting his place for twenty-five dollars a month and works as an office manager for a reporting agency. Ms. Lula Rhodes is eighteen years old and is out of Tuskegee, Alabama.

Living next door and paying six dollars in rent is Mr. Henry Lyle, sixty years old, and his forty-year-old wife Fannie Lyle. Mr. Henry Lyle does yard work for a private family. Mr. Thomas Smith is paying five dollars in rent for his place. Mr. Smith is fifty years old, single, and does yard work for a private family. Mr. William Thomas is a thirty-six-year-old colored man paying four dollars and fifty cents for rent. His wife is Jenettie, who is thirty-five as well. He is working as a yard man. These colored families and maids are living among some wealthy white men on Peachtree Road in the Cross Keys District 686. Mr. G. H. Turner is a barber and owns his barbershop.

His mortgage is $1,200. John E. Lee is a kitchen boy for the social club and pays the same mortgage. Mr. James L. Gwin is a sixty-two-year-old paying mortgage of $4,000 and is a salesman. Mr. Sam B. Haskey pays $5,000 in mortgage and works as the operator of a retail dump. Mr. Gilbert M. Stokes pays $4,000 in mortgage and is a salesman in wholesale coffee. Linotype operator for a newspaper is Mr. Waller M. Fudge, who pays $8,500 in mortgage. Mr. Yates Eaglston pays $1,400 in mortgage and his wife Mrs. Evelyn sells newspaper advertising. Mr. William Scott is a butler and his wife Fannie M. Scott is the maid for Mr. Homer A. Whitaker, who is paying mortgage of $1,400 on Peachtree Road. William Scott is forty-nine and Fannie M. Scott is twenty-five. Living a few houses down and renting their place for ten dollars are Henry Martin, a thirty-three-year-old colored man, and his thirty-eight-year-old wife Nina. Mr. Henry Martin is a porter for a filling station and Mrs. Nina is a hairdresser. Now, living in the house of Mr. William H. Slaton on West Brookhaven Drive is Mrs. Irene Ford, his maid. Mrs. Irene Ford is forty years old. Renting their place for ten dollars are twenty-four-year-old Thomas J. Hood and his twenty-three-year-old wife Doris. Mr. Thomas Hood is a cook at the social club and Mrs. Doris does housework for a private family.

Young Clifford Lindsey is thirty-one years old and is the yard boy for Mrs. Mary Thomas. She lives at the corner of Peachtree Road and Rollins or Bellsire Drive. Mr. Tom Jones a thirty-year-old colored man and he and his twenty-three-year-old wife Judie are living on West Brookhaven Drive, paying rent at fifteen dollars a month. The two of them are out of Monroe County, Georgia. Tom works as a butler for a private family and his wife does housework. Mr. Walter Turner, a colored man, aged thirty-eight, and his forty-year-old wife Mattie are paying rent at forty dollars a month and are on the corner of East Brookhaven and West Brookhaven. Moving on down East Brookhaven I come to the house of E. Thagard, a white man out of Alabama and worked as a salesman. His maid is Angie Mayfield, a thirty-seven-year-old colored lady. Mrs. Janeta Lambert is a twenty-year-old colored maid working for Mr. Maurice Golestine from Texas.

Mr. George Jackson is thirty-nine and from Alabama. Pearl Cone is a forty-year-old colored woman and cook from Tennessee working for Mr. Clyde Wilkins, also from Tennessee. Mr. Ollie Mosley is a twenty-nine-year-old colored man who pays rent at twenty dollars a month. He does housework for a private family. Lula Harmon is a maid at the age of thirty and is a widow and works for Mr. Charles Lagomaysino, a thirty-five year old advertising manager for a department store. Mr. Charles lives on Mabry Road and pays mortgage of $9,000. I believe that Mabry Road is named for Mr. John F. Mabry, a seventy-four-year-old man who is living with his fifty-nine-year-old wife Ella on Mabry Road. Moving on down Mabry Road toward the Lynwood Park Colored Community is the house of Mrs. Maggie Ezzard, who is paying rent at six hundred dollars a month. Her house is number 96 and she is a widow at forty-six. Her son Candler is twenty-five. Eugene is seventeen. Inez is fourteen. Sidney is thirteen. Dorthey is ten. Ommery M. is seven. Edward is five. Essie Parks is twenty-seven years old and a widow as well. Her grandson William S. Parks is four. Mrs. Ezzard and her family are all from Fulton County and are doing housework. Her eldest son is in construction, while the second child does yardwork.

The next house is that of Mr. Herman Quisley, a thirty-eight-year-old colored man, and his thirty-nine-year-old wife Nillie. Their daughter Ina May is twenty-three, Robert is twenty-one, Roxey may is fourteen, Homer is seven, and their grandson Robert Jones is six years old. *Here I really want to know the occupation of Mr. Herman Quisley because it was said down through the years in Lynwood Park that he was one of the biggest liquor runners in Lynwood Park. The lake that I come to love while growing up in Lynwood was called Herman Lake, named for Mr. Herman Quisley.* Mr. Herman Quisley is a butler for a private family and earns enough money to pay his rent of eight dollars a month.

Now, I am moving on to West House Road (Winsor Parkway). I am at the intersection of Mabry Road and Winsor Parkway, at the house of William Johnson, a sixty-six-year-old colored man out of Tennessee. His wife is named Lena Johnson, a sixty-eight-year-old colored woman. *I must say that I am overwhelmed with emotions to see the families that helped influence me while growing up in this place that I called home for so many years!* The next landowner is a colored man named Mr. George Allen, a fifty-five-year-old widower with a seventh-grade education. Mr. Allen pays $1,600 in mortgage. It is strange to me that he has nothing listed as his occupation. Mr. George Allen's son Thomas is thirty-seven. *Ms. Hortense, my Sunday school teacher at China Grove Missionary Baptist Church,* is twenty-three. Kite Allen is a son-in-law at the age of twenty-five. Mrs. Emily Allen is twenty-seven. She is the daughter-in-law. Thedore, his grandson, is seven years old. George hood is a lodger at the age of thirty-three. Lucy Hood, his wife, is twenty-seven. J. C. Henry is a lodger at the age of twenty-three. Rosa Henry his wife is twenty. Mr. Arthur Allen pays mortgage of four hundred dollars for his property. Mr. Arthur Allen is a thirty-three-year-old colored man with his thirty-two-year-old wife Amanda and his son Woodson at the age of eight. Arthur is seven. Mr. Clifford Sandford pays five hundred dollars a month for his property. Mr. Clifford is forty-five years old and his wife Mrs. Christine Sandford is thirty years old. Mary Ann, their daughter, is seven years old. Mr. Clifford Sandford does yardwork for a private family. Mr. Clifford Sandford's house is located at the intersection of Osborne Road and next door to him are Mr. Homer Gillard, a forty-nine-year-old man, and his forty-nine-year-old wife Mattie. Mr. Gillard is a merchant and owns a grocery store. His wife is the clerk at their store at the corner of Osborne and House Road (Winsor Parkway). Mr. Homer Gillard pays mortgage of $250. Mr. Otis Benton is a sixty-two-year-old man out of Chamblee, Georgia, and living with his fifty-eight-year-old wife Alice. Their daughter Anna Laura is twenty-eight. Mr. Benton pays five hundred a month and works as a laborer in the hospital. Mr. Miles Mosley is a forty-four-year-old colored man and his wife Flora is forty years old. Mr. Mosley is a porter in a grocery store and their daughter Mammie is twenty years old. Mrs. Sue Fleming is a fifty-five-year-old widow living alone and renting her place for two dollars. Mr. Oscar Jones is thirty-three and his wife Mrs. Bertha Jones is twenty-nine years old. Mr. Oscar and Mrs. Bertha pays six hundred dollars a month for mortgage for their property on April 11, 1940, as Mr. John Frank Bass states on the census.

Mr. Belcher Williams pays two hundred dollars for mortgage and is thirty-two years old. Lena, his wife, is thirty-one years old. Both are from Covington, Georgia. Mr. Benjamin Burson is fifty years old and his wife Lena is forty-five. Benjamin Jr. is nineteen. Fornice, their daughter, is eighteen. David, their son, is three. Reuben, their grandson, is eight months old. Mr. Burson pays eight dollars in rent for his place on Osborne Road. Mr. Burson family is all out of Gwinnett County, Georgia.

Mr. Page Usher pays one hundred dollars a month in mortgage for their property on Osborne Road. Mr. Usher is out of Atlanta, Georgia, in Fulton County and is a laborer in public works. Mrs. Ines, his wife, is thirty-nine years old and their daughter little Ms. Millard is five years old. Mr. Culler Chaney is a sixty-one-year-old man living alone and pays sixty-five dollars in mortgage. He is a married man and out of Atlanta. I do not know where his wife, Mary, is from. Mr. Raymond Akins is a thirty-nine-year-old laborer as well. Nellie, his wife, is forty-two years old and their son John is twenty-four. Viola is their daughter-in-law and is the same age as John. Carrie May is their daughter at the age of six. These two men, along with Mr. Luke Hosley, are the founders of Little Zion in the Lynwood Park Colored Community. Mr. Raymond and his wife pay mortgage of two hundred dollars a month. Bennie Banks pays one hundred and fifty dollars a month. He is a forty-six-year-old colored man and his wife Ollie May is forty-one years old. There is nothing listed pertaining to their occupation. Mr. He is thirty-nine years old and his wife Katie is forty years old. Raymond Williams is a lodger in the house at the age of thirty-six and Geneva, his wife, is thirty-three years old. Mr. Edgar Jones is out of Doraville, Georgia, in DeKalb County, and so is his wife Katie. Mr. Raymond Williams is out of Duluth, Georgia, in Gwinnett County.

Mr. Will Banks is fifty-five years old and pays one hundred and fifty dollars. Minnie his wife is forty-four years old and their children are Willie May (eighteen), Kattie B. (sixteen), Julian (ten), Roy E. (nine), and Dorthery (eight). Katie, the mother, is sixty-nine years old. Will Banks is a gardener and florist. The Banks family is all out of Atlanta.

Robert Butler pays three hundred and fifty dollars a month in mortgage. He is thirty-four years old in 1940. His wife Rosetta is twenty-eight, Robert

Jr. is eight, Elloise their daughter is six, Millie the mother is seventy-four years old. Mr. Butler is out of Atlanta and the mother is out of Decatur in DeKalb. Mr. Columbus Chatman is thirty-two years old and his wife Mrs. Annie M. is twenty years old. They pay three hundred and fifty dollars a month in mortgage on the property they own. Mr. Columbus Chatman is out of Decatur in DeKalb County and Mrs. Annie is out of Jones County. Mr. Willie Sims is thirty-nine years old and his wife Mrs. Rosa Lee Sims is thirty-eight years old. Mr. Sims owns his property and pays mortgage of two hundred and fifty dollars a month. Mr. Willie Sims is a brick mason by trade. He is employed by a building company. Mr. Sims and his wife Mrs. Rosa have Mr. Charles Worthy, a thirty-nine-year-old colored man and his family in the house with them. Mr. Charles Worthy's wife is Beatrice, a twenty-year-old. Their daughters are Sara May (eight) and Charlie Bee (seven). Mr. Will Sims, as I grew up calling him, was a long-time fishing partner of my grandfather Arthur. He would make the trip to Pensacola, to the longest pier in the world to fish. Mr. Lewis Clements is forty-seven years old and his wife Georgia M. is seventeen years old. Mr. Lewis Clements pays five hundred dollars a month in mortgage on Osborne Road. He is a yardman for a private family and his wife does housework for a private family. Mr. Robert Worthy pays three hundred and fifty dollars for his place. His wife is named Annie. Robert is forty-nine years old and Annie is forty-one. Mr. Luther Radford is twenty-nine years old. Lucile, his wife, is twenty-six. Luke is nine. Evelyn is six. Jos., the father, is fifty. At the intersection of Osborne Road and Mae Avenue *(spelled May Avenue)* Mr. Radford father last place of residence was Cobb County.

Another one of my grandfather's closest friends was Mr. Luke Hosley. In 1940 he was thirty-seven years old. His wife Lucile was thirty-three. Their children were Timothy (eleven), Robert J. (seven), Francis (six), Lula B. (five), Luke Jr. (three), and Silva Lee (one). Mr. Luke Hosley was a master bricklayer. I worked alongside him and my grandfather on many days and learned not only how to lay bricks, but also many other construction trades. Mr. Hosley's mother was born in Albany, Georgia, where I found Mr. Luke Hosley in the census ten years ago.

Mr. Leotha Glast is a thirty-year-old colored man living with his twenty-four-year-old wife Savannah and his stepdaughter Rosa Lee Scoot, who is six years old. Mr. Leotha Glast is out of Atlanta and his wife Savannah is out of Athens, Clarke County. Mr. Glast rents his place for seven dollars a month. Paying $120 in mortgage is Mr. Will Johnson, a fifty-eight-year-old, and his wife Mammie, who is forty-six. Samuel their son is twenty, Odell their daughter is nineteen, Claude their son is seventeen, Bessie is fifteen, Mr. Harold Otis Hood their grandson is two, and Charles Johnson their other grandson is seven.

Living next door is Mr. Hilton Dillard, a thirty-year-old colored man out of Griffin, Georgia, Spalding County. Hilton's wife Mrs. Lucile is twenty-eight and is also out of Griffin, Georgia. Mr. Hilton does yardwork for a private family and his wife Mrs. Lucile has listed as her occupation housework for a private family. They pay mortgage of $200 a month and their children are Nathaniel (eleven), Hilton Jr. (nine), and James Willie (eight). They have their sister-in-law Mrs. Essie Thomas in the house with them. Mrs. Essie Thomas is twenty-four years old. She has her six-year-old son Amos E. Thomas with her. Hilton and Lucile Dillard's one-year-old daughter is named Annie. Paul is their two-year-old son. Oh! Mrs. Essie Thomas was out of Griffin, Georgia, and does housework for a private family. *Mr. Hilton Dillard and the Thomas families, are kin along with the Truitts as well. The Truitts live to the left of us, the Thomas family lived behind my grandparents, and the Dillards lived on the other side of the Truitt family. I remember when I fought with Dexter Thomas and beat him, but I was cornered behind the outhouse at the back of Mema's house by the Truitts and the Dillards and I ran for my life as I was swinging and running at the same time trying to get to my granddaddy Arthur's house for safty. After a few days had passed we were all playing in the yard again, we were children! I enjoyed many days at mothers Truitt's house. I had my first taste of turtle on her front porch it was very good.*

Paying one hundred dollars a month for mortgage and living next door is Mrs. Hattie Cox, a fifty-year-old lady. There is not much mentioned about where she comes from, just that she works for a private family.

The next colored landowner is Mr. Sidney Brown, a thirty-three-year-old, and his wife Lena, who is thirty years old and the eleven-year-old daughter Mary Francis, their nine-year-old son John P., and their eight-year-old daughter Geneva. Mr. Sidney Brown and his wife are both out of Fulton County and he is a laborer in ground work.

Mr. John Brown is thirty-nine and is living next door. He pays $1,000 a month. He is from Fulton County and is a truck driver for a construction company. Mrs. Ethel, his wife, is thirty-four years old. Both she has two sons from an earlier marriage, Herman Jeter (fourteen) and Robert Jeter (sixteen). They all live at the corner of Mae Avenue and Victoria Avenue in Lynwood Park. Mr. Herman Jeter was born in South Carolina.

Also living at the corner or intersection of Mae Avenue and Victoria Avenue and paying two hundred and twenty-five dollars in mortgage is Mr. Love Jones, a thirty-nine-year-old colored man, his thirty-seven-year-old wife Elvira, Lula M. Norwood their nineteen-year-old daughter, and Ella May their six-month-old granddaughter. Mr. Jones is out of Atlanta and works as a delivery boy for a drugstore.

Mr. Dave Hudson is thirty-seven and pays $135 in mortgage for his property. His wife Phoebe is thirty-six years old. Her nephew lives with them, James Brown, who is twelve years old. They are all out of Atlanta and Mr. Hudson works as a carpenter for an outdoor surveyor. *At this house I was a very young boy who got his haircut done by Mr. Cleo Hudson. He was a short bright-skinned man with a wonderful personality. I could just see him preparing the high seat for me and asking me if I am old enough for the regular chair. This is where I got my first haircut as a little boy. I was with my mother Mary.* There are only two colored families on Victoria Avenue in 1940 and they are the families of Mr. Love Jones and Mr. Dave Hudson.

At the intersection of Victoria Avenue and Mae Avenue (spelled May Avenue) is the family of Mr. Abe Johnson, thirty-five, and his wife Mamie. They are the same age. Their children are Anderson (eleven), Theodore (nine), Catherine (seven), and Lenora (?), who is twelve. Mr. Abe Johnson and his family relocated from Atlanta and he works as a cook in a restaurant. He also does ironing in a laundry. Mr. Abe Johnson pays eight dollars in rent for his place.

While, Mr. John Lester is a fifty-year-old widower who pays $125 in mortgage on Mae Avenue. His daughter Addie Lee is eighteen, Edward is seventeen, Lucile is thirteen, James is eleven, and Thomas is nine. John Lester and his family are all out of Chamblee, Georgia, in DeKalb, and he is not working. However, Addie Lee is doing housework for a private family and Edward is a stable boy for a riding stable.

Mr. John W. Kelly is twenty-five and his wife Rhoda is twenty-seven. His father-in-law is Mr. Will Jones, a sixty-six-year-old. His wife Maggie is sixty-three years old. Their niece-in-law Annie B. Jones is ten. John W. Kelly and his household are all out of Chamblee. He works as a woodcutter for a college and so does sixty-six-year-old Will Jones just to pay seven dollars in rent.

Mr. James Jackson is sixty years old and his wife Pearl is fifty-eight. Their daughters are Ms. Mildred (nineteen) and Ms. Mozell (twenty-six). Mr. James Jackson works in landscaping for a private family and his wife does housework for a private family. *Ms. Mildred was a licensed barber and was a very light skinned woman. It was just a joyous occasion to just be in the shop and hear her give such great advice too us young preteen boys. While on our way to get our haircut at her shop, someone would ask, "Where are you going?"*

I would say, "I'm going to Ms. Moot's." They would know by her nickname that I was going to get my haircut and enjoy a wonderful conversation with Ms. Mildred! I remember one visit to Ms. Moot's barbershop was a walk with Howard White, my mother's boyfriend, who took us to Tampa, Florida, when I was very young. I was to get my haircut by Ms. Moot and the next thing that comes to mind is that I was looking out the living room window as they were using the water hose to wash the blood from the driveway after my grandfather had shot him. He was told not to come back to my grandfather's house for some reason or another. I was a very young boy when these things happened. I wouldn't ever learn to play the guitar now!

Mr. Fred Haywood is forty-one years old and is out of Alabama. His wife Elizabeth is twenty-six. Mr. Fred Haywood pays $1,500 in mortgage on the property that he owns at the corner or intersection of Mae Avenue and House Road, with Mr. James Jackson opposite him on a place he owns and pays $1,000 a month in mortgage.

Mr. Robert Ousley is twenty-one years old and his wife Ann is twenty-three. Robert L. is two and Barbara R. is a few months old. The Ousleys pay rent at eight dollars a month on House Road (Windsor Parkway). Mr. Robert Ousley is out of Atlanta and he's a butler for a private family.

Mr. Boley Gather is seventy years old and is a widower out of Atlanta. He is paying mortgage of three hundred dollars a month and is living with his nineteen-year-old grandson Fred Gather Jr. Mr. Boley Gather is an orderly in the hospital, and his grandson Fred is a new worker.

Mr. John Gilbert is paying $1,500 a month in mortgage and is thirty-seven years old. He is from Atlanta and is an orderly in the hospital as well. His wife Bessie is thirty-two, their son Thomas is sixteen, Corvin is fourteen, Jennie Woodward is a seventy-two-year-old aunt living in the house with them. Mr. John Gilbert's house is at the corner of House Road and Lynwood Drive, along with Mrs. Annie Flanagan, a colored woman paying five hundred dollars a month in mortgage. She is fifty years old and does housework for a private family. The next house is that of Mrs. Menema Baugh, a thirty-seven-year-old widow who pays $1,600 for mortgage and has with her, her brother Mr. Henry Taylor, a thirty nine-year-old widower. Both are out of Atlanta, Fulton County, Georgia. Menema does housework for a private family and he does yardwork for a private family.

Mrs. Ora Wilcox is a forty-five-year-old widow and pays five dollars for rent and her son William is thirty years old. His wife is Mrs. Catherine, who is twenty-eight. Mrs. Ora and her son are out of Atlanta and Mrs.

Catherine is out of Jacksonville, Florida, in Duvall County. She works as a teacher in the public school. The next house on Lynwood Drive is Mr. Bryant's. He pays $1,000 a month in mortgage. He is sixty years old and his wife Elizabeth is fifty years old. Their daughter Iris is twenty-five, Mildred is twenty, and Louisa is nineteen. Mr. Bryant is a private gardener.

Mr. Arch Hood is forty years old and his wife Ruth is thirty-nine years old. They pay mortgage of seven hundred dollars a month on Lynwood Drive. Both are out of Atlanta. I think that Mr. Hood is a laborer doing plumbing work. His wife does housework. Mr. John H. Barnes pays six dollars for rent and is forty-nine years old. His wife Susie is thirty-nine, Georgia E. is sixteen, Henry is twelve, John D. is eleven, Benjamin is six, Mary Ruth is four. Their son Lewis Ray Thomas (five) is with them in the Barnes house. Mr. John Barnes does yardwork for a private family.

The next colored family is that of Mr. Sam Jones, a forty-one-year-old man doing yardwork and has a three-hundred-dollar mortgage. His wife is Mrs. Ruby, thirty-nine years old. Their children are Clara (eleven), Norris S. (nine), Robert (seven), Willie B. (five), Melvin (three), and Rubie J. (six months). Eva Chandler is their sister-in-law, a forty-something. Marion their daughter-in-law is twenty-five.

Mr. Utah Clement is thirty-seven years old and his wife Eva is thirty-two. Utah J. Jr. is two years old. The Clement family pays two hundred dollars a month for mortgage. He is listed as a laborer in the natural gas sector.

Mr. Lucius Albert is a thirty-six-year-old and his wife Ola Albert is thirty-two. He is a photographer and pays a mortgage of nine hundred dollars a month.

The next house on Lynwood Drive is that of Mr. David Holland, a thirty-year-old construction worker and cement finisher. His wife Mrs. Lena Bell Holland is thirty-one. The two of them pay mortgage of five hundred dollars a month.

Mr. Charles Nobles is a colored twenty-seven-year-old born in Alabama and his wife Rea is twenty-two years old. He works as a porter for some bottling company. They pay eight dollars to rent their place. I don't know if Mr. Charles Nobles is out of Walton County with Henry Callaway or if he is out of Monroe County in Evers who buried Mary Callaway.

Charles Nobles has a lodger living with him and his name is John Hudson, a twenty-five-year-old man. His wife Constance is twenty-three. John W. Jr. is their four-year-old son. The next house on Lynwood Drive is that of Mr. Bird Dallas, a fifty-nine-year-old, and his wife Lula, who is forty. They pay rent at a rate of seven dollars a month. Mr. Bird Dallas work as a laborer on cars.

Mr. Buster Dallas is a fifty-year-old man and his wife is living next door to Bird Dallas and his wife Lula. Buster Dallas is a widower and his daughter Matilda is fourteen, Buster Jr. is seventeen, Ruth is twelve, Ernest is ten, Clifford is five and Mattie White is the housekeeper at the age of sixty-five and is a widow. Buster works as a Florist.

Major Wright is a forty two-year-old colored man out of Atlanta living with his wife Essie Wright a thirty nine-year-old from Atlanta as well. Robert L. their son is twenty, Andrew Wright their father is eighty-two years old, and the niece is Jennie May at the age of twenty. All are out of Atlanta. Major Wright is an orderly in a hospital, so he can pay his mortgage of five hundred dollars a month.

Mr. Thomas Hood is a sixty-two-year-old widower living with his children twenty-two-year-olds Louise and Thelma B., twenty-four-year-old Willie M., and a son named Colquitt, who is twenty. Mr. Hood works as a carpenter in a construction company to pay his five-hundred-dollar mortgage.

Mr. James Harrison and his wife Betty are forty years of age and pay six hundred dollars a month for their house on Lynwood Drive. He labors in public works. Mr. Balus Hood is twenty-six and his wife Catherine is twenty-four. They pay three hundred dollars a month for mortgage and he works as a yardman.

James Hood is a twenty-seven-year-old man and his wife Nolia is twenty-two. Ernestine their daughter is four, Eunice is two, and Robert is one. James and Nolia pay five hundred dollars a month for mortgage. James does housework for a social club.

Mr. Henry Wright is a forty-two-year-old man with his wife Ethel, who is thirty-six. They pay seven hundred dollars a month for mortgage. Living in the house with them are Henry their son at the age of seventeen, Ethel M. their daughter at the age of fifteen, and sixty-three-year-old widow mother Mary Ranson from Atlanta. Henry wright works a Porter. *Now, I know that there is a tie between my grandfather Arthur and Mrs. Mary Ranson who is in the house with the Wright Family in Lynwood Park. She shows up on some colored Callaways' death certificates. She also witnesses for my grandfather on his deed for his house on Mae Avenue.*

The next house heading toward the intersection of Lynwood Drive and Osborne Road, the same intersection where I lived just about all my life, is that of Mr. Luther Clemmons, a thirty-three-year-old man and his wife Emma, who is twenty-eight years old. With them is their daughter Gaynell, who is two years old. Mr. Luther pays eight hundred dollars in mortgage to keep a roof over his family's head. Mr. Luther Clemmons works as a manager at a retail coal yard.

Mr. Willie Johnson is twenty-two and is paying five dollars. He is from Milledgeville, Georgia. Mr. Johnson works as a laborer in construction. His next-door neighbor is a mysterious man or head of the house. He is forty-nine years old and he pays five hundred dollars a month in mortgage on Lynwood Drive. His occupation is working as a laborer in public works. His wife is named Mary Ella, aged thirty-nine. Their daughter is Margrett, who is sixteen. Wiley is fourteen. Marry Alice, his granddaughter, is three. His son Paul is one. One grandson is named Willie O. Wright (twenty-three) and another is John H. Wright (twelve).

The next house is that of Joseph B. Hood (twenty-four) and Mrs. Bernice, his twenty-two-year-old wife. Their son William is six, Francis is five, and Marvin is three. Joseph Hood was the janitor at the college.

Mr. Lewis Scott is twenty-seven and his wife Willet is twenty-four. They have a twenty-eight-year-old lodger, J. B. Radford. Lewis Scott pays five dollars in rent and works as a cement finisher in a construction company. He was out of Gwinnett County.

Mr. Lenard Anderson is twenty-six years old and his wife Daisy is twenty-eight. Their son Harold is five, and Lewis is a year old. Lenard Anderson pays six dollars for rent and works as gardener.

Mr. J. B. Hugley is forty years old and his wife Mammie is thirty-five. They pay five hundred dollars a month and have their mother Irene Rutledge, a fifty-year-old widow, with them. All are out of Atlanta. Mr. Hugley is a clopper for a private family.

The next three houses at the intersection of Lynwood Drive and Osborne Road are all of white renters. W. B. Davis is renting his place for twelve dollars and William Danielle is paying rent at six dollars and fifty cents. Mr. William Dleshaw is forty-five and pays the same. The next white family owns their property and pays mortgage of $3,000, headed by William Rulhumayle, a German. The next white family is the family of Fred C. Robinson, who pays $2,000. He is thirty-six years old and a carpenter.

Mr. John Frank Bass, the enumerator, is moving up Osborne Road toward Peachtree Road after leaving Lynnwood Drive. The head of the household of these white men are Edner Ross, a renter; James R. Cook, who pays $2,000; William H. Cunningham, who pays the same mortgage; Russell Cutler, who pays $1,800; Mr. Ernest Brand, who pays rent at $25; James M. Flowers, who pays $2,500; James W. Hinduer, who pays rent at $37; Othela Space, who pays rent at $12; Mr. Miller Sanders, who pays $7; Claud Tibbs, who pays rent at $6; Buck Frank, who pays $6; and Mr. Level E. Whitaker, who pays $600 a month for mortgage.

When I got to Peachtree Road, I found Mr. Lewis Jones paying rent at five dollars a month. Mr. Lewis Jones was forty-two and his wife Sally was forty. Dorthy their daughter is nineteen, and Sylvie was thirteen. Mr. Jones does yardwork.

Mrs. Mattie Fugerson is the maid for Mr. H. J. Gartner, a teacher at the college on University Road. Mrs. Mattie is thirty-four and is single.

At the intersection of Peachtree Road and Ashford Road is the house of C. H. Baldwin, a thirty-five-year-old, and his wife Cleo, who is thirty-seven years old. Mr. C. H. Baldwin has an eighth-grade education, and his wife Cleo has a ninth-grade education. He is from DeKalb County and she is from Atlanta. His fifty-six-year-old mother-in-law Frances Swient is out of Butts County. C. H. Baldwin is a chopper for what looks like a concrete company. Mr. Baldwin pays fifteen dollars for his rent.

The largest landowner whose land I believe C. H. Baldwin is on is Mr. Cobb Howell, who pays $30,000 in mortgage for property on the corner of Lake Road and Peachtree Road. Mr. Cobb Howell is sixty-nine years old with a ninth-grade education. He is with his sixty-one-year-old wife Mary. Howell, their son, is thirty-seven years old. He owns a sawmill and I believe C. H. Baldwin works in his mill as a chopper.

Living next door to Mr. C. H. Baldwin and his family are Lige Blake, a sixty-six-year-old colored man; his wife Mammie, who is fifty-nine years old; and their children Annie B. (nineteen), Will (twenty), and Ina May (eighteen), along with Mildred, their nine-year-old granddaughter. Mr. Lige Blake pays eight dollars for rent and works as a laborer in a nursery.

Roy Blake is twenty-nine and his wife July is twenty-six years old. They pay five dollars a month, and he works as a laborer in a nursery.

Mr. John Blake is twenty-nine years old and his wife Mrs. Emma L. is twenty-three. Betty A., their daughter, is eight, and Clyd is six. John Blake does yardwork for a private family to pay his rent at eight dollars a month.

The next house is that of Mr. George Truitt, a seventy-six-year-old colored man, and his thirty-seven-year-old wife Annie. With them are their twenty-two-year-old daughter Annie M., George Jr. (nineteen), Cecil (seventeen), George S. (twelve), John W. (ten), Pat R. (nine), Franklin D. R. and Jasper (twenty-one). Their daughter-in-law Odessa is fourteen, their granddaughter Frances is one, Mary E. their granddaughter is four, George A. their grandson is three, and Lena Ruth their granddaughter is two years old. John Frank Bass made this survey on April 17, 1940. Mr. George Truitt Sr. works ten hours as a well digger in construction. Mother Truitt or Mrs. Annie, his wife, does not have an occupation and only stays at home to take care of her large family. Annie M. and George Jr. work seventy-two hours a week. She does housework for a private family and he's a delivery boy for a drugstore.

Mr. William Landers is a fifty-six-year-old white man renting his place for six dollars a month. His wife Maggie is the same age as her husband and their son William is twenty-one. Estell, their daughter, is sixteen. Geraldine is thirteen. They are living at the intersection of Ashford Park and the Ashford Park Monastery property, at a little street called Church Road. However, before you get to this road you come to the house of Mr. Fred Bryant, a thirty-year-old colored man, and his wife, whose name is not quite legible. She is thirty years old as well. They pay four dollars for their rented property. Fred Bryant works as a laborer in the nursery. They are living next door to a white man by the name of Sidney Reeves at the age of forty-two. He is the manager of the nursery. Mable, his wife, is thirty-six. Ernest, their son, is eighteen. John T. is sixteen. Lura is thirteen. Frank is eleven. Mr. Sidney Reeves pays rent at $1,200.

Mr. Jasper Byrd is a colored man at the age of fifty and his wife is named Adea at the age of thirty-five. Ermles their daughter is twenty-nine, Mohalla their daughter is twenty-four, Mathew their son is eighteen, Cornetha their daughter is fifteen, Walber Barnes their granddaughter is four, and Sally Mae Barnes their granddaughter is two. Jasper Byrd pays rent at five dollars a month. He and his family are out of Hoganville in Troupe County, Georgia. He is a farmhand in the nursery. His son Mathew works at the college.

Living at the intersection of Johnson Ferry and a little street called Church Street is the family of seventy-six-year-old white man John Ellison and his wife Samantha, who is at the age of seventy. Living right next to Mr. John Ellison is Mr. Bailus Sutton at the age of sixty and renting his property at fifteen dollars a month at the corner of a road that looks like it is spelled Corner Road near Church that intersects with Johnson Ferry Road. I believe that this road is either by Blackburn Park and near Aiken Drive, where the Sutton Subdivision is located even today.

Mr. Wallace Jones a thirty-one-year-old colored man living right next door to Mr. Bailus Sutton and is paying rent at four dollars a month. His wife Mrs. Idell is twenty-eight years old and Wilber their son is nine. Mrs. Georgia Ann, as I endearingly called her growing up, is four years old and her brother Columbus Jones is two years old. My aunt Eugenia Hart Callaway knew him, I believe, before he was killed one night. I was a little boy when I heard the news of his death. I believe that Mrs. Idell's maiden name was Sutton before marrying Mr. Wallace Jones, who I believe is the son of the older Columbus Jones, who had 2,000 acres of land at the corner of Shallowford Road and Johnson Ferry Road on April 4, 1940, under Mrs. Neva Barnes McTown, the enumerator.

Mr. John Frank Bass, April 18, 1940, took this census of Mr. Balus Sutton and Mr. Wallace Jones and others at the corner of Johnson Ferry Road and Ashford Park. Mr. Clifford Sutton was forty-eight years old and his wife Kattie was forty-nine. Their son Stanton was twenty. Willie their daughter was twenty-four. Clifford Jr. is a widow at the age of twenty-five, and Edward his grandson is seven years old. His grandsons are Maxwell (five), Alvin (three), and Thomas (seven months old), who is listed as his granddaughter. Mr. Wallace Jones is a laborer for the golf course, Stanton is a caddy for the golf course, and Clifford Jr. is a laborer for the college grounds. Sixty-year-old Balus Sutton is a farmer in agriculture and works sixty hours a week. His neighbor Wallace Jones works fifty-two hours a week. Clifford Sutton Sr. is working sixty-two hours a week, while Clifford Jr. is working sixty-four hours a week.

On April 22, 1940, at the end of Johnson Ferry Road in the supervisory district number 5 and the enumerated district 44-35, the enumerator did not sign his name on the census.

Living next door to Mr. Clifford Sutton Jr. is Mr. Ollie Willingham, a forty-three-year-old and his twenty-nine-year-old wife Lizzie and their daughter Mary Hellen, who is six years old. Mr. Ollie pays two dollars and fifty cents for rental of his property and his family are all from Elberton, Elbert County, Georgia. Mr. Ollie works fifty-five hours a week as a woodcutter in the forest. Lizzie work as a laundress in house work. Mr. Ollie Willingham has been close to my Grandfather Arthur Calloway and might even be kin as Mrs. Willingham told me one day while showing me my mother's picture as a little girl in the front yard while living in the first house on Mae Avenue. Mrs. Willingham was the mother of the church at China Grove and I remember her as one of the mother during the Communion who stood by the Pastor. I remember one cold snow storm that Mrs. Willingham had to come and live with my grandfather. I found this to be very true.

Mr. William Jones is a thirty-five-year-old living with his wife Lola, who is thirty-five as well. They pay two dollars and fifty cents for rental of their property at the end of Johnson Ferry Road. Lola is out of Elberton, Elbert County, Georgia. Mrs. Pearl Strozier is a forty-three-year-old widow paying rent at seventeen dollars and fifty cents for her property. Her cousin Orien Bacon is thirty-eight, Irene Strozher her daughter is sixteen, and E. W. Bacon, another cousin, is forty. Her cousin Orien Bacon works a fifty-five-hour week as a florist. Mr. E. W. Bacon is a farmhand on a farm. Living at the end of the Johnson Ferry Road is Mr. Samuel Johnson, who owns his property and pays two hundred dollars a month in mortgage. He is fifty-four years old and his brother William Johnson is fifty-two years old. They are only ones in the house. Mr. Samuel Johnson is a farmer and works seventy hours a week. His brother William is a carpenter and does building work and works fifty hours a week.

The last place I found Mr. Ollie Willingham and his wife was in the Third Ward in the city of Atlanta on Piedmont Avenue near Chestnut Street.

On April 16, 1940, Mr. John Frank Bass signs his name as enumerator. He is at the intersection of Mabry and Osborne Road in the 686th District, Cross Keys, at the house of Mr. Robert Miller, the landowner, who pays $3,000 a month for mortgage. He is a merchant out of Atlanta. He has a twenty-eight-year-old colored woman named Eva Dunington living in the house with him and his wife. She followed them from Atlanta to Lynwood Park. She has nothing listed as her occupation while in his house.

Mrs. Nora Flanagan is a fifty-five-year-old widow living next door paying three dollars a month for rent. Mrs. Nora was last located in Rockdale County. She works as a laundress in housework.

Mr. Turner Baker is a seventy-eight-year-old man living with his sixty-five-year-old wife Sally and their twenty-nine-year-old son Columbus Wood and his wife Ruth (twenty-four) and Mojorie, their seven-year-old daughter. Doris, who is four. James R. is two and Peggie J. is six. Oscar Parker is a nephew at the age of twenty-four and Jessie Goodin a seven-year-old nephew. Mr. Columbus Wood does yardwork for a private family in 1940 before he became a preacher at Mt. Mary Baptist Church. I believe that this location is down near Brookhaven Drive. The largest landowner is a white man named Richard Hardwick, a forty-year-old agent who sales insurance. Living next door to Mr. Hardwick and his household is a colored man named Jake Samples, a fifty one-year-old, and his wife Wellena, who is forty-nine years old. He owns his property and pays two hundred dollars a month in mortgage and work painting houses.

Mr. Burtley Worthy is a thirty-year-old colored man living with his wife Beatrice, who is twenty. Susie May his daughter is eight, and Claudia Belle is seven. Mr. Worthy pays four dollars a month in rent and work as a farmer for a private family.

Mr. Henry Kellog is a seventy-three-year-old widower and his daughter Connie Samples is thirty-three. Lula Johnson his daughter is a thirty-year-old widow. Rosa M. Murky is seventeen. Mason Brown is an eighty-seven-year-old white widower out of North Carolina. With them is four-year-old colored boy Robert Brown. Mr. Henry Kellog pays four dollars a month and does housework and yardwork for a private family. The next house is the house of Cusame Brownlee, a forty-two-year-old, and his wife Thersa at the age of thirty-five, they are a white family paying rent at forty dollars a month. And living in the house with him is another white man named John Pace Mesling, a thirty-six-year-old divorced man.

Mr. J.C. Lynn

Mr. Jasper C. Lynn, for whom Lynnwood drive is named, was a very hard man to find anything about because I only knew him as J. C. Lynn. I found him yesterday, July 14, 2015, in the census book living in Atlanta next door to Ms. Emma Lou Cates at 198 West Peachtree Street. He is sixty-two years old, and his wife Maggie is sixty-one. The two of them just relocated from DeKalb County to Fulton. Ms. Emma Lou Cates is fifty-four years old and living with her sister Mays Bertling, who is fifty-six years old. They all are living at the sixteenth block of West Peachtree, where the seventeenth block begins. Oh! The year is 1940. Mrs. Mary Kate Chaplin says that it is the Third Ward.

In 1930, Jasper C. Lynn and his wife Maggie are living at 1208 West Peachtree with Mr. James L. Mason, a thirty-four-year-old plumber, his father F. W., and adopted son Samuel R. Mason. Mrs. Lynn is a housekeeper and J. C. is in construction, described as doing general building. Also sharing the same house is Ms. Sallie Fowley and her daughters Alma Jean and Eva Frances. Now, here is a reason that lets me know that my grandfather might have had a hand in the building of Lynwood Park Subdivision or Cates Subdivision. He was living with Effie in 1920 on West Peachtree as she worked for a Mr. Jack Sutler, who was kin to the McKinney family, as I am told by some of the family in a phone conversation with Mattie Hunter, the niece of Mrs. Effie. In the house of Jasper and Maggie they have a son named Melroy S. Lynn at the age of sixteen. His brother-in-law is Homer Rutledge and his niece Unice and his son Hoke. On the same street is a colored family, Rufus Bennett and his wife Lillie and Mr. Marian Harrison. The road they are living on is House Road, which leads up to Johnsonferry Road, which will become Osborne Road. House Road will become Winsor Parkway. I believe that the property that Mr. Lynn is on in 1920 is in or near Chastain Park. I say this because Mr. Jerry Hutchins, who will come to live in Lynwood Park, is living on Isom Road, the same road that Mr. R.M. Rose's brother will come to possess. Mr. Hutchins has fifteen children. Mr. Bosie Hutchins lived on Paces Ferry Road. There is one name that is in this district that I know from Lithonia and he is Mr. Oscar Center and his wife Roxy, and Ethat his daughter and Glodster who is eleven. And Annie Williams, a thirty-six-year-old widow.

Martin Mathew Callaway *is the one of the first colored Callaways that I found in DeKalb County besides C. C. Callaway in 1930. He was mainly found in Panthers Ville, Georgia, in DeKalb County. This is the same place where I found Judea and her family, with Aaron Callaway, my grandfather's grandfather. Remember I found Martin on the road gangs in 1901 at the Old DeKalb County Historical Society in Decatur.*

Martin Mathew Callaway was the second Callaway I found in Panthers Ville in Dekalb County. I found forty-five Juda and thirty five-year-old Berry and a four-year-old boy named William. William is listed as being insane and is not able to labor. Joseph Walker is the assistant marshal and the family that Juda is living next door to is that of Mr. Christopher Johnson, a twenty-nine-year-old with a twenty-three-year-old wife, Francis A. Johnson. They are keeping house with their daughter Ophelia (two) and son Nathan M. Johnson (one). For me to place where they were living at this time and in what land lot district in Panthers Ville in 1870, I must mention the white family that was living here at this time. So I will mention the family of Jennings J. Hulsey, a twenty-eight-year-old farmer and his wife Sarah E. Hulsey, who is twenty-one. Minnie B. their one-year-old daughter and William T. their three-month-old son. Now the family that owned the property that they were living on is that of Mr. William L. Williams, a fifty-seven-year-old farmer and his wife Caroline G. Williams and Penelope C. Williams, their twenty-year-old daughter. Martin Mathew Callaway married Feriby Fletcher between 1873 and 1877. Martin's son Leonard Callaway married twice, first Georgia Pope and then he married Martha Kemp. Martin Callaway will reside in Panthers Ville for quite some time before moving to Lithonia in Dekalb County. I never found a Martin Callaway in 1870 at any time but I did find him in the later years of Dekalb and in the 1880s in Fulton County.

In 1878, in the 563rd District of Panthers Ville I found Martin Callaway working with Harris Crawford, Ed. F. Cosby, Thomas Clark, Wilson Clark, William Clark, Depsey Clark, on the property of J.F. Stubbs. James English is on the property of L. Sturges with Welcome Elder, Dembo Fowler, Benjamin Fowler, Isom Fowler, Miller Farr, and Abram Fletcher,

Now don't forget that Martin Mathews Callaway married Feriby Fletcher about this same time and here we find working nearby him Abram Fletcher on the farm of L. Sturges.

In the year 1880, Martin Calaway is working for G.W. Mathews in Panthers Ville. I want to just look at who Martin Mathew Callaway is working for and try and figure out the relationship that he has with these white men in Panthers Ville. Also what comes to mind at this time while Martin is working for Mr. G. W. Mathews. Charlie and Sam Boykin, a few years later, would be arrested for breaking into the place of Huchins and Mathews in Oglethorpe County.

Between the years of 1881 and 1884

Panthers Ville 536

Mart Calaway is working with William Clark, Dempsey Clark, Henry Chamblis, Harry Crawford, Jack Daniel, Jim Deanes, Sam Dodson, and Jeff Dollar on the property of H.V. Baynes, not too far from the property of S.K. Austin. Also on the property with Mart Calaway is Ben Mattox, Brooks Mitchel, Louis Mikle, King Master, Charley Mitchell, Peter Miller, Sam Mitchel, Lavazan Pitts, and Frank Prortis. And on the property of Master Samuel is Charley Primrose, Watson Pitts, Miller Pharr, Joe Parks, Charley Pitts, George Ragsdale, and Dallas Randal.

The name that I am very much interested in is that of Mr. Charley Mitchell, who might have been the same C. C. Mitchell that was the employer of Willie Callaway when Will Callaway was in Buckhead in Fulton County. Willie Callaway was in Chamblee, Georgia, in 1917 when he was listed as working for Mr. C. C. Mitchell. I do not know if Mr. C. C. Mitchell is out of Panthers Ville or out of the third ward of the city of Atlanta. He could be one and the same like Martin M. Callaway could very well be Charlie or Burwell or even Robert. I do know if they are kin in some way or another! I say this because of Willie Howard, the grandson of Aaron, and Willie Howard being the grandson of Juda Callaway, who resided in Panthers Ville in 1870 and later resided in Puryear's District of Clarke County with Aaron in 1880 before he died. Willie Howard was living in a ward for the insane at this time. I do not know how Martin Mathew Callaway is kin to Juda or Aaron or what (white) family of Callaways resided in this part of the county of DeKalb or Henry County.

In the year of 1882, Martin Callaway is on the property of R.W. Waldrop with Andrews Crockett, Jerry Colquitt, Henry Chamblis, Dempsey Clark, Christopher Cosley, James Deaner, Samuel Dodson, Floyd Dennis, and Jessey Daniel. I found Berry Truett on the property of J.S. Fowler, with Simon Strickland, Garry Smith, Henry Smith, Jessey Smith, Levi Scott, and Henry Thompson,

In the year 1883, Martin Callaway is working with William Clark, Gid Collins, and Henry Chambliss on the property of J.G. Brown. As you can see Martin Callaway has a long-standing relationship in Panthers Ville and to see the location where Martin Callaway was living at this time as Juda Callaway in 1870 in Panthers Ville. I think they were here for quite some time because of them working in the granite mining that was taking place in the southern section of Panthers Ville in Dekalb County.

Now, in the years 1884, 1885, and 1886, Martin Mathew Callaway is missing. From 1885 to 1886, Martin Mathew Callaway is in the Third Ward near the Ebenezer Baptist Church, just off of Decatur Street in Atlanta. The street is called Airline Street.

The 1885 white defaulters: J.C. P. Johnson and I.A. Stewart in the Mill District.

However, there is no Martin M. Callaway in DeKalb. Therefore, I went to the Atlanta directory and I found Martin Callaway there. However, I think of the character of Charlie Callaway and the many times that the people that I talked with stated that he was a womanizer. He loved him some women. I not only heard this about Charlie, but also of some of his children and other colored Callaways and their white counterparts as well. Now to mention Mr. J. C. P. Johnson, the same Johnson that will come to live in Lithonia. I believe he is the same J. C. P. Johnson in Clarke County as well. I believe that Mr. J. C. P. Johnson is a very influential white man in the state of Georgia. I believe that he is the boss of the quarry in or near Lithonia and other quarries in Georgia as well.

By the year of 1893

Whites, Panthers Ville 536 district

Charles M. Calloway, Edward N. Burgess, William H. Burgess

Mr. Charles Mallory Callaway is the son of John Appleton Callaway and Penelope Austin Callaway of Henry County, just south of Panthers Ville, Georgia.

From 1893 to 1898, Martin Mathew Callaway cannot be found in DeKalb County or in Atlanta. I think that his life aligns with Charlie's circumstances in Athens and Oglethorpe County! Martin Mathew Callaway shows up in 1899.

Now, in 1893 these are the only coloreds in Panthers Ville

Nancy Avery, Joe Avery, John Avery, Anderson Bryant, Wyatt Colquitt, William Glover, John Hurd, Arch Johnson, William Lyon, Merida Lyon, Alfred Penn, John Penn, Charlie Primrose, Alfred Watkins

Look at the Lyon family, does it remind you of Collins H. Lyons? However, in 1899, look how the number of coloreds increase.

Panthers Ville 536

Martin Callaway shows up again in amidst Joseph Avery, Joe Avery (agent for Monk Avery), Nathan Albert, John Arnold, John Avery, John Brown, Ben F. Bell, Orange Bell, Wade Bowden, Jerry Brown, James T. Brown, J.T. Brown (agent for Est of Aleck Wood), Seymore Barnes, Dock T. Brown, Jerry Clark, Warren Coats, William Clark, Harvey Clark, James W. Cobb, James W. Clarke (agent for wife), Henry J. Fowler, Abe Fletcher, Ben J. Fowler, Wes Fletcher, Ben W. Fowler, Jack Gresham, Cornelius Hulsey, Sanford Hudson, Monroe Harris, Fenton Hardin, David Hardin, Andy Kirkpatrick, Aleck Lyon, Merida Lyon, James Lyon, George W. Lyon, James Lankston, Felix Lyon, Will Mitchell, Henry McGennis, James Mays, Mary Mays, Lewis Miller, Charlie Pitts, John H. Robinson, Aleck Roseborough, Elijah Stroud, Berry Shepard, Burrill Shefford, William M. Stallworth, Andrew Thompson, Tobe Thompson, Charlie White, William M. Wise, Charlie Wright, Willis Williford, Wright Williams, Oscar Williams, Alfred Watkins, Levi Wilkerson

Here in 1899 there are two sets of the Fletcher family, Abe Fletcher and Wes Fletcher in Panthers Ville

BREAKING ROCKS IN THE QUARY IN LITHONIA

In 1901, Dekalb County had a road gang that worked in sections of Dekalb County, Georgia. The coloreds that I found in Lithonia on the road gang were: Luther Albert (twenty-four), F. Albert (eighteen), F.M. Albert (forty-five), J.M. Blackman (twenty-four), L.A. J. Broadnax (forty), Lon Brooks (twenty-one), Bon Brown (forty), and H.W. Buchanan (thirty-one). All were listed as farmers. O.W. Berry (twenty-nine), Solomon Bonds (forty-seven), L.S. Boatware (thirty-eight), John Blake (twenty-eight), Dave Bonds (thirty), Boyd Brown (twenty-eight), Mr. A. Benefield (thirty), and John H. Baldin (thirty). All were listed as drillers.

E.C. Curney, a forty-three-year-old farmer

W.C. Curney, twenty-four-year-old farmer

A. Chapman, forty-four-year-old farmer

W.C. Crue, a thirty-seven-year-old farmer

George Clarke, a forty-year-old farmer

W. Clarke, another forty-year-old farmer

John Clark, twenty three-year-old farmer

P.C. Clark, a forty-year-old farmer

Willie Cruchfield, is a thirty-seven-year-old farmer

Willie Calaway, a nineteen-year-old farmer

Author Crew, twenty-one, farmer

Henry Crew, seventeen, driller

There is another Henry Crew who is twenty-five and a J.L. Crew who is twenty-nine.

M.M. Callaway, farmer, forty

Pery Carter, forty-nine, driller

Joe Clark, age not listed

Luther Clark, twenty-one

J.W. Cridle, twenty-three

Hese Center, thirty

P.J. Center, eighteen

R.A. Center, thirty-nine

Osker Dunkan, twenty-five

W. Daten, thirty-eight, truck driver

Robert Dupree, a seventeen-year-old farmer

Peter Tappen, thirty-six

John Tappen, thirty-one

Ante West, forty

W.F. Wilaford, twenty-three

P.W. Wilaford, twenty-one

W. Wilson, twenty-five

George Weather, age not listed

Allyerey Wood, eighteen

E.S. Wood, twenty-eight-year-old blacksmith.

I want to mention certain white men that are on this road crew in Lithonia as well.

W.H. Watson, twenty-two

M.D. Watson, twenty

J.W. Wiggins, twenty-three,

D.E. Wiggins, twenty

W.M. Williams, thirty-three

A.D. Williams, twenty-six

Z.O. Williams, twenty-two.

I have a feeling that A. D. Williams is out of White County. I just have a feeling that he is kin to Peg-Leg-William or Mr. Ransom A. Williams.

I have a few more names that were in Lithonia District of Dekalb County. H.C. Mariel a thirty-seven-year-old man, John Mitchell a nineteen-year-old, W.A. Meadow a forty-three-year-old black smith, H.A. Meadow a twenty-two-year-old, C.R. Meadow a seventeen-year-old, Linch Morris a twenty-eight-year-old, James Mitchell a twenty-year-old, Berry McCrey a thirty-five-year-old, Isaac Maddox a twenty-year-old, Buck Wooten a thirty-five-year-old, Author Minor a twenty-year-old, Auty Minor an eighteen-year-old, Charles Nickson a thirty-five-year-old, Lum Mongrombey a forty-four-year-old farmer, W.A. Morris a thirty-two-year-old, F. Mickel an eighteen-year-old.

The only Mitchell I found is Mr. J.W. Mitchell, a thirty-two-year-old, and he is white.

Earnest Evans a seventeen-year-old farmer, Burk Eatew a thirty-six-year-old trucker, B.A. Fowler twenty-five-year-old colored man, H.J. Fowler thirty-five-year-old colored man, Luther Fowler a twenty-six-year-old colored man, Elmer Fowler a twenty-nine-year-old colored man, John Friend a seventeen-year-old driller, Luck Flains a twenty-nine-year-old, Jack Glanton a forty-seven-year-old farmer, Frank Grissom a twenty-five-year-old driller, Sam Gwinn a thirty-seven-year-old driller, Jack Grissom a twenty-four-year-old driller, E.D. Guess a twenty-eight-year-old driller, Malent Gordon a twenty-nine-year-old driller, William Grant a thirty-five-year-old driller, H.H. Harris Jr. a twenty-four-year-old farmer, W.H. Harper a seventeen-year-old farmer, W.H. Head a twenty-two-year-old, Robert Howard a seventeen-year-old, Shurm Harris a thirty-five-year-old driller, Sam Harris a thirty-five-year-old, E.H. Harris a twenty-nine-year-old, To Halley a thirty-five-year-old trucker, George Harris a twenty-three-year-old, Dock Hinton a thirty-eight-year-old, Tom Hinton a forty-year-old, J.T. Hill a thirty-year-old, G.H. Hill a twenty-six-year-old, Will Harris a sixteen-year-old

Osker Jackson a forty-eight-year-old blacksmith, George Jordan a seventeen-year-old, Richard Jackson a twenty-two-year-old, Norm Jones a seventeen-year-old, Jobe Johnson a forty-five-year-old, S.Y. D. Johnson a twenty-one-year-old, Earl Johnson an eighteen-year-old, Joe Johnson a twenty-nine-year-old, E.D. Jones a thirty-nine-year-old

Mathew Kelley a seventeen-year-old steel totter, W.H. Lyons a thirty-one-year-old farmer, W.S. Lee a seventeen-year-old, D.J. Lee a twenty-one-year-old, Will Lawrence a thirty-year-old, Robert Lawrence an eighteen-year-old, Die Lawrence a sixteen-year-old, Dan Luck a twenty-five-year-old.

In the year of the roads being built in Georgia I found road crews in Georgia. I found one certain road crew in White County beginning in the year of 1895. This could be the reason that some coloreds came to DeKalb County from White County or it could be the liquor coming out of White County or it even could be that in 1910 the KKK forced majority of Negroes out and to move south of the Chattahoochee River. These same Negroes that were forced to move were into selling and making liquor and beer in the mountains of North Georgia and had a close relationship with the KKK.

The Jones family and the Slaton family go back to Wilkes County and the Callaway family that was located there as well. When they came to DeKalb County, they still continued this relationship. I found the divorce record of Mrs. Bertha Jones in DeKalb County.

Mrs. Bertha Jones divorce Mr. Sam Jones

1st verdict December 6, 1920

2nd verdict March 7, 1921

Order depending service September 9, 1920

Wm. F. Slaton Jr. is the attorney for Mrs. Bertha Jones case # 2356

As you can see Mrs. Bertha got Mr. Wm. F. Slaton Jr. to be her attorney in 1920. Here are a few more families that were at the DeKalb County Courthouse in the 1920's.

Mary Lester vs. John F. Ridley page 7

Ed. Lucas vs. John T. Freeman page 54

G.S. Callaway vs. Bailus Sutton pages 90–17

Alfred Truitt vs. L.L. Brooks and C.J. Lowe page 207

Bench Docket (F) Book

G.S. Callaway vs. Bailus Sutton complaint affidavit and bond garnishment filed May 25, 1921. University Garnishee filed September 10, 1921 Transferred to City Court No. 59 Case # 2853 Attorney for Callaway is Burgess, Dillard, Pirkle

And Attorney for Bailus Sutton J.J. Barge

John D. Blakely vs. Bailus Sutton Case # 2496, Complaint Personal service October 20, 1920. Answer of Defendant filed December 6, 1920 Garnishee, Answer of W.K. Durham Garnishee as Superintendent filed December 6, 1920. Answer of W.K. Durham Garnishee filed December 6, 1920 transferred to City Court No. 18.

Case # 14, Joseph M. Brown Governor vs. Moses Prittchett Principal and T.E. Anderson Security.

Case #15, Joseph M. Brown Gov. vs. John Tuggle Principal and J. Steve McCurdy Security.

Case # 16, Joseph M. Brown Gov. vs. Jim Watkins Principal John M. Beaul Security.

Case # 17 through to 26, Joseph M. Brown Gov. vs. Cal Allen Principal W.G Callaway Security, Bailus Sutton Principal and H.C. Caldwell Security, Claud Head Principal, Charlie Head, M.L. Rockmore, Ed L. Wright Security, Artis Gouldard Principal Henry C. Tuggle Security, George Malory Principal W.G. Callaway Security, Arthur Akin Principal S.E. Anderson and M.M. Akin Security, Plummer Harper Principal and J. K. Davidson Security and all are charged with

(Forfeiture of Recognizance)

Chapter Nine

Mr. Bryson Blanton in DeKalb County Georgia

Frank A. Ruggles was the son of Levi and Mary Ruggles of Toledo, Ohio in 1870 by way of Massachusetts. His father worked in construction twenty two year old Frank in a chair factory. His siblings were Emma, Charles and Clara. Eli Callaway was the son of Reuben and Biddy Callaway of Randolph County in Cuthbert, Ga. Reuben and Biddy are forty years old and young Eli is twelve. Eli siblings are Mary seventeen, Charity sixteen, Reuben thirteen, Ella eleven, Emma six, and young boy Frank at the age of four. 1910, fifty three year old Eli and his twenty two year old wife been married two years, made their way to DeKalb County with Frank A. Ruggles and his family to reside at north Howard Street in Decatur. Frank is now fifty eight and his wife Kate is forty five and their two children Clarence and their daughter Olivia. I am assuming that they helped the Ruggles make their move from Terrell to DeKalb and they made their way back to Terrell. Frank was still residing at this location in 1919. You will see the relationship that Charity and Mary will have with Mr. Blanton later on.

The first time I found Mr. Bryson Blanton was in the Cross Keys District in DeKalb County in 1893 with the following colored men.

1893, Coloreds

Cross Keys 686 District P.O. Chamblee

Bryson Blanton, Jesse Bailey, Alexander Couch, Comer Couch, Berry Green, Will Hamilton, Perry N, Hood, Thomas Johnson, Titus Jett, Ed

Jones, James Johnson, Sam Johnson, Andrew James, Preston Johnson, John Kirkpatrick, Frank Medlock, Miles McDaniel, Lawrence Mobley, George Norseworthey, William Pruitt, Henry Prichett, Wilkes Smith

Mr. Bryson Blanton might have gotten his last name from the white Blantons that were in DeKalb County in Chamblee, Georgia. While I was at the courthouse in Decatur, I wanted to see if there was a connection between the colored Callaways and Mr. Bryson Blanton and Arthur my grandfather. Mr. Bryson Blanton died January 25, 1939, in DeKalb County at the age of seventy. In the year 1918, Bryson Blanton was living in Edgewood in 1379 General Mangers District. Mr. Blanton owned a certain building in Edgewood in DeKalb County on Hardee Street. Here are a few of his ventures in the Edgewood area.

> April 16, 1923 Mortgage bond and Trust Company (Fulton County) party of the First Part (Blanton) sold land lot 207 15th district, Lots 29, 30, 31, 32. of the south side corner of Byrd and Acton Street south to west side of Byrd. Witnessed by L. B. Pascal and notary public Blanche Sallas.
>
> April 16, 1923 Bryson Blanton of DeKalb mortgage Bond & Trust Company a corporation of the county of Fulton second part. Land Lot 207 District 15 lot 21, northwest corner of Boulevard DeKalb and Bird Street D. S. Griffin Subdivision witnessed by W. D. Thornburgh and Blanche Sallas N. P.
>
> November 17, 1924, he purchased land lot 207 in the 15th district, the lot were 21, 24, and 26. These three lots were warehouses. Mr. J. L. Jones was the witness alone with Mac Alva Avery was the notary public.
>
> Bryson Blanton to S. A. Jones August 28, 1925 between Bryson Blanton the estate of S. A. Jones of the State of Georgia. $270 dollars all that parcel of land lot 207 in the 15th district of DeKalb on the east side of Anniston Avenue 246.3 ft. north of the northeast corner of Anniston Avenue. Witnessed by Edward Jones and H. W. Morris N. P.
>
> W. A. Lawson $675 land situated lying and being in the city of Atlanta land lot 207 of the 15th district of

DeKalb being lot 66 in subdivision of said property by O. F. Kauffman C. E. dated Nov. 6, 1905. Southside of Hardee Street 30 ft. thence north. Witnessed by Edward Jones and wit by Hoke O'Kelly the notary public. I think and believe that Hoke O'Kelly is out of Gwinnett County and out of Rockdale the county that was formed in 1916 on the backside of Stone Mountain.

The last two deeds are with Mr. C. A. Ruggles. Mr. Ruggles had Mr. Thomas Callaway of Terrell County Georgia who is buried in the Sardis Cemetery in Terrell County with his wife Mary.

Bryson Blanton to C. A. Ruggles of the state of New York second party for and in consideration of $1290. Dollars in hand land lot 207 in the 15th district, lot 66 in subdivision of O. F. Kauffman C. E. dated Nov. 6, 1905 south side of Hardee Street 30 ft. east of Bird Street extended along south side of Hardee Street thence 110 ft. Witnessed by Edward Jones and notary public C. R. Gholson.

July 21, 1933 Bryson Blanton to C. A. Ruggles of the state of Ga. and county of DeKalb for and in consideration of ten dollars and other valuables considerations . . . land lot 207 15th district lot 66 witnessed by Clara J. Mallard and M. A. Crumley notary public. I believe that I found another situation that ties the Ruggles to Terrell County. Terrell County 1895–1900 Superior Court Minutes. Dawson Varity Mafy. Company. vs. F. A. Ruggles. This is another situation with George Callaway in Terrell County in 1899. Shooting on public highway May Term 1899, the Defendant Geo. Callaway waives being formally arraigned and pleads guilty. John R. Irwin Sol. Gen. George Callaway receives 6 months on the chain gang. *(Clarke County Ga. Pg. 55 of 144)*

Could this be the same George Callaway on the place of William Eberhart?

Another Look at Mr. Ballus Sutton and Clifford Sutton, His Son, and Mysterious G. S. Calloway

Now, when it comes to the Sutton family, I might as well mention the Jones family as well and White County, Georgia. Let us profile Mr. Bailus Sutton a little bit closer. Bailus arrived in White County with the white family of Mr. Andrew J. Sutton between the late 1850s and early 1860s. Andrew Sutton, in the year 1860, was thirty-one years old and his wife Caroline was twenty-two. Their son William was a year old. On July 19, 1870, Mr. Bailus Sutton is thirty-eight years old and his wife Adeline is thirty-six, their son John is four and William is three. The only colored family living next door is that of Closs Fields, a forty-nine-year-old farmer out of South Carolina. Mr. Fields's wife name is Ann. She is thirty-six years old and their daughter Elizabeth is thirteen. John is twelve, Ella is nine, Charles is eight, Henry is seven, Ansel is three, and William is three as well.

On July 17, 1870, in White County, Mr. B.A. Quinn is the assistant marshal of the 135 Subdivision. I found the following white Suttons, Oriel Sutton twenty-one years old and born in Georgia, Martha who is twenty-six years old and born in Mississippi, James Sutton thirty-two years old and his wife Laura, twenty-seven. Their daughter Fanny is two. Mr. Jonathan Sutton is sixty-one. His wife Emily is forty-nine. Their son Johnathan is twenty-six, Sarah is nineteen, Manda is eleven, Alexander is seven. Sixty-one-year-old Jonathan Sutton might have come up from Monroe County, Georgia.

In the year 1880, Andrew J. Sutton is fifty years old and his wife Caroline is forty-two. Mary E. is eighteen, Carr M. is sixteen, John is fourteen, Charles C or H. is nine, James is five, Thomas F. is one. William Sutton is twenty and living next door, and Elmira is his twenty-four-year-old wife. Andrew J. their son is four. John W. is one. They are living in the Town Creek G.M District number 836 and the 189th District of White County. Mr. J.H. Williams is the assistant marshal.

In the town of Jonah 861 GM District of White County on the ninth and tenth days of June, Mr. C.P. Craig is the enumerator. Balus Sutton is thirty-eight years old and his wife Carrie is thirty-two, John is fifteen, Will is twelve, Edmond is nine, and another John is three. Ben is one and Bailus is only a month old. In 1880 the entire family of Mr. Bailus Sutton is listed as mulatto. The only colored family living near them now is not the Fields family but the Freeman family. Ed Freeman is seventy, his wife Nancy is sixty, and William is thirteen.

In Nacoochee G.M. District number 427 on the second day of June with Mr. J.H. Williams as the enumerator. I found another colored Sutton family. Mr. Aaron Sutton is a sixty-year-old colored man and his wife Cilla is thirty-five years old. Alice is thirteen, Lou is ten, and Hannah is eight years old. Mr. James H. Williams is the enumerator of Mr. Andrew J. Sutton's district as well. All three, Mr. Bailus Sutton, Aaron Sutton, and Mr. Andrew J. Sutton are in the same superior district number one and the same enumeration district number 189 in 1880. The only thing is that Mr. Aaron Sutton is living much closer to the white family of Mr. Andrew J. Sutton.

Bailus Sutton Sr. died November 3, 1927, in the county of Fulton. Bailus Sutton Jr. died February 1968 in Dekalb County. He was eighty-eight years old. In 1920, Mr. Bailus Sutton was eighty-two years old and his wife Carrie was sixty-eight years old and Hattie B. Jones their granddaughter was eighteen years old and single. Edlow Sutton was their grandson and he was five years old. All were living in White County in Nacoochee district. However, in 1910, Bailus Sutton Jr. was living in the Cross Keys District of Dekalb County on April 30. Mr. Leon P. Hudgins was the enumerator. *Bailus was twenty-nine years old and Emma B. his wife from South Carolina was twenty-three. Their son Peter S. Sutton was four years old. Mr. Bailus and Emma have been married for five years and they are listed as being mulattos.* Living next door to them is the family *of Mr. March M. Holmes,* a seventy-one-year-old colored man, and his wife Emma C. Holmes, who is seventy years old.

The family that I am interested in is the family of Mr. Robert H. Parson another colored family that Mr. Walker stated to me was a big-time liquor seller in Doraville. Only thing is that he called him Ralph Parson. He also stated that in Doraville is a street named for him as well. Mr. Robert H. Parson is forty-five years old, his wife Mandy M. is thirty-five, George W. is eighteen, Robert A. is fifteen, Hinson H. is twelve, Laura L. is nine, Julius O. their son is seven, Henry C. is five, James F. is four, Linda L. is two, and a nephew named William M. Emory is nine. I mention his name because of the fact that these men changed their names often to elude the city and state and Federal authorities for years in Georgia.

White County in 1910, Mr. Clifford Sutton is nineteen years old and his wife Bettie Sutton is the same age. Their son Clinton Sutton in 1910 is a year old. They are all listed as being mulattos. They are living next door to another set of mulattos. Their last name is Fagg. William Fagg is fifty-three, Anna is fifty, Isabella is twenty-nine. They are living between two white families. Mrs. Ella Slaton, a fifty-three-year-old widow and her daughter Jessie who is nine. The other family last name I cannot make out. *They are all in the 157th district of White County Georgia. This is the same time that Mr.*

Bailus Sutton is living in Nacoochee 427 District of White County. They also have a Slaton (spelled Slayton) living a few houses away from them. His name is William H. Slayton.

In the 427th district on April 26, 1910, Mr. Frank D. Miles is the enumerator. I found Sanford Sutton a twenty-six-year-old mulatto man and his wife Laura, who was twenty-one. Their son Willie at the age of two, and Fred who was two months old. They were neighbors of fifty-year-old George W. Westmorland. I want you to remember that Nacoochee district is the same district that R. A. Williams, a big liquor dealer, is from. I had a hard time trying to surmise if R. A. Williams is the notorious Peg-Leg-Williams for this reason.

U.S. vs. R. A. Williams principal and J.J. Holcomb and John T. Williams sureties Scire Facias. Issued 8th day of 1905

J.J. Holcomb Aerial and J.T. Williams left at residence with his mother Aeriel

R.A. Williams left at residence with his mother Feb. 10 1906 White County Ga. B.B. Landers Deputy. Charged with Distilling and working a distillery on August 12 1904.

United States vs. R. A. Williams of White county illicit distilling etc. J.M. Hudgson foreman. With: C.D Williams W.L. Richardson, G.H. Allen. I hereby certify that on the 12th day of Aug. At Hall County within my district, I did execute the within Writ by arresting the within named R.A. Williams and have him now in custody before J.B. Laston esq. W.H. Johnson U.S. Marshal by B.B. Landers Deputy

1911 Nacoochee district of White County Ga.

Mrs. M.J. Sanders, J.R. Sosbee, J.A. Underwood, J.E. Wheeler, Harry J. Williams, A.P. Williams Allen Williams R. A. Williams 75 acres number 54 district three.

M.A. Williams, G.W. Williams, Henry P. Williams 1911 tax Digest Comptrollers General's office

1910 Tax Digest White County Ga.

Nacoochee District

P.O. Sautee: J.E. Wheeler and Agent for J.L. Pitman 140 acres number 41 district 3

A.P. Williams, Allen Williams, R.A. Williams's agent for Henry P. Williams and agent for Martha W. Carrington, and agent for G.W.

Williams trustee M.K. W., and trustee for M.A. Williams, and trustee for Geo. W. Williams for M. A. W.

The moonshiners of White County were farmers and they made their way toward Clarke County by way of Highway 17 to sell in the City of Athens. In the early 1890s until 1910, the blacks in White County had migrated from White County to Atlanta and Dekalb and brought their trade with them, and some became wealthy and influential blacks in the two counties just like their white counterparts. The liquor business lethal and illegal but was not going away quietly. It had a base of people that desired the drink that went all the way back to the plantation. The black community stood alone and beside the Wets in the State of Georgia! And still at one time malt liquor and liquor and the advertisements were geared toward the black community that dated back to the plantation in the South.

Now, this is the interview and conversation I had with Mr. Bud Walker, a contractor that lived in Lynwood Park, on Sunday, August 15, 2010. Bud Walker lived and grew up next door to my grandfather on Mae Avenue. His father was named Curtis Walker and his father's brother's name was Otis Walker. He told me of a colored community called Willis Town a mile from Peachtree Street, Nichols Bottom, that was off Briarcliff Road or near Cheshire Bridge road, and Savage Ville off Paces Ferry Road, and Bagley's Park, a colored community in Buckhead.

> A few of the big-time liquor sellers that were colored were J.B. Hood, Purcel N. Hood, Bill Bryant who got their liquor from a place called Dew Drop Bottom, which is called Johnson Town near Lenox Square Mall.

I went here often with my grandfather. He would visit a Mrs. Smith and would leave me there with the older sweet mother. She would always fry chicken for me and in a way that I wasn't familiar with. She used little flour and salt and pepper and cooked over low heat. As a young boy I thought this was taking too long; however, I must say, that was some very good slow fried chicken!

The best information that Mr. Walker gave me was that of Mr. Bailus Sutton. Mr. Bailus Sutton stayed near Jim Cherry and married a white woman. Bailus Sutton rode horses into Lynwood Park and never associated with anybody in Lynwood Park, not even the colored Sutton family. He left his property to the white side of the family. Mr. Walker stated that Mr. Bailus Sutton looked almost white himself, married this white woman in the early '40s.

Now, let me tell you about another Callaway in Penfield, Greene County, Georgia. He was a very influential preacher.

THE REVEREND JESSE R. CALLAWAY AND THE JERUEL ASSOCIATION AND DAVISON ACADEMY IN PENFIELD GA.

Let's start with the death of the late great Rev. Jesse R. Callaway and surmise his many accomplishments in the town of Penfield in Greene County, Georgia, and his role in the Jureul Colored Association. I will answer the question of who started the Jureul Association. I visited Mrs. Colclough in Penfield. She had this will in her possession and was willing to share it with me. As a matter of fact, she said that she resided on the land that Jesse deeded to his children when he died. I was amazed at this mulatto lady the first time that I met her. Her house was a lively place with interesting people living with her. There was this young white boy, a Mr. Callaway, who owned the Callaway property that was in Oglethorpe County in Falling Creek, or as I called it, the Hurt house. On my first visit I noticed that the home brew was present. However, on my second visit she was just back from Bethabara that afternoon.

I noticed that her house was not as lively as before. On this visit, I had asked where the cemetery was for Bethabara. She stated that it was across the road from the church. So I went walking through the woods and I found it; however, many of the graves were unmarked and I was very disappointed! The graveyard was laid out on a hill and was terraced. It must have been a beautiful place to reconcile when the colored families that were here went to visit. I can imagine some of my relatives that might have been buried at Bethabara, the Williams, Callaways, Hurts, Smiths, Barrows, English, Colclough, and many others who died in the fields due to exhaustion after being in the hot Georgia sun all day. I remember on a visit to Mr. Rice's house and him telling me that when they died they buried them right where they fell.

I didn't too much believe him when he said this statement, because I have seen the dignity that the colored families had with their churches and their lodges in Maxey and Penfield. When I was on this path that was cut out by the forest department, I was overwhelmed by the landscape and the creeks that I came across and wondered would our young children, both colored and white, be exited to experience what I am experincing right now. To walk where their forefathers walked and where many children played. This would instill a deeper sense of value and worth in our younger generation if they were given this opportunity to walk in the footsteps of those who paved the way through hurt and pain and even death. I understand our history during the Civil Right marches but these are the black men that gave birth to the civil rights movement in Georgia and surrounding Southern states. If their belief and struggles never happened, there wouldn't have been a Civil Rights Movement! Even their humility with strength under such provocation of severe threats of death, they persevered to give birth to a king.

Jesse Callaway is not buried in Bethabara. He is buried at the Penfield Cemetery in the colored section where Dinah and Abraham English are buried. This colored historical cemetery is not kept. I had to go behind the white historical cemetery and I had to walk very careful not to step on one of the many big black snakes that I have seen quite often on my many walks through the dense Georgia woods.

At this cemetery I cried, then ran back to my truck to tell my wife what I had experienced and this time she ventured in the woods with me to see. What made and set an emotional impression upon me was that I could just see the Callaway lodge members abreast two by two and the large drum at the head of the parade of colored preachers and members that came from all over the State of Georgia and from afar to say goodbye to their members and friends and most of all their families. I was very moved to be on this colored hallowed ground. Why are we so ashamed of our past when we should embrace it for what it was? I see other white historical cemeteries honor their families and their history that is filled with stories that are full of truths and some fabricated with full of lies, but they still honor their past! Should we not give our young black children the opportunity to have more self-value and worth? They could experience what I am experiencing right now and know that they should not identify with an X. And that their last name does have real meaning, not because it was a name given to them by a slave owner but a name that was dignified by the slave that endured and struggled during slavery and reconstruction under oppression and threat of death just about every day. However, life didn't just consist of death, but for some days it was very good as well. I see the little boys and girls playing in Penfield and Falling Creek communities, swimming in creeks and lakes on Sunday. I see the families pray around dinner tables and the look on a black father's face for his family and says to God our Father thank you. I just don't see a family in a constant state of fear for their lives.

These are the burial places that could bring money into the counties and even jobs for our young children. Just let them know the story and tell it truthfully.

> The Last Will and Testament of Jesse Callaway; I Jesse Callaway of the village of Penfield County of Greene and state of Georgia being of sound mind and memory

do make, publish, and declare this to be my last will and Testament to Wit.

First; All my just debts and funeral expenses shall be first fully paid.

Second; I give, divide and bequeath the home lot house and land on this side of the road known as the home to my beloved wife Lexis Callaway as long as she lives at her death the said house and lot to be divided among my grandchildren. I have lived close enough to pay my debts without selling any of the land.

Third; I give the lot on the other side of the road Known; as the Gin House lot to my children they can keep it whole or sell it and divide it among them, this I will to Hattie Wilson and Henry Thomas

Any of the children may build on the said home lot if they can agree with my said wife Lexie if not they must move off until the said Lexis death. Charlott Callaway I will her the middle lot.

Fourth; I nominate and appoint Rev. A. C. Powers to be the Executor of this my last will and testament hereby revoking all former wills by me made. In witness whereof I have hereunto set my hand and seal this 31st day of October A.D. 1900

Jesse Callaway his X mark

Signed sealed published and declared as and for his last will and testament by the above named testor ininour presence who have at his request and in his present and in the presence of each other signed our names as witnesses is thereto. A. C. Powers M.G. Rev. Henry Daniel, John Moore, and the later two made their marks.

P.S. Fine print at the end of the will:

At the death of my wife Lexis the said house and lot to be divided among my grandchildren, names are as follows. Olie Callaway, Elrage Callaway, Armstead Callaway, Maggie Callaway, Clara Callaway, Phiner Eller Callaway . . .

> Sworn to and subscribed before me this March 4th 1907 James H. McWhorter Ordinary the last person to witness this paper is Mr. A. C. Powers of Union Point.

I wanted to find out who were the parents of Jesse R. Callaway's grandchildren. I went to the 1900 census to find this out but was disappointed when I did not find everything I was looking for.

Jesse R. Callaway was born October 1824 and was seventy-five years old in 1900. He had been married to Ann for forty-eight years. Ann was born February 1835, and was now sixty-five years old. They have had five children together, but only one child was now living. I say that is very difficult for me to believe! Now Fannie Callaway was born March 1864 and was a widow at the age of thirty-six. Now the grandchildren of Jesse Callaway are in the house of Fannie Callaway, the widow. If she was the daughter of Jesse and Ann, she would be on the 1870 census; however, for *whatever reason she is not! The only Fannie that I know is Fannie Wily who married Charlie Callaway in 1880 in Greene County.*

Ollie her daughter was born April 1882 and she is single and is eighteen years old, Eldridge her son was born September 1884 and is fifteen, Barney was born April 1888 and was twelve, Maggie was born September 1890 and was nine, Ellen her daughter was born February 1893 and was seven, and Clera was born August 1895 and was four years old. Abe Adams, I believe, is on Jesse's property. He is married to Essie and have adopted a daughter, Sallie McWhorter. On April 11, Jesse R. Callaway sold to Felix E. Boswell land. It was a b-sale and the bill of sale was in book (S) page 299. In the same year, John Daniel sold to F. E. Boswell in March 1, and Jesse to John R. Bryant and Joel F. Thornton.

I could not find this book at the courthouse in Greensboro. I had problems in trying to get access to some of the books at Greensboro and I had to appeal to Walton County to a Federal Judge to gain access. Here at the Greensboro Courthouse it was not like the Oglethorpe Courthouse. The women were black at Greensboro, while at Oglethorpe, where I thought I would have trouble, there was none. Sometime the mouth that is silent isn't always in a white face but a colored face as well. Many of the places that I visited were where people were willing to talk and they were white men like the Boswell brothers on Highway 15. They introduced me to a family member of theirs an aunt in the little town of Penfield where my wife and I had a wonderful experience on her porch and on a second visit in her living room.

On October 31, 1900, Jesse R. Callaway made out his will, on the same month that he was born seventy-five years ago. It was August 2, 1900, in the Georgia Baptist *newspaper, whose editor was Dr. William J. White. It is three months before Jesse would write out his will, and it was July 21, 1900, on which Davison Academy's celebration occurred.*

> *Georgia Baptist:* Please allow me space in your much beloved paper to say a few words concerning our little Sunday School at Davison Academy which held a grand celebration, on Saturday July 21st at 9 o'clock. Vehicles came in from all parts of the country. There were four schools represented as follows: St. Paul, Woodville, Pat Beasley, superintendent; Oak Grove, J. Jennings, superintendent, Sanders Chapel, Penfield, Rich McWhorter, superintendent; Davison Academy, Collins Smith superintendent. We had some fine Essays and Scripture questions. The forenoon was passed of in discussing questions from the Bible.
>
> 1st "What is good news and glad tidings?" by Collins Smith
>
> 2nd "What shall a sinner do to get forgiveness for sin?"
>
> 3rd "What is it that lengthens the soul to gift of enernal life?" by A. Colclough
>
> 4th "What is sin, and how shall it be put away?" by Ms. M. L. Langston
>
> Each school took a part in discussing the questions; then they were criticized by the old father Rev. G. R. Calloway (Jesse R. Callaway), after which the sisters showed us what was in each basket, for one hour's time went well from basket to mouth.
>
> Afternoon
>
> At tap of the bell, the crowd reassembled; prayer by Deacon R. Grant
>
> Song by the school
>
> Essay by Ms. Ether Wright
>
> Subject: "True Kindness"
>
> Essay by Ms. Silvia Horton

Misses M.L. Langston, of Davison Academy' Ether Wright of Penfield and Silvia Horton of Oak Grove are three worthy girls who cannot be excelled. Prof. Frank Cheney, the leader of Woodville, is worthy of note, Rev. A. P. Smith, Penfield, shot one of his big guns. Messrs. George Langston and Collins Smith deserve honor for the manner they have drilled the School. Rev. Y. Partee took an active part in the discussion. Prof. Hancock, the teacher at Oak Grove tries to be sharp. 4 o'clock closed out one of the grandest celebrations of the kind ever known in Greene County.

For the first time I have a situation reflecting the lives of the black community in Penfield, Greene County, Georgia. Besides the tax digest that just mention names and ages, I don't know why Dr. White was not mentioned in the Jeruel Association after the death of Dr. Collins H. Lyons. Rev. Jesse R. Callaway will become Moderator before the suposidly death of Dr. Collins H. Lyons in 1893. So I will start in the minutes of the Jeruel Association.

The Jeruel Baptist Association in keeping with the resolution of adjournment as passed at the last session, convene with the Thankful Baptist church at the above named place at 8:00 p.m. Thursday Sept. 24th 1891.

Brother Isaiah Thomas, opened devotional service by singing some stirring spiritual songs. Rev. W.H. Tuggle was the first to invoke the Father of Mercies to Bless, guide and prosper every interest near and dear to the . . . Many were the amens that followed his utterances. Revs. A. J. Stovall and R. D. Davis prayed most earnestly in this service.

Rev. J. R. Callaway the moderator arose in the pulpit and made some brief remarks relative to the mercies of a kind Providence, as exhibited through the past year. He then presented to the Association, Rev. Wm. Barnett, for whom he begged prayerful attention. Rev. W. S. Tate then sang the 623rd hymn, and engaged in prayer; asking the Lord to bless the brethren and deepen in their hearts the work of grace.

Rev. Barnett read 1st John 2, sang hymn 718th and preached the introductory sermon on "Christian Chastity" from 1st John 2:1; "My little children I write unto you that ye sin not; and if any man sin, we have an advocate with the Father, Jesus Christ the righteous."

Motioned that all church letters coming up during the remainder of the session be given over to the finance committee. On motion of Rev. Y. Fambro, Rev. J. S. Callaway (Jesse R. Callaway) was unanimously elected moderator. Revs. Jefferson Henry and R. Cobb were appointed to escort Rev. Calloway to the chair. Brother H.M. Smith, elected as clerk.

This is the first time I can say that Rev. Jefferson Henry of Friendship in Clarke County and R. Cobb of Bethabara in Scull Shoals are the escorts of Mr. Jesse R. Callaway. The question is why these two men? Are they close friends to Jesse R. Callaway? Do the men and their churches show the fellowship that Jesse has with the two churches, one being in Clarke and the other in Schull Shoals in Greene County?

Bethabara Baptist Church is a church that I am intrigued by because there is little information on this church where the Callaways attended and near where the Williams lived in Scull Shoals. This is the year of 1891 and Willis Williams has been dead for about seventeen years and A.D. Williams is in Atlanta or leaving the house of Mr. Maxey.

Jesse was in the company of the men who helped build and start the Atlanta University in Atlanta.

Students from 1871 To 1881

The following list of students embraces all who have been connected with the Augusta Institute and the Atlanta Baptist Seminary since August 1, 1871, when Dr. Robert took charge.

Names	*Post Office*
**F.F. Beall*	*Augusta, Ga.*
**Nathan Benjamin*	*White Plains Ga. (Greene Co.)*
**B. Borders*	*Stone Mountain, Ga.*
Jesse R. Callaway	*Penfield, Ga. (Greene Co.)*
**Edward R. Carter*	*Athens, Ga. (Clarke Co.)*

**Gad S. Johnson*	*Augusta, Ga.*
**Silas Johnson*	*Woodville, Ga.*
**J. M. Jones*	*Atlanta, Ga.*
**E.K. Love*	*Marion, Ala.*
**Thornton V. Love*	*Marion, Ala.*
**Collins H. Lyons*	*Marion Ala.*
Judson W. Lyons	*Augusta, Ga.*
Jerry Moody	*Greensboro, Ga.*
**Derry Murden*	*Crawfordville, Ga.*
**Ephraim V. White*	*Thomason, Ga.*
George D. White	*Augusta, Ga.*
**Henry M. White*	*Augusta, Ga.*
**William J. White*	*Augusta, Ga.*
(*) Ministerial Student	*(t) Deceased*

The catalogue of the Atlanta Baptist Seminary Atlanta, Georgia, 1886–1887, records the beginning of the school.

> *Founded in 1867, under the auspices of the American Baptist Home Mission Society. Atlanta, Georgia; Jas. P. Harrison & Company Printers and Publishers 1887.*

Jesse R. Callaway is a well-known member of the few colored and white men living as blacks that helped start the Atlanta Baptist College.

Jesse was mentioned in the Ebenezer Association in its early beginnings in the Georgia Association. It held its first session in Atlanta. Jesse Callaway was mentioned in the afternoons session held at two o'clock. Jesse was sent to the Presbyterian Arbor with Rev. Jefferson Milner and Rev. George Brown.

Jesse's property bordered the Sanders place in Penfield. I asked Mr. English, who lived across the dirt road and owns the property, if I could walk this place and I found an old well set in the middle of the property of Jesse Callaway at one time, which his children and himself drew water from and maybe even my grandfather as well. What made me feel nostalgic was what my grandfather's cousin told me on my visit to Michigan. I had an opportunity to talk with Howard Barnett, a World War II veteran. He told me of Mr. McWhorter, a black man who dug wells and was overcome by gasses while he was digging a well. This happened when Howard was a young man.

At one time while in Schull Shoal in the Callaway-Hurt house, I looked out from the property leading toward the road to Scull Shoal. The road was named Callaway Road, named after Jesse and his family I assume. I could only think of the many times my grandfather played up and down this dirt road as a little boy with his little sister Rosa Kate and his younger cousins. The same roads that he might have seen the fast cars going by that hauled liquor by the Smith Brothers and envied and anticipated the moment he would be behind one of these same machines doing the same business in the dark. I heard many stories of his escapades as a young man hauling the hooch!

Jesse R. Callaway Sr. in 1884 was one of two colored men that owned property in Penfield. Austin Daniel was the other. Austin had thirty-five acres and Jesse had 128. While I walked his old place, I noticed that it had deep ravines behind it. This was the home place and the house of Mr. English, whose children inherited the property in 1901. This property is on an open field. Jesse lived as the white landowners did. He had hired colored hands on his place, or sharecroppers as they were called. He even hired Mat Geer, who was in the indictments as a witness for Charlie Callaway in the year 1899, as well as Young Geer, the other person mentioned in the indictments. Working over on Mr. W. English's land were Jack English and Dan English. Jack and Dan English will eventually have their own land a few years later. Now you must remember Mr. Jesse R. Callaway is a minister. I am sure while being a farmer he also had time to marry the young colored couples in Penfield, along with traveling on the train as an agent in the 1880s and assigning preachers in the Ebenezer Association. He also cut rates for doing business with the Southern Railroad in which W. R. Callaway and Brantley Callaway had shares or stock.

Jesse R. Callaway in the 1880 census was fifty years old and Lexey was forty-three, Charlotte was twenty-seven, Jesse Jr. was twenty-one, Macon was nineteen, and Hettie is fifteen. The closest white man is Ben Spencer, a seventy-five-year-old, and his seventy-one-year-old wife Charlotte and their thirty-three-year-old daughter Fannie. Henry Smith Sr. is twenty-nine and Ellen is twenty-six. Alberta is four and Henry Jr. is two. H.M. Smith will marry Ellen J. Craddock on September 7, 1875, and the minister is none other than the largest landowner in Penfield Rev. Jesse R. Callaway. I don't quite know what the relationship between Jesse and H.M. Smith is; however, Smith becomes the secretary of the Church Association and eventually moderator. H. M. Smith and the Smith brothers become large landowners in Penfield as well. I don't know if this is the relationship and marriage between William R. Callaway and Jabez P. Smith. In the Washington, Georgia Gazette, *William R. Callaway* *is the executor of John P. Smith's estate and sold shares he had in the Georgia Railroad. Purchasing the stock were Mr. T. C. Hogue, who bought twelve, and Rev. B. M. Callaway, the brother of W.R., bought four. The stock was quoted in Augusta the same day at $147.50. William R. is the brother-in-law of J.P. Smith. I also wonder if Jabez P. Smith is any kin to James Monroe Smith and his father Zadock.*

Jesse R. Callaway might be patriotic to the Confederate cause to gain favor with the surrounding white Landowners just like Aaron in Scull Shoals. Reverend Jesse stared accumulating property in 1872 with Shelton P. Sanford of Bibb County, Georgia. Jesse didn't have to move from plantation to plantation with the favoritism he had with the white neighbors and friends. Jesse's property consisted of 39 and 6/10 acres in Penfield next to James R. Sanders and the Steam Mill Company. Jesse couldn't have a *gaming house or make any intoxicating spirits,* and if he did the property would revert to the Baptist Convention of the State of Georgia. *The Baptist Convention had reason to fear, for them to put in the deed not to have any gaming house or intoxicating spirits. The area around Penfield was nortorious for gaming and prostitution and liquor making. If this is the case, the Mercier Campus in Penfield had to move, not because of lack of access to the railroad but because of the profiteering due to the liquor and prostitution that was next door in Oglethorpe County, Georgia, and the great Watson Spring and its tavern where the young students made their way to play and frolic. I am sure that some of the young white men visited the local colored and mulatto women during the hot suppers that took place in the area around Falling Creek. What's your daddy's name? I don't know! What's your mother's name? I don't know! These are the many statements that I have noticed on many of the death certificates I found! The hot suppers were visited by the Blind Tigers in the 1870s in Falling Creek and the locals new them well. And so did the big liquor distributors of that time and so did the KKK.*

In December of 1884, Jesse R. sold to Mrs. Sarah Warner of the county of Monroe, New York State, 55 and 4/10 acres. The land was located next to J.R. Sanders place and Cynthia Sanders who helped start the Colored Sanders Chapel in Penfield. Jesse also purchased land from preacher Sam Sanders as well. The land consisted of seven acres, J. R. Sanders eight and five-tenth acres, and Shelton P. Sanford for thirty-nine and six and a tenth of an acre. All of these properties combined were property next to W. A. Colclough and Ben Spencer and south of the road from Penfield and four acres of land from Ella Grimes. Also ten acres of land from John R. Boswell and T. Langston and the same lands that he got from James and Caroline Lankford in January of 1874.

Four acres of land from the Baptist Convention in December of 1872. Jesse was probably worried about losing his land, so I am assuming that the Whites that knew him and his duties for the confederate cause saved him many times from unknowing prideful whites who despised such prosperity and a high yellow Nigger owning property. December 1884, Ella Grimes sold to Jesse Callaway for a price of $155 in the town of Penfield next to R. B. Boswell, him being on the northwest, and Jesse on the east got four acres of land on the same day. Something is going on! I don't know if Jesse R. Callaway Sr. is in trouble or Jesse his namesake is in trouble at this time. By 1885 and 1886, Jesse Callaway has only seventy-five acres of land. About this same time Charlie was arrested in Oglethorpe County with Sam Boykin. I wonder if Jesse put up property for his bail.

Now, though most of Jesse's time might have been spent accumulating land and farming, Rev. Jesse also performed marriages. One in particular was the marriage between Abraham English and Dinah Hurt, my great-great-grandparents, in 1869. The next marriage that I will mention is the marriage between Jesse Callaway Jr. and Ms. Julia Morris on May 5, 1881. This is the son of Jesse Callaway Sr., I am assuming.

Other marriages performed by Rev. Jesse Callaway are those of Moses Finch and Caroline Sander (December 20, 1875), Phillip Colclough and Julia Cornell (December 8, 1875), Seaborn Smith and Lina McWhorter (November 19, 1875), Jim Conyers and Henrietta Daniel (November 3, 1875), Perry Sharpe and Martha Smith (December 12, 1874), Solomon Janes and Harriet Broone (December 11, 1874), John Daniel and Alice Durham (February 19, 1874), and *Toney Haynes (Haines) to Nancy Favors (April 29, 1872).* On the nineteenth of April the late Jerry Moody married Henry Stephens and Minerva Barnes. *Then Rev. Jesse R. Callaway resumes, marrying Squire Haynes (Haines) and Martha Cramer on April 20, 1872;* Charles Adams and Harriet Colclough on January 3, 1872; Sam Gier and Anna Horton on February 25, 1870; Ben Wright and Mary McWhorter on February 11, 1871; *Henry White and Amanda Hurt on December 27, 1869; Allen Colclough and Charlette, the daughter of Rev. Jesse Callaway, on December 23, 1869; and* Washington Wheeler and Celeste Hester on April 5, 1872.

These are some of the colored men that work for Rev. Jesse R. Callaway: Gilford Smith, Macon Callaway, Newton Cornell, Matt Geer, Steve Daniel, Dave Lankford, and Washington Bowles. These are the colored property owners in Penfield, Greene County, Georgia: Daniel English, Butler Redd, Perry Goolsby, Jesse Callaway, Macon Callaway, Jerry Thomas, Stephen Daniel, Henry Smith, Ned Wilson, Bud Armstrong, Amariah Smith, Litha Moncrief, Newborn Grant, Lou Grant, Mont

Wilson, Pat Wilson, Kit Mitchell, Lee Mitchell, Rubin Mitchell, Sam Mitchell, Berry Mitchell, Joe Grant, Austin Daniel, and Jack Wright.

The Haynes are kin to Robert Callaway, and Robert is under the last name of Callaway and his mother's last name is Haynes. Now, I wonder does Jesse have a part in the disappearance of Charlie, his wife Mary, and Aaron, and is Charlie or Robert Calloway his son one and the same! And there is another question that I must ask myself, is Robert, who is born in 1843 and married to Anna Haynes, the son of Jesse R. Callaway or Aaron Calloway or Major Callaway? Could it be that R. C. Callaway is Robert Charles Callaway? Maybe he's not the son of either one of these colored men but the son of G. W. Callaway, a white man of Bowling Green.

Blacks have always been linked to the penal system of these United States and especially here in the South. I decided to take a good look at what was taking place just before the Civil War in Atlanta and how it was affecting the blacks in the state from a black perspective, or I might as well say my perspective on what I investigated at the Atlanta Historical Society. How were the blacks being treated by the white community in part of the colored community?

First let us look at the First Baptist Church in Atlanta and who was its first pastor and what association was the First Baptist associated with in DeKalb County, Georgia, the first Callaway family that I found in Atlanta in 1860 and their neighbors as well.

Mr. H. W. Calaway was a sixty-seven-year-old street peddler born in 1807 from North Carolina. His wife is named Martha Calaway and is forty years old and was born in the same state as her husband. John F. Calaway, their son, is twenty-one years old, born in Florida, and so was his brother David J. Calaway, who is sixteen. Adaline their sister is fourteen years old, and C. M. Jordan is a twelve-year-old and Thomas J. Jordan a two-year-old. I want to mention the Williams family in the same district. John Williams was a fifty-year-old carpenter out of South Carolina, and his wife Story Williams was forty years old, and was born in Georgia. D. A. Williams their son will sell land for Johnson Town in Buckhead and hire William Callaway during the registration of World War I.

Chapter Ten

Atlanta, a Place of Refuge

This investigation's prospective is that of an African American male born in the 1850s in the vicinity of Atlanta, Georgia. Crucial topics of interest include how the blacks were treated by the white community in Atlanta just before the war and after the war; and how the liquor trade played a part in the colored community, as well as in Atlanta. First let us look at the First Baptist Church in Atlanta, its first pastor, and the associations of the First Baptist Church. I did not just want to talk about who the plantation owner was but to also put a face on the colored men and women that he held in bondage as well!

May 8, 1848, I found the last name Waldrop in Panthers Ville with colored man Martin Mathew Callaway in DeKalb County. F. Height, L. Otumburger, Cls. Nelms, and *Mr. J. R. Waldrop*, and B. B. Tinner, were all shooting within the incorporated limits. Height and Nelms and Mr. Waldrop may have family in Panthers Ville, DeKalb County. November 18, 1849, Mr. Beard is tried before the mayor and fined one dollar. November 23, 1849, Mr. Lewis Powell is charged with disorderly conduct and fined one dollar. Also charged on November 23, 1849, were two women, Lucinda and Georgianna Burdett. Both failed to show up for court and were fined two dollars. John Tuck was also charged on the same day as Mr. Lewis Powell and Lucinda and Georgianna Burdett. John was charged with a disorderly conduct house and was fined ten dollars. He appealed to a full board and tried and fined (unreadable) by council.

The next Atlanta council meeting enlightened me on the trading that might have taken place at the Standing Peach Tree trading post. This was a trading post where the native Indians traded with the white settlers. It is located near the water shed in the tenth ward of the City of Atlanta.

City Council Room, May 27th, 1850. Resolved that the petition of Messer's Smith, Johnson and others complaining of the traffic of slaves, be referred to a committee of two consisting of Messer's Holcomb, Ryan to report an order on the subject and its kindred evils and the Mayor be added to the committee.

Resolved, that the subject of Mr. Boyd's inquiring tracking who shall be taxed for Negroes be referred to the above mentioned committee.

Council Room, June 7th 1850. Resolved, Whereas, the illegal traffic of slaves and free persons of color in the produce of the farms, poultry yards, and dairies, of this county oppression upon the citizens of Atlanta, and controversy public policy;

Resolved, that it shall be the duty of the marshal to seize and sell all such chickens, eggs, butter, pork or other produce of the farms, dairy, and poultry yards, which he may find in possession of any slave, or free person of color without legal authority exceeding the value of one dollar to be estimated by the marshal and that the proceeds of such sale be paid into the city treasury for the public use. And be further resolved that it shall be the duty of the marshal to prosecute before the superior court any and every person who shall be complained of on probably cause of having violated the 53rd of the 111 article the penal code.

July 5th, 1850. Be it ordained by the Mayor and Council of Atlanta, that all disorderly houses within said city adjudged to be such by the mayor and council upon satisfactory evidence that they are used and occupied by any person or persons as lewd houses . . . or fornication or adultery shall and may be supposed by an order . . . every marshal to suppress every such disorderly house by moving there upon the person or persons using or occupying the land provided that it shall be the duty of the marshal before summons is issued to give three days without notice to the person or persons charge to leave the city.

Sec. 2

It shall be the duty of the Marshal in every case at the time of serving Summons to delivery upon so much real and personal property of the defendant as will use his opinion sufficient the satisfy the cost that may be adjudged against the defendant.

Sec. 3

That upon a conviction of any person or persons under this ordinance for a second offense, it shall be the duty of the Mayor and Council in addition to the above penalty to find such defendant or defendants a sum not exceeding fifty dollars and cost or to cause him or them to be imprisoned in the calaboose for the period of twenty-four hours.

City Council Room, July 23rd, 1850, Atlanta

Council in Session, Present, Henry C. Holcombe, President of City Council, and Patterson M. Hodges, Stephen Biggers, John G. Humphries, and W.W. Rouak. Upon motion, unanimously resolved, wherein certain orders have been directed to the marshal of said city commanding him to remove certain persons adjudged to be disorderly house by the mayor and council of said city, for the practice therein of lewdness, fornication and adultery viz. Sarah Webster, Catherine Kelton, Mahala Leozo, and Lucinda Burdett, Georgianna Gresham, Emeline Deaton, Washington Goslin, and his wife Sarah Goslin.

Living in the same ward are Ms. Sarah Edwards, a twenty-five-year-old colored woman, and twenty-year-old Martha Noles living together. William Gofford, a forty-eight-year-old fireman, his wife Louisa Gofford (thirty), son William W. (thirteen), Martha (eleven), James (eight), Emma (six), Marion (two), and Anna (six months old). Drew Paton is a twenty-eight-year-old mulatto train man. Mr. William Gofford is a mulatto man as well and his family is listed as being black.

Still in the fifth ward I found nineteen-year-old mulatto man John Smith and eleven-year-old mulatto boy Riley Smith. Both are laborers. The two young colored boys are in the house with T. B. Daniel, a fifty-four-year-old man, and C. S Daniel, his fifty-year-old wife. Julia F. is their sixteen-year-old daughter. Charles E. Daniel is a fourteen-year-old clerk. Robert F. is an eight-year-old boy. Living in the same house or rooming house is the US marshal C. H. Chandler, a thirty-year-old man, and Julia, his twenty-year-old wife. Charles B their three-year-old son, and Claud Chandler their one-year-old son. In the fifth ward there seemed to be a lot of rooming houses and even prostitutes, both black and white.

Let's move ahead to 1866 for just a moment in the city council minutes of Atlanta to where for the first time I come across the Catholic Church coming against the liquor system that flowed in the city of Atlanta so freely after General Sherman's march through Georgia.

> A petition from Trustees of the Catholic Church and School. Praying Council to not grant license to John McMahan to retail spirituous liquors at his house on Lloyd Street.

The petition was read and upon motion the prayer of petitioners was granted. Mr. McMahan was refused a license in Atlanta, Georgia, on June 8, 1866.

Before I mention Mr. William Owen Cheney, I want to mention the first Callaway family that I found in Atlanta in 1860 and their neighbors. Mr. H. W. Calaway, a sixty-seven-year-old street peddler, was born in 1807 in North Carolina. His wife, Martha Calaway, is forty-four years old and was born in the same state as her husband. Their son is twenty-one and born in Florida, as well as, his brother David J. sixteen, Adeline fourteen, C. M. Jordan twelve, and Thomas J. Jordan two, born in Georgia.

I really want you to take notice of the next family and they are the Williams family that were living in the Fifth ward. John Williams is at the age of fifty-five and a carpenter, out of South Carolina. His wife Story Williams was forty-two and was born in Georgia. Their children are D. A. Williams, twenty-one, born in South Carolina, and works as a laborer; George

Williams is fifteen; Carolina Williams is twelve; P. Williams is eleven; James Williams is nine; Adaline Williams if five; Lenora Williams is four; and Isaac Williams is two. R. Williams is nine months old. Living in this location with the Callaway's and the Williams's are Mr. B. O. Jones, a fifty-two-year-old medical doctor and his wife S. A. Jones at the age of forty-four. Lucy Jones is seventeen. Ella Jones is thirteen. With them are also a two-year-old boy named Bart and a twenty-year-old young woman named Mittie Griggs. *There is a neighbor living next door to the Callaways named the Cozart family.* H W. Cozart is a sixty-four-year-old merchant out of North Carolina. His wife Anna is fifty-two. S. C. Cozart, daughter, is eighteen.

THE CITY OF ATLANTA BEFORE AND AFTER THE SEIGE, MAYOR'S COURT 1861 THRU 1864

Berry and Harriet, slaves of William O. Cheney, for hiring their own times and living separate and apart from their owner.

I was excited to see the first names Berry and Harriet in the city council minutes at the Atlanta Historical Society, as well as that of Mr. William O. Cheney, the same man that was living in Beardstown in Greene County and the same white man that purchased my great-grandfather Aaron, pulling his name out of a hat, in 1859. I also think that these two coloreds with W. O. Cheney might be from the estate of Isaac and Winifred Callaway. This also puts Aaron in Atlanta and DeKalb County, just before the war. Also, William O. Cheney handled the estate of Mr. Chivers, who was living in the Buckhead Community near the DeKalb County line in 1861. I believe that Berry and Harriet are off of the plantation of Mr. William Owen Cheney. William O. Cheney is the son-in-law of Rev. Enoch Callaway of Wilkes County, Georgia. The first name Berry will show up in the tax digest of DeKalb County in Panthers Ville, Georgia, with Martin Mathew Callaway. However, the last name of Berry will be under Truitt. I say how ironic that the last name of Berry is Truitt and would turn up in the same town as Mathew Callaway and Juda Callaway, and Willie Howard the grandson of both Aaron Callaway and Juda! Now, I have Aaron with Harriett in Greene County in the 147th District near Maxey, Oglethorpe County, Tissue in Clarke County in the Puryears District. Nancy was in the house of Mr. McWhorter, and Juda was in DeKalb County in Panthers Ville in 1870 and ended up in Puryears in 1880 with Aaron before she died. She was a servant in the house of G. W. Callaway in Oglethorpe County.

Mayor and Council vs. Randall a negro man slave the property of Thos. G. Sims charged with selling spirituous liquors to Isaac a slave on the 4th July 1861 July 5th 1861 Judgment of the mayor that Randall is guilty and that he be punished by the marshal or by his authority by receiving thirty-nine lashes on the bare back in the calaboose or the yard thereof and that said Sims pay the cost of this prosecution. J. Whitaker Mayor.

The Mayor and Council of the city of Atlanta vs. John a slave in the employment of Charles Beerman is charged with smoking on the sidewalk. And the evidence having been heard it is ordered and adjudged by the court that John be taken by the marshal or his officers to the calaboose and there receive twenty lashes and be discharged and that judgment be entered against Mr. C. Beerman his employer for the cost in this prosecution. Haygood and J. the city attorney . . .

Here I cannot help but think that this is John C. Callaway who will still be working for the Beermans in the 1890s. John is a hired hand to Charles Beerman. The Beermans will come to run the distillery in Atlanta.

Special session of Mayor's court at 6 o'clock P.M. Honorable Jared I. Whitaker Mayor presiding. The Mayor and Council of the city of Atlanta vs. John Barnes for furnishing a Negro slave with spirituous liquors and C. the defendant appears in court and pleads guilty to the charge. It is ordered and adjudged by the court that the defendant pay a fine of twenty-five dollars and in default thereof that he be imprisoned in the city calaboose fifteen days and there be discharged.

The Mayor and Council of the city of Atlanta vs. Bill a Negro slave owned by the estate of Mrs. Russell deceased. Bill was brought in court and pleads guilty to being found with ardent sprits about his person and C. It is ordered and adjudged by the court that he be taken to the calaboose by the marshal or his officers and that he there receive twenty-five lashes on his bare back and then be discharged.

As you can see, the colored people have had been in the city of Atlanta for quite some time. I enjoyed finding these colored men and women trying to make a living prior to the Civil War, and having to struggle so hard in such trying times before and during and after the war! The City of Atlanta did not spend money by imprisoning the Negro. The mayor would sentence them to be whipped in public on their bare backs! As I read this I just see the many images that I've seen of the scars on the back of the blacks as if they were less than human and were equated to a dog, where dogs were treated better.

John Banes having been imprisoned about seven days and having paid four dollars it is ordered discharged.

Jane, slave property of N.I. Hammond, was charged with disorderly conduct in striking a white boy. It appeared to the court that said slave is in court under arrest and no part appearing to prosecute her ordered by the court that said slave be hence discharged and this order go on minutes 9th Aug. 1861. N.I. Hammond acted as Attorney for the defendant.

The Mayor and Council of Atlanta vs. Mary Samantha Creel case charged Mary Samantha Creel as a free person of color having removed to the city of Atlanta without paying the two hundred dollars under the ordinance of the city of Atlanta. This defendant by her counsel Robert W. Sims and John Collier demurs to the above proceeding of the Mayor and Counsel of the city of Atlanta upon the grounds that it being a tax imposed by the ordinance the council could Tax the Defendant for no greater sum than that of the state Tax and therefore the Tax of Two hundred dollars required to be paid is void and without authority. Second, there is no valid or binding law or ordnances of said city which authorities the levy or collection of the defendant the sum of two hundred dollars for residing within the corporate limits of the city of Atlanta. And for plea this defendant by her counsel says that she is not a Free Person of Color as contemplated by the ordinances of said city all of which she is ready to prove and C. and prays judgment of this Court and that she may be hence discharged.

Robert. U l Sims, John Collier the Defendants. Attys.

The case was continued and it was ordered that the above stated case be continued until Saturday the 24th and that both party's plaintiff and defendant have leave to take the testimony of witnesses residing out of the county of Fulton by depositions with notice to opposite of two days with leave to cross question the witness. Jared I. Whitaker.

Special Term, August 24 1861; Mayor's court met according to an order passed on the 10th and his Honor Jared I. Whitaker mayor presiding. Coming within the limits of the city of Atlanta to live and having failed to pay to the clerk of Council two hundred dollars within ten days after having arrived in the city of Atlanta in the month of January 1861 on hearing the evidence in this case it is the opinion of the court that the said Mary Samantha Crell is not a free person of Color within the meaning of the ordinances of the city of Atlanta it is therefore ordered by the court that the said Mary Samantha Creel be hence discharged from the custody of the Officers of court. Sims & Hoyt and Ezzard & Collier.

Charles, a Negro slave owned by David Demerist is charged with quarrelling and fighting in a public street on the 2nd day of Sept. 1861. He was given twenty lashes and Mr. Demerist had to pay the cost.

The Mayor and Council vs. Dick, a Slave owned by Dr. J.W. Newell charged Disorderly Conduct by using impendent language to L.W. Yarborough and Pat Ennis 18th Dec. 1861 Defendant discharged.

Stopped on page 109

Page 112

The Mayor and Council vs. Thomas Clince for allowing your Slave Nancy to keep an eating-house & C; Defendant

> appeared and plead not guilty after hearing the evidence in this case it is adjudged that the defendant is guilty and it is ordered and adjudged that defendant pay a fine of ten dollars and then be discharged.
>
> The Mayor and Council of the city of Atlanta vs. J.L. Fears; in this allowed your slave to hire her time and enjoy the privilege of labor for herself & c. on 29 January 1862. Defendant appeared in person and by attorney and pleaded guilty; where upon it is ordered and adjudged by the court that defendant be fined twenty dollars and costs of prosecution and upon payment thereof be hence discharged . . .

The Slaves were working trying and doing just about any and everything to acquire their freedom in the city of Atlanta during the Civil War. I also believe that this liberty was given quite often to the Negroes that were of the certain higher class Whites.

> The Mayor and Council of the City of Atlanta vs. George McGinley; disorderly conduct by whipping a slave Elic, owned by Mrs. Waddail and C. on the 10th April 1862. The defendant appeared and plead not guilty and after hearing the evidence it is adjudged by the court that the defendant is guilty and it is further ordered that defendant be fined five dollars and cost and upon payment thereof he be discharged.

Page 125

> The Mayor and Council of the city of Atlanta vs. David Fraser; selling by retailing spirituous liquors in less quantities than one quart without a license from the Council and C. Defendant appeared and plead guilty exculpatory evidence being taken, It is ordered and adjudged by the court that defendant be fined the sum of fifty dollars and costs of prosecution and in default of payment thereof that he be imprisoned in the calaboose for the space of twenty-five days and then be hence discharged.

Page 129

The Mayor and Council of the city of Atlanta vs. Elizabeth Clay, Duck Clay, James Clay junior, and Eck Clay; Disorderly conduct by singing vulgar songs, using obscene language quarreling and throwing rocks & C. Defendants appeared and plead not guilty and after hearing the evidence and argument It is adjudged by the court that Elizabeth Clay & Duck Clay are not guilty, that Eck Clay is guilty but discharged by reason of his tender years being nine years old. James Clay Jr. found guilty where upon it is adjudged and ordered by the court that he be fined five dollars and cost and that he be discharged upon payment thereof.

The Mayors Court met his Honor James M. Calhoun Mayor presiding, The Mayor & Council of the City of Atlanta vs. Joseph W. Harrison; Disorderly conduct by shooting at a slave owned by J.C. Davis and otherwise being disorderly in the city of Atlanta on the 24th of April 1862. Defendant appeared and pleads guilty and after hearing exculpatory and inculcator. It is ordered and adjudged by the Court that defendant be fined twenty dollars and cost of prosecution and that he be discharged upon payment thereof.

Page 131

The Mayor and Council of the City of Atlanta vs. Thomas Bennett; Selling, given and furnishing a slave with spirituous & intoxicating liquors in the city of Atlanta on the 6th day of May 1862. Defendant appeared and pleads guilty; whereupon it is ordered and adjudged by the court that the Defendant is fined fifty dollars and cost, and in default of payment that defendant be imprisoned in the calaboose or such other place as is prescribed by laws for twenty-five days and be then discharged.

The Mayor and Council of the city of Atlanta vs. Catharine Valintino; Catharine Valintino was accused of selling, giving, and furnishing a slave with spirituous liquors & C. on 7 May 1862. Case dismissed.

The Mayor & Council of the city of Atlanta vs. J.C. Reynolds; keeping a house of ill fame in the City of

Atlanta on the July 1862 and on diverse other days before that day. Defendant appeared and plead not guilty and after hearing evidence and argument it is considered by the court that defendant is guilty and it is ordered and adjudged by the court that he be fined Twenty dollars and cost an upon payment thereof he be discharged and upon failure of payment that he be imprisoned ten days and be hence discharged.

Page 143

The Mayor and Council of the City of Atlanta vs. J. Ackerman and A. Pearlstein; Disorderly conduct by quarreling and using opprobrious word and C. on the 15th July 1862. Defendants both appeared and plead not guilty, and after hearing the evidence it is ordered and adjudged by the court that defendants are both guilty; and it is further ordered and adjudged by the court that the defendants each be fined five dollars and cost.

Page 145

The Mayor and Council of the City of Atlanta vs. Alonzo, a slave owned by B.Y. Evans, and Robert, a Slave owned by I. D. Lockhart. Defendants were charged with Disorderly Conduct by using profane language quarreling and fighting in Atlanta on the 28th day of July 1862. Defendants were arrested and brought before the court Mr. Evans present Mr. Lockhart waving the right of being present and did not appear. The defendants plead not guilty it is considered and adjudged by the court that each defendant is equally guilty, whereupon it is ordered and adjudged by the court that each of the defendants receive Thirty lashes on the bare back and that the owner of each pay the cost of prosecution, and defendants then be discharge.

Page 148

It is a shame to read the same divide back then in 1862 is still the same divide today in 2011. It was jealousy and envy then and it is still jealousy and envy now among not only the Negro race, it is in the Caucasian race as well.

The Mayor and Council of the city of Atlanta vs. Elizabeth Kissleburg; Keeping a house of ill fame in the city of

Atlanta on the 5th day of July 1862 and on diverse other days before that day. Defendant discharged upon payment of the cost of prosecution.

Page 149

The Mayor and Council of the City of Atlanta vs. Samuel B. Sherwood; Disorderly conduct by being drunk and abusing a slave & c. on the 26th day of July 1862; dismissed upon payment of cost.

Page 151

Maybe there is hope still yet in the belief of justice and the justice system on behalf of the Negro. The consciousness of these White Men should prevail toward righteousness for all Men. Who am I fooling! This will be a long time in coming!

The Mayor and Council of the City of Atlanta vs. Emily Trail; Keeping a house of ill fame in Atlanta on the 10th day of August 1862 and on other days. Defendant appeared Case Dismissed.

Page 152

The Mayor and Council of the City of Atlanta vs. Archey, a Negro Slave owned by Mrs. Mason; Drawing a knife and attempting to use the same on Dr. Fox in Atlanta on the 14th day of August 1862 ordered and adjudged by the court that the Marshall turn this case over to a justice of the peace for Trial.

Pages 152–153

The Mayor and Council of the City of Atlanta vs. Barnard Kane; Disorderly conduct by indecency, in exposing his person designedly to females citizens in the City of Atlanta on the 29th of August 1862 Defendant appeared and plead not guilty after hearing the testimony it is considered and adjudged by the court that the defendant is guilty, whereupon, it is ordered and adjudged by the court that defendant be fined five dollars and cost of prosecution and upon payment thereof that he be hence discharged.

Atlanta Georgia September 22, 1862 Mayors Court, Honorable James M. Calhoun Mayor presiding, The Mayor and Council of the City of Atlanta vs. William Owens, David Calaway, F.M. Bowen, Wit Stewart and P. N. Wade; Disorderly Conduct by quarrelling throwing rocks at each other, shooting and being drunk in the City of Atlanta on Sunday the 21st day of September 1862. Defendants all appeared and Owen, Calaway & Stewart each pleaded guilty to the charge whereupon It is ordered and adjudged by the court that each be fined five dollars and cost of prosecution and in case of default that they be put in prison two and a half days and then be discharged.

Defendants Bowen and Wade plead not guilty, after hearing the testimony it is considered and adjudged by the court that Bowen is not guilty and that Wade is guilty, whereupon, it is ordered and adjudged by the court that he be fined five dollars and cost of prosecution and in default of payment thereof that he be imprisoned two days and a half and then he be discharged.

The Mayor Court met Honorable James M. Calhoun Mayor presiding the Mayor and Council of the City of Atlanta vs. Columbus Jones; quarrelling and shooting and thereby disturbing the good order of Citizens in Atlanta on Sunday evening the 28th day of September 1862; Defendant arraigned and plead not guilty after hearing the testimony in this case it is considered and adjudged by the court that defendant is not guilty and is therefore discharged.

Page 164

The Mayor and Council vs. John Coslin, M. Cooley J.B. McCullough, and M. F. Mayson; Selling Spirituous liquors in less than one quart in Atlanta on the 1st day of November 1862. John Coslin, M. Cooley, J.B. McCollough were all fined forty dollars and discharged M. F. Mayson was found not guilty and was acquitted.

Pages 166–167

The Mayor and Council of the City of Atlanta vs. G.W. Croft; Disorderly conduct by striking and Abusing a son of Mrs. P.F. Luckie and c. on 11th of November 1862; Defendant appeared and plead not guilty; after hearing the testimony in this case it is considered and adjudged by the court that the defendant is guilty, whereupon it is ordered and adjudged by the court that the defendant be fined twenty-five dollars and cost and in default of payment thereof that he be imprisoned twelve days and a half and thence be hence discharged.

The Mayor and Council of the City of Atlanta vs. Richard Stegall, William Lemon; disorderly conduct by being drunk and cursing and abusing Mrs. Calaway at her house in Atlanta on the night of the 17th of November 1862; The defendants plead not guilty, after hearing the testimony in this case it is considered and adjudged by the court that each of the defendants are guilty whereupon it is ordered and adjudged by the court that each of the defendants be fined ten dollars and cost and that they be hence discharge upon payment thereof.

Page 170

The Mayor and Council of the City of Atlanta vs. Wesley Hudson; Retailing spirituous liquors in the city of Atlanta in less quantities than one quart without a license from the City Council on the 26th day of Nov. 1862; The defendant plead not guilty; after hearing the testimony it is considered and adjudged by the court that the said defendant be fined five dollars and cost and that he be hence discharged upon payment thereof.

Page 171

Mayor and Council of the City of Atlanta vs. James L. Grant; Allowing a slave Charles to hire his own time in the City of Atlanta on the 22nd day of December 1862; Case dismissed.

The Mayor and Council of the City of Atlanta vs. Louiza Beardin and Adaline Beardin; Keeping a disorderly house or house of ill fame in the Atlanta on the 28th day of January 1863 and C. The defendants having been duly summoned to appear at this turn of the court and having failed to do so it is therefore ordered by the court that they each be fined five dollars for contempt to the court in so failing.

Page 178

Louiza Beardin and Aadaline Beardin both appeared in court and were fined ten dollars and cost of the court and in case of default of payment that the defaulters be imprisoned in the Calaboose five days and then be hence discharged. The fine for these two ladies was remitted.

> Listen to this case that happened.
>
> The Mayor and Council of the City of Atlanta vs. Francis Nash and his wife Margarett Nash; Disorderly Conduct by cursing and abusing Mrs. Sumerlain and quarrelling in Atlanta on the 19th day of October 1862; The defendants plead not guilty, after hearing the testimony it is considered and adjudged by the court that each defendants is guilty, where upon it is ordered and adjudged by the court that Francis Nash pay a fine of ten dollars and cost and that Margarett Nash pay a fine of five dollars and cost and that each be discharged upon payment thereof.
>
> The Mayor and Council of the city of Atlanta vs. Sarah Sumerlain; Disorderly conduct by quarreling with and abusing Mr. Nash in Atlanta on the 19th day of October 1862; Defendant plead not guilty after hearing the testimony in the case it is considered and adjudged by the court that defendant is guilty whereupon it is ordered and adjudged by the court that defendant be fined five dollars and cost and be discharged upon payment thereof.

Pages 164–165

> The Mayor and Council of the City of Atlanta vs. Josephine and Betsy Negro Slaves under the control of F. N. Nash; Disorderly conduct by quarrelling at and calling opprobrious names to Rebecca McCrary and threatening to whip the children of Mrs. Sumerlain in Atlanta on the 20th day of February 1863 and at other times before. The two slaves were brought before the Mayor and after hearing the testimony in the case of each slave it is considered by the court that each are guilty whereupon it is ordered and adjudged by the court that each of the saves receive fifteen lashes on the bare back and be hence discharged, and that F.N. Nash who represented them pay the cost of trail before the delivery of the slaves.

Pages 180–181

I wonder if the war that is slowly approaching Georgia and Atlanta emboldened the two Negro women to act out or if this is a common act that plays out in the streets of Atlanta during this time. If this is true, I see a totally new perspective of the role of the colored woman in the slave society. Were these two women willing to suffer the whip or lash due to some reason or another? I asked myself this question as well, are these two women privileged in some way or another because of the color or their skin?

> *The Mayor and Council of the City of Atlanta* vs. Sarah Potter, Caroline Burk, Eliza Golsy, Ellin McHammon and Martha Thomas; Keeping a disorderly house or a house of ill fame in Atlanta on the 2nd day of March and on diverse other days before that day. The defendants above written each appeared and pleaded not guilty; after hearing the testimony it is considered and adjudged by the court that each of the defendants is guilty; whereupon it is ordered and adjudged by the court that each of the defendants be fined in the sum of ten dollars and cost of prosecution and upon payment of thereof that they be discharged and in default of payment they be imprisoned five days.

> *The Mayor and Council of the city of Atlanta* vs. W.C. Houghton; Disorderly conduct by using vulgar and profane language to Misses Willingham in the city of Atlanta on the 23rd day of April 1863; The defendant plead not guilty after hearing the testimony in this case it is considered and adjudged by the court that the defendant is guilty, where upon it is ordered and adjudged by the court that the defendant be fined forty dollars and cost and in default of payment that he be imprisoned twenty days and then be discharged.

> *The Mayor and Council of the City of Atlanta* vs. Jane a slave in charge of H.T. Jones; Disorderly conduct by using improper language and behavior to Mrs. Davis in Atlanta on the 21st day of April 1863 and at other times before that

time. Defendant through Mr. Jones her representative where upon it is ordered and adjudged by the court that the Marshal inflict twenty-five lashes on the defendant Jane and then she be discharged.

The Mayor and Council of the City of Atlanta vs. Frank a Slave of A.C. Wyly; Disorderly conduct by driving disorderly in the Streets of Atlanta on the 7th day of May 1863; Mr. Wyly the owner of Frank the defendant appeared and plead not guilty; after hearing the testimony in the case it is considered and adjudged by the court that Frank is guilty where upon it is ordered and adjudged by the court that Frank receive five lashes and be hence discharged and that Mr. Wyly pay the cost of prosecution.

Page 202

Mayor and Council of the City of Atlanta vs. C.W. Simpson; Offering for sale one Slave in the City of Atlanta otherwise than through a Negro broker or Auctioneer on the 14th day of May 1863; The defendant pleaded guilty whereupon it is considered, ordered and adjudged that the said defendant be fined five dollars and cost and be discharged upon payment thereof.

Page 203

The Mayor and Council of the City of Atlanta vs. Joseph M. Jones and Fred Coulter; Disorderly Conduct by quarrelling and fighting on the 23rd day of May 1863; both enter pleas of not guilty and Joseph M. Jones is fined twenty-five dollars and Coulter pay fifteen dollars.

Page 209

The Mayor and Council of the City of Atlanta vs. Frank Hilburn; playing marbles with a Negro on Sunday the 31st day of May 1863 in Atlanta; the defendant filed a plea of guilty where upon It is ordered and adjudged by the court that the defendant be fined five dollars and cost and in default of payment that he be imprisoned three days and be hence discharged.

Page 210

The Mayor and council of the City of Atlanta vs. L. Prince, T. Landers, Elizabeth Rice Mary Rice, I Sizemore; disorderly conduct by resisting and fighting J.M. Lester, a police officer in Atlanta, on the 4th day of June 1863. They were all found not guilty.

The Mayor and Council of the City of Atlanta vs. Philip Sheon, David Mount and James Lawshe; disorderly conduct by Squalling like cats and throwing sticks and rocks in the house of Mrs. Einstine in Atlanta on Sunday night the 7th day of June 1863; The defendants each appeared and defendants Sheon and Mount plead guilty and defendants Lawshe plead not guilty; after hearing the testimony in the case of Lawshe it is considered and ordered by the court that the defendant James Lawshe is guilty where upon it is ordered and adjudged by the court that each of the defendants Philip Shoen, David Mount and James Lawshe be fined Thirty dollars and cost and in default of payment that each in default be imprisoned fifteen days and be hence discharged.

The Mayor and Council of the City of Atlanta vs. Hannah a Slave in charge of J.D. Griffin; Peddling her own pies through the city of Atlanta on the 10th day of June 1863 and on the days before that day; The defendant was brought before the Council and Mrs. Griffin being present who plead not guilty; testimony in the case was heard by the court ; and it is adjudged by the court that the defendant is guilty, where upon it is ordered and adjudged by the court that the defendant be fined four dollars and cost and in default of payment that she receive twenty strikes and be discharged.

Page 214

I do not know if this is Hannah the mother of Aaron from Greene County or not. However, I do know that the Griffin Family is in the 147th District of Greene in Scull Shoals. And also is in the Ragan family, of which Hannah is a part of supposedly.

> *The Mayor and Council of the City of Atlanta* vs. James Banks; Disorderly conduct by being drunk taking by the collar Mr. Kiley and threatening to kill him in Atlanta on the 13th day of June 1863. Mr. James Banks pleads guilty and is fined twenty dollars.

Page 216

> *The Mayor and Council of the City of Atlanta* vs. Bob a Slave in the employment of Von Alderhoff; Soliciting and asking at the general Passenger shed in Atlanta Passenger arriving to stop at the Atlanta Hotel on the 2nd day of July 1863; The Defendant was brought before the Court being represented by Honorable D. Hammond who plead not guilty evidence was heard after which it was ordered and adjudged by the court that the defendant is guilty where upon it is ordered and adjudged by the court that the defendant Bob receive ten lashes and be discharged and that Von Alderhoff pay the cost in the case.

Thomas H. Whitaker, G. P. McNanally, Joseph Beerman Geo. F. Glazener, Paul Ryner, Henry G. Kuhrt were all charged by the Mayor and the Council of the City of Atlanta for selling and retailing Spirituous liquors in Atlanta. All were fined forty dollars or in case of default be imprisoned for twenty days.

What will become of this relationship between these men? I will tell you they will come to own or be part of the Atlanta Brewery Company at 66 Harris Street. Mr. George F. Glazener will intertwine with the Cates family that will sell part of their estate in DeKalb in the Cross Keys District to help furnish homes for the colored men and women and their families. Joseph Beerman will also employ a Colored man name John Callaway. These prominent Men will be brought up on charges with Mr. R. M. Rose in 1899 during the mass murder of colored men and the start of the disenfranchisement of the Negroes and a few Jews as well! However, the Jewish community will strive and the colored community will be decimated!

For to disenfranchise the Negro both the white community and the Jewish community will go after the Blind Tigers where a few of the prominent coloreds made great gains along with both the white and the Jewish communities in the illegal liquor business. At this time in the year of 1899 both the Jewish community and the white community tried to corner the market in the liquor and illegal liquor business, and the first casualty was the Negro Blind Tiger Organization that strived and was well entrenched in the way of life in the colored community after the Civil War. The environment that the Blind Tigers produced with sexual relationships between the races had to stop. But it had to be kept a secret that should not be talked about.

> *The Mayor and Council of the City of Atlanta* vs. Rice a Slave owned by Paul Eve; Disorderly conduct by being obstinate and using insolent language to the Clerk of the Market in the Market Yard in Atlanta on the 18th day of July 1863; The Defendant was brought in court and plead not guilty by his attorney D.F. Hammond the testimony in the case was heard by the court and it is considered and adjudged by the court that the defendant is not Guilty.
>
> Joseph Beerman, H.G. Kuhrt, P.H. Ollrech, Thomas Savage were all charged with selling and Retailing Spirituous liquors in Atlanta on the 3rd day of August 1863 all plead guilty and fined forty dollars and the cost and in case of default be imprisoned for twenty days.

This union between Beerman and Kurhrt would form the Beerman & Kuhrt by Charles Beerman and H. G. Kurhrt in Atlanta on of the largest Liquor Dispensary in the city of Atlanta. They sold cigars and tobacco, at 1 Whitehall, 1 Decatur, Kimball, and Markham House. Charles G. Beerman, with Beermann & Kuhrt, boards at Markham. Charles G. Beerman also of Beermann & Kuhrt resided at 165 Whitehall. The two men also resided at 198 Whitehall in the early years of 1900.

You will see these Jewish men become powerful in the city of Atlanta and even have streets named after them. And yet the riots in Atlanta in 1906 that took place in the colored community because of the bars and liquor and the white men and women that visited these places would spark a dark history in the City of Atlanta and the State of Georgia and yet no one blames the Rose family and other white and Jewish communities that fostered the same activity in the colored community. Hardly a voice of compassion from these two communities came forward until the death of Leo Frank! Yet their fears caused a divide in their community as well. However, the relationship between the Jewish and some white liquor runners and dealers was not diminished. It flourished well into the 1950s up until the case against Mr. Fat Hardy.

The Mayor and Council of the City of Atlanta vs. Patrick McNally for selling and retailing spirituous liquors in Atlanta on August 17, 1863. He was fined fifty dollars or spend twenty-five days in jail, for this was his second offence. *Patrick McNally will go into the real-estate business and will help design and lay-out properties in DeKalb County as well in Fulton County. As a matter of fact, the liquor business will produce a great number of realtors.*

E.J. Hunnicutt is charged with selling and retailing spirituous liquors in Atlanta on August 17, 1863, and pleads guilty and is fined fifty dollars as well or he would be forced to spend twenty-five days in jail.

James Murphy is charged with selling and retailing spirituous liquors in the city of Atlanta as well on August 17, 1863, and is fined forty dollars or spend twenty days in jail.

H. Mylius is charged with selling and retailing spirituous liquors in the city of Atlanta August 17, 1863, and is fined forty dollars or be imprisoned twenty days.

> Louisa a slave owned by Harris Fuller is charged with keeping an eating and boarding house in Atlanta on her own account or on the account of another person on the 22nd day of August 1863; The defendant plead guilty through her representative F.R. Haygood whereupon it is ordered and adjudged by the court that the said representative F.R. Haygood be fined ten dollars and cost and in default of payment there of that said slave Louisa be imprisoned in the calaboose five days and be hence discharged.
>
> Jim a Slave of John Silvey is charged with disorderly conduct by fighting with another slave on Merrietta Street in Atlanta on Sunday the 16th day of August 1863. Case dismissed.
>
> Henry G. Kuhrt, P.H. Olrich, James Murphy, Joseph Beerman, and Thomas H. Whitaker Thomas Savage, Mary Garvin, Ed Hunnicutt, George McGinley, H. Myleus, Patrick McNally, James Long, are all charged with selling and retailing spirituous liquors in Atlanta on the 21st and 25th days of August 1863.
>
> Lemuel Dean was charged with disorderly conduct by fighting Anderson Sizemore in Atlanta on the 24th day of August 1863. Case dismissed.

In September on the 7th day of 1863 the same men were back in Atlanta selling spirituous liquor in the city of Atlanta. This time they had Mr. W.I Quinn with them. Also Elias Presnell and Frank Hambree, whose case was dismissed.

> *The Mayor and Council of the City of Atlanta* vs. Charley Lester; Disorderly Conduct by quarrelling cursing and fighting in the city of Atlanta on the 7th day of September 1863; The defendant plead guilty where upon it is ordered and adjudged by the court that the said defendant be fined fifteen dollars and cost and in default of payment thereof that he be imprisoned seven days and be hence discharged.
>
> George F. Glazener was in the city selling spirituous liquors on the 7th day of Sept. 1863 and was fined fifty dollars or to spend twenty-five days in jail.
>
> Patrick McNally was in town as well, selling spirituous liquors in the city of Atlanta on the 7th day of Sept. 1863. Patrick was fined fifty dollars or to spend twenty-five days in jail.
>
> James Murphy was charged with disorderly conduct by going to the house of one Mr. Webb and forcing himself into the said house and cursing and beating the said Mr. Webb in the house aforesaid in Atlanta on the 15th day of August 1863. Case Dismissed.
>
> L.W. Yarbrough was charged with shooting at W.J. Carter with a pistol in the city of Atlanta on the 24th day of August 1863 case was dismissed.
>
> W.H. Crisp was charged on the 11th, on the 5th, on the 7th, on the 8th and on the 9th with performing Comedy Tragedy and farce in the City of Atlanta. All of the cases were dismissed except on the 9th. Mr. Crisp was charged with being disorderly.
>
> William O'Hallaran was charged with selling spirituous liquors and was charged to pay fifty dollars or spend twenty-five days in the calaboose.
>
> R. Slater, Manager and director for E. Heunt was charged with showing and exhibiting a Panarama in the city of

Atlanta on the 16th day of September 1863 without a license from the City Council.

Desly a slave owned by William Neill was charge with being found with ardent spirits about her person in the City of Atlanta on the 29th day of September 1863 and resisting the police officer when detected ordered by the court that this case be dismissed on payment of the cost.

Using colored women to sell not only the ardent spirits in Atlanta has been a long-time practice. Since the time Mayor Norcross was first elected to quell the rowdy men that did what they wanted in the City of Atlanta. At first, it was the white women and the Indian women and free colored women who set up their houses of prostitution and drink before the war came to Atlanta in 1864. It was stated by Will Samuels that Charlie Callaway in Terrell County, was born about 1854 the same time that Atlanta was ruled by rowdy white men and the white caps who tried to clean up the fragile city of Atlanta in 1854.

P. W. Bibb was charged with fighting and cutting a Negro in the Atlanta Hotel in Atlanta on the 5th day of October 1863. The defendant plead not guilty after hearing the testimony in the case it is considered and adjudged by the court that the said defendant is guilty whereupon it is ordered and adjudged by the court that he be fined fifteen dollars and cost and be discharged upon payment thereof and in default of payment that he be imprisoned seven days and be hence discharged.

Henry Johnson, Menerva Johnson, and James Banks are charged with quarreling and cursing and striking John Hammond in the City of Atlanta on the 10th day of October 1863 they are all found guilty and Menerva Johnson is fined fifteen dollars or be imprisoned five days, and Henry Johnson and James Banks be fined five dollars or spend two days in jail.

David Hollis is charged with selling spirituous liquors in the city of Atlanta on the 10th day of October 1863 and is fined forty dollars or spend twenty days in prison.

Arnold Winningham is charged with selling spirituous liquors in the city of Atlanta and he is found not guilty.

On October 17, 1863, P.M. Olrich, Joseph Beerman, Thomas E. Whitaker, William Dowling, Patrick McNally and C.T. West are in town to sell their liquor and all are charged and pleads guilty. The fine is forty dollars to fifty dollars or be imprisoned for twenty to twenty-five days.

On October 19, 1863, Shadric Walker is charged with selling spirituous liquors and is fined forty dollars or be imprisoned for twenty days.

Richard Tony is charged with selling spirituous liquors on October 12, 1863, and is fined forty dollars or be imprisoned for twenty days.

A.M. Watts is charged for not appearing in court for selling liquor on October 20, 1863.

Lucean Hollingsworth is charged with selling spirituous liquors in the city of Atlanta on November 1, 1863. He is fined forty dollars or be imprisoned for twenty days.

J.M. Lester is charged with disorderly conduct by quarrelling and fighting in the city of Atlanta on October 17, 1863, and is ordered by the court to pay five dollars.

Alfred Fowler is charged with selling spirituous liquors in the city of Atlanta on November 16, 1863, he is fined fifty dollars or spend twenty-fivedays in jail.

Joseph Shockley is charged with selling liquor in the city of Atlanta on November 16, 1863, and is fined fifty dollars or spend twenty-five days in jail.

Sim Lester and Jo Whitley are both charged with cursing and quarrelling and trying to fight in the city of Atlanta on November 24, 1863, with Andy Lambs and William Valinteno. All are fined ten dollars or be imprisoned for five days.

All are under the same indictment: Joseph Beerman, Thomas Savage, PH. Olrich, H.J. Myers, T.C. West, H. G. Hilhurt, James Long, Joseph Shockley, Lucean Hollingsworth, George McGinley, William O'Hallaran, Parick McNalley and are all charged with selling spirituous liquors in the city of Atlanta on November 28, 1863, and are all fined fifty dollars or be imprisoned for twenty-five days. And so was Mr. Thomas E. Whitaker as well, who didn't show up and was given another fine of ten dollars for contempt of court.

These men will go on in this way until the end of this log book of the mayor and council of the city of Atlanta.

As you can still see, Joseph Beerman and his friends are making a living off the liquor business in the city of Atlanta. It may be clear who would be in favor of a Wet state and who might be in favor of a Dry state in Georgia. With a large population coming to Atlanta, even Mr. R. M. Rose, and his purpose to sell the drink of choice!

Daniel a slave owned by Mr. M. Jack was given thirty lashes for fighting Jim a slave with a stick in the city of Atlanta on December 7, 1863.

Bill a slave owned by L.H. Davis was abusing Marion Smith in the city of Atlanta on the 10th day and the 11th day of 1863. The defendant pleads not guilty. After hearing the testimony in this case, it is considered and adjudged by the court that he is guilty, whereupon it is ordered and adjudged by the court that the said defendant receive thirty lashes and be discharged and L.H. Davis pay all cost in this case.

Now, the courts did not state the color of Marion Smith. I assume that she is white. I would have thought that the penalty would be death for Bill. Is the value of Bill to Mr. L. H. Davis more than the respect that Bill should have shown to Marion Smith? So when the Negro is free after the war he could be charged with death because of this offense to a white woman because he is not valuable to the white man now!

Monroe Smith was charged with throwing rocks at Bill, a slave owned by L.H. Davis, in the city of Atlanta on December 10, 1863. He pleads not guilty. They found him guilty and he would pay a fine of five dollars or three days in jail.

It looks like Bill is not off the hook so easily. Monroe Smith is seeking revenge! Is this Mr. Joseph Monroe Smith the father of Annie V. Smith who would become the wife of Stewart B. Callaway? Are they living as free coloreds in the City of Atlanta at the time of the Civil War? Or is this the Mr. Smith that sold property to the colored community in Buckhead, or is this the notorious Mr. James M. Smith of Oglethorpe County of Smithonia? Or just a relative to Mr. James M. Smith in Oglethorpe or even kin to the governor Smith of Georgia.

Jack Gober was charged with firing a pistol at Mr. Smith in the city of Atlanta on December 3, 1863, and was find five dollars or spend three days in jail.

Sim Lester was charged with cursing and slapping Mr. Turner in the face in the city of Atlanta on November 25, 1863, and he pleaded guilty and was fined fifteen dollars or be imprisoned for seven days.

On December 19, 1863, Catherine Caton was fined fifty dollars or be imprisoned for twenty-five days.

Martin Nelson was fined fifty dollars for selling liquor on December 19, 1863.

Joseph Beerman has a new man with him now. He is James Robinson and also Mr. W.H. Manning and Patrick Ennis and Charley Sheppard and Martin Nelson selling liquor.

F. Corra is charged with selling liquor on January 9, 1864, and on January 10 is charged with allowing slaves to enter his house where spirituous liquors are kept and to loiter there in the city of Atlanta. They found him not guilty.

Samuel Hoffman was charged with selling liquor but his case was dismissed

Mary Montz was charged with selling liquor on January 17 and fined seventy-five dollars or be imprisoned thirty days

F. Corra was charged with selling liquor to slaves not under his control in the city of Atlanta on January 7, 1864. They found him guilty and he was fined one hundred dollars or be imprisoned thirty days.

Hugh McTeague was charged with selling liquors in Atlanta on January 14, 1864, and was charged twenty dollars or be imprisoned ten days.

James Dickerson was charged with furnishing and selling spirituous liquors to a slave not under his control in the city of Atlanta on January 9, 1864, and fined one hundred dollars or to be imprisoned thirty days.

Mariah, a slave owned by George Gibbon, and Fanny, a slave under the control of John Bowls, was charged with quarreling and fighting and cutting each other with a knife in the city of Atlanta on the January 8, 1864. Each of the defendants pleads not guilty and was found guilty and Mariah was given thirty-nine lashes and Fanny received fifteen lashes and cost was paid by Mr. Gibbon and Mr. Bowls jointly.

Barbany Houffiman was charged with selling spirituous liquors in the city of Atlanta on January 13, 1864, and was fined forty dollars or to spend twenty days in jail

James Cay Jr., Andrew Lamb, Joshua Sewell, and William Valinino went to the store of W.C. Houghtorn and put out his light at night and threw mud on his show ase and abusing the clerk in the store on January 17, 1864. They found them guilty and fined them thirty dollars or be imprisoned for fifteen days.

Margaret Griskill was charged with selling spirituous liquors in Atlanta on January 14, 1864, and was found guilty and was ordered to pay a fine of forty dollars or be imprisoned for twenty days.

John C. Head was charged with the same offense on January 20 and was ordered to pay seventy-five dollars or spend thirty days in jail.

George A. T. Leak and William B. Cloud were charged with being drunk and fighting and abusing Nancy J. Simpson in the city of Atlanta on January 30, 1864, they pleaded guilty and George A. T. Leak was fined twenty dollars or be thrown into the calaboose for ten days. Cloud was fined ten dollars or be imprisoned for five days.

Julia Gibbs, a free person of color, was charged with going to the house of Margaret Bedford and cursing and abusing her in the City of Atlanta on January 30. The case was dismissed on payment of cash.

E. Kennedy was charged with keeping a gaming house and a gaming room and permitting persons to play and bet in said house and room in the city of Atlanta on January 20, 1864. The case was dismissed.

Paul Lemon was charged with the same offense on January 28, 1864 and the case was dismissed.

James Clay Jr. and James Evans were charged with the same offense on February 3, 1864, and the mayor and council stated that play and betting at a game were not recognized as an offence by the laws of this state in the City of Atlanta. The case was dismissed.

John Crawford and Pinch Smith were charged with malicious mischief in the city of Atlanta on December 24, 1863, by shoving over and puling to pieces a small necessary building of Lemuel Deans. Dismissed as to Pink Smith

> Thomas Chastine was maliciously doing mischief in the mutilating and cutting down the sign of Roderic a slave who was allowed by his owner to put up and have the same in the City of Atlanta on the 9th day of February 1864. The defendant pleads not guilty. After having the testimony in this case it is ordered and adjudged by the court that defendant is not guilty.
>
> Ben a slave owned by Jeptha Harris being found with ardent spirits on his person and in his house or room without the same being prescribed by a physician in Atlanta on the 11th day of February 1864. The defendant plead not guilty. After hearing the testimony in this case it is considered and adjudged by the court that the defendant is guilty and it is further ordered and adjudged by the court

> that the said defendant be whipped thirty-nine lashes and discharged and the cost be paid by Jeptha Harris.
>
> Dick Smith a free person of color being impudent and insulting to J.R. Curd in the city of Atlanta on the 26th day of January 1864 and thereby breaking the peace and good order of Citizens. The defendant pleads not guilty; after hearing testimony in this case it is considered and adjudged by the court that the said defendant is not guilty.

Could Mr. Richard Smith be governor of Georgia or out of Buckhead in DeKalb or out of Greene and Oglethorpe County?

Mary A. Ramsey, E.A. Ramsey, and John W. Ramsey were quarreling and fighting in the city of Atlanta on January 30. They were found not guilty.

Edward, a slave, owned by Mr. Ferrill was found selling and furnishing other slaves with spirituous liquors in the city of Atlanta on February 8, 1864. Edward was given thirty-nine lashes and Mr. Ferrill was to pay the cost of the trial.

Rasberry, a slave of Edwin Preost, was charged with selling and furnishing other slaves with spirituous liquors in the City of Atlanta on February 8, 1864, and he was found not guilty.

Sim Lester was charged with being drunk and striking a citizen with a stick in the city of Atlanta on December 25, 1863. He pleads guilty and was fined twenty-five dollars or to spend ten days in jail.

Stephen, a slave in the charge of Capt. Peydon, was charged with crying the hour of twelve at night and mocking the policeman in Atlanta on February 23, 1864. Stephen was found guilty and given thirty lashes and be discharged at the cost of Capt. Peydon.

Thomas Johnson was charged with quarreling and striking with a stick David Austin in the city of Atlanta on February 28, 1864. They found him guilty and fined him fifteen dollars or seven days in jail.

Kyle, a slave, owned by Mr. McKinstey was charged with fighting a slave in the City of Atlanta. Case dismissed on payment in cash.

Sam, a slave owned by C.M. Coldwell, was quarreling and cursing and fighting on February 19, 1864. Sam was found guilty and was whipped twenty-five lashes.

Henry, a slave, owned by the estate of James Loyd (deceased) was keeping a shop for the sale of fruit and other articles on his own account in the City of Atlanta on March 1, 1864. The defendant through John Loyd pleaded guilty. He received thirty-nine lashes and that Mr. Loyd pay all cost and that Henry then be discharged.

Sim Lester was disorderly and being drunk and cursing and fighting Charley Collier in Atlanta on February 21, 1864. He was fined twenty-five dollars or be imprisoned for ten days.

W.C. Houghton was charged with selling liquor in Atlanta on February 28, 1864, and was fined one hundred and twenty-five dollars or be imprisoned for thirty days.

William, a slave owned by Mr. Reynolds, was selling and offering to sell leather in the city of Atlanta on March 3, 1864. He was found guilty and whipped thirty-nine times.

Tom, Amanda, and Oliver, slaves owned by F. M. Fisk, where quarreling, cursing, and fighting in the city of Atlanta on February 19, 1864. Amanda and Oliver each were whipped twenty-five times.

Henry, a slave owned by J. D. Lockhart, was riding a horse in a gallop and in a faster gait than a walk across the bridge in Market Street, the nearest city market in the city of Atlanta, on March 20, 1864. He was whipped twenty-five times.

Jerry, a slave, and Bill, a slave in the charge of Thomas Savage, were found with ardent spirits and firearms in their possession and of furnishing ardent spirits to other slaves in Atlanta on March 22, 1864. They were found not guilty.

Eliza, a slave owned by Thomas Miller, was hiring herself out on her own time living separate and apart from owner agent in the city of Atlanta on March 23, 1864. Case dismissed.

Alberton, a slave owned by P.L. Howard, was keeping an eating house or boarding house on his own account or on account of another person in Atlanta on March 23, 1864. They didn't whip Alberton but they did fine P.L Howard fifty dollars and the cost of the court.

David Knoll was charged with selling spirituous liquors in the city on March 21, 1864, and he was fined ten dollars for contempt.

The last case was that of Mr. James Bryant for disorderly conduct on March 16, 1864. He was fined ten dollars for failure to appear. Court adjourned. N.C. Holcombe has always been the Clerk.

The Daily Herald, Atlanta Sunday Herald

R.A. Alston, H.W. Grady, I.W. Avery Alston and Co., proprietors

For Congressman Hon. M.A. Candler of DeKalb

Liquor.

The wholesale, liquor business is an important item in the trade of Atlanta. In the interest of our branch of business are we more fortunately located. We are, as it were, a center point to which is drawn the fine products of Kentucky and Pennsylvania distillers as well as the Lower Missouri and Illinois. Our merchants are therefore, enabled, and do sell their goods as cheap or cheaper than the same qualities can be bought in any market. On the lower grades of whisky, they are compelled to add the freight to the western price. The merchants engaged in this line are honorable, enterprising and industrious. They have their traveling salesmen scattered throughout the states of Georgia, Alabama and South Carolina, and have done much towards building up the wholesale business of Atlanta. We will add that in Georgia-made corn whisky and peach brandy this market supasses all others. Atlanta sells a great part of all made in this state. The sales amounted to over one million and half dollars during the past year.

Coweta County Fair!

Tuesday, October 27, 1874

The racing will be unequalled by and in the state several notorious trotters are already booked for the occasion I. H. Feathersone president J.W. Wiley sec'y

R. F. Maddox Wholesale Dealer in Tobacco, Cigars, and Liquors

M.E. Mater Wholesale Liquor dealer

The Bar Room of Frank Noonan known as Mechanic Saloon on the corner of Marietta and Bartow Street

Thomas Finley Attorney at Law

Sunday May 11, 1873

20 persons are to be hung here ¾ are of the enfranchised Black Population

February 9, 1873

The City Column

R.M. Rose and Co., Wholesale Liquor Dealers: The House that sells "O. E."

N. Lyon has a number of rooms to rent suitable for stores, shops and c. at the low rate of 10 dollars per months for the year call upon him on Decatur Street.

Liquors

Lager Beer Brewery on the corner of Collins and Harris St.

Shepard, Baldwin and Co. 11 Decatur Street

Now this is a great find! Collins and Harris Street is where the Atlanta Brewery will be located at 66 Harris Street at the corner of Courtland. The most exciting thing is that who owns the property in 1873. Mr. Baldwin and Mr. Shepard and the property in Decatur. Well this same place was owned by Mr. Charles Bangert and his wife Mary Bangert in 1885 out of Decatur, and in 1888 John C. Callaway was working for the Atlanta City Brewing Company. Owned by H. G Kuhrt the Pres. Charles Beerman the Treas. A. Flesh the Sec. the office was at 3 Decatur. The Place in 1900 was still owned by Beerman and Kurtz.

Clayton and Webb, 72 Whitehall St.

R.M. Rose and Co.

Cox and Hill Peachtree St.

Meador Bro. 35 Whitehall St.

Saloons

John W. Kimbro 5 Decatur St.

O.C. Carroll

Lee Smith Marietta St.

Paul Jones No. 39 Whitehall St. Atlanta Ga. Agent for the Sale of the Celebrated Krug and Co. Champagne, Missouri Cider, also dealer in Fine Brandies, Whiskies, Jamaica Rum, Gin, and all kind of

Fine Liquors.

The Barbarism of Public Execution: The Hanging of Susan Eberhart. Susan Eberhart a colored woman had property in Oglethorpe County Georgia before she was hanged.

The First Colored Baptist Association of Georgia

Before I go any further into the year of 1870 in Fulton County Georgia, I want to show you the minutes of the Ebenezer Baptist Association. Many of these same colored churches would be under the watchful eye of the White Southern Baptist Associations and would have a great influence in the way blacks would cast their votes that would come from the white or mulatto preachers that would influence the colored communities and all that resided on the plantations of these white landowners. And if they wanted to remain on the plantation they would vote the way the preacher says or things would go bad for his or her family. The history of the blacks in the South is centered on the church! From social events and schools and weddings and community meetings. This is why I thought the very thing that was missing in the real history of the blacks in the South is in the church life! The Ebenezer Colored Baptist Association started within the White Southern Association. It separated from it after the Civil War.

US Baptist Yearbook 1860–1869

H. H. Tucker, the president of the Mercer University and over the Theological Institution as well in Penfield Georgia in 1867. The officers of the Geo. Convention were P.H. Mell D. D. of Athens, the Pres. J. F. Dagg of Cuthbert was the Clerk, and Assistant Clerk was Rev. J. H. Stout of Cuthbert. The Callaway that were from Georgia were J. J. S. Callaway of Cuthbert, B. M. Calloway of Washington, A. R. Calloway of La Grange, J. M. Calloway of West Point, and S. P. Calloway of La Grange. Wm. Sutton of Danburg, Ga.,

American Baptist Yearbook 1887–1890

In the White Association P. H. Mell D. D. LL. D. Athens is still the president, George R. McCall D. D. Griffin Asst. Clerk Rev. E. R. Carswell Jr. Eatonton, Trea. Rev. S. A. Burney of Madison, Corresponding Secretary J. H. DeVotie, D. D. of Griffin.

The State Convention Colored: Officers were Rev. J. C. Bryan, of Milledgeville, V.P., U. L. Houston of Savannah, sec., J. H. Brown of

Savannah, asst. Sec. Rev. T. J. Hornsby of Augusta, and Treas. Rev. J. T. Tolbert of Augusta, Corresponding Sec., *Rev. C. H. Lyons, of Athens.* This was the 16th annual meeting in 1890 Rev. E. P. Johnson was in Hawkinsville Ga. J. M. Jones was in Atl. C. H. Lyons was in Athens, J. T. Thornton was in Atl. Wm. Tuggle was in Sheltonville, M. L. Williams was in Atl. Chas. Williams was in Augusta. W. J. White was in Augusta. G. B. Austin was in Jonesboro with H. Austin. William Barnett was in Winterville. No mention of Jess Callaway, S. Burges was in Perry, R. H. Burson was in Atl. In the year of 1887, C. A. Lyons is in Rome as the corresponding secretary. I believe that C. A. Lyons is Rev. Collins H. Lyons. And Jesse R. Callaway shows up as an ordained minister in Penfield.

In the year of 1874 when the Colored Missionary Baptist Convention was first held:

> The annual meeting was held at Savannah May 22, 1873. The introductory sermon was preached by Rev. Henry Jackson. The treasurer reported receipts amounting to $1, 452, 67. The missionary appointed by the Executive board reported having since his commission March 1st traveled 1,230 miles preached 31 sermons, made 4 addresses to Sunday schools, received 12 candidates for baptism, and collected $67.08. The committee on Ministerial Education recommended the members of the Convention to raise all the funds they can to provide for a Theological Institute in some central part of the State and also that they avail themselves of the present opportunity to secure as thorough knowledge as possible by attending the Augusta Institute. The next meeting will be held at Rome, Ga. May 21, 1874, the introductory sermon to be preached by Rev. Frank Quarles. OFFICERS

President Rev. Frank Quarles, Atlanta, V. P. Rev. Henry Watts, Clerk, Geo. H. Dwelle, of Americus Ga.

Georgia Baptist Sunday-school Convention Colored. This body convened for organization at Macon, Nov. 15, 1873. Twelve counties were represented. An executive committee was appointed to inaugurate and carry forward Sunday school mission work and a state missionary was also chosen. Rev. Wm. J. White of Augusta was elected President of the convention.

Chapter Eleven

FROM THE HARDSHIP OF SLAVERY, COMES THE EBENEZER BLACK BAPTIST ASSOCIATION IN GEORGIA

The Ebenezer Baptist Association was held at Atlanta, Ga., September 6, 1867 with the Constitution and Rules of Order. Printed in Augusta, Ga. by the Georgia Printing Co.'s Office 1867.

Atlanta, Fulton Co. Ga., Sept. 6, 1867.

The Ebenezer Association met at Friendship Church at 10:00 a.m.

Introductory sermon by the Rev. Henry Johnson, of Thankful Church, Augusta, Ga. Text: 1st Peter, 5th chapter, and 5th verse, and the meeting then adjourned until 3:00 p.m.

Afternoon Session, 3:00 p.m.

The meeting was called to order by Rev. H. Watts, and singing hymn 959, and prayer by Rev. Henry Morgan, after which the following brethren were appointed to read the letters form the Churches composing the association. Rev. L. B. Carter, A. Delimotta, Wm. H. Mathews. The letter of Friendship church was read by the Rev. Frank Quarles, after which the following letters were read:

Central Church, Augusta, Ga., Dead River Church, Beach Island, S.C., Ebenezer Church, Richmond Co., Ga., Springfield church, Augusta, Ga., Shiloh Church, Richmond Co., Ga., Mount Zion Church, Barnwell District, S. C., Zion Church, Marietta, Ga., Spirit Creek Church, Richmond Co. Ga., Thankful Church, Augusta, Ga., Poplar Head Church, Columbia Co., Ga., Franklin Covenant Church, Richmond Co., Ga., Greenwood Church, Warren Co., Ga.,

Brothers Joseph Jackson and Thomas Lacy were then appointed to count the ballots for the election of Moderator and Clerk. The Rev. L. B. Carter was elected Moderator, and George H. Dwell Clerk for the ensuing year.

This makes L. B. Carter the first Colored Moderator instead of Rev. Frank Quarles! I wonder if L. B. Carter is out of Clarke County. I ask this question because of the third moderator of the Ebenezer Baptist Association Mr. E. R. Carter. Could the two be related? Maybe or maybe not!

On motion the fourth clause in the Rules of Order was suspended.

On motion all brethren of the same faith and order present were invited to take part in the deliberations. The following Committees were appointed:

To Examine Letters of Application for Membership—Rev. R. Quarles, William H. Mathews, Rev. Romalus Moore, Rev. E. B. Rucker, Rev. Henry Jackson.

On Preaching—Rev. Frank Quarles, and his Deacons.

On Business—Revs. Henry Watts, Romalus Moore, Peter Johnson, Nathan Walker, and Henry Johnson.

The Committee on Preaching announce the following appointments for Friday evening: At Mount Zion Baptist Church, Brother A. Williams, of Columbus, Ga.; at the First Methodist Church, Brother Jordon Johnson; at the Second Methodist Church, brother Frank Beal; at the Friendship Baptist Church, Brother Judge Cook.

Second Day's Session

Saturday, Sept. 7th, 1867

The Association was called to order by the Moderator. The meeting was opened with singing the 389th hymn, and prayer by the Rev. Shadrack McAllister. Roll Called, and minutes read and approved.

On motion applicant letters were read, as follows: Landrum Chapel of Athens, Ga.; LaGrange Baptist Church, LaGrange, Ga.; Jackson Baptist Church Butts Co. Ga.; Covington Baptist Church, Covington Ga.; Mount Zion Baptist Church, Cartersville, Ga.; Mount Zion Baptist church, Morgan Co., Ga.; Springfield Baptist Church, Monticello, Jasper Co., Ga.; Pleasant Grove Baptist Church Warrenton, GA.; First African Baptist Church, Albany, Ga.; Bethesda Baptist Church, Stone Mountain, Ga.; Bottsford Springs Baptist Church, Burke Co. Ga.; Second Indian Creek Baptist Church, Dekalb Co. Ga.; Mount Zion Baptist Church, Atlanta, Ga.; Second Georgetown Baptist Church Quitman Co., Ga.; Flint Ridge Baptist Church, Fayette Co., Ga.; East Point Baptist Church, Fulton Co., Ga.; Stormbranch Baptist Church, Edgefield Dist. S. C.; Second African Baptist Church, Columbus, Ga.; Penfield Baptist Church, Penfield, Ga.; First Baptist Church, Columbus, Ga.; Calvary Baptist Church, Madison, Ga.; Brown Chapel Baptist Church Monroe Co., Ga.; Smyrna Baptist Church, Morgan Co., Ga.; Haynesville First Baptist Church, Houston Co., Ga.

I mentioned the body of churches to show the first churches of color to be in the first black associations in Georgia. If you take notice of your home church, you should be very proud of your forefathers who attended these churches of honor. Make these accomplishments and struggles be made known to the generations of your family to come after them. We have a colorful and powerful history besides slavery in these United State of America. We have contributed in a great way to reestablish these United States in agriculture after the Civil War and many other attributes. We deserve accolades for our achievements and progress!

Rev. J. R. Willis, of Butts County Indian Springs Church, was invited to a seat in the association. He then presented and read Indian Springs Church letter which was received. The right hand of fellowship was then extended to all the new Churches that was admitted into the Association.

Sister Maria Fields presented the Friendship Church and Association with a silver cup, which was received with thanks.

On motion two Brethren were appointed to seat visitors and keep order.

Oral application of the First Baptist Church of Rome, Ga., was received with right hand of fellowship.

The Committee on Business made a report, which was read and recommitted.

The following Committees were appointed: On Sabbath Schools, on Destitute Churches, on Temperance, on Missions, on Resolutions, on State of the Churches, and on Instructions. The meeting then adjourned for one hour.

Afternoon Session, 2:00 p.m.

The meeting was opened with singing hymn 720.

Prayer by the Rev. Mr. Epps.

Roll call and reading of the minutes dispensed with.

Brother Thomas Hardrick made an oral application for Kiokia Church, which was received, with the right hand of fellowship.

There being no business before the Association several addresses were made by the members.

The next portion of the afternoon session I find Mr. Reverend Jesse Calloway (spelled Caloway).

It was a great surprise to find him in Atlanta two years before he would marry Abraham English and Dinah Hurt in Greene County in 1869. At this time he is in the Friendship Baptist Church in the First Ward of the county of Fulton. I wonder if he is alone in his travels to the city of Atlanta. I must say that the church is the focal point in the colored community at this time. It is just about the only social gathering that takes place outside of them working together in the fields, in the houses as maids and servants. I would say that it is the only place where the landowner does not watch over them. However, I cannot say that this statement is altogether true!

On motion a letter was read from Phillips Mills Church, Wilkes County, which was recommitted. The Committee on Preaching reported as follows: Saturday Evening—At Friendship Baptist Church, 7:00 p.m., Rev. E. B. Rucker Sunday—At 11:00 a.m., Rev. L. B. Carter; 3:00 p.m., Rev. Henry Watts; 8:00 p.m., Frank Beal.

At Mount Zion Baptist Church—At 11:00 a.m., Rev. Nathan Walker; 3:00 p.m., Rev. Thomas Allen; 8:00 p.m., Rev. Henry Morgan.

At the Second Methodist Church, on Summer Hill—at 3:00 p.m. Rev. J. C. Bryan.

At M. E. Church—at 8:00 p.m., Rev. Aaron Green.

At the Presbyterian Arbor—Rev. Jefferson Milner, Rev. Jesse Caloway, and Rev. George Brown.

A letter, addressed to the Northern Baptist Board of domestic Missions, U. S of America, by the Rev. James McDonald, requesting the Ebenezer Association to endorse it. On motion his request was granted. Adjourned to Monday morning at 9 o'clock.

Third Day's Session

Monday Morning, Sept. 9th, 9:00

The meeting was called to order by the Moderator, and opened with singing the 425th hymn, and prayer by Paul Brown. The roll was called; the Minutes read and approved. The following Committees reported: On Business; On Temperance; on Instruction; on Finances; on Sabbath Schools; on the State of the Churches; on Destitute Churches.

On motion carried that the Association suspend business for one hour in the afternoon session to hear addresses from Gen. Dunn, Gen. Lewis, and Mr. E. A. Ware, Superintendent Freedmen's Schools. The Executive Board made a Report, which was received and adopted. A resolution from G. H. Dwelle was read and adopted . . .

Ebenezer Baptist Association was held with Zion Church, in Marietta, Ga. on September 8th, 9th, 11th, and 12th. The Executive Committee was Rev. Henry Watts, Rev. Aaron Green, and Henry Jackson all of Augustus Georgia. Rev. J. C. Bryan and Deacon George H. Dwelle both of Americus, Georgia. Rev. Andrew Jackson, Rev. Thomas M. Allen and Deacon J. C. DeCatur all of Atlanta, Georgia. And Andrew Wilkinson of Burke, County Georgia.

The printing was done by Franklin Steam Printing House in Atlanta, Georgia with J. J. Toon as the Proprietor.

I do not know if the Ebenezer Baptist Association had conflict with the Georgia Baptist News Paper in Augusta with William Jefferson White or not. However, I know there is something wrong. Or maybe the White communities in

Atlanta want the colored business that is being generated by the Colored Baptist growth in Georgia.

Afternoon Session, 2:00 p.m.

Appointed brothers Bryan and Tate to count funds coming up in church letters. Read letters from Zion Church, Marietta—Rev. T. M. Allen, pastor, Samuel Minns, Dennis Williams, Richard Harvey, Reuben Bennett, delegates; Keokee Church, Columbia County, Ga.—Rev. Thomas Hardwick, pastor, David Youngblood, delegates; Springfield Church Greensboro, Ga.—Rev. Levi Thornton, pastor, Frank Massey delegates; Friendship Church, Walton County, Ga.—Rev. Joshua Henderson, pastor, Terrell Abecrombie, delegates

Mount Zion Church, Atlanta, Ga.—Rev. Owen George pastor, Rev. Charles Jones, Deacon Sims, delegates; Siloam Church, Union Point, Ga.—Rev. Levi Thornton pastor, William Alexander, Buck Daniels, delegates; Antioch Church, Rocky Creek, Burke County, Ga.—Rev. Andrew Wilkerson, pastor, Daniel Berrien, delegates; Zion Hill Church, Monroe, Walton County, Ga.—Rev. Richard Sorrels, pastor, delegate; Macedonia Church, Augusta, Ga..—Rev. Aaron Green, pastor, delegate; Central Church, Augusta, Ga.—rev. Henry Jackson, pastor, Tobby Lamar, William H. Tilmon, delegates

Forest Hill church, Burke County, Ga.—Rev. Andrew Wilkerson, pastor, delegate; Ebenezer Church, Burke County—Rev. Andrew Wilkerson, pastor, delegate; Weldon Springs, Baker County—no delegate, asking for dismission; Friendship Church Atlanta, Ga.—Rev. Frank Quarles, pastor, Orange Davis, Isaac C. DeCatur, David Anthony, George McKinnie, Sandford Coles, James Tate, Hillard Darden, delegates; New Salem Church, Mitchell County, Ga.—no delegate, asking for dismission; Poplar Head Church, McDuffie County, Ga.—Rev. Benjamin Grande, pastor, delegates

Bethesda Church, Americus, Ga.—Rev. J. C. Bryan, pastor, delegate; Penfield Church, Penfield Church, Penfield, Ga.—Rev. Felix Sanders, pastor, delegate; Bethesda Church, Stone Mountain, Ga.—Rev. Andrew Jackson, pastor, Alex Potts, delegates; Springfield Church, Rock Hill, Oglethorpe County, Ga.—Rev. Felix Sanders, pastor, delegate; Mount Pleasant Church, McDuffie County, Ga.—Rev. T. M. Allen, delegate; Springfield Church, Augusta, Ga.—Rev. Henry Watts, pastor, William

Mathews, delegates; Macedonia Church, Starksville, Butts County, Ga.—Rev. James Heard, pastor, John Davis, delegates; Indian Springs Church, Butts County, Ga.—Rev. Richard Backston, pastor, Joseph Byars, delegates; Mount Pleasant Church, Dekalb County, Ga.—Rev. Mathews Mitchel, pastor, Jacob Austin, Matthew Hamons, delegates; First Church, Albany, Ga.—no delegate, asking for dismission.

In this session they appointed brothers J. C DeCatur and Rev. Robert Epps to attend the balloting for moderator and clerk. The Rev. Frank Quarles, Atlanta, was elected moderator, and George H. Dwell, Americus, was elected clerk.

Second Day's Session

Rev. William J. White was invited to a seat in the Association. Read letters from Hill's First Baptist church, Athens, Ga.—Rev. Floyd Hill, pastor,; New Concord Church, Jasper county, Ga.—Rev. Cezar Hendrick, pastor,--McDowell, delegates; Bethlehem Church, Covington, Ga.—Rev. Toney Baker, pastor, delegate; Harmony Church, Oglethorpe County, Ga.—Rev. Felix Sanders, pastor, delegate; Union Church, Jefferson, County Ga.—Rev. Daniel Rosier, pastor, George Rosier, delegates; Bear Camp Church, Burke County, Ga.—Rev. Daniel Rosier, pastor, delegate; Friendship church, Cobb County—Rev. John Moore, pastor, delegate.

These are the churches that applied for membership. Fifteen churches applied in 1871.

Piney Grove Church, Emanuel County, Ga.—Rev. Daniel Rosier, Delegate; Cumming Grove Church, Richmond County, Ga.—Rev. Henry Morgan, delegate

Mount Pleasant Church, Atlanta, Ga.—Rev. Andrew Jackson pastor, delegate

Randolph Church, Greene County, Ga.—Rev. Samuel Sanders, pastor, Joseph Fulton, delegates

Friendship Church, Lexington, Ga.—Rev. Floyd Hill, pastor, A. L. Brown, delegates; Mount Zion Church Buena Vista, Marion County, Ga.—Rev. Wyatt Bouldwin pastor, delegate

Macedonia Church, Atlanta, Ga.—Rev. George Harris, pastor, delegate

Rehoboth Church, Columbia County, Ga.—Rev. Thomas Hardwick, pastor, Thomas Cobb, delegates

Liberty Hill Church, Cobb County, Ga.—Rev. William Thomas, pastor, George Geisham, Moses Winkle, delegates

Bethel Church, Cobb County, Ga.—Rev. William Thomas Elisha Broadnax, delegates; New Hope Powder Springs, Cobb County, Ga.—Rev. Seaborn Rucker, pastor, delegate; Rock Springs Church, Henry County, Ga.—Rev. James Heard, pastor, Augustus Mansfield, delegates

Liberty Hill Church, Walton County, Ga.—Rev. Joshua Henderson, pastor, delegate; Morris Hill Church, Paulding County, Ga.—Rev. John Moore, pastor, Randal singleton, George Davis, delegates

Friendship Church, Cobb County, Ga.—Rev. John Moore, pastor, delegate

Read a report from Committee on applicant Letters, in regard to Calvary church letter, Madison, Ga.

Appointed a committee of nine to investigate the letter and matter in regard to it.

I wonder what is happening at the Calvary church in Madison that this prestigious organization would have to send a committee of nine to investigate!

Oh! Here is the situation that had unfolded concerning the pastor of the church.

The Committee of investigation of Calvary Church Letter made a report. Your Committee, appointed to investigate the matter in reference to the difficulty existing in relation to the Calvary Church, at Madison, Ga. after prayerfully considering the question and hearing all the testimony within our reach, beg leave to say that we are satisfied that brother Allen Clarke is exonerated of the charges made against him, and therefore recommend that the said church be restored into membership in this Association.

Read the letter of Calvary Church, Madison, Ga.—Rev. Allen Clark, pastor Alfred Gordon, Edmond Pace, Cyrus Hall, Henry Gautier, delegates. The right hand of fellowship was extended to the church. Read the report of the Committee on temperance:

Your Committee on temperance beg leave to report that intemperance is an evil that has already done, and is still doing, great harm among all classes of the people, and should therefore be frowned upon and encouraged by al the followers of Christ. Brethren, preach against the use of ardent spirits wherever you go. Wine is a mocker, raging, and they that are deceived thereby are not wise. Rev. Aaron Green, Samuel Minns, William Thomas, Wyatt Bauldwin, David Anthony.

William J. White made remarks advocating the Theological School at Augusta, Ga. and Henry Watts in regard to the same stating that Joseph T. Roberts, LL.D. was in charge of the school. In this same year Rev. Frank Quarles was at the Consolidated Baptist Convention at Wilmington N. C. "I call the Ebenezer Baptist Association the mother of Associations for Coloreds." A lot of associations branched off the Ebenezer and started their own.

In the year of 1872 the Ebenezer Assoc. held its session with Bethesda Baptist Church in Americus, Ga. and the only Officers were Frank Quarles of Atlanta as the moderator and George H. Dwelle of Americus as the Clerk. The printing was still done by the Franklin Steam Printing house in Atlanta. Six churches applied for membership.

Pleasant Grove, Atlanta—Rev. Robert Epps, pastor, delegate; Cedar Creek, Schley County—Rev. Wyatt Baldwin, pastor, Andrew Ellison, delegates; St. Paul, Oglethorpe county—Rev. Floyd Hill pastor, delegate; Barber's Creek, Clark County—Rev. Floyd Hill, pastor and delegate; New Bethlehem Church, Oglethorpe County—Rev. A. L. Brown, pastor, delegate. Right hand of fellowship extended delegates of New Churches.

There were several visiting white ministers that attended one such minister was the Rev. Geo. F. Cooper, pastor of the Americus, and corresponding delegate from Friendship Association, invited. He addresses the association on African Mission.

Rev. J. S. White, pastor of Presbyterian Church, invited us all to sit in their midst. The report on education was that it is much neglected in some parts of the state. And that every encouragement be given by each and every one for the institutions now under consideration by the Missionary Baptist Convention of the State of Georgia. As it is of great and vital importance that our people be educated, and more especially the ministers of the Gospel, as we find much need among those that are chosen to carry the word of God, and they that preach the Gospel must know the Gospel. They focused on missions in their association. And the state of the churches was that the north and east Georgia churches belonging to this association are all in good condition and doing well. But in other parts of the state they are not doing so well. So you can see the where the greater influence was coming from as far as the money and the affluent membership lies because of their wealthier white landowners that resided in the north and in the eastern section of Georgia!

Churches Dismissed from the Association

Friendship, Cobb County; Poplar Head, Columbia County; Calvary, Madison County; St. Peter's Rock, Monroe County; Liberty Cobb County; Morris Hill, Paulding County; Brown Church Monroe County; Mars Hill, Monroe County; Fellowship, Walton County; Mt. Zion, Monroe County, Siloam, Union Point; Springfield, Greensboro; Mt. Pleasant, Thompson; Covington Baptist Church, Covington

These are some of the colored churches that went on to start associations that were located much closer to where they lived.

The Atlanta Sunday Herald

Atlanta Ga., Sunday February 9, 1873

No. 138

Minor Topics Section:

Can we not organize a Jockey Club in Atlanta and revive the love of racing once so prevalent here? It does appear as if there ought to be enough men in our midst of standing and means who could place such an organization on a firm footing. We know well enough that there are strong objections to racing on the part of church members and no doubt. Atlanta is the most pious city in Georgia, still we think that a sufficient number of "worldly" persons can be found to make a very respectable Jockey Club, and enable us to enjoy almost the only exiting pastime which our inland situation affords us. What do you think, Mr. O. H. Jones?

I had to input this tidbit of information here because these are the few rich landowners in Atlanta and Coweta County that could live in such a lifestyle while others struggled and would be eventually left out of the economic growth after the Civil War! The Jones family that branched out from the eastern early land grants of the 1790s after the American Revolution, like so many, would have their hands in every social change in Georgia!

In the year of 1874 the Ebenezer held its session with the Friendship Baptist Church in Atlanta, Georgia on the 11th thru to the 15th of September, 1874.

This session is held in the famous section of Atlanta called the First Ward. Vine City is located here where the Historical Famous Black Colleges will come to reside and the elite of he White community would move on to Dekalb County and Northeast Atlanta.

Services started at 10:00 a.m. Rev. Floyd Hill, the founder of Hills Chapel in Athens, Clarke County, did the devotional services.

Read Letters from—

Friendship Church, Atlanta, Ga.—Rev. Frank Quarles, Pastor, H. Darden, James Tate, J. H. Delamotta, Peter Ethridge, C. S. Johnson, John Carter, J. C.C. DeCatur, H. E. Baldwin, Geo. McKinnie, delegates

Bethesda, Americus, Ga.—Rev. J.C. Bryan, Pastor, Robert Breedlove, delegate

Cumming Grove, Richmond County, Ga.—Rev. Henry Morgan, Pastor, and delegate

Central Augusta, Ga.—Rev. Henry Jackson, Pastor, Peter Battey, delegate

New Hope, Jasper County, Ga.—Rev. James Heard, Pastor, Mac McDowell, delegate

Springfield, Augusta, Ga.—Rev. Henry Watts, Pastor, Thos. McMurphey, F. P. Johnson, delegates

Ebenezer, Burke County, Ga.—Rev. Reuben Scott, Pastor, Hiram Frazier, delegate

Pleasant Grove, Douglass County, Ga.—Rev. C. B. Rucker, Pastor, W.W. Dobbs, delegates

Macedonia, Augusta, Ga.—Rev. Aaron Green, Pastor, and delegate

Friendship, Lexington, Ga.—Rev. A. L. Brown, Pastor and delegate

New Bethlehem, Oglethorpe County, Ga.—Rev. E. D. Jennings, Pastor, A. R. Davenport, delegate

Shady Grove, Clarke County, Ga.—Rev. Thos. Morse, Pastor, Ned Haygood, Early Anthony, delegates

Pine Grove, McDuffie County, Ga.—Rev. Benjamin Greneade, Pastor, Anderson McGender, delegate

Springfield, Monticello, Ga.—Rev. George W. Talley, Pastor, Henry Freeman, delegate

Newberry, Lincoln County, Ga.—Rev. Benjamin Harrison, Pastor and delegate

Stone Mountain, Dekalb County, Ga.—Rev. Richard Burson, Pastor, T. J. Brandon, H. Johnson, E. Turner, J. W. Scott, M. Harrison, delegates

*Zion Hill, Atlanta, Ga.—Robert Grant, Pastor, G. Dobbins, delegate

**This is the first time that Zion Hill Baptist church shows up in the Ebenezer Baptist Assoc. I don't know if Rev. Grant is the founder of the Zion Hill Baptist Church. However, I assume that Grant might be off the Plantation of Mr. Grant who donated land for Grant Park and donated land for Mount Zion in Atlanta as well. Another name that will come to be connected to the Hurt and Callaway house in Greene County will be Mr. J. T. Johnson. The same name J. T. Johnson will become the pastor of Zion Hill in the community of Johnsontown near the Lenox Square Mall the same mall where the Rich Black Hip Hop Moguls shop and cruse.*

Macedonia, Butts County, Ga.—Rev. John Davis Pastor, L. M. Walthal, delegates

*Mount Zion, Atlanta, Ga.—Rev. Owen George, Pastor, James Thornton, J. H. Harper, Floyd Finch, Moses Ponder, Sterling Watts, delegates.

**I do not know if Mr. Finch is the first colored State Rep. of Georgia and is attending Mount Zion.*

Mount Zion, Oglethorpe County, Ga.—Rev. Dock Finley, Pastor and delegate

Liberty Hill, Cobb County, Ga.—Rev. William Thomas, Pastor, W. P. Butler, Joseph Grisham, delegates

Mount Moriah, Appling, Columbia County, Ga.—Rev. Thomas Hardrick, Pastor, Elvin Doggett, Simon D'Antignac, delegate.

Hill First Baptist Church, Athens, Clarke County, Ga.—Rev. Floyd Hill, Pastor, Henry Horton, delegate

Macedonia, Atlanta, Ga.—Rev. Jerry M. Jones, Pastor, Douglass Craddock, Thomas Foster, Amos Weaver, Jacob Chapman, delegates

Corinth, Sumter County Ga.—Rev. David Gates, Pastor, no delegates

Randolph, Greene County, Ga.—rev. Samuel Sanders Pastor, Joseph Fulton, delegate

*Harmony, Maxey's, Ga.—Samuel Sanders Pastor and delegate

**Here is Harmony Church in Maxey which later is called Harmonia right in the mist of Aaron Callaway, and every Maxey citizens both black and white in the town of Maxey. This is the same place where you find Robert Callaway residing in 1880!*

Zion, Marietta, Ga.—Rev. Thomas M. Allen, Pastor, Chas. Thomas, Reuben Bennett, James Julian, Boston Coleman, Buck Thomas, delegates

*Pleasant Grove, Atlanta, Ga.—Rev. Robert Epps, Pastor, Benjamin Wright, delegate

**With the last name of Benjamin Wright, I wonder if he is any kin to Rev. Wright who is the pastor of Little Mount Olive on Maple Street in Vine City. Also, could it be that Little Mount Olive could have been at one time named Pleasant Grove?*

St. Paul Louisville, Jefferson County, Ga.—Rev. Andrew Wilkerson, Pastor, Dennis Ponder, delegate

New Hope—Rev. E. D. Jennings, Pastor and delegate

*Springfield, Oglethorpe County, Ga.—Rev. Wm. Tyler Pastor, no delegates

**Now here is a last name that I am very much interested in and it is Mr. Wm. Tyler the pastor of the Springfield Church in Oglethorpe County the same church that Rev. Silas Johnson would come to pastor. The reason that I am interested in Mr. Tyler is that it was Henderson Tyler the only lone colored man, alone with these White men, Felix T. Pitman, P. B. Johnson, H. H. Crenshaw, and R. H. Mathews charging Aaron with stealing a watermelon and trespassing onto Mr. Felix T. Pitman Property in Bowling Green in Oglethorpe County near the Springfield Baptist Church in 1884. This relationship between Mr. Henderson Tyler might show the relationship that Rev. William Tyler has with Mr. Pitman in the colored community that would charge Aaron with this offence. Mr. H. C. Tuck was Aarons Attorney and got him out of this situation.*

Forest Hill—Rev. Reuben Scott, Pastor, Nathan Wilkerson delegate

Mount Olive, Cherokee County, Ga.—Rev. William Thomas, Pastor, David Durham, delegate

Poplar Head, McDuffie County, Ga.—Rev. Benjamin Grenade, Pastor, Austin Brashaw, delegate

Antioch, Burke County, Ga.—Rev. Thomas Martin, Pastor, Daniel Berrien, delegate

Mount Pleasant, Atlanta, Ga.—Rev. Andrew Jackson, Pastor, R. Hall, J. Fowler, A. L. Bryant, Wm. Murphy, M. H. Bird, delegates

Jones Chapel, Jackson County, Ga.—Rev. Joseph Dowdy, Pastor, Geo. Hood, Ben Stevens, delegates

St. Paul, Oglethorpe, Ga.—Rev. Thomas Moore, Pastor, Wm. Henson delegate

Poplar Springs, Jackson County, Ga.—Rev. J. D. Dowdy, Pastor, James Jordan, Mac Rakestraw, delegates

Barber's Creek, Jackson County, Ga.—Rev. Adam Bell, Pastor, Squire Smith, Randal Craft, delegates

Lebanon, Sumter County, Ga.—Rev. Eli Smith, Pastor, D. T. Tatum, delegate

Providence, Atlanta, Ga.—Rev. W. M. Graham, Pastor, Warren Jones, W. Knox, delegates

Zion, Paulding County, Ga.—Rev. C. B. Rucker, Pastor and delegate

New Hope, Powder Springs—Rev. C. B Rucker, Pastor, Wm. Ashby, delegate

Penfield Church, Greene County—Rev. Young Partee, Pastor, Jerry Jennings, delegate

Bethel, Cobb County—Rev. Wm. Thomas, Pastor, John Burney, delegate

Rev. Allen Clark shows up and represents the New Hope Association and he is the moderator.

There were eleven new churches that joined the Ebenezer Association at this time. Some of these churches no longer exist later on as I do my research. However, they might have just changed their names or changed locations or even associations.

Catalogue of the Atlanta Baptist Seminary

Atlanta, Georgia, for the Year 1880–81

Atlanta, Georgia: 1881

376.75 At6

Historical Note

The Augusta Institute, at the desire of the colored brethren, and with the approval of the white, was removed to the Capital of the state, and its name was changed to The Atlanta Baptist Seminary. An eligible lot of about four aces was purchased, and a commodious brick building erected at the junction of Elliott and West Hunter Streets. The Georgia Missionary Baptist Convention co-operates with the American Baptist Home Mission Society in supporting the Seminary.

Instructors

President

Rev. Joseph T. Robert, LL.D.

General Assistants

Rev. David Shaver, D. D.

William R. Raymond, A. B.

Student Assistant

*William E. Holmes

Acting Librarian

Rev. Joseph A. Walker

Janitor

* Nathan Benjamin

*Licensed preachers

Calendar for the Year 1881–82

The Session lasts eight months

The First Term begins Monday, October 3, 1881

The First Term closes Thursday, December 22, 1881

Vocation of nine days

The Second Term begins Tuesday, January 3, 1882

The second Term closes May 31, 1882

The Exercises of the Institution are suspended on Thanksgiving Day, Washington's Birthday, Commemoration Day

For further information address the President,
Rev. Joseph T. Robert, LL.D. Atlanta, Ga.

Local Board of Trustees
J.H. LOW Esq. Chairman
Sidney Root, Esq., Secretary
Rev. J. H. Devotie, D. D.
Rev. W.J. White
Rev. F. Quarles

Committee of Examination and Oversight
Rev. J. T. Robert, Ll.D., Chairman
Rev. D. Shaver, D. D., Secretary
Rev. H. C. Hornady
Rev. F. M. Daniel
Rev. F. Quarles

Students from 1871 to 1881

The following list of students embraces all who have been connected with the Augusta Institute and the Atlanta Baptist Seminary, since August 1, 1871, when Dr. Robert took charge. He found no records prior to that date.

Name	Post Office
Allen, J. A.	Elberton, Ga.
Allen, Wm. M.	Athens, Ga.
Alexander, John E.	Herndon, Ga.
*Amos, A. G.	Brunswick, Ga.
Anderson, Benjamin	Waynesboro, Ga.
*Anderson, Charles	Allendale, S.C.
*Appling, Alexander	Hamburg, S. C.
*Arrington, Gilford	Augusta, Ga.
*Ashmore, Marshall	Columbia, Co, Ga.

*Baker, James A.	Atlanta, Ga.
*Barnes, Paul	Augusta, Ga.
*Battie Robert C.	Augusta, Ga.
*Beall, F. F.	Augusta, Ga.
*Beard, Thomas P.	Augusta, Ga.
Belcher, E.	Augusta, Ga.
Belcher, T. R.	Augusta, Ga.
t Bell, Florence	McDuffie, Co, Ga.
*Bell, Job	McDuffie Co., Ga.
Bell, Richard	Columbia Co., Ga.
Bell, Berren	Waynesboro, Ga.
*Benjamin, Nathan	White Plains, Ga.

*Ministerial Student t Deceased

Name	Post Office
Bentley, Edward	Aiken, S. C.
*Benton, Simpson	Augusta, Ga.
Bettis, Alexander	Edgefield, S. C.
Bins, Robert	Washington, Ga.
*Blair, Alfred,	Summerville, Ga.
*Blair, Jacob	Appling, Ga.
Boatner, Daniel W.	Herndon, Ga.
*Bohler, James	Camilla, Ga.
*Borders, B.	Stone Mountain, Ga.
Brandon, J. S.	Atlanta, Ga.
*Brewster, Henry	Augusta, Ga.
*Brightharp, Charles H.	Warrenton, Ga.
Brinkley, J. C.	Aiken, S. C.
Brodie, John C.	Lexington, Ga.
*Brown, Anderson L.	Lincoln, Ga.
*Brown, George	Atlanta, Ga.

Brown, George F.	Albany, Ga.
*Brown, George W.	Screven Co., Ga.
*Brown, Isham	Stellaville, Ga.
Brown, John H.	Haynesville, Ga.
*Brown, John S.	Montezuma, Ga.
*Bryant, John O.	Summerville, Ga.
Bugg, James H.	Augusta, Ga.
*Buoey, Harrison N.	Augusta, Ga.
Burson, G. Bartow	Stone M'ntain, Ga.
*Butler, Elijah	Warrenton, Ga.
*Butler, John C.	Edgefield, S. C.
*Byrd, Alfred	Stellaville, Ga.
Byrd, Henry M.	Berzelia, Ga.
*Byrd, Mark	Greenesboro, Ga.
Callaway, Jesse R.	Penfield, Ga.
Campfield, Mack C.	Augusta, Ga.
*Carter, Allison	Appling, Ga.
*Carter, Edward R.	Athens, Ga.
*Cassey, Arthur C.	Atlanta, Ga.
*Cassey, James	Augusta, Ga.
Chatters, O. R.	Milledgeville, Ga.

Name	Post Office
Clark, R. T.	Americus, Ga.
Clark, Rufus.	Stellaville, Ga.
Clayton, John Howard	Marietta, Ga.
*Clemons, Wm. R.	Eatonton, Ga.
Cobb, Frank E.	Augusta, Ga.
Cobb, Francis L.	Augusta, Ga.
Coles, Lemon S.	Atlanta, Ga.
Coles, Robert	Augusta, Ga.
Collier, Robert	Augusta, Ga.

Collins, Sim	Thomson, Ga.
*Conyers, Joseph F.	Atlanta, Ga.
Cooper, Alexander	Augusta, Ga.
*Cooper, Moses	Alexander, Ga.
Copeney, Marion F.	Augusta, Ga.
*Cornelius, Arthur	Pine Ridge, Ga.
*Cornelius, Sandy	Macon, Ga.
*Culpepper, Abner	Warrenton, Ga.
Culpepper, Charles	Warrenton, Ga.
Cumming, Joseph	Augusta, Ga.
*Cumming Julius	Augusta, Ga.
*Danford, Cogie	Beech Island, S. C.
Daniel, M. Z.	Atlanta, Ga.
*D'Antignac, Amos L.	Stellaville, Ga.
*Davenport, Arthur	Lexington, Ga.
Davis, David	Bartow, Ga.
*Davis, Jessie	Stellaville, Ga.
*Davy, Henry	Columbia, Co. Ga.
*Douse, William	Augusta, Ga.
*Drane, Lewis	Augusta, Ga.
Drayton, Henry	Beech Island, S. C.
Dunbar, Anderson	Millett, S. C.
Dunbar, Edward	Millett, S. C.
Dye, William E.	Eureka, Mills, Ga.
Early, J. C.	LaGrange, Ga.
Early, J. T.	LaGrange, Ga.
*Echols, P.	Lexington, Ga.
Echols, S.	Lexington, Ga.
Echols, W. B.	Lexington, Ga.

Names	Post Office
Grenade, Samuel	Thomson, Ga.

*Grinage, George	Lincoln Co., Ga.
Hall, Jerry M.	Atlanta, Ga.
*Hammond, Johnson	Edgefield, S. C.
*Hampton, Wade	Millettville, S. C.
Hanson, Edward	Lexington, Ga.
Hardwick, Thomas	Appling, Ga.
Harper, John,	Atlanta, Ga.
Harper, Thomas	Augusta, Ga.
*Harris, Wesley	Warrenton, Ga.
*Harrison, Benjamin	Appling, Ga.
Hart, James	Pope Hill, Ga.
Hart, Moses	Stellaville, Ga.
Harvey, James	Centerville, Ga.
Hawkins, J.H.	Thomson, Ga.
Haynes, Raymond	Glascock Co., Ga.
Haynes, Stephen	Warrenton, Ga.
*Hill, E. S.	Atlanta, Ga.
*Hill, J. W.	Augusta, Ga.
*Hill, Samuel,	Beech Island, S. C.
Holliman, Frank	Thomson, Ga.
Holliman, Orange	Hamburg, S. C.
*Holmes, C. G.	Madison, Ga.
*Holmes, Elias P.	Atlanta, Ga.
*Holmes, William E.	Augusta, Ga.
*Holsey, H. L.	Augusta, Ga.
Hudson, William R.	Warrenton, Ga.
*Hutchinson, David S.	Augusta, Ga.
*Ingram, Linton	Crawfordville, Ga.
*Irvine, Alexander	Hephzibah, Ga.
*Ivey, William	Augusta, Ga.
Jackson, Adams	Newton, Ga.
*Jackson, Henry	Augusta, Ga.

Jefferson, John H.	Augusta, Ga.
Jenkins, Phillip J.	Augusta, Ga.
Jenning, Eugene	Augusta, Ga.
Johnson, Ackert	Augusta, Ga.
*Johnson, Arthur A.	Augusta, Ga.

Names	Post Office
Johnson, Augustus R.	Augusta, Ga.
Johnson, A. S.	Augusta, Ga.
Johnson, Charles J.	Augusta, Ga.
Johnson, Cornelius S.	Augusta, Ga.
Johnson, Francis, P.	Augusta, Ga.
*Johnson, Gad S.	Augusta, Ga.
*Johnson, Green	Raytown, Ga.
Johnson, Gilford,	Hephzibah, Ga.
Johnson, Henry	Augusta, Ga.
*Johnson, Silas	Woodville, Ga.
Johnson, W. D.	Augusta, Ga.
*Johnson, Walker	Augusta, Ga.
*Jones, Boston	Johnston, S. C.
*Jones, C. O.	Atlanta, Ga.
Jones, Erasmus	Augusta, Ga.
*Jones, Henry M.	Elberton, Ga.
*Jones, J. M.	Atlanta, Ga.
Jones, J. W.	Madison, Ga.
*Jones, Prince	McBean Station, Ga.
*Jones, Richard	Allendale, S. C.
*Jones, Zacharias A.	Columbus, Ga.
*Jowers, John H.	Barnwell, S. C.
*Keebler, Isaac	Augusta, Ga.
Keith, Robert	Augusta, Ga.
Keller, Richard	Opelika, Ala.

Kelsey, A. T.	Warrenton, Ga.
*Kelsey, Robert	Millen, Ga.
*Kenner, Richard	Woodland, S. C.
*Key, Eli	Edgefield, S. C.
*Killgo, Levi W.	Rome, Ga.
*Lacy, Thomas	Augusta, Ga.
Ladevese, John	Augusta, Ga.
*Lanier, Joseph	Macon, Ga.
*Lark, Antony, N.	Silverton, S. C.
Lark, Nicholas H.	Silverton, S. C.
*Lawson, Andrew	Augusta, Ga.
Lawson, Solomon	Washington, Ga.
Lee, Moses C.	Appling, Ga.

Names	Post Office
*Lee, John H.	Warrenton, Ga.
Lewis, Andrew T.	Augusta, Ga.
Lewis, Andrew	Washington, Ga.
*Lewis, Gideon L.	Beech Island, S. C.
*Lewis, Thomas C.	Augusta, Ga.
*Lindsay, Richard	Hamburg, S. C.
*Love, Emanuel K.,	Marion, Ala.
*Love, Thornton V.	Marion, Ala.
*Lyons, Collins H.	Marion, Ala
Lyons, Judson W.	Augusta, Ga.
Mackey, Levi	Senoia, Ga.
*Maddox, Alexander	Columbia, S. C.
*Maddox, Matthew J.	Augusta, Ga.
McAlvie, Lewis	Augusta, Ga.
McCrary, Wesley D.	Barnett, Ga.
McCrary, Moses P.	Barnett, Ga.
McCrary, J. H.	Buena Vista, Ga.

*McHorton, Daniel	Butler Creek, Ga.
McIntosh, Seaborn	Elberton, Ga.
*McNeal, Samuel A.	Augusta, Ga.
Mapp, R. W.	White Plains, Ga.
*Mapp, W. J.	White Plains, Ga.
Martin, Seaborn C.	Augusta, Ga.
*Mathew, Luke	Augusta, Ga.
*Maxwell, Anthony R. W.	Station 3, C. R. R.
*Mims, John H.	Augusta, Ga.
*Mitchell, G. B.	Augusta, Ga.
Mitchell, Mall	Kieta, Ga.
Moody, Jerry	Greenesboro, Ga.
Moore, Nathaniel	Smyrna, Ga.
*Morgan, George A.	Edgefield, Ga.
*Morgan, Henry	Edgefield, Ga.
Morris, Ben	Thomson, Ga.
Morris, Calvary	Warrenton, Ga.
*Morton, Simon	Columbia, Co., Ga.
*Mosley, Harvey	Augusta, Ga.
*Murden, Derry	Crawfordville, Ga.
Nelson, William	Augusta, Ga.

Name	Post Office
Norris, Luke Bonnah	Warrenton, Ga.
Nun, Alexander	Gibson, Ga.
Parker, F. H.	Augusta, Ga.
*Parker James	Hephzibah, Ga.
Parker, Jerry	Summerville, Ga.
Payne, Robert	Augusta, Ga.
*Pearce, Frank	Augusta, Ga.
Pearce, Miles, C.	Effingham Co., Ga.
*Penn, Alexander	Smyrna, Ga.

*Peterson, William	Edgefield, S. C.
*Phillips, John G.	Aiken, S. C.
*Philpot, Adam	Augusta, Ga.
*Pope, Mark	Waynesboro, Ga.
Pope, Simpson	Waynesboro, Ga.
Powns, Reesen	Thomson Ga.
*Ramsey, Simeon W.	Lincoln Co., Ga.
*Rice, Luther	McDuffie, Ga.
*Richard, Dolphus	Thomson, Ga.
* Roach, Anthony	Augusta, Ga.
*Robinson, Alexander	Millettville, S. C.
*Robinson, James	Augusta, Ga.
Robinson, L.	
*Robinson, T. M.	Atlanta, Ga.
Robinson, Tony	Gum Creek, Ga.
*Rosier, S. D.	Midville C. R. R.,
*Roundfield, James	Augusta, Ga.
*Rouse, Daniel	Ellington, S. C.
*Royals, J. H.	Vienna, Ga.
*Russell, John T.	Augusta, Ga.
*Russell, J. S.	Waynesboro, Ga.
*Russell, Martin, V.	Waynesboro, Ga.
*Russell, Peter S.	Waynesboro, Ga.
Sanders, Felix	Penfield, Ga.
*Sanders, Sandy	Millettville, S. C.
*Sapp, Fane C.	Alexander, Ga.
*Saxon, George	Blackville, S. C.
*Scott, Thomas	Atlanta, Ga.
*Simmons, F. M.	Perry, Ga.

Names	Post Office
Simmons, Henry L	Augusta, Ga.

*Simpson, Crawford	Americus, Ga.
*Sims, T. H.	Newnan, Ga.
Singleton, Constantine	Augusta, Ga.
Smith, Alonzo	Atlanta, Ga.
Smith, A. P.	Woodville, Ga.
Smith, Greene	Barrett, Ga.
Smith, Hampton	Waynesboro, Ga.
Smith, John W.	Lexington, Ga.
Smith, Richard	Appling, Ga.
*Smith, Warner	Palmetto, Ga.
*Smith, William F.	
Snowden, George B.	Augusta, Ga.
Soloman, Sampson	Washington, Ga.
*Staley, Alfred S.	Perry, Ga.
*Stanley, Greene	Woodville, Ga.
Starks, Cornelius	Lincoln Co., Ga.
Starks, J. A.	Edgefield, S. C.
*Stewart, W. W.	Crawfordville, Ga.

Names	Post Office
*Stinson, A. J.	Rome, Ga.
*Stinson, S. L.	Rome, Ga.
*Street, John	Gum Creek, Ga.
Sullivan, William H.	Augusta, Ga.
*Swanson, Alexander	LaGrange, Ga.
*Swilling, A. J.	Ruckersville, Ga.
*Tate, William	Washington, Ga.
*Thomas, Aaron	Columbia, Co., Ga.
*Thomas, Walter	Stellaville, Ga.
Thomas, J. T.	Atlanta, Ga.
Thomas, Levi	
Thornton, Jesse T.	Atlanta, Ga.

*Thornton, Levi	Greenesboro, Ga.
*Tilman, William H. Jr.	Augusta, Ga.
*Tolbert, J. T.	Augusta, Ga.
*Truett, Alexander	Lawtonville, S. C.
*Turman, James	Elbert Co., Ga.
*Turner, Calvin	Augusta, Ga.
*Turner, Henry	Crawfordville, Ga.
*Turner, Thomas	Augusta, Ga.
Verden, James H.	Atlanta, Ga.
Walker, Charles H.	Bartow, Ga.
*Walker, Charles T.	Hephzibah, Ga.
Walker, J. D.	Warrenton, Ga.
*Walker, Jerry	Lincoln Co., Ga.
*Walker, Joseph A.	Hephzibah, Ga.
*Walker, Nathan	McBean Sta., Ga.
*Walker, Nelson	Augusta, Ga.
Walker, Peter C.	Bartow, Ga.
*Walker, Peter	Hephzibah, Ga.
*Ware, Decatur	Rome, Ga.
*Washington, George	Newton, Ga.
*Washington, W. M.	Rome, Ga.
*Waterman, N. W.	Thomasville, Ga.
*Watts, Henry	Augusta, GA.
*Watson, Augustus W.	Jefferson, Co., Ga.
*Way, Henry	Hawkinsville, Ga.
Wells, Jonas	Davisboro, Ga.
*Wells, Frank	Flowery Branch, Ga.
*Whatley, H.	White Plains, Ga.
*White, Ephraim V.	Thomson, Ga.
White, George D.	Augusta, Ga.
*White, Henry M.	Augusta, Ga.
*White, William J.	Augusta, Ga.

Whitmore, J. B.	Sparta, Ga.
*Wiggins, Moses	Warrenton, Ga.
*Wilkins, Cyrus, S.	Beech Island, S. C.
*Williams, Henry	Augusta, Ga.
*Williams, Frank D.	Warrenton, Ga.
*Williams, Jefferson	Beech Island, S. C.
*Williams, Lewis	Washington, Ga.
Williams, A.E.	Warrenton, Ga.,
Williams, Harry M.	Washington, Ga.
*Williams, Robert S.	Stellaville, Ga.
Williamson, N. B.	Athens, Ga.
*Willis, Noble, Ga.	Augusta, Ga.
*Wimbish, D. J.	Greenville, Ga.
Woods, Jones	Barrett, Ga.
*Wright, Alexander S.	Stellaville, Ga.
*Wright, Jackson	Macon, Ga.
Wright, James	Camak, Ga.
Wyley, George	Hephzibah, Ga.
Yancey, William	Stellaville, Ga.
*Young, Chas. A.	Stellaville, Ga.
*Young, Alfred	Stellaville, Ga.
*Young, Joseph T.	Stellaville, Ga.

Summary

Number of enrolled students	371
Of this number there are ministerial students	225
Preparing for teaching	146

Calendar for the Year 1882–83

The Session Lasts Eight Months

The First Term Begins Monday, October 2, 1882

The First Term Closes Friday, December 22, 1882
Vocation of Ten Days
The Second Term Begins Tuesday, January 2, 1883
The Second Term Closes May 31, 1883

Rev. Joseph T. Robert, LL.D., Atlanta, Ga.

Faculty
President. Rev. Joseph T. Robert, LL.D.
Professors. William R. Raymond, A. B.
Ernest W. Clement, A. B.
Rev. William E. Holmes
Acting Librarian. Rev. Joseph A. Walker
Janitor *Nathan Benjamin
*Licensed Preacher
Local Board of Trustees
J. H. Low Esq. Chairman
Sidney Root, Esq., Secretary
Rev. J. H. DeVotie, D. D.
Rev. W. J. White
t Rev. F. Quarles

Committee of Examination and Oversight
Rev. J. T. Robert, LL. D., Chairman
Rev. D. Shaver, D. D., Secretary
Rev. H. C. Hornady
Rev. F. M. Daniel
t Rev. F. Quarles

t Deceased

*Abercrombie, Terrell	Social Circle, Ga.
*Adams, Albert	Atlanta, Ga.
Allen, A. J.	Oak Bower, Ga.
Allen, W. M.	Athens, Ga.
*Anderson, J. H.	Birmingham, Ala.
*Baker, J. A.	Atlanta, Ga.
Baker, J. C.	Atlanta, Ga.
*Barnes, H. F.	Conyers, Ga.
*Battle, Julius	La Grange, Ga.
*Benjamin, N.	Atlanta, Ga.
*Beauford, S.	Eden Station, Ga.
*Bohler, James	Herndon, Ga.
*Borders, J. B.	Camilla, Ga.
Borders, S.B.	Camilla, Ga.
Brandon, J. S.	Stone Mountain, GA.
*Brightharp, C. H.	Augusta, Ga.
Brinkley, J.C.	Warrenton, Ga.
*Broadnax, S. S.	Lithonia, Ga.
*Broome, L. M.	La Grange, Ga.
Brown, G. F.	Atlanta, Ga.
Brown, John H.	Haynesville, Ga.
*Byrd, A. L.	Stellaville, Ga.
*Byrd, Mark	Mechanicsville, Ga.
Bugg, J. H.	Augusta, Ga.
Burson, F. B.	Atlanta, Ga.
*Carter, E. R.	Atlanta, Ga.
Clark, Augustus	Sumter, S. C.
*Clark, Brister	Hawkinsville, Ga.
Clark, R. T.	Americus, Ga.
*Clemonts, W. R.	Atlanta, Ga.
Cobb, W. H.	Social Circle, Ga.
Coles, L. S.	Atlanta, Ga.

Coles, S. A.	Atlanta, Ga.
*Crawford, Israel	Appling, Ga.
Crawford, J. E. D.	Atlanta, Ga.
Daniel, M. Z.	Atlanta, Ga.
*Davis, Jerry	Watkinsville, Ga.
*Delaney, M. E.	Eatonton, Ga.
Early, J. C.	Atlanta, Ga.
Early, J. T.	La Grange, Ga.
Ellington, P. A.	Crawfordville, Ga.
*Fisher, E. J.	La Grange, Ga.
*Fisher, Miles	La Grange, Ga.
Gilbert, J. W.	Augusta, Ga.
Gonder, O. T.	Warrenton, Ga.
*Goode, H. W.	Millett, S. C.
Goodwin, G. A.	Augusta, Ga.
*Graham, J. W.	Acworth, Ga.
Grant, A. L.	West Point, Ga.
*Grinage, George	Double Branches, Ga.
*Hall, Jeremiah,	Atlanta, Ga.
Harper, J. H.	Atlanta, Ga.
*Harris, J. W.	Warrenton, Ga.
*Haynes, Stephen	Warrenton, Ga.
Heard, J. D.	Atlanta, Ga.
*Heard, Larkin	Atlanta, Ga.
*Hill, E. S.	Atlanta, Ga.
*Hines, E. H.	Atlanta, Ga.
*Holland, W. J.	Jenkinsville, Ga.
*Holmes, C. G.	Madison, Ga.
Holyfield, Charles	Albany, Ala
Howard, William	Atlanta, Ga.
Hudson, W. R.,	Warrenton, Ga.

Hunt, R. Z.	Cummings, Ga.
Jackson, R. B.	Greensboro, Ga.
*Johnson, A. S.	Decatur, Ga.
*Johnson, W. G.	Hephzibah, Ga.
*Jones, A. P.	Perry, Ga.
Jones, J. W.	Madison, Ga.
Jones, Willie	Perry, Ga.
*Kellar, Richard	Atlanta, Ga.
*Lawson, Andrew	Augusta, Ga.
*Lee, John H.	Warrenton, Ga.
Lockhart, A. O.	Jonesboro, Ga.
Long, G. W.	Stone Mountain, Ga.
Long, T. R.	Newnan, Ga.
Mackey, Lm.	Senoia, Ga.
McCord, Milas	Long Cane, Ga.
McCrarey, M. P.	Barnett, Ga.
Martin, Hilliard	Madison, Ga.
Martin, Prince	Greenville, Ga.
Mitchell, J. J.	Americus, Ga.
Moore, Nathaniel	Smyrna, Ga.
Murden, G. W.	Woodville, Ga.
Norris, L. B.	Warrenton, Ga.
Parker, Mack	Jonesboro, Ga.
Potts, Ural	Long Cane, Ga.
*Ramsey, W.S.	Atlanta, Ga.
Riley, Lee W.	Perry, Ga.
*Roberts, Alexander	Crawfordville, Ga.
*Russell, J. S.	Waynesboro, Ga.
*Russell, M. V.	Waynesboro, Ga.
*Russell, P. S.	Waynesboro, Ga.
*Scott, Thomas	Toccoa, Ga.
*Staley, A. S.	Perry, Ga.

*Stewart, W. W.	Crawfordville, Ga.
*Tanner, C. C.	Stone Mountain, Ga.
Thomas, R. Lee	Kirkwood, Ga.
Towns, Johnny	Atlanta, Ga.
Turner, Spencer	Crawfordville, Ga.
Walker, George	Warrenton, Ga.
*Walker, J. A.	Augusta, GA.
Walker, J. D.	Warrenton, Ga.
Wallace, W. E.	Ellaville, Ga.
Walton, N. P.	Thomson, Ga.
Whitaker, George	West Point, Ga.
*Wilkins, C. S.	Louisville, Ga.
*Williamson, N. B.	Athens, Ga.
Williams, Charles	Camilla, Ga.
Wilson, J. H.	Atlanta, Ga.
Wilson, S.	Thomson, Ga.
*Winston, Charles	Conyers, Ga.

Ended on page 12 of the Atlanta Baptist Seminary for the year 1882–1883

Chapter Twelve

FROM THE SHARE CROPPING AND THE PLOW TO THE PULPIT AND CALLED TO CHANGE THEIR BLACK COMMUNITIES

Atlanta Baptist College, 1898 Section, Page 13, College Charter

Fourth Year in 1898 in the Atlanta Baptist College

Joseph T. Johnson, of Watkinsville Ga. was listed with Henry J. Barnett, of Athens

Jack L. Barnett, of Athens, Gardine L. Bell, of Watkinsville, Williams S. Belle, of Watkinsville, Griffith, B. Brawley of Darien, Lucus S. Durham of Athens, Daniel W. Cannon of Turin, Henry P. McClendon of Watkinsville, Sidney A. Scott of Sparta, George W. Smith of Riddleville, Charles H. Wardlaw of Greenwood, S.C.

The third year were William M. Armstrong of Shellman, James E. Brown of Shellman, Raymond H Carter of Atlanta, Henry Darden of Atlanta, John W. Eberhart of Athens, Rev. Burwell T. Harvey of Athens, Emmett

A. Henry of Shellman, Daniel Potts of Atlanta, Paul H. Weaver of Atlanta, Felton W. Wheeler of Kensington.

The second-year students were William D. Alexander of Hartwell, Issac C. Smith of Davisboro, and Isaac A. Thomas of Atlanta.

The first-year students were John Wesley Dobbs, of Atlanta, George Noble Glover of Atlanta, and Edgare G. Thomas of Lodrick.

The Theological Course students were Henry F. Barnes of Atlanta, Richard H. Burson of Atlanta, John B. Briscoe, of Lake Creek, John Y. Fambrough of Madison, William W. Floyd of Flippen, Alfred Gains of Plainville, William R. Gray of Charlotte, Lemual H. Henderson of Atlanta, Peter F. Hogans of Atlanta, Jones Kelsey of Atlanta, John T. Laster of Jones Mill, Newton T. Phillips of Atlanta, George A. Simmons of Henderson, William F. Strickland of Atlanta, John A. Trimble of Atlanta, and Pink C. Tuggle of Atlanta, and Adam D. Williams of Atlanta

In the Elementary English courses in class (A) was William Bryant of Atlanta, William Brooks of Quitman, and James H. Johnson of West Point

Class (B) Pheolian Evans of White Plains, Simon Hood of Jones Mill, Lonnie T. Jones of Doraville, Llewellyn Strange of Hartwell, Joseph Tysinger of Thunder

Class (C) James Dorsey of Atlanta, Pink Hickson of Atlanta, Green Lampkin of Eastman, Mansfield Nickols of Montezuma, Randall Sanders of Atlanta

Class (D) James E. Fisher of Atlanta, Arthur Gilmore of Atlanta, John Kelly of Norcross, Ellis West of Cuthbert, Alwyn Young of Atlanta

Class (E) Nimrod Arnold of Granville, Hugh Callaway of Atlanta, Eugene Cloud of Atlanta, John H. Curtis of Solomon, Elijah J. Fisher Jr. of Atlanta, A. B. Freeman of Atlanta, G. L. Herring of Rico, Lee R. Jones of Forsyth, Cornelius Mainor of Montezuma, James Martin of Atlanta, Victor Mathis of Atlanta, Cuba McLarin of Atlanta, Samuel Mpemba of Congo Free State Africa, D. M. Pyne, of Atlanta, Joseph Stephens of Atlanta, John Q. Swan of Garfield, Thomas Walls of Ripley, James Watson of Atlanta, Samuel A. Williams Jr. of Atlanta

Class (F) James Brooks of Atlanta, Benjamin Center of Lithonia, John Crocket of McDonough, F Rufus Davis of Atlanta, George Graham of Carrolton, Edward Grant of Atl, Charles Hickson of Atl, Jeriah Horton of Atl, Paul Howard of Atl, Edward Johnson of Atl. George Knuckles of Atl. John Love of Ralph, William Payne of Atl. John Roberts of Atl. Arizona Sims of Atl. John Thomas of Atl. Spelman R. Thomas of Atl. Scott Troy of Cooksville

Catalogue Atlanta Baptist Seminary Atlanta, Georgia 1886–7

Founded 1867, under the auspices of the American Baptist Home Mission Society

Atlanta, Georgia: Jas. P. Harrison & Co., Printers and Publishers 1887

Trustees

J. B. Hoyt, of Connecticut

J. H. DeVotie, D. D. of Georgia

E. Lathrop, D. D. of Connecticut

W. A. Cauldwell of New York

Rev. W. J. White of Georgia

Joseph Brokaw of New York

Sidney Root of Georgia

J. G. Johnson of New York

H.L. Morehouse, D. D. of New York

J. S. Lawton, M. D. of Georgia

Rev. W. H. Tilman of Georgia

Local Committee

Sidney Root

J. H. DeVotie, D. D.

J. S. Lawton, M. D.

Rev. W. J. White

Rev. W. H. Tilman

NB: The names of students pursuing studies in connection with more than one class will appear with that class in which they recite most. The names of such students as have in view the Christian ministry are marked thus (t) when occurring outside the Theological Department.

Theological Department

Full Course

Senior Class

Alfred J. Allen of Oak Bower, Hart Co.

Hardy Curry of Atlanta, Fulton Co.

Junior Class

Samuel Beauford of Eden Station, Effingham Co.

Samuel S. Broadnax of Lithonia, Dekalb Co.

Aaron B. Murden of Crawfordville, Taliaferro Co.

Jabez S. Russell of Augusta, Richmond Co.

Restricted Courses

James A. Baker of Atlanta, Fulton Co.

Pompey H. Butler of Savannah, Chatham Co.

David Dewberry of Forsyth, Monroe Co.

John B. Gibbs of Lithonia, Dekalb Co.

Robert Grant of Atlanta, Fulton Co.

Emanuel James of Atlanta, Fulton Co.

Charles O. Jones of Atlanta, Fulton Co.

Pournelle Lane of LaGrange, Troup Co.

George W. Martin of Atlanta, Fulton Co.
George Smith of Atlanta, Fulton Co.
Elbert Whaley of Thomasville, Thomas Co.

Preparatory Department
First Year
Mack C. Parker of Jonesboro, Clayton Co.
Francis B. Turner of Crawfordville, Taliaferro Co.

Elective Studies
John F. Bright of McKinny Ky.
Edward R. Carter of Atlanta, Fulton Co.

Fourth Year
James E. Brown of LaGrange, Troup Co.
Jerry M. Jones of Guyton, Effingham Co.
Ambrose M. Johnson of Appling, Columbia Co.
Jacob S. Kelsey of Wadley, Jefferson Co.
Levi M. Mackey of Senoia, Coweta Co.
John M Neal of Stone Mountain, DeKalb Co.
Edgar F. Pullum of Atlanta, Fulton Co.
Dower P. Rowe of Athens, Clarke Co.
Jerry R. Smith of Augusta, Richmond Co
Ephraim F. Smith Jr. of Kiokee, Columbia Co.
Thomas J. Turner of Stone Mountain, Dekalb Co.
Charles C. Winston of Conyers Rockdale Co.
Samuel T. Wilkins of Louisville, Jefferson Co.

Third Year
George H. Anderson of Eden Bryan Co.
Stephen H. Allen of Oak Bower, Hart Co.

John H. Avery of Clay Hill PO, McDuffie Co.
Robert L. Darden of Jones Mill, Meriwether Co.
Hezekiah H. Engram of Montezuma Macon Co.
Geo. W. Hill of Covington Newton Co.
John N. Jones of Perry, Houston Co.
Thomas C. Jones Jr. of Perry Houston Co.
David S. Klugh of Hodges, S. C.
Albert O. Lockhart of Jonesboro, Clayton Co.
Milton M. Mack of Thomasville, Thomas Co.
Hillard Marton of Madison, Morgan Co.
John H. Moore, Jones' Mills, Meriwether Co.
Carey L. Norflett of Warrenton, Warren Co.
John B. Richardson of Franklin, Heard Co.
Sheppard D. Rosier of Midville, Burke Co.
Robt. T. Schell of Atlanta, Fulton Co.
Henry T. Smith of Kiokee, Columbia Co.
William E. Wallace of Ellaville, Schley Co.
William Wynn, of Barnett, Warren Co.

Second Year
John O. Adams of Henderson, Houston Co.
John Thomas Banks of Forsyth, Monroe Co.
Henry F. Barnes of Atlanta, Fulton Co.
Jesse S. Bivins of Atlanta, Fulton Co.
John W. Center of Lithonia, Dekalb Co.
David D. Crawford of ——
Mount Z. Daniels of Atlanta, Fulton Co.
Charles S. Day of Social Circle, Walton Co.
Jason A. Deadwyler of Lexington, Oglethorpe Co.
Thomas M. Dorsey was living in Atlanta with his son Thomas A. Dorsey in 1900 while he attended school. His young son is a few months old born in 1899 and the father and his young child were in the house with Etta his

wife and Thomas brothers James and Joshua and his sister Hattie. They were living on Harris Street in the sixth ward. This area where he and his family are living near Butler Street. To the young children today who don't know about the young Thomas A. Dorsey, young Thomas wrote the son Precious Lord Take My Hand. This song is recognized around the world.

John S. Echols of Athens Clarke Co.

Albino B. Foster of Stellaville, Jefferson Co.

Wiley L. Freeman of Perry, Houston Co.

David G. Gullins of Milledgeville, Baldwin Co.

F.B. Hawkins of Americus, Sumter Co.

Wiley B. Hill of Valdosta, Lowndes Co.

Peter F. Hogan, of Leatherville, Lincoln Co.

Solomon Humphreys, of Atlanta, Fulton Co.

Lewis W. Isham of Jones' Mills, Meriwether Co.

Willis L. Jones of Atlanta, Fulton Co.

Alfred D. Jones of Perry, Houston Co.

James M. Jones of Perry, Houston Co.

Henry J Johnson of Cartersville, Bartow Co.

William Kelsey of Millen Burke Co

Judge L. Lattimore, of Social Circle, Walton Co.

John W. Long of Point Peter, Madison Co.

James W. Maddox of Cartersville, Bartow Co.

Charles McKinley of Atlanta Fulton Co.

Radolphus D. Railford of Wadley, Jefferson Co.

Elisha Reynolds of Conyers, Rockdale, Co.

Clem C. Richardson of Franklin, Heard Co.

James H. Robinson of Harlem Columbia Co.

Benjamin F. Smith of Monroe, Walton Co.

Isaac N. Stegall of Franklin, heard Co.

James H. Sutton of Henderson Houston Co.

Abram Ward of Augusta, Richmond, Co.

John F. Webb of Henderson, Houston Co.

Newton H. Whitmire of Savannah, Chaham Co.
D. A. Williams of Hamilton, Harris Co.

First Year
Sanford Alexander of Barnesville, Pike Co.
Henderson Beck of Atlanta, Fulton Co.
Dock C. Bracy of Eatonton, Putnam Co.
John A. Brown of Haynesville, Houston Co.
Tapp Clark of Atlanta, Fulton Co.
Robert H. Cody of Spread, Jefferson Co.
Thomas Coles of Atlanta, Fulton Co.
Thomas C. Combs of Cusseta, Ala.
Joseph F. Conyers of Atlanta, Fulton Co.
Oliver Crowder of Forsyth, Monroe Co.
Robert Dickerson of Millen, Burke Co.
Abraham Freeman of Senoia, Coweta Co.
John Garrison of Carrollton, Carroll Co.
Jeff Garnett of Kiokee, Columbia Co.
Alexander Harris of Savannah, Chatham Co.
Larkin Heard of Washington Wilkes Co.
William Hightower of Atlanta, Fulton Co.
Henry A. Hill of Atlanta, Fulton Co.
Thomas Hopkins of Chattanooga, Tenn.
Stonewall Jackson of Spoonsville Houston, Co.
John M. Jackson of Atlanta, Fulton Co.
Homer J. Joice of Cedartown, Polk Co.
Abel Jones of Atlanta, Fulton Co.
Edfward Jones of Oggechee, Scriven Co.
Andrew Kelsey of Millen, Burke Co.
Evans Landers of Thomas, McDuffie Co.
William Martin of Atlanta, Fulton Co.

Charles H. Morgan of Savannah, Chatham Co.
George C. McCause of Atlanta, Fulton Co.
Benjamin Oliver of Philadelphia, Pa.
Ezekiel Z. Parker o Jonesboro, Clayton Co.
Israel L. Quarterman of Louisville, Jefferson Co.
John t. Raiford of Wadley, Jefferson Co.
Anderson S. Rix of Cussa, Floyd Co.
James R. Robinson of Louisville, Jefferson Co.
William Roberts of Midville, Burke Co.
Robert Savage of Americus, Sumter Co.
Walter Scott of Atlanta, Fulton Co.
Henry Scott, of Atlanta, Fulton Co.
Charles M. Sewell of Atlanta, Fulton Co.
Jerry Shorter of Atlanta, Fulton Co.
Caleb Snellings of Waynesboro, Burke Co.
Lewis Stephens of Atlanta, Fulton Co.
Robert R. Stephens of Atlanta, Fulton Co.
Willis D. Stokes of Griffin, Spalding Co.
Richard B. Sweet Jacksonville, Fla.
Mathew W. White of Atlanta, Fulton Co.
Benjamin R. Williams of Greenville, Meriwether Co.
Archibald L. Wilkins of Louisville, Jefferson Co.
Benjamin Williams of Kiokee, Columbia Co.
Silas Wimbish of Warrensville, Meriwether Co.

Catalogue Atlanta Baptist Seminary, Atlanta, Georgia, 1887–88
The trustees and the local committee are the same

Students
Theological Department Full Course

Senior Class
Samuel Beauford, Eden Station, Effingham County Ga.
Samuel S. Broadnax, Lithonia, Dekalb Co.
Jerry B. Davis, Atlanta, Fulton Co.
Aaron B. Murden of Crawfordville, Taliaferro Co. Ga.
Jabez S. Russell of Augusta, Richmond Co. Ga.
Randal S. Snellings, Waynesboro, Burke Co.

Junior Class
Henry F. Barnes, Atlanta, Fulton Co.
James E. Brown of LaGrange, Troup Co.
Jerry M. Jones of Guyton, Effingham Co. Ga.
Ambose M. Johnson of Appling, Columbia Co. Ga.
John M. Neal of Stone Mountain Dekalb Co. Ga.
Ephraim F. Smith Jr. Kiokee, Columbia Co. Ga.

Restricted Course
James A. Baker of Atlanta, Fulton Co. Ga.
Pompey H. Butler of Savannah, Chatham Co. Ga.
Sandy Cornelius Bullards, Twiggs Co. Ga.
James T. Dunbar, Wilmington, S. C.
Raiford Gates of Americus Sumter Co. Ga.
Robert Grant, Atlanta, Fulton Co. Ga.
Isaac R. Hall of Atlanta, Fulton Co. Ga.
Griffin J. Hill, Milledgeville, Baldwin Co. Ga.
Solomon Humphreys Atlanta, Fulton Co. Ga.
Willis L. Jones Atlanta, Fulton Co. Ga.
Simon M. Mitchell, Atlanta, Fulton Co. Ga.
Chas. H. Morgan, Savannah, Chatham Co. Ga.
Frank P. Paskel, Decatur, DeKalb Co. Ga.
Howard G. Roby, Eatonton, Putnam Co. Ga.

Amos D. Reid, Hawkinsville, Pulaski Co. Ga.
Henry Sanders, Atlanta, Fulton Co. Ga.
Martin S. Scruggs, Decatur, DeKalb Co. Ga.
Eddy Smith, Atlanta, Fulton Co. Ga.
George Smith, Atlanta, Fulton Co. Ga.
Jesse J. Taylor, Athens, Clarke Co. Ga.
Elbert Whaley, Thomasville, Thomas co. Ga.
Harrison Wiggin, Seneca City, Oconee County S. C.
Henry M. Williams, Birmingham, Ala.
James Willis, Atlanta, Fulton Co. Ga.

Preparatory Department
First Year
David S. Klugh, Greenwood, S. C.
Mark C. Parker, Jonesboro, Clayton Co. Ga.
Francis B. Turner, Crawfordville, Taliaferro Co. Ga.
Thomas J. Turner, Stone Mountain, Dekalb Co. Ga.

NORMAL DEPARTMENT

Elective Studies
John F. Bright, Cartersville, Bartow Co. Ga.

Fourth Year
Stephen H. Allen, Oak Bower, Hart Co. Ga.
John H. Avery Thomas, McDuffie Co. Ga.
Robert Lee Darden of Jones' Mills, Meriwether Co. Ga.
Hezekiah H. Engram, Montezuma, Macon Co. Ga.
George W. Hill, Covington, Newton Co. Ga.
John Jones, Perry, Houston Co. Ga.
Thomas C. Jones Jr., Perry, Houston Co. Ga.

Wm. L. Johnson, Cedartown, Polk Co. Ga.
Albert O. Lockhart, Jonesboro, Clayton Co. Ga.
Milton M. Mack, Thomasville, Thomas Co. Ga.
John H. Moore, Jones' Mills, Meriwether Co. Ga.
Dower P. Rowe, Athens, Clarke Co. Ga.
Sheppard D. Rosier, Midville, Burke Co. Ga.
Jerry R. Smith, Augusta, Richmond Co. Ga.
Henry T. Smith, Kiokee, Columbia co. Ga.
William E. Wallace, Ellaville, Schley Co. Ga.
William Wynn Barnett, Warren Co. Ga.

Third Year
John Thomas Banks, Forsyth, Monroe Co. Ga.
David D. Crawford, Columbus, Muscogee Co. Ga.
William H. Churm, Atlanta, Fulton Co. Ga.
Thomas M. Dorsey, Appling, Columbia Co. Ga.
Jesse S. Durrett, Humeville, Elbert Co. Ga.
John S. Echols, Athens, Clarke Co. Ga.
George W. Foster, Agate, Floyd Co. Ga.
John W. Franklin, Stellaville, Jefferson Co. Ga.
David G. Gullins, Atlanta, Fulton Co. Ga.
Bryant Heggs, Grange, Jefferson Co. Ga.
Wiley B. Hill, Valdosta, Lowndes Co Ga.
Alfred D. Jones, Perry, Houston Co. Ga.
Frank B. Jones, Atlanta, Fulton Co. Ga.
Henry J. Johnson, Cartersville, Bartow Co. Ga.
William Kelsey, Millen, Burke Co. Ga.
Griffin D. King, Macon, Bib Co. Ga.
Mose W. Letman of Verdery S. C.
John W. Long, Mediens, Madison Co. Ga.
Charles McKinley, Atlanta, Fulton Co. GA.

Hillard Martin, Madison, Morgan Co. Ga.

Eli W. Moragne, Verdery, S. C.

Wm. L. Moragne, Verdery S. C.

Carey L. Borflett, Warrenton, Warren Co. Ga.

Limus Pickney, Verdery, S.C.

John B. Richardson, Franklin, Heard Co. Ga.

John N Sapp, Alexander, Burke Co. Ga.

James H. Sutton, Henderson, Houston Co. Ga.

Wm. B. Switcher, Americus, Sumter Co. Ga.

Abram Ward, Augusta, Richmond Co. Ga.

Geo. W. Walker, Warrenton, Warren Co. Ga.

John F. Webb, Henderson, Houston Co. Ga.

Moses Welch, Midville, Burke Co. Ga.

Second Year

Dock C. Bracy, Eatonton, Putnam Co. Ga.

Thomas W. Bryan, Americus Sumter Co. Ga.

Hezekiah Carter, Lexington Oglethorpe Co. Ga.

Wm. Crittenden, Milledgeville, Baldwin Co. Ga.

Charlie Darden, Atlanta, Fulton Co. Ga.

Jason A. Deadwyler, Lexington, Oglethorpe Co. Ga.

Robert Dickerson, Millen, Burke Co. Ga.

Oscar L. Eason of Hampton, Henry Co. Ga.

Samuel H. Henderson of Americus Sumter co. Ga.

Johnson H. Hill, Stone Mountain, Dekalb co Ga.

Stonewall Jackson, Spoonville, Houston Co. Ga.

Edward Jones, Ogeechee, Scriven Co. Ga.

Homer J. Joice, Cedartown, Polk Co. Ga.

Andrew Kelsey, Millen, Burke Co. Ga.

Evans Landers, Thomas, McDuffie Co. Ga.

William Martin, Atlanta, Fulton Co. Ga.

Wyley McAfee, Woodstock, Cherokee Co. Ga.
Wm. S. Oliver, Oxford, Ala.
Isreal L. Quarterman, Louisville, Jefferson Co. Ga.
Wm. T. Robbers, Midville, Burke Co. Ga.
Flournoy J. Shannon, Greensboro Co. Ga.
Caleb Snellings, Waynesboro Burke Co. Ga.
Williams W. Stewart, Crawfordville, Taliaferro co. Ga.
Richard B. Sweet, Jacksonville, Fla.
Anderson L. Tucker, Marietta, Cobb co. Ga.
W. D. Walthall, Cedartown Polk Co. Ga.
Archibald Wilkins, Louisville, Jefferson Co. Ga.

First Year
Sanford Alexander, Barnesville, Pike co. Ga.
Johnson Benton, Ogeechee, Scriven Co. Ga.
James Broadnax, Powder Springs Ga.
Albert P. Brown, Atlanta, Fulton Co. Ga.
Frank Carlton, Edgewood, Dekalb Co. Ga.
Henry Combs, Thomas, McDuffie Co. Ga.
Solomon Conyers, Atl.
Allen Cox, Atl.
Geo. W. Davis, Atl.
Jiles W. Drake, Greesboro, Greene Co. Ga.
Lewis Dunn, Leathersville, Lincoln Co. Ga.
Franklin Fox, Bartow, Jefferson Co. Ga.
John R. Gil, Locus Grove, Henry Co. Ga.
David A. Gordon, Sandersville, Washington Co. Ga.
Dawson Gordon, Edgewood, Dekalb Co. Ga.
Marshall H. Grier, Atl.
Nick H. Harper, Chauncy, Dodge Co. Ga.
Roland F. Hindsman, Villa Rica, Carroll Co. Ga.
Jonas T. Jones, Ogeechee, Scriven Co. Ga.

James Kelsey Jr., Millen, Burke Co.

Robert Layson, Eatonton, Putnam Co.

Walter Mackie, Madison, Morgan Co. Ga.

Jaes H. Oneal, Coosaville, Floyd Co. Ga.

Eli Z. Parker, Atl.

John Reid Hollandville, Pike Co. Ga.

Chas. H. Richardson, Ferry, Floyd Co. Ga.

Jerry Shorter, Atl.

Sandy Stevens, Athens, Clarke Co. Ga.

Lewis T. Stephens, Atl.

Handy G. Tie, Waycross, Ware Co. Ga.

Abram Turman, Mehadkee, Ala.

Sherman Turner, Conyers, Rockdale Co. Ga.

Junius Walton, Westminster S. C.

Lewis P. Walton, Westminster, S.C.

Geo. W. White, Atl

Ben W. Williams, Washington, Wilkes co. Ga.

Henry Williams, Macon, Bibb Co. Ga.

Reading Room

By the kindness of the respective publishers, The Baptist Quarterly, The Journal and Messenger, The National Baptist, The African Repository, The Musical Record, The Georgia Baptist, The Defiance, The Baptist teacher, Atlanta Herald, Youth's Companion, American Baptist, Baptist Leader and Spelman Messenger have been kept on file to be read by the students.

Catalogue Atlanta Baptist Seminary, Atlanta, Georgia 1888–89

Senior Class

Samuel Beauford, Eden Station Ga.

Jerry M. Jones, Guyton Ga.

Willis L. Jones, Atlanta, Ga.

Aaron B. Murden, Crawfordville Ga.
Randal S. Snellings, Waynesboro Ga.

Junior Class
John H. Avery, Thomson, Ga.
James E. Brown, La Grange Ga.
Robert Lee Darden, Greenville Ga.
Hezekiah H. Engram, Montezuma Ga.
David S. Klugh, Greenwood S. C.
John H. Moore, Greenville, Ga.
William E. Wallace, Ellaville, Ga.
Harry M. Williams, Washington, Ala.

Restricted Course
Sanford Alexander, Forsyth, Ga.
Cyrus Brown, Atl.
General B. Fanning, Bellwood, Ga.
Robert Grant, Atl.
Jefferson Henry, Athens Ga.
Griffin J. Hill, Milledgeville Ga.
Stewart Oliver, Anderson City S. C.
Jerry R. Smith, Augusta, Ga.
Charles H. Thaxton, Raleigh N. C.
Jesse R. Willis, Atl.
Matthew W. White, Atl.

Collegiate Deparment

Classical Course
Junior Class
George W. Hill, Covington, Ga.
John N Jones, Perry, Ga.

Thomas C. Jones, Perry Ga.
Mack C. Parker, Atl.
Henry T. Smith, Kiokee Ga.

Normal Deparment
Fourth Year
Class A
Dock D. Crawford, Columbus, Ga.
Jesse S. Durrett, Hulmeville, Ga.
John S. Echols, Athens Ga.
David G. Gullins, Atl.
Henry J. Johnson, Cartersville, ga.
Alfred D. Jones of Atl.
Griffin D. King, Macon Ga.
Henry R. Latimer, Centreville S. c.
Milton M. Mack, Thomasville, Ga.
William L. Moragne, Verdery S. C.
Sheppard D. Rosier, Midville, Ga.
Benj. F. Smith, Monroe Ga.
Richmond B. Sweet, Jacksonville, Fla.
Moses Welch, Midville, Ga.

Class B
John W. Franklin, Stellaville, Ga.
Samuel S. Humber, Tumbling Shoal S. C.
William B. Switcher, Ameicus, Ga.
John H. Wicker, Powellton Ga.

Third Year
Class A
Dock C. Bracy, Eatonton, Ga.

Thos. W. Bryan, Americus Ga.
Petr J. Bryant, Guyton, Ga.
Wm. A. Crittenden, Milledgeville Ga.
Thomas M. Dorsey, Appling Ga.
Edward Ogeechee, Ga.
James M. Jones, Perry Ga.
Jonas T. Jones, Ogeechee, Ga.
Evans S. Landers, Thompson, Ga.
Isam B. Merritt, West Bowersville Ga.
James F. Shannon, Greensboro Ga.
Jerry W. Skinner, Eastman Ga.
Lewis P. Walton, Westminster, S. C.
Abram Ward, Augusta, Ga.

Class B
Spariel V. Acrey, Cleveland Ga.
John T. Banks, Forsyth, Ga.
John G. Branham, Eatonton, Ga.
Mt. Zion Daniels, Atlanta, Ga.
Robt. W. Dickerson, Millen Ga.
Marshall M. Dickson, Augusta Ga.
David A. Gordon, Sandesville Ga.
Lemuel H. Henderson, Americus Ga.
Andrew Kelsey, Millen Ga.
Frank E. Martin, Atlanta, Ga.
Israel L. Quarterman, Louisville Ga.
Caleb A. Snellings, Waynesboro Ga.
James A. Thomas, Cleveland Ga.
George W. Walker, Warrentown Ga.
General P. Washington, Rhodes-Store, Fla.

Second Year

Class A

Jonah Broadnax, Powder Springs Ga.

Franklin Fox Barton Ga.

James H. O'Neal, Oreburge, Ga.

James W. O'Neal, LaFayette, Ga.

Major W. Reddick, Shellman Ga.

Chas. H. Richardson, Ferry Ga.

William T. Robergts, Midville Ga.

James B. Young, LaFayette Ga.

Class B

John T. Allen, Atl.

Jesse S. Bivins, Atl.

Albert P. Brown, Atl.

Allen L. Davis, Carters Ga.

Oscar L Eason, Hampton Ga.

James L. Johnson, Appling Ga.

Wyley McAfee, Woodstock Ga.

General G. McTier, Waynesboro Ga.

Walter Morton, Madison Ga.

John F. Noble, Henderson Ga.

Jerry L. Rice, Oreburge Ga.

David Stokes, Acworth Ga.

William T. Swilling, Hartwell Ga.

Cain Taylor, Lafayette Ga.

Richard Taylor, Lafayette Ga.

Ephriam V. White Jr., Thomas Ga.

Granville J. Wright, Camilla G.

Joseph C. Wynn, Barnett Ga.

First Year

James A. Austin, Jonesboro Ga.

Ephriam P. Battles, Ragland Ga.

Henry C. Gainer, Alt.

Sebron C. Peters, Columbus Ga.

Class B

John A. Allen, Atl.

Joseph S. Coles, Atl.

Marshall A. Daniels, Union Point Ga.

Dawson Gordon, Edgewood Ga.

Peter F. Hogan, Leatherville Ga.

Oscie J. Hunt, Midville, Ga.

John E. Jacobs, Ogeechee Ga.

John Keith, Chattanooga Tenn.

Stephen T. Murden, Crawfordville Ga.

Frederick D. Page, Bartow Ga.

Wm. Rainwater, Union Point Ga.

Joseph H. Townsley, Atla.

Sherman Turner, Conyers Ga.

Handy G. Tye, Norcross, Ga.

First Year

Class A

Henry H. Miller, Savannah Ga.

Class B

James Baynes, Eatonton, Ga.

Robert H. Cody, Spread, Ga.

George W. Crowley, Atl.

Cornelius R. Daniel, Dallas Ga.

Toney Davis, Atl.

Josiah D. Dogans, Raleigh, N. c.

Giles W. Drake, Greensboro, Ga.

Prince Goode, Seneca S. C.

Sherman J. Gresham, Atl.

Samuel M. Hill, Link Station S. C.

Herman Holbrook, Atl.

H. C. James, Forsyth, Ga.

Wm. A. Jones, Atl.

Josiah Logan, Brooklyn N. T.

Daniel Martin, Atl.

Lincoln A. Merritt, Albany Ga.

Josiah Paterson, Eatonton, Ga.

Albert Pratt, Hainesville Ga.

Andrew Scott, Bellewood, Ga.

Henry Scott, Franksville Ga.

George Smith, Atl.

Joseph Turner, Senoia, Ga.

Collie Warbington, Norcross Ga.

Elbert L. Whaley, Thomasville Ga.

George W. White, Atl.

Pg. 19

Historical Sketch of the Atlanta Baptist Seminary

THE ATLANTA BAPTIST SEMINARY, under the name of The Augusta Institute was founded at Augusta, Georgia, in May 1867. It was conducted under the auspices of the National Theological Institute, by Rev. J. W. Parker, D. D.

No permanent location having been secured for it thus early in its history, it was taught at night in Springfield Baptist church.

When Dr. Parker had been in charge but three months, feeble health compelled him temporarily to suspend his labors, and return North. During his absence, at his request, Rev. J. Mason Rice took the principal ship, and continued it until the following fall, when Dr. Parker returned to his post of duty.

Instruction was given by lectures to such ministers and deacons as found it convenient to attend, while two assistants taught females. In November of the same year, Dr. Parker having resigned, Rev. Charles H. Corey and wife were appointed to fill the vacancy. They retained Mr. Rice, and taught with success until July 13, 1868, when Mr. Corey was transferred to the Richmond Institute, at Richmond Virginia.

Early in the following winter, Rev. Lucien C. Hayden D. D. succeeded Mr. Corey in the management of the seminary, but as the United States Educational Bureau was then establishing schools for the Colored people, it was thought best to blend the efforts of the Seminary with those of the Bureau.

Dr. Hayden took charge of one of these schools in January, 1869. Thus, with the exception of an occasional lecture, ministerial training during that year was discontinued.

November 15, 1869, under appointment of the American Baptist Home Mission Society, Rev. W. D. Seigfried came South as the president of the Seminary. The school being still without quarters of its own, it was urged by friends that it was essential to its success that the society should purchase a site for that purpose. Accordingly, April 21, 1870, a beautiful lot in the city of Augusta, Georgia, 180 by 180 feet, centrally located on Telfair Street, was bought for cash at $5,700.

Mr. Seigfried at once removed to the premises where he had an unusually large attendance. In the summer he went North to solicit contributions to reimburse the Society for the outlay in the purchase of this property. He returned early in the following autumn; but in the course of a few months he severed his connection with the institution whose operations were a second time suspended until August 1, when Rev. Jos. T. Robert, LL.D., was appointed to its presidency. A Southern gentlemen of high culture and liberal views, Dr. Robert succeeded able to do. He conducted the school four years without an assistant. In addition to raising funds for its maintenance, he heard recitations five hours a day, and delivered two lectures a week on biblical and scientific subjects.

The fifth year he had two of his advanced students aid him in hearing classes. In the sixth year of his connection with the Seminary, Professor Sterling Gardner, an accomplished colored gentleman, a graduate of

Madison University, Hamilton, New York, was transferred from the Richmond Institute to assist Dr. Robert in Augusta. Professor Gardner was eminently fitted for the work, and did effective service, but in less than a year after a protracted illness he died. During his sickness, and after his decease, two of his pupils Collins H. Lyons and William E. Holmes, aided Dr. Robert in his work. After the death of Professor Gardner, Rev. David Shaver, D. D. Was associated with Dr. Robert as his principal assistant, for the beginning of the session 1878-'79 to the close of that of 1880-'81. A man possessed of large general information, and deeply learned in theology and philosophy, Dr. Robert found his co-laborer admirably adapted to the work he loved so well.

In the fall of 1879, the Seminary was removed to Atlanta, Georgia, and given its present name, The Atlanta Baptist Seminary. An eligible lot of four acres was purchased, and a commodious brick building was erected for its use at the corner of Elliott and West Hunter streets. Dr. Robert continued with the school until his death, which occurred March 5th 1884.

After the death of Dr. Robert, his first assistant Rev. David F. Estes, A. M. was commissioned acting president. In this capacity he served with acceptance until May 27th, 1886, when Rev. Samuel Graves, D. D. of Grand Rapids, Michigan, was appointed to succeed Dr. Roberts. Dr. Graves is unusually well qualified to discharge the delicate and difficult duties of his position, having had large experience as a pastor and educator.

Under him the Seminary has gone steadily forward; its standard has been raised, its attendance increased, and its influence widened. As the result of Dr. Graves' efforts, the American Baptist Home Mission society has been enabled to secure a lot of 14 acres, "beautiful for situation," high and healthful, in the western part of the city, for the sum of $7,500. And now a building, comfortable and convenient in all its appointments, 140 feet front, and four stories high, is in process of erection.

The corner stone of this structure will be laid in May, and the Missionary Baptist Convention of Georgia, which will then be in session here, will take apart in the exercises on that occasion. It is expected that this building will be ready for occupancy December 1889. In view of the steady and substantial progress which the Seminary has made during the twenty years of is existence, we have reason to "thank God and take courage."

In 1914 G. S. Byrd of Dawson was a colored Minister in the American Baptist year book with M. Byrd of Atlanta and S. L. Byrd of Culverson, J. R. Callaway of Penfield.

In 1915 A. M. Jones was in Smithsonia and J. R. Calloway was in Penfield.

In 1916 the White Callaway was T. F. Callaway of Macon, Thos. M. Callaway of Dawson, T. W. Callaway of Dublin. The colored J. R. Callaway was still listed as being in Penfield in 1915. and in 1916 and in 1918. However, J. R. Callaway made his will 1901 when he died.

In the year of 1919 the White Callaway's were Thos. M. Callaway of Dawson, and T. W. Callaway of Macon the Colored Callaway's were F. Caloway of Macon, J. C. Caloway of Cordele, M. Caloway of Colquitt, O. E. Caloway of Colquitt, T. C. Caloway of Bronwood, T. L. Caloway of Bronwood, W. H. Caloway of Macon,

In 1920 the white Callaways were Thos. M. Callaway of Dawson, T. W. Callaway of Macon, the coloreds were F. Caloway of Macon, J. C. Caloway of Cordel, M. Caloway of Colquitt, T. C. Caloway of Bronwood, and T. L. Caloway of Bronwood, and W. H. Caloway of Macon.

C.W. Johnson of Chamblee, E.D. Johnson of Whigha both are white, A. L. Jackson of Colquitt is colored, colored A. M. McCloud of Warwick, C. M. McCloud of Midville, W. A. McCloud of Wadley, W. H. McCloud of Dexter.

In 1922 ordained ministers in the United States Georgia. D. C. Caloway of Warwick, F. Caloway of Macon, J. C. Caloway of Cordele, M. Caloway of Colquitt, T. C. Caloway of Brownwood, T. L. Caloway of Bronwood, W. H. Caloway of Macon.

In 1923 P.C. Castleberry was in Richland; the Callaways were the same.

In 1924 D. C. Callaway is D. C. Call in Warwick. F. Callaway is in Macon, J. C. Caloway is in Cordele, M. Caloway is in Colquitt, T. C. Caloway is in Bronwood, T. L. Caloway is in Bronwood. W. H. Caloway is in Macon. In 1926 the Caloway are the same, but A. C. Calloway is in Americus

In 1927 Thomas M. Callaway is in Conyers and Ragan Callaway is in Bostwick Ga. it was in 1922 that Thomas M. Callaway was in Baconton in 1929 the colored Callaway's are in the same location.

In 1899 T. M. Callaway was living in Taladega, Alabama and P. M. Calloway Jr. was in Newton Alabama. In 1900 B. W. Calloway was in Weogufka Ala. P. M. Calloway was in Newton, T. M. Callaway D. D. was still in Talladega Ala.

In 1903 in Georgia J. J. S. Callaway was in Cumming, J. M. Callaway was in West Point, and H. S. Callaway was in Penfield, T. M. Callaway was still in Talladega Ala. There was no Thomas M. Callaway in Georgia. A white preacher named A. J. Callaway was in Louisiana in Spearsville.

BLACK COLLEGE AND A HIGHER EDUCATION AT THE BEGINNING OF DIS-ENFRANCHISEMENT OF THE NEGRO

Catalogue Atlanta Baptist Seminary, Atlanta, Georgia 1889–90

Trustees

Rev. E. Lathrop, D. D. President Conn.

Hon. W.A. Cauldwell N. Y.

Rev. H. L. Morehouse N. Y.

Hon. B. F. Abbott, Ga.

Maj. Sidney Root Ga.

Rev. Joseph Elder, D. D. N. Y.

J. S. Lawton, M. D. Ga.

Rev. N. E. Wood, D. d. N. Y.

Rev. W. J. White Ga.

I. G. Johnson N. Y.

Rev. W. A. Tilman Ga.

Joseph Brokaw, N. Y.

Local Committee

Sidney Root

B.F. Abbott

J. S. Lawton

W.J. White
W. H. Tilman

Students
Theological Department
Fall Term

Senior Class
James E. Brown, LaGrange Ga.
Robert L. Darden, Greenville, Ga.
David S. Klugh, Greenwood, S.C.
John H. Moore, Greenville, Ga.

Junior Class
Dock D. Crawford, Columbus, Ga.
David. G. Gullins, Atl.
Limus P. Pinckney, Verdery, S. C.
Wm. L. Singleon, Barnwell, S. C.
Gibson A. Turman, Bordeaux, S. C.

Restricted Course

Cyrus Brown, Atl.
Henry F. Barnes, Atl.
Samuel Bell Palatka, Fla.
Jackson C. Clark, Atl.
Robert H. Eliot, Atl.
Elijah J. Fisher, Lagrange, Ga.
Freeman Gardner, Palatka, Fla.
Robert Grant, Atl.
Isaac R. Hall, Atla.

Griffin J. Hill, Miledgeville, Ga.
James M. Jones, Forsyth, Ga.
George W. Lukes, Corinth, Ga.

Preparatory Deparment

Second Year
Class A
Ephraim P. Battles, Ragland, Ga.
Daniel Collins, Blitch Ga.
John H. Dent, Kiokee, Ga.
James H. Gadson, Savannah, Ga.
Henry H. Miller, Savannah, Ga.
Walter Morton, Godfrey, Ga.
Henry T. Redding, Juliet, Ga.
Alfred Reeves, Woodbury, Ga.
Handy G. Tye, Norcross, Ga.

Class B
Isaac Cross, Wadley, Ga.
Mansfield Crawford, Putnam Ga.
Melvin Gault, Grantville Ala.
Arthur E Drew, Clear Springs, Ga.
George Kellam, Atl.
Chas. H. Kelley, Norcross, Ga.
James W. Maddox, Centerville, Ga.
Wm. Melson, Corinth, Ga.
General G. McTier, Waynesboro Ga.
Major J. Morris, Myrtle, Ga.
Owens Nelson, Covington, Ga.
Wm. H. Riggs, Laston, Ga.

John Thomas, Blakely Ga.
George L. Weems, Atl.

Preparatory Course

First Year
Class A
William Arp, Emmerson, Ga.
Robert Brightwell, Atl.
John Chatman, Americus Ga.
James Dorsey, Appling, Ga.
Isaiah D. Dougans, Atl.
Norris W. Eason, Hampton, Ga.
Milo E. Evans, Walhalla S. C.
Solomon Fincher, Big Creek Ga.
Prince R. Goode, Birmingham Ala.
Miles Herndon, Senoia Ga.
Thomas Hines, Oconee, Ga.
Walte L. Jameson, Atl.
Wm. B. James, Bartow, Ga.
Lucius M. Kennedy, Bartow, Ga.
Emmet R. Lee, Atl.
Josiah Logan Brooklyn, N. Y.
Wm. M. Morable, Atl.
John H. Shehee, Barnesville, Ga.

Preparatory Course

First Year
Class B
John W. Bugg, Brunswick, Ga.

Wm Burroughs, Brunswick, Ga.
Noah A. Darden, Greenville, Ga.
David Davis, Atl.
Wilkins Greene, Midville Ga.
Luke Hammock, Waco Ga.
Robert Johnson, Tennille, Ga.
Freeman Jordan, Atl.
Adam Langston, Deepstep, Ga.
Walter T. Lyons, Hampton, Ga.
John M. Norris, Wrightsville, Ga.
Miles Nunnally, Walnut Grove Ga.
Jacob Richardson, Rome, Ga.
Robert Stroud, Greshamville, Ga.
Hank Wilson, Atl.
Joseph Wilson, Atl.
John L. Wilson, Atl.

1900–1901
Pg. 39

Graduates
1884
Normal Courses
John S. Brandon, Custodian Equitable Building Atlanta
Charles H. Brightharp, Pastor, Milledgeville
Richard T. Clark, Americus *1884
George A. Goodwin, Teacher, Atlanta, Baptist College
George W. Granage, Decorator, Atlanta
Richard H. Keller, Teacher, Opelika, Ala.
John J. Mitchell Clerk, Pension Office, Washington, DC
Martin V. Russell, Teacher, Marianna, Ark.

Peter S. Russell, *1895
Cyrus S. Wilkins, Pastor Thankful Baptist Church, Augusta

Theological Course
Charles H. Brightharp, Pastor, Milledgeville
Edward Randolph Carter, Pastor Friendship Church, Atlanta
George Grinage, Washington, Atlanta
Cyrus Simpson, Wilkins, Pastor Augusta

Normal Course, 1885
Alfred J. Allen Pastor, Cuthbert
Samuel S. Broadnax, Pastor, Thomasville
John H. Brown, Prin., Jeruel Academy, Athens
Henry L. Flemister, Prin., City School, Madison
Eli M. Harris*
Luke B. Norris, Prin., City School, Marietta
Jabez S. Russell, Teaching, Gurdon Ark.
John T. Russell, Teaching, Wadley

Theological Course
Charles O. Jones *1900
Jerry M. Jones *1888

------
*Deceased

1886
Normal Course
Samuel Beauford, Pastor, Waycross
James A. Bohler, Pastor
George S. Burruss, M. D. Ph.G., Practicing Physician, Augusta
Jerry B. Davis, Pastor, Thomasville

Aaron B. Murden, Pastor, Athens
Randall S. Snellings, Pastor, Macon

1887

Normal Course
James E. Brown, Prin., Bapt. Academy, La Grange
Ambrose M. Johnson, Teacher, Cedartown
William L. Johnson, Prin., Public School, Valdosta
J. Marshall Jones, Educational Missionary, Augusta
John B. Neal, Pastor, Sandersville
Mack C. Parker, Post Office, Rome
Edgar F. Pulliam *
Ephraim F. Smith *1892
Francis B. Turner, R. R. Service, Atlanta
Thomas Turner, Prin., City School, Eastman
Samuel T. Wilkins, Teacher, La Fayette

Theological Course
Alfred J. Allen, Pastor, Cuthbert
Hardy M. Curry, Pastor, Marianna, Fla.

1888
John H. Avery*
Robert L. Darden, Marietta
Hezekiah H. Engram, Teaching
George W. Hill, Prin., City High School, Washington
David S. Klugh, Pastor, Augusta
Albert O Lockhart, Physician, Atlanta
John H. Moore, Pastor, Griffin
Henry Smith, Thomas

William E. Wallace, Ellaville

Theological Course
Samuel Scott Broadnax, Pastor, Thomasville

1889

Normal Course

Doc. D. Crawford., Educ. Miss., Americus Dist., Atlanta
Jesse S. Durrett, Physician, Paducah, Ky.
David G. Gullins, Curator, Central City College, Macon
Samuel S. Humbert, School, Montezuma
Alfred D. Jones, Physician, Atlanta
Griffin D. King, Prin., City School, Macon
Henry R. Latimer, Teaching, Ninety-Six, S. C.
William L. Moragne, Honea Path, S. C.
Limus P. Pinckney, Educ. Miss., Athens Distr. Dublin
Richmond B. Sweet *

1890
Theological Course
James E. Brown, La Grange
Elijah J. Fisher, Pastor, Nashville, Tenn.
David S. Klugh, Pastor, Augusta
John H. Moore, Pastor, Griffin

1891
Normal Course
Edward Jones, Teaching, Millen
Jonas F. Jones, Teaching, Oliver

John W. Long, Pastor, Royston
James F. Shannon, Physician, Kansas City, Mo.
Lewis P. Walton, Physician, Atlanta

Theological Course
David G. Gullins, Central City College, Macon
Limus P. Pinckney Educational Missionary
William L Singleton

1892
Classical Course

George W. Hill, Prin., City High School, Washington
Alfred D. Jones, Phys., Atl.

*Deceased

Normal Course

David A. Gordon, Prin., Public School, Sandersville
Philip E. Love, Practicing Medicine, Savannah
Wylie McAfee *1900
Major W. Reddick, Prin., Americus Inst., Americus

1893

Normal Course

Henry a. Bleach, Instructor, Benedict College, Columbia S. C.
John H. Dent, Augusta
Andrew Z. Kelsey, Tutor, Atlanta Baptist College

Ulysses H. Morrison, Teaching, Thebes
William E. Rainwater, Business, Union Point
William T. Roberts, Prin., Public School, White Plains
George W. Walker *1897
James B. Young, Tidings

Theological Course
James C. Dawes, Missionary, Lagos, West Africa
James T. Hancock, Teaching, Monroe
Arnold H Robinson, Pastor, Elko, S. C.

1894.
Academic Course

Henry C. Crittenden, Atlanta
James H. Gadson, Pastor, Tuskegee, Ala.
Henry W. James, Practicing Medicine, Lumber City
Charles H. Kelley, Teaching, Owensbyville
James F. Long, Teaching, Carlton
Eli T. Martin, Pastor, Milledgeville
William L. Maxwell, Mail Clerk, Chicago, Ill.
John W. Myres, Teaching, Tullahoma, Tenn.
James M. Nabrit, Teacher, Central City College, Macon
Alfred R. Reeves, Teaching, Anniston, Ala.
Jerry L. Rice Teaching, La Grange.
Charles H. Richardson Teaching, Rome.
William H. Riggs Statesboro.
John J. Starks, Teaching Seneca, S. C.
Timothy Williams *1900

*Deceased

Theological Course

Thomas M. Dorsey, Pastor, Villa Rica
Jerry D. Gordon, Pastor, Madison
Crawford G. Holmes, Pastor, Rome
Robert R. Smith, Pastor, Columbus
John F. Webb, Pastor, Henderson
Matthew W. White, State Missionary, Atlanta

Teachers' Professional Course

Andrew Z. Kelsey, Student, Atlanta Bapt. College
William T. Roberts., Prin., Public School, White Plains

1895
Academic Course

Floyd G. Crawford, Teaching, Goggins
Theodore F. Whittaker *
Archibald L. Wilkins, Teaching, Wadley

Teachers' Professional Course
Eli T. Martin, Pastor, Milledgeville

1896

Academic Course

James G. Green, Prin., Public School, Coleman
Isaiah H. Hayes, Student, Meharry Medical School
Isaiah W. Thomas, Student, Atlanta Bapt. College

1897

Academic COURSE

Zachary T. Hubert, Student, Atlanta Bapt. College

Cornelius S. Johnson, Business, Arkansas City, Ark.

Samuel E. Lynch, Teaching, Rehoboth

John A. Mason, Student, Atl. Bapt. College

James F. Towns

College Course

Henry A. Bleach, Instructor, Benedict College, Columbia, S. C.

John W. Hubert, Teacher, Atl. Bapt. College

Major W. Reddick, Prin., Americus Institute, Americus

1898

ACADEMIC Course

B. Griffith Brawley, Student, Atl. Bapt. College

Daniel W. Cannon, Pastor, Eatonton

Henry P. McClendon, Student, Lincoln University

Sidney B. Scott, Student, Atlanta Baptist College

George W. Smith, Student, Shaw University

Charles H. Wardlaw, Student, Atl. Bapt. College

Theological Course

Henry F. Barnes, Atl.

Richard H. Burson, Atl.

William W. Floyd, Zion Hill Baptist Church, Atlanta

John T. Laster, Pastor, Mt. Zion Bapt. Church, Griffin

William F. Strickland, State Missionary

Adam D. Williams Pastor of Ebenezer Bapt. Church, Atlanta Mr. A. D. Williams the grandfather of Dr. Martin Luther King out of Scull Shoals Greene County Georgia.

College Course
James M. Nabrit, Central City College, Macon
Alfred R. Reeves, Teaching, Anniston, Ala.
John J. Starks, Teaching, Seneca, S. C.
Timothy Williams *1900

Teachers' Professional Course

Henry A. Bleach, Inst., Benedict College, Columbia, S. C.
James G. Green, Prin., Pub. School, Coleman
Isaiah W. Thomas, Student, Atl. Bapt. College

1899

Academic Course
William M. Armstrong *1900
Lawrence B. Bleach, Student, Lincoln University
James E. Brown, Student, Atl. Bapt. College
Raymond H. Carter, Student, Atl. Bapt. College
Daniel L. Potts, Teaching, La Fayette
Felton W. Wheeler, Teaching, Atlanta, Georgia

1900
Academic Course

William A. Alexander, Student, Atl. Bapt. College
James T. Germany, Student, Atl. Bapt. College
James C. Haynes, Nashville, Tenn.
Isaac C. Smith, Student, Atl. Bapt. College
Paul H. Weaver, Student, Atlanta Bapt. College

Academic Course

John W. Dobbs, Atl.
George N. Glover, Atl.
Emmett A. Henry, Shellman

Theological Course

Peter F. Hogan, Atl.
Charles S. Hubert, Atl.
Jerry F. Hughes, Atl.
Daniel Mills, Savannah
Newton T. Phillips, Atl.
John A. Trimble, Atl.

Teachers' Professional Course
James E. Brown, Shellman

College Course
Benjamin G. Brawley, Palatka, Fla.
Zachary T. Hurbert, Atl.
John A. Mason, Atl.
Sidney B. Scott, Sparta

Honorary Degrees

1900
A. M. Judson. W. Lyons, Register of Treasury, Washington, D. C.

1901
D. D. Rev. Cyrus S. Wilkins, Pastor Thankful Baptist Church, Augusta, Ga.

Prior to 1884, no student was regularly graduated. The following students are certified as to having completed the required work in the course indicated and are entitled to rank as graduates:

Normal Course

James H. Bugg D, Physician, Savannah

Wm. E. Holmes AM, Pres. Central City College, Macon

Wm. P. Hudson, Teacher, Warrenton

Augustus R. Johnson, Prin., Mauge St. School, Augusta

Charles J. Johnson, Teacher, Live Oak., Fla.

Emanuel K. Love DD *1900

Collins H. Lyons DD *1896.

Judson W. Lyons AM, LLD, Register of U. S. Treasury Washington, D. C.

Matthew J. Maddox, Pastor, Savannah

Moses P. McCrarey, Teacher, Valdosta

Gibb B. Mitchell, Pastor, Forsyth

William S. Ramsey *1901

Francis M. Simmons, Pastor, Covington

Alfred S. Staley, Prin., Public School, Americus

Jefferson D. Walker, Teacher, Ark.

Joseph A. Walker *1895

George D. White *1895

Anthony E. Williams AB, Internal Revenue Clerk, Atlanta

Nash B. Williamson, Pastor, Marietta

Theological Course

Wm. E. Holmes AM, Macon

Emanuel K. Love *1900

Collins H. Lyons *1896

Gibb B. Mitchell, Forsyth

Wm. S. Ramsey *1891

Francis B. Simmons, Covington
Charles T. Walker DD, New York
Wm. J. White DD, Augusta
* Deceased

1900

**Occasional Students

Jonas A. Grisham, Atlanta
E.H. Goodson, Atlanta
Jeremiah M Hall, Atlanta
John W. Presley, Conyers
William H. Tuggle, Atlanta
Edward Williams

**Students who entered too late in the year of enrollment in the regular classes.

1901 Rufus R. Dorsey of Atlanta joins the first-year theological courses

1903 Mr. Charles H. Lyons, the son of Collins H. Lyons, shows up in the fourth year of the academic course with Peter G. Appling of Macon, Arthur M. Jackson of Watkinsville, Monsieur U. Sanders of Eatonton; Collins is from Athens, Clarke County, Georgia

William H. Tuggle is in the D Class of 1903; he must have gotten here on time

1904 Charles H. S. Lyons is in the freshman class with Peter G. Appling of Macon; Henry E. Dean of Thomas, Georgia; Arthur M. Jackson of Watkinsville; and James G. Kyles of Milledgeville

In the first-year theological course I found John Dewberry and John Henry Jones of Forsyth; Robert T. Terrell and A.Z. Watley were from Griffin; Emmett M. Orton was from Lowndesboro, Alabama

1907–8

First year

John D. Beazley of Crawfordville Ga.

Howard Ferguson of Atl.

1910–11

Joseph T. Dorsey was in the third year of the divinity school while in Clarke County; William H. Tuggle was in his sophomore year of college

1911–12

Claud J. Cox, Atlanta

William H. Bryant, Memphis, Tenn.

Robert Shaw, Tupelo, Miss.

Winston Sims, Atl.

Herbert McFarland, Tampa, Fla.

1913 The Atlanta Baptist College has been renamed Morehouse College

1914–1915

Class C.

Walter Aderhold of Atl.

Lewis L. Bazzle, Atl.

James M. Bennett Atl

Charles H. Betts Atl.

John N. Calloway of Vernon, Texas.

Lawrence Culwell of Atl.

Channin Doyle of Milen, Moses S. H. Duncan of Atl.

Mathew Edmondson of Atl.

William E. Evans of Atl.

Robert S. Golston of Ashland

Leon W. Hill of Birmingham, Ala.

Benjamin Huitt of Atl.

McKinley Jackson of Odessadale

Robert Johnson of Cedartown, Raymond Jones of Atlanta

William Pierce of Greenville

James E. Pusey of San Andres, Colombia S.A.

Charles Reed of Chipley

Thomas C Reese of Atl.

Little Renfroe of Atl.

Maceo Tatum, of Gabbettsville

Jesse Thompson of Atlanta

C. L. Turner of Madison Ark.

Maceo White of Atl.

William Wynn of Atl.

The class John N. Calloway out of Texas was taking English Preparatory Department.

Samuel Scott Broadnax A. M. Pastor, Thomasville,

Emanuel K. Love died in 1900,

William J. White D. D. died 1913

Charles O. Jones died 1900

Jerry M. Jones died 1888

John T. Laster died 1905

I must talk about the great Dr. William J. White of Augusta before I proceed any further! He was the Pastor of Harmony Baptist Church in Augusta Georgia and ran a successful newspaper called the "Georgia Baptist" at 1339 9th street. He was a close friend to Rev. Frank Quarles of the Great Friendship Baptist Church. Rev. Frank Quarles was listed as the first President of the Colored Baptist Convention in Georgia in 1874. Dr. William J. White performed of his friend Rev. Frank Quarles to Miss.

Salina Mitchell in Atlanta on May 27 of 1880. Rev. Frank Quarles might have held his ceremony at Friendship Baptist Church in Atlanta. I gazed across the street from the Friendship Towers build many times where I and my wife minister to the needs of that retirement home before going by this church to read corner stone of this famous Black church before it was sold to make way for the new Mercedes Benz Stadium. These two famous black or white men persevered to start the famous black Morehouse College and other churches that branch off to start schools in the state of Georgia alone with Dr. Collins H. Lyons and other Black Men and Women!

Class of 1908: Charles H. S. Lyons, Teacher of Jeruel Academy, Athens and Thomas H. smith, Teacher Jeruel Academy, Athens

1917

Third year

William H. Pullen of Decatur, Ala.

Joseph Burdett of Decatur: First year

James R. Love of Columbus

Spurgeon Mayfield of Atlanta,

Class C.

Judson W. Lyons Jr. of Washington, D.C.

Henry Pullen of Newnan, Gal

Ernest L. Sutton of Atlanta, Ga.

Benjamin Weems of Atlanta Marshall M Williams of Atlanta.

1918

First Year

Simpson Calloway of Atlanta Ga.

William J. Dillard of Atlanta, Lewis Andrews of East Point, Clifton L. Wilder of East point, P. L. Jones of Chamblee

Class C.

Julius C. Sutton of Atlanta

Class of 1894 Henry C. Crittenden, John J. Starks of Sumter S. C.

1919–1920

Buford B. English of Atlanta in his first year

William M. Pulliam of Martin, G.

Henry Y. Frazier of Savannah, Philip R. Daniel of Atlanta,

O. E. Holland of Townville S. C. in his freshman year at Morehouse College.

Hammitt L. Searcy of Memphis, Tenn. In his first year at Morehouse College.

William H. Sims of Newnan Ga.

English Preparatory Department A Class

James Center of Lithonia, Ga.

George L. Pace Jr. of Atlanta, Ga.

1920–1921

Thomas M. Tuggles of Atlanta in his first year at Morehouse College

Henry Oates of Memphis Tenn. In his Freshman year at Morehouse College

Roosevelt Lyons of Athens is in his Fourth Year at Morehouse College.

Leland Crosby is out of Gainesville Ga. and is in his second year at M. C.

Charles Dorsey is out of Stilesboro Ga. in his second year at M.C.

1921–1922

Charles Wendell Holmes Memphis Tenn. In his junior class at M. C.

1924–1925

Freshman Year at Morehouse College is Clarence Lee Callaway of Selma, Alabama

Clarence Lee Callaway of Selma Ala. Is in his Sophomore

Roosevelt Geer of Penfield is in his freshman year

In his third year of class is Frank Quarles Johnson of Thomasville, Ga.

1925–1926

Clarence Lee Callaway of Selma, Ala. Is in his Junior Class with Charles Wesley Bugg of Brunswick, Howard Watson Branch of Chicago, Ill.

Thomas Charles Collins of Locust Grove, Harold Eugene Finley of Palatka, Fla.

Marcus Jefferson beavers of College Park. William Dean Pettus of Bessemer, Ala, Henry Bryant Price of Macon, Henry Thomas Sampson of Quitman, Levi Maurice Terrell of Kansas City, Kan. Jesse Love Terry of West Palm Beach, Fla.

Jams Othello Whaley Jr. of Shreveport, La. And Judson Whitlock Lyons of Washington D C.

The Freshman Class I found William Hale Eberhart of Athens, Ga.

1927–28

Clarence Lee Callaway of Selma, Ala was in his senior class

In his third-year class at Morehouse College, I found Pringle Lamar Callaway of Cedartown with James Henry Adcock of Cedartown as well. Is this the Lamar Callaway that was in the house with Rosa and John in Atlanta? I want to mention the rest of the third-year Students of Pringle Lamar Callaway in 1927: Joseph Walter Culpepper of Warrenton, Thomas Allen Dawson of Atlanta, Frederick Zimele Dube of Phoenix P.O., South Africa. George Logans, Edwards Jr. Atlanta, Rosamond Livingstone Gibson of Atlanta, Marion Hawk of Dothan, Ala. Allison Burney Henderson of Orlando, Fla. Dennis Taylor Hubert of Atlanta, Benjamin Nicholas Humphries of Rome, Sidney Harry Ingersoll of Columbus, James Augustus Joyner of Jacksonville, Fla., Robert Henry Koen of Memphis, Tenn. Henry McKinney of Waycross, William Martin of Atlanta, Rufus Sylvester Maultsby of Orlando, Fla. James Mayo of Atlanta, Augustus Gilbert Neal of Marietta, Dovdie Freeman Orr, of Crawford, Houston Person of Holcomb, Miss.; Walter Ralph Perry of Evanston, Ill. Rudolph Lawrence Powell of Deerfield, Fla.; John David Reed of Marietta, Ralph Claude Reynolds of Atlanta, William Marshall

Rice of Indianapolis, Ind. Crawford Robert of Winder, Claude Robinson of Atlanta, Robert Simpkins of Savannah, William Wallace Smith of Winnifield, La. Theodore Robert Stewart, New York City, Eugene Jay Thompson of Gainesville, Theodore Ware Turner of Rome, Andrew Frank Walker of College Park, William Melvin Walker of Franklin, Jordan Elmo Watkins of Atlanta, Eugene Benjamin Weaver of Rome, Thaddeus Edward Williams of Omaha, Neb.

In the second-year class I found Leonard Courtney Archer of Atlanta, Orion Lafayette Coker of Ocala, Fla. William Oscar English of Savannah, Lee Morris Pullins of Thomasville, Georgia.

In the first-year class, I found Paul Julius Byrd of Dawson, William Driskell Jr. of Atlanta, Texas Joseph Greenlee of Gainesville.

Morehouse College Graduates, 1928 Degrees Conferred Honorary Master of Arts

Joshua Enoch Blanton

Bachelor of Arts

Marcus Jefferson Beaves

Gosby Bell, Jr.

*Benjamin Allan Blackburn

Walter Monroe Booker

Howard Watson Branch

Burrell Hinton Brown

Charles Wesley Buggs

Clarence Lee Callaway

John Wesley Carten

*Allen Walter Childs

*Nehemiah McKinley Christopher

In the academy certificates I found Mr. Lawrence Walter Stubbs listed as dead.

Schools of Religion in the Winter Session (Unclassified)

1929–1930

Theodore Lester of Florene S. C.

Levi Rowan Patton of Alcorn, Miss.

Thomas Henry Calloway of Roanoke, Va. Of the Freshman class of M. B. C.

In the freshman class I found William Dawson McLoud of Thomasville

The School of Religion in the junior Class I found Earl Pinckney Byrd of Atlanta

1931–1932

Freshman Class

Albert Julius Calloway of Lexington Ky.

1933–1934

Anthony Thomas Quarles of Palestine, Texas

Selma University Catalogue of Students 1911–1912

Thirty-Fourth Anniversary

One name stood out in the normal department, and that was of Mr. Thomas Kirksey of Selma, Alabama. In the first-grade males I found Mr. Clarence Calloway. In the first grade females I found Myrtle Calloway. In the fifth-grade females I found Tobitha Quarles. In the sixth-grade females I found Mamie Deadwyler, Callie Gaines, Alberta Jones, Malisha Williams, J. Sturdivant, Susie Williams, Jessie Thomas, and Sallie Jones.

Alabama Baptist Normal and Theological School Selma Alabama 1881–1882

Selma Ala. Baptist Pioneer Print 1882

Faculty: W. H. McAlpine, Pres. H. Woodsmall, Teacher of Theo. and biblical interpretation

Rev. J. W. White and C.W White of Selma. Rev. J.D Dozier of Uniontown Ala.

Rev. Thos. Smith of Mont. Ala.

Theological Department

Henry Byrd of Hamburg Station, F.A. Beck of Camden, J. Curry of Shelby Iron Works, J. A. Byrd of Faunsdale, Isaac Rouse of Selma, Susie A. Stone of Selma, Mrs. A. A. Bowie of Selma, Thomas H. Pose and Wm. W Pose of Jonesboro, Margaret and Mary Oker of Randolph, Martha Loveless of Montgomery, Fannie Watson of Selma

1903–04

Senior Normal Student

Asalena Boswell of Selma, Winnie Agnew Calloway of Selma, Mary Davis Crawford of Selma, Daisy Dorine Dinkins of Selma, Gussie Calloway Fikes of Selma, Lucy Gray Goldsby of Selma, Ms. Ada F. Morgan, Precepress, Maggie Annie Martin of Faunsdale, Leila Rebecca Pitts of Lowedesboro, Leila Prentice of Selma, Julia A. Rayford of Selma, Harvey Dinkins of Selma, Nathaniel W. Huggins of Selma, Allbert Lincoln Smith of Selma, Della Mayfield of Selma

Second Year Department: Esther Kirkseyof Selma, Leola L. Johnson of Selma

Ministerial student: Alex Boykin of Perote

1907–1908

Gertrude E. Fisher of Birmingham

Mary Pace of Westbend

Henry Stubbs of Harrells

Selonia Calloway of Whitehall

Sylvia Patton of Livingston

Class of 1894
Rev. L. T. Simpson D. D. Pastor of Opelika,
Rev. C. J. Davis B. D. Pastor of Mt. Meigs
Rev. L.W. Callaway, State missionary Selma
W. White book-keeper Birmingham
Carrie A. Clark
Annie Stone works for Mrs. Murphy

Class of 1898
W. C. McCreary of Macon Ga.

Class of 1900
Rev. L.A Carter B. D. D. D Knoxville, Tenn.
Robert L. Grimes M. D. Practitioner Dothan
Rev. E. L. Randall pastor Eufaula,
Rev. J. M Coleman B. D. pastor Talladega
Rev. M. Jackson pastor Harris
Mattie L. Lipscomb (Mrs. Clark) Opelika
Mamie L. Johnson (Mrs. Burns) Selma

Class of 1902
Mabel F. Dinkins, teacher, Atlanta Baptist College

Class of 1890
R. B. Hudson A. B. principal Clark School Selma, Ala.

Class of 1907
Rev. W. L. Jeffries, B.D. pastor Marion Ala.
Rev. J. C Cunningham, B. D. pastor Snow Hill
Rev. J. Q A. Whilhite D.D president B'ham Ala.

1905–06
Rev. C. L. Fisher D. D. Chairman of the Board of Trustees
Jennie and Mabel Tate of Selma and Mattie Tate
The Pres. Is R. T. Pollard

1912
Walter A. Tutt of Selma
William A. Tutt of Pratt City

1916–1917
Pg. 50
Fortieth Anniversary
1904
Azaline Boswell (Mrs. Phillips) Birmingham
*Mrs. Winnie A. Agnew, (Mrs. Callaway)
J. C. Chandler Selma
Willis N. Huggins B. S. Normal Ala.

1916
Robert L. Champion 417-14th St. Ensley
Henry W. Terrant, 417-14th St. Ensley

1926–1927
Pg. 29
Lorenza Lambert Hawthorne of Brewton Ala.

BLACKS RAISING MONEY FOR EDUCATION FOR THEIR BLACK CHILDREN

Richmond County, Augusta, was the capital of Georgia from 1785 to 1795, and is the second oldest city in Georgia. The city was named for the

Princess of Wales. The land was ceded to the English by the Creeks in the Treaty of Savannah on May 21, 1733.

WHEREAS, The Missionary Baptist Convention of Georgia, at its Annual Meeting, June 12, 1897, and the General Missionary and Educational Convention of Georgia, at its annual Meeting, October 23, 1897, after a full and careful consideration of the suggestions submitted by Dr. Morgan, Corresponding Secretary of the American Baptist Home Mission Society, in a letter addressed to the Colored Baptists of Georgia, regarding their highest Educational interests, recommended each, as follows:

(First): That it is the plain and imperative duty of the Colored Baptists of Georgia, who have at heart the education and elevation of their race, to form themselves into an Education Society which shall systematically and effectively encourage and support all of the educational interests of the Baptists of the State.

(Second): That such Education Society, when formed, shall appoint an Educational Board which shall devote itself exclusively to the promotion of all of the educational interests of the Denomination, and which shall, for this purpose and for the purpose of co-operating with the American Baptist Home Mission Society in the financial support of Spelman. Seminary, Atlanta Baptist College, Walker Institute, and Jeruel Academy, and such other Secondary Schools as the Education Society may decide to help, appoint a competent Financial Secretary who shall devote his entire time to this work. And,

WHEREAS, Each Convention appointed a Committee of twelve to confer with each other and with representatives of . . .

A. B. H. M. S. R. G. Box 10. F 10–14, the first page

Atlanta, Ga. Sept. 25th 1894

Rev. T. J. Morgan, D. D.,

Cor. Sec. of A. B. H. M. Society,

New York.

Dear Brother:

It affords me great pleasure to inform you that the Home Mission Board at its meeting on yesterday, (24th) accepted by a unanimous vote the agreement entered into a Fortress Monroe by the Joint Committee of the Home Mission Society and the Southern Baptist Convention.

The Board desires to begin at once the duties made obligatory upon it by that agreement, and to prosecute them continuously, unless some future action of the Southern Baptist Convention, which we do not anticipate, should otherwise direct.

We would be obliged to you for such information as will facilitate the action of the Board. We especially request that you would give us the name and location of the schools of the Society, together with the names and addresses of the presiding officials.

We would also be glad to receive full information as to the mission work of the Society among the colored people of the South, and especially the names and addresses of all the General Missionaries under appointment of your Board.

We shall be pleased to confer with you in regard to plans for joint mission work among the Colored people, by correspondence, or by personal interview, if that should be more desirable.

The absence of our Corresponding Secretary during the months of October and November, in consequence of the meetings of our State Conventions, may somewhat delay the completion of the necessary arrangements for this work, but we trust that they may be perfected as speedily as possible.

The Home Mission Board is greatly rejoiced at the returning harmony among the Baptists of our whole country, and confidently expect larger prosperity and a fuller measure of the Devine blessing upon all the efforts of our churches to promote the glory of the Prince of Peace as a gracious result of their fraternal co-operation.

Your Brother,

Signed) I. T. Tichenor, Cor. Sec.

It seems to me desirable that we should secure from the Committee appointed by our Southern brethren, the following concessions;

1. The cordial endorsement of our Educational work among the Negroes, and a recommendation of it to the sympathy and co-operation of the Southern people.
2. A recommendation from them, that in each State where our schools are located the Southern white Baptists shall take a lively interest in the schools; visit them; commend them; and do what they can, publicly and privately, to promote their interests.
3. That they recommend that in each Southern State, the white Baptists shall promote the prosperity of the schools within their borders, by the erection of buildings, establishment of professorships, creation of endowments, founding of libraries; or in other substantial ways increasing the material equipment of the schools.
4. That they recommend that the Southern State Conventions shall assist in providing support for worthy young men in these schools who are students for the ministry.
5. That where it is practicable, a Fund be raised among the white Baptists in the State for the payment of the salary of one or more teachers in the Colored Schools.

I think we may concede on our part:

1. The appointment of representative Southern men, who are in hearty sympathy with our work, to positions on the Boards of Trustees of our schools.
2. The selection of teachers for these schools without regard to sectional lines, asking simply that they shall be persons who are in thorough sympathy with the Educational work and are prepared to carry it on, on conservative lines recognizing the manhood and womanhood of the pupils; treating Negro pupils precisely as they would treat white pupils.
3. So far as social equality is concerned, there should be an understanding as to what is meant by this term. The schools should be conducted so as not to give unnecessary offense to the prejudice of the Southern people, but at the same time so as not to unnecessarily offend the pride of the Negroes. They should seek to awaken in the mind of the pupils' self-respect and worth ambition to excel in life.

I. T. Tichenor, Corresponding Secretary - Ass't Cor. Sec. Walker Dunson, Treasurer.

Home Mission Board of S. B. C.

No. 52 Gate City Bank Building

Atlanta, Ga., July 5, 1895

Rev. H. L. Morehouse,

111 Fifty Ave., New York.

Dear Brother,

Replying to yours of July 2nd, permit me to say that our appointments of Advisory Committees were made last winter at a time when other matters were engaging almost the entire attention of the Board. It was not then anticipated that these Committees would take any action until the coming session of the schools.

In consequence of the decline of some of the parties appointed having ordered and the death of others, we will be compelled to revise our list of appointees. Our object has been to secure the best men we could for the purpose named.

It was my duty to officially notify you of the appointment of these committees, and I must beg pardon for not having done so. I have wondered at myself for having committed such an oversight, and can attribute it only to my being so much occupied with other things as to exclude it from my memory.

The list of Chairmen appointed have been as follows: - Washington, Rev. Green Clay Smith – Richmond, Rev. C. H. Ryland and Rev. Wm. E. Hatcher, Schools in that city – North Carolina, Rev. C Durham – South Carolina, Rev. W. C. Lindsey – Atlanta, C. C. Cox for Spelman Seminary, W. J. Northern for the other schools – Nashville, Rev. J. M. Frost was first appointed as Chairman, but when he declined on account of being a Trustee, Rev. G. A. Lefton was appointed in his place-Rev. B. H. Carroll was made Chairman of the Committee for the Texas Schools.

The instructions sent to these Committees were that they should visit the schools, interest themselves in their welfare, and make such suggestions both to the Home Board and to the Home Mission Society as they might think would prove beneficial.

We have received no reports or suggestions from any of these Committees. As soon as we revise this list we will send you a copy of it, as well as a copy of the instructions which will be forwarded to you.

Dr. Hawthorne informs me that there will be a meeting at an early day of the representative of the two colored conventions in Georgia with a view of settling their difficulties. He expects you to be present at the meeting, the time of which has not yet been determined.

Your Bro.

I. T. Tichenor

I wonder if the supposed death of Mr. Dr. Collins H. Lyons of the Jeruel Association had anything to do with this letter from I. T. Tichenor to Rev. H. L. Morehouse. Dr. Lyons dies about this same time in Clarke County. The reason that I am skeptical of the death of Dr. Lyons is that there is no mention of his death in the minutes of any association, both colored and white. Dr. W. J. White is from Augusta, where the Missionary Baptist Association formed and came into being in Augusta Georgia. Therefore, I ask you, what is the mystery that surrounds Dr. Collins H. Lyons and Clarke County? I am just going to surmise this one situation with Charlie and Mary Callaway during this same time in Clarke and Oglethorpe County. Mr. Collins H. Lyons turns up dead during 1894 and Charlie and Mary are being molested by Mr. William Eberhard.

Atlanta, Ga., Dec. 1st, 1898

To the Executive Committee of the Georgia Negro Baptist Education Society,

Dear Brethren:

After carefully considering the matters which you committed to us, we submit the following report for your approval and action.

1. we recommend that the Districts into which the State is divided be known as The Atlanta District, The Athens District, The Augusta District, and The Americus District.
2. That the residence of the Missionaries be as follows;

Rev. E. P. Johnson, Atlanta, in charge of the Atlanta District;

Rev. George A. Goodwin, Athens, in charge of the Athens District; Rev. W. J. White, D. D., Augusta, in charge of the Augusta District;

and Rev. D. D. Crawford, Americus, in charge of the Americus District.

3. We recommend that the following tables giving the population of the Counties, Cities, and Central Points for holding Ministers' Institutes in each District be placed in the hands of the Missionaries for their guidance in conducting their work; the places for holding Ministers' institutes being subject to changes as experience may make necessary.

(Title of Source: Box 10; folder 10-14 page 1 & 2 * Atlanta Ga. December 1, 1898)

These are the churches that raised money for the Educational Missionary for the Negro Educational Society. Starting with the Atlanta District and Rev. E. P. Johnson.

From the churches:

Rev. J. G. Poindexter and the Thankful Baptist Church of Rome $7.01,

Rev. S. H. Jackson and the Stone Mountain (White); $6.00

Rev. C. O. Jones and the Reed Street Baptist Church of Atlanta $10.00

Rev. A. D. Williams and the Ebenezer Baptist Church of Atlanta $4.15

Rev. R. Dorsey and the Hopewell Baptist Church of Norcross $4.00

Rev. W. A. Crittenden of Social Circle and the Mars Hill Baptist Church $1.15

Rev. F. M. Simmons of Covington and the New Hope Baptist Church $1.70

Rev. W. W. Floyd and the Zion Hill Baptist Church of Atlanta $2.66

Rev. A. P. Pratt and the Bethel Grove of Covington $1.00

Rev. J. C. Center and Lithonia Baptist Church $6.87

Rev. R. W. Watkins and the Shiloh Baptist Church of Dallas Ga. $1.30

Rev. P. J. Bryant and the Wheat Street Baptist Church of Atlanta $12.40

Rev. E. P. Johnson and the Zion Hill Baptist Church of Marietta $6.45

Rev. E. R. Carter and the Friendship Baptist Church of Atlanta $63.21

Rev. J. D. Gordon and Calvary Baptist Church of Madison, Morgan County $7.55

Rev. B. Austin of Edgefield Baptist Church of Fayetteville $1.75
Rev. Cyrus Brown and Zion Hill Baptist Church of Acworth $14.28
Rev. A. J. Allen and the Montezuma Baptist Church $1.00
Rev. J. C. Beavers and Shiloh Baptist Church of Lithia Spring $2.26
Rev. E. J. Fisher of the Mt. Olive Baptist Church of Atlanta $10.08
F. A. Lynch the clerk of Mars Hill Baptist Church of Dallas $3.00
Rev. H. Way and the Springfield Baptist Church of Hawkinsville $8.10
Deacon R. Johnson of Zion Hill Baptist Church Marietta $1.00

From Individuals
Macon County: Rev. W. G. Johnson $1.10
Augusta Ga.: Rev. T.J. Hornsby $2.00
Atlanta Ga.: Rev. K. H. Huston and wife $2.00
Atlanta Ga.: Rev. E. P. Johnson $7.67
Social Circle Ga.: Rev. W. A. Crittenden $ .70
Monroe Ga. Mr. Clemmens $ .10
Madison Ga. Mr. J. C. Paschall $. 75
Atlanta Ga.: Mr. G. H. Farmer $ .20
Atlanta Ga.: Cash $.26
Atlanta Ga.: Mr. J. W. Jones $.25
Monroe Ga. Mr. A. M. $.50
Atlanta Ga. Mrs. McNeal $.40
A Friend $ 1. 82
Augusta Ga. Rev. C. T. Walker $1.00
Forsyth Ga. Rev. A. Delamater $.56
Madison Ga. Rev. R. Simms $.25
Godfrey Ga. Rev. C. H. Young $.25
Social Circle Mr. W. Belcher $.25
Atlanta Ga. Jos. Thomas $2.50
Atlanta Ga. C. C. Beasley $1.00
Cash $.10

Cash $.15

South Atlanta Mr. Moore $.25

Vienna Ga. Mrs. A. J. Leonard $1.00

Cash $.05

Cash $.25

Madison Ga. Jeanus Madison

From Associations & Conventions

Madison S. S. Con. Social Circle, J. A. Lowe $5.00

S. S. Union, Atlanta, J. B. Brandon $7.10

S. S. Workers Con. Atlanta, A. R. Johnson $31.05

New Hope S. S. Con. Reynolds-town, H. W. White $6.35

C. C. Society A. B. College $1.03

Western Union Assoc. Newnan, Rev. J. W. Give $7.81

Madison Assoc. Farmington, Rev. E. P. Johnson $15.85

Cabin Creek Ass'n Milner, Rev. J. H. Moore $3.05

Friendship Ass'n Douglass Co., Rev. A. Penn

Carollton Union Ass'n Whitesburg, Rev. A. J. Beavers $9.20

New Hope Ass'n, Covington, Rev. J. C. Center

Minister's Institute, Hampton, Rev. G. N. Bryant $5.60

Gen. E. & M. Con. Roe, Rev. G. H. Dwelle $10.00

Middle Ga. Ass'n, Macon, Rev. F. M. Simmons $19.70

Woman's Con. Monroe, Mrs. M. Clemmons $1.50

Total $350.96

Money raised by Rev. Goodwin Educational Missionary for the Negro Educational Society of GA. Athens District

Athens:

Jeruel Academy $.83

Mt. Pleasant Church $1.07

Friendship S. S. $.81

Mt. Pleasant $.30

Elberton Ga. Calvary Baptist Church $.50

Gainesville 1st Baptist Church $1.48

Elbert Ga. Calvary $11.01

Greensboro Ga. Springfield $6.57

Monroe Ga. Tabernacle $3.36

Covington Ga. Bethlehem $.74

White Plains Ga. in Greene County Ga. 4th dist. S. S. Con. Shiloh Baptist Ch. $1.25

Social Circle Walton Co. Mod. S. S. Convention (Con.) $5.00

Covington Ga. Newton County, Bethlehem $.50

Madison Ga. Morgan Co. Calvary $8.01

Crawfordville Ga. Friendship $1.26

Union Point Ga. Greene County Springfield $1.05

Rockmart Ga. Rockmart Church $2.00

Whitney Ga. Fellowship $.71

Farmington Ga. Morgan Co. Mod. Baptist Association $10.00

Millville Ga. Flaggs Chapel $12.30

Millville Ga. Trinity C. M. E. Ch. $1.07

Millville Ga. Shiloh Baptist Ch. $.40

Grantville Ga. Rev. C. J. Gordon $1.10

G. Hunter and the N. W. Association $5.00

Atlanta Ga. Rev. C. O. Jones $.25

Ebenezer Church (spelled Eb.) $3.81

1st Baptist Church $1.71

Hills Chapel $.75

Watkinsville in Clarke County and Oglethorpe County Bethel Church $1.27

Monroe Ga. Morgan Co. Woman's Convention $1.56

Gainesville Ga. St. John $3.39

Monroe Ga. Zion Hill $10.49

Washington Ga. Wilkes Co. Springfield $6.10

Social Circle Ga. Mars Hill Baptist Church $.45

Social Circle Ga. Mars Hill Baptist Church $1.35

Crawfordville Ga. Friendship Baptist Church $1.25

Monroe Ga. Zion Hill Baptist Church $.46

Covington New Hope Baptist Church $1.28

Social Circle Ga. Mars Hill Baptist Church $4.44

Sharon Ga. S. S. convention 3rd. Shiloh $5.00

White Plains Ga. 2nd Baptist Church $.65

Siloam Ga. Siloam Church $.15

Buckhead Ga. Shiloh Association $4.63

Madison Ga. Calvary Baptist Church $1.65

Monroe Ga. Tabernacle Baptist Church $1.07

Shady Dale Ga. Greenwood Baptist Church $1.61

Millville Ga. Trinity C. M. E. Church $1.56

J. T. Singleton $.50

Monticello Ga. New Tologia $5.00

J. Hunter & S. S. N. W. Association $1.47

Royston Ga. Deacon H. Tate $3.77

Lee $10.00

Jeruel Association $4.00

Total $150.96

Money raised by Rev. J. M. Jones Educational Missionary for the Negro Educational Society of Ga. Athens District. From Churches

Ditch Pond Baptist Church, $5.40 / Ditch Pond Baptist Church $1.08

Halls Baptist Church $.2.25 / Halls Baptist Church $.25

Ditch Pond Baptist Church $20.50 / Halls Baptist Church $1.00

Maysville Baptist Church $.14 / Hurricane Grove Baptist Church $.68

Ebenezer Baptist Church $.25 / Halls Baptist Church $1.25

From Societies:

Odd Fellows Society $.35

Masonic Society $1.35

From Individuals:

Mr. C. T. Reed $.25, Mr. L. L. Ramsey $.10, Mr. E. Jones $.25, Mr. John Jones $.05, Mr. Willie Lockhart $.05, Mr. Andrew Steward $.10, Mr. W. H. Harris $.05, Pick Thompkins $.10, Mr. James Groover $.05, Mr. D. B. Young $.25, Mr. William Lyons $.10, Miss M. A. Spirers $.35, Miss M. L. Ramsey $.05, Mrs. Annie E. Fennell $.10, Total $36.40

Money raised by Rev. W. J. White Augusta District

Augusta:

E. A. Barney $.50; S. D. Walton $.10; Harmony Church $1.00; Rev. H. Morgan and the Friendship Baptist Church $2.42; Union Baptist Church $2.42; Mrs. Charity Washington $.25; Sherman Hayes $.25; Union Baptist Church $3.12; Shiloh Association Rev. S. C. Walker President $4.64; Educational Society, Walker Baptist Institute $1.13; Darien Ga. Second Shiloh Association $2.75; Zion Baptist Association $11.49.

Powellton Ga.:

Reuben Lightfoot $.01; Jeff Walker $.09; Rev. Moses Hubert $.15; Mattie Rudicle $.38; J. H. Heath $.05; Arlena Miller $.08; Julia Dixon $.21; Sallie Lewis $.06; Bessie Dixon $.09; Abbie Jackson $.07; Willie Rudicile $.08; Zack T. Hubert $.05; Eva Dee Roberts $.08; Lucy A. Barksdale $.25; Indy Hubert $.05; Mary L. Hubert $.60; Jerry Walker $.19; Mrs. Minnie C. Heath $.10; A. H. Heath $.59; U. S. Roberts $.15; Milton Castleberry $.10; F. Heath $.05; S. M. Thornton $.05; H. H. Harley $.10; Clara Barksdale $.15; Mary Frazier $.15; Mrs. Harriet Mapp $.10; Ellen Hubert $.10; Lucy Hubert $.10; A. V. Hubert $.10;

Sparta Ga. H. B. Gilbert $.06; Henry Watkins $.05; R. E. Crayton $.05; Olla S. Lewiers $.05; R. T. Battle $.05; R. S. Ingram $.10; A Friend $.10; Adeline Ridley $.25;

J. C. Clayton $.42; Rev. E. Lawrence $.09; Birdie Washington $.13; Maria Pinkston $.05; German S. Divers $.15; Augusta Richardson $.05; Addie W. B. … $.18; Ethel Stanley $.05; Anna Spence $.05; Annie Shivers $.05;

Augusta Ga.:

Rev. T. J. Hornsby Moderator and the Walker Baptist Association $5.00; Hale Street Baptist Ch. $11.65; Union Baptist Church $.92; Union Meeting St. John $.45; North Augusta Association $2.50; Noah Ebenezer Association Waynesboro GA. $1.25; Hephzibah Ga. Ebenezer S. S. $.46; Ebenezer Baptist Church $3.00; Rev. G. W. James of Kiokee Mt. Carmel Baptist

Church $10.35; Columbia S. C. and Rev. R. Carroll $5.00: Macon Ga. Capt. J. M. Barnes $1.00; Augusta Ga. and Union Baptist Church $1.25; Augusta Ga. Mr. Willie Simms $5.00; Union Baptist Church $.81; Ministers Union $1.00; Donated By W.J. White $14.13; Total Donated $142.57.

Money Raised by Rev. D. D. Crawford Educational missionary for the Negro Educational Society for Ga.

Americus District:

From Associations:

Rev. J. D. Davison and the 2nd Flint River $3.92: Rev. G. W. Martin and the Benevolence $5.00: Rev. F. M. Simons and Middle Georgia $10.00: Rev. J. B. Brinkley and Harrison Union $20.00; Rev. J. B. Green and Southwestern Union $.301; Rev. C. F. Glowers and Union Meeting Flint River Assn. $2.30; Rev. J. T. Stevens and Union S. S. Meeting of Twiggs County $2.75: Rev. W. R. Forbes and Mt. Calvary $.48; Rev. M. J. Morris Union Assn. $21.80; Rev. R. Munson and Southwester Assn. $3.25; Rev. J. H. Moon Cabin Creek $3.05; Rev. Young and Thomasville $6.10.

From Churches:

Rev. R. Dorsey, Norcross and Hopewell $1.06; Rev. A. J. Allen of Montezuma and Magnolia $5.35; Rev. P. Fann Ft. Valley Shiloh $5.35; Rev. R. S. Snellings, Macon Mt. Olive $10.61; Rev. J. Thomas, Macon Union…. $2.00; Rev. H. May, Hawkinsville; Springfield $4.07; Rev. J. R. Willis, Cuthbert; Liberty $1.80; Rev. T. M. Williams, Hebron Ga. Poplar Springs $2.51; Rev. L. P. Pinckney Sandersville; Bay Springs $2.47; Rev. R. B. Williams Tennille; Tennille Grove $4.00; Rev. H. S. Solomon, Kathleen Ga. Piney Grove $3.11; Rev. J. S. Kelsey of Columbus Ga. Friendship $.40; Rev. J. S. Kelsey, Americus Ga. Friendship $2.00; Rev. M. Gibson, Pinehurst Ga. Evergreen $.60; Rev. H. R. Bennett, Louise Ga. Mt. Zion $2.61; Rev. S. Thomas of Quitman Ga. Sweet field $1.60; Rev. A. J. Allen, Shellman Ga. New Harmony $6.72; Rev. A. King, Shellman Ga. and White Springs $.60; Rev. B. W. Davis of Pralen Ga. Benevolent $2.01; Rev. W. E. Mullen, Roanoke Alabama; 1st. Baptist Church $1.37; Rev. M. J. Morris, Cordele Mt. Calvary $18.22; Rev. J. S. Brown of Marshallville Ga. Bethel $15.17; Rev. W. G. Johnson of Macon 1st Baptist $14.05; Rev. I. R. Hall of Macon Fulton Church $3.48; Rev. J. T. Stevens, Solomon Stone Creek $11.60; Rev. J. R. Willis, Davison Sardis $8.51; Rev. S. S. Broadnax of Quitman and Beulah Baptist Church $7.81; Rev. T. M. Williamson, Sun Hck…. Green Grove $6.39; Rev. Geo. Cullins, Dwights Ga. Bold Spring Baptist Church $1.61; Rev. Geo. Washington, Warthens Ga. Middle Hill Baptist Ch. $1.37; Rev. R. S.

Smith Columbus Ga. 6th Ave. Baptist $4.06; Rev. C. H. Young, Americus Ga. Bethesda Baptist Ch. $3.11; Rev. W. F. Farver, Dixie Ga. Simmons Grove $5.00; Rev. B. W. Warren, Ft. Valley Ga. Center Union $.35; Rev. S. Thomas, Hebron Gum Hill $1.50; Rev. E. Forrest, Valdosta Ga. Antioch $2.30; Rev. A. J. Allen, Shellman Ga. Union Hill $.11.

Augusta Georgia: Rev. J. J. Lindsey of Antioch and Antioch Baptist Church $.35; Rev. W. M. Heard, Five Points Alabama and Macedonia Baptist Church $.55.

Dawson Ga. Rev. H. L. . . . McRoe, St. Mary (Freewill), $.30; Oak Grove $5.48

Caravan, Rev. W. E. Mullen, Owensbyville Ga. $1.91;

From Individuals:

Buena Vista Ga. Rev. Anderson $.50; Macon Ga. Rev. R. Marcus $.75; Macon Ga. Prof. G. D. King $.50; Norcross Ga. Dewitt Kelley $.30; Americus Ga. Steve Osten $.25; Montezuma Ga. J. W. Williams $.25; Montezuma Ga. Prof. J. G. Green $10.; Macon Ga. Rev. M. Singleton $.25; Montezuma Ga. Miss Sallie Gibson $.25; Hebron Ga. Ellis Cummings $17.; A. F. Dapl—— $.25; Hebron Ga. (last name is Moses $.25); Oconee Ga. J. R. Irwin $.05; and J. M. Reed $.12; Owensbyville Ga. Mrs. Frances G. Kelley $1.55; Marshallville Ga. Miss Rebecca Felton $.15; Macon Ga. Rev. J. Thomas $1.00; Americus Ga. M. H. Barnett $.10; Americus Ga. J. Matt. Hart $.10; Montezuma Ga. Noah Hargabrook $.05; Montezuma Ga. Chas. Felton $.05; Montezuma Ga. Jas. Wilson $.05; Americus Ga. D. H. Higgins $.10; Hebron Ga. C. Sheppard $.25; Griffin Ga. Rev. J. H. Moore $.50; Cordele Ga. R. H. Harris $.05; Tennille Ga. Levi Humphrey $.50; High Shoals Ga. T. Holliday $.10; Quitman Ga. Rev. C. C. Smith $.25; Montezuma Ga. Prof. S. S. Humbert $.90; Miscellaneous $4.21.

Total Collected on Field $269.21 Libraries Sold 14.

Money Raised by Rev. W. J. White Educational Missionary for the Negro Education Society of Ga.

Augusta District:

Rev. R. Carroll $.25; Cesar Proctor $.25; Church Collections $.57; Rev. Pinkney James $.25; Rev. F. M. Heyder $.05; Miss L. C. Laney $.23; Mrs. D. T. Hutchinson $.25; Mrs. Ida Ward $.25; Mrs. D. D. Hutchinson $.25; Mrs. Malinda Kimball $.25; Rev. Simon Morton $.25; Mrs. Eliza Elliott $.50; Chas. Bronham $.10; Lewis McKelvie $.50; Harmony Church $.50;

Rev. Chas. A. David $.50' Mrs. Martha Mock $.25; Afternoon Collection $2.50; Miss Alice Overton $.50; Collection $.12; Mrs. Mary McKelvie $.50; Mrs. Alexena Jones $.50; Mrs. Viney Horton $.25; Antioch Church $1.00; Rev. J. W. Hill $.25; Felling Spring Church $.40; Miss L. B. Mims $.25; Mrs. Kittie Robinson $.50; Mrs. Janie Mims $.10; Mrs. Nellie Stokes $.10; Dea. A. Thompkins $.10; Collections $.30; Miss Gracey Johnson $.05; Clem Easton $.05; Anderson Robinson $.25; R. B. Bussey $.25; Rev. Henry Owens $75; Tabernacle Church $.2.45; Elim Church $1.00; Sister Hankerson $.05; Rev. Wm. Russell $.35.

Augusta Ga.:

Russell & Rosenfield $1.00; Oscar Cook $.25; Cash $.05; G. H. Howard $1.00;

Savannah Ga.:

James Flournoy Mrs. Celeste King $.25

Brunswick Ga.:

S. Hodges $.10; Bro R. Carroll $.50

Savannah Ga.:

W. Collier $.10; B. Cashin $.05

Savannah Ga.:

L. J. Pettigrew $.10; Rev. P—— Hunter $.10; G. H. Eubanks $10; Rev. E. O. Johnson $.20; Wm. Durden $25; Capt. H. W. Walton $.25; Mrs. Barbara Dezara $.25; Mrs. Jas. Wells $.25; R. M. Davis $.50; Church Collection $.50; Mrs. S. B. Jenkins $.25; Mrs. Mary McKelvie $.25; Mrs. Katie Brown $.10; W. J. Cooney $.50; Savannah Rev. P. W. Jenkins $.30; Rev. B. J. Morgan St. John Baptist Church $3.50; Rev. R. B. Habersham $2.50; Lic. Julius Jackson $.50; Rev. G. W. Griffin $2.03; Rev. J. S. Irby of Savannah and 1st Tabernacle Bapt. Ch. $.50; J.H. Rockley $.25

Waycross Ga.: Rev. S. Beauford $.20; Deacon A. Smith $.25

Brunswick Ga.: Rev. G. R. Williams $.25; Mrs. E. F. Johnson $.30; Miss Mabel Coles $.10; Rev. John Williams $.10; Rev. S. Doster $.50

Shiloh Baptist Church $.50; Mrs. Indians Giles $.10

St. Simons Island: Rev. J. G. Dent $.25; New Jersey Baptist Ch. $.25;

Baxley Ga. Mrs. Harriet Hall $.15; Dr. E. M. Brawley Grace Baptist Church $2.00; Hudson Ga. Mrs. Betsie Robinson $.20; Crescent Ga. Mrs. M. Baldwin $.25; Hudson Ga. Bro. R. Lotson $.25; Crescent Ga. Bro. Cato Wilson $.10; Darien Ga. Rev. R. R. Miff—— 1st A. B. Church

$3.00; Baxley Ga. Miss Maggie A. Hall $.10; 1st A. b. Church $.1.20; Rev. R. H. Thomas of Hudson Ga. and Elm Grove Church $2.25; College Ga. Rev. R. H. Thomas $.50; Bro. A. Robinson $.25; Hudson Ga. Bro. D. L. McIntosh $.25; Crescent Ga. Mrs. L. G. Leake $.25; Brunswick Ga. Co. H. T. Dunn $1.00.

Chapter Thirteen

BLACK BAPTIST BACK IN THE HANDS OF WHITE SOUTHERNERS BECAUSE OF UNIFICATION OF THE BAPTIST!

TWELVE REASONS why every Baptist in Georgia should Support Heartily the plan of Co-operation Adopted Between the American Baptist Home Mission Society, Home Board, Southern Baptist Convention, State Board, Georgia Baptist Convention on the One Part, and The Georgia Negro Educational Society on the other,

-

----------- To: -----------

ATLANTA, GA., APRIL 28, 1899.

1. Every lover of the great Negro Baptist family of Georgia has been praying that some plan might be formulated and adopted by which, once more, with united hands, hearts and heads, the great denominational interests, committed to us by Almighty God, might that this plan has come in answer to those prayers.
2. The Missionary Baptist Convention of Georgia, in Augusta, June 12, 1897, appointed a committee of twelve to meet with a similar committee

of twelve appointed by the General Missionary and Educational Convention of Georgia, in Athens, October of the same year. These two committees representing all the Baptists of the State, met at Spellman Seminary, November 30, 1897. A large majority of each was present. After a full, free, and thorough discussion of the subject under consideration, the committee decided to call a convention February 16, 1898, in the city of Macon. There was but one vote in the negative. At the appointed time 264 churches, represented by 302 delegates, were reported. The Educational Society was organized there and then by leading Baptists from all over Georgia. It is therefore a State body and deserves the hearty co-operation of every Baptist in the State.

3. The work of this Society does not interfere with the special work of either convention. Its purpose is help, in all parts of the State, regardless of conventional lines. It will aid both Conventions in doing their educational and missionary work at the least possible cost.

4. This plan of co-operation opened to the many preachers, who have not had the advantages of the school-room, a three years' course of reading and study and has been arranged so that ten of the best books for ministerial students for the small sum of five dollars can be obtained.

5. New Era Institutes are being held in central localities in all part of the States. The best qualified preachers and laymen, white and colored give most valuable instruction to those who attend. The only opportunity many of our good men will ever have for getting help is found in these Institutes.

6. The Educational Society has as one of its objects the building up of denominational schools in all sections of the State. Last year the American Baptist Home Mission Society, one of the bodies in the co-operation gave $1200 to help three schools owned by colored Baptists and taught by colored teachers--- Americus Institutes $200; Walker Baptist Institute $500; and Jeruel Academy $500.

7. We have in this State many Baptist teachers who would be great powers in the denominational ranks if employed in Baptist schools. These young men and women, many of whom are not even known as Baptists, will be brought to the front as leaders in church work. By building up these schools the Educational Society will do a wonderful work for the denomination. All over this State there are high schools that need a helping hand to support the in their struggle for existence. If the Baptist of Georgia will rally around the Educational Society as they ought, this will be done.

8. This plan has already added four colored members to the Board of Trustees of Spelman Seminary and four to the Atlanta Baptist College.
9. A Theological department has been established at the Atlanta Baptist College. The salary of Dr. C. C. Smith, a most worth and able Christian, gentleman, is paid by the co-operative bodies. Next year, another instructor will be employed in the Theological Department.
10. Article XII of the Constitution of the Educational Society reads as follows: "The Board of Managers of the Educational Society shall have the right to nominate to the Board of Trustees of the Atlanta Baptist College for appointment on the faculty as many professors and teachers as it shall provide the money required for the payment of their salaries." From the above, it will be seen that a great opportunity is offered the Baptists of Georgia. If we furnish all the money required to run the Atlanta Baptist College, then the College will be ours to manage. Why not do this? We can if we will. Let us try it. This is much cheaper than building and running a college. First, one hundred churches would give $100 apiece yearly, another hundred $75 apiece yearly, and another hundred $50 apiece a year, the handsome sum of $22,500 will be raised for our schools.
11. This plan has brought together the strongest possible combination of Baptist forces to help us do our State work. Think of it! One hundred and eight thousand white Baptists of Georgia, the many hundred thousand of the Southern Baptists Convention, and the great hosts of Northern Baptists, connected with the American Baptist Home Mission Society, have united in this co-operative plan. The Northern and Southern Baptists, so long separated, have united their forces to help the Negro Baptists. These three bodies will give this year to the work of co-operation $3,450, next year $3,066.99, the third year $2,299.98. In three years $8,816.97
12. There is room enough in this co-operative scheme for all the Baptist leaders, great and small. All the head power, heart power, and pocketbook power in the denomination will find ample room for service. You will not be asked as to your Conventional proclivities, you will not have to tell at what institution you were educated. No one will prove to find out from what State you hail. If you are a Baptist and desire to help in the work of the denomination, the right hand of fellowship will be extended, while "Am I a soldier of the Cross," is being sung.

E. P. Johnson

General Educational Missionary of Georgia

Now, I have one question to the state that Rev. Collins H. Lyons is one of the men that took part in the two committees that came together in Augusta, Georgia, on June 12, 1897 because he helped form the Missionary Baptist Convention with Rev. W.J. White and others. The question is, did Mr. Collins H. Lyons live as a colored man and have colored children? And did he, like so many men that were white up until, frowned upon in the late 1880s and early 1900s? Are Charlie Callaway and John Austin living in the same manner as well? Or are they part of the notorious Blind Tiger Gang that was so powerful at this time in Georgia and both white and colored covered for each other in this crime and liquor organization?

There must have been an agreement between the White Southern Baptist and the Colored Missionary Convention in the Chattanooga Conference for Mr. C. S. Brown to write a ten-page letter to Rev. H. L. Morehouse. After I read this letter, I read in the Baptist newspaper coming out of Augusta by Rev. W. J. White that something was happening in the Missionary Baptist Association as well!

Listen to what Mr. C.S. Brown of North Carolina writes to Rev. H. L. Morehouse on December 21, 1900.

New York City

My dear Brother,

Your Favor of the 17th instant came promptly to me, soliciting y opinion respecting the feasibility of the cooperation approved November 23, by a conference held in Chattanooga between representatives of the Southern Baptist Convention and the National Baptist Convention. I had previously decided to write your respecting the same, and your letter only urges me to hasten forward my communication to make known my convictions concerning this new movement.

I am a cooperationist of the most radical type- I hail with delight every honest effort made to unite the races in Christian work, and believe this to be the most potent way to eradicate race prejudice and destroy hostility- I want cooperation; I want the races brought into closer relations with each other; but I want this done on terms fair and honorable to all parties concerned. I must frankly confess that I do not approve of the doings of the conference in question. From my point of view, it is but an act in a well- planned tragedy, which, if permitted to develop uncontested, will prove seriously detrimental to our work and progress throughout the

South. The drift of affairs during the past few years, the unseemly attitude of many of our assumed leaders towards the most reliable benefactors of my race, forces me to regard this movement with suspicion, and urges me also to condemn the plan. The truth is, the plan seems to be in direct opposition to the present plan of co-operation adopted at Fortress Monroe sometime ago. There an agreement was reached between the American Baptist Home Mission Society and the Southern Baptist Convention, the Contracting parties, to do mission work among the Colored People in cooperation. In several of the states, this plan is now in successful operation, and is accomplishing beneficial results. It is somewhat strange that a new co-operation should now be formed by one of the contracting parties to the previous compact, without the knowledge of the other party, and especially when the new contract contemplates the doing of the same line of work. So far as North Carolina is concerned, we are satisfied with co-operation as previously inaugurated, and we do not want, and will never approve of any sort of co-operation that ignores the American Baptist Home Mission Society. Again, I am puzzled to understand the official capacity and relationship which these new officers will sustain to the organizations creating them. Are they to be Superintendent and Secretary of the Colored of the Southern Baptist Convention? Or, are they to be paid officers of the National Baptist Convention with assumed authority to go over the county to "boss" our State conventions, associations, and Missionaries? Secretary and Superintendent of what, is the question. Now, if the brethren to be chosen are to be officers of the Southern Baptist Convention appointed to supervise them interests among my people, then we shall bid them "God speed" But, if they are to go out to represent the policy of the National Convention, which policy during recent years has been manifestly antagonistic to our Northern benefactors, then we shall repudiate the movement and brand the whole thing as an unholy conspiracy. I am not yet prepared to take a course that will be construed as hostile to the people who fought my battles for me when I could not fight them myself, who aided me when I could not aid myself, who have spent millions of dollars to educate and elevate my unfortunate people in their poverty, and whose generous offerings and self-sacrificing deeds now constitute our brightest hope for the future. I cannot feel that this new movement will meet the cordial endorsement of the brethren generally; the action is rather to suspicious to be regarded as a sincere effort to benefit my race. I wish, however, to emphasize the fact that I rejoice at every evidence of sympathy manifested towards us by our Southern White brethren, and pray to see this spirit demonstrated in a practical manner; but I want a more genuine recognition of my true manhood, the disposition to accept me on my merits as a citizen and a Christian shown, according to me the ordinary rights and privileges which belong to me as a man, before I fully and finally desert and divorce myself form those who lifted me out of wretchedness, who believe in my manhood and who are now laboring manfully to secure to me the unmolested enjoyment of my privileges. The Home Mission Society having come to our rescue in the dark days of reconstruction, has now its work thoroughly established among us—academies and colleges in nearly every state, and missionaries everywhere—and is generously spending thousands annually to carry on this great work, and has solicited the co-operation of both the White and the Colored Baptist of the south and the most generous terms to aid in the extension of the same. What has led to this new alliance? It must be that certain leaders in the Southern Baptist Convention must not be in accord with the policy of the Home Mission Society in its work among us, and takes this method to embarrass the Society; and that certain leaders of the National Convention, disgruntled for personal reasons or supposed insults, have decided to wreak vengeance on the Society by crippling its work. In Conclusion, permit me to say that North Carolina is a Co-operation State. We, both white and colored, have labored together in perfect harmony, and our intercourse had been helpful and fraternal, and the result has been gratifying to all. We shall regret seriously any action that will disturb this amicable relationship; and, knowing our position on this question of co-operation, we shall feel imposed upon to have the Southern Baptist Convention send an agent or secretary of the National Convention into our State to interfere with our work. I am further of the opinion that the white Baptists of this state will condemn the doings of the Chattanooga Conference. We shall contest with fearless determination any movement calculated to array the Colored people against the work of the Home Mission Society, feeling this to be our evident duty.

Truly Yours,

C. S. Brown.

The Atlanta Historical Society

1878 TO 1879 City of Atlanta recorder Court Docket March 16, 1878 through May 24, 1879

W.M. Carter was arrested for drunk disorderly and using profane language February 24, 1879 and was fined $10.02.

City of Atlanta Recorder Court Docket May 10, 1879 thru April 22 1880

W.M. Carter was charged with drunk on the streets July 5th 1879 and was fined July 7th $3.25

Here is a marriage that took place in the year of 1878 on the 27th day of April. Thomas Callaway a person of color married Mary Ann Chambers. Jesse M. Cush is the minister of the Gospel.

Joseph Walker married Eliza Callaway on the 1st day of June of 1878 and minister of the Gospel was Rev. J. M. Jones. J. M. Jones was pastor over Macedonia Baptist Church in the Ebenezer Baptist Association. I do not know if he is still pastor of Macedonia when he married Joseph Walker and Eliza Callaway. In the year of 1877 he was still the pastor of Macedonia in Atlanta with the following Delegates: Gordon Jackson, Jefferson McHenry, Oscar Young and Joseph Rogers.

It was about this time in the later 1870s and early 1880s that the Ebenezer Association started branching off to start associations that were closer to where the colored communities could best benefit from the association.

In the year of 1877, Macedonia Church was located at State Street northeast corner of Wallace. Rev. J. M. Jones pastor. Services 11 a.m., 3 p.m. and 7:30 p.m. Prayer meeting Wednesday 7:30 p.m. Sunday School 9 a.m. This church was located near Cherry Street, near Third Street, and near Georgia Technical College. Just about the same place where Springfield was located and Springfield Corinth Baptist is formed. These are the same churches that my grandfather is affiliated with and even C. E. Callaway as well. I am beginning to see a pattern now! Cherry Street is the same place where I found Cornelius E. Callaway and not Cornelius Callaway. I do not know where Mr. C. E. or C. C. Callaway came from. However, I have a younger Charlie Callaway in the house with Mary Callaway that lived on Maple Street! I wonder why there is such mystery surrounding the Callaways at Springfield Baptist Church.

Here is an insert from the Springfield Baptist Church Anniversary program I acquired from a member that was living at the Friendship Towers where my wife and I minister to the elder that are living there. The Corinth Baptist Church came out of Greater Springfield Baptist Church in 1922.

> Rev. W. M. Phillips was the pastor and Deacon Luther Gilliam served as Board Chairman that started Corinth in 1922. Now Greater Springfield was organized in the year of 1873 in a small house on Orme Street, now known as Techwood Drive and served that community for fifty-four years. Rev. Hill served as pastor, followed by Rev. Jeffrey, Rev. J. H. Sims, Rev. W.M. Phillips, Deacons C.H. Offord and Jake Harper served as Board Chairmen. Prior to Rev. Hardy's resignation, the church was partially torn down and condemned, in getting the church repaired. Greater Springfield is the same church that the Rev. O. C. Woods who served as pastor from December 11, 1942 until his death on December 17, 1974. He became pastor after Rev. A. J. Walker and before Rev. Walker was Rev. J. W. Johnson who came after Rev. I. S. Mack who served the church from 1923 to 1930. In Greater Springfield was the choir named the C. E. Calloway Choir. Other choirs were organized by Sis. Susie M. Carter, with the C. E. Calloway choir being organized and named for the late Mrs. C. E. Calloway. Sis. Carter and Sis. Calloway were well known pioneers of the church who served faithfully and tirelessly until their deaths. As you can see now that my grandfather must have come to know Mr. Luke Hosley through Arthur association with Little Zion Baptist Church or the Corinth Baptist Church.

I believe that this is the brother of my grandfather who is named Charlie, and sometimes C. E. Callaway goes under the name of Charles and Cornelius Charles or C. C. Callaway. In the marriage records of Fulton County at the Atlanta History Center in Buckhead I found Cornelius Callaway who married Annie May Cunningham and a Cornelius who married Johnnie Borman. In the year of 1920 I found a Charles Callaway at the age of fifty. He would have been born in 1870 and his wife Francis Callaway was thirty-eight and she would have been born in 1882. It was the seventeenth of January. Edward E. Thornton was the enumerator of the tenth ward. His house was at the corner of Willard Street and Glenn Street in Atlanta. I never found Cornelius who was in the house of

Henry Callaway in Walton County in 1910. I believe that he was in Atlanta; however, I have yet to find any concrete information on him in the A. T. L. Now, I have three supposed Callaways that could be Cornelius Callaway in 1920. One is on Connolly Street in southeast Atlanta and is married to Johnnie Callaway and the same Cornelius that is married to Johnnie Callaway living in Greene County near Richard and Emily Callaway. As a matter of fact, on May 4, 1920, Cornelius paid A F. Durham mortgage (pg. 2 of Richard and Emily Callaway). And now Charlie Callaway and Fannie Callaway are on Glenn Street. Oh yeah! Cornelius Callaway in Decula, Georgia, in Gwinnett County, who is married to Susie M. Callaway. (Charlie and Fannie Callaway on Glenn Street might be the son of Jesse Callaway and Fannie, who was under the charge of Reverend Jesse R. Callaway of Penfield, Greene County.)

Now, in 1883 there is one name on the roll of this association that produced ties to Lynwood Park and the Hope Well Association. His name is P. N. Hood, who was living in the Cross Keys District 686. In addition, W. E. Craddock and Mr. M. W. White, Cornelius Callaway, a member of Williams Chapel in Decula in Gwinnett County. Williams Chapel Church does not exist any longer. Many churches were relatively close to the New Hope Baptist Association. The other church was located in Vine City, called Little Mount Olive. There is one name that I came across that was affiliated with it and his name is I. R. Hall. Little Mount Olive does not exist any longer. However, in 1883, Pastor I. R. Hall was the pastor of Shiloh Baptist Church in Atlanta, Ga. There is another church that was located in Lithonia on the 1916 map of DeKalb County. However, when I went to look for this church no one knew anything about Antioch Baptist Church in Lithonia. Antioch Baptist Church is one of the churches that Rev. J.C. Center pastored.

Rev. E. J. Fisher also has a church in the New Hope Baptist Association as well. Rev. E. J. Fisher came out of the Western Union Association. This colored association branched off from the Western Association out of Troup County, Georgia, and had a close relationship with Coweta County and Fulton as well. However, in 1883, Rev. I. R. Hall, granted leave of absence to Rev. E. J. Fisher, who went to Atlanta to be installed as pastor of Mount Olive Baptist Church, also L. Harvey and P. M. Mobley. Now this is a strange thing. In the same year, Rev. E. J. Fisher was the moderator of the Western Union Association. He even sang the hymn "There is Work." This shows the prominence of these men in the New Hope Baptist Association with the Western Union Association that was formed in LaGrange, Troup County, Georgia.

I also wonder what is the role of Mr. I. R. Hall in the New Hope Baptist Association and his affiliation with the Little Mount Olive and A. Callaway in 1916 in Vine City.

The other church is Zion that was in Chamblee. J. W. Williams was the pastor at one time and N. H. Hayes was the clerk. I do wonder if the other Church was Thankful in Decatur. Thankful Baptist Church is the same church that C. E. Callaway joined when he relocated out of Atlanta. I also found something that was very surprising! I found Mr. M. M. Kelly who was on the roll of the association for New Hope Baptist Association in 1883, And then he shows up on a jury in 1917 in Dekalb County unless you can pass! Yes! There was a great migration to DeKalb County out of Fulton and especially out what is called the First Ward and Fifth Ward and the Second Ward, where you find Vine City and Morehouse College, Morris Brown, Spelman, and Clark Atlanta University, I can see the colored Callaways and maybe the white Callaways in this association very clearly. Even though they are not mentioned or acknowledged, they are in this association!

Rev. J. M. Jones, in the year of 1883, was now moderator of the New Hope Baptist Association. The session was held in Cave Spring in 1883 on the fifthe to the eighth of October of that year. Georgia Baptist was in charge of the print. I do not know if Eliza Callaway or Joseph Walker was a member or not. A. A. Blake is the clerk and F. B. Burson is the assistant clerk. This is the same association that has S. S. Broadnax in it. He would eventually move to South Georgia and pastor a church down there. Right now, Broadnax is living in Lithonia, Georgia. *As you may see, the ministers in the Ebenezer Association are branching off to work in other associations or starting up their own in the 1880s.*

List of Ministers and Their Post Office in the New Hope Association in 1883

Revs. J. M. Jones of Atlanta; G. B. Austin of Jonesboro: T. M. Allen of Marietta: R. H. Burson of Atlanta: J. F. Farmer of Chapel Hill; U. A. Eason of Jonesboro; C. H. Smith of Decatur; G. Valentine of Atlanta; I. Maddox of Stone Mountain; R. Avery of Campbellton; J. M. Hall of Atlanta; E. W. Harris of Marietta; R. H. Elliott of McDonough; D. Bond of Marietta; J. A. Baker of Atlanta; W. H. Knight of Cartersville; A. L. Bryan of Edgewood; J. B Gibbs of Lithonia; H. A. Burge of Woodstock; J. N. Jennings of Marietta; E. S. Hill of Atlanta; Wm. Thomas of Marietta; H. Blalock of Fayetteville; A. Knight of Cartersville; A. Penn of Smyrna; M. Scruggs of Decatur; B. Hill of Stone Mountain; J. C. Center of

Lithonia; A. A. Delamotta, of Atlanta; J. Clarke of Atlanta; J. T. Thornton of Atlanta; J. A. Blake of East Point; J. Davis of McDonough; U. Daniel of Cartersville; M. Bird of Atlanta; S. T. Thompson of Stylesboro

Licentiates

J. S. Simms of Edgewood, J. Austin of Decatur; R. M. White of Conyers; A. Crowley of Ben Hill; O. B. Blunt of Campbellton; J. Mucle of Marietta; W. P. Harper of Marietta; A. Moore of East Point; C. Moore of Chapel Hill; C. Gipson of Campbellton; M. Harrison of Stone Mountain; O. L. Beavers of Campbellton; G. W. Farmer of Atlanta; A. Rabun of Stockbridge; A. Beavers of Douglassville; M. Dalden of Wilsonville; D. Howard of Fairburn; and J.W. Graham of Atlanta.

The New Hope Baptist Association has a closer relationship with Rome, Georgia, and Dekalb counties and there are a few names related to Martin Callaway in Panthers Ville, Georgia, in Dekalb. In 1883 there is one white man named E. R. King of Cave Springs who was introduced to the association.

By the year of 1901, J. M. Jones was living in Guyton Ga. in the county of Effingham and I also found him in Rocky Ford. I do not know if this is in Tennessee or Georgia. I assume that it is in Tennessee near or just south of Knoxville. Guyton is just north of Savannah, Georgia.

**Stewart Calloway was charged with disorderly conduct and quarrelling July 8th 1879 with Henry Pullem. A warrant was issued for assault and battery on Henry Pullem, but the charges were dismissed on July 12, 1879 (page 187, Case no. 1820 and 1821). This is another great find here. Stewart B. Callaway is from Charles Callaway's side of the family that resided in Taliaferro County with his wife Louisa. He married Annie V. Smith.*

Let us turn our attention back to the Atlanta Historical Records.

Freeman Hightower disorderly conduct quarrelling and using profane language Aug. 14, 1879 fined $4.25

J.W. Hurt failure to pay Drayage August 14,1879 charges dismissed Aug. 21,1879 Stephen T. Grady was charged with keeping open doors as a dealer in spirituous and malt liquors on the Sabbath day Aug. 24, 1879 and divers other Sabbath days. Find $51.75 and remitted to $15.00 paid 36.7.5 dollars.

Jeff Calloway was charged with jumping on a Car while in motion Aug. 31, 1879 dismissed Sept. 6, 1879

Charles Smith disorderly conduct quarrelling using profane and vulgar language Aug. 31, 1879 and was fined $6.75 Sept. 6, 1879

Charles Terrell charge with failing to register and pay registration tax Sept. 1, 1879

Charges was dismissed.

Thos. F. Grady was charged with keeping open doors as a dealer in spirituous and malt liquors on the Sabbath day Aug. 10, 1879 and divers other Sabbath days. Fined $11.75

Mattie Terrell was charged with disorderly and immoral conduct and using profane language Sept. 10, 1879 fined $1.75

Nelson Calloway Loitering on the Rail Road Tracks Sept. 21, 1879 fined $2.75 and was sentenced to work on the Streets Oct. 1, 1879

Loitering on the Rail Road track with him was Neal Mathews as well.

Wade Calloway was charged with Disorderly conduct and obstructing the sidewalk Nov. 26, 1879. Also charged with him were Mat Sykes, Tarrance Jackson, James Alexander, and Gus Cody.

Charles Noble disorderly conduct and quarreling Dec. 22, 1879

D.B. Carr disorderly conduct quarrelling and using profane language De. 22, 1879

W.R. Fears was charged with Drunk disorderly and using profane language Dec. 24, 1879.

Bob Brightwell jumping on a car while in motion February 25, 1880 fined $2.75

Charles Smith charged with drunk and disorderly March 5, 1880 charges was dismissed

C.H. Willingham was charged with being drunk on the street March 7, 1880; charges were dismissed.

J.W. Rose was charged with being drunk and disorderly March 20, 1880 fined $4.00

R.M. Tuck was charged with drunk disorderly and using profane language April 5, 1880 fined $6.25

Atlanta Police Court Docket 1871 to 1872

Page 2

Louis Huff, Liza Richards, Pemelia Terrell, Stephen Jackson

Page 4

John Morris, Albert Grant, William Holly, Jack Bullock, Fannie Smith, W.H. Lee, Milton Connally

Page 6

Filmon Reynolds, Jan Sellers, Anna Johnson, Malifea Norwood

Page 8

George Washington, Henry Williams,

Page 10

Joe Stewart, Joe Martin, Thomas Howard, William Wilkerson, Andrew Hill, Henry Woodson

Page 12

Edward Thomas, John Sprayberry

Page 14

A.C. Monroe, Frank Henderson, Cicero Wyatt, Professor Chas. Evans

Page 16

Lotie Bailey, William Harris, James Parker

Page 18

Jennie Zolozo, Dick Collins, Lee Wallace

Page 20

William Smith, John Smith

Page 22

Lizzie Howard, (white); P.P. Kilby selling spirituous liquors, F.M. Jones selling spirituous liquors

Page 26

Nelson Overton, Dick Hale, Toney Dailey, Isom Logan, (white); John Stewart all but Nelson Overton were charged with getting on the cars while the same were in motion Sept. 14, 1871

Page 28

Billy Jones, Monroe Marshal, Martha White

Page 30

William Terry, Sim Braucum, John Sheppard, Jim Watkins

Page 32

Edd Ferrell charged with keeping open doors and allowing parties to assemble in a Bar Room after hours on Sept. 17, 1871

Giles Scott, William Strickland were both with jumping on the cars while the same were in motion Sept. 18, 1871, J. Leonard, (white): Charles Carter was charged with jumping on the cars while the same was in motion Sept. 18, 1871 as well as colored man Hiram Mathis, Violet North, William Knight, Edward Manning, William McKeever

Page 36

James M. Goodlett, Thos. Howard, M.C. Holloway might be colored or he might be white his description is marked thru. Jerry Thompson

Page 38

William White, Bill Gartrell, Henry Pope, Sarah Stubbs, Abe Benton, Robert McBride, George Mackey

Page 40

Nelson Bird, George Turner, Magie Johnson, Ed Jones, Mandy Dougherty

Page 42

Ed Hill, Ed Collins, Silla Collins, Frank Clemons, Aaron Smith

Page 44

George Henderson

Page 46

Jesse Brown

Page 48

William Folston, Phil Tansil, Edd Davis, (white): Edd Hartsfield

Page 50

Chas. Luckie, Jerry Walker, Henry Spear, J.T. Wright

Page 52

(white): Jane Driskill, (colored): Fannie Tolbot, Matilda Stokes, William Jones

Page 54

James Coleman

Page 58

Mary Monroe, John Tivilly, Emanuel Sanders

Page 60

Wiliam Levey, Phil Pot

Page 70

Thomas Neal was charged with Draying without a license from the city council on 19th Oct. 1871, George Kein George Simms, Morris Lane, Appleton Gay

Page 72

Joe Dobb,

Page 74

Charlotte Guggs, Henry Bailey, Richard Goldsmith, Samuel Lowe, Force Johnson, Hester Johnson

Page 76

(white) Felix Smith was charged with throwing offensive matter on the street 23rd Oct. 1871, Jackson Johnson, Ed Harrison, Robert Jones, Lizzy Berry

Page 78

Frank Lovey, Jackson Pierce

Page 82

P.S. Waters, Bud Fuller, Wiley Houston

Page 84

Malinda Stokes

Page 86

William Lewis, James Warren, Zack Rice, Bettie Johnson, Jane Carter

Page 88

Fletcher Baker

Page 90

Battle Brown

Page 92

William Walker

Page 94

Sallie Lewis, Horattio Harris, Henry Harris

Page 96

Levi Allen (white)

H.M. Grady was charged with being drunk on the street with George Peavey, A.C. Blalock

Pg. 98

Peggy Bowden, Addy Martin, Albert Roberts

Pg. 100

Lucenda Northern, Geo. Wallace, J.B. Devaux, John Ellington, Ed Ferrell

Pg 102

Thos. Harris, Robert McGuire, William Clarke, Abe Wooten

Pg 104

Charles Jones, Robt. Winbish, Zack Simms, Ann Nash

Pg. 106

James Williams, Dick Humphries, Francis McCoy, Lizzie Cooper, Charles Austin, Margaret Moore

Pg. 108

Harriet Minor, Chas. Austin

Pg. 112

Malinda Bell, Anna Dillard, Jane Craig

Pg 116

James Coleman, Ester Wilbourn, D. Marion Strong, George Pleasant

Pg. 118

Joseph Taylor

Pg. 120

Dexter Saffold, Charles Parish, Charles Austin, Clarence Herrington, Jim O'Neal

Pg. 124

Ellen Pope, Isaac Weed, James Warren

Pg. 126

Robert Webster, Ann Shields, Poney Geter (white), Matt Dewberry, John Broad, Mr. Spencer, William Kile and Joe Livsey are both charged with keeping open doors as a dealer in liquors cigars and C. on Sunday Dec. 17, 1871

Pg. 128

Sarah Newkirk, Rebecca Hollingsworth, John Jones

Pg. 132

Richard Cox, Jesse Jones, James Winship (white), Jesse Jones and William Jones charged with being drunk and being disorderly on the 25th day of Dec. 1871

Pg. 134

Anderson Ivey

Pg. 136

W.F. Carrington (white), Lou Fowland, Mr. Williams

Pg. 140

Reid Olsy (white), Henry Davis and William Jones), Seab Wright

Pg. 142

John Brown, Manerva Jackson (white)

William Wilson was charged with keeping open doors as a dealer in liquors and cigars a C. on Sunday Dec. 31, 1871

Pg. 144

Nellie Johnson, (white; W.R. Jones,), Mary Powers

Pg. 148

Jack Rogers (white)

William Wilson was charged again with the same offense

Pg. 152

James Carr, Green Rash, Hansell Hughes, William Rash

Pg. 154

Adam Chapman, Jesse Bland, John Thomas

Pg. 156

Adam Boyd

Pg. 158

J.W. Winters (white) was charged with being drunk on the streets Jan. 17, 1872

Pg. 160

Lizzie Cooper

Pg. 162

Andrew Clark was charged with running a hand cart on the side walk

Pg. 164

Henry Wade, Augustus Baugh (*Henry Wade is the servant of R. M. Rose and is in his house in the 1870s)*

Pg. 166

Edmond Johnson (white)

P.A. B. Meister allowing parties to assemble in his bar room for the purpose of drinking after hours Jan. 27, 1872

Nancy Westmoreland (white) was charged with disorderly conduct and quarrelling Jan. 27, 1872

Thomas Kilpatrick (white) was charged with being drunk and disorderly

W.J. Wooten Jr. (white) was charged with disorderly conduct and quarreling

Pg. 172

Silvey Robinson

John Eisenhert (white or Jewish) charged with disorderly conduct and using profane language

Charles Jones (white), William Little, J.G. Brazelton

Pg. 174

Solomon Everett, Nash, Florence Dimond (white)

Pg. 176

Thomas Anderson, Wm. McKeever

Pg. 178

George Coleman

Pg. 180

Richard Sheats, Lewis Thomas, Kitty Bass

Pg. 184

Gussie Brown

O.H. Jones (white) charged with riding on the side walk

Dave Allen

Pg. 186

Godfrey Herring, Jordan Farrar

Pg. 194

L. Levy (white), G. Bradley, L. Abbot, J. Johnson, J.J. Harrison, Walter Henry, R.J. White, were all charged with carrying on a system of lottery without a license from the city Council Feb. 17, 1872

Pg. 196

R.J. White (white) was charged with carrying on a system of lottery without a license from the city Council Feb. 20, 1872

O.C. Carrol (white) allowing parties to assemble in his bar room after hours on 21st Feb. 1872

Pg. 202

William Smith was charged with posting bills without a license from the City Counsel Feb 24, 1872

Sandy King, George Whitaker (white), and Charles Hetzel were charged with throwing rocks at the church Feb. 25, 1872

Pg. 204

Mary Murphy (white), Charles Smith charged with being drunk and discharging firearms Feb. 27, 1872

Pg. 208

Ed Ferrel, Josh Webb, Adam Harrison

Pg. 210

J.T. Finch (white) was charged with being drunk and disorderly

Pg. 214

Guss Geeter (Jeter) Abe Wooten

Pg. 216

Lucy Brooks

Pg. 218

Zack Rice

Pg. 224

Samuel Jackson, charged with disorderly conduct March 20, 1872

W.P. House (white) was charged with disorderly conduct quarrelling and using profane language March 18, 1872

Pg. 226

Kate Anderson, Phillis McNaught, Jack Powell, Jesse Rivers

Pg. 228

Alice Blackwall, Harrison Baker, Carrie Dupree, Eleck Wooten

Pg. 230

Charles Gilliard, Ceazar kinabroo, George Pleasant, Alvin Hutchins (white)

Pg. 232

Jim Jenkins, William Hall, Jim Apple, Harrison Robinson, Nancy Williams

Pg. 234

Marrian Jones, Jack Meriwether, Giles Scot

Pg. 242

Jack Ansley (colored) was charged with running a cart on the sidewalk April 3, 1872

Ben Harris

Pg. 248

Baldwin was charged with hitching a horse to a shade tree on April 8, 1872

Pg. 254

Simon Scott

Pg. 256

Geo. P. Barnett (white) disorderly conduct and quarrelling on the 10th day of April 1872

Margaret Walker

Pg. 274

Thos. F. Grady (white), J.L. Griffin, A. Silvey were all charged with keeping open doors as a dealer in liquors Cigars & C. on the Sabbath Day for the purpose of selling on 21st day of April 1872

Pg. 282

John Bollager (white), Stephen Strickland, W.S. Williams and James F. Callaway were all charged with being drunk and disorderly and using profane language on the 28th day of April 1872

Pg. 290

Ike Welch (white) was charged with keeping open doors as a dealer in liquors cigars and C. and allowing person to assemble in said house on May 2, 1872

David Wallace (white) was charged with selling spirituous liquors on the Sabbath April 28, 1872

Samuel Haslett (white) and Geo. Chapman were both charged with fighting chickens cocks in the Corporate limits for money on May 1, 1872

Pg. 294

Jimmie Smith (white) was charged with disorderly conduct to the disturbance of citizens on May 3, 1872 Savannah Stephens (white) was charged with disorderly conduct and using profane language on May 3, 1872

Pg. 310

L. Baldwin (white) was charged with being disorderly and using profane language on May 11, 1872, and so was W. R. Pendly

Pg. 314

Mrs. Hix (white)was charged with keeping open doors as a dealer in liquor Cigars and C. for the purpose of selling on the Sabbath day on May 12, 1872

Pg. 316

Jerry Thompson (white) was charged with selling spirituous liquors in less quantities one quart without license from City Council on May 12, 1872

Bridget Gallagher (white) was charged with keeping open doors as a dealer in Beer Cigars and C. on the Sabbath day on May 12, 1872

Pg. 320

John Coker was charged with jumping on the cars while in motion May 15, 1872

George Kile was charged with jumping on and off the cars while in motion May 15, 1872

Pg. 322–324

Lena Hogan, Copra Howard, Eva Leslie, Lottie Marsh, Emma Dixon, Jennie St. Clair, and Dora Davis, Emma Gilmore, Fannie Osborn, Julia Thompson were all charged with being an occupant of a house of ill fame and a disorderly house May 15, 1872.

Julia Thompson was charged with keeping a disorderly house and a house of ill fame and a nuisance May 15, 1872, as well as Mrs. Abbie Howard

Pg. 344

Spencer Rose was charged with being drunk and disorderly and using profane language May 27, 1872

Lizzie Watson and Mary Murphy were both charged with keeping a disorderly house, a house of ill fame and a nuisance May 27, 1872 and a divers other days before and since that time

Pg. 358

Sarah F. Rose was charged with failing to abate a nuisance after being notified to do so June 3, 1872

Ebenezer Williams was charged with disorderly conduct June 3, 1872

Pg. 362

A. Boyd (colored), A.J. Winters

Pg. 364

Ann Redding, W.S. Williams

Pg. 390

Milly Rankin, John Rankin are both charged with disorderly conduct and quarrelling June 15, 1872

G.W. Wheeler was charged with being drunk and disorderly June 15, 1872

Pg. 392

Mary Pace charged with being drunk and disorderly to the disturbance of public worship June 16, 1872, Bud Baccus, Francis Vincent, Green Irvin,

Pg. 400

D.C. Coker and Martha Coker were both charged with being drunk and disorderly and quarrelling June 21, 1872

Pg. 408

*C.D. Goode was charged with disorderly conduct and quarrelling June 25, 1872

In the year 1915, on the DeKalb County District map, Mr. C. D Goode is living near the Mount Mariah Colored Church and the Masonic Colored Cemetery in North DeKalb. Now I know that this could not be my Charles Callaway. However, I still wonder how did the McCloud family have a Martha or Mary Goode as a great-grandmother?

Pg. 414

Nathan Birge, Charlotte Birge, Dicy Birge, Camilla Jackson Joe Birge were all charged with disorderly conduct, quarrelling, and throwing rocks June 26, 1872

Pg. 420

Mark Hammond and J.W. Chase, Mrs. E. M. Ritchie were all charged with selling spirituous liquors in less quantities than one quart without license from the City council July 29, 1872

Pg. 422

E.A. Baldwin, J.W. Jones, W.B. Hurd and Frank A. Spurr were all charged with being drunk and disorderly and using profane and vulgar language July 1, 1872

Pg. 452

E.H. Smith was charged with disorderly conduct and quarrelling July 15, 1872, and so were Charles Kajar, A. Fisher, Joseph Howard, and Jasper Howard

Pg. 460

Randall Stokes was charged with being drunk in the streets

*Stephen Ryan was charged with being drunk to the disturbance of citizens

Lizzie Stokes was charged with disorderly conduct quarrelling and using profane language July 16, 1872

**The name Stephen Ryan brings back to my remembrance a Ryan that was mentioned on the Little Mount Olive Baptist church in Vine City with A. Callaway and Marshall and others in 1916.*

Pg. 472

E.H. Smith was drunk to the disturbance of citizens on July 22, 1872

B. Chaney was charged with being drunk on the streets July 23, 1872

O.H. Jones was charged with failing to abate a nuisance after being notified to do so July 22, 1872, and on divers other days before since that time

Mary Humphries was charged with keeping a disorderly house and house of Ill fame on the second day of August and divers other days before that time, and so was Jinnie Birtha

Pg. 502

James Peak had two charges against him, first selling spirituous liquors in less quantities than one quart without license from the City Council August 4, and on diverse other days before and since. Second, keeping open doors as a dealer in liquors, cigars and C. on the Sabbath day for the purpose of selling, August 4, 1872, and on diverse other days before since that time.

Next, I will show you the every day life of those who resided in the City of Atlanta in the 1880s and late 1870s. I must look at the penal system to find out a few things that went on in the city.

Hunter Street

Freeman Hightower disorderly conduct quarrelling and using profane language Aug. 14, 1879 fined $4.25

The Atlanta City Council Minute Book

July 1/83.

Pg. 119.

By Councilman Howell.

Whereas the Mayor & General Council have learned that the subject of an appropriation to purchase land for the erection of barracks in or near our city for United States troops is now pending in congress—and Whereas, this Body believes that the re-location of barracks at this point well be agreeable to our people and of benefit to the city, and is exceedingly anxious that said appropriation shall be made their fore—Resolved, That this Body extends its acknowledgements to our Senators & Representatives in congress, for their efforts in this behalf and that they be requested to continue the same until the appropriation is made.

Resolved, further that the kindly efforts of General Sherman in this matter deserve our recognition & and grateful thanks, which are hereby tendered.

Resolved further, that this action be communicated by his Hon. The Mayor to General Sherman & to our Congressional delegation. Adopted.

Before, I get into the recorder court of 1884 and 1885, I want to mention the 1880 census. These are the Callaway's that were living on Peters Street in the First district. J. H. Jones is the enumerator on the fourth day of June. I found Mr. Joshua Callaway a thirty-seven-year-old white man working as a wood molder, and his wife Elizabeth his thirty-six-year-old wife. Their children are William at the age of ten, Lena at the age of seven, Joseph F. at the age of five, Asbury at the age of three, and Martha the mother of Joshua who is sixty-seven years old. Now Joshua was born in Florida and his mother and father were both born in North Carolina. Martha is the wife of H. W. Calaway in 1860.

Here are a few of the colored marriages that happen in the 1880s. John Callaway a person of color married Mary Garland on the sixth day of February 1887. Rev. W. R. Clemants performed the ceremony. Rev. W. R. Clemants funeral service. The house was filled to its utmost. United in singing hymn 1221 led by Rev. U. Daniel; prayer by Bro. H. J. Johnson. Rev. W. H. Knight then read a part of the 1 Philipians, and took for text the twenty-third verse of the same: "For I am in a strait betwixt two, having a desire to depart, and to be with Christ; which is far better." Prayer by Rev. U. Daniel. Sang and collected $4.10; benediction by Rev. W. H. Knight.

His service was held at Mount Zion Baptist Church in Cartersville, Ga., Bartow County, Pastor, Rev. J. F. Bright; delegates J. Bird and A. Linzy. I do not know what church W. R. Clements was a pastor of; however, he marries John Callaway and Mary Garland on the sixth day of February 1887 and he dies and his funeral is held September 29, 1887. I found Amanda Callaway a thirty-five-year-old colored woman living with her son John fourteen, Wade thirteen, William six, and Louisa a twenty-three-year-old woman in the first supervisory district of Atlanta. I also found John Carter a white man at the age of thirty-two, and his wife Lou at the age of twenty-five, Carrie four, Maybell two, and Maggie Carter an adopted mulatto girl at the age of nine.

Enrollment of Churches and Delegates J. M. Jones Moderator: 1885

1. Zion Hill Baptist Church, Acworth, Ga., Cobb Co.—Pastor, Rev. J. M. Jones; delegates, J. H. Floyd, I. Ross, E. D. Taylor.
2. Stone Mountain Baptist Church, Stone Mountain, Ga., Dekalb County—Pastor, Rev. T. M. Allen and delegate.
3. Macedonia Baptist Church, Dekalb County—Pastor, Rev. J.C. Center and delegate.
4. Mt. Olive Baptist Church, Woodstock, Ga. Cherokee County—Pastor, Rev. J. Davis; delegates, David Durham, Jeff Harris, Rev. J. Davis.
5. Zion Baptist Church, Chamblee, Ga., Dekalb County—Pastor, Rev. J. W. Williams; delegates, P. N. Hood, Rev. J. W. Williams.
6. Macedonia Baptist Church, Atlanta, Ga.—Pastor, Rev. J. M. Jones; delegates, W. E. Craddock, A. Sanders, T. C. Crook.
7. East Point Baptist Church, East Point, Ga., Fulton County—Pastor Rev. J.C. Riggins; delegates, A. A. Blake, H. Duncan, J. Conley, D. Moore.
8. Zion Baptist Church, Marietta, Ga., Cobb County—Pastor, Rev. C. G. Holmes; delegates, J. Julian and W. P. Harper.
9. Mt. Zion Baptist Church, Ben Hill, Ga., Campbell County—Pastor, Rev. J. A. Blake and delegate.
10. New Hope Baptist Church, Conyers, Ga. Rockdale County—Pastor, Rev. R. M. White; delegates, J. Gay, R. M. White.
11. Pleasant Hill Baptist Church, Conyers, Ga. Rockdale County—Pastor, Rev. J. C. Center delegates, Rev. J. C. Center, M. Hull and Wm. Hull.

12. Bethlehem Baptist Church, Atlanta, Ga.—Pastor, R. M. White, delegate, O. Carter.
13. Zion Baptist Church, Canton, Ga., Cherokee County—Pastor, Rev. D. B. Bond; delegates, R. Fields, Rev. D. B. Bond.
14. Kelly Chapel Baptist Church, McDonough, Ga., Henry County—Pastor, Rev. R. H. Elliott; delegates, W. M. Reed and M. Hartfield.
15. Antioch Baptist Church, Edgewood, Ga., Dekalb County—Pastor, Rev. A. L. Bryan; delegates, S. Bond, Rev. A. L. Bryan.
16. Mt. Zion Baptist Church, Fist Creek, Ga., Polk County—Pastor, J. T. Johnson; delegate, Pleasant Glenn.
17. Shiloh Baptist C Church, Jonesboro, Ga., Clayton County—Pastor, Rev. G. B. Austin; delegates, Rev. G. B. Austin, W. A. Gay, and R. Patillo.
18. Thankful Baptist Church, Decatur, Ga., Dekalb County—Rev. M. Scruggs; delegates, L. Harvey, and Rev. M. Scruggs.
19. Shiloh Baptist Church, Stone Mountain, Ga., Gwinnett County—Pastor, Rev. B. Hill; Delegates, Rev. Hill and J. D. Hudson.
20. Flint Ridge Baptist Church, Jonesboro, Ga., Fayette County—Pastor, G. B. Austin; delegate, H. Adkins.
21. Shiloh Baptist Church, Stilesboro, Ga., Bartow County—Pastor, Rev. W. H. Knight; delegates, Rev. W. H. Knight, W. Watkins, G. P. Rogers, E. D. Billups.
22. Salem Baptist Church, Cherokee Mills, Ga., Cherokee County—Pastor, Rev. J. Moore; delegate, L. Morris.
23. Antioch Baptist Church, Lithonia, Ga., Dekalb County—Pastor, Rev. J. C. Center; delegates, Rev. J. C. Center, J. B. Gibbs, S. S. Broadnax, E. E. Phillips and J. Walker.
24. Shiloh Baptist Church, Atlanta, Ga.—Pastor, Rev. J. T. Thornton and delegate.
25. Mt. Pleasant Baptist Church, Stone Mountain, Ga., Dekalb County—Pastor, Rev. M. Harrison; delegates, Jeff Wood and W. G. Whitaker.
26. New Hope Baptist Church, Cave Spring, Ga., Floyd County—Pastor, Rev. W. H. Knight; delegates, Jerry Berry, J. D. Walker.
27. Mt. Zion Baptist Church, Fairburn, Ga.—Pastor, Rev. H. R. Bennett; delegates, Rev. H.R. Bennett, J. C. Cook.

28. Macedonia Baptist Church, Eason Hill, Ga., Polk County—Pastor, Rev. W. H. Knight; delegates, Rev. W. H. Knight, W. L. Johnson.
29. Mount Sinai Baptist Church, Taylorsville, Ga., Bartow County—Pastor, Rev. M. Davis and delegate.
30. Cedar Spring Baptist Church, Cedartown, Ga., Polk County—Pastor, Rev. U. Daniel; delegates, A. J. Daniel and C. C West.
31. Antioch Baptist Church, Atlanta, Ga.—Pastor, Rev. M.W. White and delegate.
32. Damascus Baptist Church, Bartow Iron Works, Ga., Bartow County—Pastor, Rev. A. Knight; delegates, Rev. A. Knight and R. Smith.
33. Bethlehem Baptist Church, Panthers Ville, Ga., DeKalb County—Pastor, Rev. H. Sanders and delegate.
34. Mount Sinai Baptist Church, Marietta, Ga., Cobb County—Pastor, Rev. A. P. Roberts and delegate.
35. Sardis Baptist Church, Big Shanty, Ga., Cobb County—Pastor, Rev. Wm. Thomas; delegate, J. B. Grisham.
36. Mt. Zion Baptist church, Cartersville, Ga., Bartow County—Pastor, Rev. J. F. Bright; delegate, Rev. J. F. Bright, R. Byrd and J. Benham.
37. Edgefield Baptist church, Fayetteville, Ga., Fayette County—Pastor, Rev. G. B. Austin; delegates, Rev. H. B. Blalock and Stirling Bennett.
38. Rightsville Baptist Church, Greene County, Ga.—Rev. Mark Byrd, pastor and delegate.
39. China Grove Baptist Church, East Point, Campbell County, Ga.—Pastor, Rev. H. Sanders; delegate, A. Norwood.
40. Springfield Baptist church Boltonville, Ga., Fulton County—Pastor, Rev. W. J. Scott; delegates, Rev. W. J. Scott and H. A. Bond.
41. New Salem Church, Lime Branch, Ga., Polk County—Pastor, Rev. J. T. Johnson; delegate, N. D. Brown.
42. Springfield Baptist Church, Atlanta, Ga.—Pastor, Rev. E. S. Hill and delegate.

I now want to talk about the Reverend J. T. Johnson again. Rev. J. T. Johnson is a hard man to track. At first I went looking for him in the Jeruel Association with Collins H. Lyons in Clarke County, Georgia. However, he is pastor over at two churches in the New Hope Assoc. Mt. Zion Baptist Church.

Fist Creek, Ga., Polk County—Pastor, J. T. Johnson; delegate, Pleasant Glenn

New Salem Church, Lime Branch, Ga., Polk County—Pastor, Rev. J. T. Johnson; delegate, N. D. Brown. J. T.

Johnson will become the pastor of Zion Hill in Atlanta near or in Johnson Town just east of Lenox Square Mall. The strange thing is hardly any of the members of this association are listed on the National Baptist Association. On the statistical table of the churches does not list Rev. J. T. Johnson over any churches.

New Salem has W. Johnson as the pastor and N.D. Brown as the clerk. And Mount Zion of Polk County has as its pastor G. W. Freeman and the clerk is J. River in Fish, Ga. At one time in the New Hope Association I found him listed as J. P. Johnson, and at Mount Zion in Polk County and there is no clerk listed. In the same year he is listed as J. T. Johnson over at New Salem in Polk County in Lime Branch. Another time J. T. Johnson is listed as J. A. Johnson over at New Salem in 1884. Another pastor over at New Salem is W. M. Johnson and J. H. Floyd is the clerk. It is listed as being in Cartersville. At Mount Zion in Bartow County J. F. Bright is the pastor and F. J. Johnson is the clerk in 1887.

Evans W. Callaway, a person of color, married Addie Jackson on April 17, 1884. The marriage ceremony was performed by E. R. Carter the pastor of Friendship Baptist Church. *E. R. Carter is the pastor of Friendship Baptist Church in Atlanta. I think they might have been married in this church. Ebenezer Colored Baptist Association is mentioned on page 329.*

Nelson Callaway, a person of color, married Nora Anderson on the July 14, 1880. Nelson would become a preacher and I assume that he is a Methodist because I never see him over at any church in the Baptist Association.

Tom Cater, a person of color, married Annie Callaway on the 29th day of October 1889. H. L. Underwood performed the ceremony.

City of Atlanta Recorder Court Docket October 3, 1884, Through to August 31, 1885

Abram Walker and Willis Sims charged with retailing spirituous and malt liquors on the Sabbath day and diverse other Sabbath days Oct. 19, 1884

W.O. Jones was charged with allowing cattle to roam at large in city limits fined $.75

Will Cosby was charged with loitering on R.R. Nov. 9, 1884, dismissed

Alex Calloway, obstructing the sidewalk, Nov. 9, 1884; charged or fined $2.75, Nov. 18, 1884

Joel Hurt was charged with failing to abate a nuisance on his premises, Nov. 12, 1884; charges were dismissed, Nov. 24, 1884

J.F. Calloway was charged with drunk on the street, Nov. 21, 1884, and so were C.B. Palmer and Charles Hightower and Green Daniel J.F. Caloway; charged $2.75

Roderick English was charged with disorderly conduct, quarrelling and using profane language, Nov. 24 1884

J.C. Rose, obstructing the street, Nov. 29, 1884; fined $5.75

Vinning Calloway, disorderly conduct, quarrelling and using profane language, Dec. 1, 1884; charged $10.75

W.H. Williamson, disorderly conduct and quarrelling, Dec. 15, 1884; fined $.25

W.C. Sparks was charged with failing to register and pay registration tax, Dec. 29, 1884 fined; .10 ct.

Dr. William Smith was charged with leaving team without a driver, Dec. 8, 1884, charges dismissed

Narcissa Cloud was charged with disorderly conduct and quarrelling, Jan. 12 1885, with Zack Thomas, Harriett Thomas, and Catherine Stone; all were fined $2.00

Charles Bell, Will Callaway, Dan Wilson, George Hollingsworth, Mitchell Daniel, John Thomas, and Will Brooks were all charged with disorderly conduct and obstructing the sidewalk on Jan. 28, 1885. The fines ranged between $5 and $7 dollars, and Will Callaway and Charles Bell had to work on the streets, Dan Wilson's charges were dismissed, George Hollingsworth paid his fine, Mitchell Daniel worked on the streets, as well as John Thomas and Will Brooks.

Bartow Lucas was charged with disorderly conduct and quarrelling Feb. 7, 1885, dismissed

James Smith was charged with discharging firearms Feb. 2, 1885, $5.00 fine and $1.00 bond for carrying concealed weapons

George Floyd, Elias Cook, John Carroll, and Thos. Grant were all charged with obstructing sidewalk Feb. 9, 1885; charges were $2.00 and Elias Cook paid his fine but the rest had to work on the street.

A.T. Humphries was charged with drunk and disorderly Feb. 16 1885

Henry Hutchins was charged with disorderly conduct and quarrelling, William Callaway as well. Will's charges were dismissed and Henry Hutchins had to pay a fine of $10 and a $50 bond for fornication.

Stewart Calloway was charged with disorderly conduct and quarrelling Feb. 20 1885; fined $10.00, and he paid this charge March 2, 1885, and so did Lizzie Ragland on the same day.

J.F. Callaway was charged with drunk and disorderly conduct to the disturbance of citizens Feb. 28, 1885; fined $5. He was also fined $100 for wife beating for five days and paid $3.25 on March 10, 1885.

Charles Nobles charged with disorderly and immoral conduct using profane and vulgar language March 4, 1885; fined $20.00, stayed 2 days, paid $19.00

Hamp Reid and John Callaway are both charged with disorderly conduct and quarrelling March 2, 1885 and fined $10.00; John stays 2 ½ days in jail and paid $9.50

N. Calloway disorderly conduct and quarrelling March 11, 1885; fined $3.00, paid March 17, 1885

Jas. Hudgins charged with drunk and disorderly conduct using profane and vulgar language March 10, 1885

Henry Williams, Robert Manly, and William Wright were all charged March 10, 1885 and all charges were dismissed

William Calloway charged March 25, 1885 with disorderly conduct and quarrelling; fined $5.00, paid $5.75

John Kimbro, S.W. Blanchard, Alec Wesson, Joe Clements, Walter O'Neal, Sallie Callaway charged on the 25th day of March 1885 and fined $10.00 and stayed 2 days in jail and paid $9.75

Cornelius Grimes, Katie Easley, Emma Polite, Joe Redding all charged April 15, 1885 with quarrelling and fined $10.00

Charles Terrell and John Hightower were charged with Jumping on and off trains while in motion April 29, 1885; Charles Terrell or Ferrell's charges were dismissed.

*J.C. Bridges, Wallace & Cates, Wade Merrett were all charged with draying without a license May 5, 1885 and so was A. Tuck; all paid $5.00

**J. C. Bridges, Wallace & Cates, Wade Merrett, and A. Tuck show me a relationship that was in DeKalb County in Buckhead and Terrell and Oglethorpe County and also Gwinnett as well with these white families and Charlie Callaway!*

Riley Callaway and Emma Johnston were both charged with disorderly conduct and quarrelling May 7, 1885; both charges were dismissed

Wm. Williams was charged with disorderly conduct and quarrelling May 12, 1885 and fined $12.00

Pickens Samuels charged with disorderly conduct and disturbing public worship May 20, 1885; charges dismissed

J.F. Calloway drunk and disorderly May 29, 1885; fined $3.00, paid June 2, 1885

Narcises Cloud charged with disorderly conduct quarrelling and discharging firearms in city limits May 30, 1885

Dicey Stokes, Oscar Jones, Mattie Brown, Narcisse Jones, Minnie Terrell, Lula Jackson, Annie Jones, Anna Brown, and Lula Williams all are charged with occupying a portion of a house used as a house of ill fame June 2, 1885; fined $10.00

Henry Oliver charged with disorderly conduct, using profane language and resisting an officer June 12, 1885; fined $15.00, paid $2.50 and worked on the streets for 25 days

K. Hightower was charged with violating Sec. 62 City Code June 24, 1885

E. Foster was charged with obstructing the sidewalk June 24, 1885

J.M. Smith was charged with obstructing the streets, June 24, 1885

J.M. Spencer was charged with doing business without a license June 24, 1885

James Calloway was charged with violating Sec. 409 of City Code June 27, 1885, and so was Samuel Flood; both were fined $5.00, both paid their fines July 1, 1885

W.A. Smith and Henry Elliott were both charged with disorderly conduct and quarrelling June 27, 1885

West Barnes and John Calloway were both charged with obstructing the natural flow of water July 10, 1885; West Barnes paid his fine and John paid $1.50 and worked 2 ½ days on the streets July 15 1885

Willie Callaway charged with disorderly conduct with James Tray and Stephen Ryan July 17, 1885; all paid their fines*

*This is the second time that I found the last two names of Callaway and Ryan together; the other time was on the Little Mount Mariah Church deed.

James Smith, Carrie Wilson, Henry Key, Alfred Cato, Wm. Callaway, Henry Thompson, William Holbrook, Ed Cheshire, Gus Dodd, Clarence Bell, Seaborn Durden, Lee Clay, and Samuel Simpson were all charged August 2, 1885 for disorderly conduct and charges were dismissed for William Callaway, Henry

Thompson, Wm. Holbrook, Ed Cheshire, Gus Dodd, and Clarence Bell. These charges were for slight misconduct in front of church yard and are dismissed on request of Col. Westmoreland, chairman of the board of trustees of the church on premise of young men to use discreetly in future.

Lora Callaway disorderly conduct Aug 10, 1885 fined $5.00 paid Aug 18, 1885

This is the end of the Police Court Docket. I'd had hope to revealed to you a few Black citizens in Atlanta, whom you might have never known about or have known about and see them in Atlanta about this time. Blacks have been associated with either the church or the penal system. Happy to oblige!

The first time I find Charles Callaway in Atlanta is in the year 1891. Charles and Henry Callaway are both working for the Finley Furniture Co. This company was run by William W. Finley, the superintendent, who resided at Hampton Inn Curran Street. Mr. W. R. Ware owned the property. Remember Charlie is on the run from Oglethorpe County in 1888 and I found him in Atlanta in 1890 two years later with Henry C. Callaway and I am assuming that his bride of four years Mary Hurt Callaway is with him as well his young son Charlie who was born in 1885, and maybe Willie and Howard as well, the two might just be babies. Henry C. Callaway could just be Cleveland or Clayborn who was on the Jackson plantation before making their escape to Atlanta and when he got to Fulton County Charlie might have convinced his younger brother to change his name. Because Mr. Edward Jackson was on the pursuit for his contract laborers who was on the run from Oglethorpe the county. The county where a new form of Slavery existed. I'm wondering what William Eberhart and B. B. Williams were thinking when they hired Charlie in 1892. They knew his reputation for running. Or did they hire him for another reason, maybe because of his unique technique for manufacturing beer and liquor? Or maybe he's a well-known blind tiger! I'm assuming this because of the charges lodged against him by J. R. Haynes in 1899.

At this time, the only Charles Callaway that I found was living at 15 Alice Street. The street led from Pulliam to Pryor from Rawson, in the Second Ward on the 1930 map. It was a short street. The neighbors of Charlie are M. Barr, Tom Pride, George Smith, and C. Harris. However, the first person that I found in Fulton that was related to Charlie was his wife Mary Callaway, who was listed in the phone directory in the year of 1890. Mary Callaway worked for R.L. Sibley in the rear at 13

Houston Street. The neighbors on this street were Ms. Ada F. Smith, Rev. R.S. Barrett, H.R. Powers, A.H. Cox, Mrs. C.D. Smith, Mrs. E.A. Curtis, T.M. Hall, Dr. J.G. Earnest, and Nathan Eberhart, who lived at 92 Houston. All are white. There were only two colored men that lived on Houston Street at this same time. Gus Williams was at 524 Houston and Henry Fomby lived at 443 Houston Street, and the street came from Peachtree east to limits 1 N of Wheat Street Wards 4 and 6.

In 1895 Stewart Callaway lived at 181 Houston Street. Here I will talk about Mr. Stewart B. Callaway again because he and John C. Callaway are two very interesting colored men in Atlanta! Then Mary Nesbit. I will attempt to build another profile of Stewart Callaway or Stewart B. Callaway in Atlanta, Georgia, starting in the Atlanta Directory of 1889.

> *Index to Council Minutes volume 12, pages 1–179, City of Atlanta, 1889*
>
> *Pg. 131 line 4 Annie V. Callaway: Annie V. Callaway for relief from sewer assessment on Clifford St.*
>
> *Pg. 151 line 28 Annie V. Callaway: Adverse on Annie V. Callaway's petition for relief from sewer assessment Clifford St.*

Stewart Callaway is living at house 17 on Harris Street with A. Woods and E. Westmorland and C. A. Lumpkin. All four are living on Harris Street just before you get to Ivy intersection. There are only three houses that are on this strip of property just lying west of Peachtree east of Harris to Fort and W to Marietta and one block north of Cain Street in Wards 4, 5, and 6. F. F. Hester is in house 15 east of Stewart Callaway's house and west of Stewart's house is F. T. Gather in house 29 and west of Gather is F. Bafter' in house 42. Living in the house before crossing the Ivy Street intersection is R. D. Badger, a colored man. Living in the house where the Atlanta Brewery will come to reside is the property just after you cross Courtland Avenue intersection in house 71 A. J. Kuhn, and in house 73 is Mat Schifferer. And in house 79 is Mack Cain, a colored man. This portion of Harris Street is a business section before crossing over to Peachtree Street.

I must go on down Harris Street because there are some interesting colored men and women there who will come to reside in Vine City. After going further east on Harris Street past Mack Smith's house your next colored house in order is Richmond Reed in house 95, Hilliard Hightower house 96, Samuel Watts house 97, H. Muse and I. Mitchell in house 99. Before Crossing over the Calhoun Intersection is J. C. Morgan in house 101 and after crossing Calhoun Street is the property of the Colored Presbyterian Church. J. C. Morgan, a white man, is in house 216.

All that I will mention are listed as being coloreds on Harris Street in 1889:

Scott Jordan, house 119

Tallie Morgan, house 121

Anderson Davis, house 127

Dennis Robinson, house 129

D. Franklin, house 132

Noel Mattox, house 134

House 136 is vacant

Reuben Cutwright, house 138

Henderson Davis and K. Ducan, house 139

Silvey Mays, house 140

Silas Starke, house 141

Robert Mitchell, house 143

Anthony Tuck, house 144

Fate Davis, house 145

S. H. Jackson, the Mount Olive Baptist Church, and Mary Johnson, house 146

Robert Greenlee, house 157

George Johnson, house 158

Crossing Butler Street Intersection:

A. T. Thomas, house 160

Jerry White and Robert Thomas, house 162

W. H. Harrison, house 166

J. H. Haygood, house 167

H. Marion and C. Johnson, house 170

D. Hill, house 173

Turner Rivers, house 174

Earnest Penny, house 175

John Barrett, house 177

Robert Pierce, house 178

House 180 is vacant

Alonzo Herndon (the first millionaire in Georgia) with Albert Robinson, house 181

Mary Harris, house 190

House 194 (rear) is vacant

Alex Pitts, house 196

George Boykin and Wm. Cooper, house 198

Now this street goes further west, where I found the house of Mr. R. A. Sibley, house 39, just after crossing over Spring Street and just before you get to Williams Street. Past R. A. Sibley is the same Sibley that is out of Greene County and soon will become a Federal Court judge, Mr. R. L. Sibley, whom Mary Callaway worked for. Also, Sibley will defend Johnnie Rains in Oglethorpe County in 1899!

Now crossing Orme intersection, the only coloreds on Harris street are John Humphreys (house 116) and Stonewall Jackson (house 118). In the year 1890, on Harris Street in Atlanta, E. Westmorland and A. Woods have moved on and only Stewart Callaway and C. A. Lumpkin are at 17 Harris Street.

Living in house 15 were F. F. Hester and D. T. Bradley in house 15. R. D. Badger is in house 46. Living in house 95, where Richmond Reed once lived, are Hattie New, Miami Pace, and Julia Bailey. Living in house 96, where Hilliard Hightower once lived, was R. Redwine. Samuel Watts vacated house 97 before the year came in and the house is now occupied by Eliza Morgan. House 99 is occupied by S. Watts. House 101 is where H. Muse still lived with Mitchell. J. C. Morgan. The Colored Presbyterian Church is not listed with a street number.

These are the new colored that have moved onto Harris Street in 1890:

B. Bedford, house 112

G. Holley, house 119 (he replaced Scott Jordan)

G. Miller is in the house where Anderson Davis lived, house 127

T. Thomas has moved into the vacant house 136

Reuben Cutwrigth, in what used to be vacant house 138

J. Hightower, house 140 in place of Silvey Mays

There is now no house 141, only 142, occupied S. Starke and M. Hightower; another house 142 is where S. Meys lives.

House number 143, is occupied by M. Thomas and R. Mitchell when previously it was occupied by only Robert Mitchell. However, there was a second 143 in 1889 that was occupied by Albert Thomas, so I am assuming they are still one in the same.

S. E. Smith, house 144 in place of Anthony Tuck lived

House 157 is now vacant and V. Robinson is in the house where Butler Street Baptist Church is located.

Crossing the Butler Street Intersection:

House 158 is occupied by J.T. Boring

G. Johnson is in house 158 ½

William Scott is in house 160

H. Morrow is in house 162 where Jerry White and Robert Thomas lived

In house 167 is D. Sibley, a colored man, living where J. H. Haygood lived

A. Bosrun is in house 170 where H. Marion and C. Johnson lived

Alonzo F. Herndon is still at 181 and so are T. Rivers, E. Penny, and R. Pierce

House 180 does not exist

House 190, where Mary Harris lived, does not exist

Vacant lot 194 is now occupied by George Boykin, and where George used to live, house 198 no longer exists

S. Reid is living in house 196 where Alex Pitts lived

J. Mitchell is in house 200 where Benjamin Crawford lived

In the year of 1891, Stewart Callaway was living in house 190 on Calhoun Street just after you cross Houston Intersection, with Frank Screen. James Mitchell was in house 193. Joe Blackman was in house 200 with Dill Blanton.

A. F. Herndon is at house 181 Harris Street still and T. Herndon has moved into house 185 on Harris Street. M. Marshall was living next door to A. F. Herndon at 182. G. Boykin is at house 194. I mention Boykin because of Sam Boykin, who was brought up on charges in Oglethorpe County with Charlie Callaway in 1886. W. C. Jones is at house 200. I have noticed that only white families lived at this location. House 17 is not mentioned on Harris Street before you get to Ivy intersection. Both houses 15 and 29 are vacant in 1891. However, R. D. Badger is still located in the house 46, after crossing Ivy Street. Now going west in 1891 I found a few interesting names worth mentioning: D. P. Nolan in house 34; crossing the Orme intersection I found L. Fisher, a colored man, in house 118.

In the year 1892 Mary Nesbit shows up in house 17 on Harris Street. She is not listed as being a colored woman. House 15 is occupied by J. W. Roberts, and house 29 is occupied by J. H. Malone. Now let me tell you how close Mary Nesbit, John C. Callaway, and Stewart B. Callaway were. She was living at 17 Harris Street while they were living at the corner of Peachtree Street and Harris Street. Ivy Street is now Peachtree Center Street. I drove up and down Harris Street and found the exact place they were living. I have read how Alonzo F. Herndon owned his barbershop that only catered to white social elite of Atlanta. And now I wonder if the Callaways were the owners of this property and if A. F. Herndon purchased it from the Callaways living at the corner of Peachtree and Harris Street. At this place was a bar that was owned by John C. Callaway and Stewart B. Callaway and Mary Nesbit. All three resided here in the same house!

> *From the Atlanta Historical Society:* Mr. William L. Callaway will come to be close friends with the Walden Family and the Alexander family as well. 1957 September Consolidated Mortgage and Investment Company is formed to assist African Americans in obtaining real estate, loans, collecting mortgages, buying, selling, owning, and leasing property; and making investments A.T. Walden is elected president; W.L. Callaway Executive Vice President; T.M. Alexander Treasurer. He was also photographed shaking hands with Citizens Trust Bank President. In addition, Mr. Walter H. Smith was in the picture. Walter H. Smith is the nephew of Annie V. Callaway the wife of Stewart B. Callaway the Grandson of Charles Callaway out of Taliaferro County.

The illicit use of alcohol with women was brought to light on October 15, 1900, communication from the Colored Assembly relative to women being prohibited from drinking beer in pubic restaurants and clubs, also that no lewd colored women should be allowed on the streets after 7:30 PM. A second petition for the same was issued on Nov. 19, 1900.

Councilman Hammond says the dance academy was located at 12 1/2 Piedmont Avenue. However, the directory has him living at 91 E. Cain Street in 1899. His wife Annie V. Callaway is living at 89 East Cain Street in 1895. And in the year of 1900 and the following year 1901, he is at the same location, 91 E. Cain Street. Houses 87 through 91 are in the same lot on the right side at the corner of Courtland Avenue and located across from the auto storage, which was at 77 and 83 East Cain Street. Stewart B. Callaway and Annie V. Callaway were five houses down from Hotel Moore at 63 East Cain Street. As I had stated before, it was in 1895 that I found Annie V. Callaway in the house with Louisa Grimes at 89 East Cain Street. It was in 1895 also that Mary Nesbit changed her name to Harriet Nesbit while at 17 East Harris Street. This was while John Callaway was at 125 East Harris Street just before you go past the Presbyterian Church that was at 130 Harris Street after crossing over Piedmont Avenue.

The only other Callaway that lived on Cain Street other than Annie V. and Stewart B. Callaway is Charles Callaway at 260 East Cain Street down near Phoenix Alley south of Tanner Alley. Cain Street and Harris Street both gave up portions to make way for I-85 and I-75. The place where Charles Callaway resided at 260 East Cain Street and even where Alonzo F. Herndon resided on Harris Street are gone. Even Mattie who did laundry and resided at 126 East Cain Street is plowed under. I believe that the places in Atlanta where the colored men and women lived and made their way to Decatur Street and bought their liquor at R. M. Rose at Hilliard Street comes to a dead end into the Buttermilk Bottom Community. The stigma of these communities and the Jewish and white and mulatto half-white men preyed on the colored community and is still true today, this Friday, September 16, 2011!

Now, I know the struggle that the colored colleges and churches had to deal with within the colored community and the adversities that the white and Jewish communities brought upon these unassuming poor people. It was not only the ignorant Negro, it was also those who pushed their liquor and prostituted the young colored farmgirls and even had children with them and left them to fend for themselves! I say this because of the fact that in 1891 Stewart Callaway is listed as being a white man and is a porter for R. Dohme while there are only two other colored men listed as such. Mr. Evans W. Callaway a laborer for Elsas, May & Co. Evans W. Callaway lived on Glenn Street. And James Callaway was a laborer and resides at 35 Fort Street. Now if James is living at the rear of 35 Fort Street, he is located near Decatur Street at its intersection, or at the intersection of Fort Street and Hunter Street or where Fort Street dead ends at Memorial Drive. I do not know where Evans W. Callaway was living at this time. However, in 1877 he was living at the rear of 220 Decatur Street, which might be near Fort Street, where it intersects where James Callaway was still residing in 1877. Stewart Callaway was a student at the rear of 250 West Hunter Street. Stewart resided at the house on West Hunter Street. After crossing over Maple Street, you are only four houses away from the place where he resides. You would also go past the house of Charles Callaway at one time on 35 Maple

Street, which lies between West Hunter and Mitchell streets. Stewart was living between Maple and Walnut streets.

Now I know that Henry and Will Callaway are related somehow, but how old is Henry Callaway? Moreover, is Will Callaway the same Will Callaway that was located in Dekalb County in 1916 working for C.C. Mitchell? I went looking for Mr. C. C. Mitchell and could not find him anywhere or in any system or mode of search! However, I did find a Mr. Charles Mitchell living in Terrell County near Mr. Ned Callaway in 1880.

I also found a Mary Callaway who was also a domestic worker for B.H. Austin and resided in the rear of the place on 407 Whitehall. Mr. B.H. Austin's full name was Boomer Austin. Now I will ask you this question is Gus Williams, Charlie Callaway and is Henry Fomby who might be Henry Callaway or some kind of kin to Charlie I just do not know. Nevertheless, I can say the attorney for Johnnie Raines in the August term of court at Oglethorpe in 1900 was Samuel H. Sibley! Moreover, Johnnie Raines just did not try to get Mose Sims off the plantation of William Eberhart but he also tries to get Charlie Callaway of his place just as well. Could Charlie or Mary be pulling the strings in Oglethorpe County? Is this why the White Community cannot kill this Negro Man? It could have been easy to just find a tree and do away with him as if they would normally do a Man of Color. This put Charlie in a completely new light to me! Wow! The power that is behind Charlie Callaway is it his last name Callaway!

On the other hand, even this might be the works of Mary his wife, who is orchestrating this situation behind the scene. Mary shows up in Spelman College in the basement of Friendship Baptist Church between 1885 and 1886. Now Mary married Charlie Callaway in 1884 in Clarke County.

For the first time I found Mary Calloway of Fulton County in the Preparatory class of Spelman Seminary:

Living in Atlanta: Lula Alexander, Amanda Anderson, Amy Barclay, Melinda Barron, Noona Battles, Belle Beadles, Martha Bennett, Millie Blair of Augusta, Jane Bonner of Austell, Bessie Bradford of Montgomery Ala.

Lula Brooks, Mary Lou Brooks, Maggie Bruce, Mattie Bundley, Susie Burdine, Burena Burkes, Mary Calloway, Louisa Coleman of East Point

Celestia Cosby, Emma Crawford, Missouri Dalles, Rebeca Davis, Fannie Davis, Jennie Davis, Phillis Dixon, Maria Dixon of Augusta, Ga.

Mary Echols, Alice Edmons, Nancy Floyd, Elizabeth Foster of Athens, Ga.

Rena Freeman, Ella Fritch, Mary Gessling, Mary Gibson, Effie Goldsmith, Ida Gordon, Lydia Gray, Sarah Green, Ida Green of Covington, Ga.

Missouri Hall, Laura Jane Hamilton, Mary A. Harris of Albany

Claud L. Harris, Carrie Heard, Sophronia Heard, Sallie E. Hicks, Grace Hightower, Charity F. Hill, Mamie Hopkins, Carrie Howard, Milie Hughes, Mamie J. Jackson of Madison Morgan Co., Eliza Jackson of Montezuma Macon Co., Lula A James of Rome Floyd Co., Hattie Johnson of Columbus Muscogee Co., Betsey A. Johnson of Appling, Columbia Co.

Rosetta Johnson, Mollie Johnson, Elvira Jones, Mary C. Joyce, Beatrice Joyce, Daphne P. Knox, Mollie Lee, Carrie Lewis, Leila Lewis, Popa Malone, Lucy E. Malone, Bertha Map, Lizzie Mells, Mary Menns, Dora A. McFarling, Josephine McWilliam, Lugenia Miller, Louisa Minter, Lula Mitchell, Elizabeth Moses, Anna Mosley, Omey Nealy of Cartersville Bartow Co. Josephine Osborne of Edgewood DeKalb

Carrie J. Patillo, Ida Peakes of Conyers, Rockdale Co.

Amanda A Potts, Mary Riley, Lovinia Rome, Hannah Russell, Mary A. Scandrick, Lena Sexton, Lottie M. Simms, Emma Simmons, Lena Shankle, Loila Smith, Lula Smith, Nora Strong, Mattie Strozier, Vina Thompson, Omer Thomas, Lake Erie Thomas, Hattie Tilman, Julia Turner of Eatonton, Putnam Co. America Turner of Eatonton Putnam Co. Josephine Tyes of Forsyth, Monroe Co.

Carrie Walton of Augusta, Richmond Co.

Mollie Washington, Flora Wilbor, Mary Wilder, Stella Williams Annie M. Williams of griffin Spalding Co.

Mary Willingham, Ada Wilson, Mollie Wood, Cora A. Woods

1886–7

Pg. 11

Ida A Hawthorne of Forsyth Monroe Co.

Mary Callaway is in the Normal and Preparatory course of Class A with Sallie D. Adams of Millen Screven, Malinda Anderson of Atl, Ella D. Bailey of Bailey's Mills Camden, Ammelia F. Bell of Thomson McDuffie,

Laura Bell of Atl, Donnei Brittain of Greenville, Meriwether, Maggie L. Brooks of Atl, Turlitha Brooks of Atl., Fannie J. C. Brown of Quitman Brooks Co., Lavinia A. Burkes of Atl, Lucile L. Burkes of LaGrange Troup Co.

Lucinda M Butler of Yarborough Camden Co., Mary Callaway of Atlanta Fulton Co., Emma Clark of Atl, Willie Cosby of Atl, Amanda Crook of Atl, Cora Favors of Jones Mill Meriwether, Ida S. Floyd of Atl, Hattie Foster of Birmingham Jefferson Ala., Lucy H. Garrison of Carrolton Carroll, Lulu Glassco of Atl, Elizabeth S. Gordon of Edgewood Dekalb, Mattie Greer of White Sulphur Spr. Meriwether.

Stella Gunn of Atl, Cornellia M. Guyton of Thomasville Thomas, Laura F. Harbor of Atl, Fannie Hardnett, of Hemphill Fulton Co. Margaret Harris of Atl., Idella Jameson of Jacksonville Durval Fla.

Exie Jennings of Atl, Annie C. Johnson, Betsey A. Johnson of Appling, Columbia Co.

Cora B. Johnson of Appling Columbia Co., Lula V. Johnson Chatt. Hamilton, Tenn.

Alice H. King of Orchard Hill of Spalding, Lucy King of Hawkinsville Pulaski Ga.

Laura Lemons of Atl., Julia Long of Atl, Sarah Lucas of Atl, Sarah Mercer of Atl, Annie B. Merricks of Atl, Isabella M. Miller of Atl, Maggie B. Mills of Chatt., Tenn.; Hamilton, Tenn.

Susie A. Nelson of Brunswick Glynn Co. Ada S. Pennamon of Eatonton, Emma R. Pullins of Atl, Josephine Quarterman of Atl, Chaney A. Robinson of Waynesboro Burke Co., Georgia Robinson of Atl, Irene Sanders of Atl., Katie Scott of Atl, Lizzie Scott of Bolton Ga. Fulton Co.

Mary L. Shells of Atl, Octavia Sheriff of Atl, Mindora Sorrels of Stone Mountain Dekalb,

Leila Stolls of Decatur of Dekalb, Alice Sullivan of Locust Grove Henry Co.

Carrie A. Thompson of Charlotte Mecklengurg N. C. Lula H. Thrasher of Atl, Lizzie E. C. Ward of Hampton Henry Co. Delphia Whaley of Thomasville Thomas co.

Lizzie B. White of Atlanta, Amassie A Williams of Griffin Spalding, Ema M.L. S. Williams of Greenville Meriwether Co.

Roberta E. Williams of LaGrange Troup Co.

In the Directory of Atlanta in the year of 1887 I found these colored Callaway's. Malinda Callaway a laundry worker resided at 208 Elliott Street, William Callaway was a laborer and resided at 3 C. R. R. Cicero Calloway was a laborer and resided at 13 Trenhelm, Evans W. Calloway works for the Atlanta Paper Co and resided at 222 Glenn St. *Jefferson C. Calloway a laborer resided at 21 Tatnall,* John Calloway worked as a laborer and resided at 43 Hills Ave. Sherman Calloway worked as a laborer and resided at 13 Trenhelm with Cicero Calloway with Squire Calloway as well. Martin Callaway is a laborer and lives at 1 Ella Street.

In the year of 1888 in the Directory of Atlanta, the only new Callaways that show up are Daniel Callaway a driver for John Hoffman, Emma Callaway a laundress who resides at 3 Railroad, James Callaway a laborer who resides at 35 Fort Street, and John C. Callaway who works for the City Brewery and resides at E. Harris Street. *John C. Callaway is working for one of the oldest dealers in liquor! John C. Callaway is working for the Atlanta City Brewing Co., H. G. Kuhrt, president and Chas. Beerman, treasurer, A. Flesh, Sec; office is at 3 Decatur. The Brewery is at the corner of Harris and Collins. The men of this company were in and out of the city jail in Atlanta during the Civil War. I do not know where John C. Callaway comes from however; Mr. Cornelius Callaway would come to live at Rout 54 E. Harris Street on June 3, 1917. Cornelius Calloway is twenty-four years old, he was born May 12, 1893 and was born in Woodville, Ga. and is a cook for Randolph Rose at 73 N. Pryor Street. Cornelius supports his Father, Mother, and his wife. He is short, Medium complexion, Brown eyes, and black hair. And has a broken right wrist. Now I have found Cornelius Callaway with three men that might be his father! Richard Callaway and Emily Callaway in Woodville, Greene County in 1910 and 1920, Henry Callaway in Walton County only in 1900. Cornelius is living at the same place as J. C. Callaway in Atlanta.*

Judy Callaway a domestic working for Anne Harrison, Lila Callaway who resides at 14 Jones Alley, Reuben Callaway a striker for A. B. and A. Co. and resides at 158 Gray Street. Stewart Callaway resides at 17 Harris Street.

I found Stewart Callaway a colored Student residing at 250 W. Hunter Street in 1877.

In 1878 he was listed as a colored driver and resided at 45 Windsor Street.

Let us take a very close look at what is going on at Stewart Callaways house at 17 Harris Street starting in 1884; I will try to figure out the relationship between the members of this household. (The Atlanta History Center): The Atlanta Directories for 1884, Stewart Callaway is a porter for J. Askew. I went looking for J. Askew and found James Askew Saloon at 210 Marietta Street. I found it very interesting to find out what kind of influence Stewart B. Callaway had in Atlanta. He's been a mystery to me until I found out some more about him. In 1887 on December the 2nd, the Atlanta Constitution wrote this article about him. Stewart Callaway, a Negro was arrested yesterday on a warrant charging him with malicious mischief. And on June 14, 1889 of the Atlanta Constitution at the Courthouse in the Justice Court. Thomas W. Callaway the man who sold land to Morehouse University is a contractor and resides at 240 West Peachtree. John Callaway is a drayman and resides at 287 West Mitchell Street. Mary Callaway is a cook and resides at the rear at 50 Alexander with M. Bell. There was another Mary Callaway who worked on 46 Jackson Street, starting from Foster north to the city limits east of Fort, in the 4th ward. Mary lived with A. L. Greene. W. H. McWhorter lived on the same street at this time.

In 1885, Stewart Callaway worked as a driver for D. H. Dougherty and lived in the rear of the place at 211 Peachtree. This place was located at the southeast corner of Baker Street not far from Harris Street. It was just a block north from where he was living on Harris Street. Now living at 17 Harris Street is Mary Nesbit. Mary Nesbit, I can tell you I have not found a Mary Nesbit listed with the Callaway's Colored or White at any time but now! The colored neighbors of Mary Nesbit and Stewart Callaway living next door, before you get to the Atlanta Brewing Co. at the corner of Collins is the house of Charles Bangert. And the house of Mr. G. Sig a colored man living in house # 39. In house # 46 R. D. Badger resides here, they are the only two colored families living before you gets to the Atlanta Brewing Company. The street that was before you got to Collins Street was called Ivey Street, Mary Nesbit, G. Sig and R. D. Badger are the only coloreds living between Ivey and Collins Street (Courtland Ave.) Stewart B. Callaway married into the family of Jacob Smith who lived in the fourth ward of the city of Atlanta. It was in 1870 that I found Jacob. His wife Katie was sixty years old, Anna D White was twenty, and I believe that this is Annie V. Callaway. Lewis Smith was eighteen, and Martha Davis was seven years old. They were listed at house number 680 and Mr. Anthony Graves a thirty two-year-old mulatto bar keeper out of North Carolina was at house number 686. His wife Cilie was twenty-seven, Charles was seven, Lizzie was six, Levi was four, Eunice was two, and Effie was fourteen, Sarah was twelve, and Joe was ten.

Crossing over Collins Street (Courtland Ave.) I found the first colored man Mr. E. Nelms in house # 95, 96-M. Latimer, 99- M. Adams, 101- F. Mitchell, 103-S. Johnson, 105-vacant, 119- W. Wynes a colored grocer, 127- J. R. Harris, 131-J. Graves, 132-R. Mitchell, 133- M. Redding, 134- N. Maddox, 136-J. Partee, 138-H. Hightower, 140-L Anderson, 141-M.

Butler, 145- J. Arnold, 147-R. Hall, 156-A. Soloman, 157 Zion A. M.E. Church. 158-Northeast corner of Butler, G. Johnson, 160- A. T. Thomas Grocery Store. 162- J. Barlow, 164- M. Jenkins, 166- D. Cureton, 170- J. C. Norris, 174-E. Thomas, 175-E. Penny, 178-R. Pierce, 179-M. J. Garner, 182-D. McGhee, 192-M. Harris, 198-R. Carter, 204-northwest corner Fort Street R. Carter. Now the number goes down again as we head west on Harris Street the only colored that I found were C. Lester living as the neighbor of a white man named J. Winter whose house number is 74 and C. Lester house number is 76 they live just before you get to the corner of Orme Street (now called Techwood).

Living at the northeast corner of Hayden was J. H. Stark a white man and the Negroes that lived beyond Hayden Street is E. Wilkins at house 116, at house 118 is D. Drake, and at house number 139 is J. Burgess who is the last colored man living on Harris Street. The last Whites are in house number 140 W. S. Simmons and C. C. Simmons.

The last names of the famous Clansman W. J. Simmons. Now is, Julia Callaway, Stewart Callaway and William Callaway were in Atlanta in 1885 and by 1886 they were gone! *I do not know if Julia is the daughter of Aaron that is not listed in the house with Aaron in his tax digest with the other children).* However, Martin Callaway shows up on Ella Street. That started from the Georgia R. R. north to Wheat Street north east limits in second Ward. I believe that this street is Airline Street, but in the directory it is called Ella Street. Martin Callaway is living with H. Haines a colored man and in house number 2 is W. Evans, in house 7. H. Upson, house 9. D. Cook, house 11. S. Lynch, house 13 W. Cobb, house 17. H. Reed.

Moreover, at the corner of Foster Street and Ella is soon to be famous Ebenezer Baptist Church. At house 107 is J. Bryant, house 108. H. Manor, house 110. J. Williams, house 112. M. McCarthy a white man, house 113 is vacant. House 114. Sallie Jackson, house 115. G. Henderson, house 117. W. Lewis, house 119. Martha Walker, house 120 Dora Williams and house 122 is R. Ward. I assume that Martin Callaway might be attending Ebenezer Baptist Church at this time. I mean, Martin Mathew Callaway who will return back to Dekalb County in Lithonia where Mount Zion Baptist Church is located.

Now in 1887 Stewart Callaway shows back up and is with Mary Nesbit again at 17 E. Harris Street with John C. Callaway who again does not state what his house number is on east Harris Street. Mary Nesbit is the only colored woman living on Harris Street before you cross over Ivy Street and the only colored man living after you cross Ivy Street is R. D. Bangert. Mrs. Mary Bangert is over the Grocery Store at 66 Harris Street and not her husband

Charles. Living in house number 54 where Cornelius E. Callaway in 1917 will come to reside is Mrs. L. Kutzchan. There are only six houses before going east from Stewart Callaway, John C. Callaway and Mary Nesbit.

I do know that the place of Beerman, and Kurtz and Charles and Mary Bangert are on the north end of the Colored Community while Rufus and Randolph Rose are on Hilliard Street further east. These two stores must have been competing for the business of the colored men and women in the fourth and third wards. I wonder did the Atlanta Brewery suffer the same misfortune as did R. M. Rose & Company!

The first name that I come across is C. Bangert who lives at 66 Harris Street. C. Bangert is Charles Bangert who resides at the northwest corner of Collins and the Atlanta Brewing Company in 1885. Now, John Callaway resides at or is a laborer on Lowe Street. When I went to find who John Callaway was living with while residing on Lowe Street because it did not give a house number I found these names on Lowe Alley! The house numbers are listed 1 to 18. All those that are living on this street are Colored Americans.

1. H. Fambro, 2. M. Harvey, 3. W. Queen, 4. J. Adams, 5. G. Davis, 6. L Clayton, 7. M. Kimball, 8. J. Lamar, 9. C Branham, 10. N. Hammond, 11. E. Akers, 12. J. Harris, 13. G. Johnson, 14. A. Sheats, 15. S. Carter, 16. J. McFarland, 17. H. Foster, 18. I. Grier.

I tell you this Charlie and Mary are not making it easy for me to find them in Atlanta. Now, Lowe Street runs from Carter north to Spencer, 1st w. of Maple, Wards 1 and 5. Southwest corner Spencer intersection lives T. F. Johnson, northwest corner of Foundry is W. S. McNeal, Magazine Street (Magnolia Street) lives M. Bryant and H. Mapp. All are colored men except T. F. Johnson and W. S. McNeal. Lowe Street which will become Electric Avenue where Israel Baptist Church would come to first reside. There is no 50 Electric avenue yet in 1885. However, John is listed as living at Lowe 1st south of Carter St. before you get to Lowe Ally. Somewhere before you get to Lowe Alley Israel Baptist Church would come to lie. The last name that surprised me was that of Johnson. Either Mr. T. F. Johnson or Mr. W. S. McNeal donated the land for Israel Baptist Church. However, I am just assuming this!

In 1887 Lowe Street had changed and so has Lowe Alley as well. From Carter north to Spencer west of Maple Street in Wards 1 and 5 I found in house number 1 Mr. J. A. Lafontaine. In house number 2 T. F. Johnson. In house number 3 Mrs. E. Freeman. There was not a number 4. In house number 5 is J. M. Wright. In house number 6 is M. Mitchell, the only colored man before you get to the southeast corner of Magnolia to the house of H. Mapp. On the street intersecting south of Magnolia lives N. Simmons, a colored man. In

Lowes Ally from Larkin southeast of Chapel in Ward 1, the houses are numbered 6 through 27. So the names are aligned with the numbering of the houses: H. Foster, I Henderson, Sarah Cater, vacant, vacant, G. Johnson, J. Harris, P. Scott, (white): Mrs. L. Brenham; Laura Thompson, Sarah Morris, F. Cramer, vacant; R. Mayes, Louisa Clayton, M. Queen, O. Sanders, Virie Sanders. I believe that in house 16 N. Simmons and Laura Thompson are living in the same house.

S. B. Callaway who resides at 115 E. Cain Street. In the year of 1889 in the City Directory I found a few more faces again. Annie Callaway a dressmaker boards at 115 E. Cain Street, now I know that Stewart B. Callaway is the husband of Annie V. Callaway. However this is the situation with Mr. Stewart B. Callaway! First there is Stewart Callaway a colored bar tender who resides at 17 E Harris Street. Then there is Mr. Stewart B. Callaway who is not listed as being colored but as being white working as a coal and wood man at 92 E Cain and resides at the same place. And then there is Mr. S. B. Callaway who resides at 115 E. Cain Street. Now comes Mrs. Emma Callaway living at 199 West Hunter Street, John Calloway has a restaurant at 11 W. Peters Street while A. Butler has a suit brought against Stewart B. Calloway in Judge Manning's courtroom. The Atlanta Constitution printed it like this. There was a suit brought in Judge Manning's court yesterday for seventy five cents. The suit is by A. Butler against S. B. Calloway, both colored. Calloway it is said, has valuable property in Atlanta but this is in his wife's name and safe from Calloway's debtors. In addition to this he owns property in Alabama valued at $25.000 to $30.000. He acknowledges the debt and says he will pay as soon as he is able. The State of Alabama open up a lot of mysteries to the rich landowners that migrated there in the 1820's from Georgia. This migration might have even started earlier with the Callaway's children and the Williams. I have mention Job Callaway. Now Mrs. Annie V. Callaway is sometimes white and is sometimes colored. I found her in the Atlanta City Council minutes in 1889.

Index to Council Minutes Volume 12 page 1–179 City of Atlanta. 1889

> Pg. 131 line 4 Annie V. Callaway: Annie V. Callaway for relief from sewer assessment on Clifford St.
>
> Pg. 151 line 28 Annie V. Callaway: Adverse on Annie V. Callaway's petition for relief from sewer assessment Clifford St.

Clifford Street is a street that lies south of Cain Street and north of Ellis Street and runs parallel and between Courtland Street and Piedmont. The Mayor and council do not state that Annie V. Callaway is a colored woman. There is only one other name that I can put in this general location on Clifford Street and that is Anderson Callaway in 1881 Anderson was a colored man that worked or owned part of a company of Callaway & Holmes and resided at 24 Clifford Street or Alley E. H. Holmes was his partner. In 1873 Anderson Calloway resided at 76 Ferry. Now Aaron is missing from the Tax Digest in 1874 if I recall this matter right, he was living in the 147th after working on the farm of Mr. T. M. Fambrough. Aaron was working on the place of Mr. Campbell as a white man and while there on Campbell's place, Anderson Callaway was listed in his place. About the same time Peter Callaway and his son Wash shows came up from Monroe County. As a matter of fact, Aaron and Burwell are both missing from the 147th in 1879. I also know that Aaron is a man of many names. Aaron has been working in Clarke County in 1870 under the last name of Cheney. However, I have come to think that it is Robert or Bob Callaway that is living as Aaron under this last name. Ferry Street is in or near the Third Ward where Martin Callaway, William A. Callaway the son of Robert Callaway and his wife Mary would come to reside on Richardson Street. This section of Atlanta is called the Summerhill Colored Community.

Laura Calloway does laundry and resides at Lowes Alley. *Laura Calloway is the first colored female Calloway that resides near Israel Baptist Church besides John Calloway who resided here earlier between 1885 and 1886. John Calloway would reside on Lowes Street however. This might eliminate Mary Nesbit, while living in the house with Stewart and John C. Callaway, as being the wife of John Calloway, and Laura Calloway might be the wife of John C. Calloway. Now remember Amanda Callaway the single mother with John her son at the age of fourteen, and Wade thirteen, William who was six and Laura a boarder at the age of twenty-three in the first ward of the city of Atlanta in 1880. Well, I must say this, that J. C. Callaway is doing what I see Charlie, Stewart, and George are doing! They are in the section of what is very much saturated with prostitution and liquor and gambling!*

Let us take a look at the Atlanta City Council Records and look at what some of the colored women and men and their religious organizations tried to do against this lifestyle that was very much prominent in Atlanta.

Atlanta City Council Minutes Books 1882 Through to 1886 Vol. 10

Pg. 47

Prohibiting engaging the attention of pupils in the public schools by signs &c.

Pg. 63.

Houston Street Grammar School (Colored)

Mitchell Street Grammar School (Colored)

Summerville Street Grammar School (Colored) (Summerhill)

Total Colored Grammar Schools 1,477

The average attendance of the colored Grammar Schools 93 ¼ per cent

Pg. 92.

Petitions: of S. Wylie et al. For permission to supply guards and nurses to their colored friends stricken with small pox. No response from the council.

Pg. 99

Petitions: of Congregational Church corner of Houston and Collins for curbing free.

Pg. 101 On petition of S. Wylie Et al. for permission to supply guards to their colored friends stricken with small pox—report favorable if they can furnish guards in compliance with the law for *less* price, same to be under supervision of Board of health.

Pg. 114. On petition of First Congregational Church for curbing free in front of their church, report favorable.

Pg. 27 Colored Orphan home line five. Carrie Steele for 4-acre land at stockade to build colored orphan home.

Pg. 28 line 16: Adverse to donate 4 acres land to Carrie Steele for colored orphan home.

Pg 18 line 49: Petitions H. M. Turner et al to have a colored Physician appointed to wait upon the colored sick paupers referred to relief committee.

Now, I am going to start in the year of 1916 in the Atlanta Directories. This is the year that the Liquor Ledgers in Oglethorpe County, Greene County, and Barrow County are listing the men and women both colored and whites as bringing liquor into the counties just mentioned. However, the State of Georgia is supposed to be under the Prohibition Law at this time in 1916. While at the

(Atlanta Historical Society), I found this advertisement for Randolph Rose Company. However, it did not state that it was selling liquor! Randolph Rose advertised as having

> *Pocket Billiards, Bowling Alley, Soft Drinks and Cigars. The Best of Each for Gentlemen. Randolph Rose Co. 14 Marietta Street Phone M. 216.*

I went on the search for this property and who was living around and in the vicinity of Randolph Rose Company on Marietta Street.

It was in the year of January 18, 1899, that the Atlanta Constitution printed an article that stated "The Jury Convicts Whisky Dealers." R.M. Rose found guilty other persons indicted plead guilty to the charges. J.H. Spillman W. A. Long, Joseph Jacobs, W.P. Avery, E.H. Carroll and Henry Potts pleaded guilty to the same offense as soon as the verdict against Mr. Rose was read. Mr. Rose was convicted of selling liquors on election day, two miles of an election precinct. This is well after he brings his business from Tennessee in 1888.

In the year 1899, Rufus M. Rose place of business was at 12 Marietta Street. At one time he had a place on Cone Street not far from Marietta Street. Colored man Alonso F. Herndon was at 4 Marietta Street. J. T. Alexander was at 17 Marietta Street with Raphael Genetosu. A house or work place 13 was occupied by W. L. Harden and J. R. Steele a colored man. G. H. Hancock was at 15 ½ Marietta Street with W. Finch another colored man.

> *Any Place Where Liquor Is Illegally Sold a Nuisance*
>
> *No. 292*
>
> *An act to declare as a nuisance any place where spirituous, malt or intoxicating liquors are sold in violation of law, to provide for abating or enjoining such nuisance, and for other purposes.*
>
> *Section I. Be it enacted by the General Assembly of Georgia, That from and after the passage of this Act, any place commonly known as a "blind tiger," where spirituous, malt or intoxicating liquors are sold, in violation of law, shall be deemed a nuisance, and the same may be abated or enjoined as such, as now provided by law, on the application of any citizen or citizens of the county where the same may be located.*

> *Section II. Be it further enacted, That if the party or parties carrying on said "nuisance" shall be unknown or concealed, it shall be sufficient service in the abatement or injunction proceedings under this Act to leave the writ or other papers to be served, at the place where such liquor or liquors may be sold, and the case or cases may proceed against "parties unknown," as defendants.*
>
> *Section III. Be it further enacted, that the court shall have authority under this Act to order he officers to break open such "blind tiger" and arrest the inmates thereof, and seize their stock in trade, and bring them before him to be dealt with as the law directs.*

In the year 1900, R. M. Rose was still located at 12 Marietta Street. However, at 13 Marietta Street was a colored man A. McNeal working as a barber and another colored man named W. George selling Cigars & Tobacco. Also at 13 Marietta Street is the store of J. Aquaddro, umbrella repair shop. At 17 Marietta Street is J. T. Alexander and his saloon. R. A. Broyles, grocer, was at 41 Marietta St.

I wanted to go to the year 1908, the year before the Prohibition Law went into effect in Georgia. I found the Walkover Shoe Company at 12 Marietta Street. However, at 13 ½ Marietta Street is where colored man Alfred Nash is located. Mr. Thomas Vogles is at 14 Marietta Street. I found Mr. Allen Cruickshank and Adolph Samuels. If you remember, in 1899 Mr. Sig. Samuels was charged with R. M. Rose for selling liquor on an election poll day. Here is Mr. Adolph Samuels or Mr. A. Samuels, who was selling his liquor out of Tennessee and Jacksonville, Florida, in Greene, Oglethorpe, and Barrow counties along with Mr. R. M. Rose and others.

Vol. 15 Atlanta City Council minutes index from July 2, 1894, to January 6, 1896

M. P. Callaway 16–48: Favorable for building permits as follows: M. P. Calloway 99 Trinity Ave.

William Callaway 37–239: To sell country produce

William Calloway 16–327: Adverse

P. C. Adams free peddler's license

M. Flesham, Annie Epps lunch, M. Kaplan peddlers, Mrs. Miller license to sell old clothes, W. Calloway to peddle, C. Watkins lunch license. J. E. Davison et al. to return amount paid for licenses; pg 656, line 44

J. E. Davison et al. for refund of amount paid for license; pg 727, line 36

Pg 763 line 8: Adverse upon petition of Traders Collection Agency for refund of license tax. *J. E. Davison and the Traders Collection Agency Co.

**J. E. Davison is the man whose brother will sell property to Emily Hurt Callaway the wife of Richard Callaway in Greene County in 1915. I think that J. E. Davison is in the same business as Robert L. Callaway and Peg-Leg-Williams.*

Pg. 273, line 34: Petition of the Coca-Cola Co. to connect houses on Magnolia St. with Haynes St. Sewer

J. E. Davison et al. to return amount paid for licenses; pg. 656, line 44

March 21, 1904, page 264, line 33: Petition of Willie Callaway for boot-black stand corner Edgewood and Courtland

April 4, 1904, line 21: Favorable to grant the following petitions for free licenses: N. N. Blair, Will Calaway, Mrs. S. E. Stewart, Mrs. L. E. Kirkland, and Mrs. A. E. Sallander; adopted; Pg. 486, line 9

April 6, 1903, line 32: Son Bently has heretofore been granted a license to conduct a "Dance Hall" at #95 -1/2 Peters Street, and whereas the licensee, Bentley, conducts an immoral and disorderly place, and indecent exposures of females commonly occur, and said place has become a nuisance, and should be abated. Therefore, be it resolved by the Mayor and General Council that the license granted Son Bentley to conduct a dance hall at 95-1/2 Peters St. be and the same is hereby withdrawn and the Chief of Police shall notify said Son Bentley of this action and he shall likewise see that the said Dance hall is at once closed. On motion of Councilman Harwell. Amended by revoking license granted at #95-1/2 Peters Street. Amendment adopted, and resolution as amended, adopted.

Pg. 515, February 20, 1905: Petition of citizens against the granting of license to dance halls

Pg. 520, March 6, 1905, line 7: Favorable upon petition of citizens against the granting of license to two dance halls for colored people . . .

Pg. 290, May 2, 1904, line 37: Petition of Citizens (coloreds) to break up places where colored women congregate and drink; petition of Big Bethel Church against issuance of a license to Mosely Bro; petition of H. Jacobs for wholesale liquor license at No. 29 Courtland Ave.

July 15, 1907, pg. 371, line 20: Mrs. A. V. Callaway to connect with Elm Street Sewer

August 5, 1907, pg. 376, line 43: Also favorable upon petition of Mrs. A. V. Calloway to connect with Elm St. sewer on condition that the property be responsible for the assessment when sewer is laid in Lester street; adopted

February 20, 1905, pg. 515: Petition of citizens against the granting of license to dance halls

March 6, 1905, pg. 520, line 7: Favorable upon petition of citizens against the granting of license to two dance halls for colored people . . .

The Atlanta Directories offered me a more detailed experience of the Callaways and their neighborhoods. It also told me who my grandfather was closer among other Callaways or Calloways.

Nelson Calloway is a drayman and beds at 216 W. Foundry St. Riley Calloway works at the oil mills and resides at 3 Railroad where Emma Callaway first lived before moving to 199 West Hunter Street. Martin Calloway is still here at this time after relocating from DeKalb County and is now working for R. & D. R. R. depot and resides at Ella Street (Airline Street). By the year 1915 Martin Callaway is back in DeKalb County near East Lake Drive in Decatur. I really believe that Martin M. Callaway is Robert Callaway or Bob Callaway that worked and lived with Aaron in Greene County in Scull Shoals and worked with Burrell his brother in Falling Creek in Maxey Ga. In 1880 he has two children Will Callaway born in 1879 and Mary

Now the year 1892 will tell the story! I say this because in 1892, Charlie went on record in Oglethorpe County as to entering into a Servitude Contract with Mr. William Eberhart. This was the first time that I have him entering into anything beside him being on record in Oglethorpe with Sam Boykin in 1888 for breaking into the house place of Hutchins and Mathews Store. So, in Atlanta in the year of 1892, there is no Mary Callaway nor is there a Charlie Callaway but there is a Mr. Henry Callaway and he is working as a Porter for Singer Mfg. Co. and also as a waiter for Capital City Club.

The Singer Mfg. Co. manager is Mr. John Y. Dixon and the place of business is 85 Peachtree Street. There is also a Singer and Miller (John R. Singer & Andrew C. Miller), carriage and wagon manufactures that is located at 19 Collins Street as well. Now, located at 186 Peachtree Street is the (114) Capital City Club, where Henry worked as a waiter as well.

Henry did not have to go far for either job he could have just walked a few blocks and he was on one job or the other.

In 1893, Henry Callaway resided with Wylie Willis at 166 Wheat Street. Nevertheless, I could not find a listing of the neighbors of Henry Callaway in the Directory at this time. In 1894, Henry C. Callaway boarded at 38 Howell Street with a Colored man named J.C. Starks.

Now I will just mention a few of the neighbors of Henry C. Callaway and Mr. J.C. Starks. (Whites): H.C. Terrell, J.Q. Stockman, L.A. Holley, W.R. Ray, Mrs. M.E. Snider, R.N. Smith, M.H. Newsom, John M. Hooks, Mrs. M.J. Spinks, J.N. Bartles, Oscar L. Swiney, J.G. McWaters, Mrs. L.A. Crankshaw, R.H. Duncan, J.T. Harris, Mrs. Mary Forrest, R. C. Powell, Mrs. Rachael Hughes, D.E. Brooks, William S. Gullatt and P.B. Bradley. (Coloreds): Lizzie Brandon, J.C. Starks, Henry Williams, Catherine Kirkpatrick, Christopher Robinson and Mark Dorsey all lived on Howell Street before you got to the Edgewood intersection. Now living across the intersection was L.J. Thompson, J.W. Powell, J.I. Coleman, N.J. Walker, W.L. Thompson, E.F. Harris, W.E. Chapman, I.S. Bethea, L.C. Varnado, H. Treadwell, and H.S. Ely.

Living at the intersection of Auburn and Old Wheat Street were L.B. Tedder, Mrs. A.E. Doggett the last white woman before you get to houses owned by Coloreds. F.J. Wimberly, J. Connally, M. Lounds, A. Gray, J. Phillips, J. Robinson, J. Perry, T. Coleman, T. Holmes, S. Wylie, C. Foster, W. Clark, J.C. Hudgins, J.A. Parker, W. H. Tillman, L. Fernison. J.H. Lawrence, A. Hamilton, and J. Parks. As we cross over the intersection of Irwin Street Mr. A.J. Wade, lived in the first house, W. Davis, Maria Conyers, and Mr. E. Smith. Crossing over the intersection of Houston the first house you would come to is J.C. Connally, W. T. Mooney, T. Queen, J.H. Rogers, R.F. Watkins, C.C. Gillea and R. Jackson the only colored man on the block. Crossing over Johnson Ave. the only person here is Mr. L.M. Mayne.

Henry C. Callaway was born January 7, 1866 and died in 1913. His wife Annie A. Callaway was born 1870 and died 1910. They are buried at the South View Cemetery with Willie Callaway born 1892 and who died 1954 and his wife Florence C. or Florence C. Smith who died or was born 1913. Now I have two Henry Callaways born in 1866. Henry Callaway who is buried in the Jones woods on the line between Morgan and Walton County. In the year of 1895–1896 Henry, C. Callaway boards at 38 Howell Street with J.C. Starks and resides at 23 Brooks Alley which is from Piedmont avenue east to Bell, between Houston and Auburn avenue. In 1930, Brooks Alley is Glazner Avenue.

In 1896, Henry Callaway is a cook and boards at 183 Butler Street and is working for H. Underwood; however, Mr. Henry C. Callaway is a janitor for Equitable Building. In addition, he resides at 40 Chamberlain Street. Chamberlain lies between Yonge and Boulevard. Now living with Henry C. Callaway was a man named Freeman at this address. A. L. Mason was living next door, and E. Long, William Stephens, and John Partee are the white men that were living on the same street before you got to Fitzgerald intersection. J.M. Nash, B.F. Mitchell, Mrs. A.C. Thomas, R.B. Jernigan, J.A. Webb. These are the colored men and women that lived across the road leading from Fitzgerald.

P. Strickland, G.B. Brown, G. Evans, Ella Brown, S.W. Freeman, William F. Rhodes, Frank Whittaker, and Lewis Dawson. The white men are James M. Nichols, Joseph M. Walker, and Benjamin Burkhardt.

In the year of 1896, I also found Mr. J.C. Hudgins, a colored man, at 140 Howell Street and Mrs. Annie V. Callaway, a colored woman, living at 89 Cain street but, look at her next-door neighbors: Charles Marshall, Mary Jones, J. Hightower, and a white man named J.C. Clein. They were all living between the intersection of Courtland and Clifford streets.

I need to stop here and reflect on the words that my grandfather's cousins the McCloud brothers told me that there mother had a close friend named Mary Jones. Therefore, after mentioning Mary Jones I decided to go to Maple Street to a section of Maple Street that lies between West Mitchell and West Hunter Street.

Maple started at Markham north to Spencer, 1 c of Walnut. These are the Colored people on Maple at this time in 1897. Lucious Robinson, John Drake, B. Bunley, Ed Mattox, William Roberts, W. McCurty, D. Anderson, J. Dickerson, However the next three houses are the houses that are very much interested in. House # 33; L. Dewberry, House # 35; Jane Andrews, House # 37; Clara Cunningham all lived in the short space between W. Mitchell Street and W. Hunter Street which is now part of the parking lot of a Methodist Church. You can still see the foundation of the houses that once stood there and one house still remains just behind the Church which is called The Central United Methodist Church which was founded in 1928.

After you cross over West Hunter Street, which is Martin Luther King Blvd now, the first house will be the house of Walter Manly, G.R. Beckham, and J.C. Early, David Currington, J. Murray, D. Franklin, P. Ramsey, Henry Raglin.

Crossing over Carter Street the first house will be Simon Jennings, T. Turner, Millie Porter, B. Gillard, Nettie Weems, Emma Thompson, Lula Allen, S. Jennings, Francis Maddox, and Little Mt. Olive Church. Crossing over Rhodes, Magnolia and Rigdon the next four houses belong to White Men by the names of J.W. Allen, J.H. Ruffin, J.B. Harris and W.P. Turner, and on the same block is one Colored female by the name of Clara Griffin. Now we are at the intersection of Foundry Street and the first house that you will come to is that of Mr. Ed Moore, Edward Crawford, Hester Urkwood, B.R. Mays, George Magbee, B.F. Jenkins, W. Lovelace, N.S. Blue, Newsome Jackson, George Murray, Joseph Murray, William Reese, Nannie Sanders, Mary Dezell, Mac McCarver.

Living in House # 83 in 1897 is D. Franklin, the same house that the Williams and the Callaway's will come to live in later on. Lula Duke bought this same property in 1901 from Annie V. Callaway the wife of Stewart B. Callaway out of Alabama whom I believe is a white man or a man that can live in both worlds created during this disenfranchisement era at this time. D. Franklin is another name whose last name has a tie to Brantley Callaway in Michigan. Now let us look at Humphreys Street in 1897 this is where the mysterious Susie Callaway will come to live. Humphries is from Whitehall n w to Green's Ferry Avenue and s to the city limits going north. Peters Street intersection; Ida Jackson, Lucy DeVaughn, T. Arnold, Mrs. Lizzie Brown, Emma Trimble, J.P. Ramey, Dan Oliver, (white); Mrs. R.E. Shipman, (Coloreds); R. Richardson, Emma Jones, Howard Haynes, M. Biggins, Kuhrt Street intersection: Atlanta Lumber Co. Cato Lamar, Susie and Will Callaway moves to Rome Georgia and resides there I believe until their death.

J.N. Fulton, Chapel Street intersection: J.S. Weems, Owen Poe (White), Chapel Warren (Colored), Alice Jackson (White), Mrs. Lottie Atkinson (Colored), William Johnson, Wade Griffin, J. Peters, John Howard, Janie Bridges (White), W.H. Briley, and J.R. Jackson

Liberty Street intersection: Coloreds Hannah Hadley, D. Broadnax, Ed Lowe, Lizzie Osborn, Edie Selfrige, Shep Tatum, Alex Sloan, M.W. Burch (White), James Gann.

Green's Ferry Avenue intersection toward Southern Railyard: S.H. Whatley, J. Wicker, H.P. Ashley, Bartow McEver, W.Y. Griggs, I.M. Mayer, H. P. Seay

Hightower Intersection: Mrs. L. Reives, E. Bart, Mrs. Fannie Smith, Mrs. Carrie Lee and Butler & Sloan, (Coloreds), R. Terrell, Nancy Brown (White), W.W. Butler, St. Paul M.E. Church (Colored), Charity Martin, Bettie Henderson, P. Mitchell

Living at the Wells Street Intersection: (White) Charles Minor, (Colored) D.K. Knight, Robert Jones, Lewis Warren, Seaborn Oliver, C. Jenkins, (White) W.H. Dozier, W.F. Henderson, Henry Baber (Coloreds), T. Potts, S. White

Morris Street intersection: E. Morgan, Nathan Hall, Maggie Farmer, Silla Bryant, A. Carey, Ellen Green, A. Brown, R. Moody, W. Adams, Mary Marable, I. Logan, G. Cox, Katie Crawford, Minnie Harris, W. Garr, Zion Hill Baptist Church, (White) T.J. Hightower Jr.

Glenn Street intersection; Atlanta Lumber Co., Southern Rail Yard intersection, (Whites) Mrs. E.O. Stewart, C. H. Bender, C.M. Smith, J.A. Franklin, Jacob Deckner, J.F. Milam, W.H.H. Futrell, D.M. Goodling, C.W. Wells, C.E. Sears, A.C. Kerlin, R.E. Cagle, C.M. Moon, (Coloreds) T.D. Daniel, A. Jones, and L. Daniel.

It's 1897 and we are walking down Auburn Avenue where we start at the Courtland Avenue intersection where we will start at the house of Whites living on Auburn Avenue, B.B. Hay, N.C. Lang, R.H. Lockhart, Rev. G.M. Campbell, D.B. Ladd, Mrs. H. Randall, J.M. Smith, J.M. Denson, J.S. Dorn, R.C. Kibler, Mrs. S.C. Dooley, A. Alexander, J.A. Means, J.F. Hollingsworth, J.M. Smith, J. Gifford, Piedmont Avenue intersection: K. Cillig, James S. Watson, J.T. Gordan, O.T. Watson, W.B. Kimbrough, C. Dyer, R. Ragsdale, J.W. Green, W.C. Taylor, W.P. Lother, H.J. Piggott Cycle Co., (Coloreds) Pauline Hubbard, J. Tinson, Jane Moore, C. Collier, G. Housworth, J. Kendall, D. Edwards, W. Todd, J.H. Tanner.

Ga. Tile & Artificial Stone Co. T. Goosby, Louisa Leslie, Carrie Byrd, M. Allen, Annie Chapman, Priscilla Bradford, L. Nolan, W.M. McHenry, Lucy Foster, Lucinda Jones, E. Weems, Mary Reed, B.V. Echols, Berry Echols, (Jewish) A. Kaufman, Butler Street intersection; Big Bethel A.M.E. Ch., P. Eskridge, John Brandon, J. Mitchell, C. Robinson, A. Mangrum, R. Bates, J.J. Sims, E.E. Bickers, (White); Age Southern, J.T. Mapp, (White); Tulley & Co. Bell Street intersection; (White) Holcomb Bro. (Coloreds) C.C. Cater, W.C. Redding, W.A.

Morgan, Gate City Drug Store, (Coloreds); M. Adams, Sallie Huey, (Whites) Mrs. V. Allen, S.T. Harris, R. Mitchell, Colored United Friendly Society of Am., Enterprise Furniture Co., (Coloreds) E. Watkins, E. Nicholls, E. Pace, (White) W.F. Reid, (Coloreds) Nora Williams, Bettie Hurd, Olive Heard, Nancy Smith, Benjamin Holbrooks, Elizabeth Alexander, J.M. Baldwin, Victoria Gray, Albert Wimbish, (White) R.A. Starnes

Living on Horton Street or Houghton Street leading from Fort east to Hillard 1 block north of Decatur Street. I found F. Jones, M. Nichols, and William Calloway, Maria Mitchell, William Clark and Thomas Smith J. Jenkins, William McNeice, J. Parks, J. Freeman, A.W. Mosteller, Georgia Foster, William Dansby, Houghton Street Church, S. Foster, Elizabeth Johnson, Nicie Brown, M. Meador, Henry Warner, R. Williams Mt. Moriah Baptist Church, F. Brown, Maria Boyd, Fannie Glass, (Whites) Ms. Mollie Reeves and Ms. Mamie Austin.

Living on Chamberlin Street coming from Yonge to Boulevard 1 block south of Edgewood Avenue I found these Whites living on this street. J.I. Henderson, B. Stahl, S.A. Griffin. Jackson Street intersection: Fourth Presbyterian Ch., W.G. Herndon, D.M. Holsomback, W. J. Bishop, P.B. Jernigan, *(Colored) John Partee, House # 40 F. Freeman & H. Callaway, A. Mason, R. Howard, E. Long, W.M. Stephens.*

Fitzgerald Street intersection; W.N. Strickland, G. B. Brown, Bettie Dacus, S. Freeman, Wm. Rhodes, F. Whitaker, (White) Joseph M. Walker, (Colored) L.B. Dorsey, (White) B.C. Burekhardt

Living on Ocmulgee Street in 1897 leading from Whitehall south to Glenn, between Sou. Ry. And A & WPRR: (Whites) C.O. Hardwick, F.A. Cobler, W.A. Randall, R. W. Eberhardt, J.M. Berekel, J.E. Callaway, H.P. Courtney, G. Smith, (Coloreds) Amanda Little, Wesley Callaway, R. Walker, and J. Slack.

1898 Maple Street from Markham north to Spencer, one block east of Walnut Street. (Coloreds) Mattie Keller, V. Yopp, J. Drake, B. Bunley, W.H. Clark, P. green, W. McCurty, D. Anderson, Mattie Duke

West Mitchell intersection: L. Dewberry, J. Bufford, F. Zachry, West Hunter intersection); P. Morris & J. Credille, G. Beckham, J.C. Early,

F. Cureton, F. Lumpkin, J. Murray, House # 83 G. Williams, Patience Ramsey, H. Ragland,

Carter Street intersection: T. Turner, Millie Porter, Nettie Weems, Emma Thompson, A. Johnson, S. Jennings, E. Maddox

Rhodes and Magnolia intersection: (Whites) J.W. Allen, J.H. Ruffin, J.B. Harris, J.F. Kendrick

Foundry Street intersection: J. King, E. Crawford, T. Kirkwood, B.R. Mays, G. Magby, B.f. Jenkins, W. Lovelace,

Spencer Street intersection: N. Blue, N.D. Jackson, G. Murray, Alice Post, Emma Moody, Nannie Sanders, J.C. Shelton, Rebecca McCarver, W. Collier, W. Jones, A. Hawk, W. Toliver & W. White, Laura Butler, R. Nall, B. Wright, Wright, Colored Baptist Ch.) B. Wright is the pastor of the Wright Colored Baptist Church. This church never shows up on any Association any where. I do not know why this is but it's not alone as one that is never mentioned in any Colored Association. The other church is Israel Baptist Church that was located on Lowe Street which would become Electric Avenue in Vine City in Atlanta. In 1910, Little Mount Olive is not mentioned as being in the Atlanta Directory but it is mentioned prior to 1910 in 1897 as being at the intersection of Maple Street and Spencer Street in Vine City.

Now, we will take a walk down Auburn Avenue again in 1898 starting at Piedmont Avenue. J. F. Sounders is a white man living in the first house, (Colored) Sol Winfrey, (Whites) C.H. Powell, W.B. Kimbrough, (Coloreds) J.F. Sharp, C. Dyer, (Whites) Mrs. Sallie Ellis, T. C. Williams, J.W. Green, (Coloreds) Ella Brown, M. Conway, Victoria Harris, G. Houseworth, Patsy Jones, Lanie Williams, Mary Todd, J.H. Tanner, T. Goosby, Gleaner Social, Carrie Byrd, Josephine Castleberry, (White) W.D. Brewer, (Coloreds) J. Richardson, Priscilla Bradford, (White) H.L. Dobbs, (Coloreds) L. Nolan, W.M. McHenry, Lucy Adams, Jane Story, Lucy Harris, B.V Echols, (Jewish) N. Kaufman

Butler Street intersection: Big Bethel AME Ch., P. Eskridge, J. S. Brandon, J. Mitchell, C. Robinson, Sidney Sasseen, R. M. Bates, J.J. Sims, A. Davis, F.J. Wimberly, D.F. Fisher, J.T. Mapp,

Bell Street intersection: (White) P. Jolly, (Coloreds) C. C. Cater, European Hotel, W. A. Morgan, Gate City Drug Store, R. Anton, C. Chishol, (Whites) Mrs. N.J. Riggs, Hill & Latimore, R. Mitchell, R. A. Boyd, C.V.H. Vaughn, World Bottling Co. (Coloreds) Delia Skelton, E. Watkins, (Jewish) G. B Kline, (Colored) E. Pace, (White) Mrs. L.J. Seymour,

(Coloreds) Nora Williams, Benj. Holbrooks, (White) Star Laundry, (Coloreds) D. Henry, J.H. Gray, (White) R. A. Starnes

Fort Street intersection: Colored Baptist Church, E. Wimbish, Colored Episcopal Church, (Jewish) J. Cohen, (Coloreds) H.C. Simmons St. Paul's Church, W. Byrd, William Parks, W.T. Robinson, L.G. Harris, A. Glenn, J.F. Thomas, F. Boykin, Elbert Davis, K. Darden, Terry Jones, T.W. Lewis, F.N. Landrum, Mary Walker

Hillard Street intersection: S.S. Roberts, J. Hightower, Mary Baber, C. Threatt, H.R. Butler, R. Williams W. A. Green, Harriet Williams, J.R. Porter, Sally Walton, D. Cypher, T. Benjamin, J. Robinson, W. Walton, Sally Scroggins

Yonge Street ends: A.H. Robinson, W. Jenkins, Mattie Collins, David Allen, D. Hill, (White) W.J. Grafton, (Coloreds) R. Hollingsworth, Nannie Keys, E. L. Martin, C. E. Blake, E. S. Jones, Jane Stiles, J.H. Bell, L. Shy, Matilda Franklin, Chas. Stanley, Effie Edwards, J.C. Graves, A. Hart, (Jewish) M.W. Merk, (Whites) W.J. Sharke, Connally & Connally, C.M. Perry

Jackson Street intersection: (White) O.S. Myrick, (Colored) A.J. Dedbridge, (White) P. Hampton, (Coloreds) J. Schell, Jennie Simmons, H.W. Parks, Evaline Nowell, C.J. Jones, Ella Berry, W. Jones, Lucinda Clarke, Chas. King, House # 332 Fannie McWhorter, House # 335 L.H. Holsey, House # 339 W. C. Redding, House # 342 G. Read, House # 340 S. Davis, House # 343 F. Morehead

House # 344 J. Fears, House # 345 R. Davis, House # 347 Sol Reynolds, House # 348 Elizabeth Johnson, House # 350 Henry Callaway, House # 352 G. Dennis, (Whites); F.R. Graves, and P. J. Luke. (Hogue Street intersection); House # 390 W. A. Baldwin, House # 402 W. Kerr House # 403 J.C Carter, (Old Wheat Street and Bradley Street intersection); House # 350 J. Howell, House # 452 M. A. Thomas, House # 458 M. Boyd, House # 460 A.J. Divine, (Randolph Street intersection); House # N. Smith, House # Malinda Wyatt, House # 485 Mary Kemp.

1899 Telephone Directory; H.C. Calloway is living at 138 Howell Street, T. Coleman, Sarah Davis, A.D. Hamilton, W.M. Austin, H. Crowley, Mary Holmes, C. Foster, G. Washington were a few on the same street with H.C. Callaway. On Auburn Avenue intersection and Old Wheat Street and Irwin intersection lived, H.H. Williams, Lizzie Brandon, Amanda Crockett, *J.C. Starks, H.W. Alexander, *T. Fletcher, J. Watkins, H. Hawkins, *R. Clarke, M. Dorsey, C. Robinson, L. Finlason, F.J. Wimberly, H. Sellers, A. Graves, A. Connally, G. Gray, C.G. Gray, D.

Ware, J. Phillips, F. Zachery, *J. Fears, R.M. Cheeks, G.L. Goosby, W. McCullough, W.B. Mathews, J. Aikens, J.A. Parker, J.W. Gaines, F.P. Rayford, T. Fry, R. Ferrell, J. White, St. Paul M.E. Church, A. Oliver, H. Tucker, Mary Gresling, Ninnie Brown, H. Wright, S. Burns, Rev. M.W. Travers, L. Warner, S. Oliver, C. Jenkins, W.H. Dozier, W.F. Henderson, Eunice Dozier, D. Woolfolk, T. Potts, Samuel M. White, Ed. Strickland, (Morris Intersection), Lula Cobb, J. Hinton, E. Morgan, Filla Bryant, A. Chipley, Ellen Green, A. Brown, R. Moody, Carrie Jackson, Mary Marble, W. Dennis, I. Logan, T. Jones, F. Cook, U. Bennett, A. McCoy, W. Garr, Zion Hill Baptist Church © A. McGhee. J.C. Huggins is a colored man living with S.B. Spencer on Hunter Street.

Chapter Fourteen

On Maple Street, I could not find house # 38. However, I did find # 37 where I found J.F. Fears, # 35 I found L. Dewberry, at house # 35 I found Mr. M.H. Alexander. Remember J. Fears is living on Howell Street he also has property on Maple Street and so is H.W. Alexander. The Dukes also came out of the third ward in the 1870's and Lula owns property on Maple Street.

In the Grantor Index book A-G April 30, 1901 Fulton County Georgia. The Filing

Docket Book, Lula Duke the Grantee received from A. V. Callaway et al. the Grator in District 14 land lot 83 property on Maple Street. Book 7, Page 124.

Lula Duke – Avd. State & County District 14 land lot 83 Maple Street FiFa & Levy Book 130 Page 426.

Lula Duke-Gus Ramsey district 14 land lot 83 Maple Street Book 139 Page 118

Lula Duke- by Sheriff Callaway and Simmons district 14 land lot 83 Maple Street, Book 130 Page 425.

Over on Ocmulgee I found J.E. Callaway at house # 551, J.H. King at house # 553, R.F. Winn house # 555, J.A. McCloud house # 561, and E.L. Graves.

Pay very close attention to what I am about to write. In 1894 in the Atlanta Directories Thomas Callaway a colored man who worked for George Young, and resided at 12 Piedmont Avenue. In 1899 S. B. or Stewart B. Callaway owned property at 12 ½ Piedmont Avenue. The City Court Minutes of Atlanta states that on June 19, 1899 it was Read and Adopted: On motion of Councilman Hammond the City Clerk is ordered to withdraw the licenses issued to S. B.

Callaway & Co. for a Dancing Academy at 12 ½ Piedmont Avenue same having been proven to be kept in a disorderly manner and frequented by a class who spend their time in idleness. Adopted. I could not find Stewart B. Callaway at this time in 1894. In all that is happening with Charlie and Mary Callaway they would fail to issue a license to S. B. Callaway in 1899 because of the class of people that attended the establishment. Mr. Stewart B. Callaway is a very complex person all the time I look for him in the tax digest he has his wife Annie V. Smith Callaway listed. In 1901 the only Colored Callaway listed were A. V. Callaway, Ellen Callaway, E. W. Callaway or Evan W. estate. This was the situation in the years of 1902 thru the time of her death in 1920. At times Stewart B. Callaway would be living at two locations and sometimes Annie V. Callaway would be living at one place and Stewart B. at another. Stewart B. Callaway was listed as being white and colored in the same city directory.

Living on William Street before Henry and Mattie come to live there, I found these Colored families living here in 1899. S. Scott, Lilly L. Davis, Lena Jackson, Lila Holliman, W.H. Watson, Wm. Flagg, Rena Davis, Josie Williams, Sallie Alexander, Alice Teasley, F. Holbrook, Belle Washington, Briston Alston, Lotla Mathis, I. Decatur, B. Young, (white) J. Kilgore, W. Edwards, Dollie Stroud, T. Brooklin, Cornelia Logan, Lizzie Worthy, J. Rodgers and Ada Goodman.

The year is 1900 and we might as well take a walk down Humphries Street, ten years before Susie Callaway and her husband Will arrives in 1901 and Henry C. Callaway and his family arrives in 1911. J. Jones, C. McElroy, N.W. Wright, J. Morris, Ida Warner, Lucy A. Vaughn, G. Dennis, R. M. Moore, Pansey Pendleton, Ada Grimmett, W. Rayford, Annie M. Smith, Emaline Jones, Farr Haven Tabernacle, *H. Haynes, H. Hall,* Jane Strong, C. Lamar, (white) J.A. Fulton Groceries, Chapel Street Intersection- A. Alexander, Warren Chapel, Alice Jackson, Nigle Green, W. Griffin, Minnie Smith,

J. Peters, Nancy Robinson, T. Grier, C. Kieth, Sallie Terrell, T. Williams, Hannah Hadley, Liberty Street Intersection- B. Hayes, Rev. J.L. Trimble, J.R. Jackson, S. Rosser, J. Arnold, Fannie Lathem, Price and Colored Meat Market, Mary Reynolds, R.R. Ferrell, W. Harper, A. Tuggle, a colored Fireman, T. Williams another colored Fireman, Nannie Brown, St. Paul A.M.E. Church, Charith Martin, Betty Henderson, J. Shank, Annie Morgan, Rev. H.D. Cannady, Cornelia Jackson, A. Smith, L. Little John, A. Malone, S. Oliver who owns two properties 78-80,

C. Jenkins, W.H. Dozier, W.F. Henderson, J. Stephens, T. Potts, S.M. White, A. Oliver, Morris Street Intersection- H. Mann, J. Hinton, R. Everett, Amanda Carey, J.H. Green, A. Brown, R. Moody, H. Palm a colored Fireman, W. Dennis, J Logan, J. Jones, Lucy Bruce,

H. Thomas, Nettie McCoy, W. Garr, Zion Hill Baptist Church, J. H. Sawyer a Conductor, B.S. Moore an Engineer, and J.H. McElroy is the switchman and all three that were last mention are all White Men.

Living on Maple Street in the three houses that are located between West Mitchell Street and West Hunter Street which is now Martin Luther King Jr. Boulevard I found in house # 33 C. Tonsil, in house # 35 L. Dewberry, in house # 37 A. Holley and in house # 38 Lula Pitts. Now onto the Census at this time in 1900 and these are the only ones living at this section of Maple Street in 1900. House # 35 lives Mary Callaway a 38 year old widow, whose age is really unknown, Lovett her daughter whose age is unknown, and Thomas Hannah or James Hanna a lodger who age is unknown but he is listed as being twenty-one years old, Living in house # 33 is Addie May a thirty-year-old widow and her thirty five-year-old sister Alice Tonsil and a twenty five-year-old cousin named Isabella Johnson. Now the house that is next to Mary Callaway and Addie May, that is located on West Hunter Street is the house of widow Julia Thomas a thirty eight-year-old woman, and her daughter Gurtie who is eighteen, and her son Willis who is fifteen, Albert her son who is six, and at the house on the corner of West Mitchell Street is Alice McFoley, thirty five-year-old woman and her daughter Ellen Stevens what looks like that she's the same age as her mother so her mother might be fifty five. This situation of being unknown goes to the house of Samuel Alexander a sixty five-year-old colored man and his wife Nellie who is fifty-eight and Annie Coldwell house a fifty-year-old colored woman whose husband is not in the house. However, her son Edward is in the house and he is fifteen and his sister's name is Robec who is sixteen.

In the year of 1899 Mary was living on Tatnall Street with Emily M. Cox of Cox Funeral Home. Emily Cox was living at 131-129 Tatnall Street and Mary was living at 116 Tatnall Street on the opposite side of the street. B. Burch was at 124 Tatnall, Stella Branch was at 122 Tatnall, H. Crawford was living at 119 Tatnall, D. Jones was at 118 Tatnall, N. James was living across the street at 113 Tatnall, Lucinda Wilson was at 106 Tatnall, white man J. H. Morse was at 102 Tatnall, colored man G.

Moncrief was at 101 Tatnall across the street, and colored man J. T. Drake was at 97 Tatnall at the end of the street at the intersection of Markham and Tatnall. At the southern end where I began is the intersection where Emily M. Cox resided between Walnut and Mitchell Street. As you can see the number of the houses decrease going north toward town.

Moreover, W. E. Holmes lived at 47 Tatnall, before it intersects Chapel Street. Reverend E. R. Carter the pastor of the famous Friendship Baptist Church resided at 71 Tatnall Street at this time. He lived between Mary Tidwell at 77 Tatnall and J. C. Waters at 67 Tatnall in 1899. This area is where young colored women were prostituted. This was a practice in this section well before the Colleges arrived. This is the very same element that the Colored Churches and Schools would have to fight against to raise the awareness of the colored community of the blight that was upon them with the liquor and beer and bar rooms that were set in the colored communities to further their control over the colored communities and even today this same plague still exits! If there is no desire for the very thing that destroys the mind and ignites the imagination to act on impulse, the churches and schools could have prevailed even further. The same white community then turn around in 1906 and accuses the same people with being Colored Brutes against their white women with demeaning and detrimental articles in the prominent newspapers and caused riots to justify themselves against the same unfortunate Colored Men and Women and their Children. However, they did this impulsive action while fueled by the deadly liquor to justify their actions to ease their conscious while the colored community ran and fought for their lives in 1906. Then, you would have to ask yourself who was the Brute!

Now to turn my attention to Thompson Alley, this alley was at the intersection of Fort Street and it ran east to west while Fort Street ran north and south. I had a hard time finding out whom lived on Thompson Street in the Atlanta Directories during this time however, if by chance *I came across Mr. George Callaway at the intersection of Thompson alley and Fort Street in the 1900 census report. George Callaway was born December 1858 and was forty-one years old and his wife Minnie was born January 1860 and was forty years old and Charlotte Callaway their daughter was born May 1886. George and Minnie have been married for twenty years and Charlotte is listed as being their only child since being married. This portion of Thompson runs east to west from Hilliard Street to Fort Street.* Living with George and Minnie and Charlotte on Thompson Alley are Jefferson Burks born Jan. 1830 and is seventy years old, Jefferson has been married to Bettie his wife for forty years and Bettie was born March 1841 and is fifty-nine years old, their granddaughter Mande Burks was born April 1883 and is seventeen, Beauragaurd Burks their grandson was born May 1890 and was ten. The Burks lived at house #49. Living at house #48 was the family of Mary Williams who was born December 1856 and was forty-three years old and is a widow. She had been married for seventeen years before the death of her husband. Willie Williams her son was born march 1884 and was sixteen, Clifford Williams was born May 1885 and was sixteen. Living at house #47 was Mr. Asbury Holbrook born September 1850 and was forty-nine years old and has been married to Mary Holbrook for twenty-four years. Mary Holbrook was born December of 1860 and was thirty-nine years old. Ms. Eliza Parker was born march 1830 and was seventy years old and a widow. Living in house # 46 is widow woman Patsy Mitchell who was born April 1859 and was forty-one years old. She had been married for fifteen years before her husband died. George and Minnie Callaway and young Ms. Charlotte are in house # 45. Living in the last house at the end of Thompson Alley in house #44 is the family of Homer Hargrove who was born Feb. 1862 and has been married to Susan his wife for twelve years and Susan was born Aug. 1864 and is thirty-six years old, their children are Howard born May 1893 and is seven, and Ruth Hargrove born March 1899 and is one. Living at the intersection of Fort Street and Thompson Alley is the family of Delia Johnson, who was born January 1877 and was twenty-three years old and is a widow. Delia Johnson had been married only five years before the death of her husband. Hattie Johnson her daughter was born November 1895 and was four years old. They lived in house #185 Fort Street. Living in the same house was Nettie Durden who was born May 1870 and was thirty years old and is a widow as well. Nettie Durden had been married for twelve years to her husband before he died. Her daughter Ella Durden was born December 1890 and was nine years old. Living next door to the Durden family was Emma Huges born Oct. 1868 and was thirty-three years old and a widow who had been married for nineteen years before her husband died. Indiana Huges her daughter was born March 1888 and was twelve, and Fred Huges was born Jan. 1890 and was ten. In the same house as Emma Huges at house # 181 is Richard Flemister born May 1855 and was forty-five years old and his wife Hattie Flemister was born Jan. 1874. The two has been married for six years and have four children. Winnie born March 1892 and is eight, William born Nov. 1894 and is five, Percy their son born October 1898 and is three and George Flemister born Jan. 1899 and is one.

Mr. William Betts is living in house # 175 Fort Street. William was born 1856 and is forty-three and has been married fifteen years to Georgia Betts who was born May 1863. Their daughter Lucy was born April of 1893 and was seven years old. Living in the house with William and his family is Mary Knight who is listed as being the mother in the house and was born March 1841 and was fifty-nine years old and a widow. Lizzie Moore is a boarder and was born Sept. 1845 and was fifty-four and a widow as well. The last house before you got to what looks like another alley by the name of Alemo is Mrs. Mattie Jones born March 1875 and was twenty-five years old and a widow as well. Her sister Abbie Goldsmith was born Dec. 1880 and was nineteen and single and her nephew Albert Upshaw born Feb. 1886 and was fourteen.

Across the street or at this intersection of Fort and Alimo is the houses of Stella Murry born Dec. 1870 and was twenty-nine and a widow, her son Henry Murray was born Mar. 1894 and was six years old, Willie Murray was born April 1897 and was three, Gertrude Murray was born Dec. 1899 and was a few months old, John Robinson was a boarder at the age of forty years old and was born Jan. 1860 and was single. Mr. Johnnie Walton was born Sept. 1838 and was sixty-one years old and his wife Harriet was born Dec. 1840 and was fifty-nine, and Lizzie Walton was born mar. 1870 and was thirty and a widow. This is listed as being the Fourth Ward in Supervisor's District No. 35 and Enumeration District No. 63. And John C. Newman is the Enumerator. I do not know if John C. Newman is any kin to Federal Judge William T. Newman. This could lead to the mystery of George Callaway living in at Thompson Alley on a street that never mentions its occcupants that are living on Thompson Street. The date that I find George Callaway living at this location is on June 7.

I wanted to investigate this section of the Fourth Ward of the City of Atlanta. So, I started in the year of 1889 on Fort Street in the Directories. I started at the house where I found John or James Callaway in house numbered thirty-five. The Colored families that I found in 1900 are just about the same in 1889. However, I believe that it would serve me to mention the families anyway. Starting at the intersection of Decatur going north to limits and south to Fair or Memorial Drive in the third and Fourth wards. House # 2 is vacant, 3 through 11 is the Fur Company of Trowbridge, house #6 is Jane Magee, house # 14 is Sallie Isom, house # 24 is a white man J. P. Hornsby, house 25 is colored woman Sarah J. Hightower, house #33 is R. Kelsey, house #34 is R. Jackson, house #35 is J. Calaway, house 336 is S. Kirby, and house #44 is K. D. Crutchfield and

G. Watts. J. Calaway is in the third house before you get to the intersection of Schofield.

I will move on down the road to the intersection where I found George Calaway on Thompson Alley. The Houses that were at the intersection of Fort Street and Thompson Alley are the house number starting at the corner of Old Wheat intersection. At this intersection is Mr. Jerry Moore, and on the other side of the street is Mr. F. w. Johnson at house 158, Rachael Sewell is at house 159, Malissa Davis is at 160, and house 167 is unfinished this tells me that at this time the Colored Community is building in the Third and Fourth Ward. Moving on down the road I came to the house of David Stokes at house 168. J. P. Gray, a white man, is at house 169. J. P. Gray has living with him a colored man named Jacob Speer, at house 170 ½. Now we are at the intersection where George Callaway will come to live in 1900. At house 171 is Mr. William Betts, this is at the intersection of Green and Fort Street. Samuel Stevens is living with George Johnson at house 173. Living at house 174 is Pinkney Hugley, house 175 is vacant, house 176 is George Moore and John Law. Now we are at the intersection of Thompson Alley. Crossing Thompson Alley is the house of Mary Jones at house 177, and in house 178 are Green Gates and then the junction Houston and Irwin.

In the year of 1890, starting at the Decatur and Fort Street intersection I found M. Jones in the once vacant house Mr. M. Jones, and Trowbridge Furniture Co. is at number 3, house 6 is vacant, and S. Herring is at house 8, G. Williams is at house 10, S. Johnson is at house 14, Lou Bell is at house number 16 living with Laura Barnett, and Richard Kelsey is at house 33 after crossing the Fillmore intersection and J. Callaway is at house 35, and Sarah Weeks is at house 36. Crossing over Schofield intersection is the house of William Keith, and Lizzie Smith, and Edward Dawson living in the rear of the house of Lizzie Smith. Moving to the Old Wheat intersection is the house that is numbered 138 is G. Sansom, living with William Brown, house 139 is Hannah Sewell, house 160 has Melissa Davis and A. L. Morrison, house 165, is George Moore, James Allison, Jane Glass, Aaron Henderson, and Sam Williams. House number 168 is occupied by Lizzie Andrew and D. Stokes, house 169 is occupied by Jerry Speer and J. T. Maddox, Amos Allen, Columbus Mays, and Hilliard Nolan. William Betts occupies house 171, Alonzo Wilkins occupies house 171 ½ with M. S. Garner at the intersection of Green Alley. After crossing Greene Alley, you come to the residence of Lucy Dawson at house 173 and Same Stevens is living with her along with Sallie Haygood. House 174 has Melinda Nolan with Pink Hughley, house 175 has Jennie Brown,

Lizzie Nesby, Estella Murray, John Norwood, Hattie Ragland, Lavinia Clayton, and Jane Sanders, House 175 has John Law, mamie Dokes, and Merritt Fillmore. The last three are at the entersection of Thompson's Alley. Living at 177 after crossing over Thompson Alley is Peter Lewis and living at 178 is Hattie Gates. At the junction of Houston and Irwin in house 179 is Lucy Clayton and Georgia Stephens. Ceasar Miller, S. Clark, two colored men are living with two white men J. E. Clower and W. P. Powell. This is not the end of Fort street and its residents I just chose to stop at this point of the street because as I go north up Fort Street. I go out of the Third Ward into the Fourth Ward.

In the listing by last names in the Atlanta Directories under Callaway, James Callaway is a laborer and is residing at 35 Fort Street. James is not renting the property or owns the property at 35 Fort Street he is just residing there in 1890. Under the listing of last names Callaway, I found John E., a white man and a engineer for H. Crankshaw & O. and resides at 140 Thompson. Mrs. Nettie also resides at 140 Thompson as well. Nettie's occupational trade is a seamstress. Also, living at 140 Thompson is William who works for H. Crankshaw & Company as a machine hand and only boards at 140 Thompson. The widow Martha Calloway is the widow of H. W. Callaway and is a seamstress and livies at 30 South Terry Street. Terry Street is the first place where I found Alexander Callaway living in 1870. I tie this Martha Callaway to Terrell County as a widow of H. W. Callaway. H. W. Callaway was living in Bibb County but ran a farm in Terrell County in 1860. Martha has ties to the Cates that owned property in what was called Lynwood Park Colored Subdivision in Buckhead! The property that was on Thompson Alley was owned by Mr. James R. Wallace.

In 1891, I will only mention a few names that were located in this area of research for the mysterious family of colored Callaways or Calloway in the Third and Fourth wards of the city of Atlanta! The block between Filmore and Schofield intersection are the houses of Laura Barnett, and Richard Kelsey, J. Callaway, Sarah weeks, Eliza Williams, and George Watts. Mrs. Eliza Lucas lived at 110 Fort Street at the intersection of Edgewood Ave. and on the same block or intersection is Mrs. Susan Walton. At 200 Fort Street at the intersection of Rasberry Alley is Caesar Miller and Seagraves & Ellington a colored business. This business is at the Rasberry Alley and Wheat intersection before coming to the Union St. R. R. co. Stables and J. Moore. Mr. William Betts is still located at 171 Fort Street with M. J. Garner. Moving on down up the street E. Opwell is at 173 with Same Stevens, living at 174 is Melinda Nolan, at 175 is Emma

Goldsmith with Steve Nesby. At 176 is Filmore Merritt. Thompson's Alley intersection is the place of Mary Daggett at house 177 and Hattie Gates is at 178. at the junction of Houston and Irwin is Lucy Clayton and house 200 on this street is Mr. J.E. Clower. Just a few more names that are on Fort Street are Mr. A. Beasley at 217, J. M. Ryan at 219, S. Jones 220, moving on up the road where Baker Street ends and intersects Fort Street is the residence of Rufus Dorsey. Crossing over Forest Avenue intersection is the place of Robert Epps at 350.

1892 Fort Street. At this time in just one year a major change of residence had taken place to this section of the Third and Fourth wards, starting at the intersection of Decatur Street. Residents or buildings 3 thru 11 are the property of Trowbridge Furniture Co. at house 10 at Gilmer Street intersection is the place of S. Ambrose, crossing Gilmer Street is the place of C. Combs at house 29, R. Kelsey is at house 31, M. Douglass is at house 33, M. Holmes is at house 34, Silas Blake is at house 35, and the Colored Baptist Church is at lot 37, and a white man name H. Fenneman is at lot 38, and R. L. Bryan is at lot 44. At the intersection of Old Wheat Street is the place of Emanuel Nolan at house 145, at the intersection where Green ends is house 171 with William R. Betts, Celia Hill is at 168, with Henry Tellis, and Ida Coles is at 174, and Jerry Moore is at 178.

1893 Fort Street. The section starting at Decatur Street are the lots 3–11 owned by Hass Guthman & Co. House 10 is occupied by J. Wilson, house 14 is occupied by S. Johnson, at the intersection of Gilmer Street is son Boggs at house 29, house 31 is still occupied by R. Kelsey, Carrie Johnson occupies house 33, and house 35 is now occupied by Mrs. Elizabeth Rhodes for the first time. Lot 37 is where the Colored Baptist Church is located. Lot 38 is occupied by Mr. C. M. Calloway a white bar owner. Lot 44 is occupied by W. G. Forsyth, lot 46 is vacant, lot 48 is occupied by Burns Mfg. Co. Mr. C. Eberhart is located at 145 Fort Street near Wheat Street intersection and J. Glass is at 161 across the street. Mr. George Moore is at 169, and William Sherman is at 170 near Green Alley. R. Andrews is at 172 across the street. Wm. R. Betts is at 175 Fort Street. P. Hugeley is at 180, and A. Carter is at 181, and Peter Williams is at 182. Mr. Robert Epps is gone and so is Mr. Rufus Dorsey as well. However, living at 484 Fort Street is S. Callaway a colored man and Mr. R. Payne is at 495 just before you get to Pine Street and two white men are living across the street at lot 506 Mr. J. T. Coogler and house 510 is J. H. Farmer just at Linden intersection. I do not know if this is George or not however he might be under the middle name S. whether than to go under the name of George.

1894 Fort Street. Starting at Decatur Street intersection is lot 3 American Upholstery Co. lot 10 J. Wilson, lots 25-29 Gholstin Spring Be Co. Gilmer Street intersection, lot 31 R. Kelsey, lot 32, H. Sims, lot 33, M. Avery and J. McLendon, lot 35 is Elizabeth Rhodes, and lot 37 now names the church that is located on Fort Street is Mt. Moriah Church. lot 38 is A. Finch, lot 44 is a white woman name Mrs. B. Day, lot 46 is George Moore, and lot 48 is Purity Ice Works a business owned by R. M. Rose located at 12 Marietta Street. Rose goes under the logo of "*Purity*." By all mean there must be a liquor store in the black neighborhood! Mr. Rose like so many that will come after him has found a treasure trove a means to get filthy rich by exploiting the Black Community! However, if the desire for these seductive spirits and drugs the crime rate and police would not have a perpetual presence in the black community. As those of old let us raise our standard as the churches of old tried to prevail over the week minded or week conscience the faculty which that decides right and wrong.

There is a large number of Negroes living on Fort Street at this time and do not forget that Rose also has a liquor store at the end of Hilliard Street that ends in the Colored Community of Buttermilk bottom. I assume that Rose Liquor decided to have this Purity Ice Company to have Draymen to also deliver his liquor as well. Draymen were known for this time of deliveries. Yes, the Horse & Buggy Men making their Ice runs to the many families that not only wanted just the ice but the drink to go with the ice as well! Moving on up Fort Street at Schofield intersection is E. Wilson, at house 54, I. Robertson is at house 55, S. Flood is at lot 59, W. L. Dansby is at lot 65, R. Wright is at house 69, and William davenport is at lot 71, at the Tanner intersection is white man W. J. Tanner at house or lot 93, across the street is A. Osborne at house 104, H. Washington is at lot 108, Martha Byrd is at lot 112. At the intersection of Edgewood Ave intersection is M. Stenson at lot 120, and across the street is house 121 that is occupied by Mr. W. H. Chamlee (Chamble) at the Wheat intersection is lot 158 the Atlanta Con Street Car Stables and Wheat Street Baptist church and at lot 161 is P. Lever.

At this time some of the usual names that are at the Thompson Alley section are missing and Thompson Alley does not even exist. However, William Betts is still located in the general area at house 175. John Eaves is at 174, L. Salter is at 173 and C. Hill is at 172, P. Hugeley is at 180, A. Carter is at 181, and L. Sims is at 183, Stephens Nesbitt is at 185 and J. Jones is at 186. At the intersection of Houston and Irwin is S. E. Holland

and J. E. Clower the white man and C. C. Wimbish are both there after crossing Ellis Street. At the intersection of Harris Street is Clower & Johnson at house 284 and G. Daniels is at 285. I want to see who was living where S. Callaway was living at Pine Street and I found no S. Calloway at 484 Fort Street, I did not even find a lot number 484 where he was residing. However, I did find house 481 with W. Barnes, and at 495 where R. Payne was residing I found Mr. Robert Epps. At the end of Fort Street are J. T. Coogler, J. H. Farmer, and C. Drennon, and a vacant lot. However, I did find John Callaway living at 189 Houston Street.

1895 Fort Street. At the same corner of Decatur Street are the same businesses. Between Gilmer Street and Schofield are the house of R. Kelsey at house 31, houses 32 and 33 are vacant, house 34 is occupied by J. McLendon, house 35 is occupied by Elizabeth Rhodes, and house 37 is occupied by Mt. Moriah Church, Mrs. M. L. Bersellia is in house 38, Mrs. Sallie Alexander is at 44 Fort Street, Jennie Stewart is at 46 Fort Street, and the Prurity Ice Works are at 48 Fort Street. Moving on up Fort Street toward Irwin and Houston intersections I four John Eaves at 174, I. S. Huntley at 174 ½ and Wm. Betts at 175 Fort, J. Hicks at 178, and P. Hugeley at 180, J. Barnes at 181, and C. Gates at 182 Fort. E. Stephens at 184, Stephen Nesbitt at 185, and D. Ellington at 186, Wm. Gates at 187, S. Stephens at 188, Adaline Hinton at 189, Lavenia Clayton at 190, W. Keith at 192, and L. Clayton at 194 Fort Street and crossing over the intersection you come to the house of Elsie Thomas, and a white man name R. N. Cobb and a colored man named C. C. Winbish. And a colored woman named Mary Albright, and a colored person named R. Colbert, and colored man J. M. Rayns, and the house of S. Fambro and A. Grant and then the house of Frank Zacry, and then the house of A. E. Beasley . . . Johnson and Clower are at the intersection of Harris and Fort Street in 1895. William Epps is at 323 Fort Street after crossing over Baker Street. The intersection of Pine where I found Robert Epps and S. Callaway, now Butler Williams is in the house and house 495 is vacant.

The year is now 1899 and this is the year before I find George Calaway at Thompson Alley. In the listing of the last names of Callaways in the Atlanta Directories I found George Callaway working for the Southern Rail Yard. However, I never did find out his place of residence in 1899. At this same time, I found Henry C. Callaway at 138 Howell Street, John Callaway works for Green Banks and resides at 64 Haynes Street with colored man J. Willingham.

The other John Callaway is living at 288 Butler Street and works as a waiter for Hotel Jackson. Joseph Callaway boards at 134 E. Cain Street and works as a Driver for Mrs. R. B. Blacknall. And for the first time, Mary Callaway is a washwoman and resides at 116 Tatnall and Nelson boards at 22 White Alley. I don't know if John Callaway at 64 Haynes Street is any kin to Granddaddy Arthur or not. However, this is a similarity in relationships. John E. Callaway a white man that lived on Thompson Alley. However, in 1899 he is an agent for Regina Flour Mills St. Louis and resides at 551 Whitehall. Like I had stated before there is no Thompson Alley in 1899 or in 1900 in the Atlanta Directories.

I went to look at who was living near or on the block of Haynes Street and J. Willingham living at this place and living after you cross the Walker and nelson Intersection. H. Ross a colored man is in house 66, Martha Smith is located at house 67, S. Jackson is at house 68, and 69 is vacant, Lula Jones is at house 71, G. Hurst is at 72, Susan Sarters is at 73, H. King is at 74, and Silvia Woodford is at house 75, and Ella Wilson is at house 77. Chapel intersection is next and then two vacant houses.

Back on Fort Street at the intersection where Gilmer Street dead ends to Fort, R. Kelsey still resides at 31 Fort Street, and now has R. Ragsdale living with him. House number 32 has Green Young, house number 33 has Cora Butler, house number 34 has Emeline McLendon, house number 35 has Elizabeth Rhodes, house number 37 has the Mt. Moriah Church, and house number 38 has Lavinia Williams, and Fifth Avenue dead ends to Fort Street intersects, and the house of Lucy Humphrey and is listed as house number 44, house 46 is occupied by Susie Few, and house r48 is still occupied by the Purity Works. Schofield Street begins at Fort Street and Mrs. Annie Williams house number 54 is across the street from Purity Ice Works. Margrave Harris is in house 55, and S. Flood is in house 59, and J. Tucker is in house 61, W. M. Andrews is in house 63, Kate Shakespeare is in house 65, Jane Storey is in house 67, Matthew Nichols is in house 69, J. Crane and G. Wynn are in house 71, Mary Davis is in house 73, the last five people are all white residence on Fort Street before crossing over Fain intersection. Mrs. M. V. Gill at house 75, W. E. Dunn house 78, Mrs. M. Sill house 79, and s. H. Whatley at house 83.

Moving on up the road of Fort Street to where George Callaway we will come to reside a year from now in 1900. I'll start at the intersection of Edgewood Avenue where J. Haywood lives at 123, F. Boykin lives at 125, at the Auburn avenue and Old Wheat intersection heading north is the house of Willie Wright at house 166, at the Green Street intersection is the house of O. Nash at 172 Fort Street, R. Smith is at house 173, W. Keith is at 174, and William Betts is at 175, House 176 is vacant, and 178 is occupied by L. manning, and P. Hugerly is at 180, Charles Gates is at 182, and R. Allen is at 183, Mary Tidwell is at 184, Rachel Frank is at 185, Bella McCoy is at 186, John Green is at 187, Georgia Stephens is at 188, Adeline Hinton is at 189, Eliza Reid is at 190, H. Walker is at 192, and Fannie Tell is at 194.

Crossing Irwin Street where it begins and intersects with Houston Intersection is R. D. Stinson, and at Ellis intersection is C. C. Wimbish at house 215, Lela McLendon is at 216, Wm. Reese is at 219, and D. Strickland is at 223, Belle Ryan is at 227, S. Fabro is at 228 and C. C. Beasley is at 229, and T. B. Kelley is at 232. A. E. Beasley is at 233, Fort Street A. M. E. church which is now located on Boulevard is at the intersection of Cain Street across the street of C. King at 253, and Rev. C. L. Johnson who is at 254 Fort Street. H. Riggins was residing at 264 Fort Street and Lizzie Williams was living at 266 Fort Street. Crossing over Grace where it begins and Bynum ends is the house of I. Speer living at 269, crossing over Wilson begins and Harris Street ends we comes to the house of Rachel Edwards at 283, and Clower & Johnson is at 284. Mary Lovelace is at 294, H. Bruce is at 298, W. Lee is at 308 Fort Street, and L. Anderson is at 310 the intersection of Highland Avenue begins. R. T. Davis is at 311, and T.H. Holcomb is at 312, D. Lay is at 319 after crossing the intersection of Baker Street. G. W. Williams is living at 347 Fort Street at the intersection of Chestnut Avenue where it ends. G. W. Johnson is a white man at 392 Fort Street after crossing Forrest Avenue. Fort Street ends at the intersection of Linden Street with Alice Powell a colored woman in the last house on Fort Street.

RIOT OF 1906 AND BLACKS ON FORT STREET

The year is 1900 and it is a very interesting year on Fort Street for it will be only nine years before the riot of 1906 and Fort Street will become one of the Streets that the white mob will seek out every Negro Woman and Man, Boy and Girl to kill. It was stated that the mob left Marietta Street from a bar and headed up Fort Street. As I started reading the Atlanta Directories of 1900 there are more houses run by Colored Women and it starts at the intersection of Decatur Street the same street the mob came down for Marietta Street turns into Decatur Street after crossing Peachtree Street and then the mob turned north up Fort Street and parts of Hilliard Street.

The first house that I come to at the intersection of Decatur and Fort Street are Louisa Gray at house 2, Henrietta Garner at house 4, Mollie Riggins at house 6, Mary Alexander at house 8, Mary Wilson at house 10, Ida Taylor at house 12, Mary Chambers at house 14, J. Carlisle furniture is at lots 16-18, Capitol Transfer & Storage Co. is at lot 27. Crossing over Gilmer Street ends; the first house 29 is vacant, R. Kelser is at house 31, with R. Ragedale, Hattie Grice is at house 32, Cora Butler is at house 33, Emma Blasingame is at house 33, G. Young is at house 34, Elizabeth Rhodes is at house 35, Mt. Moriah Church is at lot 37, Lavania Sparks is at the last house before Fifth Ave at house 38. Ella Jones is at house 44, house 46 is a vacant place and now the Purity Ice Company is now the Beer Ice Company at 48 Fort Street at the intersection of Schofield where the street begins. Ms. Annie Williams resides in house 54, Ms. Della Cook resides in house 55, Ms. Georgia Long is in house with Ms. Della Cook. Mr. S. Flod a carpenter is at house 59, House 61 is occupied by J. Tucker a carpenter, and so is Mr. Horton who is house 63, Mattie Banks is in house 64, with W. Ashmore. House 65 is occupied by Katie Shakespeare, house 67 is occupied by J. Bryan, and house 69 by M. Nichols a carpenter, house 71 is occupied by Mr. Martin, Parrie L. Moore occupies house 73, Mrs. M. Sill occupies house 75, W. E. Dunn occupies house 78, and S. E. Seagle occupies house 79. The last three residents are all white occupants.

Crossing Fain Street intersection, I come to the house of Rev. S. H. Whatley, a white minister, at house 83, and Louisa Mann, a colored woman, living at house 92. Louisa Mann lives between Rev. S. H. Whatley the white minister and a white woman named Mrs. Amanda Tanner for whom Tanner Street is named for. She is at the street which is named for her. Crossing Tanner Street you come to the house of C. Green at 104, Millie Vaughan is at 108, J. Roberts is at 112, M. Stinson is at 114, H. Banks is at 118. Perry Dobbs, a carpenter, is at 120 Fort Street and Edgewood Avenue intersection. John Haywood is a porter at 123. F. Boykin is at 125 and is a blacksmith. Emma Walker is at 128. J. A. Brown, a carpenter, is at 132. House 138 is the place of C. Miller, and 139 is the place of Mad Marie Laws, and 140 is the house of W. Burdy. House 142 is the house of P. Smith a colored barber and he has R. Dawson living with him. Crossing over Auburn Avenue and Old Wheat intersection house 158 is a vacant place. Mary Phillips occupies house 162 with W. Gettes, Wm.

Ashmore, and Mattie Banks, house 165 is the place of Hannah Sewell, and J. Campbell occupies house 166, B. Russell occupies house 168, house 169 is occupied by A. W. Hawkins a cook by trade, and house 170 is the place of Ms. Ada Mason, and Hattie Badger is number 171, Nora Reeder is house 172, house 173 is the place of Mattie Jones, Mattie Jones is living with Lelia Upshaw. House 174 is the place of Wm. Keith a porter and is at the intersection of Green Alley.

The next house is where Thompson Alley is located and yet Thompson Alley is never mentioned or is not listed in the Atlanta Directories in 1900. However, I know in the census at this time, Thompson Alley shows up with Mr. George Calloway as a resident. This mystery is not a mystery at all. House 175 is the house of William Betts a barber, house 176 is vacant, house 178 is the place of R. Nesbit, house 180 is the place of P. Huguley, house 181 is the place of Emma Haynes, 182 is the place of C. Hicks, 183 is the house of W. Daniel, Mary Tidwell is at house 184, W. Lawrence is at 185, house 186 is the place of W. Cochran a porter, J. A. Atkins is at 186 with W. Cochran, Georgia map is at house 187 with S. Keith, 188 is the place where Georgia Stephens lives and Pinkie Collins sharing her place with Julia Davis at house 189, Eliza Reid is at house 190, J. Wallace is at 192, and S. Hutchison is a drayman at where Irwin begins and the Houston intersection. C. Brown is the only house between Irwin and Houston and Ellis intersection. C. Brown house is listed at 213.

The first house after crossing Ellis Street is the house of R. Stinson at 214. C. C. Wimbish is at 215, Fannie Westmore is at 216, Cherry Fuller is at the same place. 219 is the place of Roberta cox and Melissa Cody, and C. C. Limbush is at 223, 227 is the place of J. Ryan, and S. Fambro is at 228, and C. C. Beasley is a Clerk for R M S, and T. Kelley is at 232, with Anna Kelley, and A. E. Beasley is a clerk for R M S and Mattie Hayes is at 235, J. McHenry is at 236, S. Jones is at 238 with E. Parks a waiter, and H. J. White at 239, W. Ward is a waiter at 242 and is in the same house is H. Allen, and in house 243 is S. minefield a carpenter, and V. Niles is in the same house as well. R. Joseph is in house 244, and at Cain intersection and crossing this intersection is the place of J. Heard a shoemaker at house 245, C. King is at house 253, and Lizzie Standard is at 255.

I believe I will stop here and tell you to go to this street and see for yourself how large this colored community was.

I also wanted to go north on Hilliard Street the same street that runs in the same direction as Fort Street and starts at the Decatur Street intersection as well. It was Hilliard Street that the white mob also went down to do harm in the Colored Section of Town. I noticed that there were a large number of Colored Families that were Porters, and Carpenters that lived on both Fort Street and Hilliard as well.

Hilliard Street: First east of Fort, runs from Decatur north to Forrest Avenue. The first is the house of J. A. Morris in 1900. J. A. Morris is the companion of Charles Malory Callaway out of Henry County or Panthers Ville, Georgia. He is living in house 10 on Hilliard Street, house 11 is occupied by A. N. Williams, house 14; P. H. Kistler, house 16; J. L. Gidias, a printer, house 17; J. J. Betty and machinist, house 19; J. L. Crowley, house 20; W. H. Blackstock, house; 23 W. J. McDonald a carpenter, house 25 J. Hadoway, house 26; D. L. Hammond, house 27; N. Nash, house 28; B. D. Crossley, house 29; W. L. Cardin. *Pitman Place intersection begins:* House 32; Mrs. Maggie Burger, house 34; T. A. Minor (a saloon), the same property is shared with J. Sprayberry a saloon owner as well, house 35; G. C Heck a bartender, house 38 is the house of M. E. Edwards and house 40 is vacant. *Schofield Ends intersection:* house 41; J. L. Epps a grocer, house 41 ½ is Mrs. S. Smith, house 43; is shared by Fannie Perkins and G. McElhaney the first Colored Families after crossing Schofield intersection. The families that are mentioned are all colored in majority on Hilliard Street. House 44 is shared property between C. Appleberry, P. Griffin, T. Polk, and house 44 ½ is occupied by Candice Wise. House 45, H. Cosby; house 46, R. Leonard; house 48, Mattie Holmes; house 49, H. Lane; house 50, Matie Mathews and Emma Jennings; house 52, P. Pace a fireman; house 53, W. Atkinson; house 55, Fannie Stokes; house 56, R. Keith a porter; house 59 is shared between E. Rogers and B. Harrington. House 60, C. Hughley; house 65, W. Carter a plasterer, he shares this property with R. R. Harris. House 66 W. Banks and W. White; house 68, S. Powledge; house 69, is a shared property between Ella McClendon and Ida Glenn; house 70, J. Mapp; house 72, W. Martin and L. Wood; house 73, Easter Jones and B. Heath; house 76, Harriet Williams and Ida Simpson; house 77, A. Jones and H. Beaver; house 79, Rev. A.A. Irwin.

Fain Ends intersection: house 80, J. L. Dunn; house 83, Anna Lesley; house 85, T. S. Tate (grocer); house 87, E. B. Gibson; house 89, H. Pleasant; house 91, Mattie Roane and R. Battle (a porter) and Fannie Brooks; house 95, Laura Wofford and Tennie Alexander

Tanner intersection and Edgewood Avenue intersection: house 114, A. Soloman and M. Boyd; house 117, Henry Smith (carpenter); house 119, W.A. Morgan; house 120, Jennie Williams and J. Magsby; house 121, Agness Pittman and Anna Williams; house 122, T. Collierl; house 123, Mary

Austin and Mary Eberhart; house 124, Josephine Collier; house 125, A. Hamilton (colored conductor); house 126, W. Marion (blacksmith); house 128, Lulu Howsworth; house 130, Emma Fields and Emma Martin; house 131, Caroline Sims and Peter Williams; house 133, Clara Hosley; house 135; Rena Davis; house 139, B. A. Reed

Auburn Ave. and Old Wheat intercection: house 153, S. Golden (grocer) and T. Parks (driver); house 154, Ella Jackson and Fannie Johnson; house 155, *G. W. Lephart (porter)

**I must stop and pause here to say I know where this man or his kin folks are buried. Mr. G. W. Leaphart is buried in the same cemetery as my grandfather Arthur Calloway in the Masonic Cemetery in DeKalb County off the North Druid Hills Road in the Mount Mariah Baptist Churh Yard.*

House 157, R. McBride; house 158, W. Bassil and H. Jackson; house 159, P. A. E. Johnson; house 160, vacant; house 161, J. H. Traylor (carpenter), (might be Taylor); house 162, Annie Simmons; house 168, W. McGee.

Lyons Avenue intersection begins: house 172; Matilda Stokes, house 174; Maria Foster, house 176; J. D. Love (porter), Sarah Ferrell, and Carrie Scott, house 177; Annie Murdock, house 180; A Cavil (porter), house 183 vacant, house 184 C. O. Gibson (painter), house 185 Lula Culham, Mattie Harrison, Sallie Brown, house 186; Harriet Clayton, house 188 C. Allen and Mary Spivey.

Irwin intersection and Houston intersection and where Ellis Ends: The next fifteen households are white occupants before crossing the Cain Street intersection. House 210; C. J. Vaughan, house 213; R. J. Henderson (carpenter), house 213; J. C. Rudisill, house 218; M. E. McGee (fireman), house 222; J. P. Pinnell (carpenter), house 226; S. P. Fincher and S. M. Evans, house 231; A. C. Elliott (conductor), house 235; J. F. Clower

I now know where Charlie Callaway was living when he was accused by the Federal Courts for receiving stolen goods in Fulton County because of the last name Clower that appeared on his documents. How old is Charlie at this time, I do not know!

House 236, R. S. Hilley and A. J. Swan; house 239, D. W. Webb; house 240, W. C. Morris

Cain Street intersection: The first five houses are occupied by white occupants. House 248; Wm. Florence (machinist) and H. Ivy. House 250; N. R. Keeling (machinery), house 254; F.J. Sharp (grocer), house 254 ½ Mrs. S. Cates. (this ends the houses where Whites occupy houses).

House 267; Rev. W. J. Alexander, house 268; J. Eason and Alice Bailey, house 269; W. J. Hogan (grocer), house 270; J. Smith (porter), house 274 is occupied by a white man name J. W. Kilpatrick (grocer). *Highland Avenue intersection:* house 305 is vacant, house 306; R. D. Singleton, G. M. Howard, and J. Bowen, house 310 Nany Cunningham, and S. Luckie, house 312; H. Luckie, house 314; W. Richardson, house 315; Ella Senior, house 316; J. L. Arthur, house 317; Eliza Davis, house 318; vacant, house 319; G. Davis, house 320; Lucy Ellis, house 321; Lucy Collier, house 322; vacant, house 324 Mittie Simmons, house 326; S Baugh, house 328; Jennie Wright, house 330; Lily York, house 330; Nancy E. Elrington, house 332; J. Holmes, house 334 Laura Clark, house 336 Mary Gibson, house 338; A. Lewis, house 344; Annie Minto, house 346; R. Hicks, house 352; G. Johnson (shoemaker) and Minnie Logan, house 353 B. Hill (carpenter), house 357; Rev. J. Williams and Susan Echols, house 358; R. Duke.

Forrest Avenue intersection: The first house 376; is occupied by a white woman named Mrs. F. 1. Burt. House 378; L. Wilson, house 382; W. Harris, house 384; vacant, house 386; is a white occupant named J. H. Conlill, and house 388 is occupied by a white man named N. Brightwell, and house 390 is where a colored man resides named J. Chandler. This ends the Hilliard Street Road that is first east of Fort Street and runs from Decatur north to Jackson Street. *At the beginning of both Fort and Hilliard Street and going north is the place where a great number of employed colored men worked for the Southern Rail Road and Carpenters resided here as well to help build the colored residences growing where the Third and Fourth Ward comes together in Atlanta. This might be the very reason Martin M. Callaway came to reside on Ella Street near the Ebenezer Baptist Church was first Located. It is called Airline Street now.*

There is another white man that briefly showed up in this area on Decatur Street and his name was J. C. Hudgins. John and Fannie Hudgens was living at 314 Decatur Street and his occupation was a being a laborer. I found a few more Hudgens as well. John N. Hudgens and his wife Carrie at 50 Hurt Street. John worked as a salesman for Everett, R. R. & Co. George Hudgens was a motorman and boards at 249 ½ Marietta Street, Henry C. and Georgia Hudgens resided at 152 Richardson Street in the Third Ward. Henry C. Hudgens worked as the manager for Trepoline Mfg. Co.

Hudgins Publishing Co. the H. W. Davis Mgr. 302 Kiser Bldg.; Clarence T. Hudgins worked as the clerk for R. J. Suber, and resided in Decatur, Ga. by 1901 J. C. Hudgins had moved on from Decatur

Street. However, Henry C. and Georgia Hudgens were still located at 152 Richardson Street.

From the listing of the Hudgens in the Directories I went to Decatur Street to see how far was the residence of John C. Hudgins was from Fort Street. His house was only a half a block away. House 314 on Decatur Street was between Bell and Fort Street. I will start at the residence of M. Z. Davis (meat market) at 282, House 283 is the residence of A. Ivey (wood turner), R. Ivey (carpenter), and H. Ivey (car inspector). J. K. Polk (furn) is at 288-90, house 298; Josie Smith (luncheon), house 299; A. Bernstein (peddler), house 300; J. H. Moore (coal), he shares the location with G. W. Lackey (cigars), house 301; J. A. Austion (carpenter), house 302; Abernathy Bros. (druggists), he shares this property with C. S. Bryon and B. S. Graves (Phys.), house 303: I. Sinkowitz (peddler), house 304-6; Adamson & Son, (grocers), house 304 ½; W. L. Smith (plumber), house 305; J. L. Austin, (blacksmith).

Bell Street intersection: house 307 J. T. Hagan (grocer), house 308; D. D. Henry (tinner), house 308 ½; J. Bruce (stove repair) and J. W. Segars (painter), hosue 309 is vacant, house 310; J. M. t. Bates, (tobacco), House 311; J. B. Ward (a colored fireman), house 312; W. A. Webb (a white shoemaker), hosue 314 is the residence of Mr. John C. Hudgins and Fannie. House 317; E. M. Forshaw (peddler), house 318; M. Tucker a colored (shoemaker), house 320; G. W. Hogarth a white (carpenter), house 322; D. McKinney (colored barber), house 323; Schoen Bros. (hides), house 324; two colored resident, J. King and Ms. Jennie Holcomb, house 325-31; F. I. Stone & Co. (hardware), house 328; Miss N. Smith (luncheon), house 330; W. H. Green Saloon, house 332; Mrs. L. Arnold (white luncheon), moving on down the Fort Street intersection I wanted to know who and what resided at this intersection in 1900. It was the establishment of m. J. Priscock and his saloon, and W. McKinney and his pool room at 342 Decatur Street, and at 342 ½ Decatur was G. Dewberry house his occupation was a (plumber).

The Atlanta Metal & Bottle Company was the next place listed at 344-48 Decatur Street. L. Cohen and his shoes was at 345, a colored woman named Fannie Strickland was at 352, J. Wallac Saloon was at 366 Decatur and he had a pool room at 366 ½ Decatur St. and a pool room at 368 Decatur St. as well. Colored woman Lucy Gay was doing laundry at 383 Decatur Street, another colored woman named Addie Tuttle resided at 409 Decatur St. and Dora Harden resided at 413 Decatur St. and H.

H. Stowers had a grocery store at 416 Decatur St. After crossing Yonge Street where it begins I found M. Morris at 420 and having a Dry Goods store. Moving beyond Jackson St. I came across G. G. Sahli at 482 Decatur Street at the intersection of Fitzgerald where it begins and he had a grocery store.

After crossing Boulevard which use to be called The Old Rolling Mill Road. I came to the house of R. B. Richardson a barber at 512 Decatur St. and a colored company of Mr. W. Murphy & Son at 514 Decatur St. White man S. J. Scott ran a saloon at 518 Decatur St. Mr. R. B. Richardson also had a barber shop at 584 Decatur Street as well next door to Mr. J. F. Roughton & Co. a white man dealing in drugs at 550 Decatur St. and at 554 Decatur St. After crossing Bradley where it begins I found the residence of G. Smtih a colored blacksmith at 572 doing business next door to Mrs. M. Underwood grocery store, at 570 Decatur St. and Mr. J. Hughes Saloon at 566 and M. Morris dry goods store at 564. At the Corner of Cornelia where it begins is I. D. Simpkins grocery and *the Southern Railway intersection intersects.* J. A. Ayers a foreman resided between the Southern Railway intersection and the Ella intersection before you got to the place of Mr. C. C. Cunningham and his feed store at 604 Decatur St. Mr. J. W. Fuller resides at 614 Decatur and worked as a blacksmith. I wanted to get to the intersection further on down Decatur Street to where I come to the place of Mrs. S A. White at 680 Decatur St. and W. D. White & Brothers Grocers at 682. At the corner of Delta Place where it begins I found Mr. J. Carter at 820 Decatur St. and worked as an editor. Mr. M. Corput worked as a civil engineer and resided next door to J. Carter the editor at 626. And at the Hurt intersection where it begins I found these important White Men as well! W. E. Hanye at 896 Decatur (Mgr.), W. T. Henry at 904 Decatur St. (bkkpr), at 950 Decatur was the place of R. Woolfolk (transfer), and at 975 Decatur St. Mr. J. W. Fielder the (Agent).

I am sure that these import white men at this time did not like what they saw by having to pass between these places of ill fame after leaving the City of Atlanta where all kinds of mixing was taking place at these two notorious intersections in 1906. These two intersection where the Colored Porters made their stop overs and had their share of the Bars and Women both Colored and White as well. Let us not forget why the Carpenters were there at this time. Mr. Hurt is just about to relinquish his prospects of building houses to Mr. Asa Candler or Chandler and these two roads Forts and Hilliard are the residence for the carpenters both black and white that started with Mr. Joel Hurt and Company! If you are a Colored Man and with a trade why not spend your time between the City Life and the Country Life where you came from and make more money doing both. I can just visualize in my mind this great amount of building material that was being transported by the Southern Rail Road Yard that is still located in the same place in Atlanta not far from the famous Oakland Historical Cemetery. This was the first City Cemetery and the citizens of Atlanta mainly in the Third and Fourth Ward residence are more than likely buried here, both Blacks and Whites. This Cemetery has a large Colored and Poor section that is unknown!

I also failed to mention that there was the Southern Rail Yard Freight Depot where Pratt Street begins. George Calloway or Calaway could have been working in this yard in 1901. I just wanted to talk about Mr. James Wallace at 366 Decatur Street and his place at 366 ½ and 368 Decatur Street. These are the same establishment that he had in 1900. He owns the property at Thompson Alley where George Callaway resided in 1900. Mr. James Wallace is or returned to DeKalb County after residing in the Third and Fourth Ward of the City of Atlanta! His place was between Fort Street and Hilliard Street just after crossing over from Mr. J. C. Hugins who was at 314 between Bell Street and Fort Street now in 1901 Mrs. Annie Nash resides at this location (white). Now, before you get to the place of Mr. James Wallace at 366 and 366 ½, and 368. I found Wallace Strickland at 350 and Fannie Strickland at 352 Decatur Street.

I went back to the year of 1899 and went ahead to 1901 to see if J. C. Hudgins and his wife were in the third and fourth ward at either time. I could not find Mr. Hudgins at any time. However, I wanted to see if Thompson Alley would be listed and it was not and I also wanted to take a look at the place of Charles M. Callaway and his Saloon on Decatur Street. Charles M. Callaway saloon was located close to Peidmont intersection and 161 Decatur Street before crossing over Butler Street. Moses Hawkins a colored man had his place at 160. And Mr. M. Kaplan was in 162, and Jacob Brown and David Zaban was in 162 ½, Mr. Morris & Carroll was at 163-165. Lynch Liquor Company was at 166 Decatur, and the Police Barracks was at 171-179 Decatur Street. Michael Cohen was at 180 and 181 ½. Crossing Butler Street intersection you come to the Exposition Hotel at 192 ½, W. Cohen was at 195 Decatur Street. Mrs. F. Boorstein and W. Cohen were at 201 ½ Decatur Street.

I wanted to go to the place where J. C. Hudgins would come to reside at 314 Decatur Street and found J. M. Terry living. I found several names whose last names are familiar to me. J.H. Bruce at 308 ½ Decatur, Colored man G. w. Greer at 309, living at 310 Decatur Street are R. L. Miller, and A. G. Tuggle, Colored man J. Ward is at house 311, house 317 is the house that is next door to the house where J. C. Hudgins would come to live in 1900. Living in house 317 is Mrs. N. Stegall, and 318 is occupied by a colored woman named Millie Tucker, house 320; Georgia Hill and in house 322; Della Hill, and 323 is the place of Schoen Bros. and J. King and T. Jones are living in house 324.

In Fulton County in Atlanta in 1900, I also found the Fulton County Convict Camp that was located in the fifth Supervisor's District of Atlanta. This is the Northwest side of Atlanta and the camp is located not too far from Crest Lawn Cemetery. Twenty-two-year-old Henry Callaway was born in December of 1877 the record states, and Daniel S. Walden is the enumerator of enumerated district 27.

From the Atlanta Historical Society): Mr. Will L. Callaway will come to be close friends with the Walden Family and the Alexander family as well. 1957 September Consolidated Mortgage and Investment mortgages, buying, selling, owning, and leasing property; and making investments A.T. Walden is elected president W.L. Callaway Executive Vice President, T.M. Alexander Treasurer. He was also photographed shaking hands with Citizens Trust Bank President. In addition, Mr. Walter H. Smith was in the picture. Walter H. Smith is the nephew of Annie V. Callaway the wife of Stewart B. Callaway.

I want to think that the first place I could find Charlie was in Atlanta, with Mary being at Spelman College. And Charles Callaway working on the Rail Road and even the first State Prison Commissioner of Georgia and was located in Atlanta! I want you to know that J. L. Beach was located in the Buckhead Community in 1900.

Now, J.L. Beach was a State Prison Commissioner between 1897 and 1898 and would have been the State Commissioner during the time Charlie Callaway and Gratlin Johnson were to appear before the Federal Courts. I found him in Fulton County in 1900 in the Peachtree Precinct in the North Atlanta Exclusive of Atlanta City and William P. Dale is the enumerator of this section of Atlanta. Mr. J.L. Beach is at the age of forty-one and was born in August of 1858 and had been married only seven years and was working as an insurance agent. His wife Francis P. Beach is at the age of twenty-seven and was born in 1870 and has four children.

Francis her daughter was born January 1894 and is six years old. Norwood their son is five years old, was born January 1895, and is five years old, Jacob was born August 1897 and was two years old, Scarlett their son was born October 1898 and was a year old, and Lucinda Bushella was born February 1870 and was thirty years old and works as their servant. They lived at the corner of Piedmont Avenue and Juniper Street. While Mr. H.R. Callaway is a white man living on Piedmont at house number 65. H.R. Callaway was born January 1856 and was forty-four years old and he is a wholesale (dry goods) is his occupation. Lula his wife is thirty-nine years old and was May 1861 and has been married to H.R. Callaway for seventeen years and have had four children and now only three children are living in 1900. Lula their daughter is sixteen and was born Feb. 1884, Grace their daughter was born July 1885 and was fourteen, Cary their son was born May 1888 and is twelve years old and Elvira Lovender is a colored female servant at the age of twenty-nine and was born June 1870. This section of town is supervisor's district number 5 and enumeration district number thirty-eight.

Vol. 19: Atlanta City Council Minutes Book March 18, 1901

Pg. 42 Petition of Citizen against Saloon at 125 Butler Street

Pg. 118, Petition of Citizens against Salon at 176 East Hunter Street.

Pg. 218 S. S. Moore: On motion of Councilman Minhimmell the petition of W. T. Flemmings et al. asking council to reconsider its actions and revoke the license of S. S Moore for a saloon at $ 151 Decatur St. was denied.

Pg. 227: Petition of Citizens to revoke beer license at # 47 Edgewood Ave.

1900–1901

J. E. Davison et al. to return amount paid for licenses Pg 656 line 44

J. E. Davison et al. for refund of amount paid for license. Pg 727 line 36

Pg 763 line 8: adverse upon petition of Traders Collection Agency for refund of license tax. J. E. Davison and the Traders Collection Agency Co.

Mr. J. E. Davison is located in Atlanta and is working or owns the Traders Collection Agency Co. J. E. Davison is supposed to be commissioner of chain gangs. However, he is part of or owns the Traders Collection Agency. I am going to go to a file in my records and pull up Emily Callaway and Richard Callaway in Greene County in 1917 the father and mother of Cornelius Callaway in Woodville, Georgia Greene County. I want to show you the person named in a deed that Mr. J. C Davison made in 1917 and Mr. J.E. Davison. Emily Calloway from C.W. Davison bond for title December 8 1917 she did this on the day of January 5, 1912 book 19 pages 254.

Now, I know that Henry and Will Callaway are related somehow, but the question is really, how old is Henry Callaway? Moreover, is Will Callaway the same Will Callaway that was located in Dekalb County in 1916 working for C.C. Mitchell? I went looking for Mr. C. C. Mitchell and could not find him anywhere or in any mode of research!

Let us go back to the city of Atlanta and see who else is living near Auburn Avenue on the N. E. side of town. I must mention Mr. John Hudgins a white man born in Alabama in May 1873 and his wife is named Francis born in the same year of 1873 in February and Lizzie May their daughter born February 1895. They are all living on Decatur Street and Fort Street. This place is near Mr. Charles M. Callaway the brother of Mr. Alonzo Callaway that came to reside in Lithonia where Martin Callaway would come back to live in 1900. *Sometimes Mr. John Hudgins role switches from being a white man to a colored.*

James C. Starks is a Colored man at the age of thirty-eight years old and he was born August 1861, his wife Lilla was born July 1863 and was thirty-six years old and they have been married for sixteen years and have had seven children and now only six are living at this time. Ethel was born June 1885 and is fourteen years old, Jennie was born October 1887 and is twelve years old, Lotte was born February 1889, Alfred was born March 1890 and is ten years old, Wyatt was born October 1891 and is eight years old and Earnest was born June 1893 and was six years old. Living in the same house with Mr. James C. Starks is Charlie Doster a colored man born February 1878 and is twenty-two years old and his wife Mammie who was born November 1877 and is the same age as her husband they have been marred for four years and have no children. Both James C. Starks and John Hudgins are in the fourth ward of the city of Atlanta.

Living in the second ward of the city of Atlanta was Mrs. Addie Callaway born April 1865 and is a thirty-five-year-old widow with two children with one that has already died. Henry was born April 1885 and

Juanita (spelled Wanetta) was born February 1888 and was eleven years old. Living in the house with her is Caleb Jackson, her father, at the age of sixty-one, and Fanny Simpleton, a sixty-year-old woman living with them on Glenn Street. Robert L. Sibley lived at 13 Houston Street still at the same place where I found him with Mary Callaway living with him in 1890. Robert L. Sibley was born December 1856 and was forty-four years old he has been married to Mary W. his wife for fourteen years and have no children. Robert L. Sibley occupation is Lawyer.

Mary W. Sibley says that she was born in Mississippi and her parents were both born in Maryland. Now she has a neighbor named Sallie Snyder born July 1861 and was thirty-eight years old and has been married for 25 years and is separated from her husband at this time, Florence L. her daughter was born April 1882 and is fourteen, Ethel S. her daughter was born August 1887 and is twelve years old, Sadie M. was born May 1888 and is twelve years old, and Marion was born April 1894 and is six years old. Also in the house is John H. Peoples her brother-in-law born August 1859 and is forty years old, John H. Jr. his son born December 1888 and was twelve, Sallie M. was born August 1896 and was three years old, Flora L. his daughter was born October 1895 and was four years old, Thomas Smith a colored man born August 1870 was thirty years old and his wife Lula was born April 1879 was twenty-one years old and they have no children. Thomas Smith house number is #15 on Houston Street.

Before I go forward on where Henry Callaway was living, I want to mention a few of the colored Callaways that are buried in Oakland Cemetery. Frank Callaway 9-4-1875 and was thirty-six years old. S.B. Callaway 9-26-1933 and was eighty-five years old when he died. Wade Callaway 6-18-1881 and was fourteen years old when he died. Siller Callaway had 1873 by her name, infant of Ruby Callaway, 7-7- 1833, three months old; infant John Callaway, 7-26-1883, one month old; infant Jeff Callaway 7-22-1881, stillborn; Grace Callaway 11-12-1881, seventy-eight years old; Eula Callaway 7-9-1880, fifteen years old; Annie S. Callaway 3-23-1920, sixty-eight years old. For Thomas Callaway, *1869* is the only thing that I find by his name. Hutchinson Callaway 11-8-1874, thirteen years old; Sylla Callaway 1833.

Now I am going off the beaten path to look at Walton County in the Richardson District in 1900. Henry Callaway was born march 1870, Rosetta his wife was born April 1875, Cornelious their son was born May 1892, Roy their son was born April 1894, Armstrong was born May 1899 and was one years old. In Wilkes County in 1900, I found Richard Callaway born July 1855 and was forty-four years old and Mary Callaway born November 1871 at the age of twenty-eight, and John Flowers born January 1870 and single. Bowling Greene district of Oglethorpe County Richard Callaway was born August 1854 and has been married twelve years to Emily Callaway born May 1848 and have had seven children, Nathan April 1889, Neal April 1897, Mahalie January 1894, Frank December 1897, George Sims (grandson) November 1897.

On the June 25, 1900, Taliaferro County 604 District I found Wylie Callaway a colored man born August 1829 and was seventy years old and has been married for 48 years to Betsy his wife who was born April 1835 and was sixty-five years old, Mariah their daughter was born January 1860 and was a single woman with one child at the age of forty, Emma another daughter of Wylie and Betsy was born December 1868 and was single at the age of thirty-one with four children with only three living in 1900, Sarah another daughter born April 1875 and was single at the age of twenty-five years old with one child, Annie May is a granddaughter born December 1891 and is at the age of eight, Wade H. is a grandson born April 1894 and is at the age of six, George is another grandson born August 1896 and is three years old Ester is another granddaughter born July 1897 and is two years old.

Charlie Callaway is also living in this district as well. He was born August 1847, was now fifty- two years old, and has been married for thirty-six years to Louisa his wife who was born April 1840 and is sixty years old with seven children with only three now living in 1900 Webster Smith is a grandson born November 1892 and is seven years old. Now Charles Callaway married Louisa Austin on the 6th day of March 1883 in Greene County and really has been married for only 17 years in 1900.

Greene County, Georgia

Greene County Courthouse Criminal Records

January Term 1917 Criminal Subpoena Docket Book

The State vs. Sam Porter

Names of Witnesses: Bob Young, R. T. Dolvin, Hershal Rhodes, Ben L. Bryon, Douglas Alexander, Cliff Willoughby, Charley Calloway, Smith Moody, and J. A. Elliott. Date Subpoena issued: 1/24/1917 Delivered to Hixon

The State vs. Robert Moore

Names of Witnesses: Marshall Finch, Willie Mae Sorrow, J. J. Sorrow, G. D. Channell, Howard Acre.

Names of Witnesses for Defense: Pat Mimes, Lee Evans, Howard Acre, Howard Bryan, John Turner, Mr. Callaway, Arthur Culver, Mrs. Barnes, Lawson Blake, Lyle, Willie Ryler, S. S. Gresham, R. T. Dalvin, Robert Johnson, and John Mullins.

The Greene County Criminal Records are the only time that I found anything with Charlie Callaway name on it. I have not drawn a conclusion on which Charlie Callaway this is. Could he be the brother of my grandfather or could he be Cornelius Charles Callaway? Now, Mr. Callaway that is in the Hopewell Baptist Association is named C. C. Calloway. Mr. C. C. Callaway attends the Williams Chapel Baptist Church in Dacula, in Gwinnett County Georgia. I caught up with Mr. C. C. Callaway in 1909 when the Association was held at Williams Chapel. Rev. L. T. Jones of 110 Mildred Street in Atlanta, Ga. was the President. W. L. Jones was moderator in 1885 and he was out of Atlanta as well.

In the 1911 directory of Atlanta I found Charles Callaway working as a butler at 201 South Pryor Street and living in the rear of the building. Living with Charles Callaway was a woman named Valita Callaway. Henry C. Callaway was living at 78 Humphries. His occupation was cleaning houses with his daughter Hattie while she is in attendance at Spelman. Now at this time, I also found a Henry M. Callaway working as a driver at Southern Ex. Co. and reside at 209 W. Mitchell. *Indiana Callaway did laundry at the rear of Conway place.* Remember S. B. Callaway who is buried in Oakland Cemetery? Well, Stewart B. Callaway is his name he is working at Coal-96 Fort Street and resides at 196 Piedmont Avenue in 1911.

Cornelius Callaway is working as a carpenter and rooms at 24 Richmond Street. Cornelius is the son of Henry and Rosetta Callaway or Richard and Emily Callaway. Cornelius is nineteen years old. In the year of 1912, I found Henry Callaway working as a driver and living at 209 W. Mitchell Street. Gus Callaway worked as a firefighter at the Atlanta Sanitary Dept. and resided at 245 Greensferry Avenue with Jessie who did laundry.

In 1913, Henry C. Calloway worked as a carpenter and resided at 78 South Humphries and Indiana Calloway did laundry and resided at 468. *Charles Calloway worked as a laborer and resided at 260 east Cain Street.* Now

Exa Calloway worked as a cook at East Eleventh and resided in the rear. *Charles Callaway lived on Cain Street between Hilliard intersection and where Dunlap begins in the fourth ward of the city.*

In the year of 1915, I have two Charles Callaway, one living at 260 East Cain Street and he works as a waiter and Charles who works for Henry Meinert. Cornelius Callaway is living at 5-a Conway Place. *Mattie Calloway does laundry and lives at 126-b east Cain Street.* Susie Calloway works as a cook 44 Colquitt avenue and lives at 160 ½ Auburn Avenue, ***Mary Callaway works as a maid and resides at 22 Bush and 455 Richardson Street. William Calloway is a laborer and resides at 22 Bush Street. Now the house that Mary Calloway owned at 455 Richardson Street is located after you cross over Martin Street and before you get to Connally Street and it is located in the same block as Richmond Street where Cornelius Callaway lived in 1911. The neighbors of Mary and Willie Callaway were living here in 1916 on 455 Richardson Street. Abbie Thomas, Cedia Miller, Mary Oglesby, Mary Norris, John Love, R. Farmer, E.J. O'Neal, J.B. White, B. Welch, James Thornton, C.F. Holliday, L. Smith, A.L. Ogletree, E. Maxey, E. Baker, M. Jackson, S. Graves, M. Young, J.H. Hunter, M. Hall, I. Bennett, F. Bradley, J. Johnson, R. Greer, and Mary Callaway.*

In the same year of 1916, Annie Callaway lived at 196 Gilmer Street at the same house that Susie Callaway owned while living at 78 Humphries Street. On page 640 I just mention the Callaway's that were in the 1916 Directory now on page 641 I'm going to mention the Calloway's but on the same page I found Wiley Callaway living at 1 ½ Alabaster Alley and working as a laborer. Andrew Calloway is living at 5 Conway Place;

*****Charles Calloway is working as a yardman for H. Meinert and resides at 17 Means Street. However, I went to find out who was living on Means Street at this time and found out that the house where Charlie was living had been vacant since March 18, 1916. Now, I have a clear picture of who this Charles Callaway is! He is Charles Cornelius Callaway that married Susie M. in Dacula, Georgia, in Gwinnett County Georgia. I say this because of the time of his absence from his location. However, I still have not figured out where he came from and who his parents are! This makes my grandfather Arthur to have a closer relationship with this Cornelius than the Cornelius that was either the son of Richard in Greene County or Henry that was located in Walton County! The Colored neighbors of Charles Cornelius Callaway on Means Street in Northwest Atlanta are S. Walton, M. Martin, J. Mills, and O. Henry. Now, Means Street* *is located in the fifth ward and not too far from Corput Street and is located just north where North Avenue crosses over Marietta Street. Also, this is the same place where Cherry Street is located. Cherry Street is where I found Cornelius Calloway living at 12 Cherry Street in the rear of the place. Means Street ran from 676 Marietta n. w. to Murphy Ave. (Bellwood), which was a paved road with Macadam from Marietta to Ponder Ave. Water from Bellwood Ave to Marietta. Sewerage Marietta to Ponders Ave. The neighbors' houses were from fifteen to fifty-six residences on Means Street before you get to Ponders Avenue intersection.*

> 12-G. T. Bradley and Bro., 15- Vacant since Feb. 24, 1916, 17-Vacant (Charlie Callaway)- March 18, 1916, 19-C. V. Pinion, 22-J. J. Finnigan & Co., 23- Colored man O. Henry, 25- Colored man J. Mills, 27- Colored man S. Walton, 33-Colored man M. Martin, 42-8-Vacant Feb. 24, 1916, 45-Vacant Feb. 24, 1916, 50-56-Golden Eagle Buggy Co. (Ponders intersection) 74-80 Standard Oil Co. Moving on down the road there are a few more Colored Families living in house 90-Atlanta Metal Bed Co., 93-Colored man L. Thomas, 95-Colored man M. Beulah, 97-Colored man J. Brown, 99-Colored man J. Little, 101-Colored man E. Thomas, 103-vacant since Feb. 25, 1916, 105-Colored man J. Little, 107-Colored man L Oliver.

I believe that Charles Callaway is living here at 17 Means Street. Why is he listed as being missing I don't know!

Take these words as a definite assumption pertaining to Charles Callaway living on Means Street off of Marietta Street and just south west of State Street where Springfield Baptist Church was located and where Corinth Baptist Church would divide or split from Springfield on State Street and near Omre which was Techwood Drive. This put Charles Callaway Jr. and his wife Emma. Cornelius E. Callaway and his wife Susie M. Callaway, Arthur Callaway at the same place as Mr. Charles Callaway who appears here in 1900. Even on Harris Street the two places have the same people living on them until 1900 during the disenfranchisement of the Negro. Something happen to Stewart, John C. and Mary Nesbit that caused them to relocate and this was at the same time Charlie Callaway and Mary Callaway and others were having difficult in Oglethorpe and

Clarke and Greene Counties. I remember Charlie saying in his statement to the Federal Courts that while he was away Eberhart raped his wife Mary between 1895 and 1896. Maybe his time was being spent between Fulton County and Oglethorpe and Clarke to visit this bar at 17 Harris Street and visit this half breed bar owner Stewart B. Callaway from Alabama and his wife Annie V. Callaway. I also have another Cornelius Callaway that was colored and he married Annie May Cunningham.

Third Ward of the City of Atlanta and Cornelious E. Callaway in 1916

I found this bit of information in 1918 about Mary Calloway living on Martin Street. Martin Street ran from the Georgia R. R. at 216 E. Hunter S to Milton Avenue 2 blocks east of Fraser and a paved with Macadam from Fair to Ormond Sewerage from Hunter to Richardson and Crumley to Georgia Avenue and Ormond to Atlanta Avenue water from Fair to Atlanta Avenue. Mary Callaway is the wife of colored man William A. Callaway the son of Robert or Bob Callaway out of Clarke and Oglethorpe County.

**Mary Callaway works as a maid and resides at 22 Bush and 455 Richardson Street. William A. Calloway is a laborer and resides at 22 Bush Street. Now the house that Mary Calloway owned at 455 Richardson Street is located after you cross over Martin Street and before you get to Connally Street and it is located in the same block as Richmond Street where Cornelius Callaway lived in 1911. The neighbors of Mary and Willie Callaway were living here in 1916 on 455 Richardson Street. Abbie Thomas, Cedia Miller, Mary Oglesby, Mary Norris, John Love, R. Farmer, E.J. O'Neal, J.B. White, B. Welch, James Thornton, C.F. Holliday, L. Smith, A.L. Ogletree, E. Maxey, E. Baker, M. Jackson, S. Graves, M. Young, J.H. Hunter, M. Hall, I. Bennett, F. Bradley, J. Johnson, R. Greer, and Mary Callaway. Living near Mary Callaway at this time in 1918 on Martin Street at the intersection Glenn and Georgia Avenue was Mary Callaway at house number 295a. Arthur Rodgers lived at 295, and James Sherman at 291a and Leila Carroll at 291. Living between Glenn Street and Georgia Avenue was Holcomb Weldon and J. C. Johnson both colored men. As you cross over Georgia Avenue Mr. Robert Norwood, Susan Vinston, Charles Cohen, J. W. James and others. However, there was one name that stood out and that was at house number 283 the house of Mr.

Charles Mitchell. House number 276 of Mr. Wesley Akins, Henry Hurt lived at the intersection of Hammock Place and Martin Street at house number 213. Henry neighbor was Mr. G. W. Crowder and David Collins and J.H. Lewis. Moreover, Clifford Bowden. This is the third ward of the city in southeast Atlanta.

I wanted to investigate this section of Atlanta further. I went to the 1920 census to see where this section of Atlanta located. It was called the third ward of the city and well known as Summerhill. Here I found a few more names and was very surprised to find Cornelius Callaway again in 1920 besides him and Johnnie his wife in Greene County and on Connally Street. While in the third ward in 1920 on the 19th day of June. Cornelius is thirty-five years old and Johnnie is Thirty years old. Their neighbors that are living next door and on the same street are, Willie Cheney who is thirty-five, and his thirty five-year-old wife Annie Mae Cheney and their son Henry who is eleven years old. Mattie Williams is a forty one-year-old widow woman living with her twenty three-year-old son William Lester. Lige C. Pace is a twenty seven-year-old cook and his twenty three-year-old wife is named Rosa. John Lewis is a twenty two-year-old fireman for an electric company and his wife Irene is at the age of twenty.

Cornelius like I said is thirty-five and his wife Johnnie is thirty. Cornelius occupation is a farmer. Bob Locket who is living next door is a street man and is at the age of fifty-two and his wife Hattie is thirty. Owen McCord is a brother living in the same house and he is fifty-four years old and Mozell his wife is fifty. I want to go down a few houses and mention Mrs. Ester Dorsey a twenty two-year-old widow woman and her sister Marie who is eighteen, and another sister named Lillie who is sixteen and Tommie L. Wilson her daughter who is three and five months old. Living on down the road on Connally is Fletch Beasley a forty-year-old mulatto man and his wife Sarah Beasley who was thirty-five. Fletch was a labor for a Contracting Co. Isaac was a nineteen-year-old brick layer and his wife Daisy was twenty-two years old, they had a daughter named Margaret who was a few months old. Annie Crowder is a forty nine-year-old widow woman living with her son Edward who is eighteen, and a daughter named Lura who is seventeen.

I also found Ms. Delia Mayfield, a widow at the age of sixty-five years old, and a Lord Mayfield, her son, who was thirty-five, Willie her daughter at the age of twenty-three and another named Bertha who was twenty-two. They lived next door to Rev. Jackson a fifty five-year-old waiter who works in a café. His wife name is not mentioned. However, her age is forty-eight. Another family here whose last name is familiar is

Miss Rena Lockhart a fifty-year-old widow and her daughter Connie and her son Albert. William Holmes a seventy five-year-old man and his forty seven-year-old wife Addie.

Now, the next name that is very close to Richard and Emily Hurt Callaway is the family of Henry Hurt a twenty-year-old widower in 1930, working as a cook in a café while living at 148 Martin Street just three houses from the intersection of Richmond Street. Henry is living with his eleven-year-old son Henry Jr. and his daughter Gladys who is nine. Also living in the same house is his brother E. J. or C.J. Jones who is twenty-three, and Horace, his twenty-one-year-old brother. Now, living in the house before you got to Henry house is the house of Mr. B. J. Jones a fifty-nine-year-old who works for the street engine company. His wife is named Lucy who is fifty years old and they have been married for twenty-one years and their son Walter is eighteen, Fannie is ten, and Luke Andre is their sixteen-year-old son. I also found a Mr. Robert Griffin who was seventy-five years old and his wife Henrietta who was sixty-five and a boarder by the name of Edward Broughton who was twenty-nine and his wife Mary who was twenty-four.

In the year of 1920 and still living on Martin Street I found Mr. Henry Hurt, a thirty-three-year-old man and his wife Mary who was thirty. Henry worked as a street driver. Living in the house with Henry and his wife Mary were Paul Jones fifteen, Edgar Jones fourteen, Horace Jones five, Evans Jones six, Henry Hurt Jr. is only a few months old. Robert Griffiths is sixty-three and his wife Henrietta is fifty-five. Mary Hurt the wife of Henry Hurt must have been a Jones before she married Henry. And Mr. Robert Griffin or Griffiths have been living next door for ten years to Henry Hurt.

Georgia Callaway who might be the sister of Burrell Calloway and the daughter of Aaron is living at 5 ½ Alabaster Alley. Nathan Callaway is living at 5 Conway place with Andrew Calloway in the Third Ward. I have a good idea who these Callaway's are that are located on Alabaster Alley. These mulatto Callaway's that I first found were in 1920 and the house consisted of Mollie Jackson at 400 Alabaster Alley with her son Willie and her daughter Irene. Mollie was forty nine, Willie was thirty one, and Irene was twenty seven. Living in apartment 401 was Wiley Callaway a forty seven year old and his twenty seven year old wife Susie, and a boarder by the name of Rosa L. Burke a twenty two year old lady. In apartment 402 is Mariah Callaway a seventy six year old woman and her daughter Susie who was twenty four. They were all dwelling in house 245 Alabaster Alley.

Henry and Rosa lived at 35 Alabaster Alley as well. The alley is named because of the complexion of the coloreds that resided there.

In 1880 in the 603 District, Wiley Callaway is at the age of forty years old and his wife Betsey is at the same age. Mariah their daughter is twenty years old, Frank is fourteen, William is twelve years old, Emma is eight years old, and a seven-month year old baby boy. In the same district of 603, I found Amanda Callaway a forty-eight-year-old colored woman and her family. Rena her daughter at the age of twenty, Frank who is seventeen, Emma or Erma at the age of fourteen, James who is twelve, Joseph who is ten, John who is eight, Mary who is six, and Ann who is one years old. Now, do not forget that Charlie Callaway was just down the road, Charlie was born August 1847, and his wife Louisa was born April 1840 and Webster Smith their grandson who was seven years old in 1900.

Therefore, I must tell you once again who was in the house with Wylie Callaway in Taliaferro County Georgia in 1880. Wylie was born August 1824 and is now seventy years old, his wife Betsy is now sixty-five and she was born April 1835, Maria L. their daughter was born June 1860 and is now forty years old, Emma was born December 1868 and is thirty-one years old, Sarah was born April 1875 and is twenty-five, Annie May a granddaughter was born December 1891 and is eight years old, Wade H. is their grandson and was born April 1894 and is six years old, George is another grandson born August 1896 and is three years old, Ester is a grandson who might be Elix, who was born July 1897 and is two years old.

Now living in the house just before you get to the house of Wylie Callaway is Judge Smith a color man born November 1874 and is twenty-five years old, and his wife Georgia who was born April 1878 and is twenty-two years old and their daughter Aurelia who was born August 1897 and is two years old. The next house is Charles Jackson who was born December 1869 and is twenty years old his wife Betsy was born October 1879 and she is twenty years old as well. Their son Frank who was born September 1895 and is four years old and the daughter Callie M. Jackson who was born April 1898 and is two years old. Also living in the same house with Jackson is Caroline Stinson, the mother-in-law, who was born June 1855 and is at the age of forty-five.

When I went looking for Henry C. Callaway in 1900, I found him living on Howell Street remember. Henry house number is 138 and he was born January 1867 and has been married to America his wife for seven years. America was born June 1869 and is thirty years old. Henry and America have had three children since being married seven years ago. Hattie who was born September 1893 and is six years old, Annie M. who was born August 1897 and is two years old and Lillian who was born August 1899 and is nine months old.

In Walton County in 1900 I found Henry Callaway who was born in March of 1870 and thirty-year-old Rosetta his wife who was born April 1875 and is twenty-five years old, Cornelius their son was born May 1892 and is eight years old, Roy their son was born April 1894 and is four years old and Armstrong Callaway was born May 1899 and was one-year-old.

Now I want to mention Mr. Jacob Smith in Atlanta. It was in 1870 that I found him in the fourth ward which this time is the Fifth Ward because there was not a fourth ward of Atlanta in Fulton County Georgia at this time. Jo S. Smith was the assistant marshal of the district. His wife Katie was sixty years old, Anna D White was twenty, I believe that this is Annie V. Callaway. Lewis Smith was eighteen, and Martha Davis was seven years old. They were at house number 680 and Mr. Anthony Graves a thirty two-year-old mulatto bar keeper out of North Carolina was at house number 686. His wife Cilie was twenty-seven, Charles was seven, Lizzie was six, Levi was four, Eunice was two, and Effie was fourteen, Sarah was twelve, and Joe was ten.

A.J. Orme a thirty-year-old white man was the richest land owner on this block valued at 30,000 dollars his wife was twenty-year-old Katy they had a fourteen-year-old young lady by the name of Bo…. Harman living with them.

In the First Ward of the city of Atlanta July 7, 1870, Mr. Jo S. Smith is still the assistant marshal. I found fifty-year-old John Caloway a carpenter living next door to Mr. Burrell Martin a twenty seven-year-old carpenter and his wife Judy who is twenty-five, and their daughter Julia who is fourteen, and John C. their son at the age of four.

Back in the Fourth Ward on August 6, 1870, I found Mr. James Caloway a fifty-one-year-old day laborer whose land is valued at $400 dollars, his wife Sila is fifty years old and Judson their son is nine years old. They are living next to a white family that is familiar to me because they are the Sheerer Family that I saw in Wilkes County. Wm. C. Sheerer is thirty years old and is a local machinist. His wife is named Harriet who is twenty-eight years old and Chas. is seven, George is four, and Armon or Aaron is two years old. In the 2nd ward June 2nd 1870 Mr. George B. Chamberlain is the assistant marshal.

E. Callaway is a thirty-year-old mulatto and works as a day laborer and his wife E. Callaway is twenty-six years old and does laundry. Ellie Dixon is an eighteen-year-old mulatto young lady doing domestic work and living in the house with the Callaways. She might be a student of Spelman. Many of the women of Spelman did laundry to work their way through the courses.

Atlanta Spelman Seminary 1881–1895

376.975

Sp3

Augusta, Ga.: Georgia Baptist Book and Job Print 1882

Faculty

Ms. S. B. Packard

Ms. H. E Giles

Ms. S. H. Champney

E. H. Kruger, Prof. of Vocal Music

Visiting Committee

Rev. J. H. DeVotie, D. D.

Rev. W. J. White, Augusta, Ga.

S. Root, ESQ., Atlanta, Ga.

Rev. D. Shaver D. D. Atl. Ga.

Rev. D.W. Gwin, D. D. Atl. Ga.

Rev. F. M. Daniels Atlanta, Ga.

Rev. H. McDonald, D. D. Atl. Ga.

Rev. H. C. Hornady, Atl. Ga.

Rev. E. R. Carter, Atla. Ga.

Rev. U. L. Houston, Savannah, Ga.

Rev. Alexander Ellis, Savannah, Ga.

Rev. C. H. Lyons, Athens Ga.

Dr. Wm. Crenshaw, Atl. Ga.

Rev. John C. Bryan, Americus, Ga.

Rev. G. McArthur, Columbus, Ga.

Rev. J. M. Jones Atl. Ga.

Rev. W. H. Tilan Atl. Ga.

Rev. J. C. Kimball. Atl. Ga.

Rev. V.C. Norcross, Atlanta, Ga.

Rev. E. K. Love Thomasville, Ga.

CHAPTER FIFTEEN

MARY AND CHARLIE AND HENRY C. CALLAWAY IN THE ATL. IN 1900

Henry C. Callaway was born January 7, 1866 and died in 1913. His wife Annie A. Callaway was born 1870 and died 1910. They are buried at the South View Cemetery with Willie Callaway born 1892 and who died 1954 and his wife Florence C. or Florence C. Smith who died or was born 1913. Now I have two Henry Callaway's born in 1866. Rev. Henry Callaway who is buried in the Jones woods on the line between Morgan and Walton County. In the years 1895–1896 Henry, C. Callaway boards at 38 Howell Street with J.C. Starks and resides at 23 Brooks Alley which is from Piedmont avenue east to Bell, between Houston and Auburn avenue. In 1930, Brooks Alley is Glazner Avenue.

In 1896, Henry Callaway is a cook and boards at 183 Butler Street and is working for H. Underwood; however, Mr. Henry C. Callaway is a janitor for Equitable Building. In addition, he resides at 40 Chamberlain Street. Chamberlain lies between Yonge and Boulevard. Now living with Henry C. Callaway was a man named Freeman at this address. A. L. Mason was living next door, and E. Long, William Stephens, and John Partee are the white men that were living on the same street before you got to Fitzgerald intersection. J.M. Nash, B.F. Mitchell, Mrs. A.C. Thomas, R.B. Jernigan, J.A. Webb, these colored men lived across the road leading from Fitzgerald.

P. Strickland, G.B. Brown, G. Evans, Ella Brown, S.W. Freeman, William F. Rhodes, Frank Whittaker, and Lewis Dawson. The white men are James M. Nichols, Joseph M. Walker, and Benjamin Burkhardt. In the year 1896, I also found Mr. J.C. Hudgins, a colored man at 140 Howell Street, and Mrs. Annie V. Callaway, a colored woman living at 89 Cain street but, look at her next-door neighbors: Charles Marshall, Mary Jones, J. Hightower, and a white man named J.C. Clein.

They were all living between the intersection of Courtland and Clifford Street. I need to stop here and reflect on the words that my grandfathers' cousins told me that their mother had a close friend named Mary Jones. Therefore, after mentioning Mary Jones I decided to go to Maple Street to a section of Maple Street that lies between West Mitchell and West Hunter Street. Maple started at Markham north to Spencer, 1 c of Walnut. These are the colored people on Maple at this time in 1897. Lucious Robinson, John Drake, B. Bunley, Ed Mattox, William Roberts, W. McCurty, D. Anderson, J. Dickerson, However the next three houses are the houses that are very much interested in. House # 33; L. Dewberry, House # 35; Jane Andrews, House # 37; Clara Cunningham all lived in the short space between W. Mitchell Street and W. Hunter Street which is now the parking lot of a Methodist Church. You can still see the foundation of the houses that once stood there and one house still remains just behind the Church which is called The Central United Methodist Church which was founded in 1928.

The first time that I find Charles Callaway in Atlanta is in the year of 1891. Charles and Henry Callaway are both working for the Finley Furniture Co. This company ran by William W. Finley who worked as the Superintendent who resided at Hampton Inn on Curran Street. Mr. W. R. Ware owned the property; Clarence worked for the Finley Furniture Company as well.

At this time, the only Charles Callaway that I found was living at 15 Alice Street. The street led from Pulliam to Pryor I s of Rawson in the second Ward.

In the year of 1887 C. or Charles Callaway was living at 21 Tatnall Street about the same time Mary Callaway was attending Spelman College!

I believe that this is the best information that I could have ever found my great-grandmother attending Spelman College.

In the year of 1899 Mary was living on Tatnall Street as a neighbor of Emily M. Cox of Cox Funeral Home. Emily Cox was living at 131-129 Tatnall Street and Mary was living at 116 Tatnall Street on the opposite side of the street. B. Burch was at 124 Tatnall, Stella Branch was at 122 Tatnall, H. Crawford was living at 119 Tatnall, D. Jones was at 118 Tatnall, N. James was living across the street at 113 Tatnall, Lucinda Wilson was at 106 Tatnall, white man J. H. Morse was at 102 Tatnall, colored man G. Moncrief was at 101 Tatnall across the street, and colored man J. T. Drake was at 97 Tatnall at the end of the street at the intersection of Markham and Tatnall. At the southern end where I began is the intersection where Emily M. Cox resided between Walnut and Mitchell Street. As you can see the number of the houses decrease going north toward town.

Moreover, W. E. Holmes lived at 47 Tatnall, before it intersects Chapel Street. Reverend E. R. Carter of Friendship Baptist Church resided at 71 Tatnall Street at this time. He lived between Mary Tidwell at 77 Tatnall and J. C. Waters at 67 Tatnall in 1899. This particular area might be called the Beaver Slide. This area is where young colored women were prostituted. This was a practice in this section well before the Colleges arrived. This is the very same element that the colored churches and Schools would have to fight against to raise the awareness of the colored community of the blight that was upon them with the liquor and beer and bar rooms that were set in the colored communities to further their control over the colored communities to become lethargic and complacent. And even today this same plague still exits! If there was no desire to eliminate the very thing that destroys the mind and ignites the imagination to act on impulse without reasoning, the colored churches and colored schools would not have prevailed. The same white community then turn around in 1906 and accused the same people with being Colored Brutes against their white women with demeaning and detrimental articles in the prominent newspapers and caused riots to justify themselves against the colored communities in the third ward thinking that their actions would ease their conscious while the colored community ran and fought for their lives in 1906. Then, you would have to ask yourself who was the brute!

Living on Maple Street in the three houses that are located between West Mitchell Street and West Hunter Street which is now Martin Luther King Jr. Boulevard I found in house # 33 C. Tonsil, in house # 35 L. Dewberry, in house # 37 A. Holley and in house # 38 Lula Pitts. Now onto the Census at this time in 1900 and these are the only ones living at this section of Maple Street in 1900. House # 35 lives Mary Callaway a 38 year old widow, whose age is really unknown, Lovett her daughter whose age is unknown, and Thomas Hannah or James Hanna a lodger whose age is unknown but he is listed as being twenty-one years old, Living in house # 33 is Addie May a thirty-year-old widow and her thirty five-year-old sister Alice Tonsil and a twenty five-year-old cousin named Isabella Johnson. Now the house that is next to Mary Callaway and Addie May, that is located on West Hunter Street is the house of widow Julia Thomas a thirty eight-year-old woman, and her daughter Gurtie who is eighteen, and her son Willis who is fifteen, Albert her son who is six, and at the house on the corner of West Mitchell Street is Alice McFoley, thirty-five-year-old woman and her daughter Ellen Stevens looks like that she's the same age as her mother so her mother might be fifty five. This situation of being unknown goes to the house of Samuel Alexander a sixty-five-year-old colored man and his wife Nellie who is fifty-eight and Annie Coldwell house a fifty-year-old colored woman whose husband is not in the house. However, her son Edward is in the house and he is fifteen and his sister's name is Robec who is sixteen.

Charles Calloway is working as a yardman for H. Meinert and resides at 17 Means Street. However, I went to find out who was living on Means Street at this time and found out that the house where Charlie was living had been vacant since March 18, 1916. The Colored neighbors are S. Walton, M. Martin, J. Mills, and O. Henry. Now, Means Street is located in the fifth ward and not too far from Corput Street and is located just south where North Avenue crosses over Marietta Street. Also, this is the same ward where Cherry Street is located. Cherry Street is where I found Cornelius Calloway living at 12 Cherry Street in the rear of the place. Means Street ran from 676 Marietta n. w. to Murphy Ave. (Bellwood), which was a paved road with Macadam from Marietta to Ponder Ave. water from Bellwood Ave to Marietta. Sewerage Marietta to Ponders Ave.

ROSE THE LIQUOR DEALER AND FRIENDS AND BUCKHEAD

> City and County Public Service Employees Union Local 17212, Chartered by American Federation of Labor Affiliated with the Atlanta Federation of Trades and Georgia State Federation of Labor Thos. E. Roberts, Fin. Sec and Treasure Bellwood Camp. Board of Trustees G. Allen Maddox, Court Hours, M.L. Mason City Hall, C.Y. Daniel 40 Delaware Ave. F.P. Whitney 54 Maryland Ave. Jake Hall Decatur, Ga.
>
> It was unanimously voted at our removing Joe Giles, a negro running a drill in the Quarry. Our committee advise that you stated to them some time ago that he would be removed, but they learn that he is still on the job . . .

Jan. 16, 1928

Georgia Masons' Association No. 1 of Georgia. Atlanta, Ga. June 19, 1929 box # 2 folder #2

Mr. Clark Donaldson Chief of Construction City of Atlanta *Mr. Clark Donaldson the Chief of Construction was receiving literature from Mr. R. M. Rose the liquor distributor out of Chattanooga Tennessee. This is what is written upon the document.*

Dear Sir: It has been reported to our organization by some of its members that they could get jobs with the construction department if they would get straight with the other union. Now Mr. Donaldson I am sure that you or your assistants do not understand our position. If you did all your Masons would be members of the Georgia Masons Association. At one time all of our members belonged to the International Union. Until about last August one of the organizers decided that the two locals the white and negro should be in the same union. Work on the same Jobs receive the same pay, something that we have not done in twenty-five years.

And for that reason we have a state charter of Atlanta white Bricklayers and Masons who are home owners and citizens of Atlanta, not floaters. Its membership consists of some of the best mechanics in the city on all classes of work. And it doesn't look just right that we should be discriminated against by one of the departments of our city government, because we feel like we are a little better than a Negro. We do not believe you or your department would do this if you knew the facts and we are only asking that you meet a committee form our Association, and we believe we can convince you that it would be to the best interest of the city and to your department to work some of our members.

As it was reported at our meeting that you had one man from Smyrna and one from Lithonia (spelled Lythona), we would be glad to furnish you with some competent men who live here in the city. The only reason they are not members of the other union at this time is they don't care to call and be called brother by a Negro. Mr. Donaldson please don't blame us for having that old southern feeling. We would be glad to hear from you soon, and meet a committee at any time and place you suggest. Five members of our union were with the construction department last year. Wishing you the best of success, we remain Yours Sincerely. H.O. Jansen Sect. 969 Moreland Ave. S.E. Pres. M.C. Bell 1716 Browning street.

Box #2 folder #4

John W. Ham Speaker

Home Address:

328 10th street N.W. Atlanta, Ga.

Evangelistic Meetings

First Baptist Church

Dr. T.F. Callaway, Pastor Thomasville, Ga. 5/23/ 1930

Committees

E.L. Wolslagel, Singer Biltmore N.C.

1. Prayer Meeting Committee:

E.W. Lumpkin, Chairman

2. Personal Workers:

Dr. W.B. Cochran, Chairman

3. Sunday School Committee: M.H. Goodwin, Chairman
4. Outside Engagements Com: J.A. White, Chairman
5. Civic Clubs Comm. D. Roy Hay, Ch
6. Schools: B.B. Broughton, Chairman
7. Publicity: Lee E. Kelly, Cha.
8. Entertainment: Mrs. J.W. Horne, Chair
9. Music: Mrs. S.W. Fleming,
10. Finance: R.G. Fleetwod, cha.
11. Delegations: J. Fred Singeltary, ch.
12. Nursery: Mrs. J.D. Smith in Charge
13. Ushers B.W. Stone, Jr. chairman

14. Secretaries: Miss Evelyn Lewis, chairman
15. Visitation Committee: Mrs. B.W. Stone chairman.

A letter to Mr. Donaldson on this letter heading of Mr. T.F. Callaway of First Baptist Church from John W. Ham of Brooklyn N.Y. box 326

Folder #7

To the members of the Fulton county delegation in the general assembly of Georgia:

The undersigned representatives of the city of Atlanta request a charter amendment of the city of Atlanta making a department of sewer and drains and providing for the election of the engineer in charge thereof . . .

The tenth ward 1927 C.M. Ford 210 Ga. Savings bank Bldg. wal-4272

T.F. Callaway 877 Tift Avenue, S.W. We -1588

Garland W. Cooper 327 Austell Bldg. Wal 3359

Little, Powell, Smith, and Goldstein

Jno. D. Little, Arthur G. Powell Marion Smith, M.F. Goldstein

Atlanta, Georgia, May 9, 1918

Senator Hoke Smith, C/o. United States Senate, Washington, D.C. Dear Father: This will introduce Mr. Clarke Donaldson of Atlanta, who is the son of Mr. Tom Donaldson, whom I am sure you know. Mr. Clarke Donaldson is an electrical engineer, and graduated from the Tech. He is above draft age, but wants to go into military service. He is now engaged as sewerage engineer for Atlanta, and is experienced in both electrical and civil engineering. I am sure the Government must need men with his training, and he wishes to ask you how to start towards offering his services. He is willing to work wherever he is most needed by the government.

Very truly yours,

Marion Smith

As I have stated before, while the Atlanta City Brewing Company was on the northern section of the Colored Community such as from Harris Street to Hilliard Street the colored community was Buttermilk Bottom. Right on Hilliard Street was the Liquor Store of Mr. R. M. Rose at the southern section of Buttermilk Bottom. May 23, 1912 the following prominent streets were Currier Street, Forrest Avenue on the south, Ripley on the west, Pine street on the north and Bedford Place on the east. Now Buttermilk Bottom was of the Subdivision of Gabbett Hill the property belonging to Parrott, Black & Mathews. Land Lot 50 in the 17th District of Fulton County. Conn & Fitzpatrick are the Engineers in May 1912. Now, knowing that Buttermilk Bottom was built as the Colored Property in 1912. Before this time what was the corner of Harris Street and Collins made up of as pertaining to Color! How did the congregational Church classify itself while in this community in Atlanta?

However, finally in 1909 Georgia went dry and the business was back in Chattanooga, Tennessee near Lookout Mountain. Let us talk about his business relationship that he had in this area in 1896. It's called Buckhead in Fulton County or the Cross Keys District of DeKalb County, not too far from the DeKalb County Line where I grew up.

> *Compliments of The Atlanta Historical Society:* The family that Rose had business with the Rolader Family. W. W. Rolader was born 1852 and died in 1924. W. W. married Arrie Cofield, T. B. Cofield's daughter, and bought fifty acres of land on Moores Mill Road in 1886 from Mrs. Clark (Mary) Howell Sr. for eight hundred dollars. Rolader's pottery shop and kiln were located to the east of the cabin that was on Moores Mill Road. The Clay was dug up at the rear of the property, then crushed by "a mule going round and round I the grinder to grid it up," Donald W. "Pete" Rolader, W. W's grandson, explained. The clay was then screened, turned into potter, and placed outside on planks to dry in the sun. "If it came up a shower, everybody'd run and take all the pottery inside the shop because the rain would ruin it." Once it had dried to the proper stage, the pottery was placed in the kiln" to be burned and hardened. The kiln would be fired late in the evening or afternoon, and we would stay up all night long stoking that kiln with cord wood to burn the pottery properly, and then it would be sealed up and kept for a day or two until the heat got out." The finished jugs, churns, flowerpots, whiskey jugs, chimney flu liners and milk containers were delivered throughout North Georgia . . .

Rufus M. Rose was a Rolader's Pottery customer who moved to Cobb County from New England before the Civil War. After the war in which he fought, he returned home and became an apothecary. "But he could not find any alcohol, so he opened up a still on the creek. Which is located on what is now called Stillhouse Road" in Vinings. William Dreger III said. When word of the still reached Atlanta, people went to Rose's business to buy their alcohol. "Later [Rose] opened up a dance pavilion . . . and it became a very popular place for the young people to come and dance and buy his alcohol," Mr. Dreger explained. When Rose realized he was making more selling alcohol than medicine, he went into the whiskey business and "marketed the liquor under the name of Four Roses." Mr. Rose lived at 537 Peachtree street, N. E. (across from the current site of the Doctors Building), in a Victorian-style house, that was built in 1900.

When Georgia went dry in 1907, Rose moved his operation to Chattanooga, Tennessee. Years later James H. Elliot Sr. operated the Atlanta Museum in the home, and a large statue of a black horse stood at the side of the front yard. The 1907 or 1909 Prohibition law initiated the demise of Georgia's folk pottery tradition, which had thrived in eight jug towns across the Piedmont area of the state since the 1820's. "Rolader closed his shop in the mid-20's he was one of the last Atlanta potters." Moores Mill Road at this time was located outside the City limits of Atlanta. I am sure W. W. Rolader got his clay from the Peachtree Creek that the Moors Mill road crossed. I do not know if the 5th ward extended out Moores Mill Road, however his property is not far from the 1st ward of Atlanta. It is in the 17th district of Fulton County called Buckhead on the eastern side of the 17th district.

Now, the statements that certain people made are in somewhat misleading because, here is an article in the Scott's Monthly Magazine-advertising sheet in March of 1868;

R. M. Rose & Co., Wholesale Dealers in Brandies, Whiskies, Gins, Rums, and Malt Liquors of all Descriptions. Brands and Grades.

To the country trade the most liberal Inducements are offered. To families and physicians we offer all the finest and purest articles in this or any other market, at prices which challenge competition. All the house desire is a trial—satisfaction and an increase of trade will follow. Store and Salerooms—In the Granite Building. Broad Street, Atlanta, Ga.

In the year of 1930 Prison Camp that was in Buckhead. Tony Chastain sold one hundred acres of his land to Fulton County for a prison camp (now the Chastain Park Golf Course), and a men's prison was built on the hill facing Powers Ferry Road, where the American Legion Lodge sits today. After a fire destroyed the building a new one was erected on the present site of the ball diamond at Lake Forrest and Wieuca roads. "One night when I was staying at my grandparents' [Mr. and Mrs. Charles W. Defoor, on Piedmont road] *when I looked at the 1930 map of Fulton County I noticed that there was a Defoor road in the same area were Moores Mill Road of the 17th district of Fulton as well, did these families originate from the same place before moving further east into Buckhead?*

That prison farm caught on fire. Papa drove us over there, as close as we could get," Marcus Cook III recalled. "The prisoners that they were not able to get unchained from their beds were burned to death. "That night, while young Marcus tried to sleep he saw from his window "the red glow in the sky, and the smoke, and my young mind was conjuring up the horrible visions of these people being burned to death."

Guy Patterson was working for Fulton County as a maintenance man at the courthouse when he was offered a job as assistant to Mrs. Jesse Boynton, manager of the alms houses on West Wieuca Road. In December of 1935 he moved his wife and four children into the white clapboard building that served as the black alms house (the current

> Chastain Art Center), and was in charge of the forty black prisoners who were housed in the rear of the building. The women, serving time for offenses such as stealing clothing from department stores, and playing the "bug" [gambling], worked in the alms houses, and on the prison farm, raising vegetables for the complex and for other prison camps in the county. "They'd work those ladies and they'd plow the mules down there just like a man," Guy Patterson said. The Women also cleaned the cemeteries at Sardis, Mt. Paran Baptist Church and a church in Sandy Springs.
>
> "All of the golf course was cornfield, Marcelle Simpson remembered. "There wasn't more than five or six houses from there to Buckhead. The Negro women convicts tilled the corn.
>
> Race Relations in Buckhead. Around West Paces Ferry Road, black citizens felt the whites were protective of and helpful to the new Hope Church community, while some residents of Johnson town felt that, though they were shielded from Ku Klux Klan activities by their white neighbors, the business district was often less friendly. The football field on the John K. Ottley estate (now Lenox Square) became a common meeting ground for the black and white children in Buckhead, Eugene Johnson said that, though the children played ball together, they "never struck up any strong relationships with the whites." "People here have been kind and supportive," Elizabeth "Mrs. Moses" Few, a member of New Hope Church, said. Ninety percent of the blacks in Buckhead served as domestic help in the houses of the white families as maids, butlers, cooks, and gardeners."

As I have said before in 1870, in the First Ward of the city of Atlanta Joseph S. Smith the assistant Marshal on the 27th day of June I found James L. Johnson out of North Carolina at the age of fifty, working as a harness and saddle maker living with his wife Lucy I who was twenty-six, Laura their daughter ten, Sarah is seven, and Donell the youngest daughter who is one. R. G. Tripple is a twenty-seven-year-old grocer and his wife S.E. who is twenty-two. R. M. or Rufus M. Rose is a thirty-four whole sale Liquor

Dealer. His daughter Fannie is seven. Kattie is twenty-three, and I believe that she is his wife. Laura is their two-year-old daughter. Mollie Kennedy is a thirteen-year-old white nurse. Anna Wade is a twenty three-year-old domestic servant and Henry is a thirty-year-old Hack Driver. All are living in the house of Mr. Rufus M. Rose. William Klitz is a twenty-four-year-old clerk in his store and is living with his wife C. L. who is twenty-three. Both were born in Germany. Another clerk in his store is O. H. Beatty a thirty-two-year-old and L. M. A. his twenty seven-year-old wife and O. W. their seven-year-old son. All are born in Georgia. The famous First Ward. There are two colored families Washington Roberts a twenty eight-year-old Carpenter born in Georgia and his wife Jane who is twenty-six. And Joseph Young, a fifty-six-year-old brick mason born in Georgia, and his sixty-year-old wife Ada Young, born in Georgia. Living with them is Rhoda Eady, a fifty-year-old laundress also born in Georgia. The next two colored people on the same street or sheet as Rose and living right next door to Rose were Della Waller a forty five-year-old colored woman doing domestic work in his house. And twelve-year-old mulatto Andrew Wright an apprentice to B—— and living in the same house with twelve-year-old mulatto Andrew Wright is a six-year-old mulatto boy named Burrell Dent both are born in Georgia. As a matter of fact, the two mulatto boys are living in house number 183, the same number as Mr. Rufus M. Rose! Yes, this the famous First Ward in ATL!

Now I know you ask what is the relationship between the Callaways and the Rose family. Well, I will show you who were working for Mr. Rose. Mr. Randolph M. Rose took over from his father Rufus when he moved to Tennessee the second time after the Prohibition laws were enacted a second time in 1909. However, he was going to get the liquor into Georgia one way or another! I mean illegally or through the Federal Courts and fight the State Dry Laws of Georgia prohibiting his liquor trade.

While in Tennessee:

> Randolph M. Rose and Company versus the State of Georgia; (Supreme Court of Georgia. October 1, 1909) Commerce (40) – Interstate Commerce Solicitation of Orders for Sale of Intoxicating Liquors. A criminal accusation charging that the defendant, who lived in Chattanooga, Tenn., solicited orders for the sale of intoxicating liquors by a circular sent through the United States mail from Chattanooga to a person living in this

> state, where the sale of intoxicating liquors is prohibited, did not set forth any crime under Pen. Code 1895 428 and was subject to general demurrer. It stated that a Tennessee corporation, engaged in business in the state of Tennessee, in pursuance of its Tennessee business, did personally and by agent, in the county of Fulton, a county wherein by law the sale of spirituous, malt, and intoxicating liquor is prohibited, solicit the sale of spirituous, malt, and intoxicating liquors, said sale to be consummated in Chattanooga, Tenn. Such solicitation having been made by defendant sending to the prosecutor, Fletcher E Maffett, from Chattanooga, Tenn., through the mails of the United States a circular letter advertising such liquors for sale, and by the words . . .

In this part of my book I'd like to put Mr. Rufus M. Rose and his son Randolph M. Rose in perspective as to how they played a role in the black community and certain coloreds in particular and how the liquor influenced the colored race. Mr. Rufus M. Rose came from Connecticut with his brother O. A. V. Rose. I found them in the county of New London, Connecticut, in 1850 with their father Ansel Rose, who was forty-five years old, and their mother Mary, who was forty-four. Their nineteen-year-old daughter name looks like its spelled Susan, Rufus M. Rose is seventeen, Origin A. Rose is eleven, May is eight, and Alma A. Rose is six, Camilla is three and their son George P. Rose is one years old.

Now the research that I did at the Atlanta History Center in Buckhead gave me a little more light into Mr. Rufus M. Rose. Mr. Bill Manning TAMS # 1603 states that Mr. Rufus M. Rose was born on May 17th, 1836 in Willimantic, Connecticut. He moved to New York City as a young man and was employed as an apothecary at the Sailors Hospital on Staten Island. While there, he studied medicine. He came to Atlanta Georgia in 1859 and entered the drug business with an uncle. When war broke out, Dr. Rose joined Company G of the Tenth Georgia Regiment CSA. Not only did Mr. R.M. Rose come to Georgia and move in with his uncle, his younger brother Origen Americus V. Rose came too. They were both down in Pulaski County, Georgia. O.A.V. Rose was twenty-five years old and was promoted to full first lieutenant on June 27, 1862. Enlisted on March 4, 1862, promoted to full captain on July 29, 1863, and mustered out on May 4, 1864. He died in his home state of Connecticut in the county of Waterford.

On the 1870 census, both Roses were in Atlanta with Mr. J. S. Smith as the assistant marshal. On the nineteenth of August, Mr. Smith was at O.E.V. Rose's house, a thirty-year-old wholesale liquor merchant. Ressie, his wife, was born in Alabama and was nineteen years old. Living in the house and working as a clerk in the store was O.K. Woodward, a twenty-two-year-old white man born in South Carolina, and James Woodward, a twenty-year-old born in Alabama, as well as Mary Smith, a forty-eight-year-old domestic servant born in Georgia, and thirteen-year-old Emma Bonner, another domestic servant born in Georgia as well.

Living next door was no other than Mr. John L. Hopkins, a lawyer born in Tennessee, and his family. They are all living in the fourth ward of the City of Atlanta. However, living in the first ward of the city with Mr. Smith as the assistant Marshal as well is his brother Rufus M. Rose and his family. Rufus M. Rose is thirty-four years old and the value of his personal estate if listed at $5000. Fannie his daughter is seven years old, Kattie I presume is his wife and is listed at twenty-three years old, Laura is two years old, Mollie Kennedy is a white nurse at the age of thirteen, Anna Wade is a colored domestic servant at the age of twenty-three, Henry Wade is a thirty-year-old Hack driver.

Living next door is the family of O.H. Beatty, a thirty-two-year-old clerk in the store of Mr. Rufus M. Rose, and his twenty-seven-year-old wife L.M.A. Beatty and their son O.W. Beatty who is seven years old. Mr. William Klitz is a twenty-four-year-old clerk in the store of Mr. R.M. Rose as well and his twenty-three-year-old wife C.L. Klitz are both born in Germany. As you may conclude that Rose is a Jew! In the Atlanta Directory, I located the business of R.M. Rose and Company.

Rose R M. & Co, wines, liquors and cigars, 5 N Broad.

Rose, R. M. R M R. & Co, wines liquors and cigars, H Forsyth H Peters and Garnett

Rose OAVRMR & Co. 5 N Broad., BDS National Hotel

In 1871, Rufus M. Rose was the only one mentioned in the directory.

R.M. Rose & Company wholesale deal's, wine, liqrs, tob'co, cigrs, 1 and 3 Broad street

Rose R.M. of R.M.R. & Co. resides at Garnett B Whitehall and Forsyth

Rufus M. Rose has his father living with him Mr. Ansel Rose. There is another Rose that is mentioned. Her name is Mrs. S.F. Rose, who resides at Rock Street with Mangum and Haynes that run in the back of Rock

Street. This is in the second ward of the city of Atlanta. I believe that she might be the wife of the uncle of Mr. Rufus M. Rose.

For the Jews were socially included and played a very important part in the Civil War. Now there was another Rose Family that was in Georgia in 1850 and they were living in Jackson, Georgia. Mr. Hardy Rose was fifty years old at this time, Mary A. Rose was thirty-nine, Hartwell F. Rose was fifteen, Benjamin W. Rose was thirteen, Sarah A.G. F. Rose was ten, Francis M. Rose was eight, Nancy M.A. C. Rose was five, Lucy Jane C. Rose was two years old and Mrs. Martha E. L. Hardy was seventeen.

Now in the First Ward of Atlanta, where Mr. Rufus M. Rose lived the family of Mr. William T. Cates also resided. I mentioned him in the Cates Family section of the book or in Dekalb County Section. This section of town is where you will find the Rolling Mill Iron Company after it was destroyed by Sherman during the War it relocated from somewhere near the Oakland Cemetery is now located to Marietta near the City Limits. A large number of Citizens of Georgia came to reside near the mill to find work like Mr. Cates and others. The strangest thing that I found that was different was both Blacks and Whites worked in the same place in the 1870's and not as I was told by the proprietors of the Roswell Mills that Blacks worked in the fields and produced the Cotton and the Whites worked in the Mills to make the Cloth for the Confederate Army. John Cates was the first Cates that is found working in the Rolling Mill while he boarded with Mr. J.W. Roberts in 1872. Mr. J.W. Roberts was a bailiff and resided at Marietta near the Rail Road. *I believe, that this was the 1st ward and also part of the 5th ward of the city of Atlanta.*

The next year, Mr. John W. Cates was working for the postal service as a clerk and resided at the Georgia Rail Road. These two families the Rose's and the Cates also lived in the 17th District of Fulton County rightfully called Buckhead or North Fulton.

Now to turn your attention to Buckhead in the Seventeenth District of Fulton County and the Eighteenth District of DeKalb County, Georgia, in the northeast side of Atlanta.

The property that I am about to show you is in the section that is now called the Chastain Park of Fulton County. It is where my cousins and I would some time walk to take a plunge off the high dive that was located there. My half brothers and sister attended the Galloway Private School that was located nearby.

By the year of 1909 he would be back in Chattanooga, Tennessee for good. Nevertheless, this will not stop the trading between Tennessee Liquor and the Citizens of Georgia!

179

State of Georgia,
Fulton County.

This Indenture, Made this First day of April, in the year of our Lord one thousand eight hundred and ninety-Six, between O. A. V. Rose of the State of and County of Fulton part of the first part and R. M. Rose Co. of the State of and County of Fulton part of the other part:

Witnesseth, That the said party of the first part for and in consideration of the sum of Twenty Five Dollars, in hand paid at and before the sealing and delivery of these presents, the receipt of which is hereby acknowledged, has granted, bargained, sold and conveyed, and by these presents do grant, bargain, sell and convey unto the said parties of the second part, their heirs and assigns, all that tract or parcel of land lying and being in Buckhead district Fulton County, Georgia, and part of Land Lot No. 138, and bounded as follows, to wit: [illegible] at a post of a plank fence on the West side of the big branch (said post sitting in the old original run of the big branch) and the line running the old original big branch run in a zig-zag course until it reaches another post of the same plank fence further down the big branch [illegible], & thence running up the said plank fence North (where the plank fence now stands) to the beginning point, containing one quarter of an acre more or less, adjoining the property of [illegible] on the West & the property of A. J. Vaughan on the East.

To Have and to Hold, The said tract or parcel of land, with all and singular the rights, members and appurtenances thereof to the same being, belonging, or in anywise appertaining, to the only proper use, benefit and behoof of the said parties of the second part their heirs and assigns forever, in Fee Simple.

And the said party of the first part, for O. A. V. Rose, for himself heirs, executors and administrators, will warrant and forever defend the right and title to the above described property, unto the said parties of the second part R. M. Rose Co. their heirs and assigns, against the claims of all persons whomsoever.

In Witness Whereof, The said party of the first part, has hereunto set his hand and seal, the day and year first above written.

Signed, sealed and delivered in presence of

J. R. [illegible]
Jos. H. Smith

O. A. V. Rose (Seal.)
(Seal.)
(Seal.)

Recorded, [illegible] Fulton Co.
April 21st 1896

G. H. Tanner C.S.C.

Mr. O.A.V. Rose owned this property in 1896 and sold it to R.M. Rose his brother and his Company. However, in 1870, O. A. V. Rose was living in the Fourth Ward of the city of Atlanta. O. A. V. Rose was thirty years old and was a wholesale liquor dealer. His wife Bessie was nineteen. Living in the same house with the Rose family was Clark Woodmond, a twenty-two-year-old clerk in the store, and Jane his twenty-year-old wife who works as a clerk in the store. Mary Smith is a colored domestic servant at the age of forty-six, and thirteen-year-old Ema Bommer, another domestic servant. A.O.V. runs the store that is located at the end of Hilliard Street south of Buttermilk Bottom. This tells me that R. M. Rose set up business on this land in Buckhead. At this time, it was located in Land Lot 138. this piece of property was located near Mrs. L.J. Blanton.

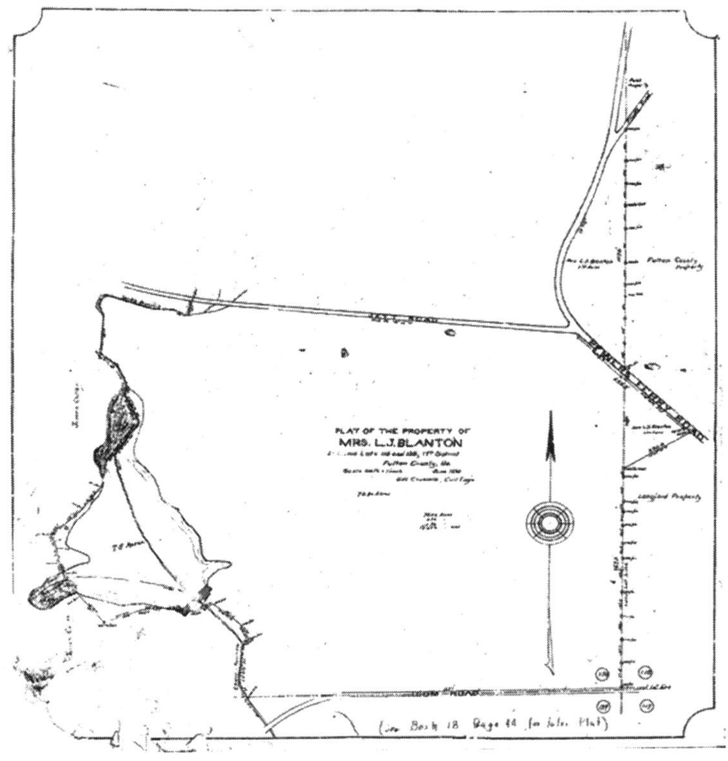

Here's a later plat of the same property with warehouses located on the property.

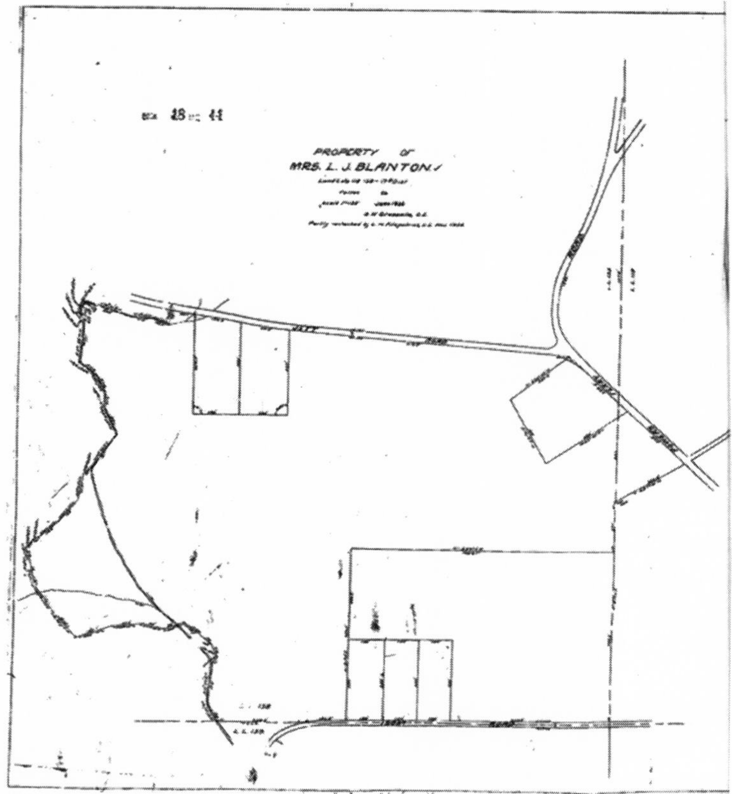

However, before buying this property in 1896, Mr. Rufus M. Rose was forced to move to Chattanooga Tennessee after the local election of 1885. Georgia voted to become a dry state. Moreover, in 1888, the prohibition experiment failed and Atlanta went wet again. Rose returned to Atlanta. I assume that he purchased this property thinking that he would be in Georgia for a while.

LIQUOR AND THE FOUR ROSES IN THE BLACK COMMUNITY

Now I know you ask what is the relationship between the Callaways and the Rose family. Well, I will show you who were working for Mr. Rose. Mr. Randolph M. Rose took over from his father Rufus when he moved to Tennessee the second time after the Prohibition laws were enacted a second time in 1909. However, he was going to get the liquor into Georgia one way or another! I mean illegally or through the Federal Courts and fight the State Dry Laws of Georgia prohibiting his liquor trade.

> While in Tennessee:
>
> *Randolph M. Rose and Company versus the State of Georgia* (Supreme Court of Georgia. October 1, 1909) Commerce (40) – Interstate Commerce Solicitation of Orders for Sale of Intoxicating Liquors. A criminal accusation charging that the defendant, who lived in Chattanooga, Tenn., solicited orders for the sale of intoxicating liquors by a circular sent through the United States mail from Chattanooga to a person living in this state, where the sale of intoxicating liquors is prohibited, did not set forth any crime under Pen. Code 1895 428 and was subject to general demurrer. It stated that a Tennessee corporation, engaged in business in the state of Tennessee, in pursuance of its Tennessee business, did personally and by agent, in the county of Fulton, a county wherein by law the sale of spirituous, malt, and intoxicating liquor is prohibited, solicit the sale of spirituous, malt, and intoxicating liquors, said sale to be consummated in Chattanooga, Tenn. Such solicitation having been made by defendant sending to the prosecutor, Fletcher E Maffett, from Chattanooga, Tenn., through the mails of the United states a circular letter advertising such liquors for sale, and by the words . . .

Now during this time of 1909 and 1930, liquor trafficking was not put on hold by any measure in Georgia! Rose would us the poor whites and colored folks to move his liquor into the state of Georgia one way or another. Now take notice when the State of Georgia finally went dry in 1909 they went right after Mr. R. M. Rose who had relocated to Tennessee. I wonder did the Atlanta Distillery or Brewery have the same controversy with the dry law of 1909. Let us look at one way Rose Distribution center in Tennessee and Jacksonville got its liquor into Georgia.

I had much travel time to do physical research of the Courthouse of Wilkes, Oglethorpe, Greene, Barrow, Oconee, Madison, and many others. However, in the courthouses of only Barrow, Greene, and Oglethorpe have I found Liquor Ledgers of Men and Women that were moving the liquors of these Companies that were located in Chattanooga, Tennessee and Jacksonville, Florida? The same two states that R.M. Rose had businesses. The first book is the Barrow County Ledger: Record of liquor deliveries in Barrow Co. You must also realize that at this time most liquors were used for medicinal reasons as well as pleasure. Not all that are mentioned here are liquor runners.

Consignee	Address of Consignee	Consignor	Address of Consignor
H.M. Oakly	Winder Ga.	R.M. Rose Co.	Chattanooga Tenn.
L.O. Sharpton	Winder Ga.	R.M. Rose Co.	Chattanooga Tenn.
H.L. Bentley	Winder Ga.	Potts Thompson Co.	Chatt. Tenn.
Lindsey Lawrence	Winder Ga.	R.M. Rose Co.	Chatt. Tenn.
Mrs. Cora L. Quattelbaum	Winder Ga.	R.M. Rose Co.	Chatt. Tenn.
G.W. D. Moon	Hoschton Ga.	R.M. Rose Co.	Chatt. Tenn.
Hobby Banks	Winder Ga.	Potts Thompson Co.	Chatt. Tenn.
Miles Hunter	Statham Ga.	C.D. Cheatham	Chatt. Tenn.
Joe Roy White	Statham Ga.	Chattanooga Sup. Co.	Chatt. Tenn.
C.E. Hunter	Statham Ga.	J. A. Kelly Co.	Chatt. Tenn.
V.O. Sharpton	Winder Ga.	R.M. Rose and Co.	Chatt. Tenn.
J.H. Anglin	Winder Ga.	National Whiskey Co.	Chatt. Tenn.
L.B. Moon	Bethlehem Ga.	Jas. Thompson Co.	Chatt. Tenn.
Gus Adams	Winder Ga.	R.M. Rose Co.	Chatt. Tenn.
Clayton Moon	Winder Ga.	R.M. Rose Co.	Chatt. Tenn.

G.L. Birts	Winder Ga.	Nation Whiskey Co.	Chatt. Tenn.
D.A. Moon	Auburn Ga.	Nation Whiskey Co.	Chatt. Tenn.
B.M. Pirkle	Carl Ga.	R.M. Rose Co.	Chatt. Tenn.
Willis Brown	Carl Ga.	Nat. Whiskey Co.	Chatt. Tenn.
Mattie Helton	Carl Ga.	Nat. Whiskey Co.	Chatt. Tenn.
A.L. Casey	Winder Ga.	R.M. Rose Co.	Chatt. Tenn.
Will Herd	Winder Ga.	R.M. Rose Co.	Chatt. Tenn.
R.D. Chaney	Winder Ga.	Haynes Dist. Co.	Jacksonville Fla.
Emory Hosch	Winder Ga.	R.M. Rose Co.	Chatt. Tenn.
J. Roy Smith	R.M. Rose Co.	Chatt. Tenn.	
W.M. Dillard	Winder Ga.	R.M. Rose Co.	Chatt. Tenn.
J.E. Barber	Winder Ga.	Jos. Thompson Co.	Chatt. Tenn.
G.P. Jackson	Winder Ga.	R.M. Rose Co.	Chatt. Tenn.
J.S. Davis	Carl Ga.	H.L. Sprinkles	Jacksonville Fla.
J.R. Coker	Winder Ga.	Jos. Thompson Co.	Chatt. Tenn.
Golden Hosch	Winder Ga.	R.M. Rose Co.	Chatt. Tenn.
W.H. McDaniel	Winder Ga.	R.M. Rose Co.	Chatt. Tenn.
G.B. Chaney	Winder Ga.	Haynes Dis. Co.	Jacksonville Fla.
J.L. Cummings	Winder Ga.	B. Reynolds	Middletown N.Y.
J. C. Orr	Winder Ga.	Universal Import Co.	Cincinnati Ohio
Truman Moon	Winder Ga.	Nat. Whiskey Co.	Chatt. Tenn.

Date of delivery was between May 3, 1916 and May 21, 1916

The carrier was So. Express Co.

Some of the drinks are rye, cabinet rye, forefathers corn, whiskey, beer, yellow corn, sweet mash corn, 4-star corn, spirituous, alcoholic, silver armor, port wine, winkers rye, p. stock rye, cider brandy,

Henry Smith	Winder Ga.	R.M. Rose	Chatt. Tenn.
Ms. Omie Dillard	Winder Ga.	R.M. Rose Co.	
Lucious Slaton	Winder Ga.	Nat. Sup. Co.	Chatt. Tenn.
Tom Daniel	Winder Ga.	R.M. Rose	
Bud Griffeth	Winder Ga.	R.M. Rose Co.	
E.O. Martin	Winder	R.M. Rose, Co.	
H.B. Swain	Auburn	Uncle Sam Dis. Co.	Jacksonville Fla.
James J. Hutchens	Carl Ga.	Haynes dist. Co.	Jacksonville Fla.
S.B. Chancey	Winder Ga.	Haynes Dist. Co.	
Green Peppers	Bethlehem Ga.	Haynes Dist. Co.	
T.R. House	Winder Ga.	R.M. Rose Co.	Chatt. Tenn.
John Cosby	Winder Ga.	National Whiskey Co.	Chatt. Tenn.
Lindsey Callin	Winder Ga.	Jos. Thompson Co.	Chatt. Tenn.
Martin Williams	Winder Ga.	Lampton & Thompson	Louisville Ky.
W.H. Bush	Winder Ga.	American Supply Co.	Chatt. Tenn.
H.B. Swain	Auburn Ga.	Uncle Sam Dist.	Jacksonville Fla.
S.F. Pirkle	Auburn Ga.	Uncle Sam Dis. Co.	

J.O. Hawthorne	Auburn Ga.	R.J. Park C	hatt. Tenn.
F.M. Stewart	Bethlehem Ga.		
Cargil Stewart Liquor Co. Chatt. Tenn.			
Warren Thompson	Beth. Ga.	National Whiskey Co.	Chatt. Tenn.
Felix White	Beth. Ga.	R.M. Rose Co.	
S.M. Stewart and Cargile Stewart Liquor Co.			Chatt. Tenn.
W.G. Stewart same			
R.D. Mack	Statham	National Whiskey Co.	Chatt. Tenn
Hoke Hopkins	Statham Ga.	Chattanooga Sup. Co.	
O.M. Hale	Statham	National Whiskey Co.	
L.H. Reid	Winder Ga.	R.M. Rose Co.	
Ed Royal same			
H.D. Bacon same			
Virginia Witt	Winder Ga.	Jos. Thompson Co.	
Pearl Bell	National Whisk. Co.		
J. Booth	R.M. Rose Co.		
Lewis Higgins Potts	Thompson Co.	Chatt. Tenn	
Thos. Couch	American Sup. Co.		
Evory Davis Potts	Thompson Co.		
F.M. Myers	R.M. Rose Co.		
W.S. Freeman	Uncle Sam Dist. Co.	Jacksonville Fla.	

Date of delivery May 21, 1916

Carrier Southern Express Co.

Will Thomas, James Patterson, Babe Simson, Tonie Still, H.T. Hendris, Davie Camp, J.W. Richardson, George Studivant, Jim HARRIS, Sam McDaniel, W.A. Brooks, Ramon Kemp, R.O. Park, R.M. Wright, Sugar Conyers, C.P. Jennings, John A. Thompson, E.C. Hill, Harry Brown, John Stanley, R.L. Sharpton, Johnny King, Lora Parks, Lindsey Lawrence J.W. Bell, Sam Smith, Judge Daniel, N.J. Willard, P.R. Chesser, John Jackson, Carrey Downing, John Meyers, G.H. Sims, Emma Bates, Tom Brittan, Bee Lawrence, Albert Long

Date of delivery May 30, 1916

A.C. Perry, S. Harmon, Emory Smith, W.D. Fergerson, Geo. Smith, J.D. Morris, Bob Slaton, S.A. Wilkins, Chas. Russell, Athie Camp, Geo. Jackson, L.H. Reed, H.C. Carruth, T.R. Roane, W.W. Patrick, W.M. Statson, St. Sturdivant, W.R. Roberts, Sallie Camp, S.A. Herd, J.W. Sheats, LL. Moane, Claud Mathis, R.H. Howell, J.W. Cooper, H.A. Carithers Jr., D.F. Thompson, Roy Smith, T.J. Austin, D.A. McDaniel, E.S. Harris, Z.N. Hendrix, A.C. Henderson, W.F. Reeves, Mrs. Cora Quattlebaum, D.W. Frye, D.P. Daniel, page 4

Page 131, Harrison Vincent Statham Ga. Solomon Shad Jacksonville Fla. Whiskey 2 qrts. S. Ex. Co. carrier

Date of delivery January 10, 1917

C.C. Williams of Winder Sol. Shad of Jacksonville Fla.

Barrow County had a large number of liquor transactions going on in 1916. I don't quite know what to say about the fact that R.M. Rose has not sold his business in 1910 to Paul Jones!

Greene County and Oglethorpe County are the next counties that R.M. Rose had a great impact. Now, you are about to see why they were calling it the "Roaring 20s." I say this because the liquor was flowing like the Oconee River that was nearby. I got these liquor consignors and the carriers out of Oglethorpe to just show you how the colored would change their names, and not only some coloreds but the whites did too.

H.H. Little had John Childers and James Childers working for him. As well as Arthur Cunningham, Will Carter, Buddie Callaway, Jimmy Crawford, Mamie Colbert, Grady Cox, Lewis Collins, Houston Colquitt,

Robert Cobb, Grant Collins, Cornelius Collins, Robert English, Charles Eberhart, Mary Eberhart, Cato Echols, and Lizzie Eberhart.

C.P. Colclough had Monroe Boykin, Will Cosby, Andrew Callaway, Buddie Callaway, Put Callaway Dilia Christopher, T. Clark, Paul Christopher, Will Crawford, Major Clark, Ed Clarke, Arthur Sims, Charlie Sanders, Charlie Smith and Wess Bugg working for him. Now, these are some of the small distributaries in Oglethorpe in 1916. W.F. Gilham, had Joe Brown selling Spirits and also E.C. Cheney, Mark Cox, and Mary Clarke. A. Flamlas & Co. out of Jacksonville Florida had T.W. Bray working for them down in Maxey. The National Whiskey Co. out of Chattanooga Tenn. had Annie Carter and Jim H. Smith working their liquor.

Voalt Applegate Co. out of Chattanooga Tenn. had W.H. Crowley running liquor for their company. H.L Sprinkler out of Jacksonville Fla. had W. D Crow and John Eberhart work their liquor for gain that was very profitable when set up near the black community, knowing that with oppression and complacency. Some knew they were going to get rich like some of the white men that owned land and worked the black community to death during slavery.

Well, let me go on, because I still have more to tell you of the Roaring 20's near the Watson Spring resort.

A.L. Oldsbrook out of Chat. Tenn. had Buddie Callaway running liquor for them. Haney Distribution Co. had Andrew Callaway working for their company. Chattanooga Supply Co. had Major Carter, Will Eberhart, Will Smith and May Shaw working their liquor. Big Creek Distribution Co. out of Jacksonville Fla. was working with Anna Callaway to get their liquor to the little General Store. Consignor A. Samuels had Ben Callaway doing their running for their company. Gabe Heiman out of Jacksonville Florida had Sara Carter running their liquor. Jos. Thompson out of Chatt. Tenn. had Lewis English driving their trucks for his small company. Georgia Whiskey Co. had Charlie Smith working and driving for them. Haynes Distribution Co. out of Jacksonville Fla. had Mamie Samuel working for them. C.D. Cheatham out of Chatt. Tenn. had J.W. Bray and R.A. Cooper working their liquor.

Now, I know that I have mentioned Mr. R.M. Rose. He was one of the biggest distributors in Georgia. As a matter of fact, he is buried in Atlanta in the Oakland Cemetery under one of the largest Grave that's in Oakland. Here are just a few of the Men in Oglethorpe that was working for Mr. R.M. Rose. Sam Brightwell, Nick Brightwell, both out of Hutchins.

Georgia. Pleas Brown, Jim Brightwell, Claud Berchmore all three out of Maxey. In fact, just about, all of the Names that I have mention come out of Maxey Ga., Crawford Ga., Lexington Ga., and Stephens, Georgia, and the surrounding districts of Oglethorpe.

However, let me finish telling you about the men and women running liquor for Mr. R.M. Rose out of Tennessee and Florida: Booker Bugg, J.H. Burgess, George Burgess, Lizie Burgess, J.A. Bray, Andrew Callaway, Ed Clarke, C.P. Colclough, Jim Cramer, John Callaway, Paul Christopher, Put Callaway, Tinsley Clark, Will Crawford, Major Clark, Frank Carter, Henry Collins, Charlie Sanders, John P. Smith, Mose Smith, Henry Smith, Eugene Smith, Will Eberhart, and George Eberhart all sold for one of the most controversial distributors in 1899.

Granddaddy Arthur had some company in Greene County when he was in the city of Greensboro running his liquor. There was Willie Criddle on Route 3, George D. Channell, Sarah Cobb, and Dock Cartough, M.P. Carrol, Will Cain, Jim Copelan, Eric Cunningham, Alf Champion Clara Callaway, she was living on Route 4 in Greensboro. Their carrier was So. Ex. Co. C.P. Callaway was in Union Point working for the H.G. Kale out of Chattanooga Tenn. and Willie Champion was working out of Siloam for the same company. Now working for the Rose Company was Robert Champion Willie Champion in Greensboro on Route 3. Now, this is where Arthur my Granddaddy was living too. W.H. Cheney was in Bairds Town, Georgia, Hill Callaway was in Woodville Ga., Jessie Champion was in White Plains, Georgia. Charlie Cato, Julia Cutwright, and R.D Calloway was all living on Route 3 in Greensboro, Georgia. Moreover, there was Charlie Champion living down in White Planes with Jesse Champion. Also living in the same area was Martha Callaway on Veazey road about a 1.5 miles south of Greensboro.

Record of Liquor Deliveries in Oglethorpe County:

John I. Callaway	Lexington Ga.	National Whiskey Company	Chattanooga Tenn.
John I. Callaway	Lexington Ga.	Rose Whiskey Company	Chattanooga Tenn.
Andrew Callaway	Maxey's	R.M. Rose	Chat. Tenn.

Andrew Callaway	Maxey's	C.P. Colclough Agent	
Buddie Callaway	Maxey's	A.L. Oldsbrook	Chat. Tenn.
Andrew Callaway	Maxey's	Haney Distribution Co.	Jacksonville Fla.
Put Callaway	Maxey's	Rose	Chat. Tenn.
Put Callaway	Maxey's	C.P. Colclough agent	
J.M. Callaway	Lexington	Rose	Chat. Tenn.
Ben Callaway	Crawford	C.P. Cheatham	Chat. Tenn.
Anna Callaway	Crawford	Big Creek Distribution Co.	Jacksonville Fla.
Anna Callaway	Crawford	Corn Liquor H.H. Little agent	
Ben Callaway	Crawford	A. Samuels	Chat. Tenn.
Lum English	Maxey's	Chattanooga Supply Co.	Chat. Tenn.
Robert English	Crawford	Chattanooga Supply Co.	Chat. Tenn.
Lewis English	Maxey's	Joseph Thompson	Chat. Tenn.
H.O. English	Crawford	A. Flauker	Jacksonville Fla.
O.N. Epps	Crawford	Rose and he also is working for C.P. Colclough	
Otis Hurt	Maxey's	R.M. Rose	Chat. Tenn.
Joseph Hurt	Maxey's	C.P. Colclough	
Guy Hurt	Maxey's	G.H. Applegate	Chat. Tenn.
Robert Hurt	Maxey's	Rose	Chat. Tenn.

Peter Hurt	Maxey's	Chattanooga Distributor	Chat. Tenn.
Will Hurt	Rose	Chat. Tenn.	
Bettie Hurt	Maxey's	Rose	
Henry Dorsey	Maxey's	Rose	
Gene Daniel	Maxey's	R.M. Rose	Chat. Tenn.
Robert Daniel	Maxey's	R. M. Rose	Chat. Tenn.
Will Daniel	Maxey's	R.M. Rose	Chat. Tenn.

Anna Deadwyler out of Stephens & Hutchins

Sam Haygood of Maxey for C.P. Colclough

Thomas Hurt, Pat Hurt, Randolph Hurt, Nannie D. Hurt, H.H. Hurt, Charlie Hurt for Tenn. Chattanooga Distribution Co. and H.H. Little as his agent

Henry Hurt, John Hurt, Will S. Hurt, Lovis Hurt, Lindsey Hurt, Ran Hurt, Jim Hurt, will W. Hurt, Gus Hurt, H. Hurt, Ela Smith, Henry Smith, Johnson Smith, Charlie Smith, Will Smith, John H. Smith, Walter Smith, Scot Smith, Lillie Smith, Lucious Sims, Fed Smith, Jessie Smith, Burt Shaw, Pope Smith, Lewis Smith, Gilbert Smith, F.D. Smith, J.T. Smith, Vane Smith, Nat Smith, Jon S. Smith, Burrell Samuel, Johnnie ?Smith, Floyd Smith, Jobe smith, Lee Smith, O.J. Sims, Roy Smith, Frank smith, John Sims, Charlie Sanders, Kissie Smith, Arthur Sims, Pete Smith, Jno. Walt Smith, Katie Sims, Gertrude Smith, Lola Smith, Tom Smith, Nora Sims

Jim H. Smith, Joe Smith, Mose Smith, David Sims, Mando Sims, Fred Smith, Lillie Smith, Jimmie Smith, Squire Smith, Alex Smith, Hudson Smith, Harrison Smith, Ralph Smith, Dilsy Smith, Judge Smith Eugene Smith, Lucas Smith, Wilie Sims, Mary Shaw, Lauren Smith, Major Smith, Hattie Lou Shaw, Bes Smith, Nellie Smith, Mamie Samuel, Orrie Smith, Plunkie Smith, Mease Smith, Rufus Smith. Stephen Finch, Bud Finch, Harry Finch, Ron Finch, Root Fair of Stephens, Luie Frazier, Della L. Finch, Perry Finch, Mary Finch, Lucinda Finch, Bill Finch, Charlie Finch, Annie Finch, George R. Finch, John Finch, Giles Finch, Jim Finch, C.L. Finch, Evie Fair, Robert Fair

Early Finch, Hattie Finch, B.S. Finch, John R. Finch, Steve Finch, Lillie finch, Rich Finch, Stephen Finch, Perry Finch, Miss Emma Finch, Lena

Finch, Jobe Finch, Sam Finch, Alice Finch, Just Finch, Hudson Finch, Clary Ann Finch, Julia Fair, Oscar Jones. Will Barrow, John Henry Barrow, Wess Bugg, Mose Barrow, Andrew Bush, Booke Bugg, Mose Broughton, John Barrow, J.H. Burges, Abe Barrow, Monroe Boykin, Kissie Barrow, Arch Brightwell, Cater Barnett of Crawford R.B. Grange of Chat. Tennessee is his agent. Jim Barnes, Lula Barrow, Elizabeth Barrow, Luc Barrow, Watt Bugg, Harrison Bugg, Mose Barrow, Jeff Bush, Tom Burges, Bil Brown, Annie Barrow, Pleas Barrow, W.T. Burchmore, Victor Barrow, Howard Barrow, Allen Brawner, Maud Barrow, Lonnie Brown. Lula Daniel, Chess Daniel, Robert Daniel, Mary Daniel, Willie Daniel, Ran Daniel, Sophie Daniel, L. Daniel, C.G. Daniel Crawford Hayner Distribution Co. Jacksonville Fla. J.G. Durden and John H. Daniel.

These names had a hand in the liquor trade in these counties where I first found the first Blind Tigers mentioned in all of my research in Oglethorpe County in the 1870's. So I assume that one of the reasons the big-time liquor dealers in Tennessee and Florida did well was because of the long standing that the black community had with the liquor trade and their power on the rich landowners' plantation in this business. The question is why wouldn't they turn to Charlie and the young twenty-year-old colored men to move their liquor!

This is one of the reasons that the poor whites and colored could not bring more than two quarts of liquor into the counties.

As you can see, Mr. Randolph M. Rose states in his advertisement,

Buy from an old reliable firm that you know will treat you RIGHT. The house of ROSE was established fifty years ago. You can only receive two quarts of Whiskey every 30 days. Why not buy the best?

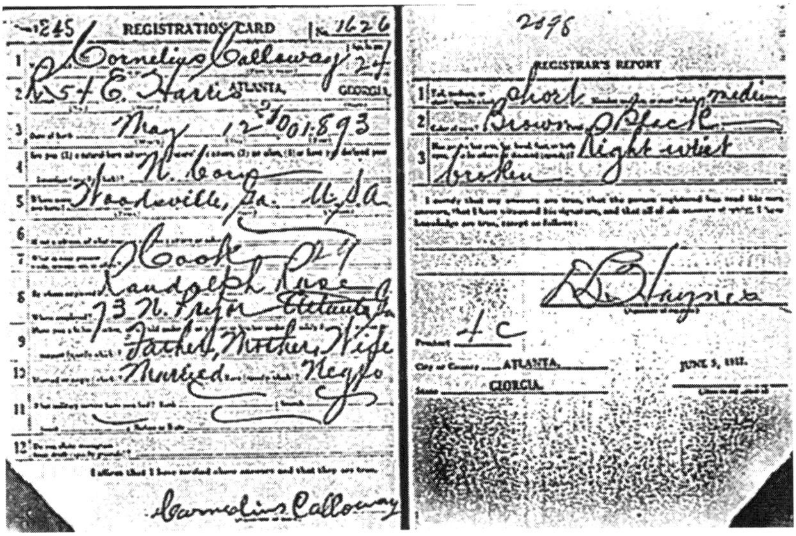
245 REGISTRATION CARD 1626
Cornelius Callaway 24
54 E. Harris ATLANTA GEORGIA
May 12 1893
Woodville, Ga. U.S.A
Cook
Randolph Rose
73 N. Pryor Atlanta Ga
Father, Mother, Wife
Married Negro
I affirm that I have verified above answers and that they are true.
Cornelius Calloway

2198
REGISTRAR'S REPORT
Short medium
Brown Black
Right wrist broken
D.L. Haynes
4 C
ATLANTA JUNE 5, 1917
GEORGIA

Cornelius Callaway is twenty-four years old and is the cook for Mr. Randolph M. Rose in 1917. Mr. D.L. Haynes is over this precinct. Now when Cornelius Callaway and Andrew and Nathan Callaway lived at 5 Conway place, they were living near Indiana Callaway, who resided in Fayetteville before coming to Atlanta with Jesse Callaway. I wonder when Cornelius said he was supporting his mother and father and his wife Johnnie while living at 54 Harris street. Who else were living in the house with him? And why can't I find in the directory any other living at this address other than Cornelius and a German brewer?

In this section of the book I will try and profile Charlie Callaway in 1918. I found him in Fulton County after traveling to the National Archives to uncover the Federal Court Case that was against him in 1918. Warrant to Apprehend was filed in the Clerk's office November 29, 1918. O. C. Fuller was the clerk. Issued the eleventh of November 1918, W. C. Carter was the US Commissioner. Howard Thompson was the US marshal and Lee Whatley was the deputy in the Northern District of Georgia. Bail was set at $300. Case No. 4392.

> The President of the united State of America, to the Marshal of the United States for the Northern District Of Georgia, and to His Deputies, or Any or Either of Them: Whereas, J. F. McGill has made complaint in

> writing under oath before me, the undersigned, a United States Commissioner for the Northern District of Georgia, charging that Charlie Callaway late of Fulton County, in the State of Georgia, did, on or about the 9th day of November A. D. 1918 at Atlanta in said District, in violation of interstate Commerce act contrary to the form of the statue in such cases made and provided, and against the peace and dignity of the united State of America. Now THEREFORE, YOU ARE HEREBY COMMANDED, in the name of the President of the United State of America, to apprehend the said Charlie Callaway wherever found in your District, and bring his body forthwith before me or any other Commissioner having jurisdiction of said matter to answer the said complaint, that he may then and there be dealt with according to law for the said offense. Given under my hand and seal this 11th day of Nov. A. d. 1918. W. C. Carter United States Commissioner.

The only thing is the warrant was not approved by the United States attorney of the Northern District of Georgia. It had to be approved to be acted upon.

Now, the Federal Courts Subpoenaed; O. M. Howell, J. M. Fluker, S. A. Ellard, J. T. McGill, J. G. Few, Nowell Houser and A. L. Glover on the sixteenth of November of 1918. The indictment charged that Charles Callaway of Fulton County knowingly having possessions of stolen interstate freight. Mr. Hooper Alexander was the US attorney and Samuel M. Castleberry was the attorney for Charlie Callaway.

United States of America Northern District
Of Georgia, Northern Division

> In the District Court of the United States in and for the division and district aforesaid, at the October Term thereof A. D. 1918; The Grand Jurors of the United States, impaneled, sworn, and charged at the Term aforesaid, of the Court aforesaid, on their oath present that Charles

Calloway on the 9th day of November in the year 1918 in the said division and district and within the jurisdiction of said Court did then and there unlawfully knowingly and fraudulently have in his possession certain goods, the same being a part of an interstate shipment of freight to-wit: 120 pounds of "Ox" brand chewing tobacco of the value of fifty cents per pound and 40 pounds of :Gem: chewing tobacco of the value of sixty cents per pound, the property of Johnson, Fluker & Company which said tobacco lately theretofore to-wit; on the 7th day of November, 1918 by a person to the Grand Jurors aforesaid unknown in said division and district had been unlawfully wrongfully and fraudulently stolen, taken and carried away from and out of a certain railroad car, to-wit; G. N. 124175, with intent to steal the same, the said tobacco then and there being a part of an interstate shipment of freight in said car contained which lately theretofore had been shipped from Winston-Salem, in the State of North Carolina consigned to Johnson & Fluker & Co., Atlanta, Ga., the said tobacco, when so stolen then and there was in course of transportation to destination and had not been delivered to the consignee. And the said Charles Calloway then and there knowing the said tobacco to have been so stolen from said car as aforesaid, did then and there unlawfully, wrongfully, fraudulently and knowingly have the same in his possession with intent to wrongfully and fraudulently convert the same to his own use. Contrary to the form of the statue in such case made and provided and against the peace and dignity of the United States.

A True Bill, October Term, 1918

George M. Browner was the foreman. These are the jurors: Richard M. Johnson of stone Mountain, John H. Buckhead of Fairburn, Walter I. Coleman of Fayetteville, Adolphus W. Ray of Atlanta, James C. Allbright of Atlanta, Moses E. Davis of Decatur, William H. Burges of Decatur, Cris H. Essig of Atlanta, Joseph w. Stuchlik of Atlanta, William B. Cummings of Atlanta, Isiah A. Christian of Forrest Park, Licurgus M. Westbrook of Fairburn, the alternates were: John E. Nesbet of Atlanta, Eugene A. Camp of Atlanta, Evelyn Harris of Atlanta,

Homer Pair of Mableton, Eugene T. Luckie of Atlanta, and David Goldin of Atlanta.

This sitting jury found Charlie Calloway, guilty! The marshal of the United States, City of Atlanta, Georgia, on the twenty-first of March 1919 was certified that he delivered the body of Charles Calloway to the warden of the United State Penitentiary at Atlanta, Fulton County, Georgia. Howard Thompson was the United States marshal and John W. Jones was the deputy. He was given twenty months in the penitentiary at Atlanta. The other strange thing about this case is that the True Bill of the Indictment (No. 2851) returned into open court by the grand jury and filed December 23, 1918, wherein the defendant is charged with violation of the act of February 13, 1913, knowingly having possession of interstate freight; plea Not Guilty March 19, 1918; verdict Guilty, March 20, 1919. I found twenty three-year-old colored Charlie Callaway in the Fulton County Jail in southeast Atlanta. This is where the Federal Prison is now located in Southeast Atlanta.

Winder News September 20, 1917

Estate of James M. Smith: Andrew C. Erwin, L.K. Smith, N.D. Arnold, Administrators J.O. Mitchell is the manager. Mr. James M. Smith had a somewhat relationship with Mr. N.D. Arnold. They both were members of the Farmers Club with Robert Lee Callaway and Mr. William Eberhart of Oglethorpe County with Mr. Eberhart as the President in 1906. And in the Atlanta Georgian and News Friday, December 24, 1909, Col. Jas. M. Smith and Mr. Nat D. Arnold were mention together as being members of the Great Southern Accident and Fidelity Company would open its offices to the world and take its place among the financial institutions of Atlanta with Mr. L. Carter of Jessup Ga. S.E. Smith of Atlanta Ga. H.H. Bass of Griffin Ga., J.M. Ponder of Forsyth Ga. Dr. S.F. West of Atlanta Ga., A.G. Campbell of Natchez Mississippi, R.H. Cantrell the President who was located in Atlanta, Col. James M. Smith of Smithonia Ga., W.G. Chipley as the Vice President of Atlanta Ga., Judge David W. Meadow of Elberton Ga. the same man that defended Mr. William Eberhart with Hamilton McWhorter in 1899 in the Federal Courts. Mr. W.C. Pitner of Athens Ga. J.R. Duvall the Secretary and the Treasure of Atlanta Ga., Ben F. Barbour of Birmingham, Alabama, and Mr. Nat D. Arnold of Lexington Ga. Could it be that Mr. James Monroe Smith has a hand in Charlie demise or relocation and name changes to keep him from the Feds! There is a large number of Charlie's children who will come to reside in Atlanta as you have seen and as I have told you about the relationship between the Cates and the Rose's and Callaway's in Atlanta and the Liquor Trade and the Blind Tigers!

There is another man that needs to be mentioned as well and he is Mr. Walter H. Johnson the U.S. Marshal at the time of Charlie's demise and relocation during his trial is located in Atlanta as well.

Walter H. Johnson is on the farm of Mr. James Monroe Smith in 1900 and would become a permanent fixture as well. It states in the Georgian that Mr. Walter H. Johnson the U.S. Marshal for the northern district of Georgia was born in Columbus Ga. and received his education at the schools near his home. When the war broke out between the states, Mr. Johnson, although quite young, joined the Confederate army and enthusiastically gave his services to his county. Shortly after enlisting, he was made a lieutenant in the Fifth Georgia reserves and all during the war he served with distinction. After the war, Mr. Johnson engaged in the mercantile business and although he was successful, he decided to enter the service of the government. Mr. Johnson has taken an active part in politics and is now looked upon as one of the Republican leaders in the South. It is largely to aim and his knowledge of politics to Georgia that such acceptable appointments have been made to Federal offices in the state. He has been recognized as a leader in Republican politics in Georgia and for that reason, he was one of the three references selected to pass upon applications for government offices in the state. He was appointed United States marshal several years ago and he has field that position since then administering the affairs of his office in a necessary than has called for words of praise. He has discharged his duties with . . . fidelity. Has conducted his offices in a businesslike manner and has (unreadable).

> Now let me show you an article of the *Georgian* newspaper that reads,
>
> The Unmerciful Beating of a Child
>
> Many Witnesses Tell of Cruelty at City Stockade
>
> Dodd says there were whippings every morning he was out there.
>
> "Dread was full of spiders and flies"

Witness Exhibits to investigating Committee Bottle of Lice Prisoners Captured while Serving Terms.

A witness called by the city at Atlanta. In the investigation into the charges made by the Georgian in reference to cruelty and mismanagement for city Stockade, a graduate physician, in fact testified to and described the most horrible details of inhuman barbarism that the people of this community have or will ever have, to listen to. He told of a little 13-year-old Negro girl being placed in the whipping chair invented by Superintendent Vinning. She was brought down stairs with only two thin undergarments on and placed in the chair. The front was fastened and it was turned over on its face as shown in the picture. A white man then whipped her with the strap about which The Georgian has told until when she was released from the chair she was hysterical. She said something to this hysterical condition, she knew not what, and superintendent ordered her placed back in the chair and again whipped.

While being beaten, she slipped her arms down through the box alongside her body, being so small that she did not fill the box of heavy plank, which tightly measures the body of an adult prisoner. She placed her hands over the parts of her body that were being beaten, trying to take some of the blows on her hands. They were soon bleeding from the blows and the doctor testified that as she went away to work that morning, the blood showed thru her clothing where the cuts had been made with the whipping strap. What will the citizens of a city like Atlanta of a State like Georgia do to bring justice to men who are so free from human instinct as to administer such cruelty. Such disgrace, such shame!

Vining-Cornett Trial on Jan. 10

Criminal Actions Against the Stockade Boss and the Guard That Does the whipping

JAMES MONROE SMITH DIES

This article is on non-other-than Mr. James M. Smith of Smithonia!

September 27, 1917 Thursday. It posts the estate of Mr. Jim Smith and his properties in other counties other than Oglethorpe.

1). Grove Creek 51 acres in the town of Sandy Cross adjoining lands of the Estate of Jim Steele, W.T. Cunningham, Stevens, Huff & Company, and W.T. Harris.

2). Lots in the town of Crawford, known as A.S. Rhodes Storehouse. Lot being 40 by 100 feet. On Depot Street, north by the Baptist Church east by street on the south by J.G. Chandler, west by Depot St. being same lots or parcel of land deeded by T.J. Shackelford receiver of A.S. Rhodes to James M. Smith.

3). Undivided one half interest of land in Lexington District on the waters of Long Creek. Known as old Joel Bacon home place containing two hundred and fifty-two acres on the north by Long Creek and lands of the estate of R.M. Bacon: on the east by lands of Mrs. E.B. Clark and W.S. Callaway, formerly known as the Hawkins Place. South by J.H. Smith, West by R.M. Bacon. Known as the Saving place. Long Creek and lands of Hamilton McWhorter Jr.

4). ½ interest in Lexington known as the Savings Place 186 acres north by W.T. Brooks and R.M. Bacon east by Long Creek land just above known as Old Joel Bacon place. And Mrs. Nora Smith, west by Mrs. Nora Smith and W.T. Brooks plat of the same made by M. S. Weaver.

5). Also the tract in Beaverdam district known as the Mitchell Place (132) acres north and west by lands of Mrs. Sam Goulding; east by lands formerly of the estate of Hal Johnson: on the south by lands of formerly of Tommie Johnson.

6). Also in Beaverdam district on Dunlap Road and Winterville known as the Mathews Place (241) acres adjoining lands of the estate of Allen H. Talmage, H.J. Meyer, and others. *W.S. Callaway is the man that is in DeKalb County Courthouse and has charges against Bailus Sutton. W. S. Callaway is also the same Callaway that helps establish the Lynwood Community in Clarke County in 1910 as well.*

7). Land lying in the counties of Oglethorpe and Madison, in Pleasant Hill and Beaverdam, on the waters of Beaverdam Creek, Big Clouds Creek and Hawks Creek known as Smithonia Plantation (7,000) acres on the north by the land of Kidd Sikes and Pharr, Waggoner, H.H.

Hampton, and Davison, on the east and north by lands of Holcomb, L.W. Collier, Chandler, Martin, J.D. Power, and J.H. Thomas. Southeast by M.V. Willingham, (deceased); J.D. Coile, and the old Johnson Place. South by George Crowley, Porterfield, Hayes, and W.J. Culbertson, southwest by T.J. Erwin, W.H. Gabriel, Lester, Freeman, and others.

As you can see the property of Mr. Hal Johnson was in the eyes of the Great Mr. James Monroe Smith. I believe that he would not have stopped until he had this property. Even if he had to murder for it and get all of the obstacles that might arise alone the way. This means if Charlie did not get on board, he too would have to be eliminated or relocated.

ATLANTA BLACKS AND WORLD WAR ONE AND THEIR CONTRIBUTION

Thursday, October 25, 1917

Night Riders and the Law (The Atlanta Constitution)

The determination and spontaneity with which the law respecting and humane white people of Houston and Crawford counties have risen to the defense of Negro Citizens against a little gang of lawless night riders indicates . . . that the flogging of hapless blacks simply because they own or drive an automobile is going to be put to an abrupt stop one cause for the many Negroes going North and hurting the southern economy which is very much needed.

Atlanta Constitution 1920s

Coming of Peace Will be Celebrated This Afternoon, Column Beginning to Move at 2:30 O'clock.

In celebration of the coming of peace, the colored citizens of Atlanta will hold an immense victory parade today. This parade, which will symbolize the splendid part that the negroes have taken in all forms of war work and the splendid service rendered by the colored troops who have fought in Europe, has been arranged by leaders of the race, and it is certain that both white and colored will view the long pageant with a sincere feeling of pride and an appreciation of the splendid service of the colored people. It is especially requested that as far as possible, employers allow their colored workers to get off for the hours of the parade. The head of column will move promptly from the starting point at Auburn Avenue and Jackson street at 2:30 p. m., and the parade will probably take about two hours to pass a given point. The line of march will be down Auburn to Ivy, Ivy to Cain, Cain to Peachtree, Peachtree and Whitehall to Mitchell, and Mitchell to the state capitol, where the parade will disband. A. F. Stewart is marshal for the parade and Tyler Grant is aide.

Formation by Divisions: The formation by divisions is as follows: First Division—United States soldiers followed by Red Cross auxiliaries. Military officers commanding, will for on north side of Auburn . . . to Jackson Street. Second Division—Officers and executive committee of the Negro division, Untied War Work campaign, in carriages, Secretary A. B. McCoy commanding, and J. C. Lindsay aide, will form on south side of Auburn avenue, leading carriage with banner, resting in front of Ebenezer Church. Third Division—Colleges and public schools, Dr. L M. Hill commanding, Professor B. T. Harvey and Professor Charles Clayton sides, will form on Jackson Street between Auburn and Edgewood. Fourth Division—Physicians and businesses men Dr. H. R. Butler commanding and Dr. J. W. Burney side, will form on Bell Street, between Auburn and Houston, leading car will banner, resting at Bell Street entrance of Odd Fellows building.

Fifth Division—Insurance Men, William Driskell commanding J. H. Starks side, will form on north side of Auburn avenue (right) resting at Gate City Drug store.

Sixth Division—Churches, Rev. Major F. T. Turner commanding, Rev. W. H. Nelson, Rev. F. E. Eberhart and

Henry Mathis aides, will form on north side of Auburn avenue (right), resting in front of Wheat Street Church.

Seventh Division—Barber and other unions, John H. Fletcher commanding M. J. Lindsay side, will form on south side of Auburn avenue (right), resting in front of Silver Moon Barber shop.

Eighth Division—Colonel John S. Bigsby commanding, Captain Oliver Moore, aids; K. of P. band and other fraternal orders will form on west side of Piedmont avenue (right), fronting at Rucker Building.

Ninth Division—Floats, Colonel J. W. Smith commanding, Captain George Shalfer and J. O. Penson, aides. All divisions must form in time to move off at 2:30 p. m. sharp, today.

Atlanta Negroes Hold Big Parade

Colored Troops, Bands, Business Men, Secret Orders and School Children Take Part in Peace Celebration.

Probably the largest parade ever staged in the city by Negroes was held in the business district Monday afternoon in celebration of the victory over Germany. Several thousand marchers were in line, including colored troop's bands, schools and Negro civic organizations, while thousands of spectators of both races crowded the downtown district to witness the celebration. A. F. Stewart acted as marshal of the parade with Tyler Grant as aide. The parade formed at Auburn Avenue and Jackson, and proceeded down Auburn to Ivy, thence to Cain, then to Peachtree and Whitehall to Mitchell, and from there to the Capitol, where the archers disbanded. The line was led by Chief Beavers and a squad of mounted officers, then came a splendid military band from Camp Gordon, followed by a number of colored veterans from overseas, and a detachment of well drilled colored troops from Gordon. Next, came a number of Negro Red Cross workers, and members of the Red Cross auxiliaries, and

Negro women's lodges. They were followed by officers and members of the executive committee of the negro division of the United War Work Drive. A large number of marchers from Morehouse College wee next in line. At the head of this delegation was a huge service flag, which contained a total of 190 stars, several of which were gold. Several hundred Negro girls and boys representing the colored schools of the city, came next, some waving "the Stars and stripes" and others service flags. A large delegation from the colored churches was followed by a number of colored businessmen and members of colored secret orders.

A. M. E. Church Fills Quota

Allen Temple A. M. E. Church, with its pastor, Rev. J. A. Lindsay, went "over the top" Sunday morning in spite of the rain for the big drive of War Camp activities now on the city. It was Allen Temple that led last June in the . . . was saving stamps- and she is pooling for the front again. Led on by its stirring committee—J. C. Johnson, E. E. Scandrett, Dollie Alexander, Annie Greene, C. C. Cade and Willie Daniels—Allen Temple will contend for her place at the front Wednesday night in the final wind-up.

In Two Counties Gifts of Negroes Pass the Quotas

Not content to wait until the official opening of the United War Work Campaign next week, the negroes in two counties of the southeastern department have already reported to departmental headquarters here that they have oversubscribed quotas assigned to both whites and coloreds.

Warren County, Georgia, and Wilson County North Carolina, are both over the top at a colored mass meeting held at Warrenton Ga. Tuesday the Negroes subscribed

$3, 350 in cash, while the quota for the entire county of Warren for both races is only $3,000.

With thirteen days remaining before November 18, when the eight-day intensive drive closes for the raising of $170,500.000 for the boys over there that the seven recognized welfare agencies may continue their war work, the colored communities of Wilson County North Carolina, has reported to the departmental colored work executive secretary Arch Trawick of Nashville Tenn., that they had over $14,000 in subscriptions and the entire county quota is for that total County Campaign Chairman T. F. Moffett of Wilson County, has wired asking that the county quota be raised to a minimum of $30,000. "President Wilson has officially stated that these seven war welfare agencies require not $170,000.000 to continue their work among our soldiers and sailors." But $250.000.000 to continue their work among our soldiers and sailors." Said County Chairman Moffett. "This is Wilson County. We are with the president and our boys. "Peace or no peace these organizations must continue their work for over a year, while the boys come home."

Georgia Makes Fine Showing on First Day of United Drive

Telegrams from county chairmen of the united War Work campaign flooded the office of Ely R. Callaway. State director, yesterday, reporting the progress made on subscriptions in all parts of the state, and indicating that many counties have gone over with their quotas on the first day of the drive, that other counties well reach their allotment with heavy oversubscriptions apparently is a matter of only of a few hours . . .

The Constitution, Atlanta, Ga., Wednesday, November 13, 1918.

Spirit of Rivalry Aiding Negroes in United Drive

The first report that was made by the two teams of colored workers in the city for the united War work campaign, showed the east side ahead of the west side by several hundred dollars. This news, when reported to the headquarters, instilled into the forces new life and a greater spirit of rivalry.

The west side held a conference of forces at Cosmopolitan A. M. E. church last evening, which brought out splendid results that will help tell a different story when the next daily report is made. Thursday evening at 6 o'clock sharp, a luncheon will be served the workers at Bethel, at which time a full report will be made of what has been done by the Victory Boys and Girls and the special workers among the young men.

The most inspiring thing of the whole campaign is the way the students in the colleges are giving. The report from Morehouse college of this city, brought forth many favorable comments. The students of this institution have pledged more than $1,500. The special committee that is handling the colleges made an appeal to Morris Brown university, Gammon Theological seminary and Clark University Tuesday, and the reports form these schools will be made before the close of the present week.

A. M. E. Conference Appointments Read

The Atlanta annual conference of the A. M. E. Church held in Cosmopolitan A. M. E. Church, corner Foundry and Vine Streets, has closed a very profitable and helpful session. Bishop J. S. Flipper read the following appointments for the next conference year:

South Atlanta District: L. A. Townsley Presiding Elder: Allen Temple: attention; J. A. Lindsay; St. Paul W. A.

Mclendon; Grant Chapel, C. G. Gray; Trinity, to be supplied: Flovilla J. E. Smith Locust Grove; E. N. Martin Jackson. J. C. Cash; Thomasville, W. C. Davis Mount Carmel, J. S. Drake West End, S. S. Maulden; Tuis and Flippen, J. Wesley Upshaw: McDoungh. A. Vaughn: Oakland C. Hamby: S. John H. J. Hall Stockbridge and Rex. S. E. Elliott; Connell and Connolley. Walter Reed: Pleasant Hill and Jenkinsburg. William Goodrum; Peeplestown. W. B. Williams, St. Matthews, L. H. Middlebrooks: Watkins Chapel. R. t. Trimble; St. Luke, Emitt Johnson; Ellen wood, H. W. Session; district evangelist, Peter Williams, S. M. Sappington Louis Smith, Andrew Wright, S. M. Turner, S. D. Green, D. C. Atwater, J. D. Render and S. B. Cary.

Atlanta District: H. D. Canady, Presiding Elder: Big Bethel Station, R. H. Singleton; Cosmopolitan, W. J. Williams Decatur, W. A. Austin; St. Phillip, J.R. Gardner; Turner Monumental, M. T. Flournoy: Morris Brown Chapel, D. R. Fobbs; Turner Chapel, M. Roberts: St. Mark, S. A. Lucas: St. James, S. M. Meadows: Conyers, M.C. Brown: Rockdale Park, R. W. Wilson; St. Peter, Horace Williams; Lithonia, J. T. Perry; Stone Mountain and Redan, J. W. Langston; Howell, J. R. Martin; Blandtown, James w. McKnight; Grove Street, R. J. Sager; Pleasant Grove, Yates Rogers; Edgewood, J.P. Davenport; Conyers, N. R. Eady; Flipper Chapel, A. U. Freeman; Holmes institute, B. R. Holmes; East Cain Street, A. H. Hardin; Jackson Street, J. B. Epperson; Scottsdale, P. W. Williams; Colyer Street, S. T. Turner; West Atlanta, S. W. Peacock; Ingleside, C. A. Clark; East Lithonia, T. H. King; North Atlanta, G. F. Patterson; Almond, S. D. Green; Rhodes Street, W. M. Nunn; Kirkwood, E. H. senior; Conference evangelists, L. Oliver, G. S. Turner and G. T. Fantroy. There are three more districts in the A. M. E. Conference; Griffin J. H. Myers as the presiding Elder, Newnan District with P. G. Simmons as the presiding Elder. Monticello District and J. A. Hadley as the presiding Elder.

North Georgia Conference

Dalton Ga. November 6. (Special)—The North Georgia annual conference. A. M. Church convenes here tomorrow in the First Church of the denomination Rev. J. T. Wilkerson pastor. The colored community is making grate preparation to entertain the session. Bishop J. S. Flipper of Atlanta, will preside. One hundred ninety-eight ministers and delegates will answer the conference roll call. Some of the pastors, college presidents and business leaders of the negro race are booked to be present on Wednesday afternoon. Presiding Eldes W. P. Talbert, Athens, District; J. R. Fleming, Marietta district, S. P. James Dalton district; W. Boyd Lawrence, Washington District D. H. Porter, Rome District are on the grounds and are having their pastors to go through their financial reports . . .

I went looking for some of the colored neighborhoods that were in Atlanta. I come across one in particular named the Beaver Slide

1950

Mount Zion Baptist Church, Atlanta, Ga. Pastor: Rev. E. R. Searcy, Messenger, Deacon J. T. Thompson.

Zion Hill Baptist Church Atlanta, Ga. Pastor: Rev. P. J. Ivory,

DECEASED WORKERS

Mt. Zion, Atlanta: Rev. J.T. Dorsey, Sister Lula Gilliam

Zion Hill, Atlanta: Sister Annie Arnold

1949

S. S. STATISTICAL REPORT

Mt. Moriah, Atlanta, Pastor: R. Julian Smith, Superintendent: Mr. Alonza Sloan, Secretary: Mrs. L.W. Beetel

Mt. Carmel Atlanta, Pastor: O. C. Woods, Superintendent: Mr. W. B. Woods, Secretary: Miss Lillie Byrd

Mt. Zion Atlanta, Rev. E. R. Searcy, Superintendent: Bro. E. D. Dorsey, Secretary: Mrs. Barbara Whitehead

B. T. U. STATISTICAL

Mt. Carmel, Atlanta, Pastor: Rev. O.C. Woods, Director: Mrs. Mattie Walker

Mt. Zion, Atlanta, Pastor: Rev. E. R. Searcy, Director: Mr. M. P. Bostick, Secretary: Mrs. Lillie B. Williams

Zion Hill, Atlanta, Pastor: Rev. L. M. Terrell, Director: Mr. L. D. Keith, Sr. Secretary: Miss Evelyn Malone

EDUCATIONAL RALLY

ENROLLMENT

Mount Zion S. S.: Bro. E. D. Dorsey, Mrs. E. L. Thompson, Mrs. Mary Hughes, Robert Hodges, Mrs. Agnes Young, Dea. M.P. Bostick, Mattie Dorsey, Mrs. Mattie Burce, Odie Waddington, Mr. J.S. Ward, Sis. Ardail Sims, Rev. E. R. Searcy.

Mount Olive B. T. U.: Doris Fletcher, Madelene Reeves, Willie Mae Moon, Miss Eula Glenn,

West Hunter S. S.: Jeradyne Hill, Gloria Mitchell

Zion Hill S. S.: A. I. Hall, Clifford Sutton, Mrs. Jewel Crawford, Mrs. Ella Chambliss, Maggie M. Taylor, Miss Nellie Woodson, Mrs. Jewell E. Terrell, Mr. J. S. Ward, Victoria Terrell, Johnnie E. Henderson, Mrs. L. D. Keith-lived in College Park., Mr. H. G. Bell, Dea. L. D. Keith,

ENROLLMENT OF CHURCHES:

24. Mt. Zion Baptist Church, Atlanta, Ga.; Rev. H. S. Stovall; Messenger, Dea. J. T. Thompson

38. Zion Hill Baptist Church, Atlanta, Ga.; Pastor Rev. L. M. Terrell; Messengers, Rev. R. A. Graves, Dea. J. C. Carnelious

1944
ENROLLMENT OF DELEGATES, ETC.

Mt. Zion:
Dea. T. D. Ealey 210 Pine St. N. E. Fulton Co. Atl. Ga.,
Rev. J. T. Dorsey 324 Angier Ave., N. E. Fulton Co. Atl. Ga.
Dea. P.W. Elliott 1508 Hardee St.
Rev. Jas. Hendrick 418 Felton Dr., N. E.
Dea. R. O. Sewell, Fairburn Ga.

Zion Hill:
R. A. Graves 31 Howell St. N. E. Fulton Co. Atl. Ga.
Dea. J.T. Harris 558 Rockwell St. S.W.
Dea. L.D. Keith 91 Haygood Ave., S. E.

Traveler's Rest:
Dea. W. Lyons, 14 Rockwell St. S. W. Fulton Co. Hapeville Ga.

Friendship:
Rev. J. R. Lovett 2069 Simpson Road P. O. College Park Ga.

U. B. Institute:
Dea. C. H. S. Lyons Clarke Co. Athens Ga.

Mt. Olive:
Dea. G. W. Partee 269 Harris St. N. E. Fulton Co. Atlanta, Ga.

ENROLLMENT OF CHURCHES:

1. Antioch (L) Baptist Church, Lithonia, Ga. Pastor Rev. J.T. Dorsey Messenger Deacon E. G. Rainwater.

20. Greater Mt. Zion Baptist Church, Atlanta, Ga. Pastor Rev. T. J Dorsey, Messengers, Deacons J. H. Hendrick, T. Ealey.

22. Mt. Olive Baptist Church, Atlanta, Ga. Pastor Rev. W. W. Weatherspool, Messenger Deacon G. W. Partee.

23. Mt. Olive Baptist Church, Fayetteville, Ga. Pastor Rev. I. P. Ward, Messengers Brothers J. T. Dorsey, Mitchell Hightower, J. H. Hood, Oscar Dorsey.

24. Mt. Calvary Baptist Church, College Park, Ga. Pastor Rev. O.S. Sutton, Messenger Deacon C. L Owens.

30. Mt. Moriah Baptist Church, Atlanta, Ga. Pastor Rev. C. H. Holland, Messenger Brother Joseph E. Howard.

48. Zion Hill Baptist Church, Atlanta, Ga. Pastor Rev. L. M. Terrell, Messengers Rev. R. A Graves, Deacon J. T. Harris.

LIST OF LICENSED PREACHERS

Brother W. Burnes of Jackson Ga.

Brother W. H. Hawthorne of Jackson Ga.

Brother John Atkins of Hapeville Ga.

PASTORS AND THEIR ADRESSES

Rev. W. H. Borders 24 Yonge St. N. E. Atlanta, Ga.

Rev. J. T. Dorsey 324 Angier Ave., N. E. Atlanta, Ga.

Rev. P. R. Geer 1001 Simpson St. N. W. Atlanta, Ga.

Rev. C. H. Holland 184 Ashby St. S.W. Atlanta, Ga.

Rev. M. L. King 193 Boulevard, N.E. Atlanta, Ga.

Rev. L. M. Terrell 272 Brown St., S. W. Atlanta, Ga.

1942 Atlanta Missionary Baptist Association, Inc. held with the Butler Street Baptist Church Atlanta, Ga.

1. Antioch (L) Baptist Church, Lithonia, Ga. Pastor, Rev. J. T. Dorsey; Messenger, Deacon E. G. Rainwater.

9. Ebenezer Baptist Church, Atlanta, Ga., Pastor, Rev. M.L. King; Messenger, Deacon J. W. Johnson.

19. Mt. Mariah Baptist Church, Atlanta, Ga., Pastor, Rev. C. H. Holland.

27. Mt. Zion Baptist Church Atlanta, Ga. Pastor, Rev. J. T. Dorsey, Messenger W. M. Ellington, C. P. Webb.

34. Reed Street Baptist Church, Atlanta, Ga., Pastor, Rev. C. N. Ellis; Messenger, Deacon L. D. Keith, Rev. R. L. Cook.

41. Zion Hill, Baptist Church, Atlanta, Ga. Pastor, Rev. I. B. Myrick; Messengers Rev. R. A. Graves and Deacon J. T. Harris.

46. Mt. Calvary Baptist Church, College Park, Ga., Pastor Rev. O. S Sutton.

STATISTICAL ORDER OF CHURCHES:

Antioch (L) Lithonia in Dekalb County the Pastor is J. T. Dorsey, no address John Dorsey is the clerk and baptized 13, received by letter -0- 3 was excluded, five has died total membership 200 and total of money $10.

Zion Hill (Atl.) Atlanta is the Post Office, the county is Fulton, J. T. Johnson is the Pastor the address is-0- the clerk is Pleas Butler the address is 1049 Coleman St 29 has been baptized, Received by letter is 13, 15 has died, total membership is 826 and total money is $15.

Mt. Zion (Atl.) Atlanta, Fulton County, J. T. Dorsey is the Pastor, 324 Angier Ave. G.A. Todd is the clerk address is 310 Piedmont Ave. 72 have been baptized, 11 have been received by letter, 27 died, total membership is 1900, total money $5.

Ebenezer (Atlanta) the Pastor is M. L. King Sr. 501 Auburn Ave. the clerk is P.O. Watson of 866 Parson. 97 have been baptized, 286 have been received by letter, 1 have been excluded, 6 have died, total membership is 2600, total money $25.

Mt. Moriah Atlanta, Fulton County, the Pastor is C. H. Holland of 184 Asby Street, C. H. Harris is the clerk of Hunter Rd.

Atlanta Missionary Baptist Association, Inc. held with the Mt. Pleasant Baptist Church, South Atlanta, Ga. 1941.

PASTORS AND THEIR ADDRESSES

Rev. J. T. Dorsey 324 Angier Ave., N.E., Atlanta Ga.

Rev. J. T. Johnson 592 Pulliam St., S.W., Atlanta, Ga.

Rev. C. H. Holland 184 Ashby St. S. W. Atlanta, Ga.

Rev. H. Lester 141 Haygood Ave. S. E Atlanta, Ga.

Rev. B. J. McCloud Lithonia, Ga.

Rev. S. B. Myrick 291 Scipleton St. N.W.

Minutes of the Forty-Seventh Annual Session of the Atlanta Missionary Baptist Association Held with Mount Carmel Baptist Church Atlanta, Georgia, October 10–12, 1950

OFFICERS:

Dr. M. L. King, Sr., Moderator of Atlanta, Ga.

Rev. C. S. Jackson, First Vice Moderator of Atlanta, Ga.

Rev. O.C Woods, Second Vice Moderator of Atlanta, Ga.

Rev. R. A. Graves, Clerk of Atlanta, Ga.

Rev. L. J. Burt, Assistant Clerk of Atlanta, Ga.

Rev. S. M. Davie, Auditor of Atlanta, Ga.

Rev. E. M. Johnson, Treasurer of Atlanta, Ga.

Place and time of next meeting: Ebenezer Baptist Church, Atlanta, Georgia, October 9–11, 1951.

ENROLLMENT OF CHRUCHES

1. Antioch (L) Baptist Church, Lithonia, Ga. Pastor, Rev. O. L. Jackson. Messengers, Deacons, E. G. Rainwater and M. B. Guthrie
2. Antioch (E) Baptist Church, Atlanta, Ga. Pastor, Rev. N. Mathis
3. Beulah Baptist Church, Atlanta, Ga. Pastor, Rev. L. J. Burt
4. Bethlehem Baptist Church, Covington, Ga. Pastor, Rev. C. W. Huff. Messenger, James Brown
5. Bethsaida Baptist church, Stone Mountain, Ga. Pastor H. J. Jackson
6. Butler Street Baptist Church, Atlanta, Ga. Pastor, J. R. Barnett
7. Dixie Hill First Baptist Church, Atlanta, Ga. Pastor, Rev. R. D. Sutton
8. Ebenezer Baptist Church, Atlanta, Ga. Pastor, Dr. M. L. King. Messenger-Deacon, P. O. Watson
9. Beulah Baptist Church, Atlanta, Ga. Pastor, Rev. E.D. Thomas
10. Friendship Baptist Church, College Park, Ga. Pastor, Rev. J. R. Lovett. Messenger, A.B. Broom
11. Kelly Chapel Baptist Church, McDonough, Ga. Pastor, Rev. N. Davie
12. Liberty Baptist Church, Atlanta, Ga. Pastor, Rev. G. w. Dudley. Deacon, Rogers Henderson
13. Macedonia Baptist, Church Atlanta, Ga. Pastor, Rev. W. W. A. Moreland. Messenger Deacon B. G. Hawkins
14. Macedonia Baptist Church, Lithonia, Ga. Pastor, Rev. E. D. Hudson
15. Mt. Calvary Baptist Church, College Park Ga. Pastor, Rev. J. H. Pullin.
16. Mt. Carmel Baptist Church, Atlanta, Ga. Pastor, Rev. O. C. Woods. Messenger, Willie Bussey
17. Mt. Moriah Baptist Church, Atlanta, Ga. Pastor, Rev. R. Julian Smith, Jr.

18. Mt. Olive Baptist Church, Atlanta, Ga. Pastor, Rev. W. W. Weatherspool
19. Mt. Pleasant Baptist Church, Atlanta, Ga. Pastor, Rev. A. V. Williamson, Messenger, L. H. Hill
20. Friendship Baptist Church Atlanta, Ga. Pastor, Rev. M. H. Jackson, Messengers, Deas. R. O. Sutton and C. A. Brown
21. Mt. Pleasant Baptist Church, Atlanta, Ga. Pastor, Rev. B. W. Bickers. Messenger, Deacon R. L. Andrews
22. Mt. Vernon Baptist Church, Atlanta, Ga. Pastor, Rev. E. M. Johnson, Messenger, A. G. Taylor
23. Mt. Zion Baptist Church Atlanta, Ga. Pastor Rev. E. R. Searcy. Messenger, Deacon J. T. Thompson
24. Mt. Zion Baptist Church, Cartersville, Ga. Pastor, rev. W. R. Dinkins
25. New Hope Baptists Church, Atlanta, Ga. Pastor, Rev. R. N. Martin. Messenger, Bro. H. Studivant
26. Pleasant Hill Baptist Church, Atlanta, Ga. Pastor Rev. U. G. Campbell
27. Pleasant Hill Baptist Church, Conyers, Ga. Pastor
28. Mt. Zion Baptist Church, Fairburn, Ga. Pastor, Rev. R. B. Thompson. Messenger, Bro. R. O. Sewell
29. Poplar Springs Baptist Church, Ellenwood, Ga. Pastor, H. Bussey. Messenger, Deacon J. A. Green
30. Providence Baptist Church, Atlanta, Ga. Pastor, L. M. Tobin. Messenger, Rev. G. C. Middlebrooks
31. Providence Baptist Church, S. Atlanta, Ga. Pastor, Rev. T. H. Blue, Jr.
32. Salem Baptist Church, Atlanta, Ga. Pastor, Rev. C. S. Jackson
33. Shiloh Baptist Church, College Park, Ga. Pastor, Rev. H. T. Thomas
34. Shiloh Baptist Church, Jonesboro, Ga. Pastor, Rev. S. M. Davie
35. Springfield Baptist Church, Scots Crossing, Ga. Pastor Rev. S. Randolph. Messenger, Deacon Troy Conley
36. Travelers Rest Baptists Church, Atlanta, Ga. Pastor, Rev. L. A. Pinkston. Messenger, Sylvester Gill
37. West Hunter Baptist Church, Atlanta, Ga. Pastor, Rev. A. F. Fisher
38. Zion Hill Baptist Church, Atlanta, Ga. Pastor, Rev. L. M. Terrell. Messenger, Rev. R. A. Graves

39. Zion Baptist Church, Jackson, G. Pastor, Rev. P. J. Ivory
40. Macedonia Baptist Church, Jackson, Ga. Pastor, Rev. C.R. Sheridan. Messenger, Deacon Thomas Taylor
41. Travelers Rest Baptist Church, Hapeville, Ga. Pastor, Rev. L. A. Jackson

MOUNT CARMEL BAPTIST CHURCH

Atlanta, Ga., October 10, 1950

At 6:30 p.m. the Executive Board of the Atlanta Missionary Baptist Association met in a business session. Rev. M. L King, presided. Song, "Jesus Keep Me Near the Cross." Prayer by Rev. H. Bussey. Moderator announced, ready for business. Board dues were collected in the amount of $12.00.

A committee on Revision of Constitution was appointed as follows rev. T. G. Blue Jr., chairman; Rev. A. V. Williamson, Rev. J. T. Thompson. They were given plenary power. On motion we adjourned. Benediction by Rev. O. C. Woods.

Rev. M. L. King, Moderator

Rev. R. A. Graves, Clerk

Night Session, 7:40

Devotions were conducted by Rev. Benjamin W. Bickers followed by a selection by the congregation. Rev. Bickers discussed the Biblical statement: "We are laborers together with God." Silent prayer by the congregation. Rev. S. J. Blue at the piano.

Remarks by the Moderator, Rev. M. L. King.

Program of the session was read by Rev. L. J. Burt. On motion it was adopted. Minutes of the Executive Board were read and . . .

End of page 7

Chapter Sixteen

THE COLORED CHURCHES AND THEIR PREACHERS

MINUTES
WOMAN'S DEPARTMENT
ATLANTA ASSOCIATION
1949

Atlanta, Georgia

October 12, 1949

The Woman's Convention Auxiliary to the Atlanta Baptist Association in session with the Beulah Baptist Church, opened with a very spiritual devotional service conducted by the Committee. Theme: "The Open Door."

Expressions from the sisters, song—"Where He Leads Me I Will Follow."

A few remarks by the president, Mrs. I. F. Henderson

Appointment of Committees.

The memorial service conducted by Mrs. Alice M. Ogletree was very touching, the eulogy was read beautifully by Mrs. P. L. Crump. Song—"Abide With Me."

Seating of delegates by counties by Mrs. N. W. Crawford. Music—"Lift Him Up," Mrs. Isom at the piano.

The president introduced Mrs. Franklin Drake, who brought a lovely message on "Paying The Price." She urged that the races get closer together and advance God's Kingdom. She introduced Mrs. Mitchell who brought greetings from W. M. U. which we enjoyed.

Mrs. Shelia of the Jackson Goodwill Center, was introduced. She also brought a grand message on "Helping Each Other."

Mrs. Isom made a few remarks on the generosity of the white missionary women.

Mrs. Geneva Haugabrooks was presented, she gave words of encouragement, and gave a donation of five dollars.

A few remarks by the president, Mrs. Henderson.

The offering for the morning was $6.30.

Adjourned for the Educational Sermon.

WEDNESDAY AFTERNOON

Joint session for the annual addresses of the moderator and the president.

Opening—"Lift Him Up." Silent prayer.

Song—"Here Is A Fountain Filled With Blood," Mrs. Terrill at the piano.

The treasurer, Mrs. Cyrus Brown, made her report of $175.99 balance in treasury.

The moderator, Rev. M. L. King, presented the president, Mrs. I. F. Henderson, for her address, she brought a deep and inspiring message from the subject What Is Woman's Work In The Church, Today?" We were inspired to do more and better work in our churches.

Comments by Mrs. Rossie P. Bivins and Mrs. Jewell Terrell.

Song—"We are climbing Jacob's Ladder."

A presentation of gifts to the president by Miss Elizabeth Whitehead, which were graciously received by Mrs. Henderson.

Moderator King commented briefly on the president's address.

A lovely selection by the Ebenezer Choir.

The vice moderator, Rev. C.S. Jackson presented Rev. L. A. Pinkston president of the state Baptist Convention, he made some . . .

End of page 28

Mrs. Crawford made a appeal for the Fifth District Work. Mrs. P.J. Ivory was appointed to head up the pageant "The Queen Contest," a committee from the various churches was appointed to assist her. This affair to be given by the next meeting in 1950. The recording secretary, Mrs. Furr, tendered her resignation. Mrs. Crawford made a statement regarding the minutes, and asked the secretary to remain in office. After some explanation she considered the matter and said she would continue to serve.

A donation of $4.00 was given to Mrs. Minnie Aiken. Then went into executive board meeting and paid off the expenses. By motion we sent Mrs. Pearl Reese, young people's directress, to the state convention, also by motion gave her $5.00 for her expense. By motion a donation of $5.00 as a love token was given to Mrs. Hattie Baker, vice president who is ill. It was also suggested we give her a card shower.

Sister Walker, the usher was given some instructions by the president regarding proper uniform. The president urged the sisters to visit Mrs. W. F. McKinney who is very ill. Closing song and parting word.

Mrs. I. F. Henderson, President

Mrs. Rossie P. Bivins, Chairman

Executive Board

Mrs. M. L. Furr, Recording Sec.

DECEASED WORKERS

Antioch, Lithonia: Sisters Louise Woodall, Velma Hall, Dea. Clifford Bullard, Rev. A. G. Scruggs

Bethlehem, Covington: Sisters Ada Banks, Marie B. Heard

Beulah, Atlanta: Sisters Bell Paschal, Savannah Ware, Rosa Moss

Greater Mt. Calvary, Atlanta: Dea. Jesse Griffin

Liberty, Atlanta: Sister Ida Brittian

Macedonia, Lithonia: Dea. M. M. Shephard

Mt. Pleasant, So. Atlanta: Sisters Lizie Ivory, Edna Freeman, Mother Daniel

Mt. Vernon, Atlanta: Sisters Gladys Hollis, Mary A. Gibson, Brother Mangum, Dea. Jordan

Mt. Zion Atlanta: Rev. J. T. Dorsey, Sister Lula Gillaim

Pleasant Hill, Atlanta: Sisters Mary Dickerson, Alice Holmes, Willie Newsome (spelled Jewsome)

Poplar Springs, Ellenwood: Sister Phoebie Shephard

Travelers Rest, Edgewood: Sisters Ovie Strickland, Mattie Latimore

Zion Hill, Atlanta: Sister Annie Arnold

ROLL OF OFFICERS

President: Mrs. I. F. Henderson

First Vice President: Mrs. Hattie Baker

Second Vice President: Mrs. Evie Thompson

Third Vice President: Mrs. Ida Wilburn

Fourth Vice President: Mrs. Henrietta Holt

Fifth Vice President: Mrs. Lula Cloud

Sixth Vice President: Mrs. Lula Hicks

Seventh vice President: Mrs. Lean Davis

Eight Vice President: Mrs. Della Walker

Ninth Vice President: Mrs. Mary Davis

Tenth Vice President: Mrs. Mary Rainwater

Recording Secretary: Mrs. L. M. Furr

Financial Secretary: Mrs. N. W. Crawford

(End of page 30)

S. S. STATISTICAL REPORT

Bethsaida Church of Stone Mountain Rev. Jackson is the pastor, the Superintendent is Mrs. Ora Woods and the secretary is Miss Walter M. Freeman.

Beulah, in Edgewood, Atlanta Rev. E. D. Thomas is the pastor, the Superintendent is Mr. Wm. Dixon and the Secretary is Miss Marthaleen Scruggs.

Beulah of Atlanta Rev. L. J. Burt is the pastor and the Superintendent (none) the Secretary (none)

Ebenezer of Atlanta Rev. M. L. King, Sr. is the pastor, the Superintendent is Mrs. Pearl Reese and the Secretary is Mrs. Sarah James.

Friendship of College Park Rev. J. R. Lovett is the Pastor, the Superintendent is Mrs. Susie Perkins and the Secretary is Mrs. V. E. Yancey.

Liberty of Atlanta Rev. G. W. Dudley is the pastor, the Superintendent is Mrs. L. E. Grier and the Secretary is Miss Robbie Bunson.

Mt. Calvary of College Park, Rev. J. H. Pullins is the pastor, the Superintendent is Mrs. Emma Jackson, the Secretary is Miss Carolyn Martin.

Mt. Carmel of Atlanta, Rev. O. C. Woods is the pastor, the Superintendent is Mr. W. B. Woods, the Secretary is Miss Lillie Byrd.

Mt. Moriah of Atlanta Rev. R. Julian Smith is the pastor, the Superintendent is Mr. Alonza Sloan, the Secretary is Mrs. L. W. Beetel.

Mt. Pleasant (McGruder St.) Atlanta, Rev. A. V. Williamson is the pastor, the Superintendent is Mrs. Mary Winfrey, the Secretary is Mrs. Allie Everette.

Mt. Pleasant (So. Atlanta) Rev. B. W. Bickers is the pastor, the Superintendent is Mr. Marion Gillman the Secretary is Mrs. Annie Jackson.

Mt. Vernon, Atlanta, Rev. E. M. Johnson is the pastor.

Mt. Zion, Atlanta, Rev. E. R. Searcy is the pastor, Bro. E. D. Dorsey is the Superintendent, Mrs. Barbara Whitehead is the secretary.

Mt. Zion, Fairburn Rev. R. B. Thompson is the Pastor and Mr. R. O. Sewell is the Superintendent and Miss Catherine Abercrombie is the secretary.

New Hope, Atlanta, Rev. R. N. Martin is the pastor and Dea. C. M. Maddox is the superintendent and Miss A. Cofield is the secretary.

Pleasant Hill, Atlanta, Pastor (none) Dea. W. McCord is the superintendent and Mrs. Carrie Betts is the secretary.

Providence, Atlanta, Rev. L. M. Tobin is the pastor.

Providence of South Atlanta, Rev. T. G. Blue is the pastor and Dea. Fletcher Nelson is the Superintendent Miss Annell Ponder is the secretary.

Salem, Atlanta, Rev. C. S. Jackson is the pastor, Dea. E. W. Stillware is the superintendent and Mrs. E. Griggs is the secretary.

Shiloh, College Park, Rev. H. T. Thomas is the pastor, Bro. J. B. Wright is the superintendent, Miss Margaret Speer is the secretary.

Shiloh of Jonesboro, Rev. S. . Davies is the pastor, Bro. Mark Wilborn is the superintendent, and Miss Nettie Walker is the secretary.

Travelers Rest, Atlanta, Rev. L. A. Pinkston is the pastor.

Travelers Rest Hapeville, Rev. F. A. Jackson is the pastor.

West Hunter, Atlanta, Rev. A. F. Fisher is the pastor, Mr. James Entaminge is the superintendent, Miss Bussey is the secretary.

Zion of Jackson, Rev. P. J. Ivory is the pastor, Dea. P. B. Barber is the superintendent, Miss Larelette Newby is the secretary.

Zion Hill Atlanta, Rev. L. M. Terrell is the pastor, Mr. H. G. Bell is the superintendent, Miss Vivian Bailey is the secretary.

B. T. U. STATISTICAL

Beulah Church, Atlanta, Rev. L. J. Burt is the pastor, there is no director, and the secretary is Mrs. C. Davenport

Beulah of Edgewood, Atlanta, Rev. E. D. Thomas is the pastor, Mrs. Ruby Langford is the director, Miss Blanche Stiggers is the secretary.

Ebenezer of Atlanta, Rev. M. L. King, Sr. is the pastor, Mrs. N. W. Crawford is the director, and Miss Era Lloyd is the secretary.

Liberty, Atlanta, Rev. G. w. Dudley is the pastor, Miss India Combs is the director, there is no secretary.

Mt. Carmel of Atlanta, Rev. O. C. Woods is the pastor; Mrs. Mattie Walker is the director.

Mt. Olive, Atlanta, Rev. W. W. Weathers is the pastor, Mr. Moses Lee is the director, and Miss Willie M. Moon is the secretary.

Mt. Pleasant, Atlanta, Rev. B. W. Bikers is the pastor, Mr. Edmonson Sims is the director, Miss Louise Fish is the secretary.

Mt. Vernon of Atlanta, Rev. E. M. Johnson is the pastor, director (none), Miss Carrie Jones is the secretary.

Mt. Zion of Atlanta, Rev. E. R. Searcy is the pastor, Mr. M. P. Bostick is the director, and Mrs. Lillie B. Williams is the secretary.

Mt. Zion of Fairburn, Rev. R.B. Thompson is the pastor, director (none), Miss Catherine Abercrombie is the secretary.

New Hope of Atlanta, Rev. R N. Martin is the pastor, Mrs. A. G. Hunter is the director, and Mr. Harold Sturdivant is the secretary.

Pleasant Hill of Atlanta, No pastor, No director, and the secretary is Miss Johnnie Dixon.

Providence of Atlanta, Rev. L. M. Tobin is the pastor, director (none), Secretary (none)

Providence, South Atlanta, Rev. T. G. Blue is the pastor, Dea. Reese Swann is the director; Miss Betty Jean Clarke is the secretary.

Salem of Atlanta, Rev. C.S. Jackson is the pastor, director(none), Miss Elizabeth Griggs is the secretary.

Shiloh of College Park, Rev. Hillie. T. Thomas is the pastor/director (none), Ms. Evelyn Cantrell is the secretary. Here I am going to mention to you who Mr. Hillie T. Thomas is. He is my grandmother Georgia Mae Callaway's uncle out of Wilkes County. My aunt Lillie Stewart told me this and so did my grandmother as well. They moved to Chestnut Street in Atlanta in 1937. My aunt Lillie was the only one to attend David T. Howard School in Atlanta with some of her classmates Catherine Wilson, Betty Sue Kelly, Mabel Collins, and Annie Eliza Crew. Aunt Lillie moved to the Lynwood Park Community in 1958. This was eighteen years after my grandfather Arthur moved to Lynwood Park. While my great-grandfather George Jones lived on Chestnut in northeast Atlanta near Alabaster Alley, they attended the Mt. Sinai Baptist Church that was located on Butler Street and their pastor at that time was Rev. H. M. Smith. The new church is now on Merrits Ave in Atlanta. My grandfather Arthur attended Israel Baptist Church that was located on Boulevard N. E. Atlanta. Hillie T. Thomas, also pastored the Rising Star on North Side Drive in Atlanta.

Travelers Rest, Atlanta, Rev. L.A. Pinkston is the pastor, Bro. H. Sheppard is the director, Ms. Ann Barksdale is the secretary

Zion of Jackson, Rev. p. J. Ivory is the pastor, the Director is Rev. W. M. Compton and Mrs. Queen Horne is the secretary.

Zion Hill of Atlanta, Rev. L. M. Terrell is the pastor, r. L. D. Keith Sr. is the director, and Ms, Evelyn Malone is the secretary.

LIST OF LICENSED PREACHERS

Bro. John Thompson of 1536 Hardee St. N. E. Atlanta Ga.

Bro. C. H. Hawks of Atlanta, Ga.

Bro. H. Taylor of Atlanta, Ga.

Bro. W. M. Purse of Atlanta, Ga.

Bro. Henry Watts of Atlanta, Ga.

Bor. L. Bell of 648 Irwin St. N. E. Atlanta, Ga.

Bro. Herman Battle of 77 Lucy St. S. E. Atlanta, Ga.

Bro. Thomas Dallas of Atlanta, Ga.

Bro. Norman Lampkin

Bro. B. W. Bickers of 583 Houston St. N. E. Atlanta, Ga.

Bro. J. B. Morton of Atlanta, Ga.

Bro. Thomas Glenn of Atl. Ga.

Bro. W. A. Dansby, Bro. Maney Brown, Sr., Bro. Ed. Rachel, Bro. H. Stephens, Rev. N. O'Neal, Bro. J.W. Walker, Bro. P. P. Epps, Bro. T. Jiles, Bro. A. G Turner, Bro. Walter Williams of Decatur, Bro. D. V. Cloud, Bro. R. L. Cook, Bro. E. Griffin, Bro. H. B. Batey, Bro. B.F. Jenkins, Bro. V. Blash, Rev. James Walker, Bro. C. V. Vaughn, Bro. James Thompson, Bro. Samuel Speer of 38 Ashby St. S.W Atl. Ga. Bro. Isiah Jones of 38 Ashby St. S.W. Atl. Ga. Bro. Clifton Hamp of 793 Beckwith St. S.W. Atl. Ga. Rev. S. B. Myrick of 291 Scipleton St. N. W. Atl. Ga.

ENROLLMENT OF CHURCHES

1. Antioch (L) Baptist Church, Lithonia, Ga., Pastor, Rev. J. T. Dorsey: Messenger, Deacon E. G. Rainwater.
2. Antioch (E) Baptist Church Atlanta, Ga. Pastor, Rev. W. W. Thomas.

3. Beulah Baptist Church, Atlanta, Ga., Pastor, Rev. B. R. Watts; Messenger, Deacon L. F. Leftwich.
4. *Beulah Baptist Church, Atlanta, Ga. Pastor, Rev. A. G. Davis.*
5. Bethlehem Baptist Church, Atlanta, Ga. Pastor, Rev. Wm. Jackson; Messenger, Brother Nelson Williams.
6. Bethlehem Baptist Church Covington, Ga., Pastor, Rev. P. R. Geer.
7. Butler Street Baptist Church, Atlanta, Ga. Pastor, Rev. J. R. Bennett.
8. Bethsaida Baptist church, Stone Mountain, Ga., Pastor, Rev. B. D. Coes.
9. Ebenezer Baptist Church, Atlanta, Ga., Pastor, Rev. M.L. King; Messenger, Deacon J. W. Johnson, and Deacon Emory Neal.
10. Friendship Baptist church, College Park, Ga., Pastor, Rev. J. R. Lovett; Messenger, Deacon W. J. Sewell.
11. Kelley Chapel Baptist Church, McDonough, Ga. Pastor, Rev. N. Davie.
12. Liberty Baptist Church, Atlanta, Ga., Rev. B. L. Davis, Messenger, Deacon Roger Henderson.
13. Macedonia Baptist Church, Atlanta, Ga., Pastor, Rev. Cyrus Brown.
14. Macedonia Baptist Church, Jackson, Ga., Pastor, Rev. C. R. Sheridan; Messengers Deacon J. O. Kelley, Deacon G. F. Fitch
15. Macedonia Baptist Church, Lithonia, Ga., Pastor Rev. S. P. Fields; Messenger, Deacon Marion Shepherd.
16. Mt. Bethel Baptist Church, McDonough, Ga., Pastor, Rev. E. M. Taylor.
17. Mt. Carmel Baptist Church, Atlanta, Ga., Pastor, Rev. O. C. Wood
18. Mt. Calvary Baptist Church, Atlanta, Ga., Pastor, Rev. B. J. Johnson.
19. Mt. Mariah Baptist Church, Atlanta, Ga., Pastor, Rev. C. H. Holland.
20. Mt. Olive Baptist Church, Flippen, Ga. Pastor, Rev. H. M. Alexander; Messenger, Deacon J. Hill.
21. Mt. Olive Baptist Church, Atlanta, Ga., Pastor, Rev. W. W. Witherspool; Messenger, Rev. Stephen Berry.
22. Mt. Pleasant Baptist Church, Atlanta, Ga., Pastor, Rev. B. W. Freeman; Messenger, Bro. William Lyons
23. Mt. Pleasant Baptist Church, Atlanta, Ga., Pastor, A. V. Williamson.

24. Mt. Pleasant Baptist Church, Atlanta, Ga., Pastor, Rev. R. H. Milner; Messengers, Deacon J. H. Freeman, Deacon S. R. Dickerson.
25. Mt. Vernon Baptist Church, Atlanta, Ga., Pastor, Rev. Wm. G. Bivins; Messengers, Deacon A. Baker, Deacon B. Hicklin, Deacon R. H. Dixon.
26. Mt. Zion Baptist Church, Cartersville, Ga., Pastor, Rev. S. M. Bryant; Messenger, Deacon W. R. Moore.
27. Mt. Zion Baptist Church, Atlanta, Ga. pastor, Rev. J. T. Dorsey.
28. Pleasant Hill Baptist Church, Atlanta, Ga., Pastor, Rev. T. H. Ford; Messenger Deacon M. Jenkins.
29. Providence Baptist Church, Atlanta, Ga., Pastor, Rev. C. D. Hubert; Messenger, Deacon Hubert Davis.
30. Providence Baptist Church, S. Atlanta, Ga., Pastor, Rev. P. R. Geer; Messenger, Deacon A. J. Merriwether.
31. Pleasant Hill Baptist Church, Conyers, Ga. Pastor Rev. H. H. Woodson; Messenger, Deacon J.A. Davis.
32. Popular Springs Baptist Church, Decatur, Ga., Pastor, Rev. S. T Rogers.
33. Rising Star Baptist Church Jackson, Ga., Pastor. Rev. T.H. Ford.
34. Reed Street Baptist Church, Atlanta, Ga., Pastor, Rev. C. N. Ellis; Messenger, Deacon L. D. Keith.
35. St. Luke Baptist Church, Atlanta, Ga., Pastor, Rev. T. J. Brown
36. Salem Baptist Church Atlanta, Ga., Pastor, Rev. C. S. Jackson; Messenger, Rev. J. H. Pitts.
37. Shiloh Baptist Church, College park, Ga., Pastor, Rev. W. T. Thomas.
38. Shiloh Baptist Church, Jonesboro, Ga., Pastor, Rev. W. G. Bivins.
39. Traveler's Rest Baptist Church, Atlanta, Ga., Pastor, Rev. O. J. Moore.
40. West Hunter Baptist Church, Atlanta, Ga., Pastor, Rev. S. P. Pettagrue; Messengers, Deacon W. H. Hutchinson, Deacon S. G. Sellers
41. Wheat Street Baptist Church, Atlanta, Ga., Pastor, Rev. W. H. Borders; Messengers, Deacon H. L. Ferrell, Deacon Joe Crawford.
42. Zion Hill Baptist Church, Atlanta, Ga., Pastor Rev. J. T. Johnson; Messengers, Rev. R. A. Graves and Deacon J. T. Harris.
43. Zion Hill Baptist Church, Rockmart, Ga., Pastor, Rev. N. T. Young.

44. Zion Baptist Church, Marietta, Ga., Pastor, Rev. A. G. Belcher; Messenger, Bro. A. B. Green
45. Zion Baptist Church, Jackson, Ga., Pastor, Rev. G. L. Allen.

personal listing spells given name Zenas Business listing spells it Zanas

Ebenezer Baptist church the church of Martin Luther King Jr. was established in 1886 and moved to Auburn Avenue from Airline Street in 1922.

William Finch the father of Negro Education in Atlanta became the city's first Black Councilman in 1870 he lived in the Auburn Avenue community on Edgewood Avenue.

Wesley Redding c. 1884 cashier and bank teller for black patrons of merchant's bank. In the 1890, he helped establish the Atlanta loan and Trust Co. and the European Hotel, the first hotel for blacks in the city.

Alexander Hamilton, a contractor, built homes for White Atlanta's and buildings in Auburn Avenue community beginning in the late 19th century. Hamilton and his family lived in the Auburn Avenue community on Howell Street.

Rev. Edward Randolph Carter's book the Black Side of Atlanta published in 1894, chronicles the achievements of many successful African Americans of the Auburn Avenue Area. Jesse Blayton the first Black certified public accountant in Georgia was a founder of Mutual Federal. He also established several businesses with Yates and Milton then, in 1949, he started WERD, the first black owned commercial radio station.

Ma" Sutton's restaurant was once the most popular eating and meeting place on the Avenue. In 1935 it was the location of a banquet honoring Poro Chain Founder Annie Malone. The Royal Peacock owned by Carrie Cunningham opened in 1949.

Mary Combs, a free black woman and the first black property owner in Atlanta, owned a tract of land at the intersection of Wheat and Peachtree Streets. Combs purchased her tract from Frederick S. Pentecost on May 7, 1856.

Real estate dealers; Walter H. Chivers, also a dealer in Real estate; G.B. Warren, Dentist: J.H. Holsey, J.W. Jones operated an employment agency.

This is the side of town where I found Charlie Callaway born in 1885 and his wife Emma who was married in Clarke County, and the mysterious Charlie Callaway, and Mr. C. E. Callaway, and later on my Grandfather will come to reside in N. W. Atlanta in Techwood with his brother Charlie on Hunnicutt Street in 1922. They lived near the Liquor and the Bar-rooms, and Pool Halls own by these Jewish or White Men!

YOUNG ARTHUR (KATOR) CALLOWAY

Arthur Calloway was born under peculiar circumstances in Athens, Clarke County, Georgia. He was raised by his grandparents Abraham English and Dinah Hurt English of Greene County, Georgia. He went with his grandmother Dinah to Maxey, Georgia, where the Maxeys and the Brightwells and Boswells reigned supreme. There, if you remained on the plantation, you could take part in the many hot suppers, where the women were plentiful and the liquor flowed on the weekends. Arthur or Kator would grow up on the Epps and Hurt plantations with his family on his grandmother's side. He left behind his two other brothers Willie and Howard in Beaverdam, Oglethorpe. However, Mr. Eberhart would gain custody of Brantley and bring Charlie, who was a servant in the Epps household and living in the house with the Epps in Maxey. Whatever the reasons, the family of Mary and Charlie Callaway had suffered during the disenfranchisement period of the Negroes in Georgia and the South. I have not quite figured out if Charlie is white or not; however, every inclination in me shouts that he is. And I honestly believe that he is!

Dinah went to court in Oglethorpe County on September 29, 1900. Arthur's birth name was Cato Calloway. He was sixteen months old in September 1900. On June 20, 1900, Kater Calloway was in the house with his grandparents Abe and Dinah in Maxey, Georgia, on J. L. Epps's place with his siblings. Kater was listed as being born January 1899 and was one years old. Note to my emediate family Kater later changed his age to his brother Brantley because Brantley had a twin sister name Annie Sib who I presume died and Kater before going into First World War change his age to Brantley and said he had a twin brother. His sister Rosa was born May 1898, his brother Brantley was born February 1896, and Lizor was born December 1893. Charlie, his elder brother, was in the house with Mr. Epps, who was just next door. Charlie was born February 1885. By the year 1910, Abe and Dina were living in Penfield in Greene County, Georgia. They only had two grandchildren in the house with them, Caleb (Kator, Cato, or Arthur) and his sister Rosa Kate. Arthur was twelve years old and Kate was now ten. Now, something is wrong. Rosa is now younger than Arthur or Kater in 1910. Brantley, is the son of Dinah and Abe, is living with John English and his wife Annie John. Brantley is fifteen in 1910. Charlie, their elder brother, is in Beaverdam with his wife Emma Crawford Calloway. Howard was in Athens with his wife Ada Harvey and her family. The only son that gives me trouble in finding is Will Calloway!

In the year 1910, I got a big surprise! Rose is younger than Arthur Callaway. I figured this because Rosa was not mentioned in any indentures for servitude anywhere. I also thought that she might be the twin sister of Kater because my grandfather told us that he had a twin. The only twins I know of in the family of Charlie and Mary are Brantley and Annie Sib, who were mentioned in the indentures in 1896 with Mr. William Eberhart.

Now, u another story that Kator told us. He said he'd been in jail for killing a man with an axe. Let me tell it as it was told to me:

> "While on the chain gang one day, I noticed that the guard was taking some of them Niggers on top of a hill and they weren't coming back down from top of the hill, only the guards were! I told myself that I be damned if I go up on that hill and die! I took a pickaxe and hit one guard on the top of his head and killed him dead whiles he was asleep and resting on that log. I told the rest of them niggers, 'Now all ya'lls is free!'"

I was told he made his way to Louisiana, changed his name to Arthur, and joined the army. I am having a hard time believing this story about the murder that supposedly took place for him to change his name in Louisiana. If he changed his name in Louisiana, why did he come back to Penfield to join the army? You would think he would have joined the army in Louisiana. Anyway, however, it did take him a long time to report for deportation. Also, I found a similar story at the Atlanta Historical Society about a colored man with the last name of English that killed a guard on the chain gang in 1900 in DeKalb County near Buckhead. I believe he was told this story and embellished upon it for himself because it might have been kin to him and his grandfather Abe who told him the story, or his uncle John might have mentioned it to him as well. All I know is he was one a chain-gang but the story was told to him.

Kator did get into trouble in Greensboro. He was in the City of Greensboro about the time he got into trouble in 1917. I know this because of his employer Mr. Felix E. Boswell, and the sheriff who got his bond, Mr. Hixon. Kator had been in the employment of Mr. Felix ever since he purchased the property of Mr. Furr. Kator went to Greensboro with Mr. Boswell when he moved his office to town and young Kator had his first experience in the city. I wonder what kind of work he did for Mr. Boswell. In the city there was no farm work to be done. I assume that he worked in the house of Mr. Boswell or drove his horse and buggy. Mr. Boswell had just one person to take with because Brantley and Charlie had already moved Clarke County. So that leaves young Kator, who just moved onto his property with his grandfather and grandmother near Boswell Chapel outside of town. I wonder what Kator might have felt moving from a poor and rural portion of Greene County and seeing young children who had shoes while he had nothing. He found himself like so many who wanted or needed but just didn't have. And looking at his circumstances, he apparently made a choice that he would come to regret. He was told of the problems that his father and mother went through by his grandmother and how he should conduct himself in the presence of Mr. Boswell! Here, what is a young high-yellow teenager barefoot in the city of Greensboro to do?

CRIMINAL DOCKET, TERM, 191 ,

Foote & Davies Co., Atlanta.

ATTORNEYS	No.	NAMES OF PARTIES	OFFENSE CHARGED
Shipley	461	THE STATE vs. Tony Edmundson	Simple Larceny
	462	THE STATE vs. Kabe Calloway	Larceny from House Shff 17.75 Clerk 6.75 Sol G 5.00 Sol 5.00
Shipley	463	THE STATE vs. Tony Edmundson	Larceny from House Sheriff 7.25 Clerk 7.45

92

GREENE COUNTY COURT.

DISPOSITION	ENTRIES
Plea of guilty - June 7 1917. 100.00 or 12 mo. 6/11/17. Chaingang	
June 7 1917 - Verdict of guilty. \$100.00 or 12 mo. 6/11/17 Chaingang	Recd of E C Hixon \$100.00 fine June Term 1917 F. A. Shipley Treasurer
June 8. 1917 - Indictment annulled Bond fixed at \$200.00	

E. C. Hixon not only got his bond once but twice. The first time was for fifty dollars.

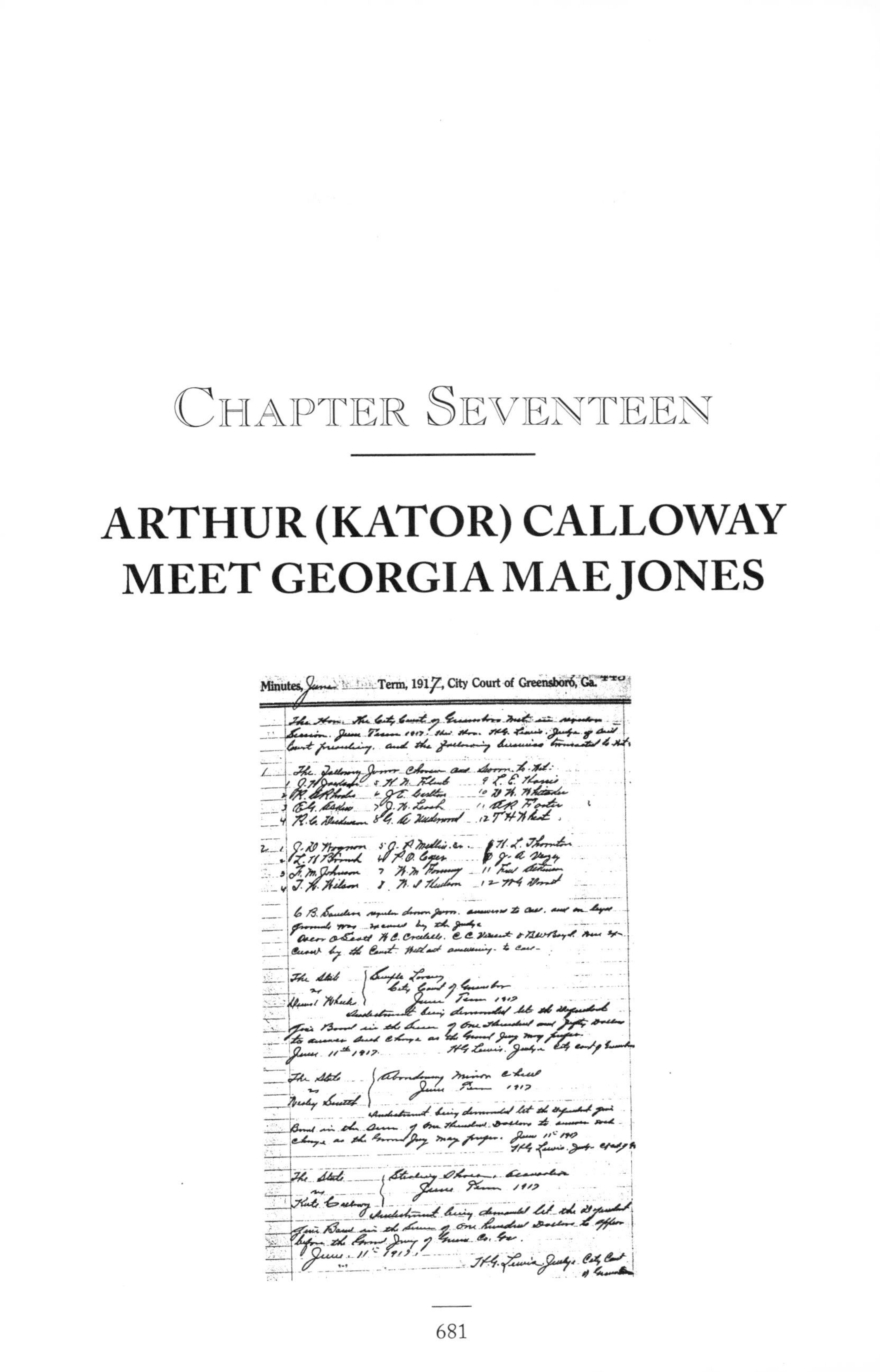

CHAPTER SEVENTEEN

ARTHUR (KATOR) CALLOWAY MEET GEORGIA MAE JONES

Minutes, June Term, 1917, City Court of Greensboro, Ga.

I do not know what role Edward C. Hixon played in my grandfather's life at this time in 1917. I do know that Kator was living in the city of Greensboro at this time, with whom I don't know. He is never mentioned in the tax digest with Abraham and his son John. I believe that he was living near Abraham English Jr. and E. C. Hixon. I remember visiting the city of Greensboro, where I met Mr. Boswell who told me about the sheriff of Greensboro who was wet. He kept his liquor in a barrel in the courthouse near his desk. I wonder if the liquor established the relationship between young Kator Callaway, his father Charlie was known as a seller of beer and liquor in Athens.

Now Arthur might have had an accomplice named Mollie Smith. She was arrested on the same day as Granddaddy Arthur, September 10, 1917, for larceny from the house. John S. Callaway got her bond.

THE STATE
vs.
Mallie Smith — Charge: Larceny from the House
In the City Court of Greensboro.

Upon inquiry before the Judge whether defendant demands a trial by jury, the defendant answers yes
In Open Court, this 10 day of Sept 1917
M. N. Lewis
Solicitor City Court of Greensboro.

Defendant waives arraignment and pleads not guilty, this 10 day of Sept, 1917
Jno S Callaway
Defendant's Attorney.

The following named jurors empaneled, sworn to try the above-stated case, to wit:

1. G. H. Eley	5. W H Wadsmore	9. N. A. Rusk
2. W H Culbreath	6. J H Bruce	10. C. C. Whitaker
3. J B West	7. M. C. Lumpkin	11. J. M. Ward
4. J Todd King	8. V. J. Merritt	12. C. C. [illegible]

We the jury find the defendant .... guilty. This .... day of .... 191..

Foreman.

Plea of not guilty 10 day of Sept 1917
Upon hearing the evidence in the above case, the defendant is adjudged guilty.
Whereupon, it is ordered that the said Mallie Smith
be, and is hereby sentenced to work in the Chain Gang on the Public Works or on such other work as the County authorities of said County may employ the Chain Gang, for the term of Eight months from the date of her reception in said Chain Gang.
The defendant may be discharged at any time before the end of said sentence, on payment of the sum of Seventy five Dollars, including all cost of this prosecution.
This, the 10 day of Sept 1917
[illegible]
Judge City Court of Greensboro.

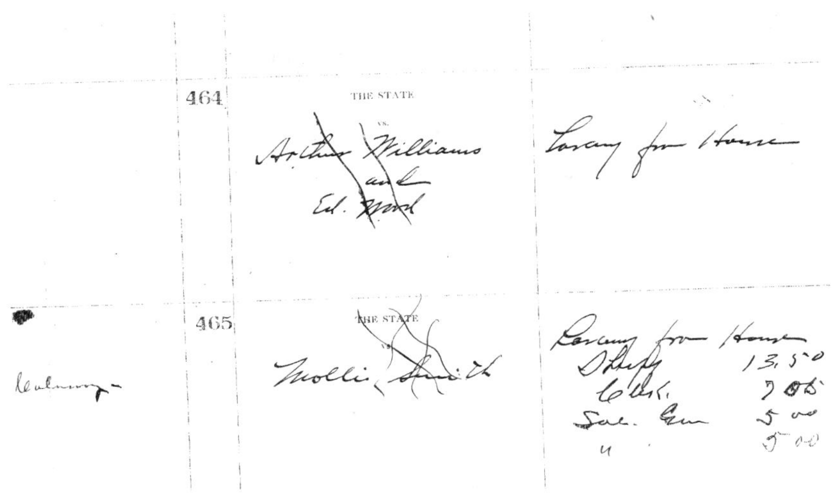
464 THE STATE

465 THE STATE

On October 29, 1917, E.C. Hixon was the chairman of the local board for Greene County for selecting men for military service for the United States. S. H. Willis was the secretary, and C. F. Thompson was the commanding major, Inf. Adjt. This was for men going to Camp Gordon in Chamblee, Georgia, in DeKalb County. However, Arthur was sent to Camp Funston. Like I had stated before, Arthur was late showing up for duty. You can see this in the report that E. C. Hixon made in the next picture. The mobilization camp report stated that "one man actually reported at the mobilization camp, that no men shown in column 6 as having been forwarded failed to report, that no men were rejected upon examination here, that one man was finally accepted into the military service of the United States, and that this Local Board has been credited on the account of quotas at the mobilization camp with that number of men by command of Maj. Gen. Swift, October 29, 1917; E. C. Hixon, chairman."

FORM 1029 PMGO.

ORIGINAL.

When completed to be mailed by Military Authorities to the Provost Marshal General, Washington, D. C.

Local Board for the County of Greene, State of Georgia, Greensboro, Ga.

10-1-36 APR 23 60

SHEET No. 1

Date, March 31st 1918

The selected men herein described, having been inducted into military service on March 31st 1918 (Date.) have this date been entrained for CAMP FUNSTON, Kansas (Camp or Station.)

This statement consists of 2 sheets.

1 Order No.	2 Serial No.	3 Name.		4 Call No.	5 Primary Industry.	6 Classification. I	II	III	IV	V	7 Failed to report to Military Authorities
2	258	Ed	Kent	92	Laborer	A					X
23	107	Corry	Caldwell	92	Laborer	A					X
48	10	Macon	Drake	92	Laborer	A					
62	739	Carmie	Terrell	92	Laborer	A					X
107	452	Ellis	Webb	92	Farmer	A					
142	1022	Ralph	Hurt	92	Farmer	A					
256	292	George	Gresham	92	Farmer	A					
257	822	Burnice	Daniel	92	Farmer	A					
263	312	Willie	Shank	92	Farmer	A					
265	90	Anthony	Dalton	92	Farmer	A					
270	753	Webster	Swaine	92	Farmer	A					
282	278	Johnie	Mapp	92	Farmer	A					
286	1172	William	Neal	92	Farmer	A					X
294	8	Lee	Heath	92	Laborer	A					
295	1160	William	Davenport	92	Laborer	A					
297	305	Antwine	Hull	92	Laborer	A					X
312	438	Ben	Eley	92	Farmer	A					
315	441	Cleft	Brown	92	Laborer	A					X
318	23	John Hart	Edmondson	92	Laborer	A					
341	1043	Jim	Pope	92	Farmer	A					
348	1273	Major	Wright	92	Laborer	A					
359	435	Joe	Jarrell	92	Farmer	A					
353	935	Manuel	Jenkins	92	Laborer	A					X
362	808	John	Broomfield	92	Laborer	A					
364	1183	Warren Henry	Stovall	92	Laborer	A					
369	940	Lee	Lee	92	Farmer	A					X
377	1107	Authur	Callaway APR 22	Y 92	Laborer	A					

Received APR 20 1918 M.G.O.

35

91

I wonder if he is the strategist behind Kater changing his name to Arthur Callaway and getting him into the military after changing not only his name but his age as well! On my grandfather's registration card he was employed by Mr. Felix E. Boswell. At this time, Felix E. Boswell was living in Greensboro and had property in Penfield outside of Boswell Chapel Baptist Church, near Richland Creek. I was shown this property by one of his cousins on one of my many visits to Greene County. So while my grandfather's grandparents Abe and Dinah were in Penfield working for Mr. Felix E. Boswell, he was in the city working for Felix as well.

Arthur Calloway was headed to Kansas. He had companions, such as Anthony Dalton, Johnnie Mapp, and Ralph Hurt, Ellis Webb, George Gresham, and many more from Greene County, Georgia. Before he left I tried to find him on someone's farm working as a servant or in the field. However, I never found Kater or Arthur Calloway in any indenture or deed with any white farmers of Greene County or Oglethorpe. So I had to track him through his grandfather Abraham, and the only document I found on Abraham English was from April 25, 1909, at the Greene County Courthouse. Abraham and Dinah and their son John H. English went to work for P. F. M. Furr, and so did Boss Durham, Charlie Lewis, Jack Love, Bill Mathis, Henry Barnhart, Abe Ellington Jr., and Joe Jeter. Some worked for the Mosley Company. This property was near the Richland Creek. This is the same creek that Granddaddy crossed to visit his soon-to-be wife Effie and to see his niece Ms. Hunter being born. He fell into the creek while on his way to the Brown house near town. This is also how he comes to work for Mr. Felix E. Boswell. As soon as they moved from Oglethorpe from the Hurt and Epps place in Maxey to Mr. Furr's place near Boswell Chapel, Mr. Felix E. Boswell bought the place and the entire chattel that was living on Mr. Furr's place in 1909. Slavery was still alive and thriving under a new system of deeds and mortgages in Georgia. This area is run and ruled by the landowners that knew how to control the labor that they need to further their farming industry of their trade and the Negroes were the pawns in the middle and were still a great necessity in the new South! These large landowners went on to public office for the State of Georgia.

I was given a tour of the property of Mr. Felix E. Boswell by a cousin that opened his house to my wife and I in Penfield. I sat in the presence of a very nice man who could have shut me out. However, he drove me in his truck and he had his hunting rifle and I assumed that was a common thing, because I was sure that you did not go alone into the woods without protection. That's why I had my pistol as well when I went into the woods looking for old abandoned cemeteries. We rode to the property of Cousin Felix, and as he spoke of him in an endearing way, I was amazed by the large places where the row houses or tenant houses were located. I fell into a solemn mood as I saw how my granddaddy, who was about eleven years old at this time, experienced a country life that was full of hard work on this place. It was the same feeling that I got quite often! I wish my other family could know this feeling!

Also, on my tour with Mr. Boswell he told me where Mose Redd's family lived on Highway 15, which I believe was called Greensboro Road in 1910. He said that Mose Redd worked for the Boswells for quite some time and he even knew the children of Mr. Redd. Mose Redd lived next door to Abe and Dinah English and their two grandchildren Kater (Arthur) and Kate (Rosa). The property was just south of the Boswell Store on Highway 15. The property was on a hill at the intersection of Boswell Road and Highway 15; an old dirt road to the right headed toward the town of

Greensboro. This property was just south of the chain gang at the Oconee River, and I must say that the Boswell brothers ran a chain gang at this location around 1915. I read articles of their convicts being drowned in the river about this time! Like I said, some of these large landowners go on to be politicians. I asked about what was told me about my grandfather, how he killed a man to escape from a chain gang and changed his name. He told me that he never heard of the story. So we drove on! I never questioned his answer because the men of these times took secrets to their graves!

Honorable Discharge

FROM THE UNITED STATES ARMY, NAVY, OR MARINE CORPS

Form 319

Certificate in Lieu of Lost or Destroyed

DISCHARGE CERTIFICATE

TO ALL WHOM IT MAY CONCERN:

Know Ye, that Arthur Callaway, a Private 1 cl of Company B Five Hundred Twenty-ninth Engineers United States Army, who was inducted on the thirty-first day of March, one thousand nine hundred and eighteen, at Greensboro, Georgia to serve for period of the emergency was Honorably Discharged from the service of the United States on the seventh day of July, one thousand nine hundred and nineteen, by reason of Demobilization.

THIS CERTIFICATE is given under the provisions of the Act of Congress approved July 1, 1902, "to authorize the Secretary of War to furnish certificates in lieu of lost or destroyed discharges," to honorably discharged officers or enlisted men or their widows, upon evidence that the original discharge certificate has been lost or destroyed, and upon the condition imposed by said Act that this certificate "shall not be accepted as a voucher for the payment of any claim against the United States for pay, bounty, or other allowances, or as evidence in any other case."

Given of the War Department, Washington, D.C., this fourteenth day of May one thousand nine hundred and twenty-eight.

By authority of the Secretary of War:

W. E. Chickering, Adjutant General

TRANSCRIPT FROM RECORD OF SERVICE

Prior service: None
Battles, engagements, expeditions: None
Wounds received in action: None
Decorations, service medals, citations, awarded: None
Service Overseas: France
Sailed from U. S. 1918
Arrived at port on return to U. S. June 27, 1919
Character given on discharge: Excellent
Certificate in Lieu of Lost or Destroyed Discharge Certificate previously issued in this case: None

Recorded May 2, 1956.
W. B. Caldwell, C.S.C.

I found Arthur's honorable discharge—well, Sheila, my wife, found the article filed under the year 1954 at the Greene County Courthouse. She just shouted and exclaimed, "Look, Derrick! Look what I have found!" This wasn't the last time this studious wife of mine would view articles and shout!

I found out that Company B. engineers were under constatant bombardment or shelling. I have much respect for my grandfather after knowing what he went through and now I can understand his stature as a man and his integrity after reading what the colored unit of World War I went throught at this time in 1918. He was one of those in the colored unit who were shipped out in a hurry because he could shoot his rifle with accuracy. I would hear stories that he could use his shotgun without even aiming and was very good at hunting rabbits, and I mean jackrabbits! I can see him as a nineteen-year-old dodging bombs and running for his life. It was told to me that he was even an ambulance driver during the war as well. I was told he would go into the fray of bullets and bombs to get the wounded soldiers, return, and go right back in! He was in the woods of Varennes-en-Argonne, Meuse, France.

He left Greene County for the first time for Kansas then Detroit, Chicago, and Canada, traveling on a big ship for the first time! What an experience for a young man for the very first time. Through young eyes he will never desire the country life in Greene County again! After returning to Greene County, he marries his first wife Effie Brown across Richland Creek.

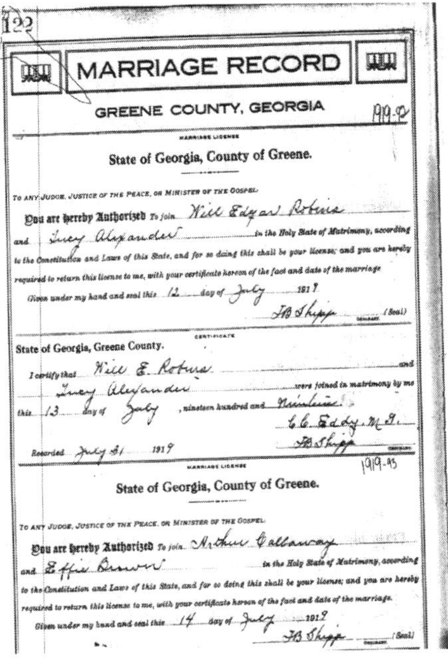
122

MARRIAGE RECORD

GREENE COUNTY, GEORGIA

MARRIAGE LICENSE

State of Georgia, County of Greene.

To any Judge, Justice of the Peace, or Minister of the Gospel:

You are hereby Authorized To join Will Edgar Robins and Lucy Alexander in the Holy State of Matrimony, according to the Constitution and Laws of this State, and for so doing this shall be your license; and you are hereby required to return this license to me, with your certificate hereon of the fact and date of the marriage.

Given under my hand and seal this 12 day of July 1919

F. B. Shipp Ordinary. (Seal)

CERTIFICATE

State of Georgia, Greene County.

I certify that Will E. Robins and Lucy Alexander were joined in matrimony by me this 13 day of July, nineteen hundred and Nineteen.

C. C. Eddy. M. G.

Recorded July 31 1919 F. B. Shipp Ordinary.

1919-93

MARRIAGE LICENSE

State of Georgia, County of Greene.

To any Judge, Justice of the Peace, or Minister of the Gospel:

You are hereby Authorized To join Arthur Callaway and Effie Brown in the Holy State of Matrimony, according to the Constitution and Laws of this State, and for so doing this shall be your license; and you are hereby required to return this license to me, with your certificate hereon of the fact and date of the marriage.

Given under my hand and seal this 14 day of July 1919

F. B. Shipp Ordinary. (Seal)

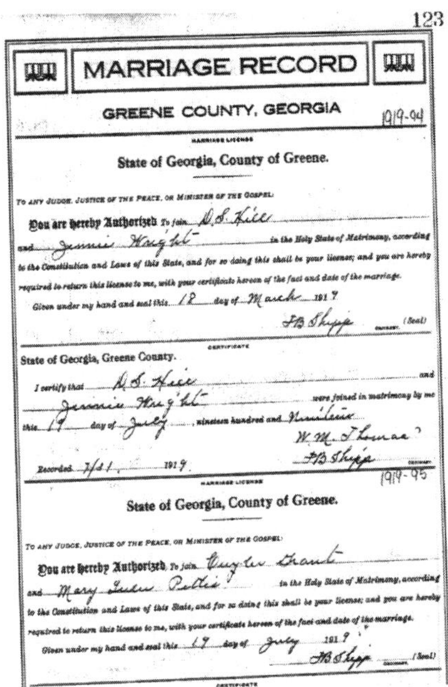
123

MARRIAGE RECORD

GREENE COUNTY, GEORGIA 1919-94

MARRIAGE LICENSE

State of Georgia, County of Greene.

To any Judge, Justice of the Peace, or Minister of the Gospel:

You are hereby Authorized To join D. S. Hill and Jennie Wright in the Holy State of Matrimony, according to the Constitution and Laws of this State, and for so doing this shall be your license; and you are hereby required to return this license to me, with your certificate hereon of the fact and date of the marriage.

Given under my hand and seal this 18 day of March 1919

F. B. Shipp Ordinary. (Seal)

CERTIFICATE

State of Georgia, Greene County.

I certify that D. S. Hill and Jennie Wright were joined in matrimony by me this 19 day of July, nineteen hundred and Nineteen

W. M. Thomas

Recorded 7/31 1919. F. B. Shipp Ordinary.

1919-95

MARRIAGE LICENSE

State of Georgia, County of Greene.

To any Judge, Justice of the Peace, or Minister of the Gospel:

You are hereby Authorized To join [illegible] Grant and Mary Lulu Pettis in the Holy State of Matrimony, according to the Constitution and Laws of this State, and for so doing this shall be your license; and you are hereby required to return this license to me, with your certificate hereon of the fact and date of the marriage.

Given under my hand and seal this 19 day of July 1919

F. B. Shipp Ordinary. (Seal)

CERTIFICATE

Arthur and Effie get married on July 14, 1919. In 1920, Arthur and Effie Callaway are living in Union Point, Georgia, in Greene County. Arthur and Effie are living next door to Mose Haynes and Adeline Haynes and a daughter named Algie and a grandson named Eulas Hall. This family is kin to Robert Callaway in Athens County and is very mysterious to me because I want to know how Robert is a Callaway when his mother's last name is Haynes. Well, after living in Union Point for a little while, Arthur and Effie moved down near Cary Station near Madison, Georgia, in Morgan County. Cary Station was a railroad watering depot. I don't know how long they stayed in Madison until they moved to Atlanta. After moving to Atlanta, they separated. I got this bit of information from a reliable source. Arthur took up with his second wife Rachel. I never found a marriage certificate with Rachel's name on it. I did find them together in Atlanta during the early 1930s, but I couldn't find them in Atlanta in the mid-1920s. Arthur and Rachel could not be foun in the directory in 1920, but Effie Calloway was. I do not know how long Effie and Arthur were in Atlanta before they separtated, but I will assume that Arthur is with Mrs. Effie Callaway on West Peachtree.

In 1930, Mrs. Effie Callaway was still at 45 Eleventh St. N.E. Atlanta at the intersection of Columbia Avenue N.E. across the street from Mr. Alfred Truitt and his wife Ida. Mr. Truitt was a white man selling hats with the white Callaways in his earlier years. Effie Callaway was a servant for Mr. Harry J. Brinsaw. Jennie M. was his wife and Mary F. their daughter. The Brinsaws were proprietors of the boarding house, with Effie Callaway (twenty-five) and James Arnold, a forty-year-old divorced colored man, working for them. After working for the Brinsaw family, Effie was still on or near West Peachtree Street in Atlanta. She shared an apartment with Rosa Lee at 1072 West Peachtree behind Mrs. R. Brawder, her daughter Mary B. Brawder, and her son Douglas and Clyde. Her daughters-in-law Eppie and Evolyn C. and granddaughter Susanne were also with her. Effie's twenty-one-year-old niece was in the house with her as well.

Effie was now listed at the age of thirty-seven. Later on she worked for Mr. Jack Sutler and his wife Lorena, a travel agent who had a house at 871 West Peachtree Street. She continued to work for the Sutler family up until she became paralyzed after she fell trying to reach an item on a high shelf.

My grandfather still visited Mrs. Effie Brown and even carried us to visit her and the McClouds, his cousins, in Decatur up until her death. She worked cleaning apartment homes on West Peachtree for quite a long time.

She was well liked by the Sulter family. I had quite a joyful conversation with the daughter of the Sulters as she mentioned her fond memories of Mrs. Effie in a very affectionate way.

Now, how did I come to know about Mrs. Rachel Calloway, the second wife of Arthur? I came to know her through my visits with Mrs. Hunter, the niece of Mrs. Effie Brown Calloway. She told me as a little girl she and Arthur and Mrs. Rachel went fishing often and she spoke of her in a very endearing and affectionate way too. I thought she might have some anger because of the relationship between who she called Uncle Arthur and Mrs. Effie, her aunt. Mrs. Hunter was very close to my grandfather because she had a lot of respect for her uncle Arthur.

I am going to start in the 1940 census and start by saying Arthur Callaway had a daughter named Liliam or Lillian. Lillian was fifteen in 1940 and her mother Rachel was thirty-four. Their house was at 400 in the Third Ward near where Arthur and Rachel live with Mrs. Wallace in 1930. Rachel and daugher Lillian are sharing a house with Richard Askew and his wife Lizer Askew. Richard Askew was in building construction, while Rachel has nothing listed as her occupation. I'm assuming that they are being taken care of by Mr. Richard Askew. Rachel might be a sister to Mr. Askew or his wife.

In 1930, Arthur Callaway is in two locations. However, the place where he was with Rachel was in the Third Ward of the City of Atlanta in the colored community called Summer Hill. Arthur and Rachel were living on Woodward Street in 1930, just behind Mrs. Emma Lou Wallace, her son-in-law W. D. Coogle, her daughter May W. W. D. Jr., Will Hill and his wife Ruby, twenty-nine-year-old Arthur Callaway and his twenty-four-year-old wife Rachel, and Mr. Ed Williams and wife Julia were the only coloreds living in the rooming house of Mrs. Emma L. Wallace. I thought it was strange that in 1930 Mrs. Wallace would have three colored families in the rooming house with a white family in a white neighborhood!

Granddaddy Arthur was a mortar maker doing construction work. This living situation tells me about the character of the roomers of Mrs. Emma L. Wallace. Rachel stays with Mrs. Emma L. Wallace and Arthur moves onto Chestnut Avenue near Courtland Avenue and Piedmont Avenue in 1940. At this place my grandfather meets my grandmother Georgia Mae Robinson and her son Wallace Robinson. Georgia Mae was nineteen and Wallace was at the tender age of one. The mother and son were living with her mother Betty Mae and Ludie Fallen, a forty-two-year-old laborer in building construction. Eulas Jones was eighteen, Lugenia was sixteen, and Lilly was fifteen. My grandmother and Aunt Lillie were working for St. Joseph Hospital as waitresses. All lived at 121 Chestnut Avenue, paying rent at nine dollars a month. They lived in an odd-numbered house on Chestnut Avenue while my grandfather lived across the street on the even side of the avenue.

Aunt Lillie told me of Mr. Ludie Fallin. She told me that Granddaddy George lived on Piedmont Avenue. I could not prove this! The census taker Dora G. Odom went down Chestnut Avenue on April 9, 1940. It was on the same day that she went down the even side of Chestnut Avenue to visit Granddaddy Arthur's house at 128b. Arthur was on one side of the house and Ida Elligan was on the other side. Arthur Calloway was listed under the first name Abe, who was at the age of forty-nine and divorced. Ida was a twenty-seven-year-old divorcee. Arthur was now working at the steel mill. This statement verifies what my grandmother told me that Arthur was working in the steel mill when she met him. When he was in the house with Rachel, he worked as a mortar mixer. I worked a wheelbarrow, mixing mortar for him as a young teenage boy growing up with my father/granddaddy.

There is one man and his family that moves wherever Granddaddy moves, and that is Mr. Oscar Stone. Oscar Stone follows him quite often from Grove Street to Techwood. The housemates of Granddaddy Arthur were Mr. Mack Smith and Mrs. Martishia Hawthorne. Now, remember my granddaddy was a colored gangster! He ran liquor and other criminal activities that a gangster did!

It was April 10, 1930 and Howard M. Fisher was the census taker for the Sixth Ward of the Atlanta Bureau on Block 76. Arthur Callaway is forty years old and Silvey his wife is twenty-six. Living with them are roomers Mack Smith and Marticia Hawthorne. Mack was thirty and Marticia was forty years old. Now, there is one family that I am interested in, that of Walter Cloud and Marie. They are twenty-two years old. Now, my granddaddy might have rented this place at 422 Techwood Drive from Ms. Francis Moody. I don't know what the relationship between the two was but I know he is never too far from the women! I assume his good looks and his high yellow complexion were very attractive to the ladies in his life, and I mean many ladies in his life! He lived in the houses of the many women and never had to use his name in the Atlanta Directory. Ms. Francis lived at 422 or 424 Techwood from 1927 to 1929, after Mr. Arthur and Silvey Callaway and Mack Smith and Martitia Hawthorne moved out in 1931. I believe that Francis Moody was close to Arthur's brother. I also believe that she grew up in Bowling Green in Oglethorpe County, Georgia, in the house of Abraham and Mary Moody, her parents, and her sister Rosa and her brother Isiah. Francis is the same age as Charlie, Arhur's brother. She was born February 1884. I assume that Arthur would come to know her through his elder brother Charlie when he moved into the Techwood area. I heard some interesting stories about his moving into Techwood in the 1920s during the height of the KKK movement. He was a veteran of World War I and knew about explosives. He rigged an explosive during one of the visits of the Clan one night after they put out notice of their arrival. He came into the black community and everyone was terrified, and he said, "What's going on?" They said, with fear in their hearts, "The KKK is a-marching." He said (with expletives not to be mentioned), "What the —— are y'all scared of? I ain't scared of no —— KKK!" That night the Clan were run out of Techwood. Now, while Arthur was at the house of Francis Moody in Techwood in Atlanta, she was living with Sam Mosley and his wife Ada on Francis Street, at the intersection of Chestnut in the First Ward. Francis is forty-five, Sam is thirty-nine, and Ada is thirty-six years old.

I don't know if Mamie Cloud is the cousin of Arthur who married George McCloud. I know Arthur is a man that is very smart at changing his name and living incognito. It was April 5, 1930 when he was in the Third Ward of Atlanta in Summer Hill. Now, the only other time that I found Arthur and Rachel together was in 1935 when they were living at 926 Grove Street in northwest Atanta, north from Pillion to Fourteenth, two blocks east of Howell Mill Road. He was not too far from the Eighth Street intersection. However, Rachel must still have strong feelings for Arthur.

After the death or surpossed death of Charlie Callaway in 1936, his brother Arthur and Rachel were now living in separate locations. And by 1940 he had been separated from her four years before marrying my grandmother Georgia Mae Robinson. Arthur was a very hard person to keep track of in Atlanta. Remember, I had him in April of 1930 in two places, once in Summer Hill district and another time at the Techwood section of Atlanta. From what I remember of what the McCloud brothers told me, he carried two pearl-handled guns, one on each side for protection while hauling his liquor and other activities while in Atlanta. He was a colored man that could pass as a white man and got out of sticky situations with the law with the help of white men! Wherever we traveled when I was growing up in his house, both white men and colored men called him Mr. Calloway!

Emma L. Wallace had some kind of dilemma at her house, and it was Rachel and Arthur Calloway. In 1931, at Mrs. Emma L. Wallace's house—according to the Atlanta Directory, at 402 Woodward Avenue—Rachel is under the last name of Calhoun. However, the gangster Arthur Calloway couldn't be found in the directory under Calhoun. As a matter of fact, when Arthur and his first wife Effie moved to Atlanta only Effie's name could be found in the early twenties! It was only in 1929 that he shows up at 444 Strong Street on the northwest side of the City of Atlanta, living was a lady named Belle. I believe that this is Rachel! Well, about the same time, his brother Charlie was at 82 Hunnicutt Street in Techwood and is on the chain gang. His wife Emma is under the last name of Webber in the directory. Arthur and Rachel are living under the last name of Calhoun from 1931 to 1934.

Arthur and Rachel were last seen together in 1935. The were living at 926a Grove Street in Northwest Atlanta. While they were living here, Arthur's brother Charlie died of a stroke and was carroed back by Hanley Funeral Home to Greene County to be buried. He had just returned from being in the prison out near the Chattahoochee River. When Charlie returned from prison, his wife Emma had moved from Hunnicutt Street to Currier Street in northeast Atlanta. I don't know why his wife of thirty-three years didn't sign his death certificate. However, Arthur signed his name as the informant.

By year 1936, Arthur and Rachel Calloway are seperated. However, while they were together they led quite an exciting gangster lifestyle together. Arthur was always under a new first name or last name in Atlanta. I found him living in 1929 in the house with a preacher that had a church in Atlanta, as well as in Athens, Clarke County. His name was Rev. Cyrus Brown at 402 Rock Street. Cozy was living at 401 Rock Street. However, there was no 401 Rock Street! He could be with Ms. Nora Knox or Ms. Katie M. Freeman. I believe that these are rooms that are being rented by Rev. Cyrus Brown.

After this, Arthur is living in two locations in Atlanta, one is in the Third Ward on Woodward Street and the other is on Omre or Techwood Drive near Hunnicutt near his brother Charlie and his sister-in-law Emma. He has in the house with him Mack Smith and Martishia Hawthorne. My aunt Lillie told me about these two people. Mrs. Hawthorne could pass as a white woman and so could Mack Smith, and they both loved to drink their liquor! Arthur might have met Mack Smith in the Sixth wWrd on Hunnicutt Street near his brother Charlie. Mack is a veteran of the war as well. He was stationed at Fort Gordon in Chamblee, Georgia. Charlie and Emma were living at 82 Hunnicutt and Mack Smith was at 85c Hunnicutt. Mattie Kendrick was 85d, with Lucy Parks at apartment 86. Robert Lattimore was at 85b, and Farmer Reynolds was 85a. Another Nora with the last name Dean was across the street from Charlie and Emma in house 84.

In 1940, Arthur's partners in liquor running are living at 9b Ripley Alley N.W. in Atlanta in the Third Ward, in block 54. I wanted to know why my grandfather would come to reside on Chestnut Avenue or in this section of Atlanta. So I took a journey through the years to see what would bring him to this side of town. In the year 1920, Mollie Jackson, a forty-nine-year-old widow had living with her, her son Willie, who was thirty-one, and Irene, who was twenty-seven. Sharing the property at house number one was Wiley Callaway, a forty-seven-year-old man, and his twenty-seveny-year-old wife Susie, as well as a boarder by the name of Rosa L. Burke, who was twenty-two. Also sharing the same property was Mariah Callaway, a seventy-six-year-old widow, and her daughter Susie, who was twenty-four. All lived at the corner of Chestnut Avenue and Alabaster Alley in 1920. I must mention the Dean family that was living on Alabaster Alley as well. Marrie B. Dean was a thirty-three-year-old widow, and her son Raymond was nine, Eugenia was six, and Lena B. was four. I mention them because in 1940 Wylie Calloway is sixty-seven and is lodging in the house with Lucille Dean on Piedmont Avenue near the intersection of Chestnut Avenue with her daughters Beatrice (sixteen) and Mercedia (fourteen).

In block 41 on Chestnut at 185 lived a younger Ollie Willingham at the age of twenty and his wife Warnell and their daughter Catherine. My grandfather's cousins the McClouds told me of the Good family, who were friends of the family. And living near Ollie and his wife were Katie Good, a thirty-nine-year-old widow, and her daughter Mary, who was sixteen, at 191 Chestnut Avenue. They had their grandmother Sarah Carter, who was eighty at this time.

Let's visit my great-grandmother Betty Mae Jones's house again. Remember she is living with Ludie Fallin in 1940. By 1941, the directory has my aunt Lillie and her husband George Stewart at 121 Chestnut Avenue with Mack Smith across the street in 120 ½. My aunt Lillie and her husband George would come to know Mack Smith and Marticia Hawthorne well because of their loud fighting. Ms. Ida Elligan is at 128 ½ where my grandfather lived and Mrs. Eugenia Coleman is now sharing the house where Arthur once resided. George Lattimore and Jos. Harper are at 130 and 130 ½. Oscar Stone is at 132 Chestnut. The Stone family somehow follows Arthur and Charlie Calloway. I believe they are part of the liquor trafficking as well. I followed them coming out of Walton County, one of the biggest wet counties in Georgia! Between 1944 and 1945, Mrs. Betty M. Jones and Lillie J. Stewart had a beauty shop at 121 Chestnut Avenue. Mack Smith and Marticia are still located across the street at 120 ½. they share a house with Nollie Finch. To tell you the truth, I had a hard time trying to figure out what is going on at 121 Chestnut Avenue. The house is now being rented by Ms. Olivia Daniels.

Mrs. Olivia Daniels is the aunt of my grandmother and her siblings. In 1930 she was living in Wilkes County with Lillie Grant, my fifty-four-year-old great-great-grandmother. Olivia was nineteen, Lillie was seventeen, M. L. Grant was ten, and adopted son Leroy Richardson was ten months old. In 1940, Granny Lilly was now sixty years old and paying three dollars for rent at her house in the Gully Town section of the City of Washington in Wilkes County, Georgia. Olivia Daniel is now twenty-nine, Lillie Grant is twenty-six, M. L. is now twenty-four, grandaughter Lillie V. Daniel is ten, and Bernice Daniel is seven. Olivia moved into the house at 121 Chestnut Avenue in 1945 with her sister Betty Mae Jones.

Now, there was another woman that my grandfather had ties to and her name was Mrs. Dora Mckinney. This lady causes me to believe that out of Greene or Walton County and Charlie Calloway Jr. are living two lives. I haven't figured out who has two wives. I strongly believe that it is Cornelious out of Walton County! I will start with this fact about Mrs. Dora Mckinney out of Gwinnett. While in 1929, she is living at 1 Irby Street. Irby Street is west from Roswell Road, north of Pace's Ferry Road. My granddad is living at 444 Strong Street in Atlanta in 1929 near Gray St. Living in house 446 is Ora Sherman, and house 447 is Lula Fisher's. Now, Mrs. Dora would live between the two places. In 1926, Mrs. Dora was living at 1 Irby Street in Buckhead. She might be living between the two places because she is having her house built or she is in the liquor business and bootlegging. She had her humble beginnings in Pinkneyville, Georgia, or Norcross, as I had always known it to be called while growing up in Buckhead myself.

In 1900, she was there with her husband Darlin and their children Sherman R., Bertha, Verla, Louise, and a lodger named Jasper Millican. However, I want to talk about Darlin McKinney first. In 1880, Darlin

McKinney was ten years old living with his father Miles McKinney and his mother Charity. Both were in their forties and living in the Berkshire District of Gwinnett County, Georgia. He was off Charles McKinney's place, a white landowner who was well up in age in 1880, living with his daughter Elizabeth and a Wm. T. Goldsmith. I assume that Goldsmith was there courting his daughter. He was a thirty-four-year-old man and Charles's daughter was twenty-seven. Darling had siblings Mathew, his elder brother, who was fourteen, Johnson who was eight, Daniel was five, and Clinton was two years old.

Now, let us turn our attention toward Arthur's brothers. I have already mentioned Robert, now I want to talk about the brother that he was closest to. His name was Charlie. In 1900, Charlie was a servant in the house of J. L. Epps at the age of fifteen years old. He was born Feburary 1885 and living next door to his grandfather Abe English, his grandmother Dinah, aunts and uncle, and his brothers and sisters. He would move from this property of Mr. Epps to Beaverdam to work on the farm of Mr. J. T. Irwin. J. T. is the same man that beat his father in Clarke County in Youngs Stables in Athens in 1899! He's better known as Tom Irwin. Young Charlie marries Emma Crawford on May 15, 1909. Rev. J. S. C. Strickland was the minister who performed the wedding. I believe that Emma was out of Lincoln County, Georgia. I found an Emma about the age of Charlie's wife in 1880 with her father Rich and mother Josephine and siblings Mattie, Lula, Hattie, Richard, Jefferson, and a seventy-five-year-old grandfather named Jackson Crawford. Emma is being raised in the same place where I found Green Callaway, the father of Charlie, and Clayborn family in 1870. As a matter of fact, this family is so close to the Reed family that my grandfather told his son Eulas that he might be marrying kin! Eulas told us this at the homecoming of his mother Georgia Mae Calloway. Charlie, after leaving Oglethorpe County in 1900, either moved to the property of Mr. Tom Irwin, one of the men indicted in the beating of his father Charlie Sr. between 1896 and 1899.

Young Charlie Callaway had to obey the order of the Oglethorpe County courts to fulfill the contract of his father Charlie and his mother Mary after the writ of habus corpus against their grandmother Dinah English. Charlie appears in Beaverdam 1906. He is there with his brother Howard. I don't quite know if Will Callaway got out with the help of Peg-Leg Williams in 1900. Whatever, he never shows up in Beaverdam even though he was to work for William Eberhart, who was now living in Cornelia, Georgia. Charlie and Howard are in Beaverdam in 1907 with

Dave Bird, Wilson Bronner, Elias Baugh, Lige Butler, Mary Butler, and others, and no Will Callaway, their brother!

I don't know what happened to Will he was in the house with Howard and Aaron and Harriet, his wife, whom I believe is Mary, the wife of Charlie, or the daughter of Aaron. Willie Howard the son of Aaron is in Beaverdam in 1900. He Will was born March 1894 and was six years old, and Howard was born May 1892 and was eight years old. Aaron was listed as being dead on the census down in Greene County, yet he's alive in Beaverdam with another Harriet who is old enough to be his daughter and his son Willie Howard who shows up for the first time as being Aaron Calloway's son! What is this confussion and why is there so much confussion. If Charley is dead, then he's just another dead Negro, right? If this is so, why all the lies?

In the year 1909, in Beaverdam, the only Callaway that resided there was Howard Callaway. Charlie marries Emma Crawford in May 23, 1909,

Charlie, died in 1935, right after he was released from the chain gang out on Moores Mill Road. When Charlie Callaway died, while living with my grandfather at 926a Grove Street in northwest Atlanta. Charlie was seperated from his wife at the time of his death. Now, in the year 1936, Charlie shows up working for a Mr. Walter H. Aiken. Walter was born in Delaware and lived in New York City. However, in 1940, Walter lived at 66 Piedmont Avenue in Atlanta with his wife Lucy, and the both of them were in their late forties. Walter worked in construction with his brother-in-law Jefferson Rucker. I am sure that Granddaddy was under his brother's name at this time. He was working in construction and the iron works in Atlanta as well. Charlie and Arthur are the only two children that I found living in Atlanta among his counsins.

I don't know if they are living with other family members of Aaron or their sisters that might be married now and under different last names. I do have a Rosa Calloway that lived in the Third Ward as well. She might have been a cousin or the daughter of Birt and Rosa in Morgan County, Georgia. She was buried by her brother Robert in Morgan County in Rutledge, Georgia.

As I have stated before, Arthur Calloway lived a very interesting life in Atlanta, like many of his family who relocated from the country to the city life! Also while living in northwest Atlanta in 1936, he is living at Corput Street with George McCloud and his wife Aunt Carrie, the cousin of Arthur. Aunt Carrie is the daughter of Sallie English and Tiller Barnett of Greene County. In 1910, Carrie was six years old in the house of her momma and daddy in Scull Shoals on the banks of the Oconee River with her brothers Walter, George, and Howard.

George Aaron McCloud was born in 1895 and living in Wilcox County, Georgia, in March 1900, with Jim McCloud Jr. and Martha, his mother. In 1910, in Turner County, George A. McCloud is twelve years old and the nephew of Isaac Fuller and his wife Vena. Vena's son is named Samuel Fuller, a stepson, and Andrew Sheild, a nephew at the age of eleven. George Jones and Mandy Jones are living next door. I do not know if they are any kin to the Fuller or McCloud family but I do know that there is a Mary Jones pictured on the wall of my grandfather's cousin's house. It was told to me that she was kin. Mrs. Jones was a full-fledged white Irishwoman! I was told this by Arthur's cousins the sons of Aunt Carrie Barnett McCloud.

BRANTLY AND HOWARD AND WILLIE IN MICHIGAN

It looks like Brantley, Howard, and Willie all moved up north to Michigan. Brantley arrived in Michigan in the early 1920s. Brantley was living in Greene County in 1900 up until 1912, before moving onto the property of J. T. Irwin with his brothers. The story goes that both my grandfather and Brantley rode Harley-Davidsons to Michigan. However, I haven't found anything definitive about Arthur being in Michigan. Now, he might have been in Michigan under a different name in the twenties when I could not find him in Georgia, and he could very well be in Virginia as well. I say this because I have not found a marriage certificate between Arthur and Rachel. Now, Brantley, before moving to Michigan, would marry Carrie Houston in Clarke County. While working for Thomas Irwin, he joined the military during World War I. He was born in Winterville, Georgia, on May 10, 1895. He had only one child. He was medium height, medium build, had black hair and black eyes. He was living in Beaverdam on June 5, 1917.

Brantley was now twenty-four years old and living with his twenty-one-year-old wife Carrie and their two children, three-year-old Perlina and nine-month-old Willoughby, in an apartment at 445 Macolm Street in Michigan in the Second District of Wayne County in apartment number 117 in the Ninth Ward on January 9, 1920. Perlina was the one child in 1917 in Winterville, Georgia.

In the year 1930, in Michigan, I had a hard time finding Brantley and his daughter Perlina. However, I did find Carrie living with a man with the last name of Gresham! The strangest thing is George Gresham is the same age as Brantley. George is thirty-eight years old and is married. Carrie is a lodger in the house at the age of thirty-two and is married. Willie B., Carrie's son, is eleven years old. John Button is thirty-seven years old and is divorced. Luther Lighton is twenty-eight and is married as well. All are living at 2716 Hastings or Hostings street, sharing a building with a Birtha Franklin, a twenty-seven-year-old, and twenty-six-year-old Lula Montgomery. Birtha Franklin is out of South Carolina and Lula is out of Alabama. They are living in the Sixth Precinct of Wayne County, Michigan, in 1930. Now, there is a situation, and it is with Brantley and his wife Carrie. It is with Mrs. Franklin, whom they are sharing an apartment with. In 1940, Brantley is living with Edward Franklin, a twenty-three-year-old colored man out of Georgia. Brantley is working as a watchman for a construction company. Edward sets pins for a bowling alley. Brantley must have learned the trade in construction while on his place in Beaverdam, Oglethorpe County, Georgia. As a matter of fact, all of the Callaways that I come across were well versed in construction. From plumbing, carpentry, and electrical work to laying foundations for houses. Brantley left his wife Carrie and son Willoughby and was now paying rent at 2239 St. Antoine Steet. He is sharing an apartment with Henry Burnes or Barnes and his wife Ruth and a lodger name Clara Carr and her daughter Alice. Henry is in apartment 91 and Brantley and Edward Franklin are in apartment 92. I believe that Brantley has two women in his life in 1930 while living under the last name Gresham.

On April 27, 1942, at the age of forty-seven, Brantley registers to fight in the Second World War. He is five feet five inches tall, and weighs 175lbs., with black eyes and black hair, and his complexion is light brown. When I was reading the description of Brantley, it was like I was describing my grandfather Arthur. Could it be that the argument that I vehemently defended against my aunt Lillie could be false and that Arthur did have a twin? Could it be true? It was in 2013 that I might have spoken to my aunt Lillie that I said to her that it was true that Arthur was born in 1899 and his mother died in childbirth. However, could It be that in changing Arthur's (Kator's) name and age they put Granddaddy Arthur in the likeness of the twin sister of Brantley, Annie Sib, who were both under contract with William Eberhart. Both were born in 1896. Either she died or they listed him as Annie Sib and not Kator as a twin. However, William

Eberhart didn't mention her in his writ of habeas corpus against Dinah in 1900. In 1942, Brantley was living at 1340 Rivard Street in Wayne County, Michigan, with Wallace Boyd out of Greene County, Georgia. He was unemployed and living in a rooming house alone and was resolved to go to war for his country once more! Brantley says that he was born in Columbia, Georgia, and more than likely raised in Clarke County, Georgia! I don't think that Clarke County has a district named Columbia. So it might be that Brantley was born in Columbia County. Brantley, in 1942, wrote on the dotted line. He wrote his name in a simular fashion as Arthur wrote his name for his brother Charlie in 1935. Now, before Brantley signs his name in 1942, his wife Carrie is living with Viola Deharry and young man Ezeikel Sinclair at 1479 Layfayette Street in the Seventh Ward of Wayne County, Michigan, while Brantley was in the Third Ward of Wayne County, Michigan, in 1940. Where he registered for the war while living with Wallace Boyd in the Fifth Ward in 1942. The question is what happened to Brantley that he would be in such a dillema and almost homeless! Is it the lifestyle that I hear so frequently about the Callaway brothers, liquor runners?

I did find out what might have happened to Perlina, the daughter of Brantley Calloway. Perlina Inez Calloway Boyd was born August 20, 1943, and died October 9, 2006. William Brantley Callaway, the son of Brantley, was born April 11, 1918. He was born in Athens, Clarke County, Georgia, to Brantley Callaway and Carrie C. Houston. He died July 8, 1996. I have never met this side of my family even though I have traveled through Athens, Clarke County, Georgia, often in my fifty-three years. I was even posted there while in the Army Reserve, near the airport. The secrets that were kept even to the grave have lasted for so long because of a generation of men, both black and white, who could not acccept the truth and still can't accept it even today that their parents might be Black and living as White or that they could have a Black father in the family or a Black Mother living as a White Woman

Now I want to talk about Howard Calloway. Howard was born in 1888 and resided with Aaron and Harriet in Beaverdam, Oglethorpe County, Georgia in 1900, with Willie, his brother, on Mr. William Eberhart's property. Aaron, their grandfather, was born March 1827 and was seventy-three years old. Harriet, his wife, was born March 1862 and was thirty-eight. William H., a son born in April 1878, was twenty-two. A lodger by the name of John Clarke was born in April 1870 was thirty years old. Charlie Eberhart was born May 1881 and was nineteen and lodging in the house of Aaron and Harriett Calloway on Mr. William Eberhart's land. Aaron and Harriet had been married only five years. Now, these are the grandchildren's mother, Mary, living with Aaron while Charlie is somewhere in Elbert County or dead! I am assuming that Mary is under the first name of Harriet in 1900 in Beaverdam, Oglethorpe County, Georgia. I say this because Mary and Aaron have a contract with William Eberhart up until 1901! The two of them are under contract and the paperwork of the contracts put them both on the property of William Eberhart farm in Beaverdam.

Georgia, Oglethorpe County.

This Indenture, Made this the 12th day of October, 1897, between Wm Eberhart and Mary Calloway of said county:

Witnesseth, That the said Mary Calloway in consideration of the promises and undertakings of the said Wm Eberhart hereinafter set forth does hereby bind herself to the said Wm Eberhart for the full term of three years from this date, 1897, and she hereby agrees and contracts with said William Eberhart to work faithfully under his directions; respect and obey all orders and commands of the said Wm Eberhart with reference to the business hereinafter set forth; at all times demean herself orderly and soberly; and the said Mary Calloway further agrees to account to the said Wm Eberhart for all loss of time except in case of temporary sickness. If such sickness should be of longer duration at any one time than six days, then said lost time is to be accounted for at the same rate per day as she is then receiving pay under the contract. And should this contract be terminated by the death of either of the parties to this indenture, then the compensation of said Mary Calloway shall be pro rata for the time completed for the year in which the death may occur. And the said Wm Eberhart in consideration of the promises and undertakings of the said Mary Calloway agrees and contracts with said Mary Calloway to furnish her with board, lodging, ~~every day wearing apparel and washing~~. He further agrees to pay said Mary Calloway annually, on the 12th day of October each year the following sums of money, to-wit:

On the 12th day of October 1898 Thirty Dollars;
on 12th Oct 1899, Thirty Dollars;
on 12th Oct 1900, Thirty Dollars;
on 12th April 1901, Fifteen Dollars;
on 190 Dollars;

and he further agrees to teach the said Mary Calloway the trade of Farming in all its details.

In Witness whereof, the said Wm Eberhart and the said Mary Calloway have hereto respectively set their hands and seals the day and year first above written.

Executed in duplicate in presence of
[illegible]
[illegible], J. P.

Wm Eberhart (L. S.)
Mary her x mark Calloway (L. S.)

Filed in office for record this 5th day of Dec. 1897
[illegible], Ordinary.

Recorded this 5th day of Dec. 1897
[illegible]
Clerk Court of Ordinary, Oglethorpe Co.

Georgia, Oglethorpe County.

This Indenture, Made this the 30th day of August 1897, between William Eberhart and Aaron Callaway of said county.

Witnesses, That the said Aaron Callaway in consideration of the promises and undertakings of the said William Eberhart hereinafter set forth does hereby bind himself to the said William Eberhart for the full term of three years from January 1st, 1898, and he hereby agrees and contracts with said William Eberhart to work faithfully under his directions; respect and obey all orders and commands of the said William Eberhart with reference to the business hereinafter set forth; at all times demean himself orderly and soberly, and the said Aaron Callaway further agrees to account to the said William Eberhart for all loss of time except in case of temporary sickness. If such sickness should be of longer duration at any one time than six days, then said lost time is to be accounted for at the same rate per day as he is then receiving pay under the contract. And should this contract be terminated by the death of either of the parties to this indenture, then the compensation of said Aaron Callaway shall be pro rata for the time completed for the year in which the death may occur. And the said William Eberhart in consideration of the promises and undertakings of the said Aaron Callaway agrees and contracts with said Aaron Callaway to furnish him with board, lodging, ~~[struck out]~~ He further agrees to pay said Aaron Callaway annually, on the First day of January each year the following sums of money, to-wit:

On the First day of January 1899 Sixty Dollars;
on 1st January, 1900 Sixty Dollars;
on 1st January, 1901 Sixty Dollars;
on 1st , 190 Dollars;
on , 190 Dollars.

and he further agrees to teach the said Aaron Callaway the trade of Husbandry in all its details.

In Witness whereof, the said Aaron Callaway and the said William Eberhart have hereto respectively set their hands and seals the day and year first above written.

Executed in duplicate in presence of
J. C. Fleeman
W. T. Carter J. P.

William Eberhart (L.S.)
Aaron his x mark Callaway (L.S.)

Filed in office for record this 2d day of Sept 1897
J. J. Bacon Ordinary.

Recorded, this 2d day of Sept 1897
J. J. Bacon
Clerk Court of Ordinary, Oglethorpe Co.

Howard married Mary Hannah Harvey in Clarke County on April 22, 1909, with Rev. J. T. Henry as the minister of the gospel. In 1910, he was living with his mother-in-law at 320 Vine Street in Athens. However, before moving to Michigan, I believe, he resided in Atlanta. In 1917, Howard was working for the Atlanta Steel Company at the Atlantic Plant near Brookwood in Buckhead. He lived at #7 Box Street with his wife. Howard said that he was born in Athens in 1888. He was not very sure.

Howard stood about five feet eleven inches, with medium complexion. By the year 1919, Howard Callaway was in Michigan. He is listed in the Michigan Directory at this time. I do not know if his brother Brantley is with him or not. While his name was in the Michigan Directory in 1919, he had been in Michigan since September 20, 1918. On this day in 1918, he married Ms. Annie Raglea, who was also born in Georgia. Howard is running from something or somebody in Georgia since the time he fills out his draft card for 1917. I say this because when he marries he says that he was born in 1870 and was forty-eight years old and his wife was forty-two. I wonder what made him flee Georgia so fast, get married so fast, and change his age so fast! Or could it be the trouble that Charlie is into with receiving stolen merchandise from the railroad in 1917? He might be dodging the draft for World War I. This could be the reason for him changing his age. When your life is in danger, fear makes many go to the extremes and do strange things! If this is the case, Kator and Howard are two different kinds of people. Kator changed his name to join up and Howard did the opposite. Howard could have left Georgia because of Mr. Tom Irwin of Oglethorpe County, Georgia. Tom was known for chasing down indentured servants to Chicago and returning them to his farm. When Howard left Atlanta, I believe that he left Mary to live in the city alone because he had to make a hasty departure for his life. Mary Harvey decided to remain in Atlanta.

The 1920 census tells the real ages of Mr. Howard Calloway and Mrs. Annie Callaway on Monroe Avenue.

Annie was married to Howard in September of 1918. By January 18, 1930, they were divorced. It took two years. She filed on November 20, 1928. Howard did not contest. She said that she was divorcing him due to extreme cruelty and abandonment, and Howard had to pay $1.00 for alimony because they had no children. On March 25, 1930, a certificate of marriage between Howard Calloway and Ms. Ada Lewis was granted by Marion A. Pettis. Howard was living at 1435 Grant Avenue. his father was Charlie Calloway and his mother was named Mary (unknown). Howard says he was born in Georgia, and in 1930 he was forty years old. Ms. Ada Lewis was living at 1445 St. John Street. Both were in Genesee, Flint Michigan. I assume that the two were waiting for a judge to come to a decision and after the divorce was finalized in January they got married in March. Ms. Ada was born in Texas. Her father was named James Lewis and her mother was unknown. They were married by Rev. C. W. James of the Shiloh Baptist Church and Mrs. Nicie James and Mrs. Minnie Reaves (Reed) witnessed this union.

Howard, on September 21, 1942, led the way for his brother Brantley to do the same thing in April. Howard was five foot six inches tall and had black hair and black eyes, and had a black complextion, or they just listed him as being black. Howard weighed 165 pounds. Now he says he was born December 25, 1897 Howard resided at 1820 Clifford Street in Michigan. Mr. Ronald Clayton, a white man, would always know his address and whereabouts. As you can see, Howard changed his age quite often. I wonder if this is the reason I can't find anything about his death. Now, during his separation from his first wife Annie and before his divorce was finalized in 1930, Howard was visiting his brother William and his wife Harriet in Sandwich, Ontario, Canada. This could be the reason Annie said that he abandond her in her divorce papers. Howard was listed at the age of thirty-five years old and was living in Monroe in Michigan and was a Baptist and a laborer. He was born in Athens, Georgia. Howard is the only Negro making this journey into Canada on April 30, 1929. Now I was very pleased while Howard and his wife Ada resided in a house at 1908 Jasmine. Howard is a factory work in the Chevolette factory and residing in the house with Howard and Ada is Mr. Robert C. Callaway an employer for the YMCA, Cafeteria. Who is this Robert C. Callaway in the house with Howard. I could only guess that it could be his brother Charlie or his father.

When Brantley seperated from Carrie in 1940, he moved back to a place he was familiar with when he first arrived in Michigan, back to St. Antoine Street.

For whatever reason, Brantley, Howard, and Willie made their way to the north. I do not know if it was by choice or from having to flee Tom Irwin's place! Could it be that they were looking for some of their families that might have left between 1899 and 1900 with the help of Peg-Leg Williams, who was operating in the areas of Clarke, Greene, and Oglethorpe counties of Georgia? And was moving Blacks to Ohio where they could have migrated to Michigan into Canada as well.

Now, I know that I haven't profiled Willie Calloway, who was in the house with Aaron and young Harriet in Beaverdam, Oglethorpe County in 1900. He was one of the hardest to profile in Michigan and even in Atlanta and Clarke County. He never shows up in the tax digest of Clarke County as a young man; neither does he show up in Oglethorpe County on Tom Irwin's place with Charlie and Brantley and Howard. I wonder where he could be during the beginning of World War I. Well, I found a Willie Calloway in Clarke County in the 220th District working for a Mr. C. E. Mathews. Willie stated that he was born on April 10, 1896. I was very happy to see this WWI record; however, the year he was born in would put him at the same age as Brantley! But the month Willie said he was born in leads me to believe that this is my grandfather's brother, because Brantley was born May 10, 1895.

Now, the only person that I have seen with the Mathews were Charley and Sam Boykins when they broke into the Mathews and Hutchins place in 1886.

I thought Willie was being raised in the house of Robert Callaway in Clarke County however Robert has his own son named William working as a farm tenant on his place. Then I thought I found him in Chamblee, Georgia, but he was born in 1874. In 1900, Willie was born March 1894 while in the house with Aaron and his young wife Hattie. However, William, the son of Robert Calloway, was born in October 1894, only months apart. The William who is the son of Robert Callaway born in October is William A. Callaway listed in the 1900 census as being born in October of 1891. At the time of his enlistment into the First World War, he was living in Jackson County, Georgia! Robert's son William married a Ms. Cornelia and later moved to Atlanta in the Third Ward.

Now, turning my attention to Will Calloway, the brother of my grandfather Arthur (Kator) in Michigan! I have to prove that he is my grandfather's brother. I have a (white) William Copelan Callaway in Michigan during registrations in 1917. He was born May 1, 1895, and was living at 355 Brush Street in Detroit, Michigan. He states that he was born in Macon, Georgia, and was single at this time. He was medium height, medium weight, dark brown eyes, and black hair. This same William joined World War II as well. He stated that he did not know his middle name. He was born on December 25, 1895 instead of May of 1895. In 1900, Aaron or Harriett stated that Willie was born in March of 1894. The Willie in Michigan and who is moving between two countries, the United States and Canada, is my grandfather's brother, whom he could not find as the stories were told by my aunt Lillie and the McCloud brothers.!

I believe that Will Calloway disappeared with Aaron and Harriett Callaway after 1901 when Mary and Aaron's contract was up with William Eberhart. For him to show up in Michigan and to be living in Canada, I was glad to research Canada's records through *Ancestry.com*. I found him when Howard was visiting him in 1929. However, I did find a William Calloway born in Georgia in 1891, but his parents were born in Virginia. I don't quite know what to think about his parents being born in Virginia, because this is the same place where my grandfather Arthur stated that he was from while living in the Third Ward of Atlanta with his second wife Rachel. Also another reason to believe that Willie Callaway in Canada and in Michigan is that he is the same age as the son of Robert C. Callaway of Athens, Georgia.

This arisocratic society that influenced the South in a great way might be where Charlie and Mary and Aaron and even Will fled to in Virginia. While living in Virginia they could very well be passing themselves off as being white. The very well could have met Charlie in Virginia maybe after his departure of the chain-gang in Elbert County. I say this because of the rail road that was there in 1899. The rail road was SAL or the Seaboard Airline Rail Road and the Southern Rail Road had an express rout from Jacksonville to Virginia. Maybe I will find out the mystery after my book goes into print and published. I do know that Howard visited his brother while he was separated from his first wife Annie. He went over into Canada to visit his brother Will and his wife Mary. Now Will, who was rooming in Michigan, was a widower rooming with a Mr. Arthur Anderson, who was born in Georgia, and his wife Anna. Also boarding in the house was Mr. Clayborn Baker and Ms. Elizabeth Baker. William was working as a porter in a pool hall.

FINDINGS AARONS DAUGHTER MATILDA IN OHIO

With Peg-Leg-Williams opperating in Ohio, I found the oldest daughter of Aaron who married Robert Williams or as known Bob Williams.

Mrs. Matilda Williams. Remember, married Robert Williams, who was from Greene County, Georgia and worked alone side of Aaron for years after marrying Matilda. I do not know if Brantley or Howard and William or even Arthur knew that she lived here or not. However, they are close neighbors. When I made my way to visit Howard McCloud, my grandfather's cousin, in Michigan, I was told he lived in Michigan by his nephews his sister Carrie children. My wife and I stopped over in Ohio for a while and it was my second time visiting. My first time was when I was in my early teens with my mother Mary and her husband Harold Waller and my two sisters to visit his relatives.

Matilda was twelve years old in 1870 . She being the eldest daughter of Aaron and Harriet Calloway kept the house in order while her parents made their way to work in Clarke County or in Beaverdam and Puryears .

She was raised on Zachariah Freeman's place in Penfield, Greene County, Georgia. By the year 1880, both she and her younger sister Julia had married and left the house of their father Aaron. Matilda had married Robert Williams. They lived in Scull Shoals in the 147th District of Greene County, Georgia not far from her father and mother. Bob was twenty-two years old and Matilda was the same age. They had a son by the name of Jasper at the age of one. Jasper died on November 1880, only six months after the census was taken on June 16 in the summer. Jasper died of pneumonia. He is more than likley buried in the Bethabara Cemetery, which is one of the largest cemteries in Schull Shoals for blacks in this general area. In the same year, Mack Smith, a three-year-old colored boy, died of diptheria. He was under the care of Dr. Willingham. I mentioned Mack Smith because my grandfather's companion in the thirties in Atlanta was name Mack Smith.

In the year of 1900, I had a hard time locating Bob and Matilda Williams in Greene County, Georgia. However, I found them in Scull Shoals with or near Alonzo Freeman and his wife Lidia and Ben and Mary Maxey. Both Robert and Matilda were listed as being born in 1850, and their eldest son Hamp was born in 1884, Turner was born in 1885, Sis was born in 1888, Plunk was born in 1889, Bosy was born in 1891, Lena was born in 1893, Willie was born in 1896, and Jennie was born in 1897.

In 1910 I found the two of them with their son seventeen-year-old Josie. They've been married for thirty-six years and have had fourteen children with only twelve living. He was fifty-six and she was fifty-eight years old. They were living on Oglethorpe Road in Penfield, Greene County. I found Hamp Williams, their son, living in Schull Shoals in Greene County. He was twenty-one years old was an employee of the General Farms in 1910, like so many that year. Remember, in Oglethorpe County and in the United States, the South was the bread basket for farming and these farmers needed the contracted black and black convict laborers to rebuild not only in the South but the North as well. And what better way than to use that which is so familiar to the South, the Negro. But first they had to reestablish control over this highly prize commodity during time of the old south! And this would come through disenfranchisement. This talk started early in the 1890s and maybe even earlier. Tom Watson was spear heading the disenfranchisement of the Negro while the Governor of South Carolina Mr. Calhoun voiced his views of disenfranchisement in 1899 with his speech in Elbert County. I wonder did Tom Watson attend this meeting as well? Blacks as well as whites who lived in both worlds had to make a choice! At this time, a large number of blacks and whites and men and women who could pass as white were put on chain gangs or beaten and threatened by the KKK to force and coerce or compel them through some kind of reasoning to make their decisions as to how they shall live. It was a new era in these United States of America, the land of the free!

In 1912, Matilda and Hamp, her son, were living at 154 Willow Street in Athens, Georgia. Hamp Williams and his mother were here when the United States entered World War I. They were residing at 161 Willow Street. Hamp was forty-two years old and born on March 3, 1876, and was a laborer for Webb Crawford Co. on Foundry Street. He was medium height and medium build, and black eyes and black hair, he fits the same physical characteristics as my grandfather and his brothers. Bob Williams might be dead by now.

By 1920, Matilda Williams was living in 161 Willow Street in Clarke County, Georgia. Bob, her husband, was dead and she was living near her in-laws at this time. Matilda is now fifty years old and her son Hamp is thirty-five, Robert W. is eighteen, and Nellie B is ten. Alfred Fears and his family are at 180. Ada is his wife and Addie is his daughter. Their young son is named Perry. Chester Williams is her fifty-year-old neighbor residing at 129 Wiillow Street with Della, who is five yeard older her husband. Their children are Nora Lee and Demp. Rev. J. Williams is living at the intersection of Broad and Willow streets in Athens. Rev. J. Williams is forty-two years old and his wife Sallie is forty-seven. A boarder named Dililiah Elder is fifty-five years old. I mention the Fears family because everywhere I found Arthur, my grandfather, in Atlanta there was a Mr. Fears living near him and even near Mary Calloway at 35 Maple Street in northwest Atlanta. There was one more William family on Willow Street in 1920 near Matilda, and he was Mathew Williams at 172 Willow Street with his wife Alma and their children Paul and Lutrell. Willow Street ran alongside the Oconee River. Can you visualize the view where these houses were lined alongside this large body of moving water and the life that they lived alongside the Oconee?

In the year 1922 at 161 Willow Street, Robert Williams Jr. died. Hamp Williams buried his brother at the age of twenty-two. The cousins of my grandfather said Ohio is one of the many places that my grandfather said he visited on his many journeys across these United States. I found that Matilda left Georgia with her daughter Lena, who married Clarence Merritt in Georgia. They made it to Cleveland, Ohio, between 1927 and 1928. I find Mr. Clarence Merritt living at 2666 East Firfty-Third Street, Cuyuhoga, County Ohio, Cleveland, in the Twelth Ward on Block 92. Later on they were living at 4520 Woodland Avenue in the 1930's and paying rent at a rate of thirty dollars a months at apartment 13. All in the house were Clarence her son-in-law at the age of thirty-three, Lena was at the age of thirty two, and mother-in-law Matilda Williams was eighty years old, widow and the daughter of Aaron and Harriett Calloway-my grandfather's auntie! Thomas Gillian, twenty-two, and Andrew Gillian, nineteen years old, are lodgers out of Georgia. Lennie Williams and his wife Nellie were living next door with their two sons Harold and Albert. Like the other mysteries that unfolded while searching for family, I found that this was the case with Matilda Williams as well I found her and her families in two places at the same time. It was in the year 1940, on East 45th street, in the 12th ward on block no. 4 lived Clearence Merritt and his wife Lena at the age of forty four. Matilda is at the age of eighty two years old. Mother Matilda has only aged two years since 1930. Willis Williams is thirt five, Lennie his wife is forty six, Robert their son is twenty, Harold is fifteen, and Albert is fouteen.

Clarence Merrett was born March of 1893.

However, in the year of 1900 he was seven years old and his wife to be Lena Williams was living in Greene County in the town of Penfield while Clarence was in the 162nd district called Credill. Clarence father was name Charles born a year after the end of the was in June of 1866. His mother was named Sarah, she was born in May of 1872. Collas their oldest daughter was born October of 1888, Filbert their oldest son was born November of 1889, Aaron was born July of 1891, Clarence was born March of 1893, Pelman their son was born December of 1892, Cleola their daughter was born May of 1899. The only other Merritt that I see in 1900 is living with the Parks family next door.

Silvey Parks is a twenty-three-year-old married woman living separated from her husband. She has in her care her daughter Lucinda, a servant named Malinda Parks, and William Merritt, born March of 1887, and is thirteen. By the year 1910, Sarah was a widow living in the Mountain District of Walton County, Georgia! She was living with her children at 405 Settlement Road. Sarah's youngest child was four-year-old Grady. Charles died just a little after Grady was born. They are all listed as mulattos. Clarence is now sixteen, Delmar is twelve, Cleola is eleven, Doyle is nine, Ella is five, and then four-year-old Grady. Sarah is living next door to her eldest son Felix and his wife Anna. Here I believe that Lena or Lenora might have come to know Clarence Merriett throught her father's side of the family, the Williams! The Williams family in Greene

County in Penfield had relatives in Walton and Morgan counties, as did many of the residents of Penfield, Greene County, Georgia.

This is a pattern that plays out in the Callaway family just as well. These two families have the same ties to the English side on Abraham's side of the family, with Creecy, who married Willis Williams, the preacher in Penfield. Bob Williams has a tie to this same family of Mr. Willis. The first person that appears with him on the tax digest in Scull Shoals is Randle, the son of Willis Williams. Robert or Bob Williams is either the brother of Willis and some kind of caretaker of Willis's children when he died. This is before Adam was under the care of the Burgess family. This is the Burgess family that has their names on the old DeKalb County Jail. This is the same reason Judge Mitchell of DeKalb County arrested Dr. Martin Luther King Jr. during the civil rights movement because of familiar family ties from Greene County in Scull Shoals. The families that are tied to Scull Shoals in Greene County leds me to believe that the KKK called upon the Ray family to handle old buisnes as usual when it comes to killing an upity N. Oh! ties that binds! And for anyone to believe that James Earl Ray didn't know the Williams family and have a hand in killing Dr. Martin Luther King is a deceiving themselves! As I set and read the stories coming out of Greene County and Oglethorpe where they took Black Men out and threw them into the Oconee after tying iron wheels around their necks and drowning them. Under the disguise of Atlanta a city to busy to hate, lul the country to sleep to commit murder as usual and get away with it!

It might be repetitive in my research and I must apologize for this being my first publication, but the Williams and the Callaways or Calloways and English families run paralell quite often. From Ned and Charlie Callaway and Peg-Leg Williams, to Harriett Callaway in Wilkes County, Georgia, and the marriage of Bob Williams to Matilda Callaway, the daughter of Aaron Calloway, etc. This is even in the liquor trade from Penfield, Greene County, to Walton County in the Mountain District that made Walton County one of the richest counties at one time in Georgia! This tie is clearly visible, along with their families that relocated in Walton County to the city of Atlanta.

I want to paint a clearer picture of Matilda, the daughter of Aaron Callaway and wife of Mr. Robert (Bob) Williams. Two years after their marriage, in 1878, Bob Williams and his wife Matilda (Callaway) Williams were living near or on the property of Mr. Samuel Sorrow, a seventy-three-year-old white farmer and his sixty-two-year-old wife Millie in the 147th or Scull Schoal. They have one son by the name of Jasper Williams, aged one, on June 16, 1880. By May 31, 1881, R. J. Haynes writes that Jasper Williams is dead. J. R. Haynes stated that Jasper died in November of pneumonia. They were living in Falling Creek of Oglethorpe County for about a year, just about as long as their son Jasper lived. And if they are in Falling Creek, they are on or near the property of Matilda's father Aaron. I say this because of the tax digest records where Robert Williams worked alongside his father-in-law in their first few years of marriage. Aaron must consoled the two newlyweds after the death of their one-year-old grandchild Jasper. Aaron, must be greiving alone with young Jasper's cousins and neices and uncles as well in Scull Shoal. It must be a sad situation even in the Williams family as well to see death come and take little Jasper.

That was not the only tragic experience in Falling Creek and Scull Shoals, these two close communities in Greene and Oglethorpe County! This situation happen a few years earlier .

> Wednesday, May 5, 1875, The Daily Pheonix, Volume XI, Numer 38; Julian A. Shelby reports: A destructive tornado passed through Oglethorpe and Greene counties Saturday afternoon, between 2 and 3 o'clock, destroying life and property to a fearful extent. Scarcely a house remains in the course. Fences were blown in every direction and the forest completely destroyed. Words cannot express the awful scenes and distress which have so soon and unexpectedly come upon the people. Those who yesterday had happy homes and plenty, are today without house, food or clothing. The following are the names that were killed, wounded, and those who had their homes destroyed in the immediate neighborhood of Maxey's, in the former county: Killed: Geo. W. Maxey and Peter Watson, colored. Wounded: William Jackson in head and hip seriously; Mrs. Mary Asbury, in head, shoulder and breast seriously; Tip Shaw, arm broken; Z. Freeman (Zachariah) arm and eye; W. A. Pugh in head and arm broken; Crawford Zuber in head and eye; A. T. Brightwell in leg; Ms. Asbury, finger cut off; John Porter in head; Mrs. John Porter slightly; Handy Pullian, colored, mortally wounded; Jane Butler, colored, mortally wounded; Frank Barnett, colored, in head; Zuber, colored, in hip; Andy Hill, colored, arm broken; Dick Smith, colored, in arm;

> Kitt Bugg, colored, in head; *Aaron Calloway, colored, in head;* Cheney Smith, colored, in shoulder; *Burl Calloway, colored, in chest.* There are others who are wounded, but we have not learned their names . . .

Living around the corner from Matilda Williams was Mattie Callaway, the wife of Abraham Callaway. I have not seen a Mattie and Abe Callaway anywhere. The only person that I have seen as Abraham was in the house of Enoch and my grandfather using the first name of Abe while living next door to my grandmother on Chestnut Street in Atlanta. Mattie Callaway was born in Georgia and was seventy-four years old in 1940, and was living with Jane Alexander, a sixty-seven-year-old born in Georgia. The two of them are living at 2669 East Forty-Fifth Street in Ohio, a few houses down from Clarence Merriett and his mother-in-law Matilda Williams. The two of them are sharing a duplex with Luther Roan and his wife Nora. Later on, Mattie will share the duplex with Columbus Cole at 2669 and Clarence Merriett will share their duplex with Mr. Arthur Dix. Two places the families of Matilda Callaway Williams resided and the mystery of why I find them in two places I just can not explain.

I was very very happy to find the death certificate of Mrs. Matilda Williams and I was very happy to find that her Father was Aaron Calloway and her mother was Harriet. Her maiden name might have been Calloway as well. She more than likely came off the Callaway plantation born in slavery. She had lived in Ohio for about fifteen years. Her husband's name was Bob Williams and was deceased. Cardiorenal disease with heart failure was her cause of death. Lena Merritt, her daughter, was the informant. You would think that Lena would know her grandmother's maiden name. At the time of her mother's death, she was living at 15920 Sullivan Drive in Ohio.

Summerhill

This area of Atlanta called Summerhill is a thriving black community even today. It was a safe haven for blacks fleeing the farms in the eastern and southern sections of Georgia. Here I found the family of Callaways that were from Oglethorpe County. This is the same area where the farmers in 1900 and 1910 would come to reside in jail after being caught selling their moonshine liquor. These were mainly white farmers. It is the same place where I found Mr. Robert Callaway between 1885 under the first name of Charles, and a lady named Mary Callaway as well. I had to work hard trying to figure out the black Callaways that resided in Summerhill, and it wasn't easy as you think. They changed their names quite often and their ages as well.

Let me start with the family of Martha Callaway, better known as Martha Lumpkin Callaway, the wife of Eli R. Callaway. Like I have stated before, W. H. Callaway was sixty-seven and his wife Martha was forty-four. John F. was twenty-one, David J. was sixteen, Adaline was fourteen, C. M. Jordan was twelve, and Thomas J. Jordan was two. All the children were born in Florida.

Now I will turn my attention back to Oglethorpe in 1850. Martha is thirty-three and Annie E. Watson, who may be a sister, is twenty-nine. Thomas Callaway is twenty-seven and his nineteen-year-old wife Lucy is living in the house with him. Eli H. Callaway is the postmaster at the age of twenty-six. Mary Watson is twelve, John Watson is ten, and James Watson is ten. Thomas P. Callaway will reside or own property in Woodstock, Georgia, in Oglethorpe County. Woodstock is the place where Aaron's, the father of Charlie Callaway, family resided. This is the place where Aaron was charged with trespassing in 1872.

Thomas and his son Shelton would run a mercantile store in Woodstock, Oglethorpe, for years and reside in Lexington, Georgia. Thomas P. Callaway had over two thousand acres of land in Woodstock near Mr. D. C. Barrow's place. Thomas P. Callaway might have accumulated some of his estate from the death of his brother Eli. H. Callaway who died November 3, 1856. Thomas P. Callaway made his way to Atlanta to bury his brother in the Historical Oakland Cemetery. This wouldn't be the last time he would have to make this trip to Atlanta. He would bury his mother Martha in 1872.

In 1870, Martha is seventy-three years old in the Third Ward of the City of Atlanta. Martha is living with twenty-nine-year-old J. M. Mitchell and his twenty-eight-year-old wife Ellen. J.M. was born in South Carolina and was living on the property of Martha, who's place was valued at $1,500. Mahalia, a servant who used to be a Park, is fifty years old and Susan Callaway is a young fifteen-year-old white girl living with Martha, the mother of Thomas P. Callaway. It was on March 16, 1872, that Martha Lumpkin Callaway made out her will and left her estate in the hands of C. M. Payne, John Cooper, and Benjamin Thurmond. She left her property, both private and personal, to her son Thomas P. Callaway of Oglethorpe County, Georgia.

However, there was another family in 1870 in the Third Ward of the City of Atlanta. Charlie Lester was forty-five years old and his wife Lucy was listed as fifty-four. Lewis Lee was thirty-two years old working for Rolling Mills, with Alfred Lee, who was twenty-three years old, and nineteen-year-old Charlie Lester. I wonder if they came across Mr. Anderson Callaway, who worked at the mill in 1870 as well. Young Charlie Lester would eventually go to work for a Mrs. Willingham in Gwinnett County in the 1880s. However, before he moves to the place of Mrs. Willingham in Gwinnett County, he will marry a lady named Mary and live on Elm Street in the First Ward, where you will find John Cloud and his family. The Cloud family will become close to Arthur, my grandfather, in some way or another. Charlie is at the age of thirty-two and Mary is twenty-three, Annie is three, Rosa is two, and little Ms. Ella was born in March and is three months old. I must mention a few of the neighbors of Mr. Lester, the drayman. One in particular is John Dobbs, a brick mason at the age of fifty and his wife Louvinia is forty years old. They have three children named William, Effie, and Howell. Now, the family of John Cloud the brick mason. John is living on Vine Street, which intersects Elm Street. John is a thirty-one-year-old mulatto and his wife Narcisa is twenty-nine. William is eight, Annie is five, Adiline four, Robert W. is seven months old and his twin brother is named William Robert.

THE LESTER FAMILY IN ROCKBRIDGE, GWINNETT COUNTY

I mention the Lester because we in some way are kin to them. Mrs. Willingham had only Charlie Lester working for her on her property. The Willinghams are kin to the Callaway family as well. I found them living in the house with C. Callaway in Wilkes County as an aunt. Charlie's neighbor was thirty-year-old Mr. Robert Hammond, Jane Williams at the age of twenty-six, George W. Hammond was three at this time, and Anne Hammond is twenty-five. Twenty-three-year-old Marrion Williams was in the house as well. Later on I found Charlie Lester Sr. in the Atlanta Directory living at 164 West Fair Street with his son Charlie Jr. working for Wylie's. The earliest time that I find young Charlie Lester is in Gwinnett County in Rockbridge. Mrs. Harriet Lester died November 2, 1904. Mrs. Lester was sixty years old. She was buried at Peeks Chapel in Rockdale. I assume that her husband is buried here as well.

Now, a few years later, about 1910, Charlie Lester will be coming from Loganville and would be shot by a young white man after passing by a school. However, he lived to make out a will for his family. Now, the strangest thing is that Hattie is listed on the census at the age of fifty-seven. What is the secret with Harriett Lester? In the 1900 census, Charlie Lester was born November 1842, and Harriett or Hattie was born July 1849 and was fifty years old. They had been married for twenty-four years. In the year 1910, Harriett is supposed to be dead and Mr. Charlie Lester has remarried to Ms. Julia. It states in the will that Julia is his wife. Yes, I know that the census is not so accurate. Whatever! I just know that there is a big difference in years from 1904 to 1910. If someone is dead in a grave with a headstone stating her death, there is no way you could be living ten years later. Maybe Hattie is his daughter! Know it states that Harriet is fifty-seven and Charlie is sixty-four years old and Dred Lester, whom I suppose is the brother of Charlie, is sixty-four and they have been married for thirty some years. Charlie Lester, before his death, was selling land to his sons. First to his son Charles Lester Jr. In consideration of love and affection, he gave land to this son on the sixth day of December in 1915. However, he sold his son Paul property for five hundred dollars on the second day of February 1916. How else does Julia play into the picture of Charlie Lester in Rockbridge or Rockdale County, Georgia? It's got to be the business of running or making liquor.

Now, Charles Lester purchased this property from Mr. Thos. D. O'Kelly in December 14, of 1911. When Charlie Lester makes out his will in probate court in Gwinnett County, Georgia, Charlie's annual returns state that his children have their own property but Mr. J. R. Still is handling his estate and not Julia. However, Julia receives one hundred dollars a month for support from his estate. Mr. J. R. Still is the man in charge. I believe that Mr. Still is auctioning off the property and while Julia Lester is receiving support, she is also being paid six dollars and twenty cents for picking cotton. Mr. I. F. Williams is paying rent and eventually will purchase Mr. Lester's property along with Charles Lester Jr.'s property.

I don't know how Charlie Lester died or when he died, but I did stumble across this situation between Charlie Lester and his son or brother Paul Lester in the Gwinnett County Courthouse in 1917. In March of 1917, Paul Lester was indicted for assault and battery of one Mr. Jeff Davis. Charles Lester paid bond for Paul Lester on February 16, 1917, and was to appear on March 1, 1917, for assault. I am assuming that Charles is the father of Paul because Paul could write his name and Charles Lester made his mark. Paul had an accomplice and his name was Shad Lucas. Shad was charged with assault and battery of Jeff Davis as well. And Sam Lucas paid his bond of one hundred and fifty dollars and so did Charlie Lester. Two black men in this time and place who could pay such a steep fine! How could they come up with so much money? Well, the man behind the scene is Mr. J. R. Still himself! Mr. Still is the justice of the peace. I guess Charlie Lester owed him a favor, so he made him the executor of his estate.

I never found a Julia Lester in Rockbridge, Gwinnett County. I only found her in Clarke County, Georgia. I wondered if she made her way to Rockbridge after the death of Harriett, or if she lived under the first name as Charlie's first wife to cover up his infidelity, which was common between the mulattoes of Georgia. What are the ties with the Calloways or Callaways in Clarke County? I had to go to the Clarke County Courthouse in Athens to find the answers to this question.

CALLAWAY'S AND LESTER BOOZE IN ATHENS

Now, what is the answer to my great dilemma about Charlie Callaway and his escape from Mr. J. C. Hudgins place in Elbert County or his death in Elbert County? I tried to tie a few names with Charlie Callaway in Clarke County, and one of the names is Robert Callaway! So I went to the criminal docket of the Superior Court of Clarke County to see if the crime of selling liquor is still prevalent in the city of Athens. I wondered if I could find something to break the mystery of Charlie and Mary, my great-grandparents. The making and selling of corn liquor on the farms of the landowners were controled by the landowner. Robert C. Callaway had this privilage as well. You could sell and buy and make liquor on the farm and the trading of the hooch was to be sold in Atlanta and other parts of Georgia by the privilaged of society with the help of the law.

Clarke County Criminal Docket April Term 1890

State vs. Aldora Huff and Dan Calloway, April 22, 1890, Nol. Pros. For defaults, felony is the charge; case # 2, attorney Mr. Richard B. Russell

State vs. Alex Winfrey (colored) misdemeanor for selling liquor, October 22, 1890.

No arrest in this case, so this case was sent to city court. Alex was charged with keeping open a tippling house on Sunday. case #14 through 20, attorney Mr. Richard B. Russell.

State vs. James Brown, adultery and fornication, Nol. Pros; being the other party to the alleged offence refusing to testify; case# 24

State vs. John Ales Winfrey, selling liquor; no arrest

State vs. Dan Callaway, charged with entering a railroad car; Aldora Huff is charged with the same offence; Richard B. Russell, Thomas & S. Morris attorneys

State vs. John Austin*, misdemeanor, October 1890, carrying pistol concealed; city court, case #5

*Does not mention that he is colored

State vs. Toney Barnett, adultery, sent to city court April Term 1891; case #28

State vs. John Austin, pointing pistol at another; case # 37–38 sent to city court 1891

Burrell Shaw, assault with intent to murder (colored)

October Term 1893

State vs. William Smith, using profane and vulgar language, etc.; city court, case # 7–8

State vs. John B. Johnson, charged with selling whiskey; case #30–35

April Term 1894–1897 no arrest

O.W. Watson charged with selling liquor to a minor and opening a tippling house on the Sabbath; attorney Richard B. Russell

Cliff Cheatham, keeping open a tippling house on a Sabbath day

Dock Strickland, keeping open a tippling house on a Sabbath Day

Jack Sailors, keeping open a tippling house on a Sabbath day

State vs. Joseph McWhorter*, playing and betting at cards, October 24, 1895; continued by Default.

*Joseph McWhorter was charged along with Fran H. Kroner, Morris Jankower, W.A. M. McElhonnon, Joseph Morgan, Jake Twedy, and R.L. Moss Jr., S. Raphael, C.L. Porter, Dr. Geo. Little, R.D. Stokely, Mordicia Marks, Dr. W.M. Willingham, Barrett Phinizy, Charlie Hodgenson, and Joe Tate.

State vs. Jim Smith, carrying pistol concealed

October Term

State vs. George Barnett, larceny from railroad car, felony; October 25, 1895

Anderson Pace, betting at cards, October 1895

Wince English, gaming, playing, and betting at cards

State vs. William Smith, murder; case # 20

State vs. Elenor Calloway, selling liquor, October 29 Special Term 1912, city court; case # 1091; attorney Mr. Walker

State vs. Mat Hamilton, alias Mack Adams, alias Mack Callaway, charged with assault to murder, April term 1917; True Bill October 17, 1923; Nol. Pros., case # 1573

State vs. Callaway Oglesby (colored), burglary, second count larceny from the house

State vs. Lee Callaway (colored), cheat & swindler, continued by default to February Term 1921, Nov. 15, 1921, May term 1921, Feb. 21, 1921; verdict of not guilty Nov. 22 1921; attorney Lamar C. Rucker

State vs. Will Callaway, having whiskey in possession, continued by default to February term 1922, Nov. 21 1921, May Term 1922, March 8 1922; bond forfeited May 26, 1922; February 28, 1923, plea of guilty and sentence deferred to November Term 1923; sentenced Nov. 24, 1923

State vs. Lee Callaway*, case # 5408, colored, having liquor, May term 1922, continued Nov. 23 1923, Feb. 21 1924, May 14, 1924

*Lee Callaway came to an untimely death in Atlanta about this same time. As you can see, the Callaways were not only in the dry goods business but in the liquor trade as well, with the Lesters and many others

State vs. Major Calloway, selling liquor, Feb. Term 1923; bond forfeited Feb. 27 1923; July 30 1923, final forfeiture

April term 1911

Case # 882 State vs. Ned Lester, George Lester, Pat Lester, Bulger Lester and Reese Wade, murder, April 17–18, 1911; do arrest or to Ned Lester verdict of not guilty; to Pat Lester, Bugler Lester and Reese Wade plea of guilty of voluntary manslaughter or to George Lester

Case # 2152: The State vs. W.H. Lester, alias Preacher Lester, charge vagrancy, 1925; attorney Preston M. Almand

State vs. Walter Calloway Sr., possessing liquor; Preston M. Almond is his attorney, case # 0771, plea of guilty; motion to revoke probation sentence denied

Case # 4772: State vs. Preacher Lester, alias Willy Lester, having liquor; plea guilty, Sept. 15 1920

Case # 4730: State vs. Will Lucas, having whiskey, continued by default to Nov. term 1920

Case # 4992: The State vs. Charlie Lester, Tom Clark, Jim Griffeth, True Bill # 1681, charged with being drunk at church

State vs. Annie Callaway, having liquor, Nov. term 1930, plea of guilty Jan. 17, 1931

State vs. Emma J. Callaway, larceny from a person, Nol. Pros. March 4, 1944

Case #7475: Callaway "Puddin" Lay, assault and battery, 1932

State vs. Spencer Lester, larceny, found guilty Feb. 9, 1922

State vs. Cleve Callaway, carrying pistol concealed (2 counts), plea of guilty, sentenced Oct. 25, 1923

State vs. James Callaway, having whiskey, plea guilty and sentenced Sept. 14, 1925

State vs. Robert Callaway, possessing and transporting whiskey, plea of guilty and sentenced Aug. 22 1925

Otis Dawson, possessing and transporting whiskey, verdict of guilty, sentenced Nov. 19, 1925

Case # 2652–2653: State vs. Robert Callaway (colored), receiving stolen goods, Jan. 16, 1930; bond forfeited, attorneys Jake Joel and Thomas J. Shackelford

Carrie Callaway divorced Walter Callaway Sr.

Marie Ireland Callaway divorced James Callaway, 1943

Fannie Callaway vs. Hocksey Calloway, alimony; dismissed April 3, 1939

Jim Callaway vs. Mary Lou Callaway, divorce; dismissed Jan. 3, 1939

Callaway & Thompson by Sheriff to C.M. Ector for $24.75 that tract of land lying in the city of Athens, Clarke County fronting on Pope Street thirty-five ft. by eighty-two ft. Recorded in book (KK) page (255 and book 6 page 394.

While in Clarke County I read through the old newspapers at the courthouse I wanted to see what the criminals was all about and who participated in the world of crime and who might have spon of Charlie Callaway and Gratlin Johnson lifestyle in the city of Athens.

The Athens Banner, May 5, 1911

Negro in car shed in Atlanta had 13 pints of booze. Atlanta has had troubles with the Walking Tigers just the same as other villages. Sunday afternoon quite a number of Athens boys were at the new Union passenger terminals in Atlanta waiting to come home. On the train, under the shed in sight of the policeman on duty about the place, a Negro canvassed for customers who wanted fire-water. He had 13 half-pint bottles of booze on his person, which he had stuck in pockets and other places about him.

The Weekly Banner July 14, 1911

For 5 or 6 nights there have been some houses entered and robbed in the limits of the city of Athens. Smooth burglar dudes all watchfulness of police dept. Mr. John White Morton latest victim—Athens is over-run with burglars! Athens not the only town.

The Weekly Banner July 14, 1911

Took Two Justices of Peace to Settle Colored Church Row (Oconee Heights)

The story of the trouble is the conduct of Negroes who attend St. James colored church. There is a good church there and the colored population is thick. Not only is it thick, but well-to-do. The town Negroes take them at good picking. Every Sunday a number of Athens Negroes catch the G.M. Train and go out to visit their cousins, carry them liquor, which they sell at Tiger prices, engage them in a game of 7-Up or Craps, take away the rest of their money and then proceed to rough house them in the region of St. James. What can I say about Oconee County, Georgia? It was a place that at one time the KKK held great power and influence over. At Jug Tavern, the boys returned home from the Civil War and the killing of Negroes in this area was a priority.

There are many good Negroes in this section who attend worship and who want peace and order, but the town elements that go for gain and for age and the young bloods of that section make a bad combination.

On the last Sunday of June, the last exhibition occurred. The congregations was largely present at the trial. The people were divided. Son Cooper was badly cut with a knife. The Negro that did the cutting was Fred Cooley. Henderson Sims was beat up and bruised by rocks, which he swore were hurled by Pleas Dyer and Son Cooper. The deacons of the church swore out warrants against Dyer, Cooper, Henderson, and John Sims. Seven or eight cases are on the docket now for gambling in the woods near St. James. Huge numbers of people at St. James was a result of it being Children's Day at church.

The Banner Friday Morning April 16, 1909

Blind Tiger fined one hundred dollars in court yesterday. Mayor Dorsey had before him yesterday morning on the charge of selling liquor one Dilmus Williams colored. The evidence was against Dilmus and he was fined one hundred dollars. It is understood that the fine will be paid.

Peonage Warrant issued for Thompson yesterday

Yesterday afternoon Charlie Horton, a Negro man, went before Judge E.C. Kinnebrew, United States Commissioner, and swore out a warrant charging Ernest Thompson of Oglethorpe County with the offence of peonage. Dr. Hamilton stated to a Banner representative yesterday that the Negro had the dropsy and was in a bad condition regardless of the beating he had received. He said that the Negro had scars across his back and had a deep bruise on his back that the Negro said had been caused by being hit with a hammer by his employer. There is also a gash across his forehead. Horton says he agreed to work a year for his employer for $65 and his food and clothes. He says that Thompson claimed that he still owed him $9.50. Horton is a half-witted Negro, below the average in intelligence. The investigation of this case will be made by the Federal Grand Jury at the session of this city.

Judge E. C. Kinnebrew was actively involved in the investigation of peonage cases during the late 1880s, with Mr. James Monroe Smith and other large landowners in Oglethorpe County. He wrote letters to the Federal government concerning the tensions that were rising in the State of Georgia in the 1890s.

The Weekly Banner, Aug. 11, 1911

Rome Negro Hauled 673 Kegs of Beer through the street and sold it. Name: Frank Murphy, a well-known Negro drayman.

The Weekly Banner, Sept. 1, 1911

23 times in chain gang only 208 times in Prison. George L. Smith from N.C. the boldest Blind Tiger man who has run every Blind Tigers in the cities of N.C.

White Woman in Jessup, Ga. running Blind Tiger out of her store on the city lines.

Weekly Banner Oct. 13, 1911

Insane with rage, he slew his wife. Young Negro Hezekiah Stevens, with stockless gun, shoots wife down and women shout and cheer when he is captured! When trial date set, he said his plea is the "unwritten law."

Nov. 3, 1911

Atlanta is a wet town. It's best to admit it rather than trying to conceal it! With innumerable clubs for all grades of society, with Blind Tigers for the Negroes, with beer saloons closing to pay even a pretended allegiance to the near part of the law, Atlanta has reached the point where a man can get anything but a mixed drink across a public bar!

Nov. 3, 1911

The Atlanta police have their hands so full with the Blind Tigers hunting game just now that other offenders can get away with almost anything they want to. 40 Blind Tiger cases have been entered on the police docket within the last few days, and the hunt is still in progress. It all grew out of a dispute between Blind Tiger leader Dan Shaw against Hub Talley, a leader of the other Blind Tiger gang.

Dec. 3, 1897

Years Commercial Club started four years ago

The Commercial Club its first officers were James F. McGowen, Pres., *W.D. Griffeth Vice Pres. T.W. Reed Sec.,* W.A. McDowell Treas. The 1897 officers are W.D. Griffeth Pres., G.H. Palmer Vice Pres., S.C. Upson Sec., and C.A. Talmadge Treas.

The Commercial Club started in 1893.

Sept. 24, 1897

Out Dispensary Liquor. A big fight is being waged in Washington, Wilkes County, to secure a dispensary there just like Athens dispensary.

Case # 5408: Lee Callaway, colored, having liquor, May Term 1922, continued Nov. 23, 1923; bond forfeited Feb. 21, 1924 and May 14, 1924

State vs. Major Callaway, selling liquor, Feb. Term 1923; bond forfeited Feb. 27, 1923 and July 30, 1923; final forfeiture July

State vs. Lee Callaway*, colored, for cheating and swindling, continued by defendant to Feb. Term of 1921 from Nov. 15, 1920, to May Term 1921 and to Feb. 27, 1921; Lamar C. Rucker is his attorney

*In 1920, Lee Callaway two years from now would be killed in Atlanta was living with his wife Leona at 1020 South Lumpkin with Herman Smith, G.W. Griffeth, and Wallace Howard. Cleveland and his wife Lizzie were living at 473 Hoyt Street with J. Hill, and Jess Callaway was living with his wife Irene at 463 Hoyt Street. Nathan Callaway was living with them with his Sallie Spratlin.

State vs. Will Callaway, having whiskey in possession, continued by default to Feb. Term 1922 from Nov. 21, 1921; May Term 1922 to March 8, 1922; bond forfeited May 26, 1922, and Feb. 28, 1923; plea of guilty and sentenced deferred to Nov. term 1923, sentenced Nov. 24, 1923

Chapter Eighteen

CHARLIE, LIFE IN THE ATL. TO DEATH ON THE CHAIN-GANG IN ELBERT CO. GA.

The first black Callaway that I find living in the Third Ward in 1890 is Robert Callaway, working for the R&D Shop. I believe that the R&D Shop is the Richmond and Danville Railroad located in Room 2 at 56 East Wall Street. The president is George S. Scott, Peyton Randolph is the general manager, E. Berkeley is the superintendent, L. L. McCleskey is the division freight and passenger agent.

While Robert Calloway was working at the R&D Shop, he was in company with some very influential white men at this time in the railroad business moving in and out of Atlanta from Wall Street. These are the same railroad shops that Charlie Callaway was charged with receiving stolen merchandise from in 1919. I also have a Robert C. Callaway at 4 Lookout Mountain in Chattanooga, Tennessee. R. C. Callaway works for Spencer & Thomas as a porter. Robert C. Callaway dies in Chattanooga, Tennessee, at the age of thirty-seven on sixteenth day of 1916 of tuberculosis and it states that he was born in North Carolina, and is buried in Chickamauga, Georgia. The death certificate does not state the month in which Robert dies.

We'll have to go back to Oglethorpe and Greene County and see who was working for the railroad in the 1880s. Charlie and Robert Callaway worked for the railroad. Charles and George Callaway worked for the railroad in Wetumka, Elmore, Alabama in 1870. Charles was thirty-five and George was an eighteen-year-old black male. Both were born in

Georgia. Charles was listed together with two other mulattoes, Alfred and Albert, twin brothers twenty-eight years old out of South Carolina. In the same year, Brantley and his brother William R. Callaway of Wilkes County held stock in the Southern Railroad. Also, Rev. Jesse R. Callaway, the black preacher of Penfield, was an agent for the Southern Railroad and for the Ebenezer BaptistAssociation as well. Robert L. Callaway, who resided here in Atlanta as well. He lived at 253 East Cain Street and worked as a salesman for M. C. Kiser and company at 14-16 Pryor Street, which intersects Wall Street in the same general area of the Georgia Railroad near the R &D Shop.

As I remember, Charlie Callaway, who lived in Fairburn, Georgia, worked for a Mr. Columbus Kiser in the 1880s in Atlanta. This reminds me. During the disenfranchisement era in the 1890s, Charlie and Mary were living between Oglethorpe and Atlanta. In his deposition before the Federal district attorney E. A. Angier, he exclaimed that in 1896 he was away from his wife and children when William Eberhart raped his wife Mary. William Eberhart and other evil disposed men were working to secure the Negroes and keep them in one place, and that was on his farm in Beaverdam, Georgia! The Callaways were envied to a fault by Mr. James Monroe Smith and others. Robert or Charles could move freely, unhindered in the South under the protection of his family, the Callaways. I believe that they found more freedom in Atlanta in the First and Second and Third wards where they had more opportunities for their children than the contracts that were made with William Eberhart and James Monroe Smith and the farmers of Oglethorpe and Greene and Wilkes counties. I believe that Charlie Callaway having ties with the Rail Road met Peg-Leg-Williams or Ransom A. Williams an agent for the Rail Road. I believe their paths had to cross at one time or another. Ransom A. Williams might be the influential man in Charlie's life that might have saved him from his demise in 1899.

Now, you may be asking yourself this question. Where is Mary in all of this? I found Mary as early as 1884 enrolled in college at Spelman. She was living near an R. C. Callaway at 107 Stonewall Street in the First Ward near the Atlanta University under the last name of English. R. C. Callaway, a colored man, was living three houses down at 117. The only other colored men that were their neighbors were M. Hall and G. Steed and A. Samuels and J. Brown. A. Samuels went on to become a liquor distributor in Atlanta and owned drinking establishments in and around the city.

Later on, Mary resided at 35 Maple Street between 1899 and 1901. Then later she moved to Tattnall Street, which was the next road over. Boomer H. Austin was at 4 Wall Street. Mary Callaway did domestic work for B.H. Austin and resided in the rear of the place on 407 Whitehall. Whitehall Street intersects Wall Street and is an extension of Peachtree Street. Charlie Callaway's last place of employment in Atlanta was with the Fenley Furniture Company before leaving for Oglethorpe County in 1892. Charlie Calloway worked alongside Henry C. Callaway.

At the time of their arrival in Atlanta, I am persuaded that Henry C. Callaway is none other than Cleveland or Clayborn Callaway. The two of them are always together except on contracts with William Eberhart in 1892 at the earliest, when the first contract was made. The last time I found Charlie and Cleveland or Clayborn was on the property of Edward Jackson in Oglethorpe County, when Charlie made his escape and was in the news as one who had left under the cover of night and was wanted for jumping contract of Mr. Edward Jackson. I believe that Cleveland was not too far behind his brother Charlie, and this is the reason he is living under the first name Henry C. Callaway in Atlanta! I believe that Charlie helped get his brother off Edd Jackson's place and then returned to Oglethorpe with Mary to work for William Eberhart!

Henry C. Callaway and his wife America Callaway were living at 138 Howell Street in Atlanta in 1900. I thought it was strange that his wife was named America. The only other time that I have seen the name America was in the family of Green Callaway, and she was his daughter. Henry C. Callaway and America's daughters were named Hattie, Annie M., and Lillian. Henry C. Callaway was listed as being born January 1867 and was thirty-three years old. America was born June 1860 and was thirty years old. Hattie was born September 1893 and was six years old. Annie M. was born August 1897 and was two years old. Lillian was born August 1899 and was nine months old.

By the year 1910, Henry C. Callaway was living at 78 Humphries Street in Atlanta; however, this is where a little mystery comes into the picture. First, the whole family is listed as being mulattoes and a neighbor moves with them from Howell Street to Humphries. Henry Callaway is forty-five, and now his wife is under the first name of Annie and not America. Annie is forty-two years old, and they have been married seventeen years and have had eight children. This means that there is an older child that was listed in the house in 1900. So the eldest child in the house in 1910 on Humphries is Hattie at the age of sixteen, then Annie at the age of twelve, Lillian at the age of ten, Henry at the age of six, Migion at the age of two, and young Willie Callaway at the age of one year and ten months. The family that followed them from Howell Street was that of George Wiley and his wife Annie. The two of them are at the same age, twenty-one. On Howell Street, the Wileys were Stewart and Elizabeth, both in their sixties. Annie's maiden name was Calhoun. Her mother Amanda was living in the house with them in 1900, aged fifty-five. Remember the last name Calhoun because I have mentioned it in reference to my grandfather Arthur's second wife Rachel.

Now, this is where the mystery starts to take place within this Callaway family, as with the family of Charlie and Mary and Aaron and Harriett Callaway. Annie will live between Humphries and Gilbert streets in the 1920s. Annie is living at 136 Gilmer Street in Atlanta. Henry C. Callaway's name is not mentioned. Living on the same street as Annie was Addie Callaway at 77 Gilmer Street. In the census of 1920, Annie was listed as Anna Callaway, a sixty-five-year-old widow living with her two-year-old niece Sally Mae Kelly, twenty-two-year-old boarder named Louise Hall, thirty-three-year-old Earnest Lassiter, and his twenty-four-year-old wife Georgia. All are located on 196 Gilmer street.

Annie had moved from 136 Gilmer within the same year. By 1929, Annie was living at 204 Gilmer Street and was taking in laundry. However, in 1928, Annie was advertising that she was a midwife at 204 Gilmer Street, along with Mrs. Eliza Jackson. Now, I don't know if Eliza Jackson is any kin to Mrs. Annie Callaway but my conversation with the daughter of Mr. Willie Callaway certainly caused me to assume so! Mrs. Eliza Jackson was living at 495 Gartrell Southeast Atlanta at the rear of the place occupied by Mrs. Carrie Gant. This place was located a few houses down from Mrs. Nora Callaway, who was living at 501 Gartrell. Mrs. Nora Callaway is out of Clarke County. I found her in 1900 in the city of Athens with her children Roosevelt (five), Fannie Lou (three), and Florence (one), as well as her brother Willie Howard, who was nineteen.

Now, the conversations with Mrs. Callaway opened up quite a bit of information that was revealing. She mentioned the Jackson family she was kin to. Here, I am going to work backward from 1940 from the house of Mrs. Florence Callaway and her husband William at 519 Roy Street in the Fourth Ward of the City of Atlanta. William Callaway is forty-four, his wife Florence is twenty-eight, and Raymond their son is four. Living with them is a niece named Mary W. Nelson. Living in the house next door, house 509, is Jesse Callaway from Lawton Street in the Third Ward with Bell Hackney. Jesse Callaway is a retired grocery store owner at the age of sixty-five and Bell Hackney is forty-seven in 1940. Jesse came to live in the Third Ward with his mother Indiana Callaway from Clayton County, Georgia. I only found her in 1900 living as a widow at the age of sixty. Indiana was born May 1860. Jesse her eldest son was born April 1877 and was twenty-three years old. Daisy his sister was born February 1881 and was nineteen years old. Mattie was born January 1883 and was seventeen. Claude, a grandson, was born May 1898 and was two years old. They were living in the Adamson District right next door to them. Yes, the Adamson family for whom the district is named. Mattie Day or Mattie Callaway died June 23, 1924. Jesse Callaway listed her father as being Jim Jackson and Indiana as her mother; she was buried in Southview Cemetery.

I just think it's strange that while talking to Mrs. Callaway she did not think that she was kin to Mr. Jesse Callaway in any way shape or form. He and his family, when she came to know them, owned and operated a store in northwest Atlanta.

I found the death certificate of the sister of Jesse Callaway who lived at 468 Lawton Street in 1924. Her name was Mattie Day born January 3, 1889, and died at the age of thirty-four as a widow. Her father was named Jim Jackson and her mother was named Indiana Callaway. esse Callaway filed as the informant. Mrs. Mattie Day was buried in Southview Cemetery by the Ivey Brothers Funeral Home. I could never find any husband of Indiana Callaway anywhere in Clayton County, Georgia. Two years later, Jesse Callaway buried his mother Indiana at Southview Cemetery as well. She died February 8, 1926. Jesse did not know her father; however, he did state that her mother was named Christal Wright. Indiana was born May 30, 1858. In 1920, the only people living in the house of Indiana Callaway were her son Jesse and a boarder named Belle Hackney.

Now I have two dilemmas in 1940! Florence Callaway, in New Jersey, living with a Cleveland Callaway and Hugh Mason, are all in the house with Waymon Hill. Cleveland is thirty-five, Florence is thirty-seven, and Hugh Mason is thirteen. Waymon Hill is the head of the house at the age of thirty-five. Cleveland is out of Georgia, and Florence is out of Pennsylvania. They are all living at 130 Pretoria Avenue. Now I did find a Will Hill living nearby from Georgia as well with Albert and Emma Mitchell out of Virginia. Florence is a cook for a private family and Will is a porter for manufacturing detergents.

Will Callaway, the son of Henry C. Callaway and Annie or America Callaway, and their daughter Harriett now have ties to Robert C. Callaway in Clarke County. I finally figured out who and where Harriett Callaway was, the Doraville schoolteacher who later became a secretary. Harriett married St. Clair Harden while at Spellman. The only other harden that was at Doraville was secretary of the Hopewell Church association, James Hardin. Now, Charles C. or Edward Callaway now has a tie with Harriett Callaway, the sister of Will Callaway that has a tie with Robert C. Callaway of Clarke County, Georgia!

Now, the question is, while Robert C. Callaway, who dies in 1944, mentions Hardin and Will Callaway in his obituary, how are they kin to each other? I know that Charles Calloway has eyes on Harriett Callaway, the daughter of Henry C. Callaway and America. In 1920, I had a hard time finding Henry C. Callaway and his wife Annie. I believe that Henry died between 1913 or 1915. Living on West Fair Street near the intersection of Vine Street in part of the First Ward of Atlanta, I found Henry C. Callaway's daughter Harriett living with her husband Engram Harden at 239 West Fair Street. Engram is thirty-four years old and Harriett is twenty-four. Lillian her sister is nineteen, and young Willie is listed under the last name of Harden in the census. Willie's last name is Callaway. However, living nearby on Vine Street is Mrs. Elizabith Callaway, who at one time went under the first name of Mary. Mary is a cousin of the Harden family. Elizabeth is a forty-three-year-old widow. Johnnie Harden is a thirty-seven-year old brass molder living with Elizabeth Callaway at 18 Vine Street, along with forty-year-old Gemble Jackson. I don't know if Gemble Jackson is any kin to seventy-six-year-old Mary Jackson living a few houses away. This might be a tie to H. C. Callaway and the Harden and Jackson families.

Now what is the relationship between Mary or Elizabeth Callaway at Vine Street and Joseph, her husband, with Robert Callaway in Athens and Mr. Charles Callaway and his wife Mary. Terrell County is the mystery that ties a Joseph and Mary or Elizabeth Callaway buried in the Sardis Cemetery. So now there is a familiarity between Terrell County and Clarke County, Georgia, and the two Callaways located in Terrell and Clarke and Greene and Oglethorpe County, Georgia, and with Aaron and Harriett and Charlie and Mary Callaway. Now in 1910, at 48 Vine Street, Elizabeth Callaway is thirty-three years old and her husband Joseph Calloway is a thirty-seven-year-old machinist on the railroad yard. Maggie Hardin is living next door and she is at the age of twenty-five. Missouri Williams is living a few houses away, a fifty-four-year-old woman with her daughter Maggie Williams and son George Williams. Elvin Carpenter is a fifty-nine-year-old man married to Francis, his fifty-four-year-old wife and their children Annie and Minnie. I mentioned the Carpenters because Julia Callaway married a Carpenter in the 1880s. Living on the campus of the Atlanta Baptist College is Mr. John Hope, the president of the college, and Mr. Samuel H. Archer. I know that Mr. Alfonzo Herndon is living near as well. The First Ward of the City of Atlanta was very prominent and more prominent than that of the Fourth Ward!

The whole household is listed as mulattoes. The family comes from a section of Atlanta that is majority mulatto in the Third Ward called Summer Hill or People's Town. Now, in 1930 I could not find Will Callaway. I did find Engram Hardin and Hattie, his sister. The two of them were living at 605 Fair Street in the First Ward. Engram is forty-five and Hattie is thirty-five, and Willie Williams is twenty years old. Winston Callaway, a brother-in-law, is four years and three months old. Now, it is surprising that Winston Callaway could be a brother-in-law at four years old. This means that Henry Callaway is still alive or Annie is having children still out of wedlock! The family is living at the intersection of Fair Street and Vine. In 1940, the situation is cleared up. Winston is at 605 Fair Street, listed as a nephew. Engram is now forty-nine and Hattie is thirty-seven years old.

Like usual I have lost contact with this source that had a little insight into a story that was told to me by family members that my grandfather was in a car accident that caused him to be paralyzed and my grandmother helped him to regain his mobility and then they married in 1940. I was told by Ms. Callaway that her dad told her that he lost a brother in a car accident or he was involved in a car accident and someone was seriously injured. There is another Callaway that is close to the Hardins living on Vine Street. Her name is Mary Elizabeth Callaway and her husband Joseph. Joseph is thirty-seven years old in 1910 and Elizabeth was thirty-three. Living in the apartment next door is Maggie Hardin. Living in the house next door is fifty-four-year-old Missouri Williams and her twenty-five-year-old daughter Maggie and her sixteen-year-old brother George. Mary and Joseph Callaway are two peculiar situations about 1904. Mary was living at 17 Vine Street and Joseph was working as a coaler for Southern Railyard Shop and resided at Wilson Street, two blocks north of Mary Street. The only child that does not live in Athens, Clarke County, or Oglethorpe County is Willie Callaway after he and Aaron and Aaron's young wife Harriett are listed on the census in 1900. I believe that Willie is living in Atlanta. I believe in 1902 Willie was in trouble and was in the newspaper. Will was charged with stealing packages valued at twenty-six dollars from Chamberlin and Johnson Department store. Willie worked for the Morrow Transfer Company at the age of fourteen years old.

I earnestly believe that this is the son of Charlie and Mary Callaway. I don't know how long Willie resided in Atlanta before moving to Michigan.

I do believe that he was here during the start of World War One. I believe that Willie arrived in Atlanta with the aid of Peg-Leg Williams with Aaron and young Harriet, who might be his mother. I believe that Atlanta will always be a mystery to me because of the many secrets it possesses!

There is another set of Callaways or Calloways in Atlanta. Their names are Albert and Maggie Callaway. I come across this husband and wife in the Atlanta Journal Constitution in September 1, 1906. The headlines read Maggie broke into church and also broke into jail. Maggie Callaway was sent to tower for ten days for contempt of court. The Saturday article states that last Wednesday she tore off three planks of the Calvary Baptist Church. Albert is from Greene County Georgia and worked alone side of Aaron Callaway. Albert also worked for P. M. Stephens alone side with Albert Haynes in Bairdstown in Oglethorpe County Georgia. Albert married first Lula Champion in 1884 in Oglethorpe County and second wife was Maggie Alexander in Atlanta, Fulton County in 1901. I don't know how he fits into the family of Bob Callaway or Robert Callaway and Aaron. However, I must say that if he is a member of the Calvary Baptist Church in Atlanta, maybe just maybe Aaron or Bob or Robert and a few more of these ties to Oglethorpe and Greene County had fellowship with Calvary Baptist in Atlanta as well. The minister that married Albert Callaway and Maggie Alexander on October 10, 1901 was the great Rev. W. W. Floyd. Now, before Maggie Alexander marries Albert Callaway in 1901 I went looking for her in 1901 and found out that she was living at 45 Trenholm Street in Atlanta with her thirteen year old niece Lilly or Lillian Callaway the sister of Hattie Callaway and the daughter of Henry C. Callaway and the sister of William Callaway. She claims the niece of Albert Callaway before she's even married to Albert Callaway and if that is the case Albert is the brother of Henry C. Callaway and Charley Calloway. This might just signify who his father is, Mr. Robert C. Callaway. There are two more time that I find the Alexander and Callaway ties and it is in Ohio and with Charley Callaway in Fairburn when he was working with Mr. Columbus Kiser. Mr. Frank Alexander was working in the old ninth ward of the city of Atlanta. Robert C. Callaway and Robert L. Callaway work for M.C. and J. F. Kiser and Co. near the intersection of Pryor and Wall Street. At this same intersection was ETV & GRR Co. the same Company colored man Robert C. Callaway worked for. What a wonderful find! Thank you Ms. Lillian Callaway. Arthur and Racheal would name their daughter Lillian while living in the house of Mrs. Emma Wallace.

Here I want to surmise Charley Callaway's experience between 1892 and 1899. I just don't know if they moved him from Elbert County to

Terrell County to the State Prison in Terrell County after pronouncing to the courts in Clarke and Oglethorpe Counties that Charlie was dead by October 3, 1899. The Story does not end here in the year of 1899 for Charley Callaway and his death in Elbert County is somewhat a mystery if it really happened.

I have my doubts of the circumstances surrounding his death and one is the signing of his mark to demurred and stating he would not prosecute against Tom Erwin and other in his federal conspiracy case. The next one is the fact that the court records in Oglethorpe county states that he was released from custody of the county on October the 17 of 1899 in Oglethorpe and the witness papers against William Eberhart and others states that he is dead. And also the Charley that was a witness in the bank robbery in Winterville who was living in Jackson County. Also the fact that Red Charley who ran Mr. James Monroe Smith's train in Clarke Co. to Union Point and the Red Moss that was living in Greensboro Penfield next to Abraham and Dinah English in 1910 and 1920's and last but not least Mr. Red Callaway in Lee County who own many businesses and Charley Callaway who was living in Terrell County and supposed to be buried in the County Line Baptist Church Cemetery.

The place located on the chain-gang in Elbert County Georgia and the date is October 3rd 1899. The Report was filed by Mr. J. C. Hudgins and O. C. Gibson that Charles Calloway was dead. These are some of the men and one woman who were on the Chain-gang with Charles. Some you will know for they are the witnesses in the Federal Case against Evil Disposed men unaware to the Federal Court case. All the convicts are from Clarke County the charges range from gambling, larceny, riot, forgery, assault, trespassing and carrying concealed pistol. There ages ranges from 18 to 52 years old, and there is only one white convict in the camp.

John Lester

will Winfield

Walter Harter

Will Dun

E. L. Barron's ?

John Bauldin

Felix Harkley

Tom Daniel

Waman Glarran ?

Frank woods

Wash Matthews

Earnest Crawford

Dave Coffer

Sam Gregory

Henry Gee Johnson his age is 26 years old was imprisoned on the 26 day of August of 1899

Rich Appleby

Oscar Walton

Gratlin Johnson his age is 35 years old was imprisoned on the 22 day of May 1899 concealed weapon. Gratlin Johnson was arrested with Charley in Athens and he want ever be seen again after leaving J. C. Hudgins chain-gang. What is this close relationship that Gratlin Johnson has with Charley Callaway? Where can I start? Let's start where Gratlin Johnson lived. Gratlin grew up in Oglethorpe County in Wolfskin district just north of Bowling Green and Bairdstown. Crawford is the post office that Wolfskin is located. There are a few white families that I will mention to try and see if I can form this relationship that the two pistol carrying gangsters have in common. The first family is Mr. Henry J. Eidson and a few more Eidson as well. James N. Eidson, Mrs. M. E. Eidon, Thomas J. Erwin, Joseph E. Eidson, William Eidson, J.M. Eidson, Landrith R. Eidson, John Y. Griffith, James T. Griffith, William T. Griffith, sixty year old J. M. Griffith, John W. Griffith, R. B. Griffith, C. J. Johnson, William Jewel, Mattie Jewel, and Margie Jewel. I mentioned the few names because of the last names that have a tie with there are a few more white men that are to be mentioned that has ties to old Aaron Callaway and his mother Hannah Callaway off of Isaac and Winnifred Callaway's estate. The families are D. C. Barrow and W. A. Pope who might be a relative to Henry Pope one of the men that is over the estate of Isaac and Winnifred Callaway. Gratlin Johnson worked on the property of D. C. Barrow in Wolfskin alone with Peter Johnson and William Johnson, Isaac Jackson, William Mitchell and William Pope. Fielding Johnson another man that was to appear on Charlie Callaway's behalf in the Federal Courts was located on the place of J. F. Dillard with Mack Johnson. I do know that Fielding Johnson has been with or in the company of Aaron or Robert or Bob Callaway and Aaron Cheney in 1870. I have established that Aaron Cheney or Aaron Callaway of Bob is the father of Charlie and with this association between the two fathers Aaron or Bob Callaway or Cheney is the tie that I was looking for. The two young pistol carrying men were childhood friends of relatives growing up in Oglethorpe and Greene County Georgia. However, there is a mystery here between Aaron Callaway the son of Hannah and Aaron Callaway Cheney of Rev. Enoch Callaway as well. The mystery is that Burrell Callaway goes to work for Mr. J. K. Eidison near N. D. Arnolds place. Wolfskin might have led Burrell father Aaron here as well. Aaron was working for Mr. William Jewell in the 1870's. This was about the time Aaron was listed as being a white man in the tax digest. William Jewell was living in Penfield with his twenty eight year old daughter Martha and Mr. Edwin Campbell twenty four, a black twelve year old servant named Ida Moore, and a ten year old white girl named Mattie Jewell, I am quoting the 1870 census about this time and William Jewell is living near Lewis Maxey and his son George Maxey a little south of Macedonia Church. Being that D. C. Barrow was a non-resident living in Wolfskin I believe at one time he either vacated the place and left the Johnson's in charge of his property in the 227th. They were Sam and Gratlin Johnson, Steve and Ed Johnson, Will and Mack Johnson and Reese Jewell lived in Wolfskin without having an employer over them! N. D. Arnold had Asbury Johnson on his place next door. The only relative that I can tell that might have ties to Mr. D. C. Barrow is A. F. Pope. After living in Puryears of Clarke County in 1880, Mr. John Austin came to work on Mr. L. F. Edwards place in 1890 in Wolfskin. While John was on the place of L. F. Edwards he was in the company of friends that might know the pistol carrying childhood friends Charlie and Gratlin. It being that Charlie was living with John Austin in 1880 in Puryears, Clarke County not too far Wolfskin which lay just south of Puryears. Peter Dent, Willie Daniels and his kin Wash and Dave Daniel, Charlie Clarke and Squire Collins, Henry Bolton and Wash Bowling and his kin Albert Bowling. The last names of the two men mentioned tells you where they derived from. Bowling Green District of Oglethorpe County Georgia! While John Austin was on Mr. Edwards place just next door was the property of R. T. Tribble who hired Seaborn Bugg. In 1880 John Austin not only had Charlie and his brother Claborn, but John has his twenty four year old sister Lou, and his seven year old sister Mary, and his six year old sister Clarrisa and a six month old brother Robert (Rob), and Angeline a four year old sister as well. John Austin and Charlie Callaway are in their early twenties and young. If I surmise, Seaborn Bugg is the step son of Henry Buggs out of Falling Creek. Is Seaborn Bugg living near his brother John Austin in 1890? And in 1880 John decided to leave the house of his stepfather Henry Buggs in Falling Creek in 1880 and came with Charley and Clayborn who is their father Aaron or Bob Callaway who once was a Cheney and is living under many names to acquire property in Clarke County? Is this how Charlie and Gratlin Johnson became close friends and pistol carrying partners because of the relationship between Fielding Johnson and Aaron Cheney or Bob Callaway or Robert Callaway, and even Aaron Callaway? I might have even found Aaron Cheney under the first name of Jesse as well in the 218th district of Clarke County near Andrew Austin and his mother. Let us take one last look at Gratlin Johnson the friend and chain-gang companion in Elbert County! He will be living in the 218th district of Clarke County Georgia in Puryears District on the property of Mrs. Mildred E. Morton. He is employed alone with Pierce Nelson, Jefferson Smith and William Smith. This property is located near Mr. William H. Dean the same man that Aaron came to work for or Robert came to work for or Aaron Cheney came to work for in 1870! When Aaron was on Mr. Deans place John Austin was on Mr. William R. Tucks place. While again when Aaron or Bob Callaway or Aaron Cheney was on William H. Deans place John Austin was working on Mr. William H. Morton's place with Edmond Jones the same place where Gratlin Johnson would come to work for Mrs. Mildred E. Morton. However, Gratlin or Gratton Johnson is the son of sixty five year old George Johnson and his mother Mariah Johnson who is forty three years old Gratton Johnson has two brothers Edmond twelve and Wade who is seven. Clem Johnson another man that showed up as a witness on Charlie's behalf in 1898 was living next door in the Puryears District of Clarke County. Clem was thirty eight years old in 1880 and his wife Ella was twenty three, they had four daughters. Lula was twelve, Laura was seven, Susie was five and Reedy was the youngest at one years old. Young Gratlin is living near the property of Mr. W. H. Morton and his mother M. E. Morton who is sixty years old in 1880. Mrs. M. E. Morton has as her servant Tish Callaway a forty year old black woman. However, in the house with her husband Aaron Callaway she is fifty four years old and he is fifty five and Hattie is now twelve. And who is Aaron and Tissue and Hattie living near, Mr. R. T. Callaway the son of George W. Callaway or Elizabeth R. Callaway of Bowling Green. They are all in the 217th district of Clarke County which some of its citizens are listed in the 218th district of Puryears in Clarke County as well. This is the relationship between Gratlin Johnson and Charlie Callaway friends for life! In 1880, young twenty year old Charlie is living with his brother Cleveland in Puryears with John Austin and fourteen year old Gratlin or Gratton Johnson is in the house with sixty year old George Johnson and his wife Mariah and brother Edmond and Wade. Now let me finish the inmates at J. C. Hudgins chain-gang in Elbert County.

Will Henry Colman

Lewis Thomas

Rosa Lee Williams

Will Griffin his age is 52 years old was imprisoned on the 12 day of Sept. 1899 concealed weapon

Oliva Allen

Frank Bagwell

Dan Winter

Charlie Callaway his age is 40 years old was imprisoned on the 23rd day of February 1899 for carrying a concealed weapon and he is the only inmate with a mark listing him as being dead. Now, if he is dead in Elbert County how could he be hanging from the tree in the front yard in Beaverdam district in Oglethorpe County as my aunt Anna told me and as it was passed down by word of mouth for years in our family. His death rang out in Elbert County and Clarke County and Oglethorpe County as well. However with such a big case in the Federal Courts of Georgia and it being reported across the other state that reported about this case from 1896 to 1899 in newspapers across the United States and not a word or follow up on the Negro Charley Callaway held in Peonage with others after 1899. It took me and my wife, while looking through the Oglethorpe "Echo" News Paper in 1999 a hundred Years ago today. It took a hundred years to pass to have a follow up on the Negro Charley Callaway and his family and other Negroes held in Peonage to be brought to the conscious and for-thought by his great-grandson.

Something was happening on October 17, 1899 about the same time court was being held in Oglethorpe County on the same day and Will Griffin knew that something wasn't right. Charley was dead in the report to the State authorities on October 3rd and on October the 17th the same time that Will Griffin was bucking coincide with the time the Court case in Oglethorpe was to take place. Maybe Gratlin was concerned for his own life and wasn't going out without a fight. Anyway, Will Griffin received 28 licks for his bucking as the report states in his demeanor as to what is happening on the Prison Farm in Elbert County. I have one question why is Charlie and the rest of the men who were witnesses in the Federal court cases in Atlanta are in the prison in Elbert county under Athens penal system being under the watch of Oglethorpe men? And how can the men of Oglethorpe take the men under Clarke County Jurisdiction out of the jail to the county of Oglethorpe. These are the men who ran the farming camp in Elbert county. Mr. W. M. Hudgens is the Captain, Honorable R. E. Amse is the ch'man B'd Com'rs. The name of the Rail Road that ran through Elberton is the S.A.L. and Southern Rail Road or the Seaboard Air Line. This railroad system was owned by John Skelton Williams. Again, a Williams comes into the picture again at the same time Peg-leg-Williams is taking and leading blacks to be relocated throughout these United States. In 1896, Williams bought the Abbeville & Waycross Railroad, which ran from Abbeville to Ocilla, and absorbed it into the Georgia and Alabama. In 1899, Seaboard bought the 1017-mile Florida, Central & Peninsular Railroad, a key part of which was a line from Savannah to Jacksonville.

On July 1, 1900, the entire system was consolidated and reorganized as the Seaboard Air Line Railway, a 2600-mile network stretching from Virginia to Florida. The Seaboard Air Line name had been used previously, but as a marketing name rather than the name of the company. (At the time, "Air Line" referred to a direct route, or at least a route more direct than that of any competitor.)

SAL bought the Lawrenceville to Loganville line from the Georgia, Carolina, and Northern Railway in 1901. The Southern Railway was already established and had its beginning with the Richmond & Danville railroad. It was in 1899 that it gained control of the South Carolina which became of the Piedmont Division. The modern Southern Railway began with the Richmond & Danville Railroad chartered in 1847 to connect its namesake cities in Virginia. Remember, the Richmond & Danville Railroad that Colored Robert C. Callaway worked for in Atlanta in the early

1880's. Could this be the express train that Charley Callaway road out of Elbert County on. It is the same train system that young Charlie Callaway in 1918 in Atlanta received stolen goods from and was sent to the Federal Prison. This train brought in Benjamin "Pitch" Fork Tillman into Elbert County from South Carolina a man that spoke on disenfranchisement of the Negro and in his state of South Carolina watched as lynch mobs killed Blacks for no apparent reason but, just that they were black! I just wonder what the purpose of inviting this racist Demigod Intel with the situation with my great-grandfather and Gratlin Johnson happening and playing out in the state of Georgia in 1899.

The conduct of Charlie was stated as being Good. Two men and the only Female tried to Escape Mr. Lewis Thomas, Will Griffin and Rosa Lee Williams. The Conditions on the Convict camp in Elbert was governed by the State and work conditions were as such. HOURS OF LABOR. The hours of labor shall be from sunrise to sunset, by the watch of the superintendent in charge, with one hour for rest and dinner at noon during the months of November, December, January and February; one and one-half hours during March, April, September and October; and two hours during May, June, July and August. Before Charlie came to his supposed demised in Elbert County the Courts in Athens had asked for his appearance in court.

The State vs. Charlie Calloway (Col.) #1136 #10 Oct. adj. Term 1898.

At Chambers, Athens Ga. Feby 10th 1899

It being made to appear to the Court that Charlie Calloway (Col) is Confined in jail under an Indictment for Carrying pistol Concealed and being unable to give bond for his appearance, will be likely confined until April at expense to the County. It is therefore ordered that the Indictment against said Charlie Calloway be transmitted by the Clerk of the Superior Court of Clarke County (together with all other papers appertaining to said case) to the City Court of Athens and there stand for trial or other legal disposition. Ordered further that this order be entered on the minutes of the Superior Court and said City Court.

R. B. Russell
Judge S.C. W.C.

The State Vs. Charlie Calloway (Col.) #1136 #10 Oct. adj. Term 1898. At Chambers, Athens Ga. Feby. 10th 1899 It being made to appear to the Court that Charlie Calloway (col.) is Confined in jail under an Indictment for carrying pistol Concealed and being make to give bond for his appearance, will be likely confined until April at expense to the county. It is therefore ordered that the Indictment against said Charlie Calloway be transmitted by the Clerk of the Superior Court of Clarke County (together with all other papers appertaining to said case) to the city court of Athens and there stand for trail or other legal dispositions Ordered further that this order be entered on the minuets of the Superior Court and said City Court. I could never find the City Court Record of this case at the Athens Clarke County Courthouse. As you can see the year is 1898 and Judge Richard B. Russell is over the case of Charley Callaway.

R. B. Russell, Judge S. C. w. C.

Two weeks later Charley Calloway waives Copy of Indictment and list of Witnesses; also waives being formally arraigned, and pleads Guilty. T. S. Mell Sol. CC Pro Term Charlie Calloway and his mark as the Defendant. T. S. Mell is another white man Charley is in contact with on his way to Elbert County chain-gang.

Where upon it is ordered that the defendant Charlie Calloway do pay a fine of Fifty Dollars and all cost of this prosecution and in default thereof within three days from this date during which time he will be in the custody of the Sheriff: It is ordered that he do work in a Chain-gang on the Public works for the full time of Twelve Months to be computed from the time said defendant is set to work in said Chain - gang unless said fine and costs be sooner paid, if he fails to pay within three days from this date it is ordered that he be turned over to the Board of Commissioners of Roads and Revenues of said County who are required to deal with said defendant in accordance with this sentence this 20 day of February, 1899. Again Charley is in the hands of Judge Howell Cobb another man that would know about Charlie Callaway and his death but nothing!

& Sons.

FOR SELLING LIQUOR.

Feb 1899

Charles Calloway, Colored, Arrested Yesterday Afternoon.

Yesterday afternoon a warrant was issued against Charles Calloway, colored, charging him with selling liquor illegally in Clarke county.

Calloway seems to be in plenty of trouble recently. He was sentenced to pay a fine of $50 a few days since on pleading guilty to the charge of carrying concealed weapons.

Now he will have to face the charge of selling liquor and if convicted he will not get off with a $50 fine.

Mrs. Nancy Hitchcock, Stanfordville, Ga., writes: My husband, Elder D. S. Hitchcock, used M. A. Simmons Liver Medicine for Indigestion, and thinks its medical properties far exceed Zelin's Regulator and Black Draught.

NOT A SOLDIER EXECUTED

Judge Advocate Establishes a Record in History of Wars.

Howell Cobb Judge & C.

Here is another question I just have to ask if Charlie got off with a fifty dollar fine in Clarke in 1899 why he couldn't appear in court in Athens on the 10th of 1899 and made it to court two weeks later to appear before Howell Cobb in the City court because maybe the men who was keeping Charlie under their control didn't want him to appear before the Superior Court Judge Richard B. Russel. Or like I have investigated the hand written letter to the Northeastern District Attorney E. A. Angier, it could be the Superior Court Judge himself in control of Charley Calloway himself. He is the man with the power of the courts and a hidden secrete society behind him as well. With his friend Henry C. Tuck who is handling a very serious situation between Hal Johnson and Charlie Callaway the servant and William Eberhart himself and other evil disposed men to the courts unknown.

Clarke Superior Court. Dec. Oct. Term, 1898 Misdemeanor Carrying pistol concealed. STATE Vs. Charley Calloway Col.

Asbury H. Hodgson, Foreman. J. C. Wheless Prosecutor. T. S. Mell, Solicitor General. WITNESSES: N. O. Henson, N. B. Davis, J.H. J. A. Smith, J. C. Wheless.

The Defendant Charley Calloway waives copy of Indictment and list of witnesses, also waives being formally arraigned, and pleads: Guilty. T. S. Mell Pro-term City Court of Athens. Charley Calloway and His Mark.

Georgia, Clarke County. In the Superior County of Said County. The Grand Jurors, selected, chosen and sworn for the County of Clarke to-wit:

1. Asbury H. Hodgson, Foreman.
2. George P. Brightwell
3. John R. Crawford
4. Charles B. Chandler
5. John R. Christy
6. Thomas J. Epps
7. Albert B. Harper
8. George H. Hulme
9. James S. King
10. Elijah S. Lester
11. John R. Moore
12. William J. Morton
13. Lewis H Nichols
14. James O Farrell
15. David E. Sims
16. James H. Towns 217th dist.
17. Samuel F. Woods
18. Joseph H. Webb
19. William T. Witcher

In the name and behalf of the citizens of Georgia charge an accuse Charley Calloway a person of color, of the County and State aforesaid, either the offense of Misdemeanor, carrying a pistol concealed: For that the said Charley Calloway, a person of Color, on the fifth day of June in the year of our Lord One Thousand Eight Hundred and Ninety Eight, in the County aforesaid, unlawfully did have and carry about his person, concealed, and not n an open manner an fully exposed to view, a certain pistol, concealed, and not in an pen manner and fully exposed to view, a certain pistol, contrary to the laws of said State the good order & dignity thereof. It took from November 1, 1898 for the deacon and friend of William Eberhart to bring this charge against my great-grandfather Charlie and I just wonder why would a misdemeanor charge of selling liquor and beer can cost a man his life. Mr. J. R. Haynes and other evil disposed men finally got their chance to end Charley! They Isolated him far from public eye and the evil disposed men unknown to the courts killed him. Maybe they did or maybe they didn't I just don't quite know!

Clarke, Superior Court, Dec. Oct. Term, 1898 J. C. Wheeless, Prosecutor. C. W. Brand Solicitor General.

In the City Court of Athens Feby. Term 1899 Warrant and Accusation for Carrying Pistol concealed plea of Guilty, Feb 20/99 whereupon it is ordered that the defendant Charlie Calloway do pay a fine of Fifty Dollars and all costs of this prosecution and in default whereof within three days from this date during which time as will be in the custody of the Sheriff; it is ordered that he do work in a chain gang on the order of this for the full term of Twelve months to be computed from the time said defendant is set to work on said Chain gang, unless said fine and costs be sooner paid, if he fail to pay within three days from this date it is ordered that he be turned over to the Board of commissioners of roads and revenues of said county who are required to do with said defendant in accordance with this sentence. this 20 day of Feby 1899 Howell Cobb. Judge and C.

Charley Calloway)
The Defendant Charley Calloway waives Copy of Indictment and list of witnesses; also waives being formally arraigned, and plead Guilty.
T.S. Mell
Sol. CC. Pro Tem
Charlie his x mark Calloway
Dft.
Whereupon it is ordered that the defendant Charlie Calloway do pay a fine of Fifty Dollars and all Costs of this prosecution and in default thereof within three days from this date during which time he will be in the Custody of the Sheriff, It is ordered that he do work in a Chain gang on the Public works for the full term of Twelve months to be Computed from the time said defendant is set to work in said Chain gang unless said fine and Costs be sooner paid, if he fails to pay within three days from this date it is ordered that he be turned over to the Board of Commissioners of Roads and Revenues of said County who are required to deal with said defendant in accordance with this sentence
This 20 day of Feby 1899.
Howell Cobb
Judge C.C.

At Chambers, It being made to appear to the Court that Charlie Calloway (col) is confined in jail under an Indictment for carrying pistol concealed and being unable to give bond for his appearance, will be likely confined until April at expense to the County; It is therefore ordered that the Indictment against said Charlie Calloway be transmitted by the clerk of the Superior Court of Clarke County, (together with all other papers appertaining to said case), to the City Court of Athens and there stand for trail on other legal disposition. Ordered further that this order be entered on the legal disposition., Ordered further that this order be entered on the Minute of the Superior Court and said City Court R.B. Russell Judge S. C. W. C.

Now, let's look at the State Warrant against Charlie Calloway the Witnesses are John Strickland and Willie Howard. John W. Wise states "I have this day executed the within Warrant by arresting, the body of defendant who is now in my custody this 22nd, day of Feb. 1899.

STATE OF GEORGIA, Clarke County. Personally Appeared J.R. Haynes who, on oath, saith that to the best of his knowledge and belief Charley Calloway did commit the offense of Misdemeanor for that the said Charley Calloway, did sell Intoxicants, in the County of Clarke on the day of November 1898 and this deponent makes this affidavit that a warrant may issue for his arrest. Sworn to and Subscribed before me, this the 22nd day of February 1899. Jos. F. Foster J. P.

(Witness, J. R. Haynes)

STATE OF GEORGIA. To any Sheriff, or his deputy, Corner, County Bailiff, Constable or Marshal of said State - Greetings: J.R. Haynes makes oath before me that on the day of November 1898, in the County of Clarke Charley Calloway did commit th offense of Misdemeanor you are hereby commanded to arrest the body of the said Charley Calloway and bring him before me, or some other judicial officer of this State, to be dealt with as the law directs. Herein Fail Not.

Given under my hand and seal, this 22nd day February 1899 Jos. F. Foster J. P. [seal].

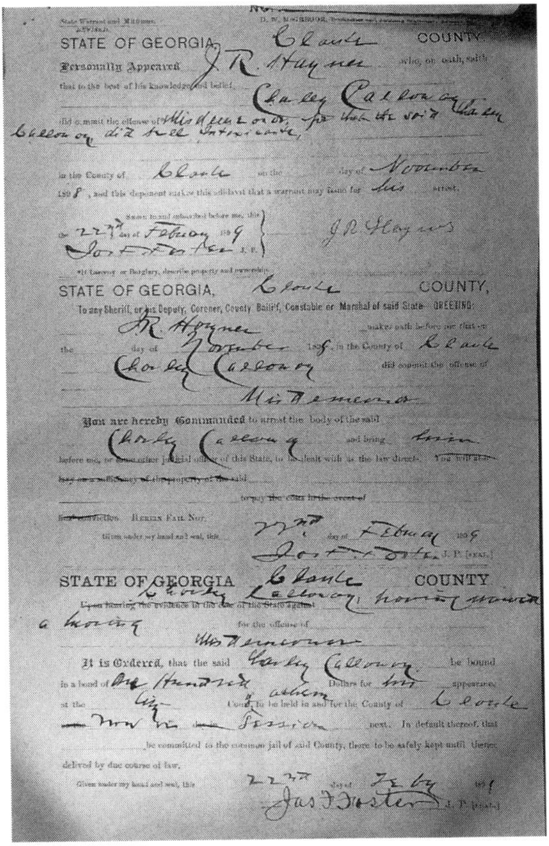

STATE OF GEORGIA, Clarke County. Charley Calloway, having waived a hearing for the offense of Misdemeanor. It is Ordered, that the said Charley Calloway be bound in a bond of One Hundred Dollars of his appearance at the City Court, to be held in and for the County of Clarke now in Session next. In default thereof, that .... be committed to the common jail of said County, there to be safely kept until thence delivered by due course of law. Given under my hand and seal, this 22nd day of Feby. 1899 Jas F. Foster.

Georgia, Clarke Co. J. R. Haynes in the name & behalf of the citizens of Georgia charges & accuses Charlie Calloway with the offense of misdemeanor for that said Charlie Calloway in the County aforesaid on the 1st day of November 1898 did unlawfully sell, barter, or exchange certain vinous malt or other intoxicating liquors, Whiskey & beer said Charlie Calloway not then & there being a Practicing Physician & contrary to the laws of said State the good order & dignity thereof-

March 12, 1899

John D. Mell, Sol. City-Court-Athens.

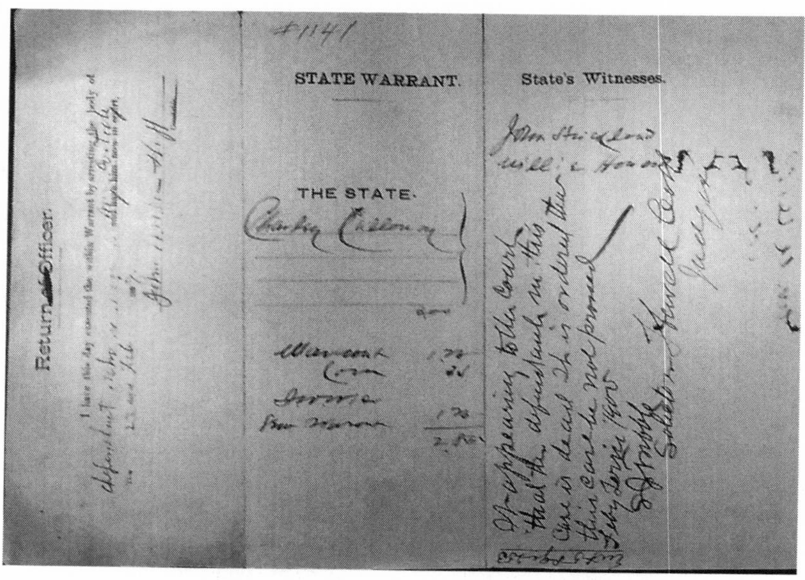

#1141

Return of Officer.

STATE WARRANT.

THE STATE.

Charley Calloway

State's Witnesses.

John Strickland

Now, I know you are supposedly asking yourself why Charlie's Received Date is is February 23, 1899 and his Crime is Concealed Pistol when he was in the custody of Sheriff John W. Wise of Clarke county on the 22nd day of February. Now, One year Later the courts in Athens Clarke County does not know that Charlie Calloway is dead on the same State warrant it states that in its own wordings ("It appearing to the Court that the defendant in this case is dead. It is ordered that this case be Nol Prosed".) I believe that the courts don't believe that Charlie is dead for they don't have the body of Charlie Calloway and Elbert County don't have a coroner's report of his death, and don't really states when Charlie died or the cause of death. So, this leads me to believe that Charlie may still be living under the watchful eye of the Secret Society the Ku Klux Klan.

Feb. Term 1900. G. J. Tribble, Solicitor.

Howell Cobb, Judge.

Now, one other thing the courts in Oglethorpe County knows Charlie Calloway is dead Two months ahead of the Courts in Athens Clarke County and they don't even have Jurisdiction or control over the body or person of my Great- Grand Father Charlie Calloway. For did Oglethorpe have a contract with Elbert county of the use of their Convict labor. No! For there was nothing in the minuets of the City council of Elbert county ever having such a contract with Oglethorpe. So, the question still is How did Oglethorpe County Courthouse and William Eberhart get informed before Clarke County and Judge Richard B. Russell Sr. when the case was in the City Courts of Clarke and Mr. Hoke Smith the 1906 Gubernatorial Candidate of Georgia who will insight riots in Atlanta that will cause Black lives to be loss by the drunken white men marching down Decatur Street to Fort Street killing Blacks as they ran for their lives, because of the rhetoric in the newspapers that would inflame the imagination of these white men whose mind was blinded with the drink from the nearby bars. The only thing I know for a fact is that the Men of Clarke County had a hand in the decision making of Charlie Calloway in Elbert county; These are some of the minuets of the Mayor and his Alderman in the City Counsel of Clarke County: the Board took a recess in order to visit and inspect the County Chain Gang located in Elbert County in charter of Mr. J. C. Hudgens; The Clerk was interested to arrange for funds to distribute the Expenses of the Board to and from Elberton.

T. P. Vincent, Foreman. G. H. Tannery, Clerk.

January 20 1899

The board inspected the misdemeanor convict camp located on the farm of Mr. J. C. Hudgins in Elbert County. The Camp was found to be in cleanly and good sanitary condition. The convict in good health and well cared for. To conform to the requirement of entered into a contract with the County Commissioners of Elbert county. As for copy recorded believe merging original contract with Mr. Hudgins into this new contract. "Contract= This contract entered into between the Board of Commissioners of Roads and Revenues or Elbert County of the one part and the Board of Commissioners of Roads and Revenue of the county of Clarke said state of the other part Witness. The party of the first part hereby heir from the party of the second part all misdemeanor convict of said county for the price of five dollars per month each until January 1st 1900 and hereby again to pay said party of the second part said same cash in hand and the time to be computed from date of the delivering of said convicts to the party of the first part of the jail in Clarke County Georgia.

Said party of the first part also agree to work and control said convict in the County of Elbert, said state under the rules and regulations prescribed by the prison commissioners of said state, and in addition hereto agree that the prison in charge of said convict shall make three monthly report as prescribed by law in St... of two: One each to be boards of Elbert and Clarke Counties and the Prison Commissioner of (of Ga.) Said party of the second part here by agrees to his all the misdemeanor convict of Clarke County at the prier heretofore named, to the party of the first part, an to deliver the same at the jail in Clarke Co; to whomsoever the part of the first part may direct. This contract both parties agree shall begin at once and expire January 1st. 1900. In writing where of the parties hereto have set their hands and affixed their official signature this January 1899. Sign in Duplicate. Board of comm. of R. R. of Elbert County. Signed by R. E. Adairs, Chm.

T. P. Vincent Chm. W. H. Woodson, J. M. Hodgson. Not one word from the commissioners of Clarke County on Charlie's where about or his death in 1899. With the case being such a high profile case. You would think T. P. Vincent also a friend of Henry C. Tuck would have stated something about my great-grandfather Charley. This is the City Court of Athens in 1899 and not one word comes from the board. You and I know that they know and so does the Superior Court Judge and the bailiffs and sheriff Mell, and others Know where and what happened to my great-grandfather. I hope that whoever read this book might have some answers to what might have happen or didn't happen in 1899 in Clarke County Georgia.

(Letter Heading) Commercial Club.

Corner of College Avenue and Clayton Street.

Elbert Co. (written in)

Athens GA. (scratched out) July, 15 1899.

Hon. E. A. Angier.

U. S. Dist. Atty.

Dear Sir; I am not imposed to prosecute any further the Case in U. S. Court in which I am prosecutor. And if it meets your approval am perfectly willing for the Cases to be nol Prosed or dismissed. I Consent to the dismissal or nol pros. (word is unreadable) it does not involve me in the payment of any Costs.

Yours Respectfully,

His Charlie (X) Calloway

mark

Witnesses: J. C. Hudgens and O. C. Gibson

Remember on page 147 Hoke Smith in Atlanta, Ga., Aug. 2, 1886 wrote to the President of the United States Mr. William McKinley , testifying to the character of Wm. T. Newman to become a Federal Judge and on Page 150; Attorney Hoke Smith gave his opinion on E. A. Angier behalf as well remember, Hoke Smith Attorney And Counsellor At Law. 10 1/2 S. Broad St. Atlanta, Ga.

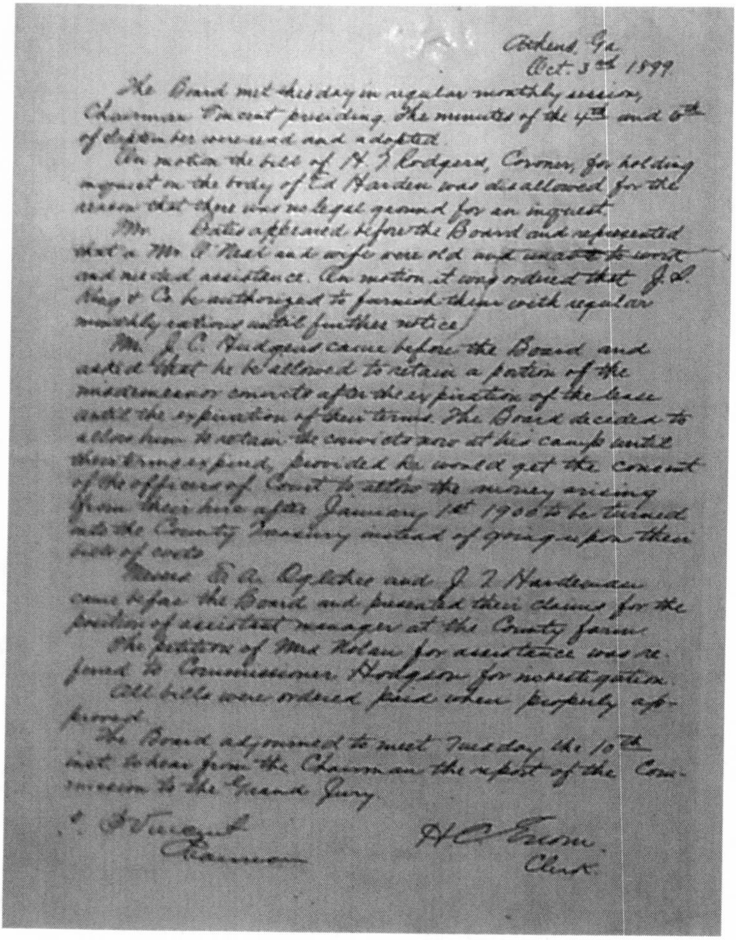

Athens, Ga.
Oct. 3rd 1899

The Board met this day in regular monthly session, Chairman Vincent presiding. The minutes of the 4th and 6th of September were read and adopted.

On motion the bill of H. T. Rodgers, Coroner, for holding inquest on the body of Ed Harden was disallowed for the reason that there was no legal ground for an inquest.

Mr. [illegible] appeared before the Board and represented that a Mr O'Neal and wife were old and unable to work and needed assistance. On motion it was ordered that J. L. King & Co be authorized to furnish them with regular monthly rations until further notice.

Mr J. C. Hodgson came before the Board and asked that he be allowed to retain a portion of the misdemeanor convicts after the expiration of the lease until the expiration of their terms. The Board decided to allow him to retain the convicts now at his camp until their terms expired, provided he would get the consent of the officers of Court to allow the money arising from their hire after January 1st 1900 to be turned into the County Treasury instead of going upon their bills of costs.

Messrs E. A. Ogletree and J. T. Hardeman came before the Board and presented their claims for the position of assistant manager at the County farm.

The petition of Mrs Nolan for assistance was referred to Commissioner Hodgson for investigation.

All bills were ordered paid when properly approved.

The Board adjourned to meet Tuesday the 10th inst. to hear from the Chairman the report of the Commission to the Grand Jury.

[illegible] Vincent
Chairman

H. C. [illegible]
Clerk

March 8, 1897 To the President, Washington, D. C.

Sir: I learn that Mr. E. A. Angier of the Atlanta Bar will be a candidate for the position of United States District Attorney for the Northern District of Georgia. Mr. Angier is a man of character and ability. He served under the previous administration as Assistant District Attorney, and performed the duties in a most satisfactory manner. I believe his appointment would be acceptable to the people of the district, and I very cordially commend him for the place.

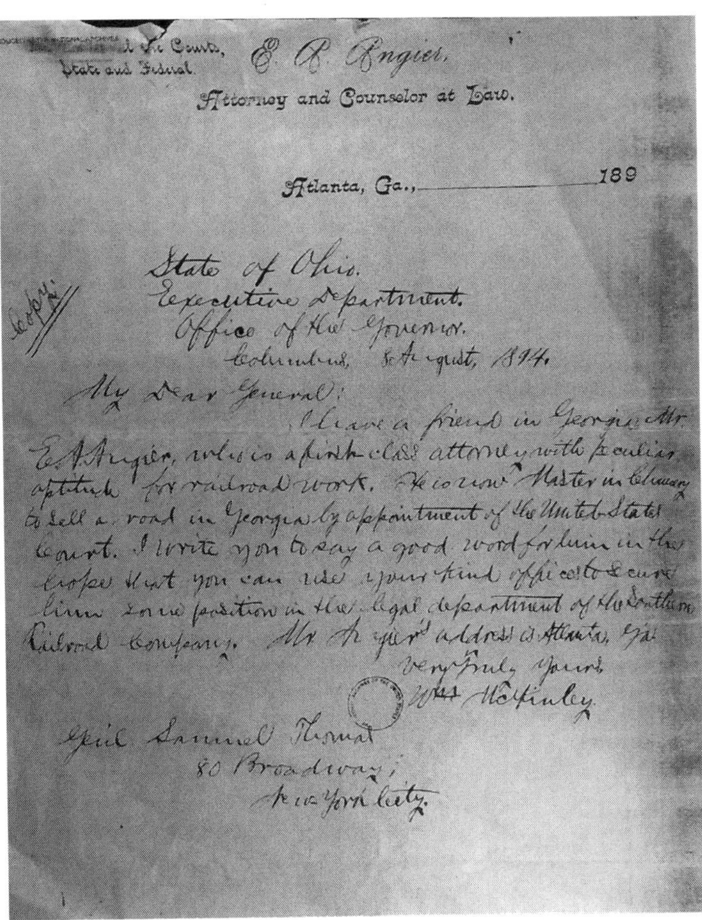

State and Federal.

E. A. Angier,
Attorney and Counselor at Law.

Atlanta, Ga., ______ 189

Copy.

State of Ohio.
Executive Department.
Office of the Governor.
Columbus, 8th August, 1894.

My Dear General:

I have a friend in Georgia Mr. E. A. Angier, who is a first-class attorney with peculiar aptitude for railroad work. He is now Master in Chancery to sell a road in Georgia by appointment of the United States Court. I write you to say a good word for him in the hope that you can use your kind offices to secure him some position in the legal department of the Southern Railroad Company. Mr. Angier's address is Atlanta, Ga.

Very truly yours,
Wm McKinley.

Genl. Samuel Thomas
80 Broadway,
New York City.

Yours very truly, Hoke Smith. Again, Charlie didn't have a chance to win this case with an attorney that more than likely has this man in his ear and the disenfranchisement sentiment filling the air with Tom Watson changing the opinion of the white men and women in Georgia permeating the simple minded who can be so easily persuaded when demoralizing the whites that solicit the votes of the Negroes by groveling and pandering. All I have written to you shows how hard the trials of the Negroes in Georgia and the struggles and achievements by these same

Negroes. I Love all Men as I have been taught of God and his Holy Words. For this is how you overcome Ignorance and that is to seek after wisdom as those of Old has taught us and let it be a garland around your neck that will bless the generation of children to come. Now, you can see why the writer in the Oglethorpe Echo and Athens Banner and Atlanta Constitution would quote Tinsley Rucker and Hamilton McWhorter that the charges against Mr. Eberhart and Albert Boykins would not be substantiated.

I did a great deal of trying to find out who is the writer of the letter on Charlie's behalf in Clarke County and I had come to a conclusion that it was Mr. Richard B. Russell Senior the Judge of Superior Court and the friend of Henry C. Tuck who was working between Oglethorpe County and Clarke County on Hal Johnson's wife situation with her brother-in-law at the same time as Charlie was going through his trials with William Eberhart and other evil disposed men unaware to the Federal Courts. I compared the written letter of Richard B. Russell who was in his chambers at Clarke County in Athens, he had stated that Charlie Callaway was dead and he was sending the case down to the City Courts of Athens. The letter written on Charlie's behalf and the hand written letter to E. A. Angier the hand writings are the same.

What was the outcome of the letter. Well, here it is. The United States Vs. Tom Erwin Et-al. True Bill Indictment filed June 16, 1899 Conspiracy. Order of Nolle Proseque It being represented to the Court by the United States Attorney that the ends of public justice do not require further prosecution in the above stated case, it is on motion of said Attorney. Ordered by the Court that nolle proseque be and the same is hereby entered in said Case. In open Court Sep 9, 1899

Wm. T. Newman U.S. Judge.

pg. (233). pg. (234) is the same Statement

Pg. 168. Monday morning July 17th 1899.

Court et pursuant to adjournment. Present the Honorable William T. Newman United States District Judge for the Northern District of Georgia presiding. Also present.

Edgar A. Angier, Esq. U. S. Attorney.

Walter H. Johnson, Asy. U. S. Marshall. The same Walter H. Johnson living on the plantation of a man implicated in these same indictments Mr. James (Jim) Monroe Smith of Smithonia. Another rich landowner or evil undisclosed evil doer that the federal courts could not account for in the federal case that was designed for the failure and demise of my great-grandfather Charlie and other blacks that were killed by lynching's across this great United States of America! In the land of the Free!

J. D. Steward, Esq. Deputy (word unreadable)

The United States vs. Tom Erwin, et-al. True Bill Indictment Filed Oct. 28th 1898. Conspiracy. Order of Nolle Proseque. In Being represented to the Court by the United State Attorney that the evidence in the above stated case is insufficient to convict, and that the ends of public justice do not require further prosecution in said Case, it is, on motion of said Attorney, Ordered by the Court that nolle proseque be, and the same is, hereby entered in said case. In open Court July 17, 1899.

Wm. T. Newman, U.S. Judge.

Evidence in the above stated case is insufficient to convict. What is the evidence? The evidence is the body of my Great grandfather Charlie Calloway what a statement to present to a Federal Judge. The Federal District attorney didn't mention the name of Charlie for one reason it is to present to the court that the evidence was not Human and to Dehumanize the man that was able to convict Tom Erwin et-al.in the Federal Courts. Tom Erwin will be brought before the Federal Courts for peonage even up until 1921. This makes believe the reason Brantley is under a disguise in Michigan in the twenties.

Commersial Club and Farmers Club and the Callaway Brothers Owners of the Callaway Merchantile buisness. By the time Chaley left Elbert co. After being there Six months the Men of Clarke and Oglethorpe counties had convinced him that it was for his own good to drop the charges against them in Federal Court so that the General Farms Inc. can move on for they needed the Negro men and women and their

Children to work in the fields as their forefathers and Mothers had done while in Slavery. The Men of Oglethrope and Clarke knew the impact the charges presented and also E.A. Angiers as well, all knew that something needed to be done about this situation with Charlie. So they presented Charlie with an option death or Land under a different name until the corporation between the two Clubs, The Farmers Club of Oglethorpe and the Commercial Club of Clarke County. Both helped form the General Farms which spread through the Southern and Northern States selling Farm products under the name of those General Stores that you see with the Coco Cola Signs upon the front and sides of these stores throughout the Country. As you know this is just history forgotten and unspoken and unwritten and I am leaving you with this, my final words from a black man from Georgia, with just a high school diploma who have made a lot of mistakes in his life and I know I might have made mistakes in this literature in seeking out this mystery of my great-grandfather Charley, but I tried! Right now I am the CEO of the Loaves and Fishes Ministry a non-profit organization for twenty five years and have been married as long, because I tried, and now I leave you with these words from Romans 14: verses 7 thru 8, we do not live to ourselves, and we do not die to ourselves. If we live, we live to the Lord, and if we die, we die to the Lord. So I say live in being truthful to God and yourselves because a liar God hates because you cannot be trusted because there is no value in those who lie and there is no value in what you say and do because you will live unto that lie and your life will never be fulfilled in Christ. God loves the truth, for in him is truth and Salvation to the new life in Christ. God Bless You and Peace be with you all, Amen. Acknowledgements: Thank you Sheila my wife, helpmate and family and also to my sister and brother in Christ, Ann and Vernon and Billy and family, I love you all very much for you kindness toward me. Thank you Granddaddy Arthur (Kator) and family, I will forever love and remember you granddaddy with an undying love for being my Father as well as my friend, you filled in the void in my life as a young boy growing up without a father. Thank you for your time and effort and guidance, patience and most of all your love! Thanks to all the men and women both Blacks and Whites that I came across while researching for the many years, your kindness toward my wife is very much appreciated. Thanks!

MONTHLY REPORT OF M

Elbert County, Georgia

Operated by J C [illegible]

NAME	County	Age	Color	Sex	Crime	Received	Term of Sentence
John [illegible]	Clark	15	black	Male	Riot	Nov 29 98	12
Will Minefield	=	35	=	=	gambling	April 9	12
Walter Harten	=	17	=	=	Larceny	Aug 26 94	10
Will [illegible]	=	28	=	=	Riot	June 8 94	12
E L [illegible]	=	28	=	=	Riot	Aug 26 94	9
John [illegible]	=	30	=	=	Larceny	Dec 15 98	12
Felix Harkley	=	22	=	=	Larceny	Sept 16 94	12
Tom Daniel	=	50	=	=	Larceny	Dec 28 98	12
[illegible]	=	36	=	=	gambling	March 7 99	10
Frank Woods	=	25	=	=	Larceny	March 28 94	[illegible]
[illegible] Mathews	=	33	=	=	trespassing	July 21 99	10
Earnest Cranford	=	18	=	=	Larceny	Oct 7 99	9
Dave Caffey	=	24	=	=	Larceny	Sept 16 94	8
Sam Gregory	=	25	=	=	Larceny	Sept 29 94	9
Henry Lee Johnson	=	26	=	=	Larceny	Aug 26	8
Rick Appleby	=	33	=	=	gambling	April 3 94	12
Oscar [illegible]	=	21	=	=	Larceny	July 21	9
[illegible] Johnson	=	35	=	=	concealing	Nov 22 94	8
Will Henry Calhoun	=	27	=	=	assault	Oct 97	36 [illegible]
[illegible] Thomas	=	18	=	=	Larceny	May 78 98	24
Rosa Lee Williams	female	19	=	=	Larceny	July 4	10
Will Griffin	[illegible]	32	=	=	concealing	Sept 2 99	12
[illegible] Allen	=	27	=	=	Larceny	Oct 15 98	12
[illegible] Bagwell	White	25	=	=	forgery	Oct [illegible]	12
Dan Martin	=	38	=	=	Larceny	Oct 29 98	12
Charlie Calloway	=	40	=	=	concealing	Feb 23 99	12

Feby Term 1900

S J Tribble
Solicitor

Howell Cobb
Judge C C

The State
v
Charley Calloway (Col)

(No 1141. City Court of Athens Warrant and Accusation, Misdemeanor.

It appearing to the Court that the defendant in this Case is dead, It is ordered that this Case be nol prossed

Feby Term 1900

S J Tribble
Solicitor

Howell Cobb
Judge C C

The State
v
J S Fletcher

No 1138. City Court of Athens Warrant and Accusation, Simple Larceny.

It appearing to the Court that the defendant in this Case is now in the U.S. Army and for other good and sufficient reasons. It is ordered that this Case be nol prossed.

Feby Term 1900

Howell Cobb

Dedicated to
(Kator) Arthur Calloway Sr., my grandfather.

Edwards Brothers Malloy
Ann Arbor MI. USA
August 21, 2017